Betrayal

Tim Tigner

This novel is dedicated to a man who never betrayed anyone, my father, my teacher, my friend, Professor Steven S. Tigner.

Copyright © 2018 Tim Tigner
All rights reserved.
ISBN: 9781729495025

For more information on this novel or Tim Tigner's other thrillers, please visit timtigner.com

Chapter 1

FBI Counterterrorism Response Team Headquarters, Quantico, VA

SPECIAL AGENT ODYSSEUS CARR looked up at the graying tiles of his boss's ceiling and began counting to ten. He almost made it to three. "What do you mean, I can't brief my men? They're putting their lives at risk, Commander. Big risk. These aren't stone-throwers you're asking us to kill. These are the guys who took out the World Trade Center."

Commander Potchak stood. He was a head shorter than Odi but built like a fireplug, and every bit as tough. "What's your point?"

Odi leaned forward and rested predatory palms on the edge of Potchak's metal desk. "My point, sir, is that we're giving up a crucial advantage if we don't rehearse. I want to give my men every available advantage. They deserve no less."

Potchak did not twitch or blink. He just stared back cold and hard for a couple seconds and then said, "If you're not up to it, Agent Carr, I'll give Echo Team to Waslager. He's been itching to go international. You can sit this one out—in isolation, of course."

Odi wanted to leap over the desk, grab his boss by the ears and put a knee through his smug face, but he knew that would not help his team. Instead he bit back his frustration and tried to suck it up like a good soldier. "That won't be necessary, sir."

Potchak turned and spat a thick river of tobacco juice into his trash can, making Odi forget his own frustration for a moment to pity Jose the janitor. "Good," Potchak said. "Now, if you'll take your head just a little bit farther out of your ass and break this task down, you'll see that I'm not ordering you to give anything up. The physics of the assault are the same whether it's Hogan's Alley or I-fucking-ran. A building is a building. A grenade is a grenade. Considering that you used to be the Bureau's top Explosive Ordnance Disposal pro, you should know that. All you need to rehearse effectively are models of the buildings and the lay of the land. Both are at your disposal, so I don't want to hear any more whining."

Odi felt his stomach quiver with a pluck of doubt. He moderated his tone and reminded himself that Potchak was usually a reasonable man. "May I ask why, sir? Why the unusual level of secrecy? Surely you don't think anyone on my team has links to al-Qaeda?"

"Oh Jesus, Carr. I'd have thought you'd understand that by now. Have you learned nothing about the way things really work these past two years? Counterterrorism is not a military matter; it's politics. By limiting foreknowledge to the mission leader and myself, some politician feels that he's protecting either his source or his ass. Probably both. I don't know who the source is, or even the politician for that matter, but I'm damn sure that whoever reconned that complex risked his ass to do it. So I'm not without sympathy."

Fighting back the urge to tell his boss what he thought of that, Odi picked up the satellite map to busy his hands. The complex in question consisted of three old cinderblock buildings in Nowheresville, Iran. It would take each of his two-man teams less than two minutes to run their building's perimeter, firing modified M441 high-explosive Rocket-Propelled Grenades. In the dead of night, it probably would not matter that the complex was in Iran. The commander was right about that. But Potchak was making a big mistake. A bureaucrat's mistake. The instant things deviated from plan—and things always deviated from plan—being in Iran would make all the difference. As a hardened field operative, Potchak knew that. This discrepancy bothered Odi, but he was not going to risk losing his team leader slot over it. "What did this secret source say about sentries?"

Potchak spat again and then sat down, signaling a truce.

Odi followed suit.

"There are usually just two men armed with AKs. One guards the entrance to the central building; the other walks a perimeter patrol. You'll have no problem taking them out with synchronized sniper shots. Use those shots as a starting gun, as your team's cue to begin the assault runs."

Odi nodded. "An eight-man team might make more sense than the standard seven. If you'll loan me Johnson, he and I could do that synchronized sniping from polar perimeter positions and then provide cover while the teams make their assault runs."

Potchak cracked a wry smile that warned Odi he would not like what came next. "You've got the right strategy, but the wrong man. You're getting Waslager. He'll be your second sniper … and your second in command."

Odi felt resentment run down his spine like boiling oil, but he could not stand up and get in his boss's face again. He had already played that card. He bit his tongue while taking a moment to analyze the situation. The core problem was that nobody on his team liked Waslager, or worse yet, trusted him. He was a self-serving loner and a politician. Odi knew that was exactly why the brass did like him. The question he should be asking, Odi realized, was: Why did they like Waslager on this mission?

He set that thought aside for later and latched onto a negotiation tactic. Since aggression was out, he would try to backpedal. "On the other hand, if I wait to shoot until the path of the second guard passes the first, I could take them both out—probably with a single shot if I use high-velocity rounds. Then we would only need—"

"Forget it, Carr," Potchak interrupted. "You're getting Waslager."

Chapter 2

Asgard Island, Chesapeake Bay

FBI DIRECTOR WILEY PROFFITT set his wineglass down a little too quickly. A drop of blood-red wine sloshed out onto the virgin white tablecloth, spreading with ominous portent. He was more nervous than he realized. He picked the glass back up and took another sip before locking his lover's gaze. "How would you like to be First Lady?"

"Of the United States?"

"Um hum." He grinned, feeling better already and enjoying the confused look that danced across Cassi Carr's amber eyes.

She instantly picked up on his mirth and mirrored it. "Does the Director of the FBI know something about Anna Beth Carver that the rest of us mortals have yet to learn?"

"Actually, it's Aaron Dish," he said deadpan.

She leaned toward him conspiratorially. "The First Lady is having an affair with the Vice President?"

Wiley shook his head. For six months he had kept his earthshaking secret, neither hinting at the future that awaited them nor alluding to his secret pact. It felt great to share the big news with Cassi at last. He decided to start with the background, give her excitement time to build. "Dish has a health condition. He won't be joining Carver on the reelection ticket."

"I see," Cassi said, clearly not believing him but apparently willing to play along. Her eyes twinkled. "So how does that make me First Lady?"

"It doesn't," he said, shaking his head as she feigned disappointment. "You're going to have to wait five years for that. In the meantime, it makes you Second Lady—come a year from January anyway."

Wiley saw a flash of confusion cross Cassi's brow. She appeared unsure if he was being goofy or serious. "Dish really is sick? Carver really asked you to join him on the ticket?"

"Yes and no," Wiley said. "Yes, Dish really is sick. And no, President Carver has not asked me to be his running mate—not yet. But he will."

"Oh, and why is that?" she asked.

Wiley leaned forward so that his lips were an inch from Cassi's ear. He paused there to inhale her sweet perfume before whispering the prophecy. She was wearing a new scent. "Because terrorism is going to top the American agenda."

She pulled back, sobered by his words. Her parents, after all, had died on 9/11. "You really are expecting an attack?"

"I am. You know all those homeland defense speeches I've been giving of late …?"

She nodded.

"They weren't just typical keep-'em-scared politics."

Cassi took a moment to chew on that one. He watched the gears spinning frantically behind her worried brow. "Maybe at one level they weren't," she finally said, thinking out loud. "But nonetheless, it is because of those speeches that you think Carver will put you on the ticket. They were what earned you the Antiterrorist Czar epithet."

Wiley raised his wine glass in a toast. "To your deductive powers."

Cassi returned the gesture, but he could see that her mind was still focused on working through the implications of his revelation. When she looked up at him wide-eyed, he knew that the other shoe had dropped.

"I'll be Second Lady?" she asked, her voice a choked whisper.

Wiley tried to smile but his lips would not move. He tried to nod but couldn't. Panic gripped him like a cold iron glove. He could not move his head.

As he struggled, Cassi continued, blissfully unaware. "Are you asking me to marry you?"

Wiley realized that a cold hand was clamped over his mouth. He endured a second of complete disorientation and then he understood. His conversation with Cassi had been a dream. The intruder in their bed, and the icy palm clamped over his mouth, were real.

Wiley's eyes bulged in horror as the dark shadow over him shifted in silence. A prickly lump filled his throat as a muscled arm drew back. Fully awake now, Wiley strained to pierce the darkness, searching for the glint of the knife that would complete the picture and end his life. All he saw were fuzzy shadows. Part of his mind latched onto the fact that Cassi was sleeping beside him. The need to warn and protect her surged within his chest, but the heavy quilt, the vise across his face and the fear in his heart pinned him like Christ to the cross.

As he prepared to buck and lunge, the bedside lamp clicked on and Wiley recognized the intruder's face. His tension drained. He should have guessed.

Wiley looked over at Cassi the instant the palm backed off of his mouth. She was sound asleep. At least she appeared to be …

"Halothane," his visitor supplied, reading Wiley's thoughts. "Like chloroform only safer."

"And more aromatic," Wiley mumbled to himself, recalling the perfume in his dream. Slowly, he returned his gaze to the midnight caller and voiced the obvious question with his eyes.

Stuart's answer was matter-of-fact. "We need to talk."

Stuart Slider was the invisible man. Compact, sinewy and average of face. Every time they met he struck Wiley as unexpectedly small. He also enjoyed the annoying ability to appear and disappear at will. Or so it often seemed. Wiley was beginning to detest that trait.

"What the devil are you doing here in the middle of the night?" Wiley asked. "Do you need another hole in your head?"

Wiley had been secretly working with Stuart for six months now, but this was the first time that Stuart had set foot on his Chesapeake Island home. Or, Wiley reflected, at least it was the first time that he knew about.

"We need to talk," Stuart repeated. "Unseen, uninterrupted and alone." He stood, canted his head toward the door, and said, "Let's go to your study. No sense giving Sleeping Beauty here bad dreams." Without waiting for a reply, Stuart reached out and extinguished the bedside lamp.

Wiley followed obediently, more out of curiosity than any feeling of subservience. They walked down the plushly carpeted hall to the room at the end. The massive oak door to his soundproofed study was ajar. An eerie glow leaked out into the hall from the 300-gallon aquarium within. The ghoulish atmosphere seemed to suit a halothane-assisted secret midnight rendezvous, so Wiley did not turn on the lights when they entered.

Sleepless fish cast darting shadows about the room as pale moonlight trickled in from the east. Wiley sought his favorite armchair, a black leather recliner. As he sat he discovered a steaming Starbucks cup waiting on the end table beside his right arm. Unbelievable, he thought. Stuart had never been to his island home before, and yet there the cup was—a low-fat latte no doubt—just what he wanted, right where he wanted it.

Setting the creepiness factor aside, the latte was both a thoughtful and insightful gesture. Yet its primary effect was to fan Wiley's flame. The invisible, unflappable Stuart Slider did not drink coffee or tea or cola. He did not smoke. He did not drink. Wiley was not entirely certain that he even slept. Yet he was always awake, alert, and controlled. What a bastard.

Wiley picked up the familiar cup, more irritated at himself for being weak than pleased to have his fix. It was still hot despite the trip from the mainland. Stuart must have planned even that detail in advance and packed a thermos. Meticulous and a bastard. Wiley took a sip, nodded a perfunctory thanks and gave his guest a get-on-with-it look.

"Is it true what I've heard about this room?" Stuart asked.

Despite the latte, Wiley wanted to go back to bed. He wanted Stuart to get to the point and then get out. But he knew from experience that playing along would get him there faster than resisting. "What have you heard?"

"I heard that the Secret Service turned your study into a fortress because you refused to have the Proffitt family's ancestral estate updated with the technology and security advances of the past hundred years."

Wiley rolled his eyes. "For an organization whose purpose is to protect national icons, the Secret Service has surprisingly little respect for history or tradition. I'm glad that I only had to deal with them that one time. They call it a panic room. It was a compromise." He reached out and picked up a large universal remote control off the coffee table. "Allow me to demonstrate. First, I'll type in the code to let the system know that this is not an emergency, and then ..." He held the square red button down with his thumb. After three seconds of constant pressure the door to the study swung shut. Hidden bolts scraped into place as titanium louvers began to lower over the bulletproof windows with a motorized hum. "Now we're safe from everything up to and including shoulder-fired missiles."

Stuart looked about the room. "You've even got a bar and a bathroom in your bunker. Not bad. What's through that door?" He pointed to the corner.

"It's just a closet."

"What about the cavalry?"

"If I had not told the system that this was a test, then the Hostage Rescue Team would automatically be summoned from Quantico by a beacon hidden in the roof." Wiley pressed and held the red square again. The lockdown procedure reversed.

Stuart nodded in appreciation and then assumed a contemplative expression.

In that dim light, with his black-clad form framed against the black leather couch, he appeared as little more than an intense set of eyes. The sight made Wiley think of an alligator in a tar pit. An alligator in a tar pit, he repeated to himself. Now there was the very definition of a Beltway lobbyist.

"I've come with news," Stuart said.

Wiley raised his eyebrows.

"I've resigned my job as executive director of the AADC to work full-time on your campaign. We decided that the time had come, now that things are underway."

Wiley did not want to talk about the American Association of Defense Contractors or the things that were now underway. In fact, he had specifically asked The Three Marks to keep him out of that loop. Thus far his only tactical contribution to things had been supplying them with a list of useful names. He hoped to keep it that way. Still, Wiley did not fail to notice that Stuart's "we" did not include him. "That's awfully generous of you. Did we agree to give you your old job back after the campaign?"

Wiley saw genuine emotion flash across Stuart's face in response to his words. That was a first. Despite playing poker for decades to hone exactly that expertise, however, Wiley could not tell which emotion Stuart had shown. Was it disappointment … or anger?

"I won't need my old job back after the campaign," Stuart replied.

"Oh? And why is that?"

"Because, after the campaign you are going to be vice president—and I am going to be your chief of staff."

Stuart's statement hit Wiley mid-sip and he choked, coughing and spraying latte over the front of his scarlet pajamas. Stuart did not bat an eye at his discomposure, and Wiley figured that the bastard probably had his timing planned. "Is that what you came here to tell me?" Wiley asked, mopping his chin with his sleeve. "Is that why you broke into my home in the middle of the night, drugged my girlfriend and dragged me out of bed—to talk about your career?"

"No."

"No?"

Stuart shook his head.

Wiley felt his stomach drop.

Chapter 3

Tafriz, Iran

AS THE WOMAN carried her daughter out, Dr. Ayden Archer wiped the sweat from his brow with a soiled rag. He still had a few clean ones left from last night's wash, but he wanted to save those for the kids. He ventured a peek into the alley before the door swung shut. The line stretched to the far end and disappeared around the corner. He knew it was time to make the mark.

"Please come in," he said in Farsi, holding open the door. The next woman in line bowed slightly, her baby cradled tight. Though she would not meet his gaze, Ayden knew that there was joy in her eyes.

"I'll be right back," he said, grabbing a bottle of iodine and stepping outside. He hated this next part of the daily ritual, but years of experience had taught him that it was the only way.

He walked east down the dusty alley, counting children as he went, offering silent smiles. It always amazed him how orderly they waited. He had not posted rules, yet the configuration never changed. Six days a week the sick children rested side-by-side along the northern wall in the thin ribbon of shade while the mothers stood across from them, baking beneath their chadors in the merciless Iranian sun. If only the women were allowed to rule the country, he mused.

When his count reached thirty children, he stopped. Five more hours at six children per hour would take him to eight o'clock. He crouched down before a two-year-old girl. Lily was her name if he remembered correctly. He said, "Hello Beautiful," and stroked her hot cheek with the back of his hand. He took the cap off the iodine and wet the tip of his index finger. He drew a semicircle on her forehead and added two dots. To him it was a smiley face, but if asked he would say it was a moon and two stars. Turning to the mother he said, "Your daughter will be the last patient of the day."

He proceeded to mark the remaining foreheads, also with a smiley face, but this time adding a third star for a nose. When he first began the practice he had numbered them, but he changed to the friendlier system when he found that no one tried to cheat. Mutual suffering bred solidarity when testosterone was not involved. As he drew he explained to the remaining mothers, "I will not be able to see your children today, but they will be first in line tomorrow. With these marks you need not come early, so let your children rest. I will see the first at eight o'clock." Ayden knew that this was like the seat belt announcement on airplanes

—everybody present already knew the rules—but he repeated it anyway. By his reckoning, little ceremonies kept you sane.

As he walked back toward the entrance to his one-room one-man free clinic, Ayden felt a chill despite the heat. The day was soon approaching when he would not draw smiley faces with noses. His funds were dwindling. After five wonderful, horrible years, his clinic would have to close.

He felt tears begin to well.

Hope had knocked on his apartment door a few months ago. He had looked through the peephole to see an exceptionally charismatic face beaming from a bush of long tousled hair and punctuated with whirlpool eyes. "Word of your good works has spread far, my friend," the man who introduced himself as Arvin had confided. "If you had the resources, the backing shall we say, would you be willing to do more?"

Looking at the stoic figures now standing patiently in the sun with sick children clinging to their legs, Ayden knew that he would do anything to keep his clinic afloat. Anything. At this point, Arvin's generous offer appeared to be his best and only chance, but he had not encountered the opportunity to earn that support. Not yet. Stepping back into his clinic, he prayed that someday soon he would …

Chapter 4

Airborne over the Turkish-Iranian Border

"WE'RE THIRTY MINUTES FROM TARGET," the pilot's voice blared over Odi's headset as the C-141 began banking north. "Potchak has just confirmed that the mission is a go."

Odi looked around. Only Waslager had heard the announcement. As deputy team leader, he was the only other team member tuned in to both the group and command frequencies. Waslager, deputy team leader, that really fried his bacon. Odi had to struggle not to show his anger to his team. They were tighter than sardines and packed just right, but Potchak had stuffed one more fish into the can. A bad one. Something was rotten in Denmark.

Odi slid his headset switch to enable the whole team to hear his voice and pushed Waslager from his mind. "Listen up. Final reminders for anyone whose thoughts are still stuck on last night's girl. That turn you just felt was our little birdie rounding the southern tip of the Turkish-Iranian border. We're flying north along that border now.

"We hit the wind in approximately twenty-eight minutes. Your chutes are set to deploy automatically at fifteen thousand, but keep your eyes on your altimeter; those puppies have been known to malfunction. You got that, O'Brian? Don't go spacing out on me."

"Aye, aye, sir. While we're on the subject, could you remind me: do I pull the black tab or the silver one?"

"Just don't pull the little fleshy one and you'll be fine.

"Anyhow, gentlemen, once you've checked your canopy, begin steering west. I'll be the first out the door and will be wearing my infrared flasher. Line up on me. Remember, the longer we ride the wind, the shorter we have to hump. And don't forget to drop your pack when you hit a hundred feet. If we've navigated right, the terrain will be bald as Mitch's head, so we won't need to worry about getting hung up in trees. If you do forget, your fifth point of contact will be a dozen grenades. Take my word for it, gentlemen. That would be enough to ruin anybody's day.

"Once you're safely on the ground, confirm with your codename designator and 'OK.' No real names. No chatter. We'll regroup on my position. Understood?"

"Understood," came six voices. Waslager just nodded.

"Good. Stick to the plan, and we'll be back in Incirlik for breakfast. Any questions, now's the time."

"What's the target?" Flint asked, mindlessly shaving the hair on his forearm with the oiled blade of his Ka-Bar knife.

Odi smiled, pleased to be able to share this information with his team at last. "In a move reflective of their devious, scum-sucking nature, our buddies in al-Qaeda have disguised a training camp as a hospital." The men all jeered—except Waslager. What was it about that guy? Odi wondered. He wished Cassi were there. His twin sister would have Waslager's number in no time. She could always read people—at least when it wasn't personal, he thought with a shrug. When it was personal, Cassi was blind as Oedipus.

"Camp al-Qaeda is located on the outskirts of what was a mining town back when there was copper in them thar hills. Now Tafriz is little more than a farming village, although it's still got more infrastructure than anyplace else around."

"How similar is the camp to the complex we've been training with?" O'Brian interrupted to ask.

"It's virtually identical. Everything will be just as we practiced. The size and layout are like our mock-ups. Their construction is cinderblock instead of wood, but that's inconsequential to your grenades.

"You'll each fire ten modified M441 grenades at ten-second intervals, spacing them at ten meters each. I know you guys could pull this off in half that time, but we've slowed it down to allow cooler heads to deal with the shit that tends to happen. So remember not to rush. You hear that, Derek. No rushing. I would hate to ruin a flawless mission with a casualty from friendly fire.

"Waslager will take out the roving sentry on the western apex of his route. That will be the starting gun, at which point I'll drop the sentry on the central door and you'll all commence your runs.

"Each team will use its first salvo to take out their building's main entrance and the floor directly above. That will seal the building up and minimize any chance for Omar to escape—not that those unlucky few who do wake up are going to have time for more than a rushed Allahu Akbar, but we absolutely cannot have any witnesses, so we're not taking any chances.

"Waslager and I will provide covering fire as you move in case anyone shows his toweled head, although I seriously doubt that there will be any need.

"If nobody screws the pooch, we should be reassembled at the fallback position just three minutes after go. Once everyone is there, I'll signal for pickup. Then we've got a two-click sprint to the other side of a nearby hill, during which a Blackhawk will skim in from the Turkish border for rapid extraction."

As Odi finished, Adam pointed over his shoulder to the jump door lights. Odi looked up to see that the pilot had changed the indicator from red to yellow. He felt the belly fish begin to thrash. "Everyone on your feet."

Chapter 5

Asgard Island, Chesapeake Bay

"YOU'RE NOT HERE to talk about your career?" Wiley asked again, trying to maintain a neutral voice.

"No."

"Then why the devil are you here, Stuart?"

"As I said, we need to talk—unseen, uninterrupted and alone. There's something I need to know. Something we need to discuss."

"Out with it then," Wiley commanded. He had had enough.

Stuart nodded once. "Very well. Are you in love with Cassi?"

"Pardon me?"

"Are you ... in love ... with Cassi?"

"I am."

Stuart gave another single solemn nod. "You started seeing Cassi six months ago, shortly after we ... began our collaboration. I didn't say anything at the time. Perhaps that was a mistake. Frankly, based on her history and yours, I didn't think it would last."

Stuart's matter-of-fact monotone bothered Wiley, but he kept his mouth shut. The sooner his campaign manager cum chief of staff got to the point, the sooner Wiley could go back to bed.

"I have to admit that this is the first move you've made that I simply do not understand." Stuart paused. He appeared to be weighing how to clarify his statement but then shook his head in surrender. "We are just twelve months out from the election now. Carver's team finalized the running mate shortlist today. It's down to three names." Stuart held up his fist, palm toward Wiley. "Jefferson Wallace." He raised one finger. "Arthur Hayes." He raised a second. "And you." He gave Wiley a gun barrel point instead of raising the third finger. Then he opened his hand for a shake. "Congratulations, Director Proffitt. You are officially in play."

Wiley smiled despite himself. He shifted his grip on the latte and took the Washington insider's cool hand, amazed that Stuart had acquired such a secret. A shortlist like that would only be known to the president and his top two or three advisers.

After they shook, Stuart continued. "Meanwhile, it's no secret that Mills will top the other ticket. And I'm ninety-five percent sure that he will select either Anders or Metcalf to run as his VP." Stuart gave an open-palmed shrug and settled back in his seat, implying with tone and demeanor that Wiley could easily fill in the rest.

Wiley drew a blank, but he was not about to let the smug SOB get one up on him. Not here. Not in his own house. He took a long sip of latte, inhaling deeply to maximize the punch of the nutty brew. He tried to think. Anders was the two-term Governor of Georgia and Metcalf was a four-term Florida Senator. Both had solid backgrounds, but neither eclipsed his two terms in Congress, four years in the Virginia governor's mansion and current service as Director of the FBI. Both Anders and Metcalf were married … Was that it? Wiley wondered. Did Stuart want him engaged? No problem. Why had he gone through all the drama to ask? Stuart was hardly the sentimental type, but then everyone has his quirks. Apparently, marriage was the one thing besides power that was sacred to the man. Wiley found that nice to know, and tucked it away for future reference.

Having discovered his reptilian campaign manager's soft underbelly, Wiley changed his tactics. He wanted the satisfaction of hearing Stuart vocalize his feelings. "Go on, Mr. Slider."

Stuart gave him a direct, icy stare. "Anders is six-foot-four, Metcalf six-five … and Cassi is six-one. You, however, are a relatively puny five-ten-and-a-half—in heels. You cannot run on a power platform while appearing substantially shorter than everyone else in the game. Try it and you will become a caricature, a political Chihuahua, a late-night joke."

Hearing those words, Wiley felt as though he had been sucker punched.

Stuart did not give him time to breathe. "I can deal with Anders and Metcalf. You won't ever have to stand right next to either of them, although I'm sure their campaign managers will try shamelessly. But Cassi … there's no way to avoid that money shot. The comparative picture of you will have longer legs than hers. 'Which Proffitt wears the pants?' 'Who's really on top?' 'Wittle Wiley Wannabe.' The tabloid headlines will be your deathblows.

"It all comes down to this, Director. Either you forget about Cassi Carr, or you forget about the Oval Office. Those are the only two options." Stuart folded his hands across his chest.

But there weren't two options. They both knew that.

Wiley closed his eyes. He would have to leave Cassi.

Stuart said, "I'll give you until Monday to do it."

When Wiley finally opened his eyes, he found that Stuart had vanished. For once he appreciated the man's magical talent.

Checking over his shoulder more than once, Wiley walked over to the wall safe, spun through the combination and withdrew a small box. It was robin's-egg blue and approximately two inches cubed. He untied the white silk ribbon, tilted back the lid and stared. It was beautiful, he thought, as unique and flawless as the woman for whom it was intended.

Wiley had found the perfect engagement ring a month ago. For weeks he had enjoyed the anticipation of a spontaneous proposal. Holding that joyous secret in the palm of his hand made him feel like a kid on Christmas morning. In fact, he had cradled it hopefully in his pocket on six separate occasions, ready to take a knee. But the moment had never been just right. His latest plan was to propose at dinner tomorrow night. He had picked the perfect restaurant and even dropped a few hints. Tomorrow was now out of the question, of course. As was the next five years …

For a fleeting second, Wiley wondered what Stuart would have done if he had already proposed. Then he remembered that Stuart had violated Cassi that very night. He had drugged her in her sleep just so that he could deliver his news with panache. Wiley decided not to pursue that line of thought any further.

He closed the Tiffany lid. It gave a final, fatal clap. He re-tied the white bow and secured the box in the safe. Turning his back on one future in favor of another, he staggered across the study to the adjacent bath … and threw up.

Chapter 6

Alexandria, Virginia

"WHAT DO WE HAVE?" Cassi asked, trying to focus on the job at hand while still reeling from a shock of her own.

Officer Foster looked down at his notebook and smiled. "We got us some fans of The King." He cleared his throat. "Elvis Aaron Adams got laid-off from the canning plant today. Came home to find his wife —Priscilla, I kid you not—in bed with another man. Now Elvis is threatening to kill them both with his shotgun. For about ten minutes he was screaming his head off and throwing things, during which the widow who lives next door called us. Then things went silent."

"Have any shots been fired?" Cassi asked, remembering that this was the second time she had negotiated with a man named Elvis and wondering if that could be pure coincidence.

"Not a one."

She nodded a couple of times as she processed the situation and then said, "Tell me about Elvis." On any other day, she would have enjoyed the humor inherent in that sentence. Today she was not feeling the least bit whimsical. Officer Foster seemed to sense her mood.

"He's Caucasian, forty-three years old. Five-foot-six. Two years ago when his driver's license was issued he weighed one-forty-five."

"Does he have a record?"

"Not even a parking ticket."

"Do they have children?"

"The neighbor says no. She says it's just the two of them living there."

"How long ago did he return home?"

"About forty minutes."

Cassi nodded as her processor kicked into overdrive. Forty minutes was a lot of cooling off time. It was also plenty of time to get worked up into a murderous frenzy or plunged down into a suicidal slump. Neither option looked good for Priscilla or her paramour. She decided to see how astute Foster was.

"Is Elvis a drinker?"

"The widow said yes, but when I pressed her on what that meant she admitted that it's just a few beers on a Friday night."

Cassi said, "Nice work," and pulled out her cell phone. "What's his number?"

"They don't have a landline and both their cell phones are switched off."

She cringed. That was bad news. "Thank you, Foster. I've got it from here."

Per regulations, Cassi knew that she should remain out of shotgun range. That would mean negotiating through a bullhorn. Whereas some of her colleagues preferred the authority of that technique, she used it only as a last resort or if drugs were involved. Her preference was always to try to connect with the perpetrator on a personal level. Without a phone, that meant she had to get close, close enough to Elvis for each of them to read the inflections in the other's speaking voice.

She had a decision to make. If her analysis was correct, Elvis was highly unlikely to shoot first and ask questions later. Yesterday that would have been good enough for Cassi. Today she was not sure. She had awakened at Wiley's feeling funny. Then she had watched with teary eyes as a white urine strip grew a blue stripe. If she risked her life today, she would be risking two.

A silenced scream emanating from the house made up her mind. She would ignore the regulation. Cassi ran to the front door and stood shielded by the frame. "Good afternoon, Elvis," she said in a loud but friendly tone. "My name's Cassandra Carr, Cassi for short. I'm here to help you. Would you please step toward the door so we can talk?" Pretty please with sugar on top.

Elvis did not offer an immediate reply. That was to be expected. He needed a minute to make up his mind. Cassi tried to focus on something else to keep from getting nervous while she waited, like whistling her way through a graveyard. It was not difficult. Her personal life had the sad, magnetic draw of the best soap operas. The irony of the latest development leapt to mind. During a recent interview on *PoliTalk*, Wiley had used the fallibility of condoms to make allegorical reference to homeland defenses—Was ninety-nine percent efficacy good enough?—unaware that one of his own little soldiers had recently crossed enemy lines. If this were not so serious she would find it funny.

How would he react, she wondered? Ex Would he be thrilled or horrified? Angry or overjoyed? Would he spurn her or propose? Surely he would propose now, Cassi figured. That was what she wanted, more than anything. But did she want it this way? The answer came immediately, soft but solid like an elephant appearing beneath a magician's wand. No. No, she did not want to get Wiley this way.

The opening of a window on the second floor shook her back to the present. She stepped back for a better view and simultaneously plotted her course of retreat. She would beat feet at the first sign of a shotgun barrel. Unfortunately, she realized with a sinking heart, there was no suitable shelter anywhere close—just a thin lamp pole and a couple of scraggly bushes. The corner of the house was her only safe bet, and that was twenty feet away. The prudent thing for her to do would be to run there immediately.

Elvis preempted her bolt. "You can help by leaving, all of you."

Cassi paused. It was a good sign that Elvis did not open with a threat. To her that indicated that violence was not the first thing on his mind. Furthermore, his request showed that he was anxious to escape. She replied, "I'd be happy to leave. So would all my friends."

Elvis did not react immediately. He was waiting for her conditions. Cassi wanted him to accept the fact that there would be conditions, so she waited for him to ask. As she stood there on the concrete stoop beside the small dilapidated house, the focus of twenty sets of battle-ready eyes and one hostage taker, Cassi's thoughts again drifted to her own condition.

She could not tell Wiley about the baby. Not now. Not until he proposed. And that meant that she could not tell her employer either. They were one and the same. Standing there in the shadow of a crime she wanted to feel good about her decision. She wanted to rest easy knowing that she had made it for the right reasons. But she did not. She felt guilty. She felt guilty because deep inside she was glad for the excuse.

Cassi was a leading contender to replace Jack Higgins at the end of the year when he retired as head of the FBI negotiations unit. Ever since he had announced his intentions she had tried not to court disappointment by thinking about it too much, but that was impossible. Running the negotiations unit was her dream job. And regardless of the psychological defenses she was trying to construct, she knew that she would be crushed if she did not get it.

Cassi did a quick tally of the math. She would be in her fourth month when Higgins' successor was announced. Since this was her first child, she could probably keep her condition hidden until then if she dressed loosely enough. She was not completely comfortable with the ethics of springing the news the same month she got the promotion, but then there was no chance that they would give her the promotion if they knew she was pregnant, and that was not fair either. Was it?

"Okay. Then go on. Leave."

Cassi snapped back into the negotiation at the sound of Elvis's strained voice. "It's not quite that simple, Elvis. First, I need you to throw me your gun."

"Don't treat me like a fool."

"I don't think you're a fool, Elvis. I think you're a good man in a bad situation. You've been betrayed. I know you're a decent guy. I know you don't have a record. I just want to keep you from acting foolishly in a moment of anger. I don't want you to do anything that would ruin the rest of your life. Let's face it. If she betrayed you, she's not worth it."

"Will you let me go?"

"I will."

"I can just get in my car and drive away and you won't try to stop me?"

"Not if you didn't hurt anybody. Not if you leave the gun behind. You didn't hurt anyone, did you, Elvis?"

"Nothing but a couple of slaps."

"Slaps they deserved."

"Damn right."

"Then you're a free man. Go ahead. Leave the unworthy bitch. Start a new life. A better life. Or wait for her to come crawling back once she realizes what she's lost. Your choice."

Again there was silence. Cassi was worried by the lack of sound coming from the house. Normally, the two hostages would be making some noise, trying to connect with the police lest they be forgotten once the bullets started to fly. She hoped that they were just scared into silence.

What would she do if Wiley did not propose soon? Cassi wondered. With the baby growing inside her, she could not wait too long. He would resent the position she had put him in even more if he found himself inextricably trapped. She knew from her counseling days that such a situation could open an emotional rift between them that would drain the intimacy from the rest of their lives.

"I'm coming out," Elvis said, his voice just behind the door.

"Smart move, Elvis. Smart move. Just do me a favor. As you walk to your car, keep your hands in plain sight."

Chapter 7

Tafriz, Iran

"THIS IS RABBIT ONE with an emergency transmission for Brer Bear," Odi said, focusing on keeping his voice down. He knew that sound would carry dangerously well through the inky Iranian night.

"Roger, Rabbit One. Patching you through to Brer Bear."

Odi hated working through the secure satellite switchboard. It cost too much precious time. He tapped a nervous foot and looked over at Adam. His best friend added to the tension by pointing to the luminous dial of his commando watch.

Odi nodded and mouthed, "I know."

Potchak has stressed that he would measure the success of their mission as much by their ability to extricate undetected as by their tactical success. He had drummed deniability into Odi's head. "Deniability tops your scorecard. Deniability is what counts. Deniability, deniability, deniability."

Odi got the message. He had to make the demolition of the buildings look like an accident, like the tragic explosion of the unstable ordnance secreted within. As mission commander, he knew that the composition of their rocket-propelled grenades had been modified with that conclusion in mind. Their equipment, their uniforms, everything was either an Asian knockoff or Soviet surplus. All of it was readily available throughout the Middle East. Including his bloody phone.

"Brer Bear here, Rabbit One. Go ahead."

Odi flashed a thumbs-up to Adam and the other six members of the assault team as they sat on their packs spitting chew and trying to look more bored than scared.

"We have a situation. The Briar Patch appears legit. Repeat, the Briar Patch appears legit. There are no sentries present, and we just observed an ambulance." His teammates all rolled their eyes at Odi's grandiose description of the donkey cart. He just shrugged his shoulders sheepishly and looked away. "It brought in a farm boy who had just lost a foot. Looked like he had stepped on a mine. He was met by medics and rushed inside. I recommend that we abort pending further intel."

"Negative on the abort, Rabbit One. You are to proceed as planned. Intel is confirmed. Don't fall for the window dressing. Skullduggery like that is what has kept this training camp operational for years."

Odi knew that Potchak was a hard ass, but he had not expected pushback. Command usually favored live input from the field over anonymous intel reports. "Sir, I'm prepared to do the recon myself, right now, alone." As he spoke, Adam snapped his fingers to get Odi's attention and then met his eye with an are-you-crazy stare. Odi turned his back. "Won't take me more than ten—"

"Negative, Rabbit One," Potchak broke in. "For one, you don't have ten minutes to throw away. You need to make it to the extraction site before first light. Secondly, I refuse to give those bastards a hostage. I'm not going to watch them cut off your head on the evening news while I try to explain that you had a hunch that the thick and exhaustive report compiled by the Middle-East desk was one-hundred-eighty degrees off the mark."

"It won't come to that, sir. I'll order my team to proceed as planned with or without me at," Odi looked at his watch, "oh-three-hundred. Just give me those ten minutes."

"You sound dead set on checking this out, Rabbit One."

"Time doesn't wash off innocent blood, sir."

Odi waited impatiently through a pregnant pause.

"Pass the phone to Rabbit Two."

Odi smiled and handed Waslager the phone as he remembered the Chinese proverb to beware of what you wish for.

As Waslager listened to the commander, Odi's team drew around, their habitually stoic faces contorted with concerned looks. "What are you planning to do?" O'Brian asked.

Odi had been in and out of the shit with these guys more times than any of them could count. With Waslager otherwise occupied, there was no need for Odi to dilute his words. "Before we propel ninety-six grenades through those cinder walls, I want to be damn sure that they're landing on terrorist wannabes, rather than sick children's heads."

The six nodded once in unison as Odi continued. "I think this is one of those situations where intelligence reported what it was asked to report, kind of like Iraqi WMD. The source of the intel was probably some Iranian kid who would make up anything for a Benjamin. And knowing how things have been going down at recruiting, that report was probably analyzed by some Pentagon conscript with three weeks on the job." Odi decided not to mention Potchak's lack of surprise at his mention of the hospital's operational status.

He removed his BDU top and untucked his tee shirt as he spoke, altering his silhouette so that it would not appear like a soldier's. He laid aside his Chinese M4 and slipped his Beretta into the small of his back. "Hopefully I'm wrong. But taking out a hospital is not something I care to live with for the rest of my life."

Odi finished the simple transformation by untucking his pant legs from his boots. Then he removed two flash-bang grenades from his pack and slid them into the pockets of his pants. "If you hear one of these, that means I'm in the shit. You are not to wait for me, and you are certainly not to come in after me. You are to move ahead immediately with the original plan." Odi met each man's eye and waited for a confirming nod.

"I don't mean to sound too dramatic. All I am going to do is take a casual perimeter walk around the two flanking buildings. I'll look for telltales of a terrorist training camp, anything military, from boot marks to bullet casings to concealed cameras or guards. Without the two sentries to worry about, Waslager can cover me through his sniper scope instead. That way we'll be right back on plan if I am challenged."

"With the exception of you hauling ass in the opposite direction, I hope," Flint added.

"Nothing I like better," Odi replied, flashing a brilliant smile. "If I don't see anything incongruent with a hospital, I'll pop my head through the central building's main door and—"

Waslager cut Odi off by clearing his gravelly throat. "Listen up," he said, in a voice that was dangerously loud. "Commander Potchak has just relieved Agent Carr. I am now Rabbit One. So get off your asses and lock and load. We're hot in sixty seconds."

Everyone turned to look at Odi.

Chapter 8

The Horus Club, Washington, D.C.

THE DEAF WAITER raised an eyebrow as Wiley polished off his Scotch.

Wiley nodded and another drink was on the way. When Stuart arrived, it would appear to be his first.

Wiley had come to their rendezvous early. He needed to decompress. Although his heart and mind were working full time on his campaign, he was still the Director of the FBI. He had another full plate.

To manage the juggling act, Wiley had hinted to his deputy director that he was not planning to stay in office very long. When the time came, he would be happy to reward Carl's diligence and loyalty by recommending his indispensable right-hand man as his clear and obvious successor. Given Wiley's close relationship with the immensely re-electable President, Carl was tripping all over himself to pick up Wiley's slack. Actually, Wiley knew that Carl slyly farmed out most of the additional load. That was not difficult. The FBI had five major departments plus a dozen or so adjunct offices and committees, each headed by a savvy bureaucrat eager to rise still higher.

The scheme was working, but Wiley still lived beneath an enormous load of stress. Stuart contributed to it. Although Stuart technically worked for Wiley, it usually felt to Wiley like it was the other way around. His campaign manager always seemed to be the one holding trump. Plus, Stuart radiated an intellectual superiority that made him awkward to command. Wiley could make requests of Stuart, but he had never managed to dictate.

Still, tonight he would try again. He had chosen the ultra-exclusive Horus Club so that he would enjoy the home-court advantage. In his heart he knew that tactical advantages would gain him nothing, but it was his habit to try. The analyst in him knew that whatever tack he chose, whatever methodology he employed, all Stuart had to do to get his way was to pull out a recording.

He might do exactly that, Wiley thought. Like a communist dictator parading his armaments for all to see. But probably not. There was no point in reminding a person of something he could never forget, and Stuart did nothing without a point.

Wiley recalled the scene as it had played out six months earlier. The AADC's lavish yacht. The three billionaire CEOs. The suspense. The arrogance. The grace. No, he would never forget their first meeting …

~ ~ ~

"It must have hurt," the fat Texan scoffed, "losing your reelection bid."

Wiley kept his eyes steady, his face void of emotion. "I landed on my feet."

"Indeed you did. Director of the FBI—that's not a bad consolation prize. Still, handing the keys to the governor's mansion over to that snot-nosed tree-hugger had to hurt."

"What's your point, Mark?"

"Relax," Mark Abrams said, his jowls bouncing grotesquely as he patted Wiley on the shoulder. "We're on your side. In fact, we invited you here to make you an offer."

Rather than ask, Wiley wedged his cigar in his mouth and raised his chin. He did not like being led down the primrose path, toyed with, or manipulated—even by billionaires. Let them get on with it.

Abrams looked him dead in the eye and locked his gaze. Without looking away he said, "How would you like to be president?"

"Of the United States?" Wiley blurted back, sending his Cohiba to the teak decking.

Mark Abrams, the head of Armed Services Industrial Supply and arguably the most powerful of the three CEOs present, flashed him a tight-lipped smile but did not say a word.

Wiley cringed inside, berating himself for his sophomoric slip even as he struggled to regain his composure. He shifted his gaze to Mark Rollins. Then to Mark Drake. And finally back to Mark Abrams. "What do I have to do?" he asked.

"Commit," Abrams replied without pause.

Wiley knew that he had asked the right question. Abrams' tone was stern but he was secretly pleased. Wiley could tell. He sensed the relief of a man who had just drawn to an inside straight.

"Irrevocably," Rollins added. "You need to commit irrevocably—both upfront and blind—that you will see the campaign through to the end."

In silence, Wiley studied Rollins, CEO of the gigantic defense conglomerate that bore his name. Rollins was the tallest of his three hosts, and like Drake was thinner than Abrams by half. None of them were puppy dogs, but Wiley sensed a genuine cruel streak in Rollins. His pampered features were pleasant enough, but the man had evil in his eyes.

Mark Drake jumped into the conversational void. "The problem is this, Mr. Director. Even with all the technological advances coming from companies like ours, there is still only one means available for untelling something." He lowered his voice. "A most primitive means."

"So before you reveal your plans, I have to sign a blank check," Wiley summarized.

"Precisely." The three Marks spoke as one.

Their proposition was clearly take-it-or-leave-it but Wiley was not sure he wanted to know what either taking it or leaving it would mean. He shifted positions surreptitiously to scan the floor behind the bar for a bucket of wet concrete. Drake and his fellow defense contractors clearly were not referring to money when they spoke of a check. Wiley wished they were.

"That check has just three words on it," Abrams added, picking up on Wiley's thoughts. "And we need to hear you say them, aloud and with conviction, before we proceed."

Wiley raised his eyebrows in query.

The Three Marks—Abrams, Drake and Rollins—clarified slowly and in unison while Stuart looked on in satisfied silence. "Whatever ... it ... takes."

Wiley took a deep breath. He thought of the White House—east and west wings—and of traveling on Air Force One. He pictured the red carpets, the gala dinners and the saluting Marines. He thought of the power. He thought about what it would be like to literally be able to summon anybody in the world to spend the weekend with him at Camp David. The offer The Three Marks made might come with a price, but Wiley doubted that there was a man alive who could resist signing that check.

As he repeated the three fateful words, never in a million years would he have guessed that the first victim of that pledge would be Cassi ...

~ ~ ~

"You're looking pale," Stuart said, jerking Wiley back from memory lane. The man had slid into the armchair across from him without Wiley's notice.

Wiley turned his eyes to meet his campaign manager's, but did not comment.

"What could be so urgent," Stuart continued, "that it could not wait until tomorrow and yet was not important enough for you to think of when we met this morning?"

Wiley hardly considered Stuart's midnight invasion of his home a meeting, but he needed a congenial atmosphere, so he let that discrepancy pass. He leaned back and tented his fingers contemplatively before he spoke hoping to get Stuart to do the same. "I want you to reconsider your position on Cassi."

Stuart did mirror his posture, leaning further back into the burgundy leather to digest the request, but he made no verbal comment.

"I'll grant you that her height is a problem," Wiley continued, "but I think it's less of a liability than going into this race single would be. I don't have to tell you that the public wants a family man in the Oval Office."

Stuart seemed to ponder the words for a moment, and then he leaned back into the conversation. "Historically, you're right. But times are changing. More and more voters are single. The divorce rate has topped fifty percent. The average American voter is personally aware of the tradeoff between work and family. Most female executives have had to sacrifice family for their careers. With the pump thus primed, it's easy to argue that twenty-first century America needs the undivided attention of its president. Your bachelor status could actually be an advantage. There's certainly plenty of room for spin."

As Stuart snatched his best arrow from the air and snapped it over his knee, Wiley felt despair creeping back into the crevices of his soul where seconds before he had nurtured hope. But he was not ready to fold, not yet. "You might be right, but you might be wrong. Surely you will agree that it would be better if we didn't have to take the chance?"

Stuart nodded once, but remained silent. He wanted more.

"I want you to meet Cassi. Get a feel for her. I think she could add a lot to the campaign. She is a psychologist and a negotiator. She is bright as the sun and she glows under pressure. Women will admire her. Men will respect her. Even kids will like her. She's gutsy—practically a hero. Talk about potential for spin ..."

Stuart shook his head. "Her image isn't nearly as important as what she does to your image. You're the one who needs the votes, not her. She diminishes you when you need to appear larger than life."

"And I'm saying that, despite the height, I look better next to her. See for yourself. Join us for brunch tomorrow."

Rather than dismissing the suggestion outright as Wiley had feared, Stuart stared at him for a minute in silence. Wiley could practically see the wheels spinning behind those dark eyes. He felt a surge of hope. Time passed. The fireplace crackled and a log fell. Finally, Stuart spoke up.

"All right. I'll take a look. I'll meet you for brunch with an open mind. But if I say no after seeing the two of you together, she's gone. No rebuttal. No tears. Agreed?"

Wiley sensed that this tenuous capitulation was the best deal he would get. He feared that it would not be enough. Once again, he was facing a point of no return. He gave a parting glance to the life he used to know and then he said it. "Agreed."

Chapter 9

Alexandria, Virginia

CASSI CONTINUED CHANNELING her frustration into sit-ups even though she was well past a hundred. At least trimmer abs would help to camouflage her condition, she thought, grasping for consolation. It looked like she was going to need it. She paused to wipe the sweat from her brow and ended up shaking her head in frustration. Despite her instincts all signaling to the contrary, Wiley had let her down again.

She had been positive that last night was finally going to be the night. Absolutely certain. The timing would have been poetic—coming the very day she learned that she was pregnant. Her intuition wasn't just the wishful thinking of a desperate woman's romantic mind, she told herself. All the signs had been there. He had reserved a prime table at La Chancery, an elegant, intimate restaurant with exquisite French cuisine. He had confirmed her availability not once but three times. And he had shown interest in what she was planning to wear. Those were objective indicators, right? Plus, she had seen him fumbling in his left pants pocket a dozen times of late, as though fondling a little treasure. A ring, perhaps? God, she hated to catch herself reading into everything like a pathetic schoolgirl. She wiped more sweat from her brow. She had already been in her gown when he called to cancel. "I'm sorry, Hon," was all he had said for an apology. "It's urgent business."

He had not even congratulated her on her successful negotiation with Elvis.

Gripping the receiver with flustered fingers, she had wanted to scream, to yell, "You promised!" But instead, she gracefully offered to cook him a gourmet brunch in the morning. By her reckoning, he had paused a second too long before accepting. But he had said yes. Thus far, she had taken everything Wiley had told her at face value. If he had said no, she admitted to herself with not a little shame, she would have spent the night searching for the other woman.

Although their discussion was twelve hours ago, her resentment still burned. She knew that it was the job and not Wiley that was to blame. She understood full well that resentment was a negative, destructive emotion. But she could not help it. She was a six-foot-one, north-of-thirty woman with a PhD and a badge. Single men who could cope with and complement that combination were rare as honest politicians.

Cassi looked at her watch and berated herself. As a result of her neurosis, he was just fifteen minutes away and she was all worked up and sweaty. Jumping to her feet she caught sight of her panting form in the mirror. It struck her that a good brunch could be even more intimate than a candle-lit dinner—given the right music, a cozy atmosphere and the proper state of undress.

She ran through the shower and then applied a dusting of makeup and a dab of perfume before slipping back into the cream silk pajamas she had been wearing an hour earlier. The lingerie was not particularly revealing in the classic sense, but it hugged her in all the right places. She had found that there was something about the way flesh bounced under silk that attracted men's eyes like a fishing lure. Twirling before the mirror she decided to go for broke and leave all but one of the buttons undone. She might as well show off her flat stomach while she could. As an afterthought, she grabbed the bottoms from a pair of pajamas that Wiley had left in her closet but never worn. Then she ran to the kitchen. She would suggest that he change.

To her own astonishment, Cassi had the candles burning and Norah Jones singing before the doorbell rang. It was amazing what you could accomplish given the proper motivation. She tossed her hair to give it extra body, checked the lie of her top and opened the door with a sultry "Good morning."

Wiley was not alone.

"Good morning yourself," Wiley said, kissing her cheek. "Cassi, allow me to introduce Stuart."

The third wheel held out his hand. "Stuart Slider."

Stuart struck Cassi as either a European gymnast or a wrestler, but given that he was with Wiley, she knew that he was neither. He wore black Bally loafers, black jeans and a black sweater that hugged his compact but muscular frame like the label on a bottle of Guinness. She recognized his casual appearance as being anything but. That man had given serious thought to his wardrobe, carefully crafting his image.

She disliked him at first sight.

Cassi shielded herself with the door as they entered so that she could discreetly button her top. When she turned back around after locking the door, Stuart held out a magnum bottle of Veuve Clicquot Yellow Label with a manicured hand while giving her a look that made her think that he could see through silk.

"Why, thank you," she said. "How considerate."

"Stuart is an old friend passing through town," Wiley said. "He called last night, but as you know, I was too busy to catch up. So I took the liberty of inviting him along this morning. I hope you don't mind?" As he finished, he apparently noted her pajamas for the first time and added, "I suppose I should have called."

"No problem," she said. "We're casual here. As you can see, I'm running a bit behind. If you'll grab some champagne flutes from the cupboard and set one more place, I'll run to the bedroom to change."

~ ~ ~

Wiley and Stuart did most of the talking during brunch. Cassi had the oddest feeling throughout that they were putting on a show, although for the life of her she could not fathom why. Adding to the strange atmosphere, she could not escape the feeling that Stuart was studying her—not as a sex object, but more as a rival. She never caught him in the act, and when he addressed her their conversation was pleasant enough, but for some reason she still felt the urge to smack those rimless silver spectacles off his taut face. That was not fair of her, she knew. It was Wiley who had done the inviting, so if she was going to be mad at anyone it should be him. But even for a psychologist, logic was not always emotion's master. She wondered if the emotional roller-coaster she had been riding these past twelve hours was the pregnancy hormones kicking in. If so, she was looking at eight long months.

The other odd thing about Stuart was that he kept taking pictures of her with Wiley. He explained it away as his hobby, his passion really was how he put it. But Cassi was not convinced. Stuart did not strike her as a passionate man.

Cassi made an effort to take her mind off analysis and back to the conversation at hand, but it was hopeless. The topics they selected were at once too deep for Sunday brunch and yet too shallow for her mood. What did she think about foreign troop deployment? Was she a defender of the second amendment? When they shifted to a woman's right to choose, she would have choked on the champagne had she not been just pretending to sip. Rather than answer she excused herself to urgent business in the kitchen.

Since she could not suddenly begin refusing alcohol without provoking the obvious question, Cassi had decided to fake it. At the table she raised the glass to her lips without actually drinking. Then she would surreptitiously soak up half her flute with her napkin and exchange the napkin for a fresh one each time she went to the kitchen. She was pleased with herself for devising such a clever ruse.

As she returned to the table with warm cinnamon rolls, Stuart turned to watch her approach and said, "I've heard of lofts, of course, but I've never actually been in one before. How long have you lived here?"

"I moved in right after graduate school, so I guess that makes it six years."

Stuart nodded. "I figured that you had been here a while. I notice that you've been watching the kids playing at the daycare center across the street. I get the impression from the emotions crossing your face that you know some of them. Am I right?"

Stuart was an observant one, Cassi thought. Perhaps he really was an avid photographer. She nodded abstractly to buy herself some time. She did not feel like revealing anything about herself to this guy. On the other hand, she did not want the conversation to lapse back into politics either. After pondering her options for a moment, she decided to risk exposing a bit of her soul to Stuart in order to see what Wiley's reaction would be to her discussion of kids. "Actually, I do know them. The red-haired one with boots is David. He likes pretending to be tough although he's really a coward. The girl with the pink glasses on the swing next to him is Rita. She falls down a lot but never cries. The little cutie in the yellow coat hanging from the jungle gym is Sammy. He's the clown. He uses humor to hide the insecurity he feels because he still wets his pants. The girl by herself on the bench is Sara. She's not interested in their games. It's because she's smarter than the others but the ironic result is that she feels inadequate." Cassi saw Wiley looking at her with wide eyes and stopped.

"How do you know them?" he asked.

She shrugged. "They're out there every weekend. Sometimes I sit and watch them as I drink my morning tea."

"So how did you learn their names?" Stuart asked.

"Oh, those aren't their real names—just the ones I use."

"Cassi was a child psychologist before joining the Behavioral Sciences Unit," Wiley added.

Cassi faked a sip of champagne to occupy her mouth. When her former career came up, people usually wanted to know why she switched. It was a story she did not like to tell. Stuart seemed to sense that, and did not ask. Instead, he inclined his head toward the daycare center and said, "It's kind of sad if you think about it. They should be spending their weekends with their parents."

It was a much more sensitive comment than she would have expected from him, Cassi thought. Perhaps there was a heart beneath Stuart Slider's dark veneer. As she contemplated that unexpected twist, he refilled their champagne flutes.

"Speaking of morning tea," she said, "I'll go brew some." Standing, she followed Stuart's gaze. He was looking at her hand as she reached for her flute and nodding to himself almost imperceptibly. He looked up suddenly to catch her expression. She felt the lining drop out of her stomach as their eyes locked. The flute slipped from her grasp but Cassi instantly forgot it. Stuart knew.

Chapter 10

Tafriz, Iran

FEELING HUMILIATED and infuriated, Odi watched from behind a sandy knoll as his team disappeared into the inky Iranian night. For a second he considered tracking their progress further with the assistance of his Unertl sniper scope, but the thought of having to look in from the outside like a wannabe voyeur just rubbed salt in his wounds. He shook his head. *What had Potchak gained by relieving him of command?* He asked himself for the dozenth time. A lousy ten minutes? Ten minutes that might have made the difference between eliminating terrorists and murdering kids? Was it extreme urgency that drove Potchak's severe reaction? Or was Odi missing something? He could not get his head around the incredible stupidity required to make a decision like that. It just did not compute. Potchak was a hard-ass, but he was no fool.

Odi had no idea why Potchak had been so quick to strip him of power. Aside from the occasional disagreement—like the one where Potchak prohibited him from informing his men about their mission—their relationship had been smooth enough. It was not a particularly warm relationship, but then The Bulldog was not a warm-and-fuzzy kind of guy. Again, Odi came to the conclusion that there were forces at work about which he had no knowledge. He hoped that once the dust settled, one of those forces would get him off the hook. As it was, Odi did not know what to hope for as he listened for the gunshot that would begin the questionable attack. His was a damned-if-you're-right, damned-if-you're-wrong situation. Either innocents were about to die, or his career was over.

Odi also worried about his team. They were doing as demanded, following orders. That was rigidly expected, of course. In fact, command repeatedly drilled in that very response in the course of some of the world's most grueling military training. But every man still had to take responsibility for his own actions, and they knew that. The guilt resultant from pointlessly killing scores of innocents could not later be ordered away—not when they had been fairly warned.

As Odi pondered that, his earphone cracked to life. Waslager's oily voice said, "All teams report."

"Red team's a go." "White team's a go." "Blue team's a go." Derek, Adam and Flint replied in sequence.

Odi ripped off his headset and threw it to the ground. He told himself that he did not want to hear anything that might later legally jeopardize his men—like them conspiring to frag Waslager for example —but in fact, he simply could not stand to listen. If the hospital did turn out to be legitimate and an investigation ensued, he would tell internal affairs that he removed his headset for tactical reasons, to better detect potential threats among the ambient noise.

It began.

The explosions reverberated like a giant's footfalls across the sleepy land. Every ten seconds there was another six-point bang as the next salvo of explosive grenades brought the suspect buildings closer to the ground. Just like clockwork. He was proud of their precision if not their mission.

Odi watched plumes of dusty smoke billow toward the inky sky, reflecting starlight back in a ghastly dance. Air that only moments ago was arid and crisp was now filled with an ominous cordite stench. He waited for the sounds of tortured screams and imploring pleas, but nothing rose above the deafening echoes of so many grenades. So much the better, he thought.

He began counting down salvos, working backward with the knowledge that there would be ten. Ten ... nine ... eight ... At two he found himself rolling across the ground with a sharp pain pulsing lightning through his left shoulder. One way or another, he had been hit. Was it shrapnel? A bullet? Divine intervention? He twisted his neck and shoulder, provoking more pain as he tried to get a look at the mysterious wound. All he could see was blood pumping through the sleeve of his shirt.

He strained to compress the wound with his chin while struggling to remove his belt with his one working hand. If only he hadn't taken his radio off, he cursed himself. Stupid, stupid, stupid. With effort he got his belt noosed around his left arm and a heartbeat later he cinched it down half an inch above the pulsing stream. He saw the flow ebb to a trickle, but it did not stop. Gritting his teeth, he cinched it further, ratcheting down until the pain was almost too much to bear. Finally, the bleeding stopped. His makeshift tourniquet would be safe for a minute or two. He only needed something to keep him conscious until his team returned. Then Adam could apply a pressure bandage and achieve hemostasis without cutting off the blood flow to his hand. He hoped he would still have enough juice in his system to run. The guys would give him grief for the rest of his career if they had to carry him to the extraction site.

Odi began laughing at the irony despite the intermittent jolts of searing pain. He could not help it. Realizing that his boisterous laughter was both dangerous and an indication of the onset of shock, he forced himself to stop. That was when he noticed the eerie silence. It would only be a few seconds now.

He pictured his teammates emerging like demons from the dark and smoke and strained to see them. He anticipated the wry smiles and jibes he would get when they saw his wound. "Can't we leave you alone for a minute, Carr?" "We should have hired a babysitter." "I think he's really a Marine."

No one came.

That was strange, Odi thought. He wondered if the loss of blood had warped his sense of time. He checked his stopwatch. Four minutes and ten seconds had passed since the first salvo. They were seventy seconds overdue.

Odi waited another fifteen seconds, but no one appeared. "The radio," Odi said, cursing himself again. He looked over to the left where he had thrown down his headset and saw a broken mess. Whatever had hit his arm had obviously demolished his headset too. The sight made him think of the magic Kennedy bullet.

Glad to have a backup, he patted his breast pocket. It was empty. Empty? Then he remembered Waslager commandeering his sat phone. "Great. Just great."

Odi was seriously worried now. If grenades were still exploding or bullets were still whizzing he would understand the delay. They would signal that his team had encountered unexpected resistance. But all was quiet. Wounded or not, Odi knew that he had to investigate. Someone might need his help.

Getting to his feet, he wondered how long it would take for local law enforcement to arrive. The complex enjoyed a peripheral location and the village itself was remote, but capture was not the only concern. He replayed the Commander's incessant order that they not allow themselves to be identified.

The protest emanating from his left fingers became unbearable. He eased the pressure off his improvised tourniquet and craned his neck to observe the sight of the wound. Crimson began to gurgle forth. He was still losing arterial blood.

He ripped his compression bandage from his pack and slapped it down directly atop his pulsing wound. The position was awkward and neck-cramping, but he still managed to hold the wad of gauze in place with his chin. Wishing he had a spent bullet to bite he cinched his belt down directly over the wound. Judging by the pain, the shrapnel was still inside. He screamed "Waslager, you bastard!" and then made for the rubble.

Odi needed only a minute to find the first man. O'Brian. He lay in a crumpled mass and was already covered with coarse gray soot. Although Odi could not see the entry wound, the expansive pool of blood beneath his body indicated that he had been hit in the head or neck. Odi felt his own pain give way to a flood of rage. Then the implications registered and he felt a chill of fear followed by a wave of guilt. Hospitals did not employ snipers.

He had been wrong.

His doubt had diminished the team's strength by nearly fifteen percent—easily enough to cost O'Brian his life.

Percolating with self-loathing, Odi began cursing himself but stopped abruptly. There was no time for that selfish sentiment now. He had to investigate. He had to see if anyone from his team was still alive.

He knew that investigating would become ever more dangerous as seconds passed and smoke cleared. Visibility was still next to nothing with the smoke blocking out the stars, but that would change with dawn's first rays. Come daybreak he would be as visible as a pimple on the prom queen's nose.

As he mentally mapped out the most efficient way to canvass the complex, he realized that there was a quicker way. He muttered a fast "Forgive me, brother," as he rolled O'Brian over to remove his radio. The sight that met his eyes was striking enough to give him pause. O'Brian's headset had also been hit. It was useless.

As alarm bells went off in his mind, Odi wondered if the al-Qaeda sniper had some new high-tech equipment that allowed him to home in on a target using radio waves. He would report that possibility—if he ever got home.

Without giving further thought to his own safety, Odi set off following a parallel trail of tracks. Twenty yards from O'Brian, Odi found Adam. His best friend also had a savage head wound, but miraculously he was still alive. Adam was just lying there, stoically silent, looking wide-eyed up at the sky as though searching for distant stars. He grew a feeble grin and groaned, "The weasel," when he caught sight of Odi.

Odi was afraid to touch his friend, afraid to make his condition worse, but as his eyes focused he realized that worse was not possible. Extreme adrenaline was the only thing keeping Adam alive.

"Swear, Odi. Swear you'll—"Adam sucked in a long, ragged breath "—get the weasel for me."

"I swear," Odi vowed perfunctorily, bending to cradle Adam's head.

"Don't let him get away," Adam gasped. Then he died.

As Odi stared down at his friend, a fetid stew of surprises swirled around his faltering mind. His sudden loss of command, his shoulder wound, the mysterious death of his friends, the solicited vow of revenge—everything collided as it tried to congeal. Something about this mission was terribly wrong.

As he tried to grasp the conclusion that was hovering at the outskirts of his conscious mind, Odi realized that his head was spinning from more than just the confluence of radical events. His vision was now blurred and the ground seemed unstable. He turned his head and strained to focus on his left shoulder. His belt had fallen to his elbow. His bandage had slipped. Before he could react his world turned gray, and then, slowly, silently, it faded to black.

Chapter 11

FBI Headquarters, Washington, D.C.

WILEY DUCKED into his private bath and closed the door to his office. He bent over the sink and splashed cold water on his face. After a couple of good dousings he straightened up and studied his reflection in the mirror. "You can do this," he said aloud. "This is nothing but a warm-up pitch. When you're in the Oval Office, you will be called upon to send thousands of the nation's sons and daughters into battles where they will lose lives and limbs, serenity and sanity, innocence and affluence. Keep your focus on the big picture. This is nothing."

He patted his face with a thick white towel embroidered with the seal of the FBI. After placing it back on the rack, he took a step back and adjusted the knot in his emerald tie, using more force than was necessary. Stuart had made it clear as they left yesterday's brunch, accenting his speech with pictures: Cassi had to go. Wiley did not agree with his campaign manager's judgment, but he accepted the wisdom of deferring to it. Stuart was the pro. He was ice-cold and impartial. Like him or not, Wiley could not deny that the invisible man was good.

For a second or two, Wiley had toyed with the thought of defying Stuart, but he knew rebellion was out of the question. If Stuart became convinced that Wiley's campaign was a loser, he could probably still convince The Three Marks to back one of the other two contenders. Wiley had to avoid that at all costs. Someday soon his campaign would cross a mutual point of no return, and then he would tell Stuart off. At least that was what Wiley told himself this morning.

The intercom on his desk beeped and his assistant's squeaky soprano shattered the silence. "Agent Carr is here, Director."

Wiley zipped over to his desk and keyed his response, noting that the knot in his throat was now as tight as the one on his tie. "Send her in, Kate."

Cassi was beaming as she walked through the door, causing Wiley to swallow hard. She really could brighten a room. She paused halfway to his desk to look around. "You know I've never been inside this office before. It looks bigger than my loft. What do you have back there?" She nodded to the door he had just come through. "The secret files, or a private bath?"

"Have a seat," Wiley said, gesturing to the chair before his desk rather than the suite of armchairs by the window to the left. He knew that it was best to be quick and clean in situations like this. Delivering bad news was like ripping off a Band-Aid.

A cloud dimmed Cassi's radiant face, but she complied without comment, sitting with her hands in her lap.

"Cassi, I—"

The intercom cut Wiley off. "Excuse me, Director. I've got Commander Potchak here at my desk. He says it's urgent."

Wiley gave Cassi an apologetic shrug. "Send him in."

As the Commander of the Counterterrorism Response Team marched into the office, Wiley could not help picturing General Patton's bull terrier. There was just something about Potchak's dull eyes and long flat nose that always invoked that particular canine image. Potchak, usually unflappable as a manhole cover, did a double take when his eyes landed on Cassi.

She stood and said, "I'll leave you two."

Wiley nodded but Potchak said, "Actually, it's expedient to have you here, Agent Carr. This concerns you as well." Potchak reached out to hold the back of Cassi's chair. She sat back down and he took a seat himself.

Wiley felt his mouth go dry. He had been dreading the breakup moment, but now that it had arrived he was anxious to plow through. Furthermore, Potchak's news was bound to be bad. Urgent news always was. He wanted to skip any further pleasantries and get this over with. "What's on your mind, Commander?"

Potchak looked uncharacteristically uncomfortable, but he nodded once and commenced. "Counterterrorism Response Team Echo was ambushed last night during a reconnaissance mission in Iran."

Wiley nodded, wearing his best poker face and keeping his gaze on Potchak to avoid Cassi's eye. "Do we know who ambushed them?"

"The details are still coming in, but since they were investigating a potential al-Qaeda training camp, our working assumption is that it was terrorists." Potchak paused as Wiley and Cassi both frowned in silence, then he pivoted to face Cassi with guilt writ large on his bellicose face. "As you must know, Echo's Team Leader was your brother, Odysseus, Agent Carr."

Cassi nodded.

"I'm afraid there were no survivors."

Chapter 12

Alexandria, Virginia

EVEN AS SHE STOOD teary-eyed before the cold oak casket and scores of familiar mourners, Cassi could not convince her psyche that she had been forever cleaved from her twin. She took a deep breath. The aromas of white lilies and freshly turned earth took her tumbling back to her parents' funeral. It seemed at once like only yesterday and yet so long ago. As then, today felt neither real nor right.

A tremble began to overtake her. She closed her eyes for a moment to calm herself before attempting to speak. She held her hand to her belly and thought of the circle of life. Odi's essence would live on—in Wiley's child.

"My brother—" Cassi choked up. She paused and readjusted her grip on the edges of the Lucite lectern. She tried to look over the crowd and block everyone out, but a small group to the far left kept drawing her eye. She wondered who they were. She thought she knew all of Odi's friends. They were not with the bomb technicians or the counterterrorism crowd. She began to take a mental tally of the other groups affected by Odi's life and the identity of the mysterious guests came to her in a flash. She smiled.

"My brother—" Cassi paused again, but this time it was for a different reason. Suddenly, her speech did not feel right. Odi had lived his life unscripted. His funeral was no place to start. She reached out and tore up the sheet of ivory paper. "I can't do it," she said. "You already know all this." She shook the shreds of paper and then let them flutter to the ground. "You know Odi was nationally renowned as a bomb technician, and considered the best in the FBI. You know he switched to the FBI's elite Counterterrorism Response Team after our parents died on Flight Ninety-Three because he felt that a reactionary job was not enough anymore. What most of you do not know is the remarkable man behind those accomplishments. I think I owe it to Odi in this final hour to tear down his modest façade.

"The real Odysseus Carr is well represented by the five mourners off to my left." Cassi gestured with her arm as she looked out to a crowd of confused faces and a subset of approving nods. "Odi was not truly a bomb technician or a professional at counterterrorist assault—any more than he was a dishwasher or a cook. Those were just functions he performed. In his heart, Odi was a scientist, a peacemaker, a humanitarian." Cassi saw more confused faces, more approving nods.

"My brother invented Divinylpolystyrene, a compound more commonly known by its trade name: ArmoWrap." Cassi saw about half the mourners' faces light up with shock and surprise. "For those of you who don't have experience disarming bombs, ArmoWrap is a quick-setting Styrofoam-like spray that encases pipe bombs in a highly adhesive shock-absorbing shield. Sixty seconds after it is sprayed onto an improvised explosive device, ArmoWrap will have cut its destructive power by an average of seventy-three percent. Every Humvee and police car operating beneath the American and NATO flags now carries a can of ArmoWrap in the trunk beside the spare, and Odi's invention is already credited with saving hundreds of lives.

"Odi developed ArmoWrap when he was just twenty-three and still working at Johns Hopkins on his first PhD. Although he never spoke of them—when was the last time one of you referred to Odi as Dr. Carr—he had PhDs in chemistry and biomolecular engineering. He could have retired on his royalty checks to a yacht or a beach to live the rest of his life in luxury and peace. But being the scholar that he was Odi chose to heed the lesson of his hero Alfred Nobel instead. He donated the ArmoWrap patent to the International Association for the Assistance of Victims of Landmines. Then he one-upped Nobel by insisting that the IAAVL keep his name out of the news. The Board of the IAAVL kept that promise, but obviously they did not forget. They are here today." Cassi nodded toward the small group as a murmur broke out in the crowd.

"I'm glad that my parents got to see Odi's triumph while they were still alive. They were very proud of him for what he did. To be honest, my reaction at the time could best be described as confused. I would never have given up a life of luxury in lieu of a dangerous job and government pay the way he did. Even though he had a twin, Odi truly was unique.

"Eventually I did figure it out, although it took me years. You see, despite his contrary outward appearance, Odi was an extraordinarily peaceful man.

"I see your skeptical faces. You're wondering if grief has somehow affected my mind. The key to understanding Odi was this: He was aggressively peaceful. Wanton violence caused him such moral outrage that he felt compelled to fight back. He did not fight for glory or medals or even the adrenaline rush. He fought for peace. Like Mother Teresa who condemned herself to living among the wretched of Calcutta, Odi condemned himself to a violent life so that others could live in peace. And he was very good at what he did.

"I will miss my brother in ways that I can only begin to express. I know that you will too."

She abandoned the lectern to stand beside the casket. Others closed in around her in a show of support. After a moment of silence, she placed a single red rose on the polished oak. "I love you, brother."

Cassi wanted to walk into the crowd and fall into Wiley's arms, but such a public display was out of the question. Oddly enough, Odi's death had pulled them apart more than it had drawn them together. Perhaps since Wiley was the ultimate man in charge of that fateful mission, she held him vaguely responsible for Odi's death. Likewise he probably felt a little guilty.

Cassi heard a chorus of distant beeps as she backed away from Odi's grave. She looked up to see a few of her HRT colleagues gathering around Jack to talk in familiar animation. Inappropriate though it might be, she felt a strong urge to throw herself back into work.

Cassi accepted a few *Beautiful eulogies* and a dozen encouraging arm pats, hugs and nods as she made her way toward the dispersing hostage-rescue team. "Jack, hold on. What's up?"

Her boss stopped the beeline he was making toward his car and turned. "We've got an incident, Cassi. Nothing for you to worry about."

"But I want to worry. I think the distraction would be the best thing for me."

"Not today," Jack said, compassion in his eyes. "You go home and get some rest. Really, that's the best thing for you. Trust me."

Cassi had half a mind to just hop in her Toyota and follow them wherever they went, but she had parked two hundred yards away by the chapel. She would never catch up. She was wearing a long dress and, on this rare occasion, heels.

So what was she going to do then? Cassi wondered. She had not thought past the funeral. Wiley had told her that he had to spend the day in the office. The last thing she wanted to do was watch the minimum-wage ditch diggers plant Odi's casket in the ground. Nor was she in the mood for more *I'll miss hims* and *I'm sorrys* and condoling pats on the back. She could call Quantico to find out where the current crisis was, but that would probably be a waste of time. The crime scene was likely a helicopter ride away. She decided to take Jack's advice and go home.

Cassi arrived at her block twenty minutes later to find a police barricade and crowded sidewalks. She felt a lump growing in her throat as she pulled out her gold shield and asked the beat cop what was up.

"We got an anonymous tip that a man was trying to break into the art restoration workshop over the daycare center. Dispatch sent two units, code two, but the perp saw them coming in time to take hostages. He's got a bomb and a couple of kids."

Chapter 13

Orumiyeh, Iran

ODI HEARD SCREAMS and moans and strange voices muttering all around him. He could not understand a word and he could not see a thing. Panic tried to seize him but he fought its grip. Was he in hell? He tried to think of the last thing he could remember. His mind was operating excruciatingly slowly, as though his synapses were sopped in molasses. He remembered the ground-shaking explosions ... and being hit in the shoulder ... and then he found Adam. He had a very clear recollection of the look in Adam's eyes as he died in his arms ... and then ... nothing else. That was all he could remember.

Odi began to scream. He did not know why. There in the dark with those voices all around it was a primordial reflex. He screamed and gasped, gasped and screamed. Finally, he felt a demon claw at his arm until the voices faded away.

~ ~ ~

Odi heard, "Wake up," and felt something moving around his head and face. "Wake up. You have to leave the hospital right away." Now someone was shaking his arm. Had it all been a dream? He wondered. Oh please, let Adam be alive.

Odi slowly opened his eyes. The light was painful, although once his eyes adjusted he saw that the room was relatively dim. Looking off to the side as he lay on his back, he saw an old rolling partition to the left of his bed, a white sheet strung in a chrome frame. It had grown gray and frayed with service and age. As he studied it a face moved in above his and Odi thought for a minute that he had been rescued by Tom Selleck—Tom Selleck holding a big wad of dirty gauze.

The face towering above him was kind and intelligent and aged about forty years—with curly dark hair, blue eyes and a thick mustache. The only thing he needed to look like "Magnum, P.I." was a Tigers baseball cap. Although Odi did not have a mustache, he too was often compared to Selleck. They shared a tall athletic frame, lively eyes and mischievous grin. For a freaky second Odi thought that maybe he was looking in the mirror. Maybe he had been asleep for years and Cassi had asked the nurse not to shave his mustache. She had always encouraged him to grow one. That ridiculous notion vanished as quickly as it appeared. The face above him was not that similar.

It dawned on Odi that the wad of dirty gauze Tom was holding had just come from around his face.

"I know you've got a lot of questions," his new friend whispered in English, "but there's no time for them now. I dyed the skin of your hands with iodine and have been keeping your white face hidden, but yesterday you began screaming in English. Word leaked quickly about an American's presence. They will be coming soon. We have to get you out." Tom withdrew a pair of sandals and a well-worn dishdasha from a cellophane bag. "Put these on. And hurry."

As Odi exchanged his hospital gown for the traditional Arab robe, he whispered, "Are you American?"

"Californian, born and raised. Now hurry up."

A lightning bolt shot through Odi's left shoulder as he pushed his left arm through. He winced without crying out. He had forgotten about his wound. Judging by the acute pain, he would not be forgetting again anytime soon.

"Ah, I almost forgot," Tom said, withdrawing a syringe from his doctor's bag.

Odi endured a flash of panic before realizing the obvious. If Tom intended to give him a lethal injection, he would have done so already.

Tom injected a clear serum above the wound.

Odi felt a warm sensation and the throbbing began to fade away. "Thanks."

Tom ignored the words of appreciation and ushered him toward the door near the right foot of Odi's bed. Odi glanced over the partition before ducking through the doorway. He had been recuperating at the far end of a long hospital ward. There must have been two dozen other beds lined up in the same room with barely enough space for a thin nurse to squeeze through between them. All were occupied. Odi had obviously been enjoying what amounted to the corner suite.

In the stairwell, Tom handed him a keffiyeh and without question Odi draped it around his head, being careful to cover all his wavy brown hair. He did not know who they were running from, but given the circumstances he was willing to accept Tom's judgment that he did not want to meet them.

They exited the hospital three stories down at ground level and walked quickly along a busy street that stank of stale urine. They turned left halfway down the block into a dusty alley and then zigzagged through a series of short and narrow backstreets for about fifteen minutes. Odi could not tell if his savior had a specific destination in mind or if he was just trying to put a labyrinth of distance between them and the hospital. He decided not to ask.

After about fifteen minutes of dusty twists and turns, Tom became particularly watchful again. Odi observed him checking over his shoulder frequently and even scanning the rooftops. A minute later they entered an apartment building. It was old but solid. Judging by the condition of the other buildings they had passed, Odi decided that this was probably one of the most desirable addresses around. In the US it would have been condemned.

Tom led him up a dim staircase littered with trash. Odi tried to ignore the olfactory assault from rotting garbage and harsh tobacco smoke. On the fifth floor they entered a hallway. A single bare bulb of not more than fifteen watts cast dim light on four hodgepodge doors. Tom stopped before one that had the number 53 stenciled on it with a ballpoint pen. He withdrew two long, double-sided keys from a deep pocket and turned each in sequence through several revolutions to unlock the door. They had not spoken since leaving the hospital and Tom did not break the silence now. He just gestured for Odi to step inside. Odi said a silent prayer and took a leap of faith.

Once Tom had shut and locked the heavy door from within, he put his hands on his knees and let out a long breath. "I've lived here for five years now, but this is the first time I have ever had to do anything like that. I hope it was the last." He held out a sweaty hand. "Ayden Archer."

Odi gave him as firm a pump as he could muster. He was winded from the walk, and really wanted to sit down. "Odi Carr. I suspect that I'm very glad to meet you. And I certainly don't want to put you to any more trouble. If you have a phone, I'll call—" Odi hesitated. He was not sure how much he should reveal.

"A friendly embassy? Your unit?"

Odi nodded without clarifying. Actually, he planned to call his sister first. He knew that Cassi would be worried sick.

"I have something to show you before you do that," Ayden said. "But first, we should get some food and drink into you. Your brain needs food. Please, come into the kitchen."

Odi realized that he was in fact ravenous. "Thank you. That would be great. You are very kind and I certainly appreciate your trouble."

They moved down a short hall past what Odi assumed was the bath to a modest kitchen with a balcony. "It's probably a good idea for you to stay inside," Ayden said, canting his head toward the balcony door. "Although you must know more about hiding out than I. The only thing I know about cloak-and-dagger stuff comes from movies and books." He let out a little nervous laugh.

Odi sat on a stool watching Ayden fill a teapot from a Brita filtering jug and then use a wooden match to ignite the stove's gas burner with a shaking hand. Once Ayden was satisfied with the level of flame, he pulled a second stool for himself from beneath the breakfast table and took a seat across from Odi. His hands were still fidgeting with the yellow box of matches.

"Are we in danger here?" Odi asked.

Ayden brought his hands together and looked at Odi with twitchy eyes. "Yes."

Chapter 14

PoliTalk Studio, Washington, D.C.

WILEY STUDIED the image in the studio mirror as he perfected the knot of his silver tie. Appearances were not particularly important to him on a personal level, but professionally he knew never to underestimate the impact of the right look. He liked what he saw. The Hickey Freeman suit fit him like a cashmere glove, accenting the breadth of his shoulders, while power radiated from his ice-blue eyes. He knew that those beamers would serve him well in the coming months as he sought to captivate, romance and cajole. Today his favorite blue shirt augmented their flair while his tie amplified their twinkle.

"Two minutes, Director Proffitt."

Wiley looked over his left shoulder and practiced his most charming gaze as "Thank you, Maxine" rolled off his tongue like warm butterscotch over a sundae. He immediately turned his head back to the mirror but watched her reaction from the corner of his eye. Bingo. It did not matter how old they were, Wiley J. Proffitt could always make the ladies blush.

~ ~ ~

"We're back with our special Terror-Strikes edition of *PoliTalk*," Jim Fitzpatrick's Irish face greeted the television crowd. "Joining us now is *PoliTalk* regular Wiley Proffitt, Director of the FBI. Good morning, Wiley."

"Good morning, Jim."

"Two weeks ago you were on our show discussing terrorism and you predicted that our number was almost up. As everyone in America now knows, one week later it was. Last Saturday, for the first time since

9/11, Americans were victims of multiple simultaneous terrorist attacks. The offices of the US Chamber of Commerce were bombed in Belgium. An American school—empty thank God—was bombed in France. And a hospital was bombed in Iran while an American delegation was present. Of the twelve Americans killed, eight were members of your Bureau, all victims of the hospital attack. Your prediction appears startlingly accurate, especially when viewed against the background of America's intelligence failures. Do you care to comment?"

"To be honest, Jim, I've been doing everything in my power to prove myself wrong. I have one of the few jobs around that rewards you for doing exactly that." Wiley looked down for a moment as if to compose himself. "The loss of those eight agents was, well, personal. The FBI is one big family, and now eight of our sons have been slaughtered. I knew several of them personally. Those fine young men were serving our country on a fact-finding mission, covertly inspecting areas we had identified as potential al-Qaeda bases. Obviously, our assumption was correct. As you and your viewers know, that particular site was ostensibly a hospital. In truth, it was an al-Qaeda training camp. Unfortunately, the terrorists somehow learned that my men were coming and they lay in wait.

"The FBI's takeaway lesson is to anticipate similar future leaks.

"The lesson for the American people is harsher still.

"Considering the calculated nature of that attack, it should now be clear to every red-blooded American that our enemies are willing to murder dozens of their own compatriots and even destroy their own infrastructure if in so doing they can also terminate a few American lives. The conventional rules of engagement no longer apply. These terrorists are not trying to win, per se. They just want us to lose."

Fitzpatrick began to comment but Wiley held up his hand. "I should add that I hope the members of the Congressional Budgeting Committee are paying attention to that particular fact. We are living in a new paradigm now. If we aim to continue the American way of life, Congress is going to have to release the purse strings. I know that the cost of protection may seem daunting at first, but I can assure you that defense is a bargain compared to the alternative. Prevention only costs an ounce."

"Reading between the lines, I take it that you're expecting more attacks?" Jim asked.

Wiley nodded somberly. "You take it right."

"Anytime soon?"

"Every-time soon, Jim. We need to remain constantly vigilant and keep striving to become ever better prepared. Tragic though they were, last week's attacks were a far cry from 9/11. By my reckoning, that trifecta was just a practice swing."

Fitzpatrick seemed taken aback. "Let me make sure that I'm getting this right," he said. "In your professional opinion al-Qaeda is just warming up?"

"I am afraid so."

Fitzpatrick let the air go silent for a moment to emphasize the gravity of that revelation. "I suspect that if you get it right again, the Press will start spelling your last name P-r-o-p-h-e-t."

Wiley struggled to keep his face as stern as a battleship prow while Fitzpatrick's comment sent a surge of elation flooding through his veins. Tomorrow, Proffitt or Prophet? would garner many a headline. He said, "Let's hope I've got it wrong."

Fitzpatrick nodded and looked down at his notes. "Now that you've warmed up, let me hit you with one from left field. There is a rumor circulating around the Beltway that Dish may not be on the reelection ticket. Another correlative rumor says that President Carver is considering you for the Vice Presidential slot. Care to comment?"

"Jim, you're the Washington expert, so let me ask you this. Would you be a wealthier man if you had a nickel for every cup of coffee drunk within the Beltway, or a penny for each of Washington's whispered rumors?"

Fitzpatrick smiled, treating the home audience to a thick helping of his Irish charm. "You've got me there, but tell me this: would the job of Vice President appeal to you?"

Wiley turned toward the active camera. "I've already got my dream job. I'm honored, thrilled and blissfully happy to be defending America from the helm of the FBI." He stopped there, even though he had more to say. He had hinted during the booking interview that Fitzpatrick should probe deeply on this issue.

Fitzpatrick's eyes twinkled. "I'm happy for you, Director, but please, tell me this: Would you accept the Vice Presidency if President Carver were to offer it?"

"It's not Carver's to offer. Only the citizens of America can do that."

"With Carver's sixty-six percent approval rating, most experts would assert that there's no difference."

"No one likes dealing with hypotheticals, Jim."

Fitzpatrick grunted knowingly.

"—But then no one likes slippery answers either," Wiley continued. "So let me say this. I will answer any call to service that the people of this great nation care to place."

~ ~ ~

Wiley found Stuart waiting for him back in the *PoliTalk* dressing room. Usually the sight of his campaign manager bristled the hairs on the back of Wiley's neck. But not today. Today, Stuart actually seemed pleased.

"He called you a prophet. That's gold in itself, Wiley, political gold. But then he went on to link you with the Vice Presidency. Congratulations. I feel like I should write him a check."

Riding the adrenaline high and hearing Stuart's words, Wiley felt a tide of courage swell within his breast. He made the split-second decision to ride it. "Thank you. Actually, I've got a little announcement of my own."

As Stuart's features snapped back to their black-granite norm, Wiley felt a wave of trepidation, but he did not falter. He knew that if he did not stand up to Stuart now, he probably never would. Since Stuart was forcing Wiley to make him his chief of staff, the least Wiley could do was teach Stuart his place. He plowed on. "I have decided to stick with Cassi. If you still think she's a liability, you will just have to find a way to make her an asset. Understood?"

Wiley thought he saw a shadow pass behind Stuart's already dark eyes, but his expression did not change. He just nodded.

Wiley continued to hold Stuart's gaze for another moment. His poker instincts were kicking in. As absurd as it seemed, he was getting the distinct impression that Stuart had not only seen this little rebellion coming, but was also somehow prepared …

Chapter 15

Alexandria, Virginia

"YOU'VE GOT to let me have this one, Jack," Cassi said, lowering her voice. "It's too important to leave to Ralph."

Jack pursed his lips, trying to ignore the last part of her comment, she supposed. "You above all people should understand that you're in no condition to be negotiating today, Cassi. Ralph will do just fine."

Cassi wanted to scream but that would just make her boss's point. She slipped into negotiations mode instead. "Forget about politics for a minute. What if they were your kids? What if that was Bobby and Becky up there? Can you honestly tell me that you would want Ralph as your point man?"

Jack shrugged. "Ralph has four times your experience, Cassi."

"Yeah, and despite that he's got triple my failure rate."

"I gave the case to Ralph. I can't take it away now—especially in order to give it to you. Go get some rest. By the time you wake up, everything will be fine."

Cassi knew that Jack was doing his best to be objective and kind. She could also sense that his magnanimity was wearing thin. She knew she should back off now and do as he asked, but the image of two little caskets pushed her on. She decided to try a different tack. "How about a deal then? I get this negotiation; Ralph gets the promotion. Just let me save those kids."

She saw surprise cross Jack's face and a flash of something else, but he just shook his head. "The job is neither yours to barter, nor mine to give away."

Cassi shot her last arrow. "Women have a thirty-percent advantage over men in negotiations where child hostages are involved. You've got a female negotiator on the scene asking to do the job. If you say no and this goes south, some ambitious reporter is going to dig that statistic up. Your judgment will be called into question, both in private with the parents of those children, and in public as the mayor conducts damage control."

Jack gave her a long icy stare. Cassi understood in that moment that she had done their relationship irreparable damage. But for better or worse, she was too spent emotionally to care.

Finally he said, "Don't screw up."

~ ~ ~

As the other agents disappeared down the stairs, Cassi looked at the photos ripped from the children's locker doors. The hostages' real names were Masha and Zeke, not even close to the Sara and Sammy she had guessed. She hoped that was not a bad omen. With two of her kids hanging in the balance and her own unborn child along for the ride, this was going to be the most important negotiation of her life.

Cassi took a visual sweep of the empty brick hallway and then brought her focus to rest on the metal door. She closed her eyes, let out a slow breath and willed her mind to drift down through the clouds into The Zone. The Zone was a mental room with a chessboard floor and black walls. This was where she studied her opponent and calculated her moves. Once in The Zone she blocked out every sound, every smell, every extraneous tick and tock. She only allowed the players in The Zone—just she, the perp and the hostages. The hostages. She hated to see those two small pieces on the board. It took a real son of a bitch to use children as pawns.

Back in the real world, Cassi pressed herself against the brick wall of the corridor. She spoke loudly enough to be heard through the metal door but in a tone that was still conversational and polite. "Good morning. It's just the negotiator, as you requested. Everyone else is gone. I've got two cups of coffee here, in case you would like one. My name's Cassandra, by the way. Cassi for short. What can I call you?"

"What you can call me is a fucking helicopter if you don't want to lose these two kids."

He was talking, Cassi thought. That was a good sign. She began her mental tally of notes. The man had gone straight to his central demand and his ultimate threat. That meant he was both impatient and scared. Both could work in her favor if she played them right. Both could get everyone killed if she played them wrong. In either case, his condition was not conducive to the standard tire-him-out routine.

Her first objective was to establish herself as his friend. The constant repetition of his name would work wonders in that area, but she sensed that he would not be inclined to give it. Perhaps she could guess. His voice was mid-thirties Italian with a Brooklyn accent. She decided to play the percentages. "You having a bad day, Nick?"

There was a long pause.

Cassi kept her focus on the chessboard, preparing the various countermoves she would use for different reactions.

"Nice try, lady. There were three Nicks on my block growing up, but I ain't one of 'em. I do respect a woman who isn't afraid of taking a chance, though. You can call me Sal."

Yes! Cassi felt the juices pumping. She was in her groove. Everything was going to fall into place. She could feel it. "You having a bad day, Sal?"

"You shouldn't be concerned with what kind of a day I'm having. I can take care of myself. You should be concerned about the kids locked in here with a bomb."

The kids were all that she cared about, but she knew that they were okay for now. She could hear their muffled sobs. Her goal was to keep them that way. She would use all her skill and experience to keep Masha and Zeke out of play for as long as Sal was in play. Her primary means of doing that would be to keep the negotiation focused on Sal until they reached agreement or it was time for HRT to intervene. "But I do worry about you, Sal. Surely, you didn't want it to come to this. Did you?"

"You got that right. This was supposed to be a quick in and out job."

"So what went wrong?"

"Humph. You showed up." He paused.

Cassi waited.

Finally he asked, "How'd you know?"

"Somebody saw you. We got a call. It happens all the time. Too many eyes in this big city. Tell me, Sal, how do you see this working out?"

"I'll tell you exactly how this is going to work out. You're going to land a helicopter in the schoolyard. I'm going to climb onboard—just me, the pilot and the two kids. We're going to take off. Once I'm sure I'm in the clear, I'll have the pilot set me down someplace I can disappear. Then he brings you back the kids and it's like this never happened. Nobody gets hurt."

"Sounds good to me," Cassi said. She put conviction in her tone, but knew that Sal's request was a fantasy. In her business someone always got hurt.

Chapter 16

Orumiyeh, Iran

"WHO ARE WE IN DANGER FROM?" Odi asked Ayden.

"I don't know."

"Then how do you know that we're in danger?"

"It's a long story."

Odi did not understand why his rescuer was being so evasive. He was obviously nervous and uncomfortable. Perhaps evasion was his default defense mechanism. Odi decided to try a different tack. "Does anybody know where we are?"

"I don't think so, but I'm not sure. I rent this place from an old lady who doesn't even know my name. Still, I'm readily identified as the tall American. It would be easy to find me by asking around."

"And who would be asking?"

"I don't know."

Odi thought about that for a moment, trying to cut through the circular logic. He did not know what was going on, so he could hardly formulate hypotheses. He decided to calm Ayden down while taking a mental inventory of things he could use as improvised weapons—kitchen knives, a broomstick, a wine bottle filled with sand. "How did I end up in that hospital? The last thing I remember was bleeding to death on a battlefield."

"Battlefield, huh?"

Odi understood he had made a faux pas but the words were out. He just shrugged.

Ayden said, "Forget it. To answer your question, I took you to the hospital. We're in Orumiyeh, by the way. It's twenty kilometers south of Tafriz—the site of the battle."

"So, are you a doctor?" Odi asked, steering the conversation toward a non-controversial subject.

"Yes. I studied at Berkeley."

"Really, Berkeley. Great school. What's your connection to Iran?"

"My father was Iranian."

Odi must have shown his surprise on his face because Ayden continued. "I know, I don't look it. I take after my mother's father, and my parents gave me her last name."

Odi nodded. "Are you here with the Red Crescent or Doctors Without Borders?"

"Close. I came here with the Peace Corps. They pulled out a few years back but I didn't want to leave. Too much work to do. Too many children left to save. So now I'm working on my own."

"Who's footing the bills?"

Ayden blushed.

"I'm sorry," Odi continued. "That just slipped out. It's none of my business. Must be the drugs."

"No. That's okay. Actually, I get by on an inheritance."

The kettle whistled. Ayden poured tea. Then he pulled a sleeve of Fig Newtons from the white chipboard cupboard hanging over the sink and set it down. "I don't eat many meals here. I hope this will do."

Odi said, "Thanks," before tucking in. After swallowing three he asked his host, "How did I end up in a hospital in … "

"Orumiyeh," Ayden repeated. "Last weekend I happened to be doing aid work in Tafriz when a couple I had helped a few times before awakened me in the middle of the night. Their boy had just gotten his foot blown off by a landmine. I stabilized the wound and directed his parents to the local clinic you know so well. About twenty minutes after they left, I remembered that Bahir, the boy, was allergic to penicillin. I went chasing after. The rest you can guess."

"What was the boy doing that he got his foot blown off in the middle of the night?"

"A lot of kids work in the fields at night to help support their families. It's cooler and that way they don't miss school. Bahir was taking a shortcut home through the woods."

Odi nodded. One more life his team was responsible for losing. "So you found me near the clinic while returning for the boy?"

"That's right. I took you back to the hut I was working from to patch you up. Your wound was not life threatening in itself, but you had lost a lot of blood. I had some to spare."

Odi tilted his head inquisitively.

Ayden nodded. "I'm O negative, a universal donor."

Odi's head began to reel from all the implications surrounding his predicament. If any of the locals learned that he was a member of the team that blew up their clinic and killed … how many Iranians? He was afraid to ask. He had other questions that he wanted Ayden to answer as well, lots of them, but he feared that time might be short.

Since the US did not maintain an embassy in Iran, he figured that he had two options. Either he could approach a friendly embassy as Ayden had suggested earlier, presumably the British or the Canadians. Perhaps the Aussies. Unfortunately, Tehran was over five hundred miles away. He could call and try to get someone to send a car. Or perhaps there was a major Western corporation that had an office near his current location. Any embassy would know. But how would he manage that without compromising the mission? He was not naïve enough to believe that any phone communication to a Western establishment would be secure. And now that the mission had gone to shit, maintaining deniability would be the prime American objective. Potchak would have a fit if he placed an unsecured call.

The alternative was to wait until nightfall and head for Turkey on foot. Since Orumiyeh was twenty kilometers from Tafriz, and Tafriz was twenty kilometers from the border, he had to be within forty kilometers of the Turkish border. Just a marathon.

"I can't tell you how grateful I am," Odi said. "Forgive me if I'm being rude, but I would hate to let someone interrupt us and spoil your work." He glanced over at his bandaged arm. "What was it that you wanted to show me?"

"Yes, of course." Ayden disappeared into a room off the entryway and returned a moment later with a burlap sack labeled "Brown Rice." He cleared the mugs and empty cellophane wrapper from the table. Then he upturned the bag. The remnant parts of eight military headsets clattered onto the Formica table. Obviously, they had come from his team. This was the last thing Odi had expected.

"Do you know how your teammates died?" Ayden asked.

"I only saw two of them. Both were shot in the head."

"I'm no expert in forensics, Odi, but I had a look at the bodies and then consulted with a friend. Your teammates were not shot. All seven were assassinated by tiny bombs. Check out the headsets." Ayden held up the remnants of an earpiece. "I found bits of this same plastic lodged in all seven head wounds."

Odi felt his skepticism kicking in. "How did you end up with the headsets?"

"I got them from the boy who scavenged them. He was playing with one while I examined him. I had already examined the bodies by then and found the strange shrapnel. When I saw the bloody headsets, I put two and two together."

Odi did not want to think about the implications of that revelation. Instead he began to examine the pieces one after the other. They had not been tampered with, that much was clear. They were still covered with streaks of blood and bits of gore. It did not require his expert eyes to see that Ayden's conclusion was correct—although he had missed it on the battlefield. Each headset had exploded from within. A tiny charge had been cleverly directed by the speaker dish into the wearer's ear.

Odi put a residual piece to his nose and recognized the distinct scent of RDX. He knew that a drop of RDX the size of an eraser head would take a human head clean off. Given the location of the explosive, just millimeters from the ear, the charge would not have had to be any larger than a match head to be lethal.

Odi set the evidence back down on the table as his head began to spin.

His teammates were not the victims of war.

They had died from assassination.

He felt the walls closing in.

Ayden bobbed nervously in his chair as Odi took a long moment of contemplative silence. Then Odi brushed the broken bits off the table with a single sweep of his good arm. He looked up at his new friend. "Why would someone rig our headsets to explode? Why would someone back at Quantico want to kill my team?"

"If yours had been the only incident," Ayden said, "I would say that someone on your team posed a serious threat to the person behind this —as in knowing something that would send him to jail—so he killed everyone to cover his tracks. But—"

"Hold on a minute," Odi interrupted. "There were other incidents? Other attacks?"

"Oh yeah. There were two. The AmCham office was bombed in Belgium, and an American school was bombed in Paris."

"When?"

"Both attacks took place the night your team was assassinated."

Odi leaned back in his chair and let out a long breath. His life was getting more complicated by the minute. Now he understood why Ayden had discouraged his making a call, but that was about all he understood.

He needed more information.

"I interrupted you," Odi said. "You were going to tell me why you thought someone had done this."

"Yes, well, I think the core reason is obvious. Why do people do anything?"

"Money?"

Ayden nodded.

"How does killing my team make anybody money?" Odi asked.

Ayden answered him with a question. A surprising question. "Do you know what the biggest industry in the world is?"

"Oil?"

Ayden shook his head.

Odi raised his brows.

"Fear," Ayden said.

"Fear?"

"Yes, fear. At the individual level, fear is sold in many forms, the most common of which is insurance: health, life, accident, theft. People are afraid that something big will go wrong, so they put their money down. At the collective level, fear is sold in the form of defense— against fire, flood, famine and crime. Of course the granddaddy of these is national defense. Mention the word terrorism and people trip over themselves to hand you blank checks."

"You're losing me. What does—" Odi cut himself off. "I'm beginning to see where you're going with this, but I'm not there yet. Keep talking."

"America's War on Terror was worth around three billion dollars a week to the defense industry. Think about it, three billion dollars a week. That's greater than the GDP of many nations. Surely you don't think the guys who were pocketing that kind of cash were happy when the gravy train stopped rolling. So why would you assume that they would just mothball the mint and walk away once the attacks lightened up?"

Odi had to accept the logic, but something still bugged him. It only took a moment for him to figure out what it was. "Ayden, with all due respect. If the defense contractors were secretly sponsoring attacks to spur demand and keep that gravy train rolling, you wouldn't be the only person to figure it out."

Ayden shook his head sagely. "Nobody else knows that someone inside the FBI planned the murder of your team. The world thinks your team was killed when you uncovered a secret al-Qaeda training camp. And even if someone suspected the truth, so what? He would have no proof. If he spoke up, nobody would listen. If he persisted loudly despite the skepticism, he would just be labeled a nut."

"But we have proof, Ayden. These headsets ... my testimony as a Federal Agent ... those are proof."

"Right," Ayden said, looking up from the floor. "Now do you understand why I'm so afraid? Now do you comprehend just how much danger we're in?"

Chapter 17

Alexandria, Virginia

STUART LISTENED INTENTLY to the complementary voice streams coming from the two speakers. Timing was everything in an operation like this, so he was glad to have bugs both inside the daycare center office and out in the hall.

Both were quiet now. Cassi had just finagled Sal's name. She was a clever one. Stuart had to give her that. If she were just three inches shorter she would be a valuable asset rather than a critical liability. Wiley had that right. Unfortunately, those three inches meant everything. It was just one more way Washington politics resembled professional sports. The difference between winning and losing often came down to fractions and milliseconds. In this case, three inches meant that he had to cut Cassi from the team—the only way that he could.

Stuart wished that there were another way. Wiley would not cooperate. Violence was never his first choice. It was too primitive. But he had no other. Cassi should not have gone and gotten herself pregnant. She had painted him into a corner and this was his only way out.

Wiley would go berserk, of course, but that would change nothing. No spark of vengeance could outshine the luster of the Oval Office. Truth be told, Stuart had been secretly pleased to see Wiley show a little spine and stand up to him on Cassi's account. The edge he displayed would serve them well in the campaign. Of course, Stuart had to ensure that Wiley never forgot his place again. Today, he would solve both issues—with the simple push of a button …

Chapter 18

Alexandria, Virginia

CASSI FELT A JOLT of excitement run through her as she considered Sal's nobody-gets-hurt proposal. Cracking a hostage situation was not unlike cracking a safe. You had to find the right combination. As soon as he said the word helicopter, she felt the first tumbler fall squarely into place. "You seem to have thought this through," she said, keeping the dial turning.

"Damn straight," Sal replied.

Giving a hostage-taker a helicopter was out of the question, but she could not let Sal know that. "If you want me to consider releasing you, Sal, you're going to have to convince me that you're a small fish. No danger to society."

"You want a reference? A note from my guidance counselor?"

Cassi was pleased to hear Sal exercising his sense of humor. That meant both that he was looking for approval and that he was not freaking out. "Tell me about this job. It was obviously well planned and highly sophisticated. Who set it up? What was the plan? Stuff like that. We've already caught you red-handed, so you've nothing to lose— except this last chance to get your freedom back. Don't try to bullshit me though. If I think you're lying, I certainly won't trust you with a helicopter, a pilot and two kids."

Sal met her request with silence. Either he was thinking, or she had pushed too hard. "I'm throwing you a lifeline, Sal. You'll be regretting it for twenty-to-life if you don't grab on with both hands.

Finally, Sal replied, his tone softer than before. "I'm just a wrench."

"A wrench?"

"A tool. Hired help. It wasn't my idea. He called me."

"What did he say?"

"He said he'd give me a million cash if I could get him the Vermeer."

"What Vermeer?"

"The one undergoing restoration on the other side of this brick wall."

"What else did he tell you?"

"Everything. He planned it out for me. Told me about a gap in the security system I could use."

"And what gap was that?"

"What's it matter? Didn't work."

"I'm trying to work with you here, Sal. You've got to work with me back. Give me the details."

Sal sighed loud enough for Cassi to hear through the door. "The art restorer uses a hyper-sophisticated security system. Detects vibration, body heat, shit like that. I can't disable it locally because it arms and disarms according to a remote timer. On at eight every night. Off at eight every morning. Every morning. Since they open late on Sundays, there's a ninety-minute window before anyone shows up. Nothing to worry 'bout from eight to nine-thirty but the normal door and window whistles. The brick wall the studio shares with the daycare center gave me a foolproof way to get around them."

"Go on."

"I broke into the daycare center last night and hid in the storage room, that's where the shared wall is. Eight-fifteen I start drillin' brick, knowing that all them kids running and screaming below will cover up the muffled noise. I'd almost got a hole big enough to wriggle through when I sees colored lights reflecting off the wall. I go to look and see the pigs pulling into the yard. There's nowhere to run so I snatch a couple kids. The rest you know."

Cassi did know. Sal had been set up. There was no Vermeer. There was no sophisticated alarm. There was definitely more to this than met the eye, and she wanted to know what it was. "Now for the most important question, Sal, the one your future rides upon. Who gave you the contract?"

"I knew you was going to ask that. I don't know."

"You know more than you think," Cassi said. "What did he call himself?"

"X."

"X?"

"Yep."

"What else can you tell me about X? Was he working from the inside?"

"I'd say so. He had everything: blueprints, details of the security system, and, of course, he knew 'bout the painting."

Cassi saw a picture rapidly taking shape. "Did he mention the kids?"

"Yeah. He said their screams would cover up the noise. Also suggested that if the shit hit the fan they'd make good insurance."

"He said that?" Cassi asked, filling in the final strokes.

"Yeah. See. Takin' hostages wasn't even my idea. I'm no threat to nobody."

"And how did he get you the blueprints?"

"Mail."

"And how were you going to get him the painting and collect your cash?"

"He was going to call me once the job was done to work that out."

The results of her interrogation were not perfect, Cassi thought, but the police were still going to be pleased. More importantly, Sal was now convinced that she was receptive to his escape plan. It was time for her to rescue the kids.

From his explanation of the job, she knew that Sal was quick on his feet. From his vocabulary and syntax, she knew that he was intelligent but not formally educated. From his escape plan, she gathered that he was meticulous. She had to assume that Sal had studied hostage negotiation techniques. That made her job more complicated, if not more difficult.

Given his current state of mind, Cassi knew that Sal might react violently if he caught her manipulating him with standard procedure. That meant she would not be able to play this one by the book. Still, she could not abandon negotiation's central tenets. She would still keep him off balance, but in an unorthodox way.

"You know what I'm supposed to do now, right Sal? You've seen the cop shows. I'm supposed to tell you that you can't take the kids. Make you release one now. Tire you out. But I can tell that you're too smart for that. So here's what I'm going to do … Oh, hold on a second, I almost forgot. You said you have a bomb, right? What kind is it?"

"What's it matter?"

I want to make sure that it won't go off when we shoot you, she thought. "I need to make sure there are no electronics around that might accidentally trigger it."

"It's plastique—not military grade, the homemade stuff. X sent it to me in case the drill wasn't enough for the wall or I couldn't crack the restorer's safe."

"How much?"

"Enough to do the kids is all you need to know."

"Don't talk like that, Sal. Don't blow it now. I can tell that you're a reasonable man at heart, not some violent psychopath. I am prepared to get you what you want. I'm going to call for your helicopter now. All you have to do for me is put the kids in the bathroom to keep them quiet and out of the way while we wait."

"These kids are staying right next to me. If you're worried about them, you'll get the helicopter here that much faster. Meanwhile, they're going to make sure that you don't get any bright ideas. I do like the idea of keeping them quiet though. Hold on a minute."

Cassi felt spiders in her stomach as she heard the screech-rip sound of duct tape. Once. Twice. Then the soprano sobbing peaked and stopped. Her nerves began to kick in, yanking her out of The Zone. Suddenly, she was acutely aware that two beautiful kids, her unborn child and her career were riding on the next sixty seconds of her performance.

"Okay, Sal. I've put in the request for the helicopter. It won't be long. Now, convince me that you're not going to harm those kids."

"What can I say? I was just trying to steal a painting. That's just larceny, not a violent crime. It ain't a big deal to have me out on the streets. I'm a teddy bear. And like any bear, I'm no threat if nobody spooks or threatens me."

Cassi noted that a desperate twang had crept into Sal's voice. She kept quiet, pressuring him to continue.

He did. "I don't want to harm these kids. But if you threaten me, then that's what I'm going to do. I'm sure you agree it would be much better to let me fly out of here than to let it come down to that."

"Absolutely, I see your point. Oh, hold on ... It's here, Sal. Your helicopter is here."

"In the yard?"

"No, there wasn't room with the telephone wires and the jungle gyms. It's up on the roof. You're going to have to use the fire escape." This was all bullshit, of course. As soon as Sal put his head above the roof he would get a bullet between the eyes. Cassi could not let herself think about that, however. She could not let treachery tweak her voice.

"Okay, here's the deal," Sal commanded. "Everybody clears out. Everybody but you. Nobody is in the yard. Nobody but the pilot is on the roof. When you've made it that way, you let me know."

Cassi felt the warm glow of approaching victory when her ears seemed to erupt inside her head. Before the sound could register she found herself flying backwards through the air, borne toward the bricks with great force by a giant bubble of heat.

Chapter 19

Lake Maroo, Virginia

ODI BOLTED UP IN BED, awakened by chirping birds. He had slept well, even with his ears perked like a German shepherd's.

Two weeks had passed since his auspicious awakening in the Iranian hospital ward, and in that time his outlook on life had swung one-hundred-and-eighty degrees. Betrayal changes a man. Betrayal makes him worry about things he never worried about before. It makes him worry about things like self-preservation. Ponder motives. And plan his revenge.

Realizing that going public with their knowledge would put them squarely in the assassins' sights, he and Ayden had inevitably settled on the only course of action that was both honorable and expedient. They had chosen to hunt the killers down. Actually "they" was a generous term. Odi was the soldier. He was going after them alone.

He had entered the US using Ayden's passport in order to preserve his greatest tactical advantage: the fact that everyone still believed him dead. He had used discretion and disguise to keep it that way, and he would continue to do so for as long as it took to neutralize all the people who conspired to murder his team. Once his mission was complete, he would just wake up in Iran. A coma was an airtight alibi. And he had a credible doctor to corroborate.

Slipping out of bed fully dressed, he pulled on his hiking boots and looked out the bedroom window. Dawn's first light was just breaking over the lake. The water took on a golden shimmer and seemed to summon all living creatures to come forth for a dip. Lake Maroo was a pristine paradise. He could see why Commander Potchak spent virtually every weekend here in his cabin. It was just what one needed to balance out a Quantico workweek. At least it would have been for Odi. Obviously, Maroo's charms were insufficient to stifle Potchak's ravenous greed.

Odi emerged from the cabin's only bedroom to inspect the status of his project. Potchak was still there, of course. He was standing exactly as Odi had left him eight hours earlier—suspended on his tiptoes by the noose around his neck.

Odi walked to the center of the room to appraise the condemned man. The fact that this was the traditional time for military hangings had not been lost on his prisoner. Potchak's face was beaded with sweat despite the morning chill and he had dark bags beneath his bloodshot eyes. Physically, Odi thought, he looked just about right.

Odi stretched his arms over his head and let out a contented yawn as he studied Potchak's eyes. It was a tactical ploy, designed to stress the contrast of their relative positions while simultaneously giving Odi time to evaluate his opponent. Odi liked what he saw. He could begin—but he wouldn't. Not just yet.

Odi had not said a word to his former boss since capturing him at dusk. He would say nothing now. Better to let him stew a few minutes more. He took a moment to reflect on the events that had transpired, letting tension mount.

Capturing Potchak had been surprisingly easy. When the commander returned to the rustic cabin from a day of bow hunting, Odi was waiting, hidden behind the dense foliage of a Fraser fir. The moment his boss turned his back to unstrap the buck from the hood of his Jeep, Odi Tasered him in the back. As Adam would have said, it was a piece of pumpkin pie.

~ ~ ~

When Potchak awoke to a choking sensation, his first crazy thought was that the deer had somehow turned the tables on him, for he was the one who had been strung up. He had no idea how he had gotten there, but there he was, hanging by his neck at the end of a rope in the main room of his cabin. He reached for the noose around his throat as his feet sought the floor but found his arms bound tightly behind his back. His toes made blessed contact and he pressed down vigorously and managed to ease some tension out of the rope. Potchak gasped a few breaths and sought to maintain his balance. A few seconds in that position were all it took to realize that remaining elevated and balanced enough to breathe was going to inflict a constant mental and physical strain.

He immediately recognized this as a stress position. The kind often used in interrogations. But his mind did not dwell on that. For as surprising as his new predicament was, the next sight that met his eyes as he glanced around was even more so. He found himself looking at a ghost.

Odysseus Carr was dead. Yet there Odi was, sitting beside him in an armchair, casually reading a book. Was this hell? Was this to be his special torment? Was he doomed to spend eternity struggling to breathe while his victims looked on in peace?

Potchak groaned through the duct tape that gagged his mouth.

Odi continued to read in silence without looking up.

~ ~ ~

After finishing Follett's latest thriller and breaking for a dinner he did not share—fresh venison steak—Odi retired to Potchak's bedroom without a word. He was anxious to get started but knew that the interrogation was more likely to succeed if he gave his captive's fears a chance to percolate. He wanted Potchak to contemplate the reversal of their positions as his terror fermented and his physical strength dwindled away.

Appraising the situation anew that morning, Odi found himself intrigued by the thoughts that must be going through Potchak's mind. He reasoned that his boss must have spent much of his tiptoe time trying to guess the angle that would give him the best chance of saving his own neck—praying all the while that Odi would give him a chance to speak before he hoisted him up that last lethal inch. Odi was curious to learn what strategy Potchak chose, what ploy he would invoke. Potchak's choice would tell Odi a lot about how he was perceived.

Would Potchak attempt to sway him through pity, through fear, or through greed? Would he offer Odi money? Apologies? Information? Sex? Would he try a power play and issue threats? Would he claim to be a victim himself? Or would he just beg?

Appraising his captive, Odi decided that it was time to find out. He grasped the rope that ran upwards from Potchak's neck over the central rafter and down to a cleat that Odi had screwed to the far wall. He twanged it as though the rope were the string of a giant guitar. Potchak's heels lifted further off the floor. Twelve hours of stretching had made no difference to the rope. It was still taut as a sumo's loincloth.

Odi walked over to the cleat and partially unwrapped the end—just enough for it to slip. He added enough slack to let Potchak slump from his tiptoes onto the balls of his feet and then re-secured the rope. Satisfied that Potchak remained utterly helpless but would now have the mental bandwidth to focus on something other than balance, he spoke for the first time since the capture. "Lest you get any bright ideas, the noose is tied so that it cannot be loosened or removed."

Potchak grunted. Odi took this as a submissive sign. He untied Potchak's left hand and used the extra rope to secure his right hand to the back of his leather belt. Then he ripped the duct tape from Potchak's mouth in one swift move. It left a nasty red rash, but Potchak still looked relieved. Odi smiled with satisfaction. Then he walked behind Potchak and into the kitchen without another word, no doubt leaving his prisoner even further confused.

He watched Potchak through the doorway as he brewed a pot of strong coffee. Potchak did not try to turn around or speak. The former did not surprise Odi. His prisoner had no doubt suffered from a misstep or two during the night and learned to leave well enough alone, even now that he was down on the balls of his feet. As for the latter, the silence, that, Odi was sure, was about to change.

When he returned with two large steaming mugs, Odi found Potchak looking much better. The smell of fresh brew, the glimmer of hope, the setting and the free hand were all having their effect—exactly as planned. He handed Potchak a mug and said, "Lots of milk, lots of sugar."

Odi's knowledge of how the commander liked his coffee was a poignant reminder that, according to the soldiers' code, Potchak was guilty of worse than murder. He was guilty of betrayal.

Odi thought he saw a streak of guilt cross Potchak's face as he mumbled "Thanks." But before he could be sure, Potchak dove into his mug. Odi positioned a worn old leather armchair to Potchak's left and plopped down, sending stuffing sprouting out a slit in the side like hair from an old man's ear. After settling in comfortably, he took a sip of his own black brew and began. "So, after eighteen years with the FBI you suddenly quit to work for Armed Services Industrial Supply. What was that I read in the paper, you start Monday as Vice President of Government Relations? That plum assignment must be worth quite a bump in pay. I'm curious, what were the lives of my team worth? Three-hundred grand? Half a mil?"

"I didn't know anyone was going to get killed," Potchak said.

As an opening line, Odi thought it wasn't bad, but he was still ready with a retort. "Other than the doctors, nurses and patients at the hospital, of course. But they were Iranian civilians, so I suppose they don't count. We killed more people liberating Iraq than we lost in Vietnam, and nobody seemed to notice, so you figured, what the hell…"

Potchak closed his eyes for a long second, then continued. "When they gave me the headsets, they said they were just so they could listen in, so they'd know if you suspected anything and could decide if it was necessary to pull the plug."

"And once we were all dead, well, you were already in too deep."

"Exactly," Potchak said. Then he finished off his coffee as though the meeting were over.

Odi looked at him and thought, if you only knew … He took back the mug and grew a broad smile for what must have appeared to be no apparent reason. Potchak smiled back, trying to act chummy—for the first time in two years. He did not even resist when Odi rebound his hand.

"Do you remember what I used to do before joining CRT?" Odi asked.

Potchak's face registered the odd combination of panic and relief. He was wary about being let off the hook. As an avid fisherman, he knew that this was often the last thing that happened before the man who caught you cut off your head. "Yeah, of course. You were with the bomb squad. You shocked us when you requested a transfer to CRT because you were EOD's golden child."

Odi did not comment immediately. Instead he walked to the closet and withdrew a tripod and a video camera. He began setting them up as he spoke. "I've been fascinated by explosives ever since I got my first firecracker as a kid. Long story short—we don't have much time—before I was done at Johns Hopkins, that fascination led to PhDs in Chemistry and Biomolecular Engineering. But you know that.

"What you don't know is that I did a lot of research, a lot of tinkering in the lab during graduate school. I even came up with a couple of groundbreaking inventions." Odi spoke calmly, his tone dispassionate, very matter-of-fact. "The first invention you may have heard about. The trade name is ArmoWrap. It's a defensive tool, kind of like a fire extinguisher for bombs. The second invention is at the opposite end of the spectrum. It is a devious weapon. I call it Creamer, although since I am the only person on the planet who knows about it, the name has the irrelevance of a tree falling in an empty wood. Anyhow, sparing you the technospeak, Creamer is a bio-reactive explosive." Odi paused to study Potchak's face. His expression did not change. The words bio-reactive explosive had not tipped him off. That was just as well, Odi thought. He wanted to capture Potchak's initial comprehension on tape.

Now that he was done revealing personal information, Odi stood up and turned on the video camera. He pointed it directly at Potchak's strung-up head while making sure that his own chair was nowhere in the frame. Then he did a test with the microphone to make sure that the oscillating sound filter he had attached over the mike sufficiently altered his voice. Satisfied with the arrangement, Odi hit the record button and continued where he left off. "Aside from a slightly oily sheen, my creamer looks like ordinary coffee creamer. Thus the name. Mix it in equal parts with Half and Half, add a little artificial flavoring, and it tastes that way too."

Odi licked his lips as he watched Potchak's face contort into a mask of terror. Then he continued in the same, soft pedagogical monotone. "Creamer is a stable, inert liquid until it is placed in an environment with a low pH—like your stomach, for instance. Once swallowed, the hydrochloric acid in your stomach catalyzes radical hemophilic adhesion. In other words, the liquid explosive draws together as though magnetized to form an ever-denser solid. It is kind of like milk curdling, but in the extreme." Odi stood up, careful to keep out of the video, and began to pace as he continued the lesson with the aid of his hands. "Once the Creamer compacts sufficiently, it begins to sweat a polymer. That polymer further interacts with the hydrochloric acid, encasing the explosive in a tough shell. Picture a loaf of baking bread, only with a crust as tough as iron. And that's only the half of it. To continue the analogy, the yeast in the batter continues to rise long after the solid crust forms, increasing the pressure within that shell. As the pressure of that confined space rises, so does the heat—that's the first law of thermodynamics, you may recall. The pressure keeps building and the temperature keeps rising until it reaches one-hundred-ten degrees centigrade. That's the tipping point where the internal pressure becomes too great for the shell to withstand. Wanna guess what happens then?"

Potchak mouthed, "It explodes," but no sound came out.

"That's right. The explosive self-detonates."

Odi smiled at Potchak. "The whole reaction takes about thirty minutes in pigs. As for humans, well, you'll be the first to know."

Whatever psychological ploy Potchak had been planning as he stood there on tiptoe through the night, a revelation like this had not factored into the equation. He began to shake.

"We'll know that you have about ten minutes left when your breathing becomes rapid and shallow and your lips and fingernails begin turning blue. That's on account of the polymer the explosive sweats—it's extremely destructive to hemoglobin."

Potchak was writhing like a worm on a hook, Odi noted with satisfaction. When Odi finished speaking, Potchak made a visible effort to bring his body under control.

Odi waited.

When the condemned man finally opened his mouth again, his voice was surprisingly stable. "Is there an antidote?"

Odi cocked his head to the side and winked. "Who asked you to do it?"

Chapter 20

The Mall, Washington, D.C.

WILEY STUDIED his own reflection in the black rain-streaked granite as he walked the length of the Vietnam Memorial. He was not satisfied with the countenance staring back. It did not look tough enough for the meeting he was headed for. Nor did it exude his usual fire. He held out his right arm as he approached the memorial's western end and ran his fingers along the cold chiseled surface, attempting to leach courage from the hallowed stone.

"You called," Stuart said, appearing beneath Wiley's umbrella as if conjured from the wind.

Wiley stopped walking and turned toward his campaign manager, angling his body to force Stuart to face into the gusting drizzle. "I know it was you. Cassi's accident. I don't know how you did it—and I probably never will—but I know it was you."

Stuart removed his misted silver spectacles once Wiley had finished. He stared back at him eyeball-to-eyeball with those cold reptilian eyes. "If you know so much, then you're also aware that her misfortune is your blessing. The albatross has been blown off your neck. With Cassi out of the picture, Carver doesn't have a single objection to inviting you to join his ticket. I know. I asked. I have also been getting great traction off Fitzpatrick's Prophet quote. The media are eating it up. Everything is coming together for the Antiterrorist Czar. And I'm glad you know whom to thank."

Wiley felt conflicting emotions churn. He was thrilled with the career news but was not yet done lashing out. "What if I was to tell you that I'm sticking with her?"

Stuart scoffed. "I'd say that you might as well keep walking—right past the Lincoln Memorial and into the Potomac. After blackmailing her boss, breaking protocol and costing two children their lives, your girlfriend is political cyanide."

During the half-second it took Wiley to compose his barbed retort, his cell phone began to ring. He knew by the tone that it was Carl Jenkins, his Deputy Director for Operations and second in command. He hated to see Stuart saved by the bell, but he had to take the call. "Good evening, Carl."

"I'm calling with bad news, Wiley. Former CRT Commander Potchak is dead."

Wiley felt his stomach shrink to the size of a walnut. "Potchak is dead?" He repeated the words back to Carl while activating the cell phone's speaker for Stuart's benefit. "He just retired to work for ASIS last Friday. That can hardly be a coincidence. What do you know?"

"ASIS called us when Potchak failed to show up for his first day of work this morning, thinking that maybe old habits were hard to break and he'd driven to Quantico instead. He didn't, of course. He was not at home or reachable on his mobile phone, so Agent Dobrinovitch drove out to his hunting cabin. It's way out in rural Virginia on Lake Maroo."

"I know it."

"Yes, well, Potchak was there, in his cabin. Or at least that's what we think."

"I don't follow."

"The remains we found were severely scattered. The victim, who we're assuming was Potchak for now, was either hit center of mass by the equivalent of an antitank weapon or he was forced to swallow something akin to a hand grenade."

Wiley stared blankly at the leaden clouds streaking across the sky, trying to grasp the implications. Finally he asked, "Was there anything like a Mafia signature in the room? A dead fish, a horse's head, a black spot, a white rose … ?"

"If there was, it wasn't prominently displayed. At the time of the explosion, however, Potchak had a noose about his neck. Maybe that's the same thing. I'll run the MO past Edwards in Organized Crime."

"I take it we don't have any leads on the killer yet?"

"Actually, we do. We know from splatter voids on the wall and footprints that a six-foot-one male with an athletic build and size eleven shoes was present with Potchak in the room. He arrived and left on a cross-country motorcycle. Our preliminary analysis indicates that he was not injured in the blast, although he must have been drenched in Potchak juice. We'll know for certain once we get the blood work back."

"No other clues to the killer's identity?"

"None. All the windows and doors were left open, and it was a windy, rainy weekend, so we've got a highly contaminated scene. The place was wiped clean of prints. Osborn says the guy was a pro so forensics is not expecting much."

"Thank you for giving it to me straight."

"There's one other thing," Jenkins said. "The killer was using a tripod for something. We're guessing it was either to support the weapon or to capture the explosion on video. Winslow in Behavioral Sciences says that in the latter case there's even money that the killer will send us a copy as a gauntlet of sorts—either in the mail or over the web."

Wiley considered that. "As long as we don't see it on the news first."

"There's no way any public network could show this."

Wiley cringed. "Keep me posted on every significant development, as soon as you have it, day or night. The word on the street needs to be clear: the FBI takes care of its own."

"Of course."

Wiley closed the clamshell phone with a trembling hand and studied Stuart. They were obviously thinking the same thing. One way or another, this was related to Wiley's campaign. Not only was someone aware of their conspiracy, but he was out to stop it, to stop them. Potchak's death might be just the beginning.

Chapter 21

Alexandria, Virginia

CASSI OPENED HER EYES to an unfamiliar face: mid-forties female, thin to borderline gaunt, scraggly black hair, boring brown eyes, white smock. She was looking at either a mortician's assistant or an unfortunate nurse. "What happened?"

The nurse bent over and used icy fingers to pry her left eye farther open. "Follow my flashlight," she said, moving the light back and forth, up and down.

"What happened, Gretchen?" Cassi repeated, once her eyes had recovered enough to read the nurse's name tag."

"You were in an explosion. You suffered multiple abrasions and a serious blow to the back of your head, but—"

The hallway scene came back in a flash the moment Gretchen said explosion. "What about the children?" Cassi interrupted, trying to sit up.

Gretchen pushed her firmly back and then shook her index finger in silent warning. She was not to move. "I can't discuss other patients."

Cassi was about to make the request in an official capacity when she was struck by another thought and her whole body went cold. "What about my baby?"

Gretchen gave a compassionate frown and shook her head. "I'm sorry, dear. You miscarried."

As Cassi's head reeled, Gretchen placed one cold hand on her arm while reaching for the IV with the other. Using her thumb to crank up the sedative drip, she said, "You need to get your rest."

~ ~ ~

Cassi drifted back into consciousness as a nurse rolled a noisy patient past her room. Her throat felt like sandpaper and she could swear that someone had used her head to break bricks while she was asleep. She opened her eyes to see that Gretchen was there, poised like a sentry. In reaction to Cassi's movement, Gretchen shoved a straw into her mouth. Cassi drew in a sip of warm water and her throat immediately felt a little better. She spent the next thirty seconds clearing her head and draining the cup.

"Is it true? Is my baby really gone?"

"I'm afraid so, dear. But there's no reason you can't have another. You're still healthy and young."

Cassi was not so sure.

Where was Wiley? she wondered. More than anything, she needed him with her at that moment. There were flowers all over her room, and no doubt some were from him, but those were hardly consolation. She needed flesh and blood to cuddle and hold. She needed reassurance, support and consolation. She understood that he could not possibly afford to sit watch at the foot of her bed, but she felt that he had slighted her all the same. Her and their baby.

"How do you feel?" Gretchen asked, nudging the discussion in a different direction.

Cassi decided that a change of subject probably was for the best. "Like I was hit by a truck."

Gretchen nodded. "In a Newtonian sense, you were."

Cassi wasn't sure what that meant. It sounded like something Odi would say. "What time is it?" she asked.

"Six o'clock, Monday evening. You've been asleep for nearly twenty-four hours. Are you hungry? I've got orange Jell-O and some tasty applesauce that will both go down nicely."

Cassi was not in the mood to eat, but she knew she should build up her strength. "That would be nice. I would also appreciate whatever you can give me for my headache."

Gretchen mumbled something in response as she walked out the door.

Cassi was anxious to learn about Masha and Zeke. She would watch the news during dinner. If she could not find coverage of the explosion, then she would find a phone and call over to the pediatric wing. Meanwhile, she tried to recall the details of what happened.

She remembered blackmailing Higgins into giving her the reins of the daycare center negotiation. She remembered Sal's explanation of the job and her conclusion that he had been set up. She remembered convincing Sal that a helicopter was waiting for him up on the roof. She remembered being certain that Sal would have to expose himself to HRT sniper fire as he climbed the fire escape to the roof. She had effectively saved the children. Then, for some unforeseeable reason, the explosives he had brought for the safe exploded. One of the kids or even Sal himself must have accidentally triggered the detonator.

Gretchen returned with a plastic tray and set it on the table beside her bed. Cassi looked over to see a mushy meal and a little paper cup with two Tylenol. Gretchen refilled her water from a plastic pitcher and handed Cassi the cup. Once Cassi swallowed the pills, Gretchen said, "Your boss is here."

Cassi perked up. Jack was there. That was good news. He would tell her about the kids. She felt a wave of nervous tension run up her spine.

What would she do if they were not okay? She had a sudden urge to look in the mirror, but realized that was silly. She had a thick cap of gauze wrapped around her head. Besides, how she looked was the least of her problems. "Has he been waiting long?"

"No. He called earlier and we told him when the medication was likely to wear off. He has been here about fifteen minutes. You don't have to see him if you don't want."

Cassi got the impression that Gretchen enjoyed sending people away. "No, that's okay. Please send him in."

It was not Jack Higgins who walked through her door. It was Wiley. Wiley was there!

"It's great to see you," she said, accepting a mixed rose bouquet and a kiss on the cheek. The cheek. That was disappointing. Perhaps her lips looked like an old hen's.

"I'm glad to see you too."

"When the nurse said that my boss was here, I was expecting to see Jack Higgins."

"Actually, that's part of what I needed to talk to you about," Wiley said, pulling the chair up beside the bed.

"I owe him an apology. I know. But—"

"Jack's not your boss anymore," Wiley interrupted. "He had to resign. Ralph Unger is the new Head of Hostage Negotiations."

Cassi felt the blood draining from her face. "Is that ... Is that my fault?"

Wiley nodded. "Jack took your bullet. But as you know, he was about to retire anyway."

"And thanks to me, after thirty years of distinguished service he went out under a cloud." Cassi bowed her head as tears swelled in her eyes. That was a double blow, straight to the heart. She needed some good news. "What happened to the children, to Masha and Zeke?"

As Wiley shook his head, Cassi thought she would faint. She was already numb when he spoke the dreaded words. "They didn't make it."

She gripped the rails of her bed like lifelines as Wiley continued. "As you might guess, their deaths have been all over the news."

Grasping for straws, Cassi asked, "Do we know what happened yet? Why the bomb went off?"

"We don't. The forensics team thinks it was an accident—homemade plastique is notoriously unstable—but that's almost irrelevant. This is a political football now, so it's sensation not science that counts.

"Look Cassi, I'm sorry to hit you with this first thing after waking up. I thought it was important that you understand what's going on. The minute word gets out that you are awake, the press are going to be trying to get to you, and they can be pretty slippery. I wanted to make sure that you were forearmed."

"Thank you," Cassi mumbled. "So what is going to happen to me?"

"Ralph's first act in his new role was to place you on thirty-days medical leave and suspend your negotiator status—indefinitely."

Cassi felt the world closing in on her. The injustice of it all was overwhelming. It was not her fault that an unstable bomb had exploded. She had successfully negotiated Sal out of the room with the children unharmed. Ralph, on the other hand, had blown dozens of cases. This was so unfair. She had—

"Cassi, there's more."

"More?"

"I don't know how to say this other than to come right out with it." Wiley stood up and began to pace. "Vice President Dish has an inoperable aneurism. He can't stand with Carver for reelection, and it's looking like I have a serious shot at his slot." Wiley bowed his head and spoke with a soft voice. "It's an opportunity I can't let sail past."

Cassi felt the floor giving way, but she managed to hold on. She knew that this discussion, in fact this whole chapter of her life, would only last a few seconds more. Wiley was going to make a run for the White House—and she was now too heavy to carry along. Part of her wanted to scream at him and make him feel bad, but after a moment's repose she realized that that was the smaller part. In her heart of hearts she hoped he would succeed. She decided to make it easier for him. She said, "I understand. Air Force Two is like the Concorde—you have to check your baggage at the door."

Chapter 22

Wilmington, Delaware

AVAILING HIMSELF of the bridging cover provided by his chauffeur's upheld umbrella, Defcon4 CEO Mark Drake stepped quickly from the portico of his Delaware mansion into the back of his custom Bentley limousine. He had a meeting with the Italian Ambassador that morning and did not want a single drop of October rain to blemish his dove-gray Versace suit.

As he settled into the buttery black leather, the chauffeur pulled the limousine around the circle and headed down the gravel drive. Mark listened to the bulletproof tires crunching out the sound of wealth on the tiny stones. It was music to his ears. The drive to work was often his favorite part of the day. It was forty-five minutes of refined luxury and productive peace.

He plucked the steaming latte from the heated cup holder in his armrest and savored the day's first sip. He loved the nutty warmth and the ensuing rush, the more so on dreary mornings like these. He smacked his tongue. Today's brew left a funny aftertaste. Had William used his own off-the-shelf grounds, rather than the custom order Blue Mountain beans? Drake wondered. He was about to buzz William to lodge a complaint when his eye fell upon a headline on the front page of The Wall Street Journal: Pentagon Budget Woes. He unfolded the crisp paper, swallowed another sip of latte, and began to read.

Some twenty minutes later Mark heard a television monitor spring to life. He looked up to see the limo's large central screen glowing blue. He reached for the remote control but found the holder empty. Vexed, he pressed a burl wood button and activated the intercom. "I say, William, the tele has just come on and I'm missing the remote."

William did not reply. That was the problem with these high-technology cars, Mark thought. A twenty-five-cent fuse could bring them to their knees. For three hundred thousand you expected better. That thought made him smile proudly. For that amount of money a government did get absolute reliability, in the form of one of his FreedomSeeker missiles.

Only when he glanced out the window to find an unfamiliar road did he get the feeling that something more serious than a technical glitch might be afoot. As if in answer to his unvoiced question, a video began to play. If he'd had any latte left, he would have choked. The screen showed a bulldog of a man hanging on to life at the end of a rope. His toes were barely touching the floor and his hands appeared to be bound behind his back. The man was looking at someone whom Mark guessed to be seated below the camera, although no part of him could be seen. The narrator could, however, be heard. "Aside from a slightly oily sheen, it looks like coffee creamer. Mix it in equal parts with Half and Half, add a little artificial flavoring, and it tastes that way too."

Mark watched the hanging man's face contort as he reacted to the words. Then Mark heard the narrator describe the chemistry of an explosive he called Creamer. When the description was over, the video paused. Mark wondered if this was some strange form of marketing video, a new explosive for Defcon4 to manufacture. Slipping it into his limo's DVD was a bit aggressive, but then his was an aggressive business.

Engrossed as he was by the morbid show and tell, Mark had not noticed that his limo had parked. Looking out the window he was surprised to see the Delaware Valley below. They were at one of those scenic pull-offs beside a hillside road. It was not very scenic now, however, on account of the rain.

Mark tried the door but it was locked. He pushed the unlock button and found that it had no effect.

Panic seized him.

He pushed the intercom button frantically but received no response. He began screaming William's name. Nothing. The inescapable conclusion hit him like a punch in the gut. He was a captive, albeit in a burl wood and leather prison.

The video monitor came back to life and Mark refocused his attention on the pitiful wretch hanging by his neck. "Who asked you to do it?" the unseen narrator asked.

The wretch shook his head a few times as though coming to accept his fate. That action must have caused him considerable pain, though he seemed beyond the point of noticing anymore. His neck was already rubbed raw and blood had discolored the bottom of the coarse noose. Finally, the man grew a resigned grimace and looked directly into the lens.

The camera zoomed in.

Mark began to tremble.

The shaking started deep in his bones and worked its way out through his limbs in an uncontrollable spasm. He recognized the face.

The death mask before him belonged to the FBI Commander he had to hire as part of his contribution to Stuart Slider's scheme. It was the man Wiley had given them to work the inside angle. Potchak.

"Who asked you to do it?" the narrator repeated.

Potchak spoke just two words, but they came out clear and strong. "Mark Drake."

~ ~ ~

Odi stopped the video. He wished he could have seen Drake's face at the moment Potchak pronounced his name, but his hidden camera only provided a profile view. He turned to face the rear of the car and lowered the partition halfway. The pallid CEO of Defcon4 stared back at him, a look of absolute horror on his aquiline face.

"You're not William."

All things considered, Odi found that a ridiculous thing to say. "No, I'm not. Care to guess who I am?"

"No, I don't care to guess. Now let me out of my car."

"Let you out? Do you know how many lives were sacrificed to provide you with this opulent ride? The least you can do to respect their memory is to enjoy it."

"God damn it, I said let me out! I insist that you let me out of here—right now."

Odi said, "If you don't adjust your attitude, Drake, you may never leave." He raised the partition to cut off further protest.

Odi fast forwarded the DVD to the climactic scene and pushed play. The explosion happened so fast that you missed it if you blinked. One second Potchak was there, then you heard a sickening ka-woomf, and the next second you found yourself looking through a misted red lens at an empty pair of boots. After enough time passed for your mind to register what your eyes had not seen, a cloth wiped the lens, providing a clear view of the grisly remains and the blood-drenched, gore-splattered room. The video showed that medieval picture for a full thirty seconds before it stopped.

Odi gave Drake a minute of silence before flicking the intercom switch with his leather-gloved hand. "Potchak got testy too. He didn't have your advantage though. He didn't have the visual of what happens to people who don't fully cooperate. Tell me, Drake, are your fingernails turning blue?"

Again, Odi wished he could see Drake's face, but he did not dare to lower the partition a second time.

"Oh my God. You've got to give me the antidote." His voice was no longer the haughty drone of a faux-British aristocrat. It was a nasal whine born of horrified desperation.

Odi let him dangle for a moment longer at the end of his metaphorical rope and then asked, "Does that mean you're willing to cooperate fully?"

"Yes, yes, of course I'm willing to cooperate. Just hurry. My fingers. My fingers are already blue."

Odi smiled. He was not enjoying the violence. He wasn't the sadistic type. But he loved it when everything went precisely according to plan.

"Who are you working with?"

"Mark Abrams, Mark Rollins and Wiley Proffitt." Drake spit out the words as if they were poison.

The first two names Odi had expected. Together with Drake they rounded out the Wall Street darlings known collectively as The Three Marks. The third name stole Odi's breath away. He was glad that the partition was raised so Drake could not see him shake. Wiley Proffitt was seriously involved with his sister. In fact, if her prediction was correct they were already engaged. What possible motivation could Wiley have for getting in bed with Defense? He had his own island for chrissake, and was the Director of the FBI. What could The Three Marks possibly offer him that he did not already have? "Tell me why," Odi commanded.

Odi listened to Drake's panicked account of the defense contractors' plight, of how the river of cash from the War on Terror was drying up, and they were desperate for another Iraq. It was precisely as Ayden had hypothesized, but Odi still found himself amazed at both the brashness of their plan and the depth of their greed. He was also stunned by the personal connection. The fact that the consortium had selected Wiley for its White House puppet was an amazing coincidence, and Odi did not believe in those. Drake, however, knew nothing about Cassi. Nor did he recognize Odi's face or name. The investigation of that coincidence would have to wait.

"Now give me the antidote," Drake implored, his voice accented by an adolescent crack.

"Coming right up."

Odi scanned the scenic pull-off again to ensure that they were in fact as alone as you would expect at a location like this come seven A.M. in the rain. They were. He opened the driver's door and went around to the trunk. He pulled wet-weather clothes on over his chauffeur suit and then pulled a small motor scooter from the trunk as Drake pounded away at the windows.

He spoke into the intercom before riding the scooter away with the limo's keys, leaving Drake locked inside.

"Drake?"

"Yes!"

"Adam Brazer, Flint Mulder, Jeremy Jones, Mitch O'Brian, Derek Doogan, Tony Oritz and William Waslager."

"What?!"

"Those are the names of my teammates. Those are the names of the men you killed."

Drake could not get any paler. He just looked up with pleading eyes, and said, "The antidote ... you promised."

"There is only one antidote for Creamer...and that antidote is death."

Chapter 23

The Horus Club, Washington, D.C.

AS THE GRISLY IMAGE of Potchak's boots faded to black, the four men stared silently at the blank screen. They did not know Potchak personally, but they knew Drake. Now they also knew the circumstances of their friend's grisly end. Now they also understood the true horror of the threat. And so they sat there, motionless, silent. None wanting to meet another's eye. None wanting confirmation that the nightmare was real.

Wiley was not surprised that it was Stuart who eventually broke the silence, but nonetheless his words left Wiley choking on his Dalwhinnie.

"It must be Odi Carr," Stuart said.

Every time, Wiley thought, wiping his chin. He does it to me every frigging time. "Why do you say that?"

"Yes, why?" Abrams echoed, incredulity in his voice. "Carr is dead."

Nestled amidst the sea of embassies in Dumbarton Oaks, the exclusive club Wiley had selected for their meeting was a flashback to a time when men of extraordinary privilege and means routinely gathered to exchange news and talk business at the end of the day over grossly priced brandy, the very best imported cigars, and whatever else men of unlimited means might desire. The only indulgence not offered at The Horus Club was whores. The deficiency was not a morality statement. It was just their stubborn adherence to a policy maintained for over two hundred years. Horus was for gentlemen only. As General Manager Oliver Appleton loved to point out whenever he could do so with discretion, even Supreme Court Justice Sandra Day O'Conner's application had been denied.

Abrams turned to Wiley. "You're sure we can talk here?"

Wiley took a long, contemplative puff on his cigar. He wanted to present himself as cool and composed while his friends were still reeling from the shock of the video. "Absolutely," he replied, blowing out a long stream of smoke. "The waiters, you know, are all deaf."

"That's ridiculous," Rollins chuffed.

"Not at all," Wiley said, teasing out the moment by pretending to study his cigar. "They read lips."

Rollins and Abrams both raised their brows and nodded.

Wiley savored the moment before continuing. "Still, given this day and age, I brought in the Bureau's best technician one evening to perform a surreptitious electronic sweep. Rives declared the club to be clean as a virgin's sheets." The men nodded their approval, teeing up the kicker. "On the way out that evening, Oliver Appleton pulled me aside. Despite Rives' expertise, his actions had not gone undetected. Oliver told me that he recognized what my guest was doing because he did it himself—twice a day."

Wiley accepted another round of kudos, noting that even Stuart actually looked impressed for once. "So yes, I am sure that we can talk. Stuart, you were going to tell us why you think our troublemaker is a dead man."

Stuart took a sip of his twelve-dollar club soda. "Whoever killed Potchak and Drake was obviously very familiar with explosives. I'm no expert, but I work in defense and I've never heard of anything like the device that was used. Yet the killer was familiar enough with the explosive to stay in the room. That requires both intimate knowledge and humungous balls."

"Like the balls of a CRT leader," Abrams added.

Stuart nodded and continued. "Odi Carr not only has every reason in the world to kill those two men, but he is also one of the world's leading explosive ordnance technicians. Furthermore, only seven bodies came back from Iran. Potchak assumed that Carr's body was incinerated in the explosion, given that there were no reports of survivors. In retrospect, I concede that perhaps that was wishful thinking. At the time it seemed the most reasonable conclusion."

"It still seems a stretch," Abrams said.

"Perhaps," Stuart agreed. "But there's more. I didn't mention this before, but Potchak actually had to remove Carr from command mid-mission."

"What?" Wiley asked.

"Apparently, Carr figured out that it really was a clinic and not a training camp. When planning the attack, we figured that there would be no activity in the middle of the night, but were unlucky. A peasant boy got his foot blown off harvesting at night and showed up in an ambulance just as Echo Team was prepping for the attack. Anyhow, when Carr's body was not with the others and not a peep was heard from him, Potchak assumed that he must have tried to rescue some locals and either succumbed to the smoke or got caught up in the blast."

"That's a lot of assumptions," Rollins said.

"He has paid for his mistake," Wiley replied.

Everyone nodded somberly.

"What about the letter?" Abrams asked after another protracted silence.

"Read it again," Stuart said. "Aloud."

Abrams picked up the note that he and Rollins had each received with their copy of the Potchak execution video and read its single sentence. "Come forward, confess all, and resign within twenty-four hours of receiving this, or share the same fate as Potchak and Drake." Abrams put down the note as everyone pictured the smoking stumps. Then he said, "I don't see any clues to the author's identity."

Wiley was most curious about that himself.

Stuart said, "Carr was the leader of Counterterrorism Response Team Echo. Consider what that tells you in terms of character profile. He is a man of action, violent and intense. You are all defense guys. You know that Special Forces soldiers tend to be men of few words. I'm sure that is exactly the kind of letter that an FBI profiler would expect Odi Carr to write."

Wiley nodded in response to the other men's inquisitive looks.

"So what do we do?" Abrams said. "I sure as shit am not going to resign and turn myself in."

"Nor I," Rollins said. "But I'm not going to be fatally egotistical about this either. If he could get to Potchak and Drake, we should assume that he could get to us too."

"You have several advantages they did not have," Stuart said. "First of all, you know that someone is after you. Potchak and Drake were caught unaware. Secondly, you know your stalker's identity. That means that we can launch both offensive and defensive countermeasures."

"I've got no problem with that," Rollins said. "Defense is what I do. But I don't want to have to hide out forever. Bunkers are boring."

"I second that thought," Abrams said. "I don't know if Hitler gave up or he just needed a change of scenery."

"What do you suggest?" Wiley asked Stuart.

Stuart told them.

When he finished, Abrams said, "I like your approach, Stuart, especially your clever use of that secret weapon. If you are confident that it will work, we are willing to go along—but only as long as Rollins and I are not the only ones with skin in the game."

Wiley met Abrams' eye with a calm gaze, although he knew the coming words would shake him to the core.

Abrams continued. "We won't be organizing any more terrorist attacks until you take Odi Carr out of play—and put him in a box. Consider your campaign on ice."

Chapter 24

Alexandria, Virginia

AN ADRENALINE SURGE accompanied the doorbell's chime, making Cassi feel an odd mixture of longing and fear. She missed Wiley dearly despite his decision to sacrifice their relationship for his political ambition. She got up from the sofa, set down the latest issue of *The Journal of Child Psychology*, and walked to the door.

The last time she had seen Wiley she was still in the hospital, confined to a bed and sporting an inch-thick cap of gauze on her head. He had left her after saying that he needed to let things cool down before he would attempt to salvage her career, and she had not seen him since. Then out of the blue he had called an hour ago to say that he was coming over with news. Did that mean she was in the clear? Or declared radioactive?

Cassi had struggled to get through the job suspension with her sanity intact. With no Wiley or work to distract her, she had been alone with the demons of her mind—and the ghosts of two dead kids. Every time she looked out her window, she only saw what wasn't there. She loved her loft, but she was going to have to move. Her family, her career and now her home—she had lost them all. Yet as depressing as her situation was, when she thought of Masha and Zeke, Cassi knew that she was better off than she deserved.

She opened the door to find Wiley wearing what she had come to know as his politician's face. That was not a good sign. With little else to do but sleep in, read books and watch the news, she had been following the rumors of his impending campaign—rumors that she knew to be true. She still had mixed thoughts.

In her heart Cassi hoped that Wiley would not get the job. She wanted him for herself. She acknowledged that this was selfish, but knew better than to try to deny her own emotions. It did not look like she was going to get him, however. Since the recent round of terrorist attacks—the same blitz that took her brother—Wiley's name recognition and public opinion ratings had soared. She tried to be happy for Wiley, but it was no use. For a woman with her daunting profile, finding a meaningful match was a next-to-impossible task. This was a once-in-a-lifetime opportunity for Wiley, no doubt about that, but it might be for her as well. "Are you alone, or did you bring the Secret Service?"

Wiley chortled as he stepped through the doorway. Then he gave her a single, soft kiss on the cheek. He never did that when they were dating, she noted, kiss her while they were standing up. She figured it was his subconscious aversion to having to tilt up his head.

Cassi procrastinated receiving news of her own fate by preemptively asking about Wiley's. "So, is it going to happen? Will President Carver offer you the job?"

"I have no idea what the President intends," Wiley said dismissively. "Mind if I take a seat?"

"Of course," she said, leading him to the armchairs she had repositioned before her indoor waterfall. This was her new favorite sitting spot, now that the view of the playground was out.

She had a bottle of Chablis cooling in an ice bucket. She wished she had thought to turn on music as she poured them each a glass. The silence was awkward. "Cheers."

"I've come with good news," Wiley said without taking a sip. "The FBI is not going to force you out. In fact, I've already got your new assignment."

Wiley's words seemed to open a curtain, and Cassi felt sunshine come streaming into her dark world. "Oh, Wiley, that's wonderful. Thank you. Thank you so much."

Wiley spread his arms and bowed. "Anything for you."

Oh, if only that were true, Cassi thought. "What's the assignment?"

"Well, it's an unconventional role—for political reasons—but I'm sure you're going to like it."

"An unconventional role," Cassi repeated, not liking the sound of that. "What does that mean, exactly?"

"Two children died, Cassi, so it's going to have to look like you're being punished. Officially, you're going to be swept aside into a back-office research role."

Cassi wanted to protest that it wasn't fair, that Masha and Zeke's deaths were not her fault. But to be honest, she could not even convince herself. She had to consider herself lucky to be getting anything but sacked. In fact, she realized, lucky probably wasn't the appropriate word. Wiley must have gone to bat for her big time. "And unofficially?"

Wiley brightened. "I know your passion lies in counterterrorism, so that's what you'll be doing. In fact, you'll be in charge of a very important case."

Cassi felt a surge of warmth growing in her belly. That sounded wonderful—too good to be true. Alarm bells started to sound but she stifled them. "A terrorist case?"

Wiley nodded and dove in. "A terrorist case. And a highly classified one at that."

"And I'll be in charge."

"You will, although it's just going to be a one-woman team."

Cassi bit her lower lip and considered this. Although physically surrounded by others while working, she had always managed her negotiations alone. "I'm okay with that. Tell me about it."

"In a nutshell, a terrorist has begun assassinating US defense contractors. Your job is to catch him."

"How can that be a one-person task? Is this just a theory I'm to prove?"

Wiley shook his head gravely. "Last Friday the CEO of Defcon4, Mark Drake, was murdered."

Cassi nodded. "I saw that on the news. Someone put a bomb under his car. They said a major investigation was underway by both the local police and the FBI, on account of his being a prominent British citizen." Cassi read Wiley's expression and her mind raced ahead. "But that's not what's really going on, is it?"

"It is as far as the public, the police force and even the FBI are concerned. But no, it's not. Believe it or not, I got a call from the director of the CIA. It seems they have a mole highly placed within al-Qaeda who says that Drake's death was an al-Qaeda hit. In fact, that mole told us that Drake is just the first of many. Apparently, al-Qaeda has hired a professional assassin, and they've given him a list."

"A hired assassin," Cassi interrupted. "Why would al-Qaeda hire an assassin?"

"You're the profiler. At least you used to be. Consider the profile of the average assassin, and then compare it to the average al-Qaeda operative. I'm sure you'll see there's quite a difference."

"A difference that circumvents half our screening and security measures," Cassi thought out loud while nodding appreciatively.

"The CIA mole has no idea who the assassin is, but he was able to get us the names of his next two targets."

Cassi's adrenaline continued to surge as issues and ideas began colliding in her head. This was getting very deep very fast.

"Here's the rub," Wiley continued. "The CIA is desperate to protect the fact that they have a mole. In fact, sacrificing the next two victims is a price that they are willing to pay. They need their source in place to give them notice of the next mass attack, the next 9/11."

Cassi was beginning to understand. "So you can't let the public know that you know Drake's death was the first in a series of planned terrorist assassinations."

"Correct. And it gets even more complicated than that. The CIA mole says al-Qaeda has a highly placed source within the FBI, although again he doesn't know who it is. That leak led to the ambush that killed your brother. Al-Qaeda knew that Team Echo was coming.

"Needless to say, I can't let anyone in the agency know what I've just told you. Furthermore, whoever the mole is, he is willing to kill to protect his identity. Commander Potchak was murdered by the same means as Drake, presumably because he saw or heard something that made the mole uncomfortable." Wiley stopped talking and raised his eyebrows, waiting for her reaction.

Cassi struggled to separate the flood of emotion from the wave of information. She would digest the facts later. For now, she was just pleased to understand her new role. "Thus you need a low-profile, one-person team. Someone you know you can trust. Someone you can reassign without raising any alarms."

"Precisely."

"So what, exactly, am I to do?"

"The first thing you have to do is meet with the next two people on the assassin's list and make them hard targets. They, like Drake, are both defense corporation CEOs. One is Mark Rollins, CEO of Rollins, and the other is Mark Abrams, CEO of ASIS. Wall Street knows them collectively as The Three Marks."

The irony of the moniker was not lost on Cassi. She nodded. Her task sounded simple enough.

Reading her mind, Wiley said, "It's not going to be an easy sale. First of all, I can only send you, which implies that the FBI is not overly serious. And, of course, you can't let them know that they're on a list or even that we have inside knowledge, for the reasons already mentioned. But at the same time, you have to get them to take this seriously enough to agree to some highly inconvenient lifestyle changes."

"So basically, you're placing their lives in my hands, but they're not allowed to know it."

"Precisely."

Cassi thought about what that would mean in practical terms. She did not know anything about Rollins or Abrams, but she could guess that billionaire CEOs would be arrogant and cocky and would have a child's immortality complex. Her assignment was not going to be easy. Then she thought of Masha and Zeke and decided that saving these two might be her best chance to begin making amends. She drew her gaze from the slate waterfall back to Wiley. "I'll get the job done."

"I know you will, Cassi. That's why I was thrilled to come by the opportunity to give you this job. I think it's a perfect fit, given our circumstances."

"Any suggestions on where I should start?"

Wiley opened his briefcase and withdrew five thick folders. "This is everything we have from Potchak's and Drake's murder scenes, as well as background information on Drake, Rollins, Abrams and their companies. You are to use this to create a profile on the assassin and then use that profile to make specific security suggestions to Rollins and Abrams—all the while being careful not to betray the fact that we have a source."

Cassi nodded. She understood. "Thank you, Wiley. I'm your agent. What's the timeframe for the profile and plan?"

Wiley flashed her a guilty look. "I hope this leave has given you a chance to catch up on your sleep, because you may not be getting much until you catch the assassin. You're presenting to Rollins and Abrams in Wilmington—tomorrow afternoon."

Cassi grimaced. Profiles usually took weeks to compile and then got sent off in the mail. She would be hopping on an airplane to present hers in less than twenty-four hours. "Tomorrow afternoon. Great."

"That's not all," Wiley continued. "Once you've gotten Rollins and Abrams squared away, your real job begins—"

Cassi raised her chin.

"You're to use that profile to anticipate the assassin's moves ... and lure him into a trap."

Chapter 25

Chesapeake Beach, Maryland

SITTING ON A DARK PORCH in a white wooden rocker, Odi nursed a beer and stared at the glow of his laptop computer screen. He hoped Ayden would come online as promised. He had a lot to get off his chest.

He was holed up in his Aunt Charlotte's summerhouse. He found it the perfect place to plan his moves and hide out between hits. There were few residents on her stretch of the Chesapeake shore this time of year. Most sought warmer climes, including Charlotte herself. She was in Phoenix.

He drew comfort from the surroundings. Their familiarity was a soothing balm, given that everything else in his life had changed. His family had enjoyed many a summer there with Charlotte when he and Cassi were kids. Her cottage was a modest, wooden structure built largely by his uncle in the mid-sixties. Odi had not noticed back then just how modest it was. He reflected on how wonderful it was to be an unspoiled kid. He closed his eyes, leaned back in the rocker, and listened to the rhythmic clang of a neighboring warning buoy. As a kid he had fallen asleep to that sound a hundred times.

A different sound interrupted his reverie. His computer had chimed ta-dong, indicating that Ayden had arrived online. Odi leaned forward and pressed send, dispatching the message he had prepared.

Two minutes later, he heard a friendly zzhing announcing the arrival of an instant message. He looked down and read Ayden's reply. "Saw your video. Unbelievable. That Creamer of yours is powerful stuff!"

Odi gathered that the gory shots had not repulsed his friend. That was no surprise, his being a doctor in a violent region, but it was still a relief. Ayden had helped to put together the general plan, but Odi had not decided on his tactics before leaving Iran. His e-mail package to Ayden contained a brief explanation of the Creamer along with ten seconds of highlights from the Potchak video clip. "So you approve?" he typed.

"Sure. Where did you get the explosive?"

"I made it," Odi typed with some pride. "I went back to Johns Hopkins and used the same lab where I invented the stuff—working at night, of course."

"No risk of getting caught?"

"Naw. I'm still young enough to be mistaken for a graduate student if someone sees me, and the graduate chemistry lab has used the same formula for their door code for years."

"Formula?"

"It's the square of the numeric value of the month converted from Centigrade to Fahrenheit."

"Pardon?"

"This is October, the 10th month. So the code's 212. That's 10 squared times 9 divided by 5 plus 32."

"Okay ... Anyway, your explosive is brilliant. Brilliant and chilling."

"Thanks. Let's hope that it's chilling enough to catalyze the desired reaction." Odi leaned back from the keyboard feeling better for having shared his experiences. His newfound sense of relaxation and relief made Ayden's next message all the more disturbing.

"You're going to have to kill them all. It's naïve to think that those kings are going to walk away from their thrones. That isn't the way of the world. Never has been. Never will be."

Odi tried to think of a clever retort. It only took him a second. "Attorneys make deals every day for the sentence of life behind bars when the alternative is the electric chair or the needle."

"Nice analogy," Ayden replied. "But it only applies to people who have been caught. These guys don't consider themselves caught yet. Your proposition is nothing to them but an invitation to a game of cat and mouse."

"I've got claws."

"Maybe, but kings like these are going to consider you a mouse."

Odi felt his excitement deflating. He thought he had found a way to render true justice, to get the truth out and put the bad guys behind bars. In fact, judging by the rich-and-famous cases that had made it to court in recent years, he considered his solution to be the only way that an American billionaire would ever be exposed to justice. He owed his fallen comrades that justice. He pounded his response into the keys. "One way or another, I am going to dethrone those kings—starting tomorrow night."

Chapter 26

The White House

"THANK YOU, GENTLEMEN," President Carver said, rising from his chair.

As Wiley filed out of the Roosevelt Room with the other members of the committee, the president's aide took hold of his elbow. Jerome Murphy would normally have been one of those guys you loved to hate. He had a brilliant mind, a Herculean build, and exceptional good looks. But he was so unassuming and nice that you could not help liking him instead. Still, Wiley had no doubt that Murphy had his eye on the boss's office, so he was ever on guard. Vigilance was Wiley's watchword around men of ambition.

Wiley allowed Murphy to escort him silently through a couple sets of guarded doors and the chief of staff's office into the president's private study. "Please, have a seat," Murphy said. Then he walked out and closed the door.

Wiley had grown up wealthy among men of power, so titles and architecture did little to impress him. He knew that the president pissed yellow just like everyone else, and he saw the Oval Office as nothing more than a famous arrangement of bricks and mortar. Still, he got a thrill out of this first visit to the president's private study. Rumor had it that this was where presidents conducted much of the business unsuitable for the official record. Had Marilyn Monroe waited here as he did now? Naked?

As he sat down to wait, Wiley felt butterflies begin to dance. His subconscious was voicing the words his conscious did not want to hear. Whatever happened next would be either very good, or very bad.

President Carver entered the study almost immediately through another door. Wiley caught a quick glimpse of the Oval before it closed. "Thank you for staying, Wiley. Please, remain in your seat."

The windowless study had royal blue carpet and white plaster walls. The furnishings were handmade from gold upholstery and rich mahogany wood. Wiley was pleasantly surprised to detect the scent of cigar smoke, though the cleaners clearly tried to overpower it with room freshener and furniture polish. He always found deep satisfaction in the discovery of another man's peccadilloes.

As Carver sat opposite him in a matching chair, Murphy entered with two glasses of freshly squeezed orange juice. Wiley would have preferred another cup of joe to the president's favorite drink—the only

C Wiley ever craved was caffeine—but he accepted it with a grateful smile, saying, "Perfect," after savoring a sip. He set down the glass, smiled at Carver and tried to relax.

"A privilege of the office," Carver concurred. Then he hardened his features and cut to the chase.

"We didn't predict the fall of the Berlin Wall or the collapse of the Soviet Union. We didn't foresee 9/11 or Hamas. Yet even with all that precedent, I'm going to look like one of history's greatest fools if al-Qaeda pulls off something major on US soil after my own FBI Director has spent the year blasting the airwaves and editorials with predictions of an impending attack."

"With all due respect, Mr. President, that's not necessarily true," Wiley interrupted. "You just need to be seen taking a firm and active stand."

Carver paused to consider Wiley's words, but then forged ahead on a predetermined course. "I trust you didn't hold anything back earlier in your briefing. You really have no idea when or where the next attack will come?"

"I could give you the techno-fluff we feed the media about increased chatter and prime targets of attack," Wiley said, "but that won't get you further in practical terms than a little common sense."

"Still, you're predicting that the next attack is coming soon, say within a few months?"

"I am, Mr. President."

"Please elaborate."

Wiley knew that he was on dangerous ground. He had to remain vague yet valuable, coy yet credible. "I wish I could, but all I have is intuition—the confluence of thousands of subliminal clues gleaned from the endless stream of reports crossing my desk." With someone else, Wiley would have repeated the same statement another way, adding no facts while making his answer seem more complete. But he knew that tactic would not fool Carver, so he stopped.

Carver stared at him, and then seemed to make a decision. His stern look evaporated into his trademark smile and he said, "Well, it's good to have a prophet on my team."

"Thank you, Mr. President," Wiley replied, struggling to suppress the glee erupting within at Carver's choice of adjectives.

Wiley thought that was the end of the meeting, but then Carver continued. "If there's one thing the base likes, one thing that will drive them to the polls next November, it's a hellfire-and-brimstone prophet —assuming, of course, that terrorism still piques their interest."

With that repetition and embellishment, Wiley felt a hot surge of adrenaline rush from his heart to the far ends of his body. Carver had said it. He had actually said it. Only thanks to a lifetime of practice was Wiley able to keep his poker face un-cracked.

Carver seemed to be reading his expression anyway. The president flashed him an amused smile. "I understand Stuart Slider is consulting for you now."

Wiley was shocked. Carver was throwing all subtlety aside. This was unbelievable.

"You're not my only source of information," the president continued. "Anyway, I was glad to hear that. Stuart is very, very good."

"Thank you," was all Wiley could think of to say. He was elated beyond words, at least until his eyes drifted to the doorway of the chief of staff and remembered the price he had to pay.

Chapter 27

Annapolis, Maryland

STANDING THERE in the ASIS boardroom, Cassi could not shake the feeling that the two CEOs had something dubious to hide— especially Rollins. He looked positively evil. She could tell that both men were a lot more scared than they were letting on and her instincts were screaming that that was important. But she had yet to pinpoint why. Were they just being coy because they were mighty captains of the defense industry and she was a woman? That was possible, but Cassi did not find it likely. Given the context, she felt that the very fact that they were trying hard not to betray their fear indicated a sense of guilt. Still, she was not there to investigate collusion, be it with Drake or against him. She was there to salvage her career and save two lives.

So far, Cassi did not have the impression that she was doing well on either account. She would know for certain soon enough. She concluded the formal portion of her virtually impromptu presentation with what she hoped would be a provocative line. "One thing we do know for certain is the nature of the beast. Mark Drake was killed by a professional."

Abrams and Rollins both continued to lean back in their leather chairs as she finished. Cassi felt a chill of disappointment. Her lure had not brought them forward. "But you don't know which professional," Abrams said after an uncomfortable silence. It was a statement of fact by a man unimpressed. "Nor do you know whom he was working for."

"Or why," Rollins added. "Yet you chose to warn us. That's quite a leap."

"Might even border on harassment," Abrams said.

Cassi bit her tongue, reminding herself to stay on target even as she felt her FBI career slipping from her grasp. Their skepticism might not be personal. Perhaps these guys had endured a recent proctologic exam courtesy of another federal agency, perhaps the IRS. In any case, she had to deduct that her feed-them-the-facts approach had failed to light their fires. The fact that she'd had only hours to prepare it would not buy her any slack in Quantico. Whatever goodwill she had previously enjoyed, the daycare disaster had destroyed.

She weighed her options and decided to regroup to launch a second offensive from more familiar ground. She closed her eyes for a second, just long enough to slip into The Zone. She pictured Rollins and Abrams on her chessboard, looking like Laurel and Hardy. She leaned forward toward the obese Abrams as the fire reignited in her eyes. "You're right," she said. "There are dozens of reasons why someone might want to kill your colleague that have nothing to do with either of you. Why, there could be a hundred. So for the sake of argument, let us suppose that there is only a one-in-a-hundred chance that Drake's killer is planning to shove a grenade up your ass. Are you willing to accept those odds, gentlemen? Are you willing to risk everything on a single roll of the dice? Or would you rather work with me to keep your proctologist happy?"

Rollins' gaunt cheeks assumed a lemon-like pucker. He turned to Abrams, who shrugged his fleshy shoulders. "What do you know about the assassin, Agent Carr?"

That was more like it, she thought. She decided to skip the usual statistical qualifiers and give it to them with both barrels. She needed to make the assassin's threat seem credible. To do that she needed to make the assassin feel real to them. Besides, if she got something wrong, nobody would know it until she caught him, and then no one would care. This time she leaned toward Rollins. "We're looking for a white male in his thirties. He is a large man, about six feet tall, with an athletic build. He keeps his hair short and does not wear glasses. He is skilled as an actor, and capable of convincingly altering both his appearance and his voice. He works alone on the basis of meticulous advance planning. He is highly disciplined, highly educated and exceptionally creative. He is a techie, comfortable with everything from digital cameras to laptop computers. And he is a chemist, capable of brewing sophisticated original ordnance. He is knowledgeable of investigative procedures and forensics. He is passionate about his work and yet coldly detached. In short, gentleman, he is as serious as the death he deals. Of all the profiles I've worked over the years, this is the man I would fear the most if he was after me."

During her speech, Cassi was delighted to see both faces begin to crack. Now she leaned back in the plush chair and hoped for an inviting fissure.

Abrams offered one. "What are you asking of us?"

"I want free rein to work with the heads of your corporate security to augment your personal protection. I want them and everyone working for them to know that my orders are to be accepted without pushback."

"We're a defense contractor," Rollins said. "Our security is already top notch. You must be aware of that." Then he walked right into her trap. It couldn't have happened to a nicer guy, she thought. "I'm sure that even with your gold shield you didn't get your gun past my men."

Cassi smiled and opened her purse. "You're right. They asked me to leave my firearm at the door." She withdrew three lipstick tubes from a side zipper pocket. Then she added, "Hexamine, nitric acid and ammonium nitrate," as she set each down like a missile on Rollins' precious table. "I may as well be packing a rectal grenade."

Rollins grew a shade paler, but he was not finished yet. "Do I understand that it's our personal safety rather than our companies' security that you are worried about?"

"That's correct."

"Well, then you needn't worry about me. I'm scheduled for two weeks of annual leave starting Monday. There's no reason I can't start a few days early. I will be staying at my Florida beach house, which may as well be Fort Knox. It's built to withstand Category 5 hurricane winds, and the security system is state of the art."

"That sounds like a promising start," Cassi said. "The important thing in the short term is to get you out of your usual routine. Do you have room at your beach house for a contingent of guards?"

"As many as you'd like."

"Tell me about the place."

"I've got two acres of oceanfront property on a semi-private beach."

"Semi-private?"

"Velveteen Beach is a three-mile-long, one-bridge island separated from the Florida mainland by the intracoastal waterway. The houses on Velveteen are few and far between, numbering only eighteen in total."

Cassi nodded. "Very well. I'd guess six guards should be able to secure a location like that around the clock. With your permission, I'll ask your director of security to make those arrangements."

Rollins nodded.

Cassi turned to the larger CEO. "What about you, Mr. Abrams? Do you have any vacation coming?"

"No, and I'm afraid that taking leave is out of the question at the moment. But I can confine myself to my home and the office, with a short helicopter ride in between."

"I'll need to inspect both sites. Will you be flying home tonight?"

"Yes."

"May I join you?"

Abrams stroked his chin between a pork-chop thumb and two sausage fingers.

"I'll only need a couple of hours if your majordomo will cooperate," Cassi added.

"All right."

"So we're agreed then," Rollins said. "I'll leave immediately on vacation in the company of the dirty half-dozen. And Miss Carr will accompany Abrams home tonight to help wall him in."

As Cassi concurred, Abrams asked, "Agent Carr, I'm assuming that you will be able to wrap this up in a week or so. Is that correct?"

Cassi attempted to give a nod that conveyed more confidence than she felt.

"Then I'll give you my full cooperation—until a week from this Friday," Abrams said. "If I haven't heard the all-clear by then, I'm going to make a call to your boss."

As he spoke those closing words an odd look passed between Abrams and Rollins. Cassi did not know what it meant, but she left the meeting with an unsettling impression. It was almost like she was being used …

Chapter 28

Velveteen Beach, Florida

ODI PAUSED with his finger on the trigger. Something did not feel right. He squirmed to adjust the pile of sand beneath his chest and then added a few scoops. He wanted to take more weight off his elbows, leaving his arms completely relaxed. Satisfied with his position, he closed his eyes and focused on the ocean's swishy roar as he slowly inhaled and exhaled a deep breath of salty air. It was time.

He refocused his gaze on the laptop lying before him on the dune and squeezed the joystick's trigger. Four yards to his left the rotor of a remote-controlled helicopter spun to life, kicking up a cloud of fine white sand. Odi squeezed harder and the craft began to rise. He took it straight up, easing off on the trigger only when the altimeter display on his computer screen indicated a height of forty feet. Forty was what he needed to clear the neighboring rooftops with a margin of safety.

Focusing on the screen's main display, he watched his own prone form come into focus as the helicopter leveled off. There between the rolling dunes of Velveteen Beach he looked like a single hotdog in a sea of buns. He smiled, pleased that the hobby shop salesman had not talked him out of an extra four-hundred bucks in vain. Even at night the picture quality transmitted from above was remarkably clear. He could trace the individual camouflage splotches on his desert BDUs.

He used the joystick's thumb lever to orient the helicopter due south and then pushed the handgrip forward. The bird responded like a dream. It was both nimble and quick.

Odi had positioned himself three houses down from Rollins' place where he still had line-of-sight to the CEO's third floor across half a mile of sea oat-covered dune. He had reconned the beach from Charlotte's cottage using Google's keyhole satellite shots. With those photos, it took him just ten minutes to find what looked from above like the perfect spot, and the reality on the ground had not disappointed him.

He had exercised extreme caution getting to Velveteen, especially for the last few miles. Odi reasoned that if he were in charge of Rollins's security, he would have a man watching the bridge through a long-distance lens. So he parked his rental car at a motel on the mainland and crossed the river on the bridge's scaffolding just as the sun was going down. It was the time of day when everyone's eyes played tricks and the ground was still hot enough from the Florida sun to make infrared binoculars worthless.

Once on the island, he low-crawled sniper style most of the way from the bridge to his chosen location, taking his time, moving bush to bush when no one was around. The size of the pack he had carried would have earned him a kick in the balls from every drill sergeant he ever knew, but for this operation he needed every bit of the bulky cargo stored therein so he had risked it. If detected, he had planned to pretend to be the nephew of a local resident, a soldier on leave preparing for upcoming Special Forces training. But he made it to the beach without incident or challenge. Once settled into his pre-selected spot on the dunes, he had spent six virtually motionless hours studying his target through a telescope lens while struggling to ignore the constant nipping of sand fleas.

The presence of attentive guards working three-man shifts bothered Odi. It was not that they posed any particular threat or challenge. He had built his plan around them. Rather, he was irked because their presence reconfirmed that neither Rollins nor Abrams intended to come forward and confess. That was a disappointment if not a surprise. Ayden had predicted as much, but it still blew Odi's mind. How could the condemned men ignore him once they had seen the explosive video of their lackey and the encore with their colleague? Odi retained hope that Abrams would come forward tomorrow after Rollins's death, but he would not hold his breath.

Odi tracked the helicopter's position by comparing what he saw on the laptop screen to the printout he had made from the Google satellite shot. As the neighbor's swimming pool disappeared from the screen, he felt the thrill of the end game kicking in. A moment later the helicopter was over the target.

Rollins' beach house was a beautiful three-story white structure, with multiple balconies and lots of floor-to-ceiling tinted glass. Looking at it from his flea-ridden dugout in the sand, Odi could not help remembering that he had passed up the opportunity to spend his life in one of those. He had passed on the beach to work for Potchak. The thought set his blood aboil. Only with effort was he able to push his feelings of betrayal aside and refocus his attention completely on the mission at hand.

He could see the whole oceanfront side of the mansion from his position in the dunes. When the guards were out of sight, it looked more like the setting of a romance novel than a thriller. "Except for the damn fleas," he added aloud, swatting for the thousandth time. Once the sun had set and the lights had gone on, it had not taken him much time with the telescope to figure out which balcony belonged to the master bedroom. Now that the lights were out, he steered the helicopter to where they had been.

He tried to position the helicopter directly over the master balcony, but gusting winds were creating a dangerous stability challenge. For this to work he had to align it midway between roof and rail and perpendicular to the master bedroom's sliding glass door. He cursed himself for forgetting to factor wind into the equation when designing the payload. If, after all he had gone through to get here, he had to abort his beautiful plan on account of something as mundane as wind, he would go berserk. That would be like scrapping the moon shot for a flat tire.

Three minutes and five aborted attempts later sweat was rolling down his face despite the evening chill. After six he began to worry about running out of fuel. After seven he was weighing the risks of a frontal assault. On the eighth he managed to hold the bird in place just long enough. The instant he had the position right, he brought the bird straight down. Given the position of the camera on the belly of the craft, all Odi saw for the last couple of feet of descent was a quickly rising floor and then a close-up still shot of tile grout. Tactically, the landing was perfect. He hoped it had not made too much noise. That was another oversight, Odi realized with a groan—not installing sound. For all he knew, a guard could be studying the helicopter right now, asking his boss via radio what he should do. Live and learn.

He pushed the silver button on the joystick's base, causing the cargo clamps beneath the helicopter to disengage. The camera jiggled a bit and Odi let out a sigh of relief. He had successfully separated the cargo from the bird that had delivered it.

Odi lifted his night vision binoculars, located the porch and felt a wave of relief. No guard. No lights. Time for stage two.

He fine-tuned the focus on the binoculars and then, still holding them in his left hand, squeezed the joystick trigger again with his right. He watched with satisfaction as the helicopter rose straight up into the air above the roof while the image transmitted to his computer screen remained unchanged.

He continued to take the unburdened helicopter up to a height of fifty feet where, using the binoculars and joystick's thumb toggle, he pointed its nose out to sea. He pushed forward fully on the stick, sending the helicopter racing out over the water. Without any cargo, it streaked like a missile across the sky. He let it fly until it was little more than a dot on the horizon. Then he released the trigger. The rotor stopped, and the helicopter dropped like a bagged duck into the waves. Speaking to no one but the sea, he said, "Stage two, complete."

Odi withdrew a second remote from his backpack and lay back down between the dunes. Once settled, he returned his attention to the computer screen. He had custom built the robot that now graced Rollins' balcony using a remote-controlled toy jeep as a base. It rolled on four suction cup-covered wheels and had lots of sophisticated robotic equipment attached. He turned on the joystick and gave it a short forward nudge to confirm that it was operational, sighing with satisfaction when the camera image moved. So far, so good, Odi thought, knowing that the real tests of his engineering prowess still lay ahead.

He used the run of the grout to position the robot so that it was perfectly perpendicular to the sliding door. Then he drove it forward. The image shook back and forth after a couple of feet and then the view jumped to show the weak reflection of moonlight off heavy glass. Odi felt the thrill of the hunt coursing through his veins. He was almost there.

He propelled the robot up the sliding glass door to a height of six feet and then released the joystick with a silent prayer. From his practice sessions on Charlotte's door he knew that this was a tender moment, but the technology did not fail. The robot stuck.

He toyed with the focus, trying to get a good look inside the bedroom. With the helicopter gone, there was not much he would be able to do if the robot was in the wrong place. Odi was sure that he had the master bedroom, but there was still the chance that Rollins had swapped rooms with a guard as a security measure. All Odi could do about that was hope that Rollins was too stubborn or the guards were not that good.

He adjusted the focus, taking the image a couple of turns in the wrong direction before finally getting it right. Once the image crystallized he felt another satisfying surge. Mark Rollins was sleeping beneath a white duvet on a raised platform bed. Odi used the computer to zoom in on the face just to be sure. The meticulously parted dark hair and long patrician nose of the master of the house greeted him. "Bingo."

He pressed a black button on the joystick, engaging the robot's auxiliary suction cups. Now even with the activities to follow, the robot would not slip.

Panning back out to a wider view, he saw something that made his heart skip a beat. There was a brassiere on the floor. Unless Rollins had a habit of cross-dressing, he was not alone in that big platform bed.

Odi would not allow collateral casualties to taint what Ayden had facetiously dubbed Operation Just Revenge. He would not be able to live with himself after that. He also felt certain that his fallen comrades would not want their revenge at that price. If the woman buried beneath that king-sized duvet did not remain motionless during the next few minutes, Odi would have to abort. To minimize the chances of that happening, he decided to sacrifice caution for speed.

He pushed a yellow button on the remote control, spraying concentrated hydrofluoric acid onto the glass a couple of inches below the anchoring suction cups. Hydrofluoric acid was especially potent on glass. It would dissolve a baseball-sized hole in less than a minute, even in Rollins' hurricane glass. The hole would both help to direct the explosion and make the entire window weak.

Odi watched the duvet while he worked. Nobody stirred. Full speed ahead. He pressed the orange button exactly sixty seconds after the yellow, holding it down. He smiled with satisfaction as the camera began to respond with a slight, rhythmic shake. The orange button controlled a pecking device, which was now double-tapping every other second against the glass. Tap-tap ... tap-tap ... tap-tap ... After half a dozen pecks, the duvet began to stir.

"Attaboy."

After a few more taps, Rollins rolled cautiously out of bed.

Odi let off on the button and the pecking stopped.

As Mark Rollins stood up and looked around, Odi's eyes were drawn to the gun in his hand. "Excellent," he mumbled. "With a 9mm Beretta in your hand, you're not feeling the need to call for help."

Odi glued his eyes to the screen as Mark surveyed his room. Each time Mark turned his head from the balcony, Odi gave the button another quick press. After the third salvo Mark raised his gun and walked directly toward the camera, tilting his head from one side to the other as though trying to focus. He was probably wondering if it was possible for a seagull to fly fast enough to imbed itself in hurricane-proof glass.

Odi would have enjoyed watching the doomed man's confused face, but he forced himself to keep his focus on the duvet. He prayed the owner of the brassiere would stay fully covered for another two seconds. She did.

Pictures of Odi's fallen friends flashed through his mind: Adam, Derek, Flint, Jeremy, Mitch and Tony. Finally Rollins' inquisitive face got so close that Odi could see nothing else. He said, "You should have confessed," and then pressed the red button.

Chapter 29

FBI Headquarters, Washington, D.C.

WILEY LOOKED OVER at Stuart, pleased to have his campaign manager's company for once. Stuart seemed to sense Wiley's gaze even with his back turned. When he looked over his shoulder, Wiley said, "I've finished with London Heathrow. A dozen were close, but none were close enough. I've got nothing."

With Drake and Rollins now dead, Abrams was the only defense CEO they had left. That made Wiley nervous. Though Stuart would not show it, Wiley was convinced that his campaign manager was feeling the butterflies. While the CEOs replacing Drake and Rollins would surely give Wiley's campaign their financial support, agreeing to stage terrorist attacks was an entirely different matter. Abrams insisted that he would be able to bring the new CEOs on board with the plan, but he refused to make a move until Odi Carr was on a coroner's slab. The man was adamant. "No toe tag, no dice."

Wiley silently cursed his partner in crime although he could hardly blame Abrams. The man's ass was now squarely in a clever assassin's sights. Of course, Abrams wanted the Director of the FBI fully focused on catching the bastard. Who wouldn't? As part of that focus, Wiley had broken with discretion and brought Stuart to the Hoover Building to help him scan immigration videos. Misery loves company, and Wiley could think of little that was more miserable than spending midnight to dawn studying an endless stream of faces.

Video of every passenger arriving to the US from Europe and the Middle East during the four weeks between the Iranian mission and Potchak's death was queuing up to parade past their tired eyes. It was a monstrous task. Even with the aid of the FBI's sophisticated software, which Wiley had programmed to fast forward the video past women and children and men too short or tall, they still had tens of thousands of faces to study. They were dredging in an ocean rife with weeds but containing only one fish. And the election clock was ticking.

Given the time pressure presented by the election cycle, Wiley was thrilled to have devised a two-pronged approach to killing Odi. While he and Stuart chased Odi from behind, Cassi was out in front of him ready to intercept. Talk about a secret weapon. Whatever disguise Odi chose to use to try to get close to Abrams, there was little chance that Cassi would not recognize him—even though she did not know that it was Odi she was looking for. Yes, Wiley thought, they would get him. The question was, would they get him soon enough?

"What country's next?" Stuart asked.

"I'm thinking Germany. How much Turkey do you have left?"

"I've got sixteen more flights," he replied, stretching his arms over his head.

"Can you believe that there are people who do this all day, every day? You'd think they'd go nuts."

"Or blind."

"What if we can't find Odi before he gets to Abrams?" Wiley asked, noting that his use of we left a bitter taste in his mouth. "You helped plan the first series of attacks. Could you do it again without a CEO's help?"

Stuart shook his head. "I was able to set that up because I had cushy jobs to offer our coconspirators. Without the defense contractors backing us, I don't have anything to offer besides cabinet posts, and that would be too risky."

"But we're so close. You should have heard the president. It was as though Carver took the words right out of your mouth. He said, quote, 'It would be good to have a prophet on my team, assuming terrorism still piques the voters' interest come Election Day.'"

"Well then, let's hope your ex comes through," Stuart said. "I'd love to be a fly on the wall at that reunion."

Wiley imagined that scene—Cassi learning that her twin was alive but a terrorist assassin. Talk about a double-edged sword. He wondered if it was possible to feel like even more of a shit.

"I've got him!" Stuart said, shooting out of his chair.

"Odi?"

"Odi!"

"What name did he use?"

"Hold on. It will take a moment for me to query using the time and station code."

"He flew in from Turkey?"

"Yep. And the name on the passport he used is ... Ayden Archer."

Chapter 30

Annapolis, Maryland

CASSI WAS BACK in the ASIS boardroom, bracing for another fight. As she sat there on eggshells she found herself feeling woozy. Her head had not seen a pillow since Wiley visited her apartment two days before, but she knew that a lack of sleep was only marginally responsible for her imbalance. Her incompetence was the real problem. She had lost yet another life entrusted to her care. Wiley and the FBI had given her a second chance, a shot at redemption—and now Rollins was dead. The fact that she was one person assigned to protect two people would be but a footnote beneath that glaring headline. All her excuses, legitimate though they might be, were not going to keep Rollins' corpse off her performance record. Her only chance of salvation now would be to catch the assassin—while Abrams was still alive.

As she struggled to force her latest failure from her mind, Wilbanks and Abrams entered the boardroom and took their seats without a word. She had spent every minute since their last meeting on plans to enhance Abrams' security. It was time for her report.

Wilbanks, ASIS's chief of security, opened the dialogue. "So you've completed your appraisal?" He asked, leaning back with his arms folded defiantly across his chest. "I trust my men were helpful."

"I have and they were," Cassi replied, understanding at once that there would be no mention of Rollins today. His death was still too fresh, their emotions too raw.

Cassi studied her fencing partner. He had thick white hair which he wore cropped short like a general. Normally this made him look fierce, but today it just presented a strong contrast to the dark bags beneath his eyes. Cassi found herself feeling for the man despite finding him to be a self-promoting prick. Nobody liked an outsider poking around in his affairs, especially when that outsider's job was to tell your boss everything you were doing wrong. She surely wouldn't.

Last night while weighing her options on how to proceed after what was probably the worst first-day on FBI record, Cassi realized that the potential longevity of her relationship with Wilbanks added constraint to complication. She was going to be working closely with him until she caught the assassin. That meant she had to avoid alienating him as she ripped his organization to shreds. She knew that in similar circumstance most people would say, "Screw it," and then blast the guy. But the psychological nuances of daunting situations like these actually fired her up. They also played to her strengths. So she had formulated a teardown-buildup plan.

"Tell me, Special Agent Carr," Abrams said, joining the row, "what exactly did you find?"

"Your complex is a fortress," she said, watching from the corner of her eye for Wilbanks to give Abrams an I-told-you-so nod. He did not disappoint her.

"Wonderful," Abrams said.

"No, it isn't. Not really."

On cue, Wilbanks fired back a petulant, "What's wrong with a fortress?"

Cassi stood and leaned forward, bracing her palms on the gleaming table. "Fortresses are essentially walls meant to keep people out. They will intimidate some, but in fact they are useless once someone gets in."

Wilbanks waved a hand dismissively, though his body language showed that he was worried. "That's like saying a safe is no good if someone opens the door."

"Perhaps, except that in your case tens of thousands of people have the combination." Cassi held up her temporary identity card. Then she withdrew a stack of two-dozen duplicate cards and slid them onto the table where they scattered across the polished surface like a plague. "I made these while I was at lunch."

Wilbanks' face dropped, but his response remained aggressive. "We can't run a company if nobody can come to work."

Now for the build-up, she thought, retaking her seat. "No, you can't. For that reason, security at ASIS is similar to what you find at most major corporations. In fact, you've done a better job than most."

Wilbanks' posture relaxed a hair.

"Tell me what needs to be done to make it better," Abrams said.

"To continue the analogy I started earlier, what you've got now with your electronic card-key system is the equivalent of a computerized wall. It's good at fending off a straightforward frontal assault, but like a brick-and-mortar wall, a computerized wall is useless if the enemy can find a way to open the gate or walk around."

"Or tunnel under," Abrams added. "Yes, I got your point. Tell me about our holes."

"Every card key is a hole, and there's little you can do to make it difficult for an assassin to obtain one of those. All he has to do is snatch a purse or break into a house. If he's clever about it, he'll duplicate the card key and return it without the owner ever noticing that it was gone."

Abrams sighed. Cassi continued. "Then of course there's hacking. Someone could break into your system and authorize his own card. Theft and hacking are just a couple of the many electronic means available. A less sophisticated assassin could simply apply for a job on your maintenance or security staff, or with one of your subcontractors."

Cassi paused to study Abrams. "I can see by the look on your face that you're beginning to understand the problem."

"What am I going to do?" he asked. "I can't raise the drawbridge."

"For starters, you need to put humans in place at all entrances to compare photos to faces."

Abrams looked at Wilbanks who nodded. "Done."

"Next, you need a redundant procedure at the entrance to the executive tower. That guard will also verify everyone's business. Furthermore, you need to make the tower off-limits to all subcontractors and anyone with less than a year on your payroll, including maintenance. Don't allow any service people into the tower, including deliverymen, exterminators, or gardeners. Bring those functions in-house. Even emergency service personnel like police, firemen and paramedics need to be held at bay until their identities can be verified. In essence, you're only to allow known people through that door."

"HR will have a fit, but I can live with that. Anything else?"

"Yes," Cassi pressed. "I know you like to mingle with the troops, but that's going to have to stop. Until we catch this guy, everyone comes to you, here on the twelfth floor. We'll put a guard in each elevator and only allow people on your appointment schedule to access the twelfth floor."

As she finished she saw Abrams preparing to object when a shadow suddenly crossed his face and he gave a single nod. He had obviously remembered Rollins. Cassi continued. "Other than the two glass elevators, the service elevator, the stairway and the helipad on the roof, is there any other way to access the twelfth floor?"

Abrams and Wilbanks both shook their heads.

"I'll have the stairway and the service elevator locked," Wilbanks added. "Fuck the fire inspector. And I'll let my men know that we're not expecting any window cleaners."

"Excellent ideas," Cassi said. "And you might want to put steel bars over any large ventilation ducts."

"Agent Carr?"

"Yes, Mr. Abrams."

"While everything you're suggesting makes sense, I have to wonder if any of these measures would have helped Mark Rollins?"

Cassi felt her stomach drop. "I don't know," she answered honestly. "We still don't know the exact nature of the device used to kill him. The current theory is that the assassin waited in an offshore boat for Rollins to approach his bedroom window and then fired a light antitank weapon (LAW), but that's just a preliminary analysis. The guards swear that they kept watch on the ocean and saw nothing. But the fact is

Mark's dead. And you're right, nothing I've suggested thus far would protect you from a LAW. Are you sure you won't reconsider taking a secret vacation?"

Abrams shook his head. "I'm in the defense business, and as with every business, image is crucial. I can't be seen running with my tail between my legs."

"Well then, I'll work with Wilbanks to get spotters in place by both helipads, and I'll talk with your pilot about varying your route. Other than that, you'll need to keep clear of windows."

"What's to keep the assassin from firing a dozen LAWs into my office?"

Cassi cocked her head. "Two things come to mind. First of all, there's practicality. The odds are slim that he's got that many LAWs. But more importantly, there's his modus operandi. All of the killings thus far have been surgical affairs with no collateral damage. He didn't kill Drake's chauffeur in order to replace him. He just knocked the man out. And he didn't kill Rollins' girlfriend despite the nature of the method. That indicates highly discriminatory behavior."

"In other words, I should keep my assistant close."

"So long as you make me your assistant," Cassi said.

Abrams smiled weakly and then said to Wilbanks, "Why don't you take Agent Carr down to the cafeteria for lunch? You can go through the details of her recommendations, and then spend the afternoon implementing. We can meet up at four o'clock for the flight back to my place. I can hardly wait to see what changes are in store for me there."

~ ~ ~

Four hours later, Cassi was feeling better. Wilbanks had proven to be cooperative, and most of her suggested security measures were already in place. The rest would be implemented by morning. She doubted that the assassin would have had time to plan and execute his next hit within twenty-four hours of the Rollins job, so she felt Abrams was reasonably safe.

Riding up to the twelfth floor in one of the glass elevators that overlooked the flower-and-fountain festooned ASIS quad, Cassi was pleased with the agreement that Abrams would no longer be riding them. If she were the assassin, her tactic would be to watch them through the business end of a sniper scope, waiting for Abrams to step aboard. Killing him here would be like shooting a big fat fish in a small glass barrel. With that thought, Cassi realized that this might be the perfect place for her to set up a trap. Her weary mind kicked back into overdrive.

She looked up at the other glass elevator as it descended a couple of yards away. There was a lone soul riding in it now. If she were the assassin, he would be toast. Surely she could make that work in reverse —if she knew what the assassin looked like. Cassi was confident that her profile was accurate, but it was not discriminate enough to be the basis of a kill shot. Statistically speaking, all that she had done was whittle the US population down to about ten thousand contenders.

As though sensing her stare, the man in the other lift turned to face her. They locked eyes and stared, neither one believing. A second later the elevators' opposing movements cut their line of sight like an umbilical cord. Cassi's heart began pounding, as it never had before. She continued to stare downward in disbelief as conflicting emotions took the fight from her knees. She sank to the floor with a pathetic thud. She had just seen a ghost.

Chapter 31

Chesapeake Beach, Maryland

AS THE HANDS on Charlotte's antique clock lined up on twelve, Odi heard a friendly ta-dong from his computer. He smiled. Midnight on the Chesapeake Bay was seven-thirty A.M. in Tafriz. Ayden was now online. He took his feet off the kitchen table, leaned forward in his chair and typed, "I'm screwed."

A second later he heard the zzhing announcing the arrival of Ayden's reply. "What happened?"

"Abrams just beefed up his security. This morning all I had to do to get into ASIS was swipe an employee ID. This evening they had guards in place checking photos. I got out just as they were sealing the executive tower."

"So Abrams is scared, but not scared enough to come forward and confess," Ayden summarized.

"He's hiding behind an army of corporate security."

"You'll think of something."

Given a little time, Odi knew that he would think of something. Strict procedures were good for the weaker links, but they conditioned brighter people to stop using their heads. That created new opportunities and opened new gaps. It would not take him long to identify a snafu that he could exploit.

If only it were that simple.

He typed, "I was spotted."

"You know someone at ASIS?" Ayden asked.

"It was my sister. Wiley must have brought her in. The bastard. That means he's figured out it's me."

"Did you speak to her?"

"No, but that doesn't matter. She saw my eyes. In her mind, there's no question. Now my airtight alibi has a leak."

"Only if she tells someone."

That was true, Odi thought. He was not sure what Cassi would do with the news. She would certainly feel torn. "I saw her eyes too, Ayden. I saw her emotions change from shock to jubilation to horror over the course of two seconds. She thinks I'm a cold-blooded killer." His fingers trembled as he typed.

Ayden's reply was mercifully swift. "Only because she's ignorant. She doesn't know about Iran, about Adam and Flint and the others. Look Odi, I see children stare at their parents like they're Benedict Arnold every time I pull out a needle. The kids scream of betrayal but the parents always go through with the shot. They accept the temporary emotional backlash because they know that the pain is for their child's own good."

Odi stared at the keyboard and thought about that. Ayden had a good point. Still, he was not sure he could go ahead with the Abrams execution, much less Wiley's. The danger was at a whole new level now, and with his sister aware and watching, it just did not feel right. He contemplated that for a moment longer with his fingers poised over the keys. Finally, he typed, "I think I'm through."

Ayden took a long time to write back. When he did, he said, "Don't quit just because it's getting hard. You owe it to your men to see this through to the end."

Ayden's encouragement helped, but Odi needed more. He typed, "Abrams is in a vault now, and he knows I'm coming. There's a good chance that I'll get caught, which is the same thing as being killed. Remember, since I'm already dead, they can kill me with impunity. Besides, maybe the pressure will get to Abrams and he'll come forward and confess—now that Rollins is also gone." Odi fully expected Ayden to retort with a scornful assault on his continued naïveté. Instead he got a shock.

"I can handle Abrams."

"What?"

"It turns out that I have a friend who can get close to him, close enough to slip him some Creamer. All you need to do to be rid of Abrams is get her a dose."

Odi stared at his computer screen. Tactically, that would be perfect. Strategically, it was dubious. He ran the back of his palm over his sweaty brow. Ayden's plan meant that somebody else would be involved. By involving a third person in their plans, they were multiplying the risks exponentially. What was that old saw: three people can keep a secret—as long as two of them are dead. With nervous fingers he typed, "Tell me more."

"I don't think that's a good idea. The less you know the better. Better to just leave a dose of Creamer at a drop and move on to your next target."

Odi was relieved to find Ayden half-a-step ahead of him. He asked himself what he had to lose—and came up empty. Besides, he was anxious to get back to Iran and wake up. Still, he had promised himself never to give Creamer to anyone else. It would be a disaster if his invention ever got released to the world.

He stared at the cursor for a long minute, weighing the pros and cons with a heavy heart and a troubled mind. Finally, he typed, "Agreed."

Chapter 32

The Horus Club, Washington, D.C.

WILEY WAITED for the Horus Club's deaf waiter to set down their drinks and turn his back before giving Stuart the news. "Ayden Archer is a real man."

Stuart raised his eyebrows, as if to say, Is that all the Director of the FBI was able to learn in twenty-four hours. "Is that surprising?" he asked. "I assumed Odi just stole the passport, or maybe bought it. Either would be easier than trying to generate a fake."

Wiley enjoyed watching Stuart take the hook. Now he had to make him swallow. "Even overseas, in Iran? Don't forget, passports have a photo."

"That's hardly an obstacle. If I were Odi, I would find a place that serves alcohol—a five-star hotel or an expat function—and look for someone who resembled me. Then I would get him drunk discussing war stories, and pick his pocket."

Wiley had often found geniuses to be incompetent if asked to perform a hair's breadth outside their area of expertise, so he was pleased to hear that Stuart's talents extended from politics to the dark arts—not that that was much of a stretch. His campaign manager was about to need that additional competence.

Wiley pulled a photo printout from the breast pocket of his blazer and handed it to Stuart. "This is Ayden Archer."

Stuart accepted the photo and studied it under the soft light of a reading lamp. "You've just made my point. He looks like Odi would, if Odi were trying to pass as Tom Selleck."

Wiley took the printout back, crumpled it and tossed it into the fire. "I went through Ayden's FBI and CIA files."

"Let's hear it."

Wiley savored a sip of his Dalwhinnie and began. He remembered everything without his notes. "Ayden was born in California in 1968 to an American mother and an Iranian father. Given that he had his mother's complexion and that they were both well aware of the benefits of having an Anglican name, they gave Ayden his mother's name.

"Ayden Archer lived in California until he was six, when his mother died from cancer. Then he moved with his father, Tigran Taronish, back to Iran. Tigran worked for the Shah as a royal engineer. When the Shah fell in 1979, Tigran took his son and fled to Turkey, where he got a job expanding our air base in Incirlik. He and Ayden lived there for two years until Tigran was injured in a construction accident and died.

"Are you with me?" Wiley asked, noting that Stuart was staring into the fire.

"Ayden's Iranian father died when he was 13, orphaning him." Stuart replied without shifting his gaze.

Wiley took a second to check Stuart's math in his head and found it accurate. He was impressed, but did not show it. "Here's the rub. Tigran's accident should not have been fatal. A chunk of concrete fell on him, breaking some ribs and damaging a lung, but he could have been saved through a routine procedure. Since he was not American, however, Tigran was denied treatment at the air base's modern hospital —the very air base he had worked two years to construct. He died from internal bleeding while waiting for an operating room to open at the local Turkish hospital."

Stuart looked up from the fire with interest radiating from his eyes. "That's how terrorists are made."

Wiley nodded. "Ayden got himself arrested the day of his father's funeral for throwing rocks at the base commander's jeep.

"After being assaulted by a teary-eyed thirteen-year-old American boy, the Air Force General looked into Ayden's story and recognized a potential PR nightmare. He shipped Ayden back to California posthaste to live with his grandparents.

"Back in the US, Ayden behaved himself. The FBI stopped keeping tabs on him four years later when he entered Berkeley.

"Both Ayden's grandparents died while he was at college, leaving him an estate worth a couple hundred grand. He graduated in 1989 with a philosophy major and then used half his inheritance to get a medical degree at UCLA. Instead of doing a normal residency, however, Ayden went straight into the Peace Corps. He worked for them in the Middle East for eight years and then quit to stay behind when the Ayatollah got unruly and the Peace Corps pulled his group out of Iran. He has been living in Iran doing his own thing ever since. As a low-priority case, there is not much else in his file, but there are indications that he has been acting as an international aid coordinator of sorts and running a mobile clinic."

"Who pays him?" Stuart asked.

"Good question. As far as we know, he's living off his inheritance, or rather the interest from it. That amounted to just five-hundred dollars a month, but to the best of our knowledge he managed to survive on that amount for years in Iran."

"You're speaking in the past tense," Stuart noted.

Wiley jiggled his ice cubes. "Ayden's situation has changed. About a year ago he began to draw down his capital, dipping into the original hundred grand. Since then, he has been withdrawing ever-increasing amounts. It looks like he's getting desperate. As of yesterday, his balance was down to forty-one thousand."

"But you don't know what's changed?"

Wiley shook his head.

"One man's problem is another man's opportunity," Stuart said.

"I was thinking the same thing."

"Do you think he sold Odi his passport?"

"Perhaps," Wiley said. "But I suspect that their relationship is deeper than a purely financial one. Since everyone else on Odi's team was killed, it is reasonable to assume that he was seriously injured. Given what we now know, I think our working hypothesis should be that he fell into Ayden's care."

"I think I see where you're going with this," Stuart said. "All of a sudden, Odi is back in the US on a multiple-assassination mission. He's using Ayden's passport. Meanwhile, we know that Ayden has reason to hate America, that he is sympathetic to Iran, and that his life has destabilized of late. You think Ayden has morphed into a terrorist mastermind, and Odi—motivated by betrayal and rage—is his gun." Stuart nodded subconsciously as he thought out loud, obviously intrigued. Perhaps even impressed.

Wiley felt an unwelcome sense of pride as he noted Stuart's reaction. "I'm not sure whether Ayden himself is the mastermind or he too is being used. It would not be unusual for terrorist recruiters to keep an eye on Americans in their midst, looking for opportunities to leverage. If such a person were monitoring Ayden's financial situation, he would have pounced. In either case, whether Ayden is master or pawn, we could probably benefit from cooperation."

Wiley could see the gears whirring behind Stuart's dark eyes. He was doing what he did best—figuring out the most productive way to use a man.

"Where is Ayden now?" Stuart asked.

"Since his passport is here, I assume that he is still in Iran ..." Wiley trailed off the end of his sentence.

Light dawned in Stuart's eyes. "You want me to find him, don't you? You want to find him and recruit him to our cause. Give him some spiel about differing ends requiring common means."

Wiley shook his head and smiled inside. It felt wonderful to be in strategic control. "Not exactly. I want you to find Ayden and feel him out. If he is everything that we suspect he is, tell him that the Director of the FBI would like to meet with him. Keep it general. Just tell him that I'm interested in working with him to achieve mutual goals."

Chapter 33

Alexandria, Virginia

"FORGIVE ME, FATHER, for I have sinned. This is my first confession," Cassi spoke into the grate. After the first remark, she expected to have to explain that by faith she was Presbyterian. But the priest just said, "Go ahead," and she concluded that she was not the first non-Catholic to seek holy release.

"I don't really know how this works."

"Why don't you just tell me what brought you here."

"I saw you preach once. I was here with a boyfriend. He didn't stick with me, but the wisdom of your sermon did, that and the kind crinkles around your eyes."

"I see. Well, what I meant to ask was, what have you done? What do you need to confess to our Lord and Savior?"

Cassi felt her face redden and was glad to be sitting in the dark. She sat back and faced the door. "It's not so much what I've done, as what I fear I'll have to do."

"I see," the priest replied. "The confessional is not really the place for counseling. I would be happy to sit down with you for that purpose in my office."

"Thank you, Father. That's a kind offer. But I need the sanctity of the confessional."

Cassi heard rustling sounds coming through the grate. She was making the priest uncomfortable. She began to have second thoughts about coming here. Part of her wanted to flee, but she had nowhere to run. And she had to get this out.

Finally, the priest said, "Go on."

Cassi had spent the last eighteen hours in agony, torn between two masters. She quickly determined that she could not share her shocking discoveries with anybody. She would never forgive herself if Odi got killed because she made a call. At the same time, the decision she now faced was too momentous for her to make alone. Around two A.M. she had been struck by the brilliant insight to consult a priest. The very thought of unburdening her soul to a wise man with whom she could speak with impunity had made her feel better and gotten her through the night. But now that she was in the confessional, she did not know what to say. Not so brilliant.

"You may proceed," the priest prompted.

As she tried to formulate her opening words, Cassi realized that describing her situation in a roundabout way was not going to be so easy. She could hardly tell the priest that she thought her twin brother was assassinating people, even though he was legally dead. The priest would be morally obliged to call either an asylum or the police.

The priest rustled some more. She concluded that what it all boiled down to was this: Someone was either going to slap the cuffs on Odi, or pull a trigger. As painful as that moment would be, and even though it would give her nightmares for the rest of her life, Cassi was damned if she was going to let it be anyone but her. At last she spoke. "I may have to betray someone I love, harm him ... severely."

"Can you tell me more?" the priest asked.

"I don't know how much more I can say."

"I'm here to save souls, not to judge."

"I'm conflicted by clashing loyalties. I would do anything, anything to help this person, but he has done ... he is doing something terribly wrong. And it's my duty, both contractual and moral, to stop him."

"In other words, you feel that you have to betray either this person, or yourself, and you want to know what Jesus would do."

"Exactly," Cassi said.

"Are you sure there's no way to be faithful to both?"

"I fear not."

"I see ... Then my advice to you is simply this: Whatever you do, do for love. Vengeance, my dear, is the Lord's."

Chapter 34

Chesapeake Beach, Maryland

ODI WAS HUNKERED DOWN at Charlotte's cottage, again planning his fifth and final hit. "Fifth and final hit," he said out loud, his feet up on the computer desk, a cup of strong coffee in one hand and a notebook in the other. "Commander Potchak, Mark Drake, Mark Rollins, Mark Abrams and soon … Wiley Proffitt." His words came out as a yawn. He emptied his hands and rubbed his eyes.

He considered the list an honor roll, but it was easy to picture a prosecutor reading the names as a list of charges. That thought was undoubtedly torturing Cassi at this very moment. Odi wanted desperately to call her to explain everything and relieve her misery, but he could not permit himself that luxury. Just the sound of her voice might make him weak. He needed to be strong, he reminded himself. For just a few days more he needed to be strong.

Odi knew that security made Wiley an even harder target than Abrams, but he was undaunted. By sinking so low as to deploy his own sister against him, Wiley had Odi doubly committed. Given that they were on to him, however, he had decided to break the pattern. He would not be using sleight of hand or remote bombs. Before he sent Wiley Proffitt to meet his maker, the two of them were going to have a long talk—man-to-man, tête-à-tête.

He stood, turned up the volume on the TV and walked out onto the porch. There, beneath whitewashed rafters and a rusting ceiling fan, he paced in the cool sea air with one ear tuned to the news and the other to the sea.

He was expecting word of Abrams' assassination to break any minute, and the waiting was driving him nuts. He hated to have an operation so completely out of his control. Yet it wasn't relinquishing the operation that flustered him now. The fact that he had left a dose of Creamer at a dead drop for Ayden's friend was what had his nerves tied in knots. Some anonymous woman now had two ounces worth of his secret explosive, the same amount he had used on Potchak and Drake. The quantity was perfect if you wanted the deterring effect of dramatic, blood-drenching, bone-scattering explosions. But it was much more than you needed simply to kill a man. Half a cc might not completely disembowel a person like a swallowed hand grenade, but it would certainly puree his internal organs and achieve an equally lethal result.

Pacing the porch, Odi worried that Ayden's contact might figure that out and cut the dose like a cocaine dealer. It pained him to think what such a person would then do with the remainder of the dose. In the best case she would use it to kill just one other person. If she was more entrepreneurial, she might take it to a lab. Then the world would never be the same. Once released, a secret like Creamer could never be put back in the bag. It was Pandora's Box. The thought made Odi shiver.

He had taken measures to prevent exactly that. He had stressed to Ayden that Creamer became inert after twelve hours. Twelve hours did not leave enough time for a lab. Furthermore, to keep her from breaking up the dose, he had explained that the victim had to drink the full two-ounce dose because the reaction required a critical mass. Odi figured that his bluff sounded credible enough to pass muster with both laymen and chemists alike—but he could not be sure.

With those two bases covered, there was still the possibility that Ayden's friend would take the Creamer and run, planning to use it on an ex-lover or boss. But Odi reasoned that his contingencies could only go so far. At some point he had to trust the judgment of his new friend. Odi did trust Ayden. He would feel the pain in more ways than one if Abrams was not killed tonight.

He continued pacing the balcony while repeating, "Come on" to the news. After a few minutes Odi realized that he was timing his laps to coincide with the nearby warning buoy, doing exactly one length between each bong. His conformity reminded him of a scene from the movie *Dead Poets' Society*. It was odd, he thought—that innate urge to conform. He altered his pace.

Despite all his worries, Odi liked it out there on the porch. He decided that if he lived through this and kept out of jail, he would take a long vacation and come back to do some reading and make some repairs—assuming that the cottage was still standing. He had installed a sophisticated booby-trap to deal definitively with intruders. He armed it each time he left on a mission. He had enough on his mind without the added worry of returning home to a trap or leaving damning evidence behind. He did feel badly about endangering Charlotte's cottage, but as with the Creamer, there was only so much he could do. Perhaps that was why he wanted to return on vacation and fix the place up. It would be a karma-balancing act. He figured—

"This just in," the news anchor announced. Odi turned to see the red Breaking News banner filling the bottom of the screen. He ducked through the open window without taking his eyes off the TV. "While the details are still foggy, we have just learned that an explosion in an exclusive Annapolis suburb claimed two lives this evening. We take you live to the scene where Bob Kenny is standing by.

"Bob." The image cut to a man broadcasting from atop a news van parked near the lofty iron gate of an enormous estate. Red and white lights were spinning across the stone edifice of a mansion at the distant end of a long drive. Odi recognized it immediately as Abrams'. "Thank you, Rita. Mark Ezekiel Abrams III, the billionaire CEO of ASIS whose Annapolis estate you see behind me, was killed here moments ago by an explosion in his bedroom. The police have yet to issue a statement, but sources say that he was in the company of a young woman whose identity is not yet known. While the possibility of an accident has not been ruled out, as our regular viewers will know, Mark Abrams is the third defense CEO to die a fiery death this month, so the authorities are approaching this as a double homicide. We go now to—"

Odi felt his stomach drop and his knees began to shake. *In the company of a young woman.* "Cassi! Oh God, no." He pulled the throw-away phone from his pocket and dialed Cassi's mobile number with a trembling hand.

Chapter 35

Washington, D.C.

WILEY LOOKED IMPATIENTLY at his Patek Philippe and cursed under his breath before downing his last sip of Dalwhinnie 1981. He felt tense enough without being kept waiting on pins and needles. He caught movement in the corner of his eye and turned his head, pleased to have finally caught one of Stuart's approaches. Disappointment struck. It was just one of the Horus Club's observant waiters. Wiley nodded—yes, he'd like a refill—and returned his gaze to the fire.

A voice to his left broke the silence. "I'm sorry to have kept you waiting. I was just getting out of the limo from Dulles when the story hit Headline News, so I stayed in the car to watch the whole report."

Stuart must share a bloodline with Houdini, Wiley concluded, vexed at being caught yet again unawares. "What story?"

Stuart arched his eyebrows behind his rimless silver spectacles. "Abrams is dead."

The news hit Wiley like a bat to the chest. This time he didn't have a drink to spill, but he almost would have welcomed that momentary distraction. Abrams' death might mark the end of his presidential aspirations. Hell, he thought, it might even signify something worse than that. Much worse. Although he had not received a video and ultimatum like Rollins and Abrams, Wiley could not rule out the possibility that one of the victims had exposed his involvement. He knew that the wise move was to assume as much. He gulped involuntarily. With Abrams dead, the odds were fifty-fifty that his was the next name on the list. With a dry throat, he asked, "Was it another bomb?"

Stuart nodded, and then added, "There's more. An unidentified woman was also killed in the explosion."

Wiley felt an arctic chill sweep over the desert in his mouth. "Cassi?"

"It could be. I don't know."

Wiley studied Stuart's face and decided that he was telling the truth. He really did not know. "I don't think it's her," Wiley said. "Odi wouldn't kill his own sister. Of that I am totally sure. Still, accidents do happen. I better call to find out."

As Wiley reached into his breast pocket for his cell phone, Stuart's arm shot forward fast as a cobra strike to grab his wrist. "Not now. You are about to receive a very important call." Stuart stared at Wiley until he got it.

"Your meeting went well?"

"Excellent."

"Tell me."

"In a word, he's perfect."

Wiley arched his eyebrows in appreciation. Stuart was hardly predisposed to superlative compliments.

"Ayden has brains and charisma and a deep-seated hatred seething within. He could easily be the next Bin Laden—given a little guidance, and the proper financial backing."

"And he's about to call me?"

"In precisely two minutes. As you requested, I have arranged for the two of you to meet. This call is to work out the details."

Wiley felt dizzy, as though the air pressure had changed in the room. This was it, he realized, capital I, capital T. He had been committed before but this took his campaign to a whole new level. By personally conspiring with a terrorist, he would be crossing a different kind of line, entering a whole new level of the political game. There were only two doors at the end of that road. One led to the Oval Office, the other to the electric chair.

"It's the only way—now that Abrams is gone," Stuart said, reading Wiley's face.

Wiley expected Stuart to pull a voice recorder from his pocket and play his "Whatever it takes" quote. But he didn't. He just added, "Picture the plane."

Air Force One immediately popped into Wiley's head. He hated the fact that Stuart read him so well. Air Force One was the image to which he fell asleep every night—that open door and staircase with the red carpet and presidential seal. Still, he had a pretty darn good life already. Given the increasing possibility of door number two, Air Force One was no longer enough.

Before he could say no, Stuart continued. "Ayden is not only the best chance we have of catching Odi. He is also the perfect man to coordinate the future terrorist attacks. We need someone like him, now that Abrams is dead."

Wiley was about to concur when his phone began to ring. He looked down at it and then over at Stuart. "One door closes and another one opens …"

Chapter 36

Annapolis, Maryland

CASSI POURED the last drops of Barolo into the hotel's oversized wineglass. Then she lit a fresh candle with the remains of the first and plopped back down into the tub. She knew she should have been working out rather than drinking to relieve her stress, but the room service menu had been at hand, while both energy and willpower had seemed well beyond her reach.

She took another sip as Andrea Bocelli's *Viaggio Italiano* began its third repeat and contemplated adding more hot water to the cooling tub. Her marathon of indulgence had thus far yielded neither rest nor peace and she did not relish the thought of seeing her breasts prune, but she had neither the energy nor the desire to move.

Both of her charges were gone now. Dead. Caput. Rollins and Abrams had quite literally been blown to bits—as had her career. A week ago, she would have considered this the worst thing that could possibly happen. Now the anticipation of being fired in disgrace barely raised her pulse. Odi's bomb had done more than break bones and boil flesh; it had shattered her faith.

The ring of her mobile phone eclipsed Andrea's swooning voice, and Cassi looked over her shoulder to give the intruding device a forlorn stare. That would be Wiley, she thought, calling to inform her that she was fired. He would apologize for using the phone, explaining that the folks in public relations could not wait. For the good of the Bureau, they had to be swift and decisive and all that, blah, blah, blah. She decided to let voicemail take the call. That would make it easier on both of them. If she ever emerged from the tub, she would text message her resignation.

She drained the last sip from her glass as she waited for voicemail to kick in. This was the first time in her life that she had drunk a whole bottle of wine. Staring at the bottom of the glass, she realized that she would be screwed if Wiley chose not to leave a message. She would never be able to get to sleep then despite the Barolo's depressive effect. She would just lie there staring at the phone, willing it to emit a dreaded ring. She decided to get it over with now, while the wine was still rendering its full numbing effect.

"Hello."

"Cassi?"

The voice was unusually weak but intimately familiar. She nearly dropped the phone in the tub. "Odi, oh my God."

"Thank God you're alive. I was so scared."

"Odi, what are you … why …how could you do this? Why are you doing this? To them, to me, oh my God, I—"

"I can't explain that now. But I can explain it later. You're just going to have to trust me on this. I'm a patriot, Sis. Don't doubt it. Despite all appearances I have not changed."

Cassi got out of the tub but didn't towel off. She wanted the sobering effect of the chill, and she wanted to pace. "I love you, Odi. You're a good man. Fight the evil. You're sick. You need help. Let me help you. Just tell me where to meet you, one-on-one. I'll—"

"I can't do that. Not yet. There's something I need to do first."

"Odi, you mus—"

"I love you, Sis."

Chapter 37

Chesapeake Beach, Maryland

ODI PACED before his computer screen, waiting for Ayden to come online. He was in a hurry to get to the lab, but he had to get this out of the way first. Brewing Creamer safely required absolute concentration, and he knew that would not be possible until after they spoke.

During a contemplative walk, he had found a pink rubber ball on the beach. He gave it a thousandth bounce against the kitchen's linoleum floor. He was not panicked anymore, not now that he knew Cassi was alive. But he was still upset that Ayden's friend had caused collateral damage. He needed to know who the dead woman was—or more appropriately, who she had been.

His fingers flew from the ball to the keyboard the second the ta-dong announced Ayden's arrival online. "Your friend pulled it off, but a woman was also killed. Did she tell you what happened?"

"Abrams requested the company of an escort for the evening from his usual service."

"So the dead woman was a prostitute," Odi thought out loud, his fingers poised motionless above the keys. A desperate life had met an unfortunate end. The thought made Odi sad until he considered the caliber of woman a billionaire would choose to buy. It would not be a destitute drug addict or a white slave. She would be someone Abrams could pretend was a date. She would be a classy-looking educated girl—polished, refined ... and very highly paid. Prostitution would be the life she chose.

That deduction took the edge off Odi's pain, but he still felt terrible that a bystander was now dead. Then Ayden sent a follow-up message that stole Odi's breath.

"My friend paid the girl to take her place."

Odi stared at the last sentence. This had gone from bad to worse—with a very unexpected twist. He typed, "A suicide bomber?"

"It's not what you think. She was an old friend of mine from the Peace Corps, a beautiful, brilliant woman—with an inoperable tumor."

Ayden did not add further detail. He must have figured—correctly—that Odi could fill in the rest. As a man who had risked his life for others hundreds of times, Odi understood the oxymoronic serenity that one derived from being willing to die for a cause. He was about to ask how Ayden knew about Abrams' penchant for escorts when Ayden surprised him yet again. "How do you feel?"

The question struck a chord and Odi typed an honest response without thinking. "I thought I'd feel a sense of satisfaction, accomplishment and relief once the CEOs were dead. But the truth is, I don't. I just feel dirty."

Ayden's reply came back surprisingly fast. "That's because you haven't wrought any permanent change."

Odi stared at Ayden's words, unsure how to react. Eventually he typed, "How can you say that?"

"There's an endless supply of people with equally dismal moral fiber lined up for those CEO slots. The day after tomorrow they will be back to business as usual at Defcon4, Rollins and ASIS. To create lasting change you have to be more creative. You have to think big picture …"

Chapter 38

Washington, D.C.

"WHERE WAS THE BLOODY ORANGE PHONE?" Wiley cursed as he inspected the hissing labyrinth. Embarrassing as it was to admit, he had never before ridden the Washington Metro. Was the *orange phone* something all regular Metro users would know, like the Green Monster at Fenway Park? It was worth a try. He said "Excuse me," to a well-dressed young man walking past with a lawyer's briefcase. "Do you know where I can find the orange phone?"

The man said, "Try Toys"R"Us," without slowing his stride.

Wiley raised his arm and said, "Thanks."

The three pay phones visible from the base of the F Street escalator all appeared to be the standard stainless steel and black. Was he missing something? He repeated Ayden's order again to himself from memory. "Use the F Street entrance to Metro Center. At precisely six o'clock, approach the orange phone. I'll instruct you further on our meet."

Approach the orange phone, Wiley repeated. That seemed unambiguous enough.

Given the simplicity of this mundane meet, he was beginning to appreciate the strain that sophisticated deep cover ops must put on his men. He was starting to lose it and he was the bloody Director of the FBI. By the same token, Ayden must be a wreck.

Looking around, Wiley concluded that Ayden had probably given the staging of this meet some serious thought. Perhaps he had just read a few John Le Carré books, watched a few James Bond videos and worked it out from there. Or perhaps he had been coached. In either case, if Ayden knew the truth he would be much more relaxed. Despite Wiley's title, this was the first time he had donned an operative cloak, and he did not even own a dagger.

Wiley circled the station, getting increasingly flustered as he searched for a less-obvious fit—a picture, a toy, two orange juice cans and some string. He found nothing that fit any variant of the orange phone description while circling Metro Center, so he returned to the base of the F Street escalator. Then he saw it. While he was away, someone had placed an orange sticker on the receiver of one of the pay phones he had first seen. "Of course."

Ayden must have arrived early, waited to see if Wiley was alone, and then watched to see if he spoke into his collar or anything like that as he walked around in frustration. Once Ayden was comfortable that

Wiley was truly alone, he put the sticker on the pay phone. He had probably hopped straight onto the up escalator from there, and was now poised to make a call from the busy bank of phones up top. Wiley looked up the tunnel just in case, but all he saw was the backside of a dozen raincoats. Ayden had set up a good meet, ideal really for one man working alone.

Wiley guarded the orange phone, waiting for it to ring. He did not have to wait long. "Hello."

"What's your favorite color?"

"Orange."

"Give the boy your cell phone battery and put on the pink carnation." Ayden hung up.

Wiley looked around for a boy and spotted a twelve- or thirteen-year-old in a dirty green coat riding down the escalator and holding out a flower. Little Green Coat walked over to Wiley and held out his empty hand. Wiley released the battery from his cell phone and handed it over. The boy said, "Thank you," and gave him the pink boutonnière. As Wiley pinned it on, the boy pulled a slip of paper from his pocket and read. "Ride the last car of the blue line to Capital South, get off and wait right there on the end of the platform."

"Can I have the note, I might forget?" Wiley asked.

The boy said "No," and shoved it in his mouth.

Wiley was glad to see Ayden taking precautions. Ironically, Ayden's paranoia made Wiley less nervous. Still, he was glad that he had chosen to wear one of the special suits the Secret Service had tailored. It was lined with a fabric that could not be punctured by small-arms fire. A bullet fired at him could still pierce his flesh, but the fabric would catch it before it penetrated very deep. He also sported his never-walk-the-street-without-it bulletproof vest. Wiley smiled at the boy and said "Tasty?" before turning to do as he was told.

Nobody was waiting for him at the Capital South Metro stop, so he stood alone at the end of the platform and waited as instructed. He was getting tired of breathing the stale ozone air when the arrival of another train caused him to hold his breath. The last person to get off that train was another boy. This one wore a faded Mighty Ducks cap and held a yellow rose in his hand.

The Mighty Duck spotted Wiley's pink carnation and approached. "Trade you, Mister."

"Okay."

Wiley gave the boy his pink carnation and pinned on the rose boutonnière. Once he was suitably attired, the boy said, "I have a message for sale. The price is twenty bucks."

"Did the man tell you to say that?"

The boy nodded.

Wiley hated to take his wallet out in a place like this, but he and the boy were the only people at that end of the platform. He gave the Mighty Duck a twenty-dollar bill and received a horse-like flash of white teeth in return. The boy then cleared his throat, but instead of pulling a slip of paper from his pocket, he read a message off the palm of his hand. "Exit to First Street and walk north to Union Station. Enter the Metro, find the phone and answer it before the second ring."

Wiley nodded.

The boy licked his hand and rubbed it on his jeans.

It took Wiley twenty minutes to reach Union Station by foot on a route which took him between the Capital and the Supreme Court. Even in October this really was a beautiful city, he noted, promising himself to walk more often.

This time the orange phone was ready and waiting. Two minutes later it rang. "Hello."

"What's on your lapel?"

"A yellow rose."

Ayden said, "Take the Red Line to Rockville—sit in the last car," and hung up.

Wiley was getting tired of this, but he focused on the bright side. This experience would help him relate to his field agents. Ironically, it would also help him relate better to the men they were trying to catch. Wiley felt afraid for his life, and he was just going to a talk. Thieves and drug dealers went through this routinely to swap their duffel bags of contraband for briefcases of cash. Both parties in those transactions had to have either a gnat's brains, a shark's nerves, or a bull's balls. It was no wonder someone often freaked out during a swap and provoked everyone to empty his weapon into his neighbor.

Three stops into the trip the mechanical voice announced "Next stop, Metro Center." Only then did Wiley realize that he had completed a triangle. Now he was being sent to the suburbs, having been deemed clear.

Rockville was still thirteen stops away, so he sat back to wait. Everyone not standing was either reading, sleeping, or listening to music. He had neither book nor radio, so he tried to blend in by closing his eyes. That also made it less conspicuous for him to keep his hand in the pocket of his wool overcoat—wrapped tightly around the walnut handle of his Colt.

Wiley wondered why he had not been disarmed along the way, at least not yet. He decided that Ayden must have figured that whatever he did, the Director of the FBI would have access to enough special gadgets to get something past him. And he was right. Given that, Wiley reasoned, Ayden would just level the playing field by showing up armed as well. He might even try to tilt the odds in his favor by bringing a friend ...

Wiley opened his eyes in reaction to that last thought. What if he was simply walking into the sights of Odi's next hit? He wondered, realizing that he had been so caught up in his own moves that he had not given much thought to Ayden's. It was the same amateur mistake he always made in chess.

Wiley was considering calling off the meet, just standing up and getting off the metro at the next stop, when the Rastafarian sitting across from him reached out and put his hand on Wiley's knee. Wiley pulled the trigger in shock. He heard an empty click. Thank goodness for safeties, he thought. He peered through the disguise of the man he might have killed and recognized a familiar face.

"So, what is the mutual interest your aide said you were so eager to discuss?"

Chapter 39

Annapolis, Maryland

CASSI LOOKED OVER at the bedside clock. It was two A.M. Her mind and body were exhausted but her nerves forbade sleep. She had nearly drifted off a few times only to be awakened by the annoying bing of the elevator bell. She would be sure to request a room farther down the hall next time, although that was little consolation now. Judging by the elevator traffic, there was some kind of party happening on her floor. She closed her eyes and waited for the next installment of the business traveler's equivalent of Chinese water torture, the cursed elevator bing.

She eventually drifted off again, dreaming of endless dark hallways and brightly lit elevator doors. Then lightning struck as one door opened and she bolted upright in bed. She knew where Odi was hiding! The clue had been there in the background during his call, a very different kind of bell.

~ ~ ~

Two hours later Cassi parked her rental car at the Lever's, knowing that Thelma and Morton were always in Fort Myers this time of year. She had driven the last quarter mile without the aid of headlights, but she still gave her eyes a few minutes to adjust to the darkness after slipping quietly from the car. The sea breeze, the pine scent, the rustling of reeds and sea grass—everything about this place was calmingly familiar. Only the man now sleeping in Aunt Charlotte's bed had changed.

She stuck to the moon's shadows as she crossed the three intervening lawns and made her way silently toward Charlotte's long front porch. She was afraid that Odi would slip away if he heard someone approach, not realizing that it was her. There were boat, truck, trail and even hang glider options available for escape. Odi would surely have an evasive route or four planned.

She studied the two visible sides of the cottage as she executed her silent approach. No lights were on, the shutters were closed and nothing was parked in the drive. Cassi began to worry that she had dreamed the buoy sound. Lord knows she had been sufficiently drunk on wine. What would she do if Charlotte's cottage was undisturbed? She had not a clue, but guessed that it would involve puddles of tears.

As her spirits fell, Cassi realized just how desperate she was to see her brother. She needed him as much as he needed her. Over this past month she had endured more shock and disappointment than one person should ever have to bear. She needed this victory, this confirmation, this release. And she needed to bury herself in Odi's problems so that she could forget about her own.

Cassi bypassed the second stair knowing that it liked to squeak and stepped silently onto the wooden porch. She stood there in silence for a moment, listening to the night. She took a deep breath, and tried to steady her nerve. So far, so good. She reached behind the decorative net and red-striped buoy hanging on the wall and felt for the crevice in the cork that concealed the key to the front door. She found it. The key's presence was good news, but a bad sign.

She kissed the key before sliding it slowly into the lock. In the early morning quiet she could hear each individual click as it displaced the five spring-loaded pins. She turned the handle slowly and then applied pressure to the door while willing the old hinges to refrain from protest. As the door cracked beneath her gentle touch, a fragrant whiff told Cassi that she had gotten it right. The garlic and sausage scents of Odi's famous spaghetti sauce greeted her nose. Another drop of adrenaline hit her blood. Despite her tension and exhaustion, she began to smile. Some things did not change.

When the opening was about a foot wide, she slid sideways through the gap and pushed the door quietly closed behind. She found the inside of the cottage darker than it was outdoors, as the hurricane shutters were closed all around, blacking out the moonlight. So she stood motionless with her heart pounding and ears peaked, waiting for her eyes to acclimate.

Aware that the information flow was still one way, Cassi moved with caution. "Odi? Odi, it's me, it's Cassi. I'm alone." She spoke softly at first and then raised her voice, not wanting to startle him awake. "Odi, it's Cassi. I just came to talk. I'm alone." Her ears strained to detect the slightest noise or pressure shift coming from the hall that led to the master bedroom, but nothing seemed to change. Keenly aware that her brother had always been the type to set booby-traps, she realized that she would be foolish to grope around blindly in the dark. She reached back slowly with her right hand and turned on the overhead light.

As the light went on, Cassi heard a scraping sound behind her and spun about only to find that nothing was there. The noise must have come from the other side of the door. She reached instinctively for her gun but found herself grabbing at air. Her mind caught up with her hand as it patted her side and she remembered that she had intentionally left her weapon in the car.

She tried to crack the door to find the source of the sound, but the door would not budge. The sound had been a bolt, a bolt that locked her inside. Cassi felt like a rat suddenly trapped in an oxygenless cage. She needed to escape.

Escape might not be easy, she realized in a panic. In response to the wild hurricane seasons of recent years, Charlotte had installed storm shutters, the tough metallic kind that roll down from above. They were designed for keeping two-hundred-mile-an-hour winds out, but they could just as effectively keep people in. She moved to the window beside the door and felt for the shutter switch without taking her eyes off the hallway to the bedroom. Cassi found the switch and slid it up. Nothing happened.

What did you expect? she wondered.

As she stood there cursing her bad luck, the sound of a computer booting up drew her gaze back to the kitchen. She began to tiptoe in that direction. "Odi, what's going on?" She asked, her voice just below a shout.

An annoying "beep ... beep ..." from the computer was the only response.

Cassi spotted a laptop sitting on the kitchen table. For some reason, the sight of it sent a chill scurrying up and down her spine. She assumed that her reaction was just the paranoia born of too many late-night movies—until she moved around the counter and got a look at the screen. Then she learned that it had been intuition.

The computer displayed the picture of an antenna with green waves radiating out. Cassi recognized the enlarged icon. A wireless network was in use. The other image on the screen indicated the reason. To the right of the icon were the cascading red digits of a large digital clock, followed by the words, "Seconds until BOOM."

Cassi felt her intestines turn to water as she stared in shock and disbelief at her brother's devious work. 00:53 ... 00:52 ... 00:51 ...

Chapter 40

Baltimore, Maryland

"TWENTY-FIVE. TWENTY ... FIVE." Odi kept repeating the number to himself, shaking his head as he worked. That was a lot of senators.

Tearing a paper towel off the roll without removing his protective yellow gloves, he dabbed the sweat from his brow. Time was running short. Dawn was approaching and he needed to be gone by first light. He wished he had not had to come to Johns Hopkins a second time. If it weren't for the need to super-cool the nitric acid, he could have used Aunt Charlotte's kitchen instead of the graduate chemistry lab.

He had perfected the Creamer's formula while preparing for the Potchak hit. He had the chemistry down cold. So aside from the potential of being blown to bits, he found no excitement in the task. Although the final product was magical, the production of Creamer felt mundane as chicken à la king. It boiled down to measuring and mixing, heating and cooling, filtering and separating—for hours on end. Because he had a lot of things to occupy his troubled mind—twenty-five to be exact—neither the tedium nor the physical danger bothered him. Still, he was afraid. He was afraid of getting caught. Although breaking into his old lab was not a serious crime, if caught he would be identified. Then his Iranian alibi would dissolve faster than the sugar he now poured, and he would go to prison for murder.

Odi tried to focus on the bright side as he stirred. The graduate lab had state-of-the-art equipment, so it was faster and easier to make Creamer here. It had temperature-controlled variable-speed mixers, electronically calibrated pipettes and programmable centrifuges—everything required to get each stage of the twelve-step process just right. Working in a proper lab was safer than a basement too, and that was of no small concern. His perspective had been changed by his government's betrayal, but he still valued his vision and thumbs.

An added bonus of working here was that the university lab stocked many of the ingredients he needed, including distilled water, concentrated nitric acid and acetone. He had acquired the rest for cash at area drug, hardware and grocery stores, under the cover of a simple but effective disguise. Those purchases included hexamine, urotropine, methenamine, calcium-magnesium powder, powdered cream, sugar and the omnipresent artificial flavoring.

He watched with satisfaction as the viscous white mass began to bubble slowly in the thick 10 liter beaker. It looked like a bleached lava lamp and it certainly was volcanic. Come to think of it, Odi thought, so was Ayden's plan.

Ayden had a sympathetic friend who was an aide to a senior member of the Senate Armed Services Committee. Sheila, he claimed, was certain that she could exchange the Half and Half served at a committee meeting for Creamer.

"How soon will she be able to do it?" he had asked Ayden.

"The Senate Armed Services Committee is going to be locked in conference tomorrow evening. It's a marathon effort to finalize the naval budget before recess. Everyone will be there, and unless something changes they will be alone in the building. It's perfect."

Odi thought that it sounded almost too good to be true. Still watching the bubbles, he wondered if there were video cameras in congressional meeting rooms. He had not thought to ask about that although Ayden probably would not know. He doubted that there were. Few people treasured their secrecy more than elected officials. But then, politicians also loved their security. He decided that there would likely be video surveillance, but no sound.

Waiting for stage eleven to ferment, Odi tried to picture the scene that would unfold that evening. Having been on many a stakeout, he found himself taking the security guard's point of view. The guard who drew duty the first evening of recess would be sitting with his black shoes propped up on a gray metal desk littered with Styrofoam cups containing the cold dregs of bad coffee. There would be a box of donuts somewhere off to the side. He would check it three or four times, although the last cruller would have vanished long ago. Most of the monitors before him would be devoid of life, unless you counted the drone-like cleaners vacuuming rugs and polishing floors. The exception would be the conference room with twenty-five famous faces. That was where the guard would direct the eye not tied to the *Post* crossword puzzle. If he were new he might even find it interesting, watching famous faces doling out billions to their pet constituents in the name of national defense.

About forty-five minutes into the meeting, the guard would see a pale senator pause mid-tirade to rub his stomach. If that was interesting enough to draw both eyes, he might even notice that the bellyacher's fingertips had turned blue. Then the senator would disappear in the blink of an eye. For the attentive guard it would be a perplexing version of now-you-see-him, now-you-don't.

The alarm would begin to blare a second later, once the blast blew the windows out. In shock, he would knock the coffee cups off the desk with his feet. Meanwhile, the senators sitting closest to the deceased would keel over, their bodies impaled by shrapnel made from splintered rib. The non-veterans would scramble up from the floor, their minds failing to comprehend the chaos that engulfed them. Then a second senator would explode in their midst and complete pandemonium would erupt. Slack-jawed but on his feet, the guard would now be struggling to make sense of the muted drama playing out before his eyes.

Seconds later the conference room doors would crash open and other guards would rush in only to be shoved aside by terrified senators running out. As the guards looked blankly at each other, clueless about what to do, the explosions of the white coffee-drinking senators would continue in polished mahogany elevators and on stately marble stairs.

Within hours the world would begin scrutinizing how the SASC carved up the lion's share of the national budget. Would that change anything? Odi was not sure.

Although taking out The Three Marks had served justice and satisfied the debt of honor Odi owed his fallen friends, it would not create permanent change. Ayden had been right about that. But making the public aware of how they had been duped, and why ... that just might make a lasting difference.

The big beaker stopped bubbling as Odi pondered that thought, indicating that the penultimate reaction was now complete. For the final stage of the brew he had to slowly mix in a liter of super-cooled nitric acid. Very slowly. This was by far the most dangerous step. This was how many an anarchist had met his maker. He gripped a huge flask with a pair of heavy tongs and prepared to stir its acidic contents into the beaker on the hot plate. Once the two containers were mixed and cooled, he would have just over two gallons of Creamer. Eight liters.

"Why does she need two gallons?" Odi had asked. "I'd think a quart would be more than enough. Surely twenty-five senators won't consume that much cream in their coffee?"

"She can't control which carton of Half and Half Senate Food Service will take from the fridge," Ayden had replied. "So she will have to replace them all."

"Tell her to find a way. I can't have six or seven unused cartons lying around. I don't want any innocents accidentally killed."

"We're lucky to have Sheila, Odi. Let's not push it. I'll get her to promise to go back to the kitchen and replace the Creamer with the original containers once the conference room is set up. That will have to suffice."

Odi saw Ayden's point, but he did not like it. "Can't she just replace the cream after it's already set up in the room?"

"I asked her that too. She said it was too risky. Compared to the kitchen, the conference room is much more secure."

Odi shook his head. "Okay. But she has to promise to pour the remaining Creamer down the drain right there in the kitchen."

"No problem."

"And Ayden, I am going to have to insist on delivering the Creamer to Sheila personally, so I can make that point."

There was a longer than usual pause before Ayden typed, "As you wish."

As Odi began pouring the large flask of super-cooled nitric acid into the beaker, the pager in his front jeans pocket began to vibrate. Maybe it was the fact that he had been up all night. Maybe it was because his nerves were already at their end. Whatever the cause, the shock of the pager was too much. Odi's hands trembled from the jolt and the liter of super-cooled nitric acid plummeted from the tongs.

Chapter 41

Baltimore, Maryland

AYDEN BOUNCED up and down on the balls of his feet, listening to the symphony of beeps and boops that indicated his international call was going through.

"Royal Falafel."

"Do you have fresh tabouleh?"

"Just a moment. Who's asking, please?"

"Dr. Jones."

Ayden stopped bouncing and took a deep breath to calm his nerves. This was really intense.

"Dr. Jones, how nice to hear from you. Where are you calling from?"

"I'm at Johns Hopkins University. I ... I'm not sure I can go through with this." There, he had said it.

When Arvin's voice came back on the line half a beat later, it was calm as ever. "Of course you can, Ayden. Just look at what you've already accomplished. Why, just six months ago you were a desperate doctor burning through his bank account in a noble but doomed attempt to single-handedly bailout an ocean of poverty with a leaky thimble. This evening you had a private meeting with the Director of the FBI to discuss the future of the planet. In the next twenty-four hours you will do more to alleviate world suffering than you could have done in ten lifetimes back in Iran. And that brings up a key point for you to remember, Ayden: you are no longer alone. You have friends now, comrades in arms, support."

Ayden found Arvin convincing, but he was not yet there. He decided to lay it all on the table, hoping that his sponsor would erase all his doubt. "I've gotten to know Odi over this last month. He has become a friend."

"Friends die in war, Ayden. It's sad, but true. I have lost many. Unless you can get Odi to back off his demand to meet the woman you invented—Sheila was her name as I recall—you have to go through with it. He would see through an imposter, and his Creamer is crucial to our plans. I'm sorry, but there's just no other way. I truly wish there were."

"I just don't know. I am a doctor, after all. I took an oath."

"The men whose corruption you are fighting took an oath as well. Because they have forsaken theirs for years, you must set yours aside for a day."

"I'm not sure that I can."

"Look Ayden, I know the burden is heavy. But do not let it slip from your shoulders. By seeking to get out from under it, you will only crush yourself. Think about it. You are one of the few Western doctors who have seen the pitiful, imploring looks epidemic in Third-World children's eyes. If you turn your back on them now, you will never forgive yourself. Nor will you be able to go back to your old life. If you tried, you would be paralyzed by debilitating guilt. Every time you encountered a child suffering from preventable disease and facing a shortened life of grinding poverty, you would feel responsible. No my friend, your only real option is to move forward."

As Ayden reflected on the wisdom of Arvin's words, his sense of purpose returned like a torch reignited. "Will this really make—"

"Of course it will make a difference, Ayden. Of course it will," Arvin interrupted. "If there is one thing that Americans are good at, it's standing on a pedestal and making noise. Once you rivet the world's attention to the congressional budget for defense, there will not be a literate man, woman, or child on Earth unaware of the poverty and suffering the United States could alleviate with the resources it now dedicates to war. Public opinion will force them to beat their swords into plowshares. Unfortunately, this is the only way to usher in a peaceful new world. These are their rules, not ours."

"But it's so violent, so … counterintuitive," Ayden pressed.

"Think of it as chemotherapy. Yes, when viewed in isolation it is caustic. But the cancers that your therapy ultimately cures will salvage countless lives. This is the day you'll paint a hundred million smiles."

"You know about that?" Ayden asked.

"Of course."

Ayden consciously recognized that the man he knew as Arvin had done a fine job of pushing his buttons, but it did not matter. Arvin had said exactly what he wanted to hear. He did not really want to back out. He just had a case of the jitters, he told himself. Like a bride on her wedding day.

He thought back to the evening when Arvin first knocked on his door. Arvin had asked him, "If you had the resources, would you be willing to do more?" With those words Arvin had given him hope, hope that kept him going while his resources diminished. And faith, faith that was rewarded when Agent Odysseus Carr landed in his lap. He remembered the pride and trepidation he felt when he used the coded exchange at Royal Falafel for the first time.

He had made his first call to Royal Falafel just seconds after treating Odi's shoulder wound and getting him stable. His initiative had paid off. Arvin's subsequent investigation had revealed circumstances that could not have been more perfectly suited to their cause. Eighteen hours after Ayden had picked up the phone, Arvin had personally delivered the telltale headsets to his door, and the recruitment of Odi Carr had begun.

Because of his courage that day, three defense industry CEOs, three men who ran cruel and exploitive companies like the one that killed his father, were no longer of this world. By contributing to their demise, Ayden had done right by his father. He had avenged Tigran Taronish. Thinking about that, Ayden realized that he felt better than he had in over twenty years. By honoring his father he had cured himself of a chronic disease. With a flash of blinding clarity he understood that he could not shy away from the opportunity Arvin now presented. This was his destiny.

"Tell me about your meeting with Director Proffitt," Arvin continued, sweeping Ayden back into their present discussion. "Was it successful? Did he get you the list?"

"Your insight proved accurate. Proffitt's approach is analogous to a pharmaceutical corporation's. He is making a career of treating the disease of terrorism. So, contrary to the FBI Director's vociferous rhetoric, the last thing he truly wants is a cure. Yes, he got me the list."

"Excellent. When you have the Creamer, call me back. I'll give you instructions for meeting with my twenty-five volunteers."

"Twenty-four," Ayden corrected.

"There are twenty-five senators on the armed services committee, my friend," Arvin persisted.

"I know, but you need supply only twenty-four volunteers. I would consider it an honor to be the twenty-fifth. I will take out the chairman."

Chapter 42

Chesapeake Beach, Maryland

00:53 ... 00:52 ... 00:51 ... Cassi stared at the screen, counting in disbelief as the final seconds of her life vanished into the ether. An overload of emotions bore down on her as she stared, squelching her ability to think. She wondered how Odi managed it—working under such conditions. As a psychologist, she knew the human species to be remarkably resilient, but fifty-three seconds hardly gave you time to acclimate. Then it struck her. Perhaps Odi had not acclimated. Years of this strain could explain why he had snapped in Iran. It only took a final straw to break a camel's back.

00:50 ... 00:49 ... 00:48 ... From her discussions with Odi and the occasional glimpse over his shoulder, Cassi knew much more than most on how to disarm bombs. But this was not a bomb. This was just a computer. The bomb could be anywhere within wireless range. Forty-eight seconds was not going to cut it.

00:47 ... 00:46 ... 00:45 ... Still mesmerized by the screen, Cassi flashed through her alternatives. Her best move would be to break out of the cottage, but Odi had prevented that by disabling the shutter mechanisms. He had probably accomplished that by simply removing a fuse, or—more cleverly and thus more likely—replacing a good fuse with one that looked good but did not work. Regardless, with just forty-five seconds left on her life's clock, Cassi did not have time to run down her hunch.

00:44 ... 00:43 ... 00:42 ... Cassi recalled that the shutters could also be operated with a crank key. It was a safety precaution for times when the power was out. Cassi dashed around the cottage, scanning each window for the presence of a crank key and pummeling all the other switches, just in case. Failing to produce any result, she returned to the computer cursing herself for thinking that Odi could be so easily outmaneuvered. The fanciful flight had cost her a priceless twelve seconds.

00:30 ... 00:29 ... 00:28 ... Realizing that escape was no longer an option, Cassi ran to the bedroom and pulled Charlotte's quilt off the bed along with three thick decorative pillows. She hauled them to the bathroom and leapt in the tub, burying herself like a mole beneath. Then she remembered the door. It was not solid wood or anything close—just two thin sheets of masonite—but every little bit helped. While climbing out of the tub to close it, another thought came to her.

She should pull the mattress off the bed, drag it into the bathroom and lean it over the tub. How long did she have left?

As if answering her question with "not much" the computer began an accelerated beep. Was it the final countdown, or something more? Cassi had no time to think, she could only react. She glanced fleetingly toward the mattress as though Brad Pitt lay naked there, and then ran for the kitchen.

00:08 ... 00:07 ... Cassi saw at once that something had changed. The maddening beep had ushered in a new message. Seconds until BOOM had been replaced by a trick question. She read it aloud. "What's the best size?"

Chapter 43

Baltimore, Maryland

EVEN AS THE FROSTY FLASK of acid slipped from his grasp, Odi contemplated the pager's implicit message. Someone had entered Charlotte's cottage. The bomb was now armed. In one minute the sanctuary of his youth would be reduced to matchsticks and his research would be turned to dust—along with anyone caught inside.

The heavy Pyrex flask crashed down on the desktop gas valve even as Odi lunged to catch it with gloved hands. As it shattered, he rolled to his left and dove for the floor. The reflex saved his face, but acid rain deluged the right side of his torso.

Odi heard his clothing begin to sizzle and felt his right shoulder start to burn. He scrambled to his feet and made a screaming beeline for the chemical shower by the door. Yanking on the dangling chain like Quasimodo incensed, Odi prayed that he would not emerge looking like the bell-ringer too.

He had seen acid burns before. Many times. A friend of his from this very lab referred to the cheese-grater scar on his cheek as his birth-control wound.

Twenty or thirty gallons into the drenching blast, Odi peeled off the protective goggles and heavy gloves. After a quick inspection of his hands, he tore off his shirt.

His right shoulder had borne the brunt of the splash and even it had seen worse. The blood-pocked patchwork reminded him of a gravel slide he had suffered after falling off his dirt bike as a kid. If the acid had not been super-cooled or the shower seconds away, it might have eaten through to the bone. Still, between the shrapnel wound in his left shoulder and the acid burn on his right, he would not be breaking down doors anytime soon. Given his luck and the way things were going, that ability was probably about to become important.

He stripped off the rest of his clothes and stood there two minutes more, using one of his socks as a washcloth to scrub. He was going to be cold and conspicuous crossing campus soaking wet and shirtless in the middle of October. But that beat looking freakish for the rest of his life—assuming that the rest of his life lasted longer than a few hours.

Odi wrung out his clothes as best he could and got dressed. He tried to be mad at himself for screwing up, but found himself feeling grateful for his blessings instead. "Ten fingers and two eyes," he repeated aloud, recalling his earlier musing.

Looking over at the smoking green tile floor, Odi remembered the vibration that catalyzed the reaction and his heart sunk. He dug anxious fingers into the wet front pocket of his jeans and withdrew the little black box. The pager was dedicated to the intrusion alarm on Charlotte's cottage, so its vibration yielded only one conclusion. Boom.

"Unless someone had dialed a wrong number," Odi thought aloud. The display dashed that hope. It read 843-7448, the numeric equivalent of THE SHIT, which, as his British colleagues loved to say, he was now in. Barring a robbery or some other equally unlikely coincidence, someone was on his tail. The obvious conclusion was that Cassi had talked.

The loss of his childhood getaway was a psychological blow, but in practical terms it did not matter. Not in the short run, at least. Come this time tomorrow he would be headed for Iran where he would miraculously awake. Cassi's split-second sighting would be attributed to a grieving mind playing tricks. No jury in the world would be left without a reasonable doubt. But that was all in the distant future, Odi reminded himself. Today, he had one final but crucial stop to make.

Though the tabletop and floor were now etched with nitric acid, the big Pyrex beaker full of Creamer base sat undisturbed. He could still salvage this batch. That was important. He had a rendezvous with Sheila.

Thirty-two minutes later the recipe was complete. After curing for an hour, the Creamer would be ready. He emptied the eight liters of Creamer into two gallon jugs and had about a pint of Creamer left over. Rather than pouring it down the drain, he emptied his sixteen-ounce bottle of Dasani into the sink and poured the remaining Creamer inside. He put the Dasani bottle back in his jacket pocket and then secured the gallon jugs in his backpack. The sound of the backpack's zipper was a welcome one. He had come close to disaster tonight, but in the end he had pulled it off.

With a spring in his step, Odi opened the laboratory door and nearly walked into the man waiting silently in the dark.

"Hello Odi."

Odi jumped. "Ayden?"

His friend's face was shadowed, but the corridor's emergency lighting reflected off the gun in his hand. The surprising scene took too long for Odi's tired mind to compute. By the time the threat had registered, he was flying backwards through space as an explosion of pain ripped through his body from the center of his chest. Agony racked him with an almost physical grip until his whole world was reduced to a blinding white light. Then everything went black.

Chapter 44

Washington, D.C.

"I TOLD YOU never to call me here," Wiley said, his voice raspy from lack of sleep. "It's too dangerous."

"You're in the office at five in the morning. You didn't leave me much choice," Stuart replied. "Check your Hotmail account. I'm sending a file."

Wiley bit his lower lip and did as he was told. The subject line on the message from SSSlick1@hotmail.com was "FBI's Most Wanted." There was no text, but it contained an attachment. Wiley double clicked. A second later he was looking at a composite picture of Odi's face. "Where did you get this?"

Stuart scoffed. "The important question is why did I get this. The answer is that it's time to turn up the heat."

Wiley looked back at the message header. "You want me to make Odysseus Carr one of the FBI's most wanted?"

"Don't be daft. Odi Carr is dead. I want you to make someone who looks like Odysseus Carr—someone who is impersonating a fallen federal officer—one of the FBI's most wanted."

Wiley bristled but managed to control his temper. He knew that Stuart was up to something, and Wiley had yet to figure out what it was. "Impersonating a federal officer isn't a big enough crime to warrant that."

"No, but assassinating the CEOs of three major US defense corporations is."

"True, but what good is that going to do us?" Wiley asked.

"For starters, it's going to make it a lot harder for Odi to get to us."

Wiley smiled, pleased that Mr. Slider was nervous about that too. They had not discussed it, but both men knew that they were prime candidates for Odi's next attack—and the man was batting a thousand.

"Furthermore," Stuart continued, "by proactively framing those murders as the acts of a look-alike foreign assassin—someone whose employer is intent on weakening the US defense industry—you divert the authorities from resurrecting the real Odi Carr and searching for his motive."

"But what happens if they catch him?"

"Think, Wiley, think. You don't wait around passively. You stack the deck against Odi to ensure that doesn't happen. Paint him as a treacherous enough bastard that officers will shoot first and ask questions later. Tell them he's prone to booby-trap himself, and that he has sworn to never be taken alive. Tell them not to take any chances."

"That may take care of the police, but what do I tell my own people?"

"You're not thinking," Stuart repeated, adding a soprano lilt to give his words extra dig.

Wiley still drew a painful blank.

Stuart prompted him. "How many departments do you have?"

Of course, Wiley thought. He could classify the source of the intelligence as compartmentalized information. Bob would think that it came from Bill and vice versa and so on. He could come up with an excuse to introduce the APB to the system a few layers down the chain of command so that nobody would turn to him for details. The ideas were coming fast now—thirty seconds too late. Leo Tufts would be perfect for running the look-alike assassin case. He would run with it like the wind, assuming incorrectly that it was a test prior to promotion.

Wiley tightened his grip on the receiver. "Very well, Stuart. It will be done."

Chapter 45

Chesapeake Beach, Maryland

00:08 ... 00:07 ... "What's the best size?"

The trick question struck Cassi like a balmy Hawaiian breeze on a bitter winter night. She spoke the answer aloud. "A cubic centimeter." She typed "CC" into the computer. The countdown stopped with four seconds left.

Growing up in a family of scientists, her initials had spurred both a nickname and a longstanding family joke. How could someone so big, be so small? Odi had posed a question that both she and Charlotte could instantly answer, but which would dumbfound anyone else.

Eight hours later, Wiley pulled his black Escalade into Charlotte's drive.

Cassi remained seated on the front porch, ostensibly enjoying the late afternoon sun. In truth she wanted to watch Wiley's approach. She was expert at reading body language, especially on people she knew well. Wiley, however, habitually maintained control over his face, eyes and hands. He was a natural-born poker player. Cassi had discovered his tell, however. It was his walk.

A lump grew in her throat as Wiley trampled grass beneath a testy stride. She knew she had tried his patience by asking him to drop everything and drive out there without explanation. Apparently, the drive had not mellowed his mood. "Thank you for coming. I know it's ... awkward."

"You said it was important." Wiley's words were much softer than his stance, an indication that he was trying. "What happened? You were, shall we say, uncharacteristically nebulous on the phone."

"Nebulous. I don't think anyone has called me that before," she said, trying to lighten his mood.

"So what's the urgent matter you summoned me to Crisfield for?" Wiley said. He did not alter his stance.

"Come inside," she said. "There's something I need to show you."

She led him into the kitchen and pointed at four folders she had found hidden between placemats in the credenza. She was certain that one of the reasons Odi had booby-trapped the cottage was to destroy these files. No doubt he also wanted to destroy his laptop computer, but she was not about to touch that. The first thing she had done after stopping the countdown was re-enable the storm shutters. As she had guessed, Odi had disabled them with a faulty fuse. Unfortunately, she had not guessed or discovered where he had hidden the bomb. Until it was disarmed, she would treat the computer like the Ebola virus.

"What's in those?" Wiley asked.

Cassi pushed the manila stack toward him. "Take a look."

Wiley took a half step back after opening the top folder, as though he were afraid it might bite him. Staring up at him from a glossy page was Mark Drake's smiling face. The posed headshot was part of a *Car and Driver* article entitled *Drake's Gallant Steed*.

Wiley scanned the article and then read aloud the caption beneath the picture of the automobile that now occupied an FBI forensics garage. "A bulletproof chariot drawn by five hundred horses, Drake's custom Bentley is large enough to accommodate six knights and their round table." The next page showed Drake entering the Bentley before his Petite Versailles mansion. Wiley was about to flip further when the chauffeur's familiar features caught his eye. It was obvious to Cassi that that very picture had been the catalyst for Odi's assassination plan. Wiley seemed to draw the same conclusion too, as he said, "I'll be damned."

Cassi watched Wiley flip quickly through the remaining pages of the file, having already ascertained its gist. The remainder consisted of similarly laudatory stories from other distinguished periodicals. *Business Week*, *Inc.*, and *American Rifleman* each had feature articles with pictures and useful biographical details.

Wiley set the first file aside and opened the second. This one led with an *Esquire* article entitled "A King and his Castles." The title was splashed above Mark Rollins' headshot, which was flanked on four sides by four royal residences: a mansion in Suffolk County, a penthouse in Manhattan, a ranch in Montana and a beach house on the Virginia coast. "Son of a bitch."

Cassi did not comment. She knew that the assassin's mother was anything but a bitch.

Wiley slid the second file off the stack and then paused with his fingers on the third. He pushed it aside as well, apparently grasping the significance inherent in the quantity of folders. Only three murders had been committed thus far—aside from Potchak, whom Odi had no need to research. He looked up at her before opening the fourth. Cassi clenched her jaw and nodded.

The fourth folder led with an article from the *Rappahannock Record* entitled "Celebrity Getaways." Odi had circled a paragraph in the middle with a red pen. According to Reedville Coffee Stop owner Norm Evans, Director Proffitt never misses the chance to clear his head of city smog and fill his lungs with fresh Chesapeake air. This was doubly true, Evans noted, on the weekends Proffitt was scheduled for a Sunday morning talk show appearance. "There's nothing like a Chesapeake morning to put you at your best."

Cassi felt hot tears running down her cheeks as Wiley studied the words. When he finally looked up, she had no idea what to say.

"So I'm next?" Wiley asked.

Cassi slowly nodded.

Wiley handed her a handkerchief and she dabbed at her eyes. Up until this moment, she had been working alone, feeding off adrenaline. Now she felt like collapsing, knowing that Wiley was there to keep the world from crashing down around her. This was no time to slack off, however, so she closed her eyes and made a determined effort to pull herself together. "Fitzpatrick's website mentions that you'll be his guest on *PoliTalk* this Sunday."

Wiley nodded somberly. "So you think the assassin will come for me at Asgard?"

"Yes."

"Why me? I'm not a corporate CEO."

Cassi had spent the afternoon walking the bluff, thinking about that very question. A satisfying answer, if one could possibly be found, had eluded her grasp like a wisp of smoke. Still, she knew that her conclusion was correct, so she was going to act on it. The motivation would eventually be revealed. "I'm not sure why he's after you, but I have discovered the assassin's identity, so I'm sure that it's my fault."

Chapter 46

Baltimore, Maryland

ODI DREAMT OF SNAKES. He was trapped among them, paralyzed in their dark midst as they writhed and hissed. He had harbored an irrational fear of snakes since his eleventh year when a corn snake surreptitiously shared his sleeping bag. It had awakened him after a dormant night while slithering to escape across his naked thigh. At the time, his groggy mind was unsure whether he had imagined the sensation or not. When the movement repeated he lay paralyzed with fear until the scaly head emerged an inch from the tip of his nose and broke the spell. The other Scouts found him at the base of the hill, still kicking and screaming and trying to break free of his sodden sleeping bag. Twenty years later Odi could still hear their incessant laughter.

Today, his dream recycled as nightmares often do, playing over and over again accompanied by a ceaseless hiss until at last a bolt of pain lanced through his acid-burned shoulder and jolted him awake. The first thing he noticed as his mind pierced the fog was a familiar smell. Once it registered, everything became clear and his eyes shot open like blinds released. He was back in the chemistry lab. The hissing was real, but the source was not snakes. It was gas.

A sea of green met his eyes. Tile. He was on his stomach with his left cheek resting numbly on the cold laboratory floor. His arms were tied behind his back. Ayden.

Complicating his predicament, Odi did not know exactly where the truth ended and the fiction began, but one sad fact was blindingly obvious. Once again, he had been betrayed. Ayden's motivation was also obvious. He wanted two gallons of Creamer. He was left feeling foolish that it took a Taser blast to bring him clarity. No doubt Ayden had invented the story about Sheila and the SASC to accomplish that end. The big question was why. Why did Ayden want an arsenal of Creamer? He had only learned of the Creamer a few days earlier. Before then nobody but Odi knew of its existence. That was hardly enough time to orchestrate a grand plan. Odi supposed that it was possible that Ayden had simply opportunistically inserted Creamer into a preexisting framework, but that seemed farfetched. Or perhaps Ayden had simply grasped the black market demand for such a weapon and greed had overwhelmed him overnight. Two gallons was the equivalent of two-hundred-and-fifty-six invisible hand grenades. He shuddered to think what the likes of Bin Laden could do with an arsenal like that.

His thoughts returned to Ayden. There had to be more behind his actions than greed. Ayden had abandoned his values. He had turned on his friend. That did not happen in a day. Or did it? Odi asked, turning a mirror on himself.

As uncomfortable questions rolled in, Odi tried to push them aside so that he could focus on the present. Although his hands were bound behind his back, he could tell by the way his legs were sprawled that his feet remained free. Had Ayden gotten sloppy, he wondered, or did that anomaly signify something else? Perhaps Ayden was still in the room.

Wary now, Odi rolled slowly over, trying to get a better look around. As his hands rolled beneath him, he heard a soft metallic click. A shiver shot up his spine as he froze. Nothing focuses an explosive ordnance disposal technician's attention more acutely than an unexpected mechanical sound. Either he had just rolled onto something metallic that Ayden had placed on the middle of the tiled floor, or a device of some kind was strapped to his arms. Both possibilities yielded the same horrifying conclusion. The room was a gas-fueled bomb, and he was the trigger.

Filtering out the hissing of gas overhead, Odi tried to replay the sound in his mind. He had heard a hollow clack followed by a metal-on-tile scrape. It was mysterious, but mysterious was better than the all-too-familiar arming click of a pressure switch—probably.

He considered screaming for help, but given the hissing jets that might be the worst thing he could do. If Ayden had rigged him to be a trigger, he had probably rigged the door as well. If anyone barged in responding to his call before Odi evacuated the gas, both he and the Good Samaritan would go up in flames.

Odi summarized his situation. If he moved or called out for help, the gas would ignite and he would suffer an excruciating death. If he did nothing, he would suffocate once the gas filled the room. It was not going to be a feel-good day.

He raised his legs slowly until they were perpendicular with the floor. Then, clamping his eyes shut in a grimace, he brought his legs down so that their momentum sat him up without the use of his hands.

No Boom.

He looked over his shoulder to inspect the floor. He saw nothing but tile. That narrowed down the possibilities. Slowly Odi worked his feet beneath himself and stood up, being careful all the while not to move his hands. He tiptoed over to the wall mirror beside the chemical shower. He found the smell of gas much more intense while standing and his head began to swim. He knew he did not have much time before succumbing to the fumes.

The mirror revealed that Ayden had not strapped a bomb between his arms. He had, however, done the next best thing. Ayden had duct taped one arm of a gas-igniting sparker to each of Odi's wrists and used a third strip of tape to bind his wrists together, leaving the sparker cocked. If Odi pulled his hands free, he would release the tension holding the sparker's arms together. Then the flint would scrape back across the scratchpad and emit a deadly shower of sparks. Odi pictured his life ending with a sucking whoosh and a searing boom.

Perhaps that would be for the best, he thought. Poetic justice. Just what he deserved for releasing two gallons of Creamer into the world, endangering innocents and disgracing his family. A surge of emotion swept over him. He had allowed himself to be used, and in so doing he had betrayed everyone he knew. A fiery death was too good for him after that. Besides, how many times had he cheated Prometheus while working EOD? A dozen? Fifty? A hundred?

Staring into the mirror, his suicidal thoughts disappeared as quickly as they came. He was not one to take the coward's way out. Speaking of which, now that he understood his predicament, his first impulse was to open the door and run, to get the detonator strapped between his wrists well beyond the reach of the gas. But years on the bomb squad had conditioned him not to yield to rash impulses. He turned his eyes to the exit and spotted the redundant detonator at once. As predicted, Ayden had rigged another sparker over the door. Fortunately, disabling it would be simple—once Odi had the use of his hands.

His mind raced to find a solution, aware that it was competing with a hissing clock. If he passed out now he would never awake. Did he have seconds? Minutes? One? Two? Five? Ten? There was no way to tell. One moment his head would start to spin and the next he would fall. Whoosh-boom.

Although he had disarmed hundreds of bombs, Odi had never been trapped inside one before. Being part of the mechanism brought him a whole new perspective, but it did not help.

He tried to take a mental step outside the box, to approach this bomb like any other EOD problem. The objective was the same. He had to prevent the detonator, the sparker, from exploding the ordnance, the gas. The question was how. He had only very limited use of his hands, and the gas was everywhere. He could not clip a wire or divert a circuit or place a circuit breaker between the sparker and the gas.

Or could he?

Careful not to put pressure on his arms, Odi walked to the nearest lab station and squirmed onto the countertop. The noxious smell was strongest here. He felt his dizziness begin to spike. He bit down hard on his tongue in an effort to stay awake while arching his back and lowering his hands into the sink in an attempt to engage the stopper. As he reached for the faucet, he tasted blood and his vision began to blur. The solution was in his grasp, but he was already too late.

To buy a few seconds more he pressed his leg against the nozzle of the closest jet, plugging the deadly flow. This was like playing a demented game of Twister—without the girl. Keeping pressure on his leg, he strained forward so that his bound hands could reach the faucet and turned on the cold water.

The wait for the sink to fill seemed the longest of Odi's life. His shoulder burned, his head pounded, his tongue bled, his arms cramped, and oblivion was just a spasm or twitch away. He used the time to slowly, deliberately shut off the nozzle he had been blocking with his leg. Now he only had nineteen gas jets to go.

Once the water was sufficiently deep, Odi leaned back and plunged his hands to the bottom of the sink. He yanked his wrists apart the instant the sparker was submerged. As the tape ripped, he heard the sparker's flint scrape across the scratch pad but the water rendered it impotent. It was the first time he had used that word with a smile.

With a sigh of relief contrary to the physical pain he was feeling, he rolled his wrists to peel off the tape, losing the hair on his forearms in the process. God, what was he going to look like when this was all over? he wondered. Then he laughed at himself. Anything but a cinder would do.

He tossed the sparker back into the water and sprang to the floor. He closed the remaining gas jets in less than a minute and enabled the smashed ventilation switch in a few seconds more. The noise of the overhead vent sucking gas into space was the sweetest sound he had ever heard.

After thirty seconds of breath-catching, oxygen-sucking rest, Odi sprayed the second sparker with the fire extinguisher. Then he removed it from atop the door and tossed it into the water beside its twin. He grabbed his jacket from the stool on which it was draped and was further relieved to feel some extra weight. He checked the pocket and felt a further surge of relief. The Dasani bottle full of Creamer was still there. As the sight of it registered, so did the outline of his next moves.

Chapter 47

The Grand Hyatt, Washington, D.C.

AS AYDEN WATCHED the crowd of young men growing around him, filling the suite, he felt a warm glow percolating inside. These martyrs were nothing like the barbaric, deranged, ignorant thugs the manipulating politicians and sensation-seeking press liked to finger with upturned noses. These were clean-cut, crystal-eyed, educated leaders, soberly making the ultimate sacrifice for a charitable cause. Tomorrow, the establishment's propaganda tricks would backfire. Homeland Security would never see his soldiers coming.

Before they dispersed, however, Ayden knew that such a quantity of Middle Easterners was apt to draw attention from a wary populace. To counteract any suspicions that might arise, he had let it slip that he was auditioning to fill a dozen minor roles in a new Tom Clancy movie. The bellboy's eyes lit up as they strayed from the platter of sandwiches to the videotaping equipment. "How exciting. You know, I was once in a —"

"Well, now that I've taken you into our confidence," Ayden interrupted, brandishing a crisp Benjamin, "I'd appreciate your keeping our presence quiet. These days everyone thinks they can act, and the last thing we need is a line of Tom Cruise wannabes at our door."

The bellboy made the c-note vanish faster than a chameleon's lunch. Then he bowed and offered an obsequious, "But of course."

Ayden looked out at the crowd and nodded. Arvin's twenty-four volunteers had arrived at odd intervals over the previous two hours and now they filled the two-thousand-dollar-a-night Hyatt suite. Their air was more jovial than somber, but Ayden could sense the tension percolating just below the surface. Suppressing that tension was half of today's job. The other half was locking in their resolve.

As he took a seat atop the granite counter of the sitting room bar, the chatter trailed off and the room grew silent. He rolled his shoulders once and began. "We are strangers united by our mutual commitment to a great cause. That makes us friends. Friends, please listen to me now, for I have much to reveal.

"To my left you see a stack of envelopes, to my right," he ceremoniously lifted a black cloth, "one hundred mini-bar beverage bottles. Four for each of you." Ayden held up one of the fine linen envelopes and withdrew a 3-ounce bottle of Baileys Irish Cream from the case. "These are your mission and your means. I will begin by explaining precisely how and when the Irish Cream is to be used. Then after lunch, each of you is going to make a video, a video that will make your family proud for countless generations to come ..."

Chapter 48

Asgard Island, Chesapeake Bay

AS THE NORSE WIND approached Asgard across a choppy bay, Cassi walked out to stand by the rail. She caught some spray on her face. It tasted bitterly cold and very salty—not unlike her present predicament.

She traced the yacht's heading to the coastline ahead. She had not studied Wiley's tiny marina on her previous visits. There had been no need. For the next twenty-four hours, however, Wiley's island was going to be her battleground. She began to study it as such. "Tell me about the marina," she shouted into the cabin.

"It can handle yachts up to 120 feet in length," Wiley yelled back, his voice buffeted by the wind. "The two central lifts are powerful enough to raise sixty footers completely out of the water. That isn't usually necessary, but it's nice to have when seas get rough."

Cassi knew that they would not be using a lift now. Per their agreement, Wiley was not even going to cut the motor. He was just dropping her off.

"Is something wrong?" Wiley asked. "You seem to be staring."

"No. I'm just getting a tactical perspective. Is this the only place a boat can safely land?"

"Sure is. The rocks will shred your hull if you try to tie-up anywhere else."

Cassi realized that she had never seen the island from the eastern side. They always approached from Virginia. "So the whole circumference looks like this—rocky cliffs rising from water?"

"Yep. Geologically speaking, Asgard is a rocky mountaintop protruding from the bay. The average drop is over thirty feet, and nowhere is it less than twenty."

"So why did you build the dock here? Why not closer to the house?"

"This is the best-protected spot on the leeward side of the island."

Cassi nodded and studied the scraggly cliffs. "When I look at it from a tactical perspective, it kind of reminds me of Alcatraz."

"My grandfather would have banished you forever if he heard you say that. We Proffitts prefer to think of our island as Valhalla."

Their banter was growing lighter as each tried to cover the growing awkwardness of their situation—the nervousness, the guilt and yes, the sexual tension. They were not taking the familiar trip to make love in the clover on the bluff or to walk through the sculpted gardens kissing and holding hands. They were colleagues on a mission, nothing more, she realized. It hurt. "What's the circumference of your earthly heaven?" she asked.

"Just over two miles. The island covers roughly one square kilometer, although it's not square. As my grandmother used to say, Asgard is shaped like an open-mouthed smile."

Or a frown, Cassi thought, depending on your perspective. "With the marina for its front teeth?"

"And the house as a dimple."

Cassi continued to study the marina as Wiley masterfully maneuvered the forty-eight foot yacht toward an iron berth. The last time she had been here, she had been with Odi. Odi would come this time too, but this time she would be against him.

Wiley drifted in alongside the dock, gave the twin engines a second of reverse, then put the motor in neutral. The Norse Wind halted as though on wheels. "Are you sure you want me to leave, Cassi? I would much rather stay. I don't feel good about leaving you here alone."

The woman in her yearned for him to stay, but today the agent prevailed. "I am sure. I have to handle him myself, one-on-one."

Wiley shook his head. "What if he doesn't give you that chance? What if there's a bomb waiting up there, like the one he left at your aunt's cottage? Or what if he changes MO's and uses a sniper rifle?"

Cassi looked down at the sea to hide the doubt in her eyes. "I'm not just his twin sister, Wiley. I'm also a profiler. I'm convinced that Odi won't do that."

"How can you be so sure when you don't even know his motivation? He has obviously changed. Who knows what happened to him over there. Maybe he's hearing voices or taking his orders from a dog."

Wiley was playing to her emotions effectively. She knew that she had to keep it professional or she might crack. "Because whatever his reason, the first killings show that this is very personal to him."

"We don't know that," Wiley shot back. "I'm not a defense contractor. Even if the others were personal, this one could be different."

"I appreciate your concern, Wiley. Really I do. But we agreed on this hours ago, and you promised to let me do this my way. I'm getting off the boat now. I don't want to see you again until this time tomorrow."

Chapter 49

Asgard Island, Chesapeake Bay

ODI FELT AN ADRENALINE KICK as the rising sun crested the island bluff and sent rays of golden light through the bulletproof windows. He knew it would not be long now. Wiley was a creature of habit.

Odi had given up on trying to guess Ayden's intentions for the Creamer in order to focus on a sure thing. He could not allow a traitor like Wiley to assume the second highest office in the land, but he could not expect to stop him either—at least not with political or legal means. Wiley was far too rich and powerful for conventional measures like that. Fortunately, Odi was an unconventional kind of guy—and he still had a Dasani bottle full of Creamer.

He bent over to touch his toes, holding the stretch for a ten-count to warm his muscles. Wiley did not heat the manor house at night. Odi was not surprised. Despite his wealth, Wiley struck Odi as the traditionally frugal New England flannel-pajamas-and-thick-comforter type. That really sucked when your body was as sore and cold as Odi's was after his pounding midnight Jet Ski ride. But he was not complaining. He had come a long way to reach this final phase. After weeks of struggle, he had just one battle to go.

Odi studied the room through the crack in the closet door. This was something he had not been able to do in the dark of the night. Wiley's enormous study looked exactly as it had the one time he had visited with Cassi. Windows along the east side of the room, a long aquarium along the west, with a sixty-inch screen on the far wall and a suite of matching black leather furniture in the middle.

At the far end from where Odi hid, a bar occupied one corner and a large glass desk the other. Behind the desk a Plexiglas lectern faced out the window. Odi had asked Wiley about the lectern's odd placement. "It helps condition me to ignore diversion and distraction," Wiley had explained. "Both are key to Beltway survival."

The lectern was the focus of Odi's attention now. It was the lure that would draw his rat to the trap—sometime soon from the sound of it, he noted. The pipes had just come to life. He guessed that Wiley was taking a shower.

He caught sight of the large remote control next to the marble ashtray on the end table, the one Wiley had used during their last visit to activate the panic room. He should have hidden it as a precaution,

Odi realized, but he did not want to risk retrieving it now that he knew Wiley was awake. It probably didn't matter anyway. There was no button you could push when you had a bomb in your belly—except perhaps game over.

Odi was still contemplating the irony of setting a trap in a panic room when Wiley walked in. That was quick, he thought, but then Wiley had obviously come straight from the shower. He was wearing Scottish flannel PJ's and a thick white robe with a hood that made him look like a prizefight boxer approaching the ring. He supposed the analogy was suitable. The lectern was a politician's arena.

Wiley crossed the study to his practice lectern without so much as a glance toward the closet, and began to practice for his upcoming *PoliTalk* appearance. "It's a pleasure to be back on *PoliTalk*, Jim."

Odi slipped silently out of his hiding place.

"I'd like to be the bearer of good news today," Wiley continued, "but from where I sit the situation looks bleak."

Odi raised two Berettas toward Wiley's back and said, "It does indeed."

Wiley said nothing in response. He just froze.

Odi thought he detected a tremble. "Look at me," he commanded.

Slowly, very slowly Wiley turned around while using his left hand to remove his hood. First Odi saw the voice recorder, then he saw the face. The person in the bathrobe was Cassi.

Chapter 50

Asgard Island, Chesapeake Bay

"COME ON, SHOOT HIM," Stuart whispered, staring at the security monitor. "Shoot the bastard."

"You're dreaming," Wiley said without averting his eyes. "Cassi's not going to shoot her brother. There was a chance that he might have shot her in the back thinking she was me. Then we might have gotten really lucky and seen him shoot himself after discovering his mistake, à la Romeo and Juliet, but that chance is gone. It's up to us now."

They had just watched Odi's Berettas slip from his limp hands to the floor as Cassi produced a Colt .45 from her bathrobe pocket. Now the twins were just standing there, her tears flowing, his mouth agape, neither knowing what to do next.

Stuart said, "You better get over there now before they figure things out," but Wiley was already gone.

~ ~ ~

Wiley wondered how it had come to this as he slipped out of the security closet and slunk down the hall. He knew the answer, of course. He had made a Faustian exchange, his soul for the Oval Office, when he committed to The Three Marks to do whatever it takes. He realized now that he had been a fool to think that he could pull it off without genuine sacrifice—as had they.

Peering around the doorway, Wiley could see Odi's back and the top of Cassi's head. She was holding her brother in a supportive embrace, although the Colt remained in her hand.

Cassi spotted Wiley as he entered the room and she backed away from her brother.

"What is it?" Odi asked, obviously studying her face before turning to look around.

"I couldn't leave you alone in your time of need," Wiley said, before Cassi could comment. "I was worried. I'm glad to see that you've got things under control. Shall I leave the two of you alone?"

Before Cassi could reply, Odi interjected, "Shoot him now. Don't let him get to my guns."

Wiley almost smiled when he heard Odi's words. It was as if he was reading from Stuart's script.

Odi's guns lay on the floor in front of the closet. They were a yard to Wiley's left, and a full twenty feet from the Carrs. Wiley held up his hands. "Hey, I'm not the one who came here to shoot anybody. In fact, I'm the only one walking around unarmed—and this is my house."

"Don't listen to him, Cassi," Odi interrupted. "He has killed lots of people, including Derek, Flint and Adam."

Keeping his voice soft and in check, Wiley said, "You're sick, Odi. Deranged. Mentally ill. What happened to you over there in Iran? What did they do to you?"

As he spoke, Wiley watched Cassi look back and forth, her face a mask of anguish and apprehension. Sensing her indecision, he held out his hands and said, "Let's defuse this situation. We don't want anyone doing anything stupid." He slowly bent down and grabbed the barrels of each of Odi's Berettas between thumb and forefinger without taking his eyes off Cassi's face. Moving slowly, he walked over to the aquarium and dropped the guns in, saying "sorry about this, guys," to the fish. The Berettas sank quickly through four feet of water and clanked against a white coral reef at the bottom.

Wiley said, "Why don't we all sit down and talk."

Cassi looked from Wiley to Odi to Wiley again. She blinked once and then walked toward Wiley with the Colt raised in her hand. Her face was puffy and her eyes were void of expression. In that moment, Wiley realized that he had underestimated the strength of the love that bound the twins. He had bet that Cassi would prefer to believe his trauma-victim explanation over Odi's deeply wounding truth. He had lost.

Wiley's mind raced through alternatives as Cassi drew closer. He could bolt from the room, or he could try to snatch the gun, counting in both cases on her reluctance to shoot him. As she closed the gap he decided on the latter. He wanted this mess to be over. Just before he pounced, Cassi transferred the Colt to her left hand, grabbing the barrel between thumb and forefinger.

Odi yelled, "No!" as Cassi held it up to her left and added it to the fish's collection. "Yes," she said, obviously trying to keep her voice calm. "Let's sit."

As Wiley stared at the three weapons resting impotently on the floor of the tank, he felt a surge of relief and a wave of elation. He had won.

Chapter 51

Asgard Island, Chesapeake Bay

CASSI LOOKED OVER at Odi through tear-soaked eyes, afraid that her heart would break. Although upset at first, she was now glad that Wiley had broken their agreement and returned early. She did not want to go through this alone. She dropped her weapon in the tank where it settled next to Odi's and then walked over to the couch. Wiley followed.

Odi looked back at her from the other side of the room, his face a mask of desperation. She felt an inexplicable surge of guilt, followed by a sense of foreboding. He walked slowly toward the armchair with his feet shuffling and his head bowed low, the epitome of a beaten man.

In a split second, he changed everything. As Odi drew beside the chair he scooped the marble cigar ashtray off the end table and whirled around like he was holding a discus. He completed one full turn and then launched the rock straight into the center of the aquarium.

The enormous glass panel cracked into a spider's web as the ashtray soared through. There was a catastrophic crash followed by the sound of three hundred gallons of furious water and a hundred doomed fish spewing onto the beige carpeted floor. Cassi and Wiley both shot out of their chairs as the living rainbow began to thrash and flop.

Odi dove into the writhing school toward the nearest Beretta. Cassi heard a gunshot as the Beretta jumped off the floor an inch before Odi's hand. "Don't move, Carr," a new voice shouted from the doorway. "I never miss."

Cassi turned toward the voice as Odi froze.

Stuart was standing there, dressed head to toe in black. Aside from the handgun and accompanying snarl, he looked exactly as he had when Wiley brought him to her loft for brunch. His dark eyes flashed with cold intensity behind silver spectacles as he spoke. "Lie on your stomach with your hands behind your back. If you try another funny move, I'll put the next bullet in your sister."

Cassi looked from Stuart to Odi to Wiley. "Wiley, what's going on? Tell your friend to put his gun away."

Wiley rose and picked the three wet guns off the floor. "I'm sorry," he said, not meeting her eyes. "You should have listened to your brother."

Cassi felt the blood drain from her face. The room began to spin. It couldn't be. Wiley couldn't ... Wiley wouldn't ... "Wiley ... ?"

"I didn't expect it to come to this. Your brother is a little too resourceful." Wiley slipped the two Berettas beneath his belt and used the Colt to motion Cassi toward the floor.

Cassi had no strength to resist. Stuart pressed her face into the saturated carpet as he bound her hands using thick black zip ties extracted from his pocket. A dying fish gasped for air an inch from her face. She knew exactly how it felt.

She turned to look at Odi. Stuart had him similarly bound and positioned. He was drenched and bleeding from a dozen cuts, some still embedded with aquarium glass. Guilt overwhelmed her as she asked her brother, "What resourcefulness are they talking about?"

Odi said, "I've been a fool. I've been used." He looked up at Wiley. "What are your plans for the explosive?"

"What explosive?" Cassi asked, now totally confused.

"He's referring to the two gallons of custom brew that he gave our mutual friend," Stuart said, unzipping Odi's backpack and pulling out a bottle of what looked like milk. "What he really should be concerned about is this pint." He shook the bottle as Odi groaned. Then Stuart produced a long funnel and Cassi saw tears appear in her brother's eyes. She had not seen Odi cry since the day their parents died. The sight curdled her rage into fear.

"Your brother really is a remarkable cook," Stuart continued. "I think it's time you enjoyed a taste."

Chapter 52

Asgard Island, Chesapeake Bay

ODI GAGGED on the end of the funnel as Stuart forced the tip into his throat. He was pinned on his knees with Wiley behind him and Stuart in front. Wiley had a knee planted between his shoulder blades and was pulling back hard on his elbows to incapacitate him. Meanwhile, Stuart kept one foot on Odi's crotch for insurance as he prepared to pour. Odi sensed that Stuart would joyfully transfer his weight if he resisted, however Odi was not about to do that. He had lost the will to fight the moment they emptied half a pint of Creamer into his sister. He clenched his eyes and listened to the upturned bottle gurgle as his stomach accepted the cold-flowing liquid death.

"You're working with Ayden, aren't you?" Odi asked Wiley, once the bottle had been emptied and the funnel withdrawn from his mouth. "Were you working with him from the start?"

"No, we have you to thank for introducing us," Stuart interjected.

Odi kept his eyes on Wiley. "I figured it all out, everything except one key question."

Wiley raised his eyebrows.

"Why do it? You have so much to lose."

"Let's just say that I'm a hero in need of a war."

As Wiley spoke, Odi saw Cassi staring at him, tears still running down her eyes. Odi could not begin to imagine what she must be feeling. Perhaps the Creamer was a blessing. All her sorrows would vanish in about thirty minutes.

Odi had brought the Creamer to Asgard to use on Wiley, so he accepted this turnabout as fair play. Part of him even thought that he deserved it. But he could not accept what Wiley was doing to his sister. She had given Wiley nothing but love and devotion. Now she had eight grenades worth of explosive sloshing around in her belly as thanks.

"The plan to assassinate the Senate Armed Services Committee—was that real, or another red herring?" Odi pressed.

Wiley grew a wry smile. "Oh, the idea Ayden presented was very real. I fear, however, that our mutual friend misled you on the tactics."

"How so?" Odi asked.

Wiley looked over at Stuart, who had been standing there silent and expressionless with a gun gripped professionally in each hand.

Stuart nodded, his message clear. With the Creamer already congealing in their opponents' bowels, they had nothing to fear from that revelation.

"Do you know what day it is?" Wiley asked, turning back to Odi. "What date?"

"October twelfth," Cassi interjected with venom in her voice.

"Precisely. First there was 9/11. Now there will be 10/12. Just as The Prophet warned."

Odi had not caught on to the calendar aspect, but otherwise he was not surprised. "So it's even bigger than what Ayden proposed? Bigger than the SASC? What are you going to do, take out the Capitol? Two gallons of Creamer is a lot, but it's not nearly enough for that."

Wiley returned an amused smile. "The SASC won't be in the Capitol this afternoon. They're going home. They're flying home."

Odi felt a frigid iron vise take hold of his heart and begin to squeeze. His parents had died aboard a plane on 9/11. So had many others. "Twenty-five airplanes," he thought aloud. "That's thousands of innocent souls."

"We're hoping to get six thousand—double the casualties of 9/11— but we expect it will turn out closer to five. A lot depends on where the planes hit the ground. In any case, it won't make a good advertisement for Baileys Irish Cream." Wiley paused to admire his own wit. "Oh, and just to be accurate, it's only going to be twenty-four planes. SASC Chairman Marshall is not flying home. He's taking a cruise. The senator is going to England, aboard the Queen Mary 2 no less."

Odi cringed but did not comment.

Wiley continued. "There is one particular operational detail that I'm sure will hold your interest. Believe it or not, Ayden is going to handle Marshall personally. He considers it an honor." Wiley chuckled. "Actually, Ayden's mission will bring terrorism to a whole new level, an elite level. What location could strike closer to home for the world's elite than the fanciest suite on the most luxurious ship? The QM2 may not sink, but a terrorist attack aboard it will strike home with the rich and evoke a tidal wave of campaign donations."

"How could you, Wiley? How could you become such a monster?" Cassi spit the bitter words through her torrent of tears. "You were a good man, a decent man ... I loved you."

"Love often requires sacrifice, my dear. To answer your question, only a man in full control of his emotions can hope to survive the electoral process. It's part of the hazing ritual. To join the fraternity of presidents, one must prove himself capable of despicable acts—and for good reason. You see, for all their wealth and position, the American people can't afford the luxury of a Commander-in-Chief who will waver when the time comes to pull the nuclear trigger."

It was obvious to Odi that Cassi wanted to retort, but apparently the words would not come—only more tears.

"We're going to leave you now," Wiley continued, picking up the remote control. "Stuart and I have much to do. You two enjoy the rest of your lives."

Chapter 53

Ronald Reagan Washington National Airport

AYDEN FELT his anxiety peak as he watched Amir reach the front of the security line. He looked perfect. Polished shoes, a crisp navy suit topped with rimless spectacles and platinum tie. A *Wall Street Journal* adorned with a Grand Hyatt sticker completed the disguise. But the scanner would not be looking at the man …

"Your identification and boarding pass, please."

Amir handed the requested documents to the TSA officer. It was ridiculous how many times you had to do this, Ayden thought. Did the bureaucrats really think that terrorists could not afford to go online and buy a ninety-nine dollar ticket?

The Idaho driver's license Amir presented was not real, of course. For that matter, the matching boarding pass was unlikely to be used. The twenty-four martyrs had checked-in online the day before. Each had booked himself on three or four sequential flights under differing aliases. Although Director Proffitt had supplied Ayden with the list of the SASC senators' flight reservations, plans were known to change as meetings ran long or finished unexpectedly short. With multiple tickets, each martyr would be ready to board with his assigned senator no matter which flight His Honor actually took.

Ayden watched Amir's progress over the shoulder of the lady in line between them. His colleague was a rock, or perhaps more appropriately, a rolling stone. He acted respectful but bored as the guard finished his perfunctory perusal. Then he put on the requisite thank-you-officer smile as the guard nodded like a dog approving of his biscuit.

Amir put his bag on the scanner belt.

The lady who had been separating them in line stepped aside unexpectedly as her cell phone rang. Suddenly it was Ayden's turn. It took all his willpower to keep his nervous eyes off the guard inspecting Amir's bag as he handed over his boarding pass and driver's license.

Ayden had run each refilled miniature Baileys Irish Cream bottle through the dishwasher six times, so he was confident that the agents, their bags and the bottles themselves would pass a random swab test. The luggage scanners might be a different story.

During his discussion with the woman pretending to be Sheila, Odi had asserted that Creamer would pass through security scanners like a bottle of milk. Ayden had repeated Odi's claim with certainty to his twenty-four friends, although as his sweaty palms now testified, he had serious doubts. It was highly unlikely that Odi was up to date on the latest scanning technology. The field was changing too fast. Yesterday, Ayden had pushed that worry aside because he had no choice. Now that the ball was in play, he felt weak in the knees.

As Ayden walked through the metal detector, his heart jumped into his mouth. A guard had picked up Amir's plastic quart bag as it emerged from the scanner. Ayden walked to stand behind Amir, straining to hear while trying to make nervous look like impatient. He wished he had taken one of the diazepam tablets that Arvin had him give the martyrs. His nerves were not well suited for this kind of work.

"Do you have anything unusual in here?" the guard asked, no sign of alarm in his voice.

"No," Amir said, "just toiletries … and uh, my breakfast."

As the guard held the bag up, his face registered comprehension. "Expecting a tough day at the office, eh?"

"You have no idea," Amir replied, his tone remarkably cool.

The fat guy putting on his shoes in front of Amir looked back, saw the bag full of miniature bottles of Baileys, and nodded appreciatively.

Amir was quick on his feet, Ayden noted, not without a touch of pride. He also had a gift for words. Ayden had not told the martyrs what to say in the testimonial videos each had made for release in the coming days. He had just told them to tell the American people why they had chosen to do this. Arvin had pointed out that their testimonials would be much more persuasive if the world could see the un-coached conviction in their eyes and sense the sincerity in their voices. If Ayden had written a text, however, it would have read like Amir's. His arguments were an oversimplification, to be sure, but political sound bites always were. He wiped a tear from his cheek as he remembered the words delivered by the handsome, well-coiffed man before him in flawless American English.

My friends and I do not wish to die. Quite to the contrary, we want the same thing as you. We want to better our children's lives. Unlike you, however, our situation is desperate. Desperate enough to do … this.

You all harbor a deep desire for world peace. It's in America's blood. It's the default answer in every religious sermon, political race and beauty pageant. Yet despite all your means and rhetoric, all your promises and potential, and all your fine examples of individual and private efforts, your government is actively working against it.

Your politicians are the problem.

Our action today is a result of their inaction yesterday. We do this destructive act in the hope of building a better tomorrow. My colleagues and I are executing the twenty-five members of the Senate Armed Services Committee in order to shed light on their crimes. The American voters deserve to see the enormous gap that exists between these politicians' promises and their deeds.

They spout bromides about Christianity, democracy, education and world peace much as a fountain does water—with great volume and much show but little thought. Then they quietly shovel billions out the back door and into the pockets of their war-mongering corporations in exchange for campaign contributions.

We hope that the sacrifice we make today gives the good people of America the chance to reevaluate the world, to see it not as the 'Us' and 'Them' politicians peddle, but for what it really is: one people under God.

Chapter 54

Asgard Island, Chesapeake Bay

CASSI WATCHED open-mouthed as Odi sprang from the floor, instantly recognizing the desperate act of a man with nothing to lose. She remembered his line from the Potchak video: The only antidote to Creamer is death. Since Odi's hands were bound behind his back, he tried to ram Wiley with his head. Cassi wanted to join him but before she could rise, she saw Stuart's Beretta flash and heard the sickening crack of metal on bone as he brought the butt down on the back of Odi's charging head.

"You bastard!" she screamed.

Stuart turned to point the Beretta at her face.

She ignored the gun barrel inches from her nose and gave Wiley a contemptuous stare. He and Stuart backed out the door. As Wiley lifted the remote control, Cassi screamed, "Wiley, for God's sake, don't do this!"

"It's already done," Wiley said. Then he dialed the non-emergency code and pressed the red panic button.

The door slammed closed and Cassi heard bolts sliding into place. Titanium shutters began rolling down to cover the bulletproof windows. In seconds, the study would be a fortress. For the second time in as many days, she was locked in a room with a bomb. At least this time she was not alone. And for better or worse, she could not see the clock. On the downside, she was the bomb. Escape was not an option. Strangely enough, Cassi found that fact calming.

She struggled to her feet and used a shoulder to turn on the lights as the shutters dropped into place. She walked over to Odi and knelt down beside him. He had a nasty lump where Stuart's pistol butt had cracked the back of his head, but he was breathing.

"Odi ... Odi wake up ... Wake up. I need your help."

He did not respond.

She repeated herself, louder.

Still nothing.

She gave him a vigorous nudge with her knee and then turned her attention to the floor. She needed to find a piece of glass sharp enough to cut her bonds. Unfortunately, the aquarium had shattered like a car windshield. It lay strewn about the floor in a thousand little pieces. She knew that this was a safety feature, but in her case it would do more harm than good. Most of the pieces were far too small to be of use.

After brushing a dead fish aside with her foot, she spotted a triangular piece wedged into the thick carpet pile. It was more round than pointed, and each side was less than two inches long. Still, it was better than any other piece available, so it would have to do. She squatted and found it with her fingers. Picking it up, she rotated it to feel each side. The edges were only mildly sharp. "No problem," she told herself. "You can compensate for sharpness with force." A few seconds later she knew that she had spoken too soon. It was too small and slippery to afford a forceful grip.

She stood and walked over to the desk and leaned against it so that if she dropped the glass, it would not fall far. As she scraped the edge against the tough zip tie, she continued shouting Odi's name. She knew that he would not be able to change their lot. Death was the only antidote. But that was not the point. Odi would want to face his fate head-on, teeth gritted and eyes opened wide. Since she had put him in this position, she owed him that final wish. For her part, she wanted to go out of this world as she had come into it—holding her twin brother's hand.

Trying to sever her bonds, Cassi lost her grip on the shard more often than not. Each fumble rewarded her with another gash in her palm or wrist. Adding insult to injury, the slippery blood made it even harder to work. She ignored the pain and kept at it. What else could she do? After two more fruitless minutes, however, Cassi realized that her current approach was not going to work. At least not in time. She needed to find another way to free her hands.

She considered slitting her wrists and lying down to die beside her unconscious brother—but only for a second. Wiley had her ire up. She wanted to go out fighting. She wanted to leave a note, an accusatory message from the grave. To do that properly, she had to free her hands.

Cassi turned and began looking about Wiley's desk for something sharp. The desk itself was glass, so there were no drawers. She looked into his pewter FBI pencil holder. It held a miniature broadsword that functioned as a letter opener. Her hopes jumped until she saw that it too was made of pewter, a soft metal. She dumped the pencil holder out onto the desk to test the edges, just in case. They were dull as Des Moines. She studied the remainder of the spilled contents. There was the usual assortment of short wooden golf pencils and logo-stamped ink pens. Her eye jumped to the single shiny object and she felt a glimmer of hope. Winking at her from the desk was a pair of nail clippers.

She found it slow going, trying to maneuver the tiny object behind her back with slippery fingers and bound hands. Oddly enough, it even left her struggling for breath. She did not care. It was working. The nail clippers were making headway against the tough plastic. She had gotten nearly halfway through when her eyes darted from the zip tie to her hands. The sight she saw brought the terror of the moment crashing home, provoking a guttural scream. Despite the blood she could clearly see that the tips of her fingers were blue.

Chapter 55

Asgard Island, Chesapeake Bay

ODI JOLTED AWAKE to the sound of his sister screaming. He looked in the direction of her voice and asked, "What happened?"

As he spoke, Cassi's hands flew out from behind her back and a shiny object soared across the room. It splashed down near his feet. "Odi, thank God you're awake. Stuart pistol-whipped you."

"Right after Wiley told us of his plans," Odi said nodding, wishing all the while that he could rub the back of his head.

"And made us drink your Creamer," Cassi confirmed.

The urgency of their predicament struck him like a hammer. "How long ago was that? How long was I out?"

"It was about fifteen minutes ago, I think. Look at me." Cassi held up her bloody hands and Odi saw the discolored fingertips. His stomach dropped. They did not have long. The explosive was already sweating, and they had each swallowed the equivalent of eight hand grenades.

"There may still be hope," he said, trying to sound more optimistic than he felt. "Can you free my hands?"

Cassi looked at him with wide eyes and then grabbed the nail clippers off the floor. Ten seconds later Odi's hands were also free.

"We've got to purge our stomachs. Use your finger. Gag yourself." Odi got up on his knees as he spoke and then plunged a finger into his throat after noting that it was not yet blue. The gag reflex came on fast and strong. His throat protested but his stomach began to heave. He ignored the pain. His mind was working overtime now, churning as fast as his stomach. He was desperate to prevent 10/12. He was willing to endure anything for that shot at redemption. He was straining to think of how they could possibly pull off such a miracle when an idea came to him. He pulled his finger from his mouth and shouted, "Wait!"

Cassi looked over at him, obviously scared.

Odi got off his knees and retrieved the plastic wastebasket from the bathroom. After emptying its contents onto the floor, he set it down before her and said, "Vomit into this."

Cassi looked at him funny from the corners of her bloodshot eyes but did not question why.

Over the next couple of minutes they knocked heads a few times over the can, but eventually all their heaves were dry. Cassi had expelled three or four marble-sized chunks whereas Odi's effluent looked more like milky peas.

"I've got nothing left," Cassi said, her voice hoarse. "Is it safe to stop?"

Odi was not sure. It did not look like they were accomplishing anything, and there appeared to be roughly a pint of effluent in the bucket, but the penalty for underestimation was severe. "Let's give it a couple more tries."

Thirty seconds later he said, "That's enough."

"Is it really that simple?" Cassi asked.

"I don't know. Probably not. It only takes a few drops to provide a bomb with critical mass. It's time for phase two."

Odi pulled a line of clear plastic tubing from the ruins of the aquarium. "You have to swallow one end. Once you've got it down the right tube, I'll push it all the way down and suck the remaining contents out. It will hurt like hell, but it beats the alternative."

Cassi grew a shade paler, but nodded stoically. His sister was the best.

The next couple minutes went by in a disgusting, painful blur as Odi purged Cassi and she returned the favor. He kept stealing subtle glances at the tips of her fingers, and was encouraged to see that they had gotten no worse.

With phase two complete, Odi ran back to the half bath and flung open the medicine chest. He saw aspirin, Band-Aids, Triaminic and Mylanta. "Bingo." He grabbed the green plastic bottle and gave it a good shake. It was nearly full. He tossed it to Cassi. "Drink this. The acid in your stomach catalyzes the reaction. No acid, no explosion. In case we didn't get it all, this should neutralize any Creamer that's left."

Cassi drank half the bottle in the time it took Odi to walk back to her. She gave the Mylanta back to him. Odi guzzled the rest and wiped his lips with the back of his hand.

"What do we do now?" Cassi asked. "We're still stuck here in Wiley's panic room, completely incommunicado. Six thousand people are about to die. Tell me you have a plan."

"Of course I have a plan, Sis. That's why we threw up into the wastebasket. You can help out by getting me some coffee filters. There should be some under the bar."

While she searched, he took the basket off Mr. Coffee. Then he grabbed the wastebasket and set it next to the bar's small sink.

"Here you go. What else can I do?" Cassi asked.

Odi put two clean filters into the basket and positioned it over the sink. "You hold the filter basket," he said. "I'll pour."

The milky liquid seemed to take forever to drain through the filter. As it dripped out the bottom, Odi studied Cassi's hands. They were regaining their original color. His had never changed. Although he had no empirical evidence, intuition told him that this was a very good sign. "Why don't you wash up and make use of the Band-Aids. To get out of here, you're going to need your hands."

"Okay," Cassi said. " But while I'm doing that, will you tell me what's going on?"

"The acid in your stomach causes the explosive to congeal like curdling milk. As the process progresses, the curds combine with one another. Eventually, only larger curds are left and they form a crust. The crust sweats a substance toxic to hemoglobin. That is why your extremities turn blue. By drinking the antacid, we raised the pH in our stomachs, halting the reaction. Now all we need to do is keep the pH in our stomachs neutral until everything passes into the small intestine, where the pH is too high to catalyze the reaction."

"But the explosive is still there," Cassi said, panic apparent in her voice.

"Yes, but there's nothing to set it off. Think of it as a hand grenade with the pin still in. It's safe to carry around." The thought of adding just don't fart flashed across Odi's mind, but he thought better of it. His sister did not always appreciate his humor.

He used a few more filters to dry out the congealed explosive further. "Is my memory right? Do the bolts on the door enter the frame on both sides?"

"That's right."

Odi began inspecting the frame, looking for the bolts between the cracks. "But not on the top or the floor?"

"I don't think so," Cassi said. "Definitely not on the floor."

"Let's hope you're right. There are only two lamps."

"Huh?"

"There are three ways to detonate most explosives: chemistry, pressure and electricity."

Odi took a brass lamp off the desk and its twin from the end table as he spoke. He removed the white shades, the shade supports and the bulbs. He cleared everything else off Wiley's desk and said, "Grab that end. We need to set this down in front of the door."

Cassi assisted without question.

Once the desk was flush against the door, Odi took the lamps and laid them sideways. He lined up the sockets so that they were directly in front of the door bolts. Then he bent the lampshade and used it as a prop to get the level just right.

Once satisfied, he split the explosive in half and then halved it again. Cassi watched him pack one quarter of the explosive putty between the door and frame at the location of each bolt, leaving a protuberance.

With that accomplished he packed each empty light socket, again leaving some run-over. He laid the lamps on the desk once finished, and slid each carefully toward the door until the bits of explosive made solid contact.

"Bring me that extension cord," he asked Cassi, pointing toward the desk. She did so and Odi plugged both lamps into extension cord sockets. "Now comes the fun part."

Being careful not to disturb the lamps, Odi trailed the extension cord into the bathroom, and then motioned for Cassi to join him. Once she was inside, he closed the solid door. "Crouch down in the corner with your knees covering your chest," he pointed, "and plug your ears." Cassi did not require any explanation. She rushed to do as she was told.

Odi placed the end of the extension cord over an outlet and then looked over at her. "Here goes ..."

Chapter 56

The SS Norse Wind, Chesapeake Bay

WILEY LOOKED DOWN at his hands as they gripped the yacht's wheel. No white knuckles, no jitters. He had gotten through the Asgard confrontation distancing himself from the spasms of his own heart. He had frozen his emotions, and they had yet to thaw. It had still been the most difficult five minutes of his life. But he had known going in that the third-person approach would be the only way to get through it, and he had prevailed. He had prevailed without a hint of weakness because Stuart had been by his side.

Now that it was over and Cassi's blood stained his hands, Wiley had expected to be feeling sick. He expected to be spending this boat ride back to the mainland retching over the rail while Stuart looked on in disgust. But he was not sick. He had not thrown up over the rail. In fact, he wanted breakfast. Looking from his hands to the mainland he felt only one emotion: relief.

Emboldened by this discovery, he allowed his thoughts to wander to the Tiffany box and the promise it held. It seemed a distant memory now, like a fond but forgotten childhood memory. He pondered this unexpected emotional twist, searching for deeper meaning as the Norse Wind cut through the waves. As they neared the marina, he figured it out. Cassi had been spoiling his dream. This was supposed to be the most magical time of his life, a time of self-realization and tremendous professional growth. Instead, he had been stuck in a quagmire of doubt, bogged down by worthless guilt. With Cassi gone he was unencumbered, free to grow. Her death had lifted a tremendous weight from his back. Destiny was once again marching by his side. He felt powerful, purposeful and brave.

With Cassi and Odi both out of the way, he expected smooth sailing and clear skies—at least metaphorically speaking. The rising sun had ducked behind a thick bank of clouds shortly after it cleared the horizon. Now the temperature was beginning to drop.

He saw a dock boy standing ready, eager to be of assistance, and for a second his mind flashed to the Marines ever guarding the president. He saluted the boy and eased off on the engines. As the yacht dropped lower in the water, Stuart gave him a funny look. Stuart knew what he had been thinking.

Wiley looked at his thick titanium watch. It was early enough that he could still make it to the office on time.

While tossing a line to the dock boy, a shocking thought blazed through his mind like lightning from above. He let fly a panicked "Shit!"

The dock boy jumped back.

"What is it?" Stuart asked.

Wiley stepped back into the cabin and lowered his voice. "Can you handle the boat?"

"Yes. Why? What happened? What's wrong?"

"We forgot the security video."

Stuart's jaw dropped.

Wiley stamped his foot three times on the deck. "Damn, damn, damn!" He looked at Stuart. "You have to go back!"

"Okay."

"You have to go back to Asgard right now and get the recording!"

"Okay."

"That video will show everything. You have to get it now. The panic room is engineered to withstand assault, but we used a lot of Creamer. If someone heard the explosion or saw the smoke they might have called the Coast Guard to check it out. You have to beat them to it. Hell, you have to be gone before they arrive."

"Okay, Wiley. Get out of here. Go be seen in the office. I'll take care of it."

"The recorder is right above the monitor we watched. It's in the cupboard on the wall. Actually, every monitor has its own recorder. You better take all the DVDs just to be safe. Plus, that way I can say I never got around to reloading the recorders after the last batch ran out."

"Will do."

Wiley picked up his duffel bag and jumped onto the dock. He handed the dock boy a twenty and said, "You can leave us now. He's going back out."

As the boy ran off, Wiley looked back up at his coconspirator. "Don't come back without that video, Stuart. You know what happens to people like us in prison."

Chapter 57

Asgard Island, Chesapeake Bay

CASSI CLOSED HER EYES and held her breath as Odi plugged in the extension cord. She heard a sputtering sound come through the closed bathroom door and wondered if it was the last sound she would ever hear. She had already survived one explosion of late. Was two too much to ask?

Odi tightened his grip on her shoulder. Then she heard a deafening boom. A hard rain of debris followed. It sounded as though a giant were whipping handfuls of pebbles against the walls. Cassi guessed that the stones were really glass shrapnel from Wiley's desk.

Odi held her in place for a few seconds more until everything settled down. A wisp of smoke crept under the bathroom door as they waited. Cassi worried that the house might be on fire. Odi shook his head as though reading her mind. He said, "The smoke is just a byproduct of the blast. It's not a threat." Then he released her arm, stood and opened the door.

The first thing she saw was a big hole in the wall in the place where the door had been. She shuddered at the sight, joyful though it was. The bomb that wrought that destruction had been inside her body. She would never feel pure again.

Looking around, she felt like an evacuee returning home after a hurricane. There were a thousand little rips in the black leather couch and pockmarks all around the walls. Cassi looked back at the door to the bathroom. Bits of glass were embedded like cupcake sprinkles all up and down the wood. The result was a cross between modern art and a medieval torture device, although structurally it was not damaged. The windows had also held. She realized that without Odi's bomb, they would never have escaped.

"Let's get out of here," Odi said.

"You read my mind," Cassi replied. "Just give me a second to swap Wiley's wet pajamas for my regular clothes."

While zipping up her jeans, Cassi had a thought that would not wait. She picked up her shoes and ran barefoot down the hallway to the security closet. She flung open the door to see six flat-panel monitors, each showing a different room. She found the recorder for Wiley's study and rewound the video for thirty seconds. Before pressing play, she glanced upward in silent prayer. The monitor came back to life with the picture of Odi hurling the marble ashtray into the aquarium. This was better than great. It was fantastic. "I can't believe they forgot this," she called.

"What?" Odi asked, running to stand beside the closet door.

"See for yourself. It's all here. What they did to us is all video recorded."

Cassi sat down on the floor and quickly tied her shoes. Finished, she looked up at her brother and lost her smile. He looked pale. "What's wrong?" she asked, standing up and ejecting the DVD.

"That video may cook Wiley's goose, but it also blows my alibi."

"Your alibi?"

"I was planning to wake up from a coma in Iran once my mission was complete." Odi made quotation marks with his fingers as he spoke.

Cassi understood. She looked down at the DVD in her hand and thought about his situation for a minute. She had temporarily forgotten about Odi's earlier murders. "We'll figure something out later. Tempting though it is, nailing Wiley and Stuart is not our top priority. Stopping 10/12 is. To do that we have to get off this island. How did you get here?"

"Jet Ski."

"Will it fit two people?"

"You bet."

Cassi smiled. "Finally, we catch a break."

Odi led her across the lawn in the opposite direction from the marina. They moved at a slow run, discussing strategy and the events of the last few weeks as they went. Once they cleared the manor house lawn they entered a deciduous forest. A few of the birches still had golden leaves, but most of the limbs were bare. It was beautiful and innocent, the polar opposite of how she should have felt, yet something about being there with Odi gave her hope.

Odi lurched to a halt after about five minutes. Cassi was surprised to find that the forest went right up to the cliff's edge and realized that this was no place to be running blind. She peered over the edge and saw the Jet Ski below.

Odi said, "Oh shit."

"What is it?"

"The keys are gone. I started to take them with me but then figured that they would be confiscated if I was captured, so I left them right here on this rock as insurance." He pointed to a flat-topped boulder. "Now they're gone." He bent down and began searching the grass around the rock. Cassi joined him, searching the side of the cliff as well. After a few minutes they decided that it was hopeless. The keys were gone.

"Do you think Wiley took them?"

"If he saw me coming he would have. But I don't think he did. My money is on one of those crows." He pointed at three black figures on a neighboring tree. "I thought I was being clever, but it appears that I was outwitted by a bird."

"What do we do now?" Cassi asked

"Go back to the marina and wait for the Coast Guard."

"What makes you think they're coming?"

"I'm going for a swim."

Cassi could not believe what her brother was proposing. "You can't do that. You'll freeze."

"I've got a wetsuit, and the eastern shore is much closer than the western one. It looks like it's only a mile."

"Tell that to the sharks."

~ ~ ~

On any other day, Cassi would have found Odi's plan preposterous. Today, it was de rigueur. After watching him disappear into the waves, she walked back through the woods. She heard every cracking twig and each rattling branch but no squirrels or birds. Even the crows were gone. The forest that only moments ago had seemed so refreshing, now felt dead. She found herself acutely aware of being alone. She knew that she had better get used to that feeling. The man with whom she had planned to spend the rest of her life was now destined for disgrace and prison. Or was he? she wondered, feeling a sudden chill.

Cassi drummed her fingers on the DVD in her pocket. She would let Wiley walk if that was the only way to save her brother. There was no question about that. Unless ... Cassi asked herself what she would do if it looked like Wiley would actually become vice president. Would she sacrifice Odi to prevent that? She would have to. No, she corrected herself. What she would have to do was find some other way of stopping Wiley. Some other way ...

She walked past the manor house without stopping and headed straight for the marina. She never wanted to set foot in Wiley's home again. As she stepped onto the cobbled walk, she wondered if she would ever truly understand what had happened. Wiley's actions were so far removed from her current comprehension that she did not know if her mind could twist to an angle that would allow it to make sense. Of course, she would have said the same thing about Odi a few hours earlier and now it was clear that he had charted a rational course. However, Wiley's case was different, she decided. He had confessed.

Still drumming her fingers on the DVD, Cassi wondered what it was that had turned Wiley from her? From the life they had, a life that most people would consider ideal? She still believed that he had truly loved her once. Some life-altering event must have occurred. For her sanity's sake, she needed to know what it was. She refused to believe that anything that felt so real could be faked. She suspected that Stuart was the key. She wondered who he really was. Clearly, Stuart was not the old college friend that Wiley had portrayed him to be over brunch. Perhaps he was the corrupting influence. Come hell or high water, Cassi promised herself, she would find out.

As Cassi followed the cobbled walk toward the top of the marina's stairs, she looked out across the water. A boat was approaching. Could it be the Coast Guard already? Odi would have to be one hell of a swimmer. But then he was a lot of things. Her heart leapt until she got a better look, then it dropped to her stomach as she dropped to the ground. Wiley was returning.

Chapter 58

Chesapeake Bay

ODI FELT THE COLD WATER of the Chesapeake draining his life —despite his exertion, despite the wetsuit. The bay water could not be more than forty-five degrees. Each time he rolled his face back into the water after sucking in a breath, it felt as though someone were driving a wedge between his eyes. At least the wind was light and the waves were small—for now. The sky was darkening by the minute.

Once his muscles finally warmed and he got up to cruising speed, Odi set his body on autopilot and attempted to focus on the problems before him rather than the deathly cold. He had a cart-full. He had to stop bombings on twenty-four airplanes and one cruise ship. He had to rescue Cassi. He had to catch Ayden, Stuart and Wiley. He had to do it all in a matter of hours. He had no money, no transportation, no disguise and no weapon.

Trying to piece together a plan, Odi took a nose full of brine as yet another obstacle marched across the battlefield in his mind. Whatever he did, he was going to have to do it without being identified or even seen. That was no short order. Cassi had told him that Wiley had issued an APB for a terrorist who matched his description and was using his name. It was a clever move. It blocked Odi from approaching the media, the press, or any government officer—at least today, given his time constraints. With one clever move, Wiley had isolated his opponent and forced him to work alone.

Odi began to prioritize as he stroked and kicked. The first thing he needed was a solid timetable. Wiley had indicated that the bombings would take place "that afternoon." That gave him hope. If it were true, then there should be time for him to call the Coast Guard, for the Coast Guard to rescue Cassi, and for Cassi to call the FBI in time to stop the suicide bombers.

To confirm the timing, Odi planned to pull the schedule of the Senate Armed Services Committee off the Internet. He would also check the Queen Mary 2's schedule to see when she was scheduled to depart New York. Once Cassi got out word of the attack, the chairman of the SASC would either be pulled off the QM2 or guarded by the Secret Service. Ayden, however, would not know that. He would still board the ship. Odi would board it too. Ayden was his.

Odi had no doubt that Ayden had purchased his ticket under an assumed name. Odi did not have that option. He did not have time to generate a fake ID with matching credit card. Stealing a set was also out for obvious reasons. He decided that his best chance of getting aboard the QM2 would be to mug and replace a sailor.

The more he thought about it, the more he decided that mugging was the way to go. It should not be too difficult, he tried to convince himself. He would just hang around near the NYC Cruise Terminal looking for a tall white guy with a QM2 duffel bag. Psst. Hey, bud ...

Now that he knew how to leap the highest hurdle, he began thinking about the hurdles that were closest at hand. He still had to get from the middle of the Chesapeake Bay to Manhattan. As Odi considered his options he felt something brush by his foot. It brought him out of his autopilot trance. Sharks were not unknown in Chesapeake waters. He recalled Cassi's warning but brushed it off. What were the odds? He had already been Tasered, left to burn in a gaseous explosion, and filled full of liquid explosive today. The rule of three worked against adding "shark attack" to that list.

He looked up to take note of his position and scan the waves for fins. He had swum further than he thought. That was the day's first pleasant surprise. A few hundred more bits of good news and he would be even.

Odi was able to make out the details of waterfront houses now. They appeared to be very nice, much nicer than Charlotte's modest cottage. As he stroked on, a plan began to take form. He changed his course slightly, heading directly for the nearest bay-front residence rather than the vacant lot he had been targeting. He estimated that he would reach the shore in ten minutes at about eight o'clock. Some of the locals should be leaving their houses at that time, heading for work ...

Chapter 59

Near the New York City Cruise Terminal

ONCE THE WAITRESS finally set down their espressos and departed, Ayden asked Arvin, "How did you enter the country?" He heard relief and surprise in his own voice, and tried to mask it with a calmer clarification. "I mean, aren't you on a list or something?"

The Iranian smiled a bemused smile. "Lists only catch people who don't know they're on them. Once you know, they pose no problem."

Ayden wanted to know the specifics of Arvin's assertion, but he was afraid to ask. He did not want to seem naïve. Despite everything that he had already accomplished for Arvin—recruiting Odi, guiding him, deceiving him, supporting him and finally killing him—Ayden still felt a compulsion to prove himself to Arvin. The man had incredible charisma.

Either Arvin read his face or he just happened to be in a pedagogical mood, for he did go on to explain his assertion. "I flew into Toronto and drove down from there." He grinned and shook his head in amusement. "I barely had to slow the car at the border as I waved a fake passport. If they had turned me around I would have flown into Mexico and crossed via the tomato-picking pipeline. Or," he nodded his head back toward the dark mountain of steel resting in the harbor behind them, "if I felt like crossing the border in style and didn't mind spending some cash, I would have flown to a Caribbean island and convinced a passenger to let me replace him for the homebound stretch of the cruise."

Ayden nodded. You heard so much about border security these days that he had just assumed that entering the US illegally could not be easy. "So all the hype about border security, all the boarding-pass checks and Homeland Security measures ..."

"They're just for show. Keeps the voting taxpayers docile while rewarding campaign contributors with fat homeland defense contracts."

"Still," Ayden pressed, "I don't understand why you risked coming personally?"

Arvin reached out across the tiny table and put his hand on Ayden's shoulder. Then he flashed a smile that made Ayden feel warm all over. "This is your big day, Ayden. I'm proud of you. The son of an orphaned Iranian immigrant is about to change the world. This is an historical moment. I want to be able to say that I was there with Ayden Archer on 10/12."

Ayden saw tears forming in the corners of Arvin's mesmerizing eyes. He looked down, embarrassed.

"I've heard from the other twenty-four," Arvin continued after a moment's pause. "Each is in position near his assigned gate. No one had an issue with security. Meanwhile, the SASC is still in committee, so you should be able to get to the chairman before his colleagues begin falling from the sky. And," he brought his palms together, "there's more good news. I finally learned the details of Marshall's diet. He goes through a gallon of coffee a day—lots of cream, lots of sugar. So you won't need to mix Creamer into gravy or soup."

"How on earth did you learn that?"

"I had a friend seduce one of his administrative assistants. They're all trained never to mention business, but it's natural enough to joke about bringing the senator his coffee. She said that everyone on the staff brings him a fresh mug whenever he summons them to his office. It's an unspoken rule."

Ayden nodded appreciatively and Arvin switched gears.

"This is for you," Arvin said, handing over an envelope and a small suitcase. "The envelope contains a British passport with your photo and a matching ticket. You're booked into the suite next to Marshall. There's also a credit card for incidental expenses."

"And the suitcase?"

"It contains the uniform of a QM2 steward. I don't have a weapon for you—that would be too risky—but you can use a wine bottle or a Plexiglas towel rod to knock out the steward bringing Senator and Mrs. Marshall their dinner. Then all you will need is Creamer. How much do you have?"

"I've got a whole pint."

"Excellent. That's enough to fill two little pitchers and spike the soup, just in case."

The way Arvin said it made it seem so easy, Ayden thought. Assassinating the Chairman of the Senate Armed Services Committee, getting your car washed, one and the same. He hoped Arvin was right. In any case, Ayden thought, he was about to find out.

Chapter 60

Asgard Island, Chesapeake Bay

CASSI HUGGED the ground behind a sculpted hedge and watched the Norse Wind arrive. It was approaching much too fast. The engines roared into reverse as it neared the dock, making the water boil. The yacht bucked in response but it was too little too late. She watched it career into the iron dock with a deep thud and a grating scrape. Wiley was obviously upset—but he had nothing on her.

The image of Stuart forcing Wiley to do what he had done flashed through her mind, extending a ray of hope. She caught herself grasping for it and shook her head in self-rebuke. She was a professional psychologist, not a teenage girl. She had to face it: the man she loved, the man she had pinned her hopes, her dreams, her very heart on, was a worm.

Stuart jumped onto the dock alone, making Cassi feel all the more foolish. Then insight overwhelmed shame and she understood. They had remembered the surveillance video.

She wondered if Wiley was waiting on the yacht, too racked with guilt to move, or if he was back on the mainland. Sadly enough, she would have to bet on the latter. Wiley was acting purely as a politician now. He would contract out his dirty work.

She continued hugging the hedge until Stuart jogged past, praying to the god of invisibility. Then she low-crawled to the top of the stairs and studied the yacht from above. All appeared quiet, but light was reflecting off the windshield, making it impossible for her to see if anyone was on the bridge.

Grabbing the base of the railing for support, she pulled herself over the cliff's edge until she was dangling beneath the stairs. In that position her feet were still hanging twenty feet above unfriendly rocks, but she was out of the yacht's view. The new vantage gave her a shot of insight. She anchored her feet and pulled the video recording from her jacket pocket. She kissed it and then wedged it into the gap between the top of the cliff and the underside of the highest stair. Now she would have leverage if they caught her. If they didn't, she could always come back for the video. It didn't matter if DVDs got wet, did it?

She brushed that fear aside and began working her way down the underside of the stairs again, aware that Stuart would be returning any second. There was quite a latticework under there. Whoever built the stairs had built them to last. At the bottom she used the dock's bracings to keep above the freezing water. The posts were six feet apart there, so twice she had to stretch her legs in a full split to reach. This left her terribly vulnerable for about five seconds each time, but it was better than getting wet in this weather. Poor Odi. She prayed that he had survived the swim—and summoned the Coast Guard.

She pulled herself up onto the cold iron dock where she was out of view from the bridge and listened. She heard nothing but water lapping the yacht's hull and crashing against the rocks. There was no sign of Wiley but that did not mean that he wasn't there. She wondered how much time she had left. Stuart had undoubtedly reached the security closet by now. He would be less familiar with the system than Wiley, so it would take him a minute to orient himself. He would also note that the explosion had blown out the door to the study and he might take the time to investigate. She wondered if he would note the lack of gore and realize that neither she nor Odi had hosted the blast. If he did, he would bolt for the yacht straight away. She wished she had checked her watch as he walked by. With all the adrenaline now coursing through her system, it was hard to estimate time.

She crawled toward the back of the yacht and pulled herself through the aft gate. After another short pause to listen, she crept to the companionway that led up to the bridge. She crouched there for a moment, trying to picture the contents of the cabin above. She was mentally searching for a weapon. Wiley's binoculars leapt to mind. He had the heavy nautical kind with a thick leather strap. She tried to imagine the scene, mentally practicing her moves. She would barge through the door, grab the strap and spin into a swing. If Wiley was there, she would knock him out before he had time to react—unless he was ready for her. If she allowed herself to be seen or heard, she would be running into the barrel of a gun.

Cassi took a deep breath and sprang up the stairs as quickly as a frightened cat. Bursting onto the bridge she grabbed the binoculars by the strap and began to pivot. The cabin was, in fact, empty. Stuart had returned alone.

She scanned the bridge for a handgun, just in case. Then she checked the drawers. Nothing. A weapon would have been comforting but it was not crucial. She was about to strand Stuart on the island.

Cassi had little experience behind the wheel of a yacht, just a few playful minutes with Wiley by her side. But she was not concerned about damaging his yacht or any other, so she did not care. She studied the controls for a second to re-familiarize herself, focusing on the throttles and the wheel. Then she pushed the starter. Nothing happened. She pushed again. Zip.

Frustrated now and more than a little bit nervous, she studied the rest of the controls. She saw screens and knobs and switches with labels. She pounded the wheel and cursed the wind. Where was the bloody switch marked go?

She remembered the ship-to-shore radio and enjoyed a flash of hope. She could call for help and get instructions on how to start the bloody boat. She reached up for the mike and caught empty space. Her eyes began to tear as she stared at the socket.

She thought of everything she had been through during this last hour: Wiley's betrayal, Odi's Creamer, the retching, the explosion. Then she thought of Odi plowing through that freezing surf. After all that, she could not allow herself to be foiled by something as simple as the failure to find a switch.

As Cassi considered the option of flipping every switch and hitting each button, she spotted an empty chrome hub to the right of the wheel. The sight of it made her collapse into the captain's chair. Stuart had taken the keys. "The mike and the keys," she muttered. He was one meticulous bastard.

As she flopped backwards into the captain's chair, Cassi heard a sharp crack coming from inches in front of her face. She snapped her head up and saw a spider's web of cracks in the windshield. The web had a hole in the center. The agent in her recognized the hole as a 9mm—not that it really mattered. Stuart had returned. The angle of the sun must have changed, allowing him to see her from the top of the marina's stairs. Obviously, he had decided to fire straight off, perhaps thinking that she had a spare set of keys.

She rolled out of the chair and onto the floor as she heard another crack and saw a second spider web appear. He was definitely firing from atop the stairs. His intentions and tactics were abundantly clear. Since she did not have keys, the boat was a dead-end trap. Cassi had just one move.

She leapt down the yacht's aft companionway in a single bound and sprinted for the stern. She pumped her arms as she ran, forcing oxygen deep into her lungs. She wanted to glance back to see if she had been spotted, to check if life-threatening bullets were about to fly, but she did not dare. Milliseconds mattered. Without hesitation or a second thought, she sprang with all her might and dove headfirst over the rail.

Chapter 61

Asgard Island, Chesapeake Bay

STUART HEARD the splash and knew instantly what it meant. He bounded down the remaining stairs a half-dozen at a time and ran down the dock toward the back of the yacht, arms pumping, finger wrapped around the trigger guard. Cassi was nowhere to be seen and the turgid waters told no tales. He tried to guess what direction she would swim, hoping to head her off. If he guessed wrong, she would escape onto the island. Then he would have a hunt on his hands. Hunting Cassi represented an unexpected complication, but the thought was not entirely unpleasant.

Stuart scanned the deck. He had not seen Odi on the bridge, but there was even money that he had been on the Norse Wind too. Perhaps he still was. Seeing no signs of life, Stuart returned his gaze to the churning water. He knew what he would have done in their place. He would have created a false trail. He would have thrown something heavy overboard and then hidden below deck, hoping to attack his pursuer unawares.

He spun back toward the main cabin and raised his Beretta. He saw nothing but a pair of seagulls. He waved the gun to shoo them in frustration. They ignored him. He considered shooting one to vent his rage, but only for a second. He had never let emotions get the best of him in the past. This was not the time to start.

As he did a quick sweep of the luxurious craft, checking all possible hiding places, he considered his predicament. Until he destroyed that recording and silenced the Carrs, everything he had spent his life pursuing would be up in the air.

So what was his best move? Stuart wondered. His thoughts returned to Odi. Was Odi with his sister, or elsewhere? Thinking about it, he decided that he had only heard one splash. The odds of their hitting the water at the exact same second were slim. Perhaps Odi had left the island the way he had come—either abandoning Cassi in anger or being unable to take her. The latter and more likely option implied that his boat was too small. In any case, Stuart had to hope that the video recording was still on Asgard. If that murder scene ever made it off the island, Stuart would lose his job, his career and his very freedom. He had to prioritize his actions in order to prevent that from happening.

He decided to circle the island at full speed on the Norse Wind in hopes of intercepting Odi. If Odi's craft was too small to carry Cassi, it was probably also slow. Perhaps it was even a rowboat. Oh, let it be so. Stuart realized that regardless of the craft, he had a chance of catching the seemingly indestructible agent if he hurried. And if he was wrong and Odi was still on the island, well, they would still be there when he got back.

After fishing the keys from his pants pocket with a satisfied smile, he raced to the bridge and brought the powerful engines to life. Without so much as a backward glance, he thrust the throttle into full reverse and sent the Norse Wind surging backwards into the bay. Though his piloting was careless, his search for Cassi was not. He scoured the surrounding cliffs as he backed the yacht away, hoping to see a flash of flesh or a scurry of movement between the slippery rocks. His adrenaline spiked momentarily when he thought he saw a bobbing head, but it was just a cormorant. No matter, he consoled himself. She was not going anywhere. Soon she would be a dead duck. He turned the wheel and pushed the throttle forward to full, roaring after Odi.

By the time he was halfway around the island, Stuart understood that Asgard was crescent shaped, with the marina in the center of the concave side. It faced west across the bay toward Reedville, Virginia, where he had just dropped Wiley. Now that he was on the other side for the first time, Stuart saw that it was much closer to land. His spirits sank. The southern end of the Delmarva Peninsula was just a mile or so to the east. Even in a rowboat, Odi could already have made it.

Something white caught Stuart's eye as he glanced back at Asgard. It was bobbing near the base of the cliff. Was it another bird? he asked himself. No, this was too big. He gave the eastern horizon a quick scan for other craft and then turned the yacht back in that direction. He picked up the binoculars and directed them toward the object. His heart leapt as a Jet Ski came into focus. That discovery solved the mystery of Odi's arrival and ruled out his departure. But why were they still on the island? he wondered. The Jet Ski even had two seats. The answer came to him as he piloted the yacht in that direction. Odi must have stolen the Jet Ski when it was low on gas. Now it was out. The Carrs were stranded on the island. And more importantly, so was the video.

Just to be meticulous, Stuart put a bullet through the Jet Ski's ignition switch and another through the gas tank. No sense in taking chances. Perhaps Cassi had been on the Norse Wind looking for gas.

He gunned the yacht's motor and raced back toward the marina. This time he studied the island rather than the waters around. He felt like a knight preparing to siege a castle. He was just one man, but he had the only weapon, and the king and queen could not cross the moat.

As he rounded the southern tip of the island, Stuart caught sight of another vessel. When he saw that it too was making waves for the Asgard marina, he was glad that he had not wasted ammo on the seagulls. Then he saw the orange stripe and felt a tightening in his chest. The approaching craft belonged to the Coast Guard.

Stuart weighed his options. They boiled down to fight or flight. The Coast Guard vessel was smaller than the Norse Wind, but given that it was the maritime equivalent of a State Trooper, it undoubtedly had powerful engines. Flight would be his last resort. That suited Stuart just fine. He was a fighter. He wondered how the Carrs had summoned the Coast Guard, and more importantly, what information they had conveyed. Had they been able to send a detailed message, he wondered, or just a simple SOS? Stuart knew that it was a dangerous proposition to intercept the Coast Guard without that knowledge, but he really had no other choice. His goose was cooked if they got that video. He would just have to make good use of his favorite weapon. He would have to rely on guile.

Stuart raced the Norse Wind to the midpoint between the Coast Guard and the marina and brought his motors to idle. He was about a quarter mile off shore. He knew that if the sailors were veterans, they would recognize this as a military move. To counterbalance that, he walked out onto the deck, assumed a casual stance and waved. Body language would be the key to the next few minutes, both his and theirs.

There were only two sailors aboard the Coast Guard craft. The captain had thick white hair and a leathery face, whereas his younger mate sported red hair and freckles. Both men appeared tense. As soon as they were within earshot, Stuart started to fish. He looked at freckles and asked, "I say, are you headed for Asgard?"

Freckles responded without deferring to rank, much to Stuart's relief. He said, "Yes. We got a call."

Stuart had hoped for more information than that. We got a call was a little too vague. He would have to reply in kind. "I'm glad the call got through. Our radio died."

"Was it you who called?"

That was better, Stuart thought. "I'm Stuart, Director Proffitt's Personal Aide. We thought we were stranded but as you can see we've got the yacht running."

"I recognize the Norse Wind. It's one of the finest on the Bay," the captain said. "Would you mind if we had a look?"

The captain had a friendly expression on his face, but Stuart read business in his eyes. These guys would want to tread lightly with someone as powerful as Wiley, but their trepidation would only get Stuart so far. He knew it would be a mistake not to indulge them. He could always shoot the sailors in a pinch, he figured, but only as a last resort. They would be missed with the first unanswered call, and then the heat would really be on. "Sure, you're welcome aboard."

No sooner had he spoken the words than Stuart remembered the bullet holes in the windshield on the upper bridge. If the Coast Guard saw them, the gig was up. He would have no choice but to shoot them then. He had to try to keep them away from that part of the yacht.

The two sailors conferred and then the captain climbed aboard. Stuart cursed in silence. Killing them had just become twice as difficult. "It's important that one of us stay with the radio," the captain said, inclining his head toward Freckles.

Stuart extended his arm in a sweeping gesture. "Please, enjoy yourself. She's a beaut."

He sat on the stairs to the upper bridge such that the captain would have to ask him to move if he wanted to ascend. He tried to look relaxed as he waited for the captain to complete the fifty-cent tour and chatted idly with Freckles. It took the captain less than two minutes although it seemed like forever. As he approached, Stuart wondered if it would be better to offer to show the captain the upper bridge if he liked, or if he should wait for the captain to ask. When the captain returned, Stuart tried to read his expression, but got nowhere. The salty old dog kept his features neutral. After a moment of awkward silence, the captain placed his hands on his hips, sighed and said, "This is exactly how I'd like to retire."

Stuart returned a genuine smile. The captain was not eyeing the top of the stairs. "I hear you. Say, I'm sorry if we caused you any trouble. Given Mr. Proffitt's job, we're sometimes quick to panic."

"Say, where is Walter? He on the mainland, or the island?"

"You mean Wiley, I assume. I just dropped him on the mainland."

The captain relaxed with that response. "So what caused your problem? Did you figure it out?"

"Sure did. A battery cable worked its way loose. We routinely disconnect it whenever we know that we won't be taking her out for more than two weeks. Last time we must not have reattached it tightly enough."

The captain nodded. Apparently, he had come across that before. "Please give the governor Captain Latimor's best."

Stuart inclined his head.

He did not relax until the Coast Guard boat grew small on the horizon. Then he checked the magazine of his gun, found it nearly full, and smiled. He had more than enough ammunition to wreck a couple of Carrs.

Chapter 62

Crisfield, Maryland

CROUCHED BEHIND the rear passenger tire of a shiny blue Buick, Odi had to struggle to keep his teeth from chattering as he watched his mark lock the front door of his house. The rotund middle-aged man carried a travel mug of coffee with a muffin balanced on top in one hand and a generic black briefcase in the other. He shuffled unenthusiastically, and the vacuous look of routine was readily apparent in his eyes. Eight o'clock in the morning and the poor soul was already bored. Odi was about to change that.

The man unlocked his Buick with a remote and hopped into the driver's seat. He placed the travel mug in its holder, lay the briefcase on the passenger seat, and set the muffin on top. Blueberry. Odi slid into the back seat as the man reached out to close his door.

The man jumped at the sound of Odi's door closing as though a rattrap had clamped on his ass. He let out a startled cry.

"Good morning," Odi said, trying to sound friendly. "Where are you going?"

"Who the hell are you?"

Odi changed his tone sharply. "I'm the man with a gun to your back. That was your last question. Understand?"

The man turned to face forward and nodded.

"Now," Odi continued, "what is your name?"

"Les."

"Okay Les, let's drive to work."

"You want to go to my office?"

"No questions," Odi said, pushing his fingers deeper into the upholstered back of the seat. "No noise. Just drive."

The man reversed down his driveway and turned the Buick north.

"Where is your office?"

"Laurel."

"Is that on the way to the Big Apple?"

Les hesitated, then let out a weak, "Yes."

"The fastest way?"

"Yes."

"How far is Laurel from here?"

"About an hour."

"And New York City?"

"Four to six hours, depending on traffic."

Odi nodded to himself. "Do me a favor, Les, and turn the heater on full. I caught a bit of a chill swimming into town."

Les complied without comment. He was a quick learner.

Odi watched the street signs in silence as Les followed his routine. A few miles down Highway 13 they passed a sign that said Laurel 29 miles.

"I need your cell phone," Odi said.

Les hesitated for a second, and then he reached into his breast pocket and produced an iPhone.

Odi accepted it and said, "I'm going to let you off at your office. Afraid I'll be needing your car from there. Meanwhile, I don't suppose you happen to know the number for the Coast Guard?"

Chapter 63

Asgard Island, Chesapeake Bay

CASSI FELT a sense of dread as she watched the Coast Guard ship head for the western horizon. She cursed herself. She might have been able to signal it if she had been just a few seconds faster.

After pulling herself from the freezing water and watching Stuart race off in the Norse Wind, she had run straight for the house and a hot shower. She had indulged herself for too long, soaking the cold and tension away under the hot shower while the Coast Guard approached and then departed. Now she was trapped in another nightmare—with Stuart.

The Norse Wind was still out there, idling in the bay. Cassi watched it as she contemplated her predicament. She had expected this to be the worst day of her life, knowing that she would be arresting her brother. As it turned out, that was only the beginning. The opening course. The appetizer. Since then she had also been betrayed by her lover, imprisoned in a panic room, forced to swallow a bomb, and left to explode. She had pumped her stomach, dangled off a cliff and dodged bullets. Then she had nearly frozen to death while swimming for her life while under fire amidst jagged rocks. And it wasn't even noon. If only she had shown Odi a little more faith, everything might be different.

As horrible as all of today's experiences had been, and regardless of the fact that each would haunt her for the rest of her life, Cassi knew that they were all about to fade to insignificance. She was currently empowered to prevent the next 9/11. She had information that would save thousands of lives. And she was helpless to deliver it.

Any fantasy of trying to swim to shore without a wetsuit had vanished the moment she plunged into the Chesapeake's frigid waters. She had survived the five minutes it took to evade Stuart, but hypothermia would surely suck the life from her bones long before she made it to the nearest shore.

The Norse Wind taunted her, scoffed at her, winked. It was only a quarter mile away out there in the bay, but it might as well be on Mars. She could never reach it. Could she? Could she survive a quarter mile swim in that water? Could she then climb stealthily aboard the yacht and overpower Stuart, an armed man, despite her hypothermic state? She estimated that the odds were a thousand-to-one against her. In fact, she reasoned, that was probably why Stuart was idling there. Flushing her out was exactly what he wanted to do. But despite all that, what choice did she have? She could not sit there safe but mute while twenty-four planes were bombed out of the sky. She would never forgive herself. She would rather die trying.

"She would rather die trying," Cassi repeated out loud. It was so commonplace to utter those words. Did she have the courage to live them?

The Norse Wind roared to life as she pondered that thought, sparing her the opportunity to test her mettle. Her flash of relief vanished as quickly as it appeared, however, when Stuart turned the bow toward the marina. The sight filled her with an odd mixture of hope and dread. She was going to get the chance to save the twenty-four planes. All she had to do was get the keys away from Stuart—before he shot her dead.

Chapter 64

The SS Queen Mary 2

AYDEN LEAPT BACK from the suite's peephole as though it was trying to bite him. He could not believe his eyes. From a distance he had found the tall silhouette and confident walk familiar. Now that the man was closer, Ayden could verify the face. Despite the glasses and slicked-back hair there could be no mistake. Odi Carr was walking down the corridor—directly toward his suite.

How did he get free? How did he find me? What is he planning to do? The questions came to Ayden easily. The answers did not. He had no time for interrogatory now anyway. He had to act.

He backed into the bathroom, a champagne bottle clenched in his white-knuckled hand. He tried to think. He had been planning to whack the steward over the head with the bottle when the steward brought the Marshalls their meal. Could he do the same to Odi? He did not see how. He would have lured the steward into his neighboring suite with a desperate plea—then replaced cream with Creamer and delivered the Marshalls' order himself—but he had no chance of catching Odi with such a simple ruse.

Ayden looked down at his hand, noting that it was beginning to sweat. While the hefty champagne bottle would have been fine for a surprise attack on an unsuspecting steward, it was a pathetic weapon against a primed combat veteran like Odi Carr. But what choice did he have? Odi had come to him. Think, Ayden. Think! What would Arvin do? He asked himself. The answer came as though God were whispering in his ear.

Ayden ripped the do-not-disturb sign from the door handle and slid it between the doorframe and the lock, disabling the latch. Satisfied that the door would now swing open beneath a firm knock, he grabbed the extra polyester blanket from the closet. He folded it in half and placed it on the parquet floor like a rug, a very slippery rug. It would not look right if studied, but Odi was hardly going to be paying much attention to the suite's furnishings as he burst into the room. Ayden would sweep the rug out from under Odi before he realized that he was standing on slippery ground, and then he would give him the good news with the bottle.

Ayden returned to the bathroom and picked up the champagne bottle, certain that he had not a second to spare. "Come on, come on," he mouthed, wiping his sweaty palms on his black steward's pants as he shifted the bottle between hands.

The knock did not come. Nor did Odi attempt to use a key. Ayden waited and listened, assuming that Odi was out there doing the same. After a moment he loosened his tie, hoping to get more blood to his brain. He waited some more. Nothing. Not a sound. Finally, unable to take it anymore, he flung open the door, holding the champagne bottle high.

The corridor was empty.

He backed into his suite, puzzled but relieved that no one had seen him. Then he got it. So much for God's whisper. Odi did not know that he was there. He had come to warn the man in the neighboring suite. He had come to warn Marshall.

Ayden decided to go out onto his terrace. From there he might be able to see if all hell had broken loose in the senator's suite. Ayden knew that would be a bold and risky move—windows worked both ways—but he figured that the pouring rain would help to camouflage him. In any case, everything he did would be risky for as long as Odi was still aboard. And besides, he was in uniform.

He grabbed a black QM2 umbrella from the closet and slipped out the sliding glass door.

The sky was dark as midnight and the rain was coming down in a torrent. Ayden did not care. He walked all the way to the edge and crouched down with his back to the rail. Despite the downpour, he could see clearly into Marshall's suite due to the lights inside. He saw one end of a dining table through the parted curtains. Mrs. Marshall and a female guest were seated there, drinking red wine and talking with friendly animation. Odi did not appear to be inside. Nor, it seemed, had he raised an alarm.

Ayden was puzzled. Was it possible that he had imagined the sighting? Could his eyes be playing tricks? "No," Ayden muttered to himself. He had no doubt.

Although Odi's plan of action remained a mystery to Ayden, the fact that he now had to switch tactics was clear. Perhaps he could just push Marshall overboard. All he needed to do was get him out on the terrace alone. Of course, given the weather that would require one hell of a trick.

As Ayden sifted through the possibilities, he felt another doubt tugging at the back of his mind. After a few minutes, it came forward. If Odi had come to save Marshall, then he was likely to have warned the authorities about the other bombers.

He sank down beneath the weight of the world until his butt rested on the wet deck. That last thought had taken the wind out of his sails. The flamboyant execution of all twenty-five members of the Senate Armed Services Committee would have captured the world's attention for months if not years to come, just like 9/11. Now that it might not happen, Ayden felt as though he was about to let down a hundred-million kids. That thought was too much to take.

He groped frantically at the corners of his mind, seeking some solution. Nothing came. He watched the rain beat down on the deck around him. Each drop sent a tiny fountain into the air. Would taking out the chairman garner enough attention if the remaining members of the SASC lived? He wondered. The answer came immediately. No. To rivet attention he needed something huge, something personal, something rivaling 9/11. The modern world was numb to anything less.

Sitting there beneath the black sky and pouring rain, he felt as desolate as his surroundings. The emotional roller-coaster ride was not helping. For years he had struggled to make a difference, day by day. Each day had given him little rewards in the form of tiny upturned faces. But the hopelessness of the big picture had always loomed as large as the mob outside his clinic's door. Then Arvin had walked into his life and talked of creating a world where the strong helped the weak and the rich cared for the poor.

Arvin had given Ayden hope that he could actually help cure the world's manmade woes. The tipping point was near, he preached, his eyes sucking Ayden in. Mankind had the technological means within its grasp. All the shift required was the right catalytic act. Today he, Ayden Archer, was to have tipped the balance. Today he was to have opened the door to a better world. Now everything that moments ago had seemed so certain was suddenly up in the air. Ayden began to shake with a fear that he was about to fail the children.

"No," he said aloud. "Not without a fight." At the very least he would take out the chairman. Perhaps the other twenty-four would also find the means to prevail—at least a few of them. His mind racing, Ayden spied a thread of hope. He was aboard the new Queen Mary. Nearly three thousand of the world's elite were there with him, plus a thousand crew—and he had a lot of Creamer. Given that combination, the power to focus the world's attention had to be in his grasp. Ayden felt it in his bones. He just had to think—think and then act.

He began running through the ship's systems in his head. He knew the vessel's construction inside out. He could not use the airplane approach and make the ship itself the weapon. The heavy oil powering the ship would not explode. But cruise ships were some of the largest, most complicated machines on earth. There had to be another way ...

Ayden was soaked to the bone by the time the solution came to him, but it was a grandiose, eloquent, audacious plan. Getting excited, he reminded himself that radical action might not be necessary. He had seen no commotion in the chairman's suite. For whatever reason, Odi might not have sounded the alarm. Perhaps he was afraid of prison. Or perhaps he had tried but been ignored. The why hardly mattered.

However, now that he had devised a grand solution, Ayden found that his original plan held far less appeal. Simply assassinating the chairman of the SASC seemed so uninspired.

The question he had to ask himself now was: Did he have the courage? He decided to put off handling that prickly pear for now. Better to see how Plan A turned out.

He was about to get up and head for the bar where he could check CNN and weigh his options, when movement crossed his peripheral vision. He refocused. Someone was rappelling down from two decks above. Someone was attempting to drop onto Marshall's veranda.

Ayden smiled with great satisfaction as he recognized the figure. Once again, Odi Carr had dropped into his lap.

Chapter 65

The SS Queen Mary 2

SEARCHING THE LAVISH CORRIDORS, Odi was trying hard to look like a privileged vacationer rather than a hired gun. As tired as he was, he was finding it increasingly difficult to pretend. Still, he knew that Ayden was somewhere in the honeycomb of those thirteen decks, plotting away, so he would not stop.

His plan for getting to New York and sneaking aboard the ship had worked, but it had been hard on both body and soul. Poor Kostas Tzemos, the assistant ship's engineer whose identification Odi now wore, would soon awake to a pounding headache and a nasty lump. Odi vowed to make it up to him, along with the others. He cursed himself as he thought of that growing list, ashamed of the gullibility at the root of it all. How bloody naïve he had been, naïve and blinded by revenge.

Odi was not sure where this was all going, or how it was going to play out. An hour earlier, he had watched with surprise as Senator Marshall and his wife boarded the ship. He had expected them to cancel after Cassi put out the word. Yet there they were. There were plenty of possible explanations for their presence, he knew, the most likely being that they were just used to living with threats. After two decades in the senate collecting a hundred threats a year, virtually anyone would be numb. As he mulled that over, Odi quickly latched on to the upside of the Marshalls' nonchalance. Without the Marshalls aboard, he was searching for a needle in a haystack. Now he had a magnet for Ayden.

Walking past Marshall's suite again, Odi knew that he was pushing his luck. On his first pass, he had been surprised to find that they did not have a Secret Service Agent posted in the hall. He knew that one was undoubtedly on lookout either via a hidden camera or from the peephole of the suite, but he had expected one in a more visible spot as well. This made it less awkward for him to roam the surrounding halls, but it would still be the third time he pinged the Secret Service's radar by passing Marshalls' suite. He knew that was a mistake for any man, much less one with a wanted face, but he had no choice.

Odi was racing against a clock. Although the voyage to Southampton would take six days, he had to find Ayden before Mr. Tzemos awoke and sounded the alarm. Once the alarm went out, his freedom would last about twenty seconds. He imagined that the conversation would go something like this:

"He's about thirty years old, six foot one with broad shoulders, thick dark hair, steely gray eyes, and—oh yeah—he stole my glasses."

"Hey Lou, that sounds like the APB we got from the FBI."

"Did he look like this guy, Mr. Tzemos?" the police officer would ask, producing a poster.

"That's him! That's the thief who took my ID and stole my clothes ..."

Odi's own wanted status was not the only complication on his mind. The Marshalls' nonchalance continued to nag at him. He had called the Coast Guard as agreed, and sent them to Asgard for Cassi. Was it possible that they had ignored his call? He wondered. Probably not. Could the Secret Service have ignored Cassi's warning? Again Odi's answer was no. The threat was too serious, and she was an FBI Agent. Odi concluded that his concern was the result of exhaustion combined with an over-stimulated imagination. Still, he hated to take the risk of having two corpses prove him wrong.

With the third pass of Marshall's suite yielding no sightings of interest, he went to the Future Cruises boutique and took a virtual tour of the Marshalls' split-level suite on an interactive screen. He paid particular attention to the windows, doors and terrace. Then he turned his attention to the rest of the ship. The Queen Mary 2 was enormous. It covered an area equivalent to four city blocks and carried 3,900 souls. With just one man looking, Ayden could stay hidden there for months.

As he clicked from screen to screen, Odi became increasingly nervous about spending time away from the Marshalls. Ayden had fooled him. He might also be able to fool the Secret Service. Still, Odi knew that knowledge of the ship's floor plan would be invaluable if he had to pursue, escape, or hide. He bit his lip, rolled his shoulders and decided to invest ten minutes in cramming the floor plans into his head. Fifteen minutes later he shoved a map in the pocket of his slacks and headed for deck eleven.

Odi pressed the button that opened the sliding door to the promenade, and walked into the darkest, wettest day he could remember. Never before had he considered such misery so perfect. He walked all the way to the rear of the eleventh deck and stood alone by the whirlpool. He looked over the edge. The terrace of the Marshalls' Balmoral Duplex beckoned to him from two decks below. He pictured the Scottish residence from which the suite drew its name and decided that it was time to storm a castle.

The whirlpool may only have been three feet deep but the railing beside him still proffered a life ring. He took the measure of the rope. The Atlantic raged a hundred feet below and there appeared to be enough rope to reach it. Certain that there were the fifty feet he needed, Odi removed the coil from the hook. He wrapped the ringed end twice around a post and tested the friction. It felt right. He tucked the ring between his legs and hopped over the rail.

The rain beat down upon him and the wind tried to steal his balance, but Odi was not deterred. Stopping Ayden was something he was prepared to die for. He rappelled down just far enough to see through the wet glass of the Balmoral Duplex's picture windows. He saw the companionway connecting the two floors immediately before him. Beyond it he could see through the open door of the master suite. Judging by the visible portion, the top floor was deserted. So far, so good.

He rappelled halfway down to the terrace, stopping at the blind spot between the ninth and tenth decks. He adjusted his grip on the rope, and wiped the rain from his face with his free hand. He tried to think of the rain as refreshing, but in truth it just made him cold. He still had that Chesapeake chill. What a day this had been.

He surveyed his surroundings while evaluating his next move. If the Marshalls were home, they would be just below him on the other side of the glass. The dark and rain might hide him from their view, but it probably would not. He was too close to the glass. He decided to jump backwards, out away from the wall. This was the kind of move his CRT colleagues called brave but he knew was decidedly stupid. Today it was par for the course.

He picked his target landing spot and practiced bending his knees twice before finally pushing off. Landing close to the window was dangerous, but there was a bigger penalty for going too deep. The rope made a zipping sound as he flew back in a relatively controlled drop toward the puddled terrace. Two breathless seconds later he landed squarely on his feet between two lounge chairs. He felt an impulse to take a bow but crouched instead. The life ring was still between his legs. He tucked it behind the leg of a lounger where it would be handy for his retreat.

He studied the sliding glass doors three paces before him, the lighting working in his favor. The Marshalls were there. His rainstorm rumba had not been in vain. The distinguished couple was drinking red wine and chatting animatedly with another elegant pair. No one else was visible in the suite. Odi's stomach did a nervous somersault. Where was the Secret Service? Something was either very wrong or very right. Perhaps Ayden had already been apprehended.

Straining to keep his nerves under control, Odi continued to examine the scene. The dining table before the Marshalls held several plates and bowls. The second he saw them, Odi knew he needed to see what was inside. If something was cream based, he was going to have to make a very awkward knock on their rain-streaked sliding door. He decided to sneak closer.

Dropping to his belly, he low-crawled through puddles to the wall. Then he slid sideways until he could peer around the edge of the curtains. The first thing he did was study the occupants, paying special attention to the hue of their fingers. Everyone looked fine and festive. Mrs. Marshall wore a red silk dress with a matching manicure, her companion a jungle-patterned pantsuit with gold jewelry and matching shoes. The men both sported dark suits with bright shirts sans ties. Their gaiety presented a harsh contrast to the torrent outside, and ran contrary to the danger lurking within.

Odi didn't get it. How could they be so nonchalant? He stood up and turned his attention to the table, his stomach seizing that joyous moment to remind him that he had not eaten in twenty-four hours—excluding the Creamer. One of the bowls closest to him held mouthwatering strawberries, the other tempted him with mixed nuts. Further back was a crusty French baguette on a cutting board and a large wedge of ripe Brie. As his stomach grumbled, his heart rejoiced. There was no chance of secreting Creamer in any of those. The Marshalls were safe for now.

While considering the option of knocking on the glass and confirming that Ayden Archer had in fact been captured, a squeak emanated off to his right side. As he pivoted to investigate, someone plowed into his stomach, sweeping him off his feet and into the air. Odi felt himself being carried backwards on his assailant's shoulder but his exhausted mind took a second too long to react. Before he could gather his wits he was falling backwards through space. That sensation and a fleeting glimpse made everything instantly clear. Ayden had just hurled him overboard.

Chapter 66

Asgard Island, Chesapeake Bay

AS THE COAST GUARD VESSEL dropped over the horizon and Stuart piloted into the marina, Cassi sprinted for the house, running as she never had before. Wiley kept a pair of miniature walkie-talkies in the coat closet by the front door. She needed them. As the Norse Wind's motors had roared to life, she had cobbled together the components of a desperate plan.

She grabbed the pair of Motorolas and was out of the house within ninety seconds of Stuart revving the motors. He would be docking by now, she figured. She tested the batteries as she ran to the garden and found them strong.

Flanking the south side of the manor house was a mature and elaborate garden an acre in size. It ran all the way out from the porch to the cliff. According to Wiley, twelve generations of Proffitts had spent their declining years tending to that garden. Wiley was not declining yet, he had told her, so he employed a gardener. It was spectacular during the summer when the flowers were in bloom and the fountains were running, but even this time of year the ancient fruit trees and manicured maze of hedges gave it an elegant grace. This morning, however, Cassi did not notice the aesthetics. This was a battlefield.

She crashed through a hibernating rose thicket, ignoring the protesting thorns. Once she reached the garden's center, she plunged one of the walkie-talkies into the dense branches of a spherical sculpted hedge. She secured it at chest level, gauging the distance to be about twenty feet from the front corner of the porch. She turned it on, cranked the volume up to high, scampered back out of the thicket, and said, "Testing." Her voice came back loud and clear. Motorola made great equipment. For a moment, she had the feeling that this was actually going to work.

She turned and dashed for the back of the garden, keeping an eye on the marina path as she went. She clutched the second walkie-talkie in her left hand like a lifeline. The garden ended with a thick row of hedges at the edge of the cliff. Wiley's forebears had planted it generations ago for erosion control and to act as a natural fence. Cassi dropped to the ground when she reached them. Then she peeked back over the surrounding bushes and caught sight of Stuart.

He was a couple hundred yards away, moving toward the manor house with a determined stride. To Cassi it appeared as though his forehead was being pulled by a rope, but her eyes were drawn to his hands. He held a Beretta pointed straight down in each. It did not take a psychiatrist to read that body language. He was a man on a mission, and that mission was her death.

She zipped the walkie-talkie inside her jacket's breast pocket and then climbed over the cliff's edge and began working her way toward Wiley's yacht.

She moved more quickly over the slippery rocks than any sane person would consider safe, knowing that it would not take Stuart more than five or ten minutes to determine that the house was vacant. Even scampering at a dangerous clip, it still took her the better part of five minutes to reach the Norse Wind. Once aboard, she began hastily collecting the few tools her plan required. Her first stop was the closet in the guest stateroom, where she procured the Ping driver that Wiley used to launch old golf balls into Chesapeake Bay. Next she ran to the master bath where she raided the emergency kit for an air horn and a roll of medical tape. She stashed the three items near the aft gate and then ran up two flights of steps to the upper bridge. She grabbed the binoculars off the captain's console, slung them around her neck, and then used a windowsill to climb up onto the cabin roof.

Standing on the slick white roof with the radar station by her knees, her head was about thirty feet above sea level. If she strained her neck, that put her just high enough to get line of sight over the cliff to the front of the house. She had guessed that right. Two seconds into her watch, however, Cassi understood that her perch was both awkward and precarious. The rooftop was swaying beneath her feet, amplifying each little wave. After a couple of minutes of straining her eyes for Stuart, Cassi realized that her previous assessment was wrong. Precarious was an understatement. A single unexpected gust of wind could steal her balance and send her toppling over the edge and into a fall that would likely break her neck. She had not considered that aspect of the danger when formulating her plan, but she was not going to change horses in the middle of the stream. She did not have another horse. She would have to risk breaking her neck. The passengers on twenty-four planes were depending on her.

She began to wonder what other unanticipated dangers awaited, but stopped herself. She could not afford to ponder them now. She could let neither her mind nor her gaze wander, even for an instant. If she was not alert during the second it took Stuart to walk through the front door, he was likely to spot her first. Then he would shoot her off the roof of the yacht like a carnival toy. "Come on, Stuart," she muttered through clenched teeth. "Come on."

She heard a motorboat in the distance and her hopes began to rise. Perhaps the Coast Guard was returning. It sounded like a big boat, but she could not risk a look back over her shoulder, at least until it got closer. Stuart would also want to investigate the noise. She continued to study the front of the house, darting her gaze back and forth between the windows, the porch, the front yard and the big green door. All appeared quiet. She began getting nervous. Had she missed him? Cassi knew that it was all over if she had. She was a standing duck.

The tone of the distant motor changed, bringing the approaching boat back to the top of her thoughts. It was not a change in speed that caused the shift. It was the Doppler effect. The motorboat had continued past the island and was now receding. Cassi was about to turn to see if there was any chance she could signal the captain when she caught sight of Stuart.

He appeared to be more of a shadow than a man at first, all clad in black and darting. She kept the binoculars trained on him with her left hand as she used her right to reach for the walkie-talkie. She brought it to her lips and pressed transmit. "Stuart!"

She saw him drop to one knee as he pivoted to his left. She saw him bring both pistols up smooth as silk and then she heard them bark. As she brought the walkie-talkie back to her lips, the Norse Wind was hit by the wake of the passing boat. The rocking motion caught her distracted and unprepared. As her balance faltered she flailed her arms to compensate, but it was no use. With visions of the jagged rocks and cold water below, Cassi toppled over the edge.

She saw a flash of white light and felt a searing bolt of pain shoot out of her upper left arm. She heard her humerus snap like a breaking bat. She fell a few more feet and landed with a thud on her back. Shocked though she was, Cassi managed to bring her right hand to her mouth to muffle her scream.

She rocked back and forth for a moment, trying to ease the pain. She was aware that she was lying on the main deck, twenty feet below where she had stood a second before. It took her a second to realize what had happened. She had fallen and landed sideways on the port rail, snapping her humerus. Fortunately, she had bounced back onto the main deck rather than into the freezing waters of the bay. Even in her agony, Cassi also knew that she was lucky to have landed as she had. If she had hit her neck or back or head on the rail she would already be a corpse.

Still fighting back screams and moans, she brought her eyes to rest on the walkie-talkie. She tried to focus on it and nothing else. It lay six feet away, further aft on the deck. She wriggled in that direction as though it were a desert oasis, her broken arm pulsing fire as she moved. She thought of the fire about to engulf twenty-four airplanes. That image fueled a reserve of strength. After seconds that seemed like hours, her hungry fingers enveloped the Motorola. She sucked in a deep breath and brought it to her lips.

Chapter 67

The SS Queen Mary 2

ODI HEARD the churning of seawater and the pounding of his heart. He smelled lilac perfume, cigar smoke and brass polish. He felt a thousand drops of rain. Nothing focuses the mind or sharpens the senses like falling helplessly through space.

As the rail disappeared above him, he flipped and flared faster than a falling cat, moving with the reflexive conditioning of a hundred parachute jumps. Something red entered his visual field, eliciting a primitive reaction. His arms thrust out of their own accord even before the memory of a lifeboat canister flashed through his mind. His fingertips made contact but the surface was slick and curved so his hands slid impotently down its side. His panic peaked. He was still gaining speed. Knowing that the canister rim was the only thing between him and a watery grave, Odi curled his fingers into butchers' hooks and willed them not to bend. They struck the rim an instant later.

Odi stared up his hands in gratitude and wonder as they clenched the lip where the two canister halves joined. Meanwhile, his legs continued to move as momentum swung them under the enormous canister. A split-second later the shock of his legs impacting the side jarred his right hand loose. Dangling on just four slim fingers, Odi felt gravity pulling his body downward as the driving rain pushed him from above. He teetered outward and caught a frightful glimpse of the churning black waters seven stories below. Fear fueled his left hand, turning it to stone. Swiftly but smoothly he brought his right hand up beside its brother.

Thirty seconds after Ayden hurled him over a guardrail, Odi dropped back onto the safe side. His hands continued to tremble as he crouched there on the rain-swept deck, letting it all sink in. Despite being safe for the moment, he felt winded and shaken. He stared through the rails at the bottomless waters below, knowing that for the second time today he was supposed to be dead. He looked up at the huge protruding canister that had saved his life. Its red underbelly was slick with rain, and the droplets scurried across its surface, propelled by the gale.

Odi knew that his survival was a miracle. He felt touched by the finger of God. He did not have to question the intervention of the

Almighty. Odi understood. God had a purpose, and Odi knew exactly what that was.

He shook off the water as best he could and brushed back his gel-slicked hair. Kostas's glasses had fallen into the drink, but at this point that hardly mattered. To stop Ayden, Odi had to come into the open. He had to surrender his alibi.

Chapter 68

The SS Queen Mary 2

AYDEN PLAYED with the condensation on the side of his frosty mug, waiting for Breaking News. There had been no word of a threatened terrorist attack, and now that Odi was dead Ayden knew there would not be. He checked his watch and smiled. The planes were in flight. He was moments from making a difference to the world, moments from saving the children—if the bombers had gotten aboard; if they had the courage to swallow; if the Creamer worked; if, if, if …

He took a long swallow of Boddingtons and looked around the modern nightclub of the grandest vessel ever to grace the seven seas. Club G32 was dimly lit but brightly furnished. Colorful roving lights moved randomly around, pulsing and flashing with the hypnotic music. Why they called the club G32 Ayden neither knew nor cared. His only interest in G32 was the bank of television monitors it sported on one wall, one of which was tuned to CNN. Even sitting just a few feet away, however, he could not hear the broadcast over the blaring music. He knew that would all change soon. Soon the world would stand on its ear and he would be able to hear a pin drop.

With the announcement of the first exploding airplane, someone would turn the volume up. When the second aircraft blew, even the deaf DJ would take notice and turn the music off. By the third everyone would be standing openmouthed, staring at the reports jamming every screen. That was why Ayden had come to G32 rather than watching in his own suite; he did not want to witness the birth of the new world alone. Oddly enough, he wished Odi could be there, Odi and Arvin.

But he was alone, and that was just as well. He could not permit himself more than a few minutes' celebration. He still had work to do. Once the pattern was established—only SASC-member planes—

Marshall's phone would start ringing off the hook. That was when he would order coffee. That was when the chairman would get his Creamer. That was when—

A red banner began flashing on the CNN screen. Ayden stared at the welcome words: Terror Strikes. He stood up and moved to within inches of the hanging screen. There was a volume button on the bottom edge. He turned it up. "... more than a dozen flights. Though details are still sparse, CNN has just received an amateur video. We need to warn our viewers that it contains graphic content." Ayden caught himself grinning ear to ear at the prospect of seeing the first pictures, not for what they would show, but for what they would represent. He wondered what the image would be. A flash in the sky? A plummeting plume? A smoking crater? Or all of the above?

Chapter 69

Asgard Island, Chesapeake Bay

LYING IN A CRUMPLED HEAP on the deck of her ex-lover's yacht, Cassi prayed that his shadowy accomplice was still on the front porch. She screamed into the walkie-talkie. "You're too late, Stuart. Odi's already gone. He swam to the mainland—with a waterproof bag tucked inside his wetsuit. Wanna guess what was inside?"

It was a short message, but it ought to be enough—she hoped. When Stuart's reply came, it was not what she expected. "It was me, you know. Not Sal. Not an accident. I played you like a violin. I—"

She turned off the walkie-talkie. Stuart could troll all he wanted; she would not take the bait. It did not faze her that the daycare center bombing was a setup. That incident was trivial compared to what lay before her now.

She permitted herself a long moan. Her left arm was in agony. She rolled her head and used her right arm to pull her shirt away from her body. She inspected the damage. Her arm looked like a garden snake that had swallowed a mouse. The swelling was intense, but concentrated. Her humerus had obviously broken clean through. The bone was not protruding through her skin, however, and given the level of bruising, her veins and arteries appeared to be intact. She would live. She wished she were as optimistic about the twenty-four planeloads of passengers whose lives hinged on her performance over the next few minutes.

She allowed herself one final sobbing wail, then she steeled her will and said, "No more."

Using her right hand to keep her left arm steady, Cassi rolled up onto her feet. White-hot bolts of pain radiated sporadically from her shattered arm. She did her best to ignore them. The painkillers in the first-aid kit she had raided earlier beckoned her with a Siren's song, but she had no time for such a diversion. Stuart's search of the garden would not last forever. Once he satisfied himself that she was no longer there, he would understand that her taunt had been a diversion. He would make a beeline for the boat. She had to be ready.

She staggered to the aft gate where she collected her stash of supplies—the driver, the air horn and the tape. Once on the hard dock, each footfall sent a shockwave trumpeting up her spine and down her arm where it detonated an explosion. She looked ahead at the marina's staircase, and winced. Each of the thirty-six steps represented a mountain of pain she had to climb. Cassi wedged the driver between her teeth in place of the proverbial bullet, and had at it. At one point she saw a flash of white light and felt herself starting to faint. Still she moved on. She could not help but picture jagged bone grating nerves and slicing flesh. Still she moved on. As excruciating as it was she knew that worse was yet to come. Still she moved on. "Twenty-four planeloads," she repeated to herself. "Twenty-four."

Eighteen stairs into her climb she had to stop. Sweat was gushing from her face. Her heart was pounding two hundred beats a minute, and her arm was so swollen she thought that it might explode. She took a deep breath, and continued, counting each stair off like a battle won. When at last she got high enough, she peeked over the cliff's edge. Stuart was nowhere in sight. Relief swept over her like a warm wave. Her struggles had not been wasted. The passengers still had a chance— if she hurried. Stuart would be coming any second now. He knew the yacht was what she wanted.

She took the Ping driver from her mouth and laid it down along the base of the fourth stair down from the top, noting with satisfaction that the handrail's supporting brace camouflaged the protruding club head. She withdrew the air horn from her pocket and unrolled a foot of medical tape. She looked down to take a deep breath and saw that a puddle of sweat was forming between her feet. This was it, she realized, the point of no return.

She risked another peek over the top of the stairs and saw him. Stuart was just leaving the garden, walking briskly in her direction. She shot back down, ignoring the jolt of pain. She did not know if he had seen her too. At this point, it did not really matter.

Using her chin and knees and one good hand, she positioned the cardboard roll over the air horn's button. She pressed down on the roll. The air horn began to blare. She knew the sound was coming but it still frightened her it was so loud. Wrapping as fast as her awkward appendages were able, she tried to lash the roll down so that it pressed the button, but the jet of air caught her jacket and the air horn flew from her grasp. Reflexively, she grasped at it with her left arm. Flames erupted around the break and again a searing flash consumed her eyes, but she caught it. She knew that Stuart was just seconds away. She could not fold. Summoning all her reserves of willpower and strength, she continued wrapping until the roll was secure. She scooted four steps lower and stood. She aimed for the roof of the yacht and lobbed the air horn toward the sky with the arcing throw used on hand grenades.

Cassi ignored the missile the instant it left her hand. For better or worse, her only die was already cast. As it arced through the air, she slipped under the staircase rail and climbed beneath the stairs. Endorphins were overriding her pain at last. Her body knew that it was do or die. She heard the horn clatter onto the cabin roof as she reached up for the Ping. She followed the sound of the horn as it slid off the roof and plummeted to the main deck where it continued to emit a muffled wail. Stuart would be running full out with the assumption that she was signaling a passing boat.

She strained to hear the sound of pounding of feet. Only then did Cassi realize that her ears were still ringing from the air horn's close-up blast. She felt a surge of panic. She was lost if she could not hear Stuart's approach. She closed her eyes and tried to control her breathing as she focused on nothing but her ears. Better.

Fishing line! The thought leapt unbidden into her head. She should have used fishing line. Now it was too late.

She felt the stairs vibrate before her damaged ears registered the accompanying noise. The muscles in her shoulder went tense. She only had one chance to pull off a split-second move. If she got it wrong, Stuart would shoot her at point-blank range. Twenty-four planeloads of people would die. Battered body or not, she felt primed like never before.

His foot hit the top step hard enough to make it clang. She sprang the millisecond she heard the second footfall—hitting three steps lower than the first. She thrust the shaft of the driver upward along the railing posts until the handrail supports blocked its ascent on both sides. The shaft of the driver now spanned the stairway, creating an unbreakable tripping force. She braced herself.

Chapter 70

The SS Queen Mary 2

SOAKING WET AND WILD-EYED, Odi attracted inquisitive glances as he ran through the corridors and down the stairs to the third deck. As he entered the grand atrium, his eyes flashed about in search of a phone. To his left a bartender polished glasses. She was trying to look perky although she was obviously bored. To his right a hostess sat bent over a map, assisting an elderly couple with their shore plans. Aside from them and a half-dozen sad souls mindlessly pouring money into melodious slots, nobody else was around.

The bartender gave him an odd look—half smile, half inquisitive stare—but did not comment. Odi turned his back to her and picked the phone receiver off a table.

"Ship's operator. How may I help you?"

"The Balmoral Duplex, please."

"One moment, please."

After three rings a woman's voice greeted Odi. "Hello."

"Good evening, Mrs. Marshall. Would you kindly hand the receiver to an agent of the Secret Service?"

Mrs. Marshall did not reply at once. She paused, then said, "Just a minute."

Odi heard the scrunching sound of a hand covering the phone followed by muffled voices.

"Who's calling please?" Said a different voice, a voice Odi recognized.

"Good evening, Senator. My name is Odi Carr. I'm a Special Agent with the FBI. Is there a Secret Service Agent with you?"

"If you are who you say you are, Agent Carr, then you should know the answer to that."

"I know that you're not usually under guard, Senator, but tonight should be different given the threat."

"I'm always under threat, yet here I am. Tonight is no different."

Odi felt the walls closing in around him. This virtually confirmed his worst fear. Cassi had either not been believed, or more likely had not gotten through. At least Ayden had not yet gotten to the senator. Or had he? Had the senator's voice sounded strained? Odi was not sure. "I'll call you back in a minute, Senator." Without waiting for a reply, Odi hung up.

He ran up the six flights of stairs, ignoring another series of murmurs and stares. He hoped that the body heat this generated would help him dry off. He wished he had a gun.

He kept his eyes peeled for Ayden the whole way, but did not know what he would do when he saw him. Attack like a dog, he supposed. Once he reached Marshall's suite, he stood to the side of the door. He reached over to knock, but paused. If Ayden was in there, he realized, he would shoot on sight. "So be it," Odi muttered. He had no choice.

He knocked.

"Who is it?"

Odi recognized the senator's voice. "Senator, it's Special Agent Carr."

"Hold your ID up to the peephole, Agent Carr."

"I'm undercover, Senator. I don't have my ID. I don't have my firearm either, sir." Odi backed up, raised his arms and spun slowly around. "Senator, it's crucial that we talk. Thousands of lives depend on it—including your own."

The senator opened the door. He held a nickel-plated semi-automatic in his hand and wore an expression that made it clear he wasn't afraid to use it. "You've got sixty seconds."

Chapter 71

The SS Queen Mary 2

AYDEN CLUTCHED his sweating beer glass in both hands as he watched the picture shift from the news anchor to the amateur video. His first reaction was surprise. The video was shot from inside a plane. The oxygen masks were down and flailing as wind whipped through the cabin with hurricane force. Although no hole was visible on screen, the Creamer had obviously blown through the fuselage.

The picture was bobbing left and right, the camera obviously held by a trembling hand. No surprise there, Ayden thought. The operator panned left from the oxygen masks to expose a crowd of writhing men. The elbow of the nearest one, a crew-cut bull with his back to the camera, kept popping up into the air. Though the view was blocked by his rocking back, the crunching sound clarified his unseen movements. He was pummeling someone's face. After a dozen wallops the beating ceased. The bull stood up and hefted a limp form over his shoulder. Despite the bloody nose and swollen bruises, Ayden recognized Khalid's unconscious face. He felt as though he had been kicked in the gut. They had found out one of his bombers.

The camera panned wider to expose an open exit door and the ground a couple thousand feet below. The bull approached it and flopped Khalid forward. Another large passenger took Khalid's hands while the bull retained his feet. Then the cabin grew silent but for the billowing wind and the two burly passengers heaved Khalid out into space. The instant Khalid hit the jet stream, his body disappeared from view behind the airplane. A flight attendant closed the exit door and the passengers began to cheer.

The screen cut back to the news anchor as Ayden felt the floor dissolving beneath his feet. "That remarkable scene took place just minutes ago after authorities learned that a passenger had swallowed a bomb that was set to go off before the plane could land. Sources in the Department of Homeland Security have confirmed that suicide bombers are believed to have targeted twenty-four planes. In fourteen other cases, the bombs—secreted in miniature Baileys Irish Cream bottles—were confiscated before being armed. As of this moment, we have no reports that any of the remaining nine bombs have exploded. I repeat ..."

Ayden looked away and saw that talking heads now filled every monitor. He took a step back—onto the lizard-skinned boot of a barrel-bellied man. The man did not notice. Like everyone else in the room, his attention was riveted to a monitor. Everyone in G32 had converged on the monitors and the crowd now penned him in. Ayden began to panic. He turned back toward the talking heads and tried to pull himself together. He had to decide exactly what this meant.

The conclusions crashed down on him like falling boulders. The assassination of the SASC was a bust. There would be no grand public investigation. The martyr videos would never be played on the air. The defense budget would not be publicly examined. A billion swords would not be beaten into plowshares. Nothing would change. He had failed the children.

Ayden suddenly felt much older than his thirty-nine years. Arvin's words came back to him as he stared at the depressing report on the screens: "I want to be able to say that I was there with Ayden Archer on 10/12." Ayden felt ashamed. He could sum up his startling new predicament in a series of No's. He had no money, no job, and as of this evening, no friends. He had eliminated Odi, but not soon enough.

His depression mounted until it became too much to bear. A better world had been yanked from his grasp. He could not face the old one. He was ready to take a dive off the bow when he remembered his alternative plan. Hope lifted the rocks from his heart. Desperation lent him courage. He felt born again as he pushed his way through the crowd. 10/12 could still eclipse 9/11.

Chapter 72

Asgard Island, Chesapeake Bay

NO SOONER HAD CASSI LOCKED the Ping into the crook of the rail than she felt its shaft flex and heard Stuart's startled shout. She released the quivering club and popped her head out from beneath the stairs in time to see his airborne body begin to tumble. Stuart must have been sprinting, she decided, because his trajectory was taking him well beyond the steep staircase's base. She watched him windmill his hands in a fruitless attempt to halt his forward somersault as he plummeted through twenty-five feet of empty space. He careened face-first into the iron dock, his outstretched arms snapping like twigs beneath the momentum. A fleshy thud and the sickly sound of snapping bones met Cassi's ears as Stuart's terrified scream transformed into an agonized howl. Stuart was tough, Cassi thought, but he was no match for cast iron. "That's for Masha and Zeke," she said with grim satisfaction.

Cassi made a visual inspection of Stuart's hands to confirm that neither held a Beretta before gingerly pulling herself up onto the stairs. Noting that his agony made her own pain easier to ignore, she descended the stairs with slow, measured strides. Stuart looked helpless as a two-pound kitten in a fifty-gallon drum, but she kept the Ping driver cocked back over her head, just in case. She was not going to end up like a movie chick.

Her eyes drank in the climactic scene as she descended. Both of Stuart's forearms lay splayed at grotesque angles as though he had been born with a freakish extra joint. That illusion shattered a second later as she watched. While Stuart squirmed a white bone ripped through the black wool of his sweater to glisten like the Grim Reaper's only tooth.

Cassi stood over him, club still poised. She met his eye, and smiled.

With an effort that exhibited tremendous power of will, Stuart brought his wailing under control and began to mutter. "You bitch. You bitch, you bitch, you bitch ..." He continued to wriggle belly down on the dock as he cursed. When Cassi made no reply his words degenerated into moans.

She lowered the club. He was no threat. He seemed unable to move his head but he continued to look up at her with one beady eye. She stifled the impulse to poke it out with the butt of the Ping, choosing to set the club down instead. She used her one good hand to reach into his right pants pocket. Finding the yacht's keys, she pulled the ring out and gave it a jingle. Then she stepped over Stuart's wrecked body and hopped onto the prow of the yacht.

Stuart managed to roll his head so that he could keep her in sight. Apparently, he was not paralyzed, Cassi noted. That was just as well. He parted his mouth and looked as though he wanted to say something clever, but neither the wit nor the energy were present. He remained silent.

In stark contrast, Cassi knew exactly what she wanted to say. "You can spend the rest of your life in a six-by-eight cell, or you can roll a few feet to your right and drown. I don't give a damn either way. I'm done with you."

Chapter 73

The SS Queen Mary 2

ODI PULLED A FIRE AXE from the wall as he entered the engine room. One way or the other, he knew it would all end here.

It was a different world from the glorious one he was leaving. Dim lighting bathed the pale green walls. The air was thick with the smells of grease and diesel. The temperature was at least ninety degrees. Odi found it hard to hear himself think over the mechanical noise. The only pleasant surprise that side of the sealed door was the absence of workers. He realized that technicians must be monitoring everything remotely from an engineering room. "So much the better."

Odi had gained admittance to the lower decks by using Kostas's card-key ID, which had yet to be cancelled. He was not sure how Ayden had gotten into the restricted area, but he knew that his traitorous friend was here. He felt it in his bones.

Twice he had tried to lure Ayden to Marshall's suite by ordering pots of coffee. But his nemesis had failed to appear and both times the cream that accompanied the order was normal. That was when Odi concluded that something bigger was up. It did not take him long to figure out what that would be. Or at least where. On a ship, bigger was most likely found in one direction.

Convincing the senator to put down his big nickel-plated gun and let him go was not so easy.

They had spent a few very tense minutes together while Senator Marshall verified his story. Three questions into the interrogation, Odi understood that the Chairman of the Senate Armed Services Committee had an excellent technical grasp of weapons. Apparently, he actually read the briefs and stayed awake during meetings. Realizing that, Odi shifted gears immediately and gave a detailed explanation of how his invention worked. Between the Creamer's chemistry and its creator's conviction, Marshall was convinced.

Once sold, Marshall got the Director of Homeland Security on the phone without further delay and dictated his marching orders. Odi was impressed.

"The SASC Senators are all flying home at this moment," Marshall said. "The planes they're on are all carrying bombs. These are very special bombs, so listen close. They're disguised as mini bottles of Baileys Irish Cream. Looks like each terrorist has four.

"While you bring each plane down immediately for an emergency landing, you've got to have the air marshal aboard make an announcement over the PA. He's got to recruit every passenger to help him find those four bottles. If the Baileys is found before it gets drunk, you're in the clear. If not, the situation becomes more complicated."

Odi nodded as the senator spoke, reassuring him that his understanding was correct.

"Once the contents of one or more Irish Cream bottles gets ingested, the drinker becomes a very powerful chemical bomb—with a timer of less than thirty minutes. If you can't land within ten minutes of the first sip passing lips, you're going to have to throw the imbiber off the plane—mid-flight."

There was a pause while the Homeland Security Director questioned what he had just heard.

The senator said, "I've got the man who built the bombs with me here. He says there's no other way. I believe him.

"If you don't find the Baileys bottles right away, or you find any empties in the trash, you need to have everyone look for a passenger developing blue fingertips. That symptom is your warning, but it only appears shortly before detonation, meaning that once you find it you will only have seconds to act. If you see blue you've got to get that person off the plane immediately, or everyone is lost. Have the air marshal open the cockpit door and throw the bastard into Allah's arms."

Despite what he and the senator had watched transpire over the next hour on TV, Marshall had held Odi under arrest. The Director of Homeland Security had informed him of the APB. When neither Ayden nor his Creamer materialized during that time, Odi had insisted on hunting him down.

When he finally stood and moved toward the door, the senator did not shoot.

Five minutes later, Odi was scanning a dim jungle of churning metal in search of Ayden. Due to the time constraint, he did not have the luxury of sneaking around. He had to walk the aisles, exposing himself to fire. He had no doubt that Ayden would shoot him on sight. He just hoped that his old friend did not have a gun.

The glowing flicker of a flare caught Odi's attention, coming from a dozen steps ahead and twenty feet to his left. It came from the far side of an iron tank the size of a submarine. As Odi read the label he cursed under his breath. Ayden had targeted the ship's thermal oil boiler.

Odi knew the mechanics of how ships like this were powered, having studied petroleum chemistry ad infinitum. The heavy oil they used was virtually non-reactive at room temperature. It was the rough equivalent of asphalt. To turn heavy oil into the combustible fuel the ship could use for power, it has to be primed—heated over many hours to liquid form at a temperature of six-hundred degrees. Six-hundred degrees, Odi repeated to himself. This was not going to be pretty.

He peeked around the edge of the thermal oil boiler, and spotted Ayden there. He was sitting in the narrow service passageway between the boiler and the hull. Oddly enough, one of his hands was handcuffed to a feeder pipe. He held a burning flare in the other. Odi saw that he had a dozen more flares gripped between his thighs. He was in the process of lighting them.

Odi stepped halfway out from behind the corner.

"Hello Odi. Did you decide to join me? I'm afraid I drank all the Creamer myself, but if you sit close," he shrugged, "what's the difference?"

"I'm not into suicide."

"This isn't suicide. It's a mission of mercy. The thousands who die today will save millions of lives." He produced the key to the handcuffs as he spoke and then placed it ceremoniously on his tongue as he finished. He swallowed.

Odi could not help but notice the maniacal look in the eyes of his former friend. He did not know what to say.

As it turned out, Ayden was not finished. "In a few minutes the Queen Mary 2 will be rechristened Titanic 2, as she sinks with most of her thirty-nine hundred souls. Oh, some will survive on lifeboats, I'm sure, but given the speed she'll go under it won't be a thousand. 10/12 will still eclipse 9/11. As the media sifts through the wreckage, world attention will finally be brought to focus on the issues that matter most. The money will follow."

"You're only going to kill yourself, Ayden," Odi said, shaking his head. "Heavy oil won't explode."

Ayden scoffed. "Coming from the man who invented Creamer, your thinking is surprisingly conventional. I'm not counting on blowing a hole in the hull, even though there is that possibility—I did down a whole pint. No, my friend, I'm going to burn one." Ayden gestured with the flare.

"A whole pint!" Odi sputtered, unable to contain himself. That much actually might blow a hole through the hulls if the boiler banked the energy of the explosion just right. Ayden's stomach now held the Newtonian equivalent of sixteen hand grenades. Odi dwelled on that image until he remembered the last part of Ayden's sentence. He was counting on burning a hole through the hull.

Odi thought aloud. "When you explode, you'll rip open the side of the thermal oil boiler. Ten thousand gallons of superheated oil will gush out, hit the flares and ignite. In that quantity, the oil will burn at a temperature of around three thousand degrees. Iron melts at twenty-eight hundred ..."

Ayden looked at him and smiled. Then he held his lit flare to the tip of another and it too burst into flame. The extra light revealed the blue tinge of Ayden's fingertips.

As if reading Odi's mind, Ayden shook his left arm, rattling the handcuff against the pipe. "Sorry. I'm not going anywhere."

"I'm sorry too," Odi said, bringing his right hand into view. "But I must insist."

Ayden dropped his jaw as Odi hefted the axe.

Chapter 74

PoliTalk Studio, Washington, D.C.

WILEY WAS ON TOP OF THE WORLD. Tonight he would solidify his position as America's go-to man on terrorism at the very moment that terrorism returned to the pinnacle of American attention. His move to the White House was but a hop, skip and a jump away.

Fitzpatrick had invited him to record a profile interview for a special extended episode of *PoliTalk*. Fitzpatrick would use it on Sunday, during his comparative analysis of the leading contenders for the presidential election tickets. He was gunning to become the preferred source for election coverage, and that suited Wiley just fine.

They had just finished twenty minutes of raw video when Fitzpatrick held up one hand indicating that the camera should cut as he placed his other hand over his right ear. As Fitzpatrick listened to the news coming over his earpiece, Wiley's cell phone began to vibrate—right on cue. Once his expectation was confirmed by the pallid look on Fitzpatrick's face, Wiley surreptitiously switched off his phone. He did not need to answer it to get the message.

"There's breaking terrorist news," Fitzpatrick said, looking up from the notes he had just scribbled. "Are you okay with going live?" His face was rife with excitement.

This was no coincidence, of course. Wiley had timed things to a tee. His speeches were prepared and his messages ready. The Proffitt-for-Vice-President Campaign was about to launch into the stratosphere. The confluence of events was beautiful. He would not even have to feign surprise at the images of exploding planes and flaming corpses. This was the attack The Prophet had been predicting. He gave Fitzpatrick a take-it-or-leave-it answer: "If you'll cover my back, I'll cover yours."

Wiley knew that Fitzpatrick would hate to surrender his boxing license even for an hour, but he had little choice. To have the Director of the FBI live in his studio at a time like this could make him a network news anchor if not a legend. Nonetheless, Wiley thought that Fitzpatrick said "Deal" a little too quickly. Seconds later, he understood why.

The suicide bombers had failed.

For an hour, Wiley had to sit there looking perky and satisfied as amateur videos showed air marshal after air marshal apprehending Ayden's bombers. It was not hard for Wiley to spin this battle in his favor, but behind his flashing teeth and glowing eyes, he knew that this public-relations victory might cost him the war. For terrorism to top the election agenda, the voters had to be scared. These videos not only calmed them, they gave the whole country the cocky jubilation of the winning Super Bowl team.

"Well, your prediction came true, Director. The Prophet epithet holds. And even more impressive and important than your ability to predict this attack was your overwhelming success in defeating it. We calculate that thirty-eight hundred souls were aboard those twenty-four planes. You saved them all—not to mention their families and the casualties spared on the ground. Why, by this time tomorrow, most Americans will have looked up at the sky and understood that without Wiley Proffitt, a plane might well have crashed on them. Please accept my professional congratulations and my personal thanks."

Wiley was about to comment on the value of a team effort and the dangers of dropping one's guard when Fitzpatrick held up his finger and pressed his earpiece. "We've got more breaking news—also with amateur video." He pointed to the studio plasma screen. "This video was shot just minutes ago aboard Cunard's luxury cruise ship the Queen Mary 2 as it sailed a hundred nautical miles from New York. Like the other videos we have shown you this evening, this was streamed to us from a camera phone. Our apologies for the low resolution and the jerky quality—the photographer was running while shooting. When you see it, you will understand why."

The monitor cut from Fitzpatrick to the scene of a man running up a set of ornately carpeted stairs. He carried another man over his shoulder, and that man's wrist was spurting blood. His hand had obviously just been severed at the wrist. The camera angle shifted to center on the victim trying to stem the bleeding from his stump. His efforts were not doing much good, and his moans were becoming feeble. Wiley recognized Ayden.

The running man was shouting, "Make way!" and "Move!" while the amateur videographer kept repeating "Oh my God."

As the crowd of gowns and tuxedos parted, some cursed while others screamed. The bobbing camera kept tight on the running man's heels as he exited onto the ship's promenade. Without pausing, the running man dumped his handless hostage over the rail, soliciting a gasp from the audiences in the studio and on the video. Ayden's screams crescendoed and faded as the camera followed his plummet. Then the audience lost sight of him among the churning waves.

The operator panned the camera back to the perpetrator's face and everyone went silent. Wiley felt his blood thin as the camera zoomed in. He was looking into a dead man's eyes.

No sooner had the camera focused on Odi's panting face than the speakers were filled with a water-muffled boom. The camera whirled about to reveal a geyser of seawater. Ayden had exploded a good hundred yards behind the ship, but the blast was still big enough to be both heard and felt.

The studio monitor cut back to Fitzpatrick who was eagerly waiting. "We have learned that the Chairman of the Senate Armed Services Committee, Senator Lawrence Marshall, was aboard that ship and is presumed to have been the bomber's primary target. Would you care to comment, Director Proffitt?"

Wiley's mind was redlining as it raced toward the distant light he sensed at the end of this tunnel. He sat there motionless for several seconds with the camera on him. Finally, he nodded as though making a decision and looked into the lens. "Well, now that the cats are all out of the bag, I may supply additional detail without endangering ongoing operations or innocent lives. Your assumption that Senator Marshall was the target is correct. In fact, the twenty-five members of the Senate Armed Services Committee were the primary targets of all of tonight's attacks. Al-Qaeda will stop at nothing to murder defenders of freedom.

"The man you saw throwing the bomber over the rail of the Queen Mary 2 was FBI Special Agent Odysseus Carr. Agent Odi Carr and his sister, Agent Cassandra Carr, have been working undercover in a top-secret operation to combat a specific al-Qaeda cell. Due to potential agency infiltration, their mission was so secret that the brother-and-sister team reported exclusively and directly to me." Wiley paused to let this fact sink in.

"You will recall that three defense corporation CEOs have been executed during this last month." Wiley held up three fingers on his right hand. "That was the work of this same terrorist cell. Those operations showed inside knowledge, as did the attack on our envoy to Iran. So in order to avoid the chance of any leaks in this highest-priority mission, I worked exclusively with a couple of expert field operatives whom I knew I could trust.

"While investigating those killings under deep cover, Odi Carr learned that the next 9/11 was pending. Unfortunately, he was not close enough to the terrorist mastermind to learn the details. In an effort to win him the terrorists' confidence, I added Agent Carr to the FBI's most wanted list. That ruse succeeded, if only just. Technically, this operation was a resounding success, but as you saw we were nearly too late. We need to get even better."

"Amazing, truly amazing," Fitzpatrick said. "I certainly thank you for your unprecedented candor, Director. I find it refreshing."

Wiley nodded and relaxed inside as a warm glow suffused him. He had done it! He had covered his ass with the sweetest perfume, and the scent would never wear off. Nobody picked through glowing successes. The fine-tooth comb was reserved for political failures. Of course, there would be those in the Bureau who would suspect foul play, but they would not dare to question him now, much less point a finger. This coup gave Wiley the power to castrate his opponents with a flick of his golden wrist.

All he had to do to get the keys to 1600 Pennsylvania Avenue was win over the Carrs. That should not be too hard. He had Odi cold for the CEO murders. Besides, his story made them national heroes. They would be fools to contradict it. Hell, he could even marry Cassi now if he wanted. Even Stuart could not object to having a bona fide hero as First Lady. No one could attack her without reminding everyone of Wiley's finest hour.

The thoughts were coming so fast and furious that Wiley momentarily forgot that he was on TV. As he turned to refocus on Fitzpatrick, Wiley caught sight of Cassi standing at the corner of the soundstage. His bowels turned to water as they locked eyes. As he read the intentions telegraphed by her expression, Cassi held up a DVD.

"... don't you think?" Fitzpatrick asked.

Wiley forced his attention back to his host. "I'm sorry, could you repeat the question?"

"Well, it's good to see that you are human. I was beginning to wonder. I asked if you would be content with the VP slot on the ticket after today. Perhaps you'll consider challenging Carver for president?"

Cassi waved the DVD behind Fitzpatrick's shoulder and gave the thumbs-down sign with her other hand—although that arm was in a sling.

Wiley made a split-second decision—not that he had any choice. He refocused on Fitzpatrick. "No, no. I'm not so ambitious. In fact, I informed the president earlier today that I would not consider running for any office at all."

"Really!" The unflappable Fitzpatrick seemed genuinely shocked.

Cassi nodded but kept waving the damn recording. The message was clear: she wanted more.

Wiley felt an irresistible urge to strangle her but he had to sit there looking affable on the air. He thought of everything he had sacrificed in the course of giving whatever it takes. He thought of Potchak, Drake, Rollins and Abrams. He thought of a yacht on the Chesapeake, a cabin on Lake Maroo, a clinic in Iran and a daycare center in Baltimore. He thought of Stuart's smarmy smile, Cassi's agonized eyes and Odi's brilliant Creamer. He thought of Air Force One, the White House and the Presidential Seal. He saw his dreams flash brightly before his eyes and he saw his future fade to black. He looked directly at the camera. "Yes. In fact I've decided to let this last operation be my crowning achievement. At that same meeting I informed the president that I was retiring from the FBI. This was my last day in the Director's chair."

Epilogue

Six weeks later, Arlington, VA.

"ARE YOU SURE this is the right place?" Odi asked the government driver while studying the unfamiliar brownstone.

"Yes sir, this is it. Number twenty-one."

"What's here?"

"I don't know any more than you do, sir," the driver replied.

Odi slid out of the black Lincoln, pulling his duffel bag behind. The brownstone certainly looked more inviting than the suburban Maryland safe house he had been locked away in for forty days and nights while patiently waiting for the powers that be to decide his fate. But looks could be deceiving. Had the offer been a ploy? He wondered. Were they about to take him out?

Standing there on the elm-lined curb watching the Lincoln disappear, he realized that he was alone outdoors for the first time since throwing Ayden from the Queen Mary's deck. It felt good. Whatever his fate, he would embrace it.

He closed his eyes and let the late afternoon sun shine down on his face for a minute. For six weeks he had been chomping at the bit, frustrated by the slow spin of bureaucratic wheels. Once everything fell into place, however, things started moving very fast. One minute he was sitting in his cell, the next he was getting an overview of his new assignment. Five minutes after that he was sitting in the back of the limo.

As he reached for the bell to number twenty-one, his eyes fell on the brass plaque beside the door. He sprouted a satisfied smile. Now he understood.

A grandmotherly lady with lively eyes answered his ring. "Good afternoon, Odysseus. My name is Mary. Please, come in."

Mary ushered him into a cozy parlor appointed in yellows and greens. He took a seat in a soft armchair across the coffee table from an attractive woman of his own age. Once Mary disappeared, the woman asked, "Since you're alone, I assume that you're here to interview the doctor?"

Odi chuckled to himself at that notion. "In a manner of speaking."

"She's wonderful. My Stephen was having the worst nightmares and," she lowered her voice, "wetting the bed. She cured him in just three sessions. I was going to stop coming after that but Stephen threw a tantrum. He actually looks forward to their talks. Can you imagine? A six-year-old looking forward to talks? The first time I brought him here he was screaming murder. I'm Melanie, by the way." She held out her left hand rather than her right. Odi understood the eccentricity when he saw that her ring finger was bare.

"Odi. I'm glad to hear that you're so pleased. Actually—"

The thick wooden door at the end of the room flew open and a boy with carrot-colored hair came rushing in, cutting Odi short. As Stephen hugged his mother, Cassi stepped into the doorway. She looked radiant.

Odi excused himself and walked into his sister's new office. They embraced the moment she closed the door.

"I can't believe that you left the FBI, Sis, but I'm so glad that you did. You look great."

"I feel great. Better than I have in years. Better than any time since mom and dad died."

Odi raised his eyebrows inquisitively.

"My life is about compassion now—rather than hate. But enough about me. How about you? The isolation must have been terrible. I knew that you'd be okay though, being so tough." She took two steps back and appraised him in full. "You look good, even great."

"I had the use of a small gym to while away the hours."

"I was assured that you were being taken care of, but other than that I was kept in the dark. Then the new Director called me personally yesterday to say that you had reached a mutually beneficial settlement. I appreciated the courtesy, but would have preferred the details."

"Mutually beneficial, eh?" Odi mused. "I guess that's right. I can't say that I'm entirely comfortable with their decisions, but I agree that the country will be best served in the end."

"You sound dubious."

"Ayden is getting posthumous blame for my killings. They will release the story of his father's unfortunate death as motive and try to keep the profile low. Meanwhile, to complete the whitewash, I'm receiving the Presidential Medal of Freedom for my deep-cover work—and a new job."

"Can you tell me what it is?"

Odi nodded. "I'll command a group of high-tech operatives tasked with identifying and counteracting soft spots in homeland security."

"That's wonderful, Odi. I'm happy for you."

Cassi motioned him to take a seat and then asked, "What's happening to your Creamer?"

"That was both my biggest bane and my best bargaining chip. For a while, I was worried that they would make me disappear in order to make it disappear. In the end, I gather they decided that such an approach would be shortsighted. If I could concoct Creamer, so could someone else. I'm to work with industry experts to design a means to detect and neutralize it. Ayden's contact in Iran knows that Creamer existed, but he doesn't have any technical details, so we should have detection equipment in place long before he or anyone else is able to recreate it.

"But enough about me. I didn't have any access to news while in isolation, and my handlers never answered a single question unless it suited their purposes, so I'm more curious than a boy scout in a brothel. Seeing as how you are doing so well, I guess I'll start with the big one. What happened to Wiley?"

A shadow crossed Cassi's face, but it vanished in an instant. "The official word is that he went overseas for an extended vacation—something about visiting Norway and Scotland to track down his roots. I don't know anything more than that."

"Do you believe it?"

Cassi shrugged. "I try not to think about him."

"And Stuart?"

"There's been little mention of him in the press, and no mention at all of his connection to Wiley. The bottom line is—he drowned. A fisherman found his body. He had two severely broken arms and the autopsy revealed a broken back. The Reedsville Police are assuming that he fell off a cliff onto some rocks and his body washed out into the bay."

"I get the impression that you know better?"

"Some things are better left unsaid."

"I see," Odi said. "So tell me about your new practice. How's it going? From the looks of things, I'd say great."

"It is. I'd love to tell you more but I can't."

"What do you mean you can't?"

Cassi blushed. "I have to run, Odi. I have a date."

AUTHOR'S NOTE

Dear Reader,

THANK YOU for choosing to read BETRAYAL. I hope you enjoyed it and will review it accordingly.

Are you curious about what happens to the characters next? Want to learn about my other novels? If you email me at Betrayal@timtigner.com, I will keep you informed of my new releases and reply with the surprising story behind BETRAYAL and my unpublished thoughts on what happens to its characters.

Thanks for your kind reviews and attention,

Flash

Tim Tigner

This novel is dedicated to the Beta Readers from my early years: John Chaplin, Christophe Martin, Janet Nelch, Cheryl Rennecker, Elena Tigner, Gwen Tigner, Rob Tigner, Steve Tigner, and Mark Tower, with everlasting gratitude.

Chapter 1

Spoons

TROY AWOKE to the sound of screaming. That was not unusual for a combat surgeon, but hearing soprano was.

He opened his eyes to utter blackness and a monster headache. What the hell was going on? His memory was failing him and he felt oddly unsure of … anything.

He self-diagnosed a concussion, but sensed that it was the least of his woes.

This premonition proved correct a moment later when he tried to sit up—but could not. A cold steel ceiling pressed down on his left shoulder. He also felt walls abutting his back, head and feet. As Troy strained to wrap his mind around his baffling predicament, his nose upped the ante.

Hesitant fingers groped to confirm the stench.

He was lying in a pool of blood.

Troy knew that this was the moment most people would begin to scream and flail, their fight and flight reflexes tripping all over one another. He remained motionless. Analyzing. He had learned at a very young age the wisdom of lying low and keeping quiet. In orphanages things had usually worked out better that way. In the army they still did.

He reached a steady hand into the darkness before him. Cool flesh met his bloody fingers just inches from his face. He had found the bleeder—or at least one of them. He checked the flabby neck for a pulse just to be sure. Definitely dead. "Better and better," Troy whispered to himself.

Another soprano salvo erupted from the darkness, making his heartstrings resonate. Those were not wails of pain he realized, but cries of fear.

"Hold on! I'm coming," he shouted back. Troy did not know if he was coming, of course. Aside from being boxed up with a corpse he had no idea where he was or how to get out. But he knew that hope had a power all its own. Best to offer it for now and figure the rest out later.

The screaming stopped. Then the box shook with a familiar rhythm. The motion snapped the puzzle pieces into place. He was in the trunk of a car.

The sound of an opening car door confirmed his hypothesis.

Troy strained his ears.

"Who said that?" a woman asked, her voice soft but clear.

Troy stifled his habitual Captain Troy response, giving his alternative title instead. "Doctor Troy. I'm in the trunk. Are you in danger?"

"I'm not at a party. What are you doing in there?"

For a dumb question, that was a really good one. "I have absolutely no idea. Ask the Taliban. But please let me out first."

The woman remained silent for what seemed an eternity. He appreciated her dilemma. Curtain A or curtain B; the proverbial lady or the tiger. Picturing her trying to decide, he realized that if he got lucky and she pulled the trunk release rather than running off, his appearance might send her over the edge. He would look more like a feasting vampire than a valiant knight as he leapt to her rescue. Granted, she did not seem to be expecting a fairytale moment, but he decided not to risk it and added, "Don't be scared by what you see."

More silence ended with a cautious, "What do you mean?"

"I'm not at my best. I'm really much more charming than my present appearance might suggest."

The car jiggled some more and then the trunk sprang open with a thwang and a woosh. Brave woman, Troy thought, scrambling to climb out before she caught sight of the corpse.

"Freeze!"

Freeze was a command one quickly learned to respect when working in a country rife with landmines. Troy turned his muscles to stone, but shifted his eyes toward the source of the command. What he saw both pleased and disappointed him. A petite beauty stood by the passenger door, knees bent slightly in a classic shooter's stance, revolver leering at him from between two steady hands. She wore a white blouse, pink shorts, and white tennis shoes—all spattered with blood. Definitely not Taliban, but hardly Cinderella either.

They were in the corner of a parking garage illuminated only by emergency lighting. As he raised his hands up slowly over his head, Troy scanned the shadows cast by concrete pillars and parked cars. They appeared to be alone.

"I'm frozen," he said, trying to sound disarming.

She stared at him in silence.

He stared right back at her. It was not unpleasant. She was short, and slender everywhere a woman was supposed to be, while generously rounded on top. He was not sure how his mind could focus on attributes like that at a time like this, but it did and he was glad for it. Stop to smell the roses and all that.

She spoke at last. "You're all covered in blood."

"You noticed that too," Troy said. "But then it appears that you use the same designer."

She did not look down at herself. No doubt the sight of her blood-spattered blouse was what had initially sparked her screams.

Troy did look down in an attempt to appear less threatening only to find himself out of uniform. That was odd, but not his chief concern. Priority number one was pacifying the pixie with the gun pointed at his chest. Hardware aside, she did not look like a killer, but then mental illness could be a master of disguise. Looking back up he said, "It's not my blood," and motioned toward the trunk with his head. "Speaking of which, would you mind putting your finger outside the trigger guard?"

Tinkerbell craned her long neck to glance into the trunk but then looked quickly away. "What happened? Who is he?" she asked, her arms starting to tremble. Her finger still on the trigger.

"I'm a bit curious about that myself," Troy said, deciding to focus on the latter question first. "His uniform looks a bit like Marine dress blues, less the jacket. But he's much too … squishy to be a jarhead, and that's not the Marine crest on his shoulder boards. Mind if I take a closer look? We've been sleeping together and I don't even know his name."

"Don't move!" she said.

"Sounds like you've got my headache," Troy replied. "I woke up with a real humdinger."

His comment mollified her expression. "Me too," she said. Then she beckoned with the gun. "Go ahead and have a look."

Troy pivoted back toward the trunk and went to work. The shoulder joint creaked as he moved the corpse's arm out of the way, indicating that rigor was setting. Troy knew that meant he'd been dead for three to four hours. Nice to have a timeline. For the moment he had little else.

He spotted two bloody holes and a name tag on the corpse's chest. "His name tag reads Evan Johnson, Detective Sergeant. That's an imperial police rank."

"Imperial?"

"As in British empire. A number of those former colonies are part of the coalition."

Her look did not telegraph comprehension, but Troy returned to the search anyway.

Evan was not wearing his utility belt, so he had no handcuffs, nightstick, or phone. Troy could guess where his handgun was—as well as two of its bullets. Still concerned about the possibility of experiencing the third, he kept his movements slow and steady before the woman.

He slid his hand gingerly into Evan's front right pocket and pulled out a set of car keys—Fords, like the car. Next he reached around and pulled Evan's wallet from his back pocket. He flipped it open and read from the identification card. "Detective Sergeant Evan Johnson, Royal Cayman Islands Police (RCIP). Boy is this guy a long way from home." Troy realized the obvious as he spoke. "But then, so are we I suppose."

"What do you mean, we're a long way from home?" Tinkerbell asked.

Troy turned back toward her. "Judging by your alabaster skin, green eyes, and state of dress, I'm guessing you weren't born in Afghanistan."

"What does Afghanistan have to do with anything?"

The look of sincere confusion on her face gave Troy pause. "Where do you think we are?"

"South L.A., I'm guessing."

"As in Los Angeles?"

"Of course."

Troy felt his stomach begin to constrict. He reached for his own billfold but found his pockets empty. He reopened Evan's wallet and pulled four bills and a receipt from the main compartment. The bills were ten-Cayman-dollar notes.

He took a step back to study the other cars in the garage. All had RCIP logos and right-side steering wheels. Strike two.

His stomach shrank to the size of a walnut.

"What is it?" the woman asked.

Troy ignored her and turned his attention to Evan's petrol receipt. Between juvenile detention and foreign tours, medical school and war, Troy had encountered some of the worst humanity had to offer. Nothing he'd seen had shaken him like the flimsy piece of paper he now held in his hand.

The woman spoke again, but all Troy heard was fuzzy background noise.

Not wanting to believe his eyes, he retrieved Evan's identity card in hopes of finding contrary information. Confirmation greeted him instead. Strike three.

Feeling dizzy, he turned his attention back to the petrol receipt. He mouthed the words as if testing to see if they were real. Thirty liters, forty-eight Cayman dollars, September third, two thousand ... eight.

He had not just forgotten the last few hours.

He was missing seven years.

Chapter 2

Loss

EMMY WATCHED the man's face pale as he studied a document from the dead cop's wallet. "Will you kindly tell me what it is?" she repeated.

He continued to ignore her, even though she was the one holding the gun. She was holding the gun, Emmy repeated to herself. What was going on? Ten minutes ago she had awoken in the front seat of a cop car with the worst headache of her life, a huge silver pistol in her lap, blood spatter all over her blouse, and no idea what had happened. Then some guy locked in the trunk and claiming to be a doctor told her to "ask the Taliban." Was he insane ... or was she?

Now she watched wide-eyed as he pulled his shirttails out of his shorts and began inspecting his own stomach. Drug addict was her first assumption, but his washboard abs belied the user life. When he wiped the blood from his flesh, she saw his jagged scar. It looked like the doctor had once removed his own appendix with a pocketknife. He spread the skin taut around the scar and poked at it as though trying to confirm its authenticity. Then he looked away and sank to his knees.

"What is it? What did you find?" she asked.

After a long tense silence he regained his feet and locked her gaze with disbelieving eyes.

She tried to read his thoughts but found only confusion.

"Will you answer one simple question for me?" he asked.

She wanted to say, "Hey buddy, how about answering my question first?" But his grave expression caused her to nod in silence.

"What year is it?"

She knew then and there that she should run. She had hoped that the doctor would have some answers, be her defender, ally, and guide out of this mess. But he was talking gibberish. Still, something in those cobalt blues gave her pause.

She took a moment to analyze him as she would a client—from the outside in. He wore an olive safari shirt, khaki cargo shorts hanging from a silver-buckled belt, and running shoes. Practicality was clearly his chief wardrobe concern, but he knew what style fit him. Definitely ex-military. An officer.

At about six feet, he was taller than eighty-eight percent of his peers and would be accordingly overconfident. He was fit and broad of shoulder. A man's man, used to command. A ladies' man, used to getting his way. His face was handsome, but marred. Two angry v-shaped scars peeked down from above the thick dark hairline over his right eye. Probably a war wound. Possibly an accident. Definitely traumatic.

His most distinctive feature was a big dimple in the center of his chin. It reminded her of the actor who played Spartacus. But unlike Spartacus, she noted, violence was not Troy's default reaction. He used humor to defuse tension.

He was college educated, highly intelligent—although quite possibly demented, and a wisecrack. She put the odds that he was a doctor at fifty percent.

"What year is it?" he repeated.

She decided to chance a few seconds more to see where this was going. Keeping the gun pointed straight at his chest, she said, "It's 2002. June fifteenth or sixteenth."

"You're sure it's not November 2001?"

"I'm sure," she said, backing up a step.

"Or September 2008?"

"What's this about?"

"Check out your reflection," he said. "You can still keep the gun on me if you want, but crouch down behind the car door and take a good look at your face in the side mirror."

"Why?" she asked. "What would I be looking for?"

He stepped forward until the barrel of her pistol pressed into his chest. Then he held the receipt up before her eyes while placing his free hand softly on her shoulder. "Six lost years."

Chapter 3

Flat

THE WOMAN seemed to spend forever staring into the patrol car's side mirror. When she finally straightened back up to look at him, her posture drooped. The Colt dangled from her arm like a burdensome weight. Tinkerbell had run out of pixie dust.

She looked blankly in his general direction, tears flowing freely down her troubled face. Despite his own problems, despite their impending peril, Troy's predominant emotion was the urge to wrap her in his comforting arms. He was glad to find his hormones still working at the ripe old age of thirty-eight, but resisted the chivalrous impulse nonetheless. When a patient was in shock, it was best to tread lightly. Then there was the gun.

She opened and closed her jaw a few times before producing any sound. When at last she managed, her voice was but a whisper. "Two thousand eight. Are you sure? This can't be."

"My last memory is taking shrapnel from an Afghan IED. Now I have a scar that's long healed. What's the last thing you remember?"

"I don't know. Nothing as crazy as a terrorist bomb. Business as usual, I guess. I'm having trouble remembering. Everything feels hazy … forced."

"I feel the same," He said.

"Six years … Is that possible, doctor?"

"Medically speaking, yes. But it's highly improbable."

His bedside manner seemed to calm her a bit. She wiped her tears and none replaced them. "You think we're in Afghanistan?" she asked, like Alice to the Cheshire Cat.

"I did when I first woke up. Now I think we're in the Cayman Islands."

Her expression conveyed the same *anything can happen in six years* acceptance that he felt. "Where are the Cayman Islands?"

"In the Caribbean. Between Cuba and Jamaica—I think."

"I've never been to the Caribbean. I've never even left the United States."

Troy did not know what to say. He shrugged.

"How did this happen?"

"I don't have a clue." He stepped forward and put a reassuring hand on each of her shoulders. "But whatever happened, happened to both of us. You are not alone."

He watched his last words pour life into her like a magic elixir. Her face blossomed and her eyes regained some twinkle.

She dropped cross-legged to the concrete floor, set the gun down in her lap, and began to massage her aching temples. "So what's our next move?"

Normally, Troy would have sat down with her, but this was neither a pickup bar nor a yoga class. "We run."

"Run? Where?"

"I don't know. Anywhere. We need to put distance between this corpse and ourselves. Nothing good can come from being discovered with a dead cop."

"You didn't …?"

"Of course not." He paused, catching himself. "At least I don't think I did. I can't be sure—and neither can you." She started to speak but he pressed on. "For that matter, we can't answer any questions, provide any alibi, or put up any kind of a legal defense. The I-have-no-recollection line only works if you're the president or someone in his favor. Now, maybe the last seven years have been really good to me … but I'm guessing not."

She did not get up.

He stepped toward her and held out his hand.

She looked up at him. Now that her tears had stopped he could almost see the processor spinning behind her clear emerald eyes.

"We need to run," he pressed, reverting to operational mode.

"That will only make us look guilty," she said, still ignoring his hand.

"I think we've already got looking-guilty covered. It's a question of getting caught. The way I figure it, either one or both of us did kill him, or—much more likely—someone wants it to look like we did. I'd say they've done a pretty good job."

He braced for blowback.

She just nodded in silence for a moment and then, much to his surprise and delight, completed his own thought. "And in either case, we're better off disappearing until we can figure things out. Okay, let's get moving." She took his hand and added, "With my luck it's time for a shift change and a division of cops is about to come barreling through those doors."

"If I were behind this," Troy agreed, "that's exactly how I would have planned it."

As he pulled her to her feet, Troy noted that she could not weigh much more than a hundred pounds, if that. There was no way she had lifted Evan into the trunk. Even drained of blood he was at least a deuce.

Troy started toward the garage door but she stopped him with "Wait."

He turned.

"Shouldn't we, you know, try to clean up? Get rid of fingerprints?"

"In an ideal world I'd like to take a shower too." He gestured the length of his blood-soaked body. "But we're a long way from ideal."

"We can't walk down the street looking like this," she replied, mimicking his gesture. "You look like you just sprang from the Devil's womb and I don't look much better."

"It's after midnight," Troy said, pointing to his Ironman watch.

"So much the better. Let's take the car and solve two problems at once. We can drive to a car wash—pop the trunk and ride through on the hood. It will be a hoot."

Smart lady, he thought. Smart, cool, and quick to rebound. "You're right."

She looked surprised to have won without more of a fight.

He backtracked to the car and slammed the trunk. He pulled Evan's keys from his pocket and slid into the driver's seat. "Well let's go then."

The woman walked around the car and hopped in beside him.

Troy turned the ignition, but nothing happened. He tried the dome light and then the headlights. Nothing. "The battery is either dead or disconnected."

"You really a doctor?" she asked. "Not a mechanic?"

Troy guessed it was the first time in history that a woman had asked that question and hoped to hear mechanic. He gave her a wry smile and popped the hood. "I'm a combat surgeon. That's more like a plumber, but I'll see what I can do."

While looking beneath the hood with a beautiful woman waiting in the car, most guys pray that they will find a big red wire hanging loose from its connector. Troy found exactly that. "The positive terminal has been disconnected from the battery," he said, pushing it back over the battery lead.

The door chime engaged, applauding his efforts.

As he lowered the hood slowly back into place, his gaze fell on the front passenger tire. It was completely flat. A picture of the spare—lying in a blood-filled tire well beneath Evan's blubbery corpse—flashed before his eyes.

"What?" she asked, reading his grimace.

He walked around and opened her door. "Get out. We have to walk. We have a flat."

She did not move. Instead she said, "I can change a tire in five minutes. Surely you can manage it in three?"

He stared at her a moment, trying to pierce her resolve with his eyes.

She did not flinch.

"I'm not sure about three minutes, but I expect that I can change a tire faster than I can change your mind."

"You are quick."

"Soooo, as long as you're willing to help, go ahead and pop the trunk."

The word trunk made the connection for her. Her face puckered, but she quickly swallowed the lemon. She reached across the driver's seat for the release lever and then joined him around back. She had the Colt tucked beneath the waistband of her pink shorts where it looked ridiculously large. Her eyes avoided the trunk.

Troy rotated the body until he could grab it beneath the shoulders. Evan had definitely taken full advantage of the free-doughnuts perk. "Help me do this right," he said. "We need to flip him over onto his left side so he doesn't leave an enormous bloodstain on the floor."

"I'm not good with blood," she said, her eyes locking onto his like a life preserver.

"How are you with jail?" Troy asked, regretting the words even as they left his mouth. "Sorry. Look, you don't have to do any real lifting. Just keep his feet from flailing as I flip the body."

She nodded.

Troy was still trying to hoist Evan over the trunk's lip when he heard footsteps behind them and the overhead lights blazed to life. He turned to see a police officer walking carrying a can of Coke in one hand and jingling his keys with the other. Although he was dressed like Evan, the lean captain was the yin to the hefty detective's yang. He had a beak of a nose and an Adam's apple that was nearly as prominent. His straight sandy hair parted in the middle of his forehead and hung surprisingly long for a ranking cop. He froze mid-step as his eyes came to rest on what must have been an unbelievable sight.

Before the captain had a chance to react, Tinkerbell had the Colt leveled at him. She was good with that thing, Troy marveled. And for someone so petite, she could muster quite a commanding voice. "Down on your knees! Now! Hands behind your head!"

Chapter 4

Countermeasures

TROY HASTILY DUMPED the corpse back into the Ford's trunk. "And so the chase begins."

He had been hoping to clarify a few basic aspects of his situation before running from the law—things like the year, and what continent he was on, and whether or not the woman with him was a murdering psychopath. Looking over at his pistol-packing coconspirator, Troy knew that was not going to happen.

She held the weapon steady and pointed at the name tag on the officer's chest. Troy was glad not to be on the receiving end this time, but sorry to see all chance of an anonymous escape evaporate.

Captain Honey had instantly dropped his keys and his Coke out of shock. Now he was sinking to his knees as ordered. No surprise there. After seeing his blood-soaked captors pawing at his colleague's pale corpse, it was a wonder Honey's pants were still dry.

Troy shut the trunk—gently so as not to startle the woman—and walked toward the captain without a word. He arced his route to keep well clear of Tinkerbell's firing zone. She looked cool on the outside, but he knew from experience that she was panicked on the inside and thus likely to be jittery around the trigger.

Speaking in an Irish brogue, he said, "Ya do as ye're told, captain, and we'll be out of here in two shakes. Ya try to be smart, and we'll be with ye for eternity."

Honey nodded weakly.

After pocketing his gun, Troy used Honey's own handcuffs to secure his hands behind his back. Then he grabbed the collar of Honey's shirt in one hand and lowered him face down onto the cola-covered floor.

"Use his shoelaces to bind his ankles together," the woman suggested, her accent suddenly Irish as well. "Then truss 'em to the cuffs. That'll keep him put. An' don't be forgettin' to stuff a stocking in his gob."

My kinda psychopath, Troy thought, as he followed her suggestion. Quick, decisive and bold.

Satisfied that Honey's bindings would buy them a modest head start, Troy ran back to Evan's car, slid in behind the driver's seat, and turned over the engine.

Tinkerbell slid in beside him. She still looked cool, but in the close quarters he could smell her sweat.

Captain Honey stared at them in silence.

Troy threw the patrol car into gear and hit the gas. The flat tire thunked but the car still rolled. They only needed a mile or two, and he prayed the spent rubber was good for as much. The garage door opened automatically as the car approached, revealing a curtain of wind-driven rain. "How did I know it would be raining," he said.

When no comment came, Troy looked over at the woman who had hitched her wagon to his. She stared back at him, eyes wide and blazing. This seemed a good moment to put her in the right frame of mind.

"The chase begins the moment we roll out that door," he said.

She did not seem to be breathing.

"They are going to catch us, eventually, you know."

She remained silent, but paled.

"Now that Captain Honey has seen us, our only chance of living out the rest of our natural lives beyond bars is to figure out what really happened. We've got to solve this before they catch us."

She nodded and finally spoke. "I know."

"It will likely take us weeks, maybe months."

"I understand."

"From this moment forth, we've always got to be thinking in terms of countermeasures: escape, evade, and confuse. We make one mistake, and it's life without parole."

"For chrissake, I'm with the program. That should already be obvious. Now hit it."

Troy punched the gas and the Ford surged out into the storm. He turned right to keep the weight off the bad tire and then gave the motor its head. The road was short and winding. The buildings around them were commercial in nature, but not in the Fifth Avenue sense. They were cheery wooden structures, gaily painted behind wide sidewalks. The scene reminded Troy of the Deep South. Definitely not Kandahar or L.A. Grand Cayman it was.

He heard a thud inside the car. He looked over to see that the woman had dropped the Colt on the floor. Darting his attention back and forth between her and the road, he saw her kick it away with her foot. So comfortable with the weapon just moments ago, she now seemed disgusted by it, like a reluctant actress whose tasteless scene was done.

"You did great back there," he said. "I was thoroughly impressed."

"We've got to get rid of this car," she replied. "The police will be looking for it in no time."

"I know."

"They can probably track us with GPS."

"On an island? I can't see the taxpayers springing for that expense."

"Maybe it's not so expensive in two thousand eight."

Troy caught her eye. He had not thought of that. "Good call."

Their road dead-ended at a T intersection, forcing him to hit the brakes when every instinct demanded that he floor the gas. A car shot past in front of them and the woman said, "We're driving on the wrong side of the road."

"Good thing we're in a cop car then," he said, turning left toward the ocean.

"Look for a big hotel," she said. "We can leave the car in a busy corner of the parking lot. If we roll down the windows and pop the trunk, the wind-driven rain should be as good as a car wash."

It was not a bad idea, Troy thought, but he had a better one. Seconds later they hit another T intersection, this one with a traffic light. Across the road a large pier disappeared into the harbor. He looked down the road to the right and then the left. Nobody appeared to be about, but then no sane person would be. "I've got another idea. Hold on."

He drove straight across the intersection toward the opposing curb. The deflated left side of the chassis bucked and protested loudly as it passed over the hump, but the wind swallowed the noise and the powerful engine barreled ahead, pushing the car forward with rear-wheel drive.

Like much of the surrounding architecture, the pier appeared to be constructed entirely of wood. Troy propelled the Ford out to the far end where it widened into a viewing platform. He put the transmission in park and looked back over his shoulder. Between the darkness and the rain, the only things visible on land were the streetlights, and they were a blur.

Looking forward again he inspected the railing before them—just boards and nails.

He turned to Tinkerbell. "Get out."

"You're not going to—"

"The tidal salt water will destroy our DNA and fingerprints." Troy pressed buttons to lower all four windows as he spoke. "Now for the tricky part. I really do suggest that you get out."

She did.

Troy threw Honey's Colt onto the floor next to Evan's, hoping to sever all links to both guns. Then he put the Ford in reverse and backed up until the front bumper was about thirty feet from the railing. Pressing his foot down on the brake, he shifted the cruiser into drive and pushed his door all the way open. This would be a first.

"It can't be as easy as it looks in the movies," the woman shouted.

"Nothing ever is—but we're doing okay so far."

Holding the doorsill with his right hand while grabbing the edge of the roof with his left, he shifted his foot from the brake to the gas. The car shot forward. He pulled with his left hand and pushed with his feet until he was standing up on the doorsill. He jumped backwards and away, hitting the boardwalk as the cruiser crashed into the rail. He heard the sound of wood splintering over his own grunts and groans, but by the time he had stopped rolling and regained his feet, the cruiser was already submerged.

The woman stood by the gap in the rail, watching the tail disappear beneath the waves. "It barely made it through," she said. "Then it dropped like a rock and flipped upside down. With the rail in this condition, they will find it come first light."

"The salt water will have done its job by then," Troy said.

"So, what now?" she asked.

"Now we find a hotel and go for a swim."

She stared at him with incredulous eyes. "Perhaps a massage while we're at it?"

"That would require registration," he said with a wink.

Her expression changed. "The chlorine ... The bloodstains ... Got it," she said.

"You need to do one thing first, though."

"What's that?"

"Tell me your name."

She smiled for the first time. It was a beautiful smile; one of those smiles that used to make men pick up swords and storm castles. "Emerald, my name is Emerald Green. My friends call me Emmy."

Chapter 5

Out of the Frying Pan

FARKAS CURSED the weather as he drew the emery board across his fingertips. First a few freak murders, now a tropical storm. What was next, swarms of locusts? He wished the police would get their act together so he could get back to business as usual. Tying up loose ends was not his forte.

He rubbed the pads of his fingers together, testing for the slightest ridge. Nothing. Smooth as silk. He returned the emery board to his shirt pocket without taking his eyes off the rain-soaked garage door. He would leave no prints on this job site, but then he never did.

As he slid back in the saddle, his satellite phone began to vibrate. Farkas cringed. He knew who it was without looking.

He removed the ear bud connected to the police scanner at his waist and gave the canal a scratch before activating the wireless satellite phone receiver in his other ear. "Yeah."

"Are we happy?"

"Not yet."

"Tell me."

"Call me back in an hour. We should be happy then."

"Tell me now."

Farkas was not in the mood for this, but he knew who buttered his bread. "A fight broke out at some hick bar named Moonshines. It ended with two dead teenage tourists and a roomful of drunken locals all pointing the finger at each other. The entire third shift of the George Town Police Department was called in early and asked to report directly to the scene."

"The entire third shift?"

"That's only half-a-dozen cops. Oh yeah. Did I mention the bloody hurricane?"

There was a long pause, followed by, "Where are you now?"

"I'm staking out the police garage from a bus stop across the street."

"A bus stop? You're not in a car?"

"They've been using a scooter, so I have been too. Only way to match their maneuverability. Bloody things are everywhere here, and fortunately they fit under bus stops."

Again a pause. "So our friends are in place, but undiscovered?"

"Right," Farkas said. "I expected discovery over an hour ago. Who would have predicted a double-homicide in paradise? I mean, what are the odds?"

"Tell me you set the flasher to max and erased the full twenty percent?"

"I did. These two are much too clever and resourceful to play patty-cake with. Troy will have lost about seven years of memory, Emmy six. Poor bastard will think he's still in the army. She'll believe she's still eking a living off the streets of L.A."

"Good. How long since the flash?"

"That's the problem. Three hours."

"Shit."

"Yeah. I've been monitoring the police scanner. They're wrapping up at Moonshines. I'm expecting a full house any minute, but we're cutting it close." As he spoke, the streetlight above the garage began to dance. For an instant Farkas thought it was an optical illusion caused by wind and rain, but experience quickly superseded. He cursed. His blood sugar had dropped dangerously low.

Farkas had passed out a few weeks back in a Chicago hotel lobby. He'd been waiting for the elevator after an early morning run when the room started spinning. Then the marble floor hit him in the face. He woke up in the hospital with a raging headache and a pancreatic tumor. An insulinoma. Benign but requiring regular and frequent anti-insulin injections to avoid hypoglycemia. Operable in the long term and not a big deal in the short. He already carried an insulin injection kit. Camouflage for the tool of his latest trade. All he had to do was exchange the insulin for anti-insulin and then actually start poking himself four times a day.

"I gotta go," he said, hanging up on his boss without waiting for acknowledgement.

The reminder alarm on his watch had startled him just as he was liberating the cop's soul from his body. He had twitched and nearly put a bullet into Troy as well. With Troy dead or injured, all his trouble would have been for naught. Farkas had slapped the beeper off without thinking—three hours ago.

Eager to correct his mistake, Farkas pulled a black leather pouch from the left cargo pocket on his shorts, unzipped it, and laid it open on the seat of the scooter between his legs. He selected the silver injector pen—not the black; even in a hypoglycemic haze he could never make that mistake—and cocked the mechanism.

His satellite phone began to buzz again.

He ignored it.

He was pulling up the tails of his black silk shirt to expose his favored injection site when the light across the street actually did start flashing and the garage door began ascending.

"Govno!" Farkas cursed in his native Croatian. He stuffed his shirt back into his shorts as he studied the opening door. Could Troy and Emmy really be escaping? He would prefer swarms of locusts.

The anti-insulin would have to wait.

He dropped the injector pen back into the pouch and stuffed the pouch back into his pocket without taking his eyes off target. He pushed the starter and brought the scooter to life. For what seemed a full minute the garage door stood open but empty, like a hungry mouth. Farkas was about to move in for a closer look when a squad car tore out and turned in his direction. Number thirty-seven. Detective Sergeant Johnson's. Flat tire and all.

As the car raced past him, Farkas caught a glimpse inside. Troy was no longer in the trunk. He was at the wheel, with Emmy once again by his side.

It was a shame, Farkas thought, pulling the scooter out in dark and silent pursuit. He had gone to some trouble to get the meddlesome pair life in prison. By fleeing the scene, Troy and Emmy were only outsmarting themselves. They had just upgraded their sentence to death.

Chapter 6

Radiation

THE RAIN DIMINISHED to a light drizzle while they bathed off their bloodstains, but the wind refused to let up. Now the gale threatened to blow Emmy over as they trudged the waterfront in search of safe harbor. She was tempted to walk behind Troy, to use his broad shoulders as a windbreak. But she had been burned before by taking the back seat, so she stayed by his side, confronting the elements head-on and taking three steps for every two of his.

"You're pretty handy with a weapon," he said, his eyes continuing to sweep their surroundings, his tone inquisitive.

Truth be told, Emmy was baffled by her own behavior, and more than a little scared. "To the best of my knowledge, that was the first time I ever touched a gun."

"Really? You fooled me. And Captain Honey too."

"I just did what they do on TV."

Troy shook his head. "There was more to it than mechanics. You radiated enough competence to bluff Dirty Harry."

Emmy debated how much to tell her accomplice as they crunched along the roadside stones. It did not take her long to conclude that the biggest secret of her life was already on the table. "I've been doing that since I was fourteen. Had to … to survive."

"Doing what?" he asked, turning toward her with a hint of understanding in his eyes.

His expression encouraged her to open up more than she generally would. "Radiating competence," she replied. She was about to elaborate when he grabbed her arm and pulled her further back from the road with a shush.

They crouched behind a cluster of palms.

Ten seconds later a police car drove slowly by, lights off. Troy obviously had excellent hearing. Or, she reevaluated, perhaps his mentor had focused on skills very different from radiating competence.

"How far do you think we've come?" she asked, as they resumed their trek.

"The swimming pool's just over two kilometers to the southeast."

"Sounds far enough to me," she said, pointing ahead to a pink neon vacancy sign.

The Seagull's Nest was on the cheaper side of the road, away from the water. To her it looked perfect. Not too big. Not too small. Not too fastidious.

Troy scanned the area before returning his gaze to her. "Too risky. The police will be checking all the hotels. Besides, I only have eighty Cayman dollars. I'm not sure what Cayman dollars are worth, but judging by the prices posted at the Gas-N-Go next door it's less than an American dollar. We'll probably need all eighty for food and a change of clothes." He nodded, implying game, set, and match, and turned to continue their march.

"Hold on a minute," she said. "You've been calling the shots ever since you got behind the wheel and I relinquished the gun. I've been happy to go along this far because you seem to know what you're doing and I didn't have a better plan. But now I do have a better plan."

He stopped and turned, thrusting his dimpled chin forward like a lance. "What's your plan?"

She did not really have a plan yet, per se. But she had needs. "I don't care about food or clothes. I need someplace to gather my thoughts in peace. I need to get dry and I need to get some rest."

"If you don't change your clothes, you're going to be gathering your thoughts in prison and getting nothing but rest. Those pink shorts you're wearing mark you. Mark us. Don't worry though," he said, his expression softening. "I will find us someplace safe to get some sleep. You'll feel better once the sun comes up. Then—"

Troy stopped talking as a couple emerged through the motel's lobby door twenty yards ahead. They faded back into the palm copse and watched as the young woman made her way to one car and the older man unlocked another. The couple was obviously done, with each other —and with their room.

Now Emmy had a plan.

"I'm going to get us a room," she said, leaving no uncertainty in her voice. "Anonymously. And I won't need any of your money." Without waiting for his reaction, she turned her back and began unbuttoning her shirt.

Emmy knew she looked a mess. She was still completely drenched from the rain and their blood-cleansing dip. Her hair was flat and damp, and she bore not the slightest remnant of makeup. But she also knew that most men would not notice those finer details if something more alluring was on offer.

She took off her shirt and then her bra. She gave both a good wringing and then donned her shirt while holding her bra between her knees. She fastened only the middle button and then tied the shirttails so that they knotted just under her breasts, augmenting her cleavage while exposing her toned midriff. Her breasts were not huge, but they were large and pert enough to make a wet white shirt an irresistible attraction for most pre-geriatric men. Checking the results in the reflection of a parked car's window, she decided that if six years had indeed passed, they had not been overly cruel. She turned back around to test her hypothesis.

Troy did not disappoint her.

"Hold this," she said, handing him her wet bra. "I should only be a minute."

Emmy turned back around before Troy regained enough composure to comment, and headed for the lobby door. She used the interval to put herself in the proper mindset. She was cold, drenched, exhausted, and beyond confused, but she needed to appear sexy and carefree. That would hardly be a piece of cake, but Troy's flaring irises helped to boost her confidence. And, after all, she had been there before.

Emmy gave the outside of the motel the once over. If this were a corporate hotel or normal operating hours, she would have done some reconnaissance before plunging in. She would have tried to get a look at the key rack, or the logbook, or she would have walked the grounds to determine which of the two-story complex's forty or so rooms were occupied. But she was too tired for that, and frankly, she did not feel the need. It was approaching 03:00 on a tropical island: amateur hour.

She breezed into the lobby and made straight for the bell on the counter. After confirming the location of the key-drop slot, she adjusted her cleavage while the air-conditioning did its trick. Then she slapped her cheeks to add some color, read the name plaque on the wall, and gave the bell a jingle. Twenty seconds after her second ring, a sleepy-eyed forty-something male emerged from the room behind the counter. The instant she caught his eye Emmy knew that her assumptions were correct.

"May I help you, Miss?"

Emmy put her hands on her hips, arched her back and shook her head in self-reproach. "I'm so sorry to disturb you at this hour, Anton. Problem is, I've been such a fool. I just tossed my key in the drop slot but left my purse in the room. Would you mind fishing it out for me?"

"Ah ... sure. What was your room number?"

She had no idea what room the prostitute and her John had enjoyed, but she suspected that a military-minded man like Troy would want the high ground if there was a choice. "Oh, I don't remember. Twenty-something I think. It's on the key."

She stood on tiptoe and leaned over the counter toward him while inclining her head toward the drawer that caught the keys. Anton pretended to be considering her request as he soaked up an eyeful, but then pulled open the drawer without further comment. After a second glance at her soaked shirt and a quick appraisal of her pouty lips, he fished out the only key. "Twenty-seven?"

"That's it. Thank you, Anton. You're a doll."

Chapter 7

Into the Fire

FARKAS SKIDDED the black scooter to a stop on the gravel lot of Whitfield's Fish Market & Restaurant. He dismounted in the shadow of Whitfield's delivery truck and removed his helmet. The air had gone sweet again after the storm but the smell of yesterday's fish lingered here. It was unpleasant, but nonetheless reminded Farkas that he was hungry.

He unslung a long slim case from his shoulder and slid it atop the truck. He was about to follow it when his satellite phone began to buzz. He checked the luminescent dial of his watch. Three AM. Luther had waited two hours—double the time frame promised. Farkas had to answer. He activated the wireless unit in his ear. "Yeah."

"Are we happy ... yet?"

"Very happy."

"Tell me."

Farkas backed away from the truck for a slow three-sixty audiovisual scan before uttering another word. The wind brought him snippets of banter from a few distant beach bums, but no other signs of life. This section of the coast was delightfully deserted. "You will recall that the original plan was to have them caught covered in blood in the dead cop's car, with the murder weapon and corpse and gunshot residue on their hands?"

"But no alibi," Luther added.

"Right. A perfect frame but for the lack of witnesses and motive."

"Go on," Luther said.

"We now have a witness, an ideal witness—not to the murder itself, but close enough. They restrained another officer at gunpoint during their escape."

"Excellent. Did the security camera catch it on tape?"

"No. The cameras are on the outside of the garage, angled to capture faces as people enter and exit. But the officer they humiliated was a captain. Head of the second shift."

"Does he have them now?"

"Not yet. I'm about to see to that. Although from what I've been hearing between the lines on the police scanner, this has become a shoot first, ask questions later scenario. The captain's account of what he saw them doing to Detective Johnson really shook everyone up."

"How long until they're caught?"

"Fifteen minutes."

"No chance of their escaping—again?"

"Not a prayer."

"I want details," Luther said.

As a rule, Farkas never shared the details of his work with anyone, but the fresh taste of crow loosened his tongue. "I'll do you one better. You can listen in—quietly. It might do you some good to get a taste of life in the field."

"Listen in on what?"

"You'll see."

Farkas crossed the dark road to the pay phone in the Gas-N-Go parking lot. He practiced speaking with a raised voice and island twang before dropping in three coins. "Yes, hello officer, this is, well, I'm not sure I want to say. I've been listening to my police scanner—you see I have this condition that just doesn't let me sleep. My husband, he says that, well, it doesn't matter. I was calling to say that I just saw a couple whose description exactly matches the fugitives you described in connection with the 11-99. Clothes, color, height, everything. They just walked into the Seagull's Nest Motel on South Church Street. If you hurry, I'm sure you can catch them."

He cradled the receiver without waiting for the inevitable questions. Then he gave the receiver a superfluous wipe. No sense tempting fate.

"Nice," Luther said. "What now?"

Farkas had been so focused on his work that he had forgotten Luther was listening. "By my calculations, the first squad car will arrive within three minutes. I've got to hurry into position."

"Position for what?"

Farkas said, "Plan B," as he jogged back across the street to Whitfield's parking lot. He used his scooter as a step stool to climb atop the delivery truck without leaving a telltale print on the hood. Odds were, Mister Whitfield would drive his truck to the docks before dawn, taking the crime scene with him, but Farkas liked to be meticulous.

"I'll be using the new toy you bought me," Farkas clarified, pulling the silenced Heckler & Koch sniper rifle from its custom carrying case. Remaining prone on the roof, he twisted the stock into place, then attached the trigger unit and Hensoldt scope. He slapped in a five-round magazine, put a couple of beanbags under his forearms for support, and sighted in on the Seagull's Nest. The lobby's aluminum door handle looked close enough to touch. "If our friends outmaneuver the cops again—there's no way I can miss."

Chapter 8

Pride

CAPTAIN HONEY leaned over the pier's broken rail and watched the dark waves slap the barnacle-crusted supports. His flashlight revealed no sign of Evan's car, but he knew it was down there all the same. Honey reached again for the weapon that wasn't there and cursed. He crouched to diminish his profile, keyed his shoulder mike and spoke through gritted teeth. "Molly, this is Honey. I'm at the end of the harbor pier. Looks like our perps took Evan's car for a swim."

"You think they drowned?"

"I'm not that lucky."

"You want me to wake up Sherwood?"

"Oh yeah. Nobody's sleeping until that couple's in jail. Have Sherwood bring diving gear for me too. Tell him I want to be in the water in fifteen minutes." Honey would gladly get wet for the chance to recover his Colt before submitting his report.

"Will do," Molly said. "Does that mean we can release the suspect couple Huey brought in?"

"Hell no! Not till I've seen them. Give 'em coffee and tell them I'll be there as soon as circumstances—"

"Hold on," Molly interrupted. "I've got an emergency call coming in."

Honey stood and wiped the drizzle from his face with a soggy handkerchief. What a miserable night. His first week wearing captain's bars and he ends up with his pants around his ankles.

He looked back down at the water. In all likelihood, his former partner was down there sloshing around in the submerged trunk. A friend and family man with twenty years of service reduced to fish food. How fragile we are …

He shook his head. Esther was a widow now. Martha had nearly become one too; Honey wasn't kidding himself about that. That pixie of a woman had seemed eager for the trigger. If his bladder had not been empty, forensics would now be cataloging his puddle of piss. Retirement would have been his only escape from that humiliation.

"We got a break, Captain," Molly's voice came back on, all squeaky and excited. "A woman monitoring police channels just reported seeing a couple matching your description enter the Seagull's Nest Motel on South Church."

Honey's hopes surged for a second but then his brows narrowed. "That's awfully convenient," he said. "Let me guess; she called from a payphone and didn't tell you her name."

"Right on both accounts. What you want to do?"

Honey thought about it for a moment before answering. In all likelihood, it was a diversion. The woman who called was probably the perp herself. "Which payphone did she call from?"

"The one in front of Gas-n-Go, right next to the motel."

"Really? Well, all right! Tell Sherwood to dive without me. Have Leroy and Bobby join me at the motel. Tell them to come locked and loaded."

Chapter 9

Dive

TROY FELT the dynamic of their situation change as he swung the privacy lock into place behind the door to room twenty-seven. Until that moment, all his thoughts had been on escape and evasion. But now that he was no longer moving, he could feel his mind shifting gears. He was eager to begin unraveling the mysterious ball of twine that entangled him and his remarkable companion.

As he scanned the room hoping to find a coffee pot, an eruption of gushing water broke the silence. "I hope you don't mind if I go first?" Emmy said, her voice echoing off the bathroom tile. "I really need a hot soak."

"Don't you think we should discuss things first?" Troy asked—biting back an offer to join her in the tub.

"You already told me that you don't know anything."

"Yes, but—"

"I've got a six-year memory void," she pressed. "I don't know anything either—except that I'm in no condition to be playing Sherlock Holmes. I'm cold, tense, and scared. I doubt that there's anything you can say or do to alleviate the scared. A long hot bath, however, will do wonders for the cold and tense. So, I'm going to have a good soak, and then I'm going to get some sleep while my clothes dry."

Troy stared in disbelief while the mirror fogged, digesting this unexpected twist.

"Then in the morning," Emmy added, "when our minds are fresh, we'll sit down over breakfast and try to figure things out. How's that for a plan?"

Troy searched for the right words, but apparently his muse was still stuck in the trunk. In frustration he voiced the first coherent thought that popped into his head. "This isn't British colonial warfare we're waging. We can't just lay down our sabers and muskets to enjoy a refreshing cup of afternoon tea, confident that our enemies will be similarly distracted. Captain Honey, the man you brought to his knees with your gun, you can bet that he's not taking tea. Nor are his subordinates. Nor are the people who left us with the corpse in the car."

"Look," Emmy said, hands on the curve of her hips, chin jutting forth in a defiant stance that seemed strangely familiar. "Thanks to some bold moves on both our parts, we are finally out of immediate danger. It's three in the morning and nobody has a clue where we are—ourselves included. Now, I'm no doctor or expert on British colonial warfare, but it still seems pretty obvious to me that the smart move is to use this time to recoup and reconnoiter so that the next move we make is not straight into a waiting trap."

Although her words carried weight and her posture remained aggressive, whatever spark she had shown the night clerk had extinguished. She looked to Troy like a half-drowned kitten. The sight punctured his resolve and he nodded. "Go ahead."

She said "Thanks."

Troy found himself looking into the mirror on the back of the bathroom door. His thirty-eight-year-old hair wasn't sprinkled with grey yet, but crows had begun scratching around the corners of his eyes. The big change was on his forehead. Two v-shaped scars descended below the hairline over his right eye, one for a centimeter, the other for nearly two. Their color was still an angry red, meaning they weren't more than a year old. He probed them with his fingers. A few months, he guessed. Half a year. They ran for another couple of inches under his hairline. "One more reason not to go bald," he muttered. Since he did not know his parents, he didn't know what hairline to expect as he aged, but so far, so good.

Turning from the mirror, Troy looked around their sparse room. It appeared darker without Emmy's presence. There was no television to offer company or news. He put the heat on high and set the blower to full. Since he was too wound-up to begin recouping, he slipped behind the curtains for a little of that reconnoitering Emmy had vaunted. The window turned out to be a sliding glass door. It opened into the waist-high railing of a faux balcony.

The road they had trudged in on was to his left, and there was a Gas-N-Go to the right. He did not know what lay further down the dark street beyond, but he should. He needed a map—and he knew where to get one.

He said, "I'll be right back," to the bathroom door, getting only a relaxed "Mmmm," in response. He found the lobby dim and quiet but for the night clerk's snoring. He was halfway to the rack of advertising brochures when a kaleidoscope of red and white lights erupted on the wall before him.

The sight sent another traumatic jolt down his spine. He snapped reflexively into a defensive posture, but quickly recovered his poise. He crept forward and peeked out the lobby door just as two police cars slid to a stop on the motel's gravel lot.

Troy reacted so quickly that he probably made it back to the room before the cops had set their parking brakes. He ran straight to the bathroom and threw open the door. Emmy was still in the tub, with only her face and knees above the water. Her eyes had been closed but now they were open wide. "The police are here! We have to go—right now!"

He grabbed her sopping clothes off the floor and bundled them up in a towel as he spoke. She was still lying wide-eyed in the sudsy water when he finished so he reached in, not knowing what part of her he would get. "We'll jump out the sliding glass door. The main entrance is already covered. Get your shoes on—the rest can wait."

She scuttled into her Reeboks as he pulled her toward the sliding door. They slipped behind the curtains and he carefully slid open the door. There were three police cars outside the lobby now, a mere fifty feet away. The few palms and bushes that haphazardly marred the parking lot between them promised pitifully little cover, but the Jeep parked below their window offered some hope. "I'll lift you over the rail and lower you down," he whispered.

Before he could act on his words, she jumped up and over the top rail, using her left arm as a fulcrum. She ran her right hand along a supporting rail to control her fall and then dropped seamlessly from the bottom rung. As she hit the ground, a bullet punctured the stucco where her head had just been.

Troy knew that the cops had not fired. After two tours in a combat theater he had a sixth sense about such things. He also knew better than to waste a single second searching for the sniper. He just dove.

Chapter 10

Opportunity

FARKAS PEELED BACK his eyelids to see stars. Real stars. As his vision adjusted and his mind sought solid ground, a dark face moved into his line of sight, replacing Orion's belt with a knit cap and dreadlocks. "You okay, mon?"

The peculiar dialect snapped Farkas out of his daze. Where was he? The last thing he remembered was taking a shot at Emmy from atop a delivery truck. Had he been flashed? Had Luther finished with him and decided to cover his tracks? No, Farkas concluded. If that were the case, he would have no memory of Luther or mind-flashing or the woman. "What happened?" he asked.

"You passed out, mon."

"That much I understand. What I want to know is why."

"I dunno fa sure," the Rastafarian replied, his tone more amused than concerned. "I was walkin' along mindin' my own business when I saw you lyin' besides da truck. I didn't see no bottle or smell no booze, so I went to check your pulse and saw da medical alert bracelet. I fightin' da sweet-blood myself." The Rastafarian held up a wrist to reveal his own red aluminum band. "So I guessed yous ran outta juice. It happens on da islands when people get to drinkin'. I gave you a dose from one of da needles in your pocket."

"Which syringe did you use?" Farkas asked, his eyes flaring wide.

"Calm down, eh. I understand dese mattas. De vial in da silva pen had a Lilly label. De vial in da black one had no markins at all, just de unusual red color. Never seen dat before, and I seen a lot."

"What did you—"

"I gave you da silva. Like I said, mon, no worries." The Rastafarian handed him back his pouch. "Perhaps you'd like ta share da black?"

Farkas accepted the pouch. It was zipped up, but he could feel both injector pens through the leather. He had been a fool to let this happen. If "Rasta" had not wandered along and taken an interest, he might have slipped into a diabetic coma. It was an amateurish mistake, getting so caught up in the thrill of the chase that he forgot to take his meds. He looked up and met Rasta's eye. "Thank you, friend. But believe me, you don't want to be sharing the black."

Rasta held up his hands. "No worries."

Farkas got slowly to his feet, pretending to be short of balance so he could scan the area surreptitiously. First he checked to be sure that the two of them were alone, then he swept the ground for signs of his sniper rifle. That eighteen pounds of fine German craftsmanship was worth a cool twelve grand. And it was nowhere in sight. Either Rasta had stashed it, or it had slipped from his grasp before he toppled from the roof of the delivery truck.

He reached into his back pocket and withdrew his wallet. The fact that it was still thick more or less confirmed that his rifle had not been purloined. First things first, right? He pulled out five one-hundred dollar bills and handed them over to his new friend. "This has been embarrassing," he said. "I'd like to forget the whole evening ever happened—especially if anyone should come around asking questions."

Rasta enthusiastically nodded his complete agreement. "I hear ya, mon. Consider it forgotten."

Farkas would, but not because he trusted in solidarity among society's outer fringe. Rasta would undoubtedly spend the next twenty-four hours smoking, shooting, or snorting his new wealth. For short-term memory loss, that was just as effective as a NATO 7.62 mm round—or a shot of Luther's 456.

Rasta left quickly once the money was in his hand, no doubt worried that Farkas might realize that the bills were hundreds instead of tens. Fifteen minutes later, Farkas, Heckler & Koch checked into the Starlight Motel as Mr. and Mrs. Smith.

The room's phone caught his eye the moment he opened the door, and he felt a twinge in his stomach. He looked at his watch. Four AM. What the hell.

Farkas had never met Luther. He did not know what he looked like or where he lived. He assumed that Luther called the United States home since all of their business was there, but in the electronic age he could just as well live in Australia or Switzerland. In any case, Luther's secrecy gave Farkas the luxury of ignoring time zones when he called.

Luther picked up on the second ring. "Tell me what I want to hear."

"I can't do that yet. I ... had a problem."

"Spare me your excuses and cut to the chase. Where are they now?"

"I don't know."

"You don't know? Well, that's just great. That sounds like the same kind of carelessness that cost you your medical license. No wonder your people always lived under the heel of someone else's boot. Some folks just never learn."

Luther liked to hurl emotional barbs. Farkas was immune to them. He had seen too many bones broken with sticks and stones. "Relax, Luther," Farkas said, his voice as calm and icy as a frozen lake. "We have nothing to worry about. They have no resources, no clues, no idea what's going on. The only thing they do know is that they have to avoid the police. They are either going to get caught, or they are going to disappear and then do everything in their power never to be heard from again. Either way their investigation is kaput."

Luther chuffed. "Is that your stellar insight talking? The same prescient voice you've been listening to all night? Well, let me assure you that one can always find a third option if he gets creative enough. And since Troy and Emmy have shown themselves to be a cross between Sherlock Holmes and Leonardo DaVinci, here's what you're going to do. Are you listening?"

"I'm listening."

"Good. For the next two days, you are to keep your eyes glued to the entrance to Solomon's. The way I look at it, within forty-eight hours they're either going to get caught or they're going to flee Grand Cayman. There just aren't enough places on that tiny island for them to hide with the police believing that they've killed a fellow cop. So, if they don't show up at Solomon's by close of business Friday, then we'll assume they've fled. Until then, you're on lookout. Got it?"

"Got it. What then?"

"Then you're to get your ass on a plane to Las Vegas. Check into the Bellagio and wait for instructions."

"You got a new case?"

"I've got reason to believe one is coming."

"In Vegas?"

"In Vegas."

Farkas smelled an opportunity and seized it. "All right. But as long as we're painting by numbers now, why don't you tell me exactly what you want me to do if Troy and Emmy make a miraculous appearance?"

"We're done with half measures. You're to make use of your new twelve-thousand-dollar toy."

Bingo. "Fine. I'm willing to play it that way, if that's what you want. But given the potential need for clean up that might involve, you'll need to send me more 456."

There was a long pause on the phone before Luther said, "I'll send you the dose you'll need for the job in Vegas. That will give you two in hand. If you end up using both on Grand Cayman, I'll send another one to Vegas with the file."

Farkas knew that Luther hated to part with 456. His boss feared that he would set up his own business on the side. He was right to be paranoid, but wrong in his assumption. Farkas had grander plans.

Oddly enough, it was not the threat of competition itself that worried Luther. The market could absorb a thousand times what he supplied. He was just paranoid that word of his secret memory-erasing concoction would leak.

Farkas decided to play one fear against another. "That's not good enough, Luther. To guarantee that I can keep things totally quiet, I should have at least four doses at my disposal. Better six. We've never had to deal with a situation like this before. It's unpredictable. Without 456 it could get messy. Raise uncomfortable questions."

Luther forced another long pause. Farkas knew that he had him. "All right. I'll overnight you three more doses. But I expect regular updates. Every six hours. Agreed?"

"Agreed."

Chapter 11

Form

TROY AND EMMY did not speak during their desperate sprint from the Seagull's Nest. All oxygen went to fueling their legs, and fear froze their tongues.

After ten breathless minutes of putting turns and obstacles between themselves and their hunters, they emerged from a tropical forest onto a crumbling old access road behind a small strip mall. Troy slowed to a walk and Emmy bent over to gulp air with her hands on her knees. He was glad to find that he had maintained a marathoner's legs over the past seven years. Emmy, too, was in remarkable condition—not to mention spectacular form. "You're in better shape than most of the soldiers I know," he said. "I'm impressed. Really."

She shifted her gaze up from the ground to meet his. Her emerald eyes were skeptical but they brightened when she saw the sincerity on his face.

He smiled, adding, "You're much stronger than you look." He extended the bundled towel holding her clothes. "Slip between those dumpsters and get dressed," he said, gesturing. He pulled his olive safari shirt off over his head and held it out. "You can use this to wipe the muck off your legs."

"That's a nice gesture, Troy, but I can just use the towel." She waggled the bundle of clothes.

"Oh, right ... well ... I'll just climb up onto the mall roof then— make sure that they're not tracking us."

"Tell me one thing before you go," Emmy said. "How did you handle it—waking up locked in a cold dark box full of blood with a corpse? I thought I was going to lose my mind and all I had was a gun and a bit of blood on my clothes."

Troy cocked his head. "Tommy McGuffin locked me in the kitchen dumpster on the eve of my ninth birthday—the start of Labor Day weekend. I spent two dark days and three darker nights terrified that worms would wriggle into my ears or I would suffocate from the gas of rotting cabbages. Can't say that I considered what Guffy did a favor at the time, but ..." He shrugged. "Now clean yourself up. It may seem like we've been through a lot, but I suspect that our adventure has just begun."

When he dropped back to the ground a few minutes later, Emmy was dressed. "Coast's clear. We should get moving, but I'll need your watch first."

She handed her Tissot over with a query in her eyes.

"I assume we were simply followed to the motel by whoever actually killed Detective Sergeant Johnson, but we may have been tracked by electronic means." He threw her watch into the woods, followed by his own. "I also need your shoes."

Emmy's look turned to one of horror. She was no doubt imagining what their mad dash would have been like barefoot. "Don't worry," he said. "I didn't have the tools necessary to open the watches, but I can visually inspect the shoes. You'll get them back."

As he busied himself washing the muck off their shoes in a puddle, she said, "Who shot at us?"

"It wasn't the police. They use pistols and shotguns. That was a silenced rifle shot."

"You could tell?"

"I've been to war."

"Don't the police have snipers?"

"They do in big cities. I doubt they would have one here, not a pro anyway. Plus the cars I saw were obviously reacting to a tip. Whoever shot at us was already in position when they arrived—no doubt because he called them."

"So our troubles have doubled—and just when I thought they couldn't get any worse."

"In the short term, perhaps," Troy concurred. "But this is actually great news."

She looked up at him with shock in her eyes. "By what convoluted reasoning is having a sniper after us good news?"

"I'll tell you later," he said, finishing with her shoes. "You can put these back on."

"No concealed tracking systems, explosives or microphones?"

Sweet and saucy, Troy thought. "No, nothing but foam. We can keep moving. Now that we know they can't locate us electronically, our best move is to put quick distance between ourselves and the Seagull's Nest. We're ahead of them for now, but that advantage will evaporate if they bring in dogs." He looked up from tying his laces. "Island cops probably have helicopters at their disposal too—commandeered from all the sightseeing tours."

"So where do we go? How do we hide from helicopters and fool dogs?"

"We double back in the direction we came from and steal some boardwalk bicycles from a beachfront hotel. Then we cross to the other side of George Town and head for Seven Mile Beach while it's still dark."

"And then what?"

"Don't worry. I have a plan."

Chapter 12

The Postman Always Rings Twice

FARKAS STUDIED the whitewashed four-story residence with an assassin's eye. Deep shadowed balconies with walled sides faced the wide avenue from every apartment, and the northern exposure meant the sun was always to its back. The building was perfect.

So were the people.

Unlike the guarded luxury high-rises that fought the hotels and restaurants for space along Seven Mile or West Bay, or the cheap-but-cheerful inland complexes rented by the poor-but-proud working class and secured by Smith & Wesson, number twelve Elisabeth Avenue housed the locals who had managed to climb to the middle rungs of island society. They were the shop owners, junior bankers, and real estate agents whose toil created the backbone of the Cayman economy. For the next two days, one of their quiet, undefended, unsuspecting homes would host his surveillance operation—and maybe more.

After a final glance at his watch, Farkas drained his espresso and stood. He had waited until nine-thirty to make his move so that most of the residents would be gone for the day. This left him only thirty minutes to get into position before Solomon's opened, but he liked working under pressure.

He had narrowed the selection to three apartments on the second floor. Each boasted a balcony that suited his needs, offering both the concealment and the alternate egress without which he would not operate. The final choice would depend upon the occupants.

His earlobes and fingertips began to resonate with a familiar tingle as he crossed the palm-lined avenue. The moment had come to pick the winner.

He timed his approach up the cobbled walk to hold the front door open for a housewife exiting with her dog. He gave her a friendly nod as she passed, and then stepped into the empty foyer. Certain that there were no security cameras inside, he removed his sunglasses but not his Kangol cap. Along with the beard, it would remain in place until he left the island.

He put his duffel bag down on the clay-tiled floor and set to work on the locks of the mailboxes for units 2A, 2B, and 2C. They were typical five-pin cylinder locks. Each presented not more than a few seconds' challenge for the tension wrench and pick held in his smooth, practiced fingers. Having warmed up on the first two, he even got the third plug to turn with nothing but the initial rake of the tumblers. Oh, that the rest of the day would go so smoothly, he mused.

Thanks to what must be the world's most ambitious postman, Farkas found letters in each of the first two boxes along with advertising flyers. The third had already been cleared out. He picked the three most personalized letters from the first two, returned the rest, and closed the boxes.

So far, so good.

He took the stairs to the second floor and then spent a minute listening at the doors of all three apartments. He heard a child crying in 2B, the unit that had already collected its mail, and ruled it out. Either 2A or 2C would have to do.

His knock on 2A was answered in short order by a woman whom he took to be the maid. "Mrs. Rocha?" he inquired, not sure if he should be pronouncing it with an h or a k.

"No," she said without further explanation. "What do you want?"

Farkas spotted a yellow banana peel in the bag of trash beside the door and decided that this was not just a monthly maintenance cleaning. Someone would be coming home this evening. "This letter was placed in my box by mistake. I'm new to the building so I thought I would take the opportunity to meet my neighbors."

"Do you not think that tactic would work better in the evening, when people tend to be home?" she asked, accepting the envelope.

Farkas's desire to fade quickly from memory overruled the impulse to crush her larynx, so he simply said, "Yes, I suppose you're right. Sorry to disturb you."

He turned and headed up the stairs, making enough noise that she could not help but hear. He waited on the third floor landing for ten seconds after hearing her door close and then walked quietly back down to 2C.

"May I help you?" asked the withered woman who opened to his knock. Before he could respond, an equally gaunt gentleman joined her. Mr. Wooten was naturally much taller than his wife, but osteoporosis had bent his spine into a question mark, so he peered out through the crack at shoulder level.

"Good morning. You must be Mrs. Wooten. I'm Warren Christopher." Farkas repeated his previous spiel and then proffered the letters with an expectant smile. With his peripheral vision he spotted a little cart for wheeling groceries propped off to the side of the entrance hall—evidence that they got by without outside assistance. Excellent.

"You get Jamison's old place?" Mr. Wooten asked, his voice crackling but friendly.

"I believe so."

"He was a good man, Jamison. Why there was a time—"

"How about a cup of tea?" Mrs. Wooten interrupted, opening the door wide.

"Why, thank you. That would be lovely." Farkas lifted his duffel bag up from behind the doorframe and entered. "Is it just the two of you living here?" he asked, setting the bag down inside before turning to bolt the door.

"For forty-two years now," Mr. Wooten said, obviously pleased to have the opportunity to take the lead in the conversation while his wife studied the bulky bag.

Forty-two years, Farkas repeated to himself. The teakettle wasn't even on the stove, and he had already learned everything he needed to know. "I'm afraid I have some bad news for you …"

Chapter 13

Charles

FOUR HOURS AFTER their mad dash from the police and sniper at the Seagull's Nest, Troy and Emmy were looking at what he suspected was the finest hotel on Grand Cayman: The Imperial. A taxi had just disgorged an elderly couple dressed to the nines, indicating the arrival of the morning's first flight. As The Imperial's bellhop busied himself loading the extravagant vacationers' seven bags onto a trolley, the valet waited patiently by the curb, no doubt hoping that the next guests would arrive by rental car. Troy sympathized.

He rose from the park bench where they were seated, smoothed the front of his shirt, and said, "I trust you'll think of something clever if this goes wrong."

"Have I ever let you down?" Emmy asked, also rising.

"Not that I remember."

They both stood in silence for a moment, digesting the new meaning of that everyday remark. Then Troy rolled his thick shoulders, turned and made a beeline for The Imperial's valet as the bellboy followed his patrons inside.

Noting his purposeful approach, the valet came out from behind his gazebo. Troy realized his mistake a second too late. To the locals this was paradise, not a combat zone. He needed to act relaxed, to take the snap out of his stride. Of course, this time around the cat was already out of the bag. He had about a second and a half to find another way to keep the valet close enough to the wall that no one could spot them from the lobby. Recalling another trick from his youth, he held up his left hand in a vague gesture.

The bellboy paused, his face crinkled in confusion.

Once Troy had narrowed the gap to three steps he looked up at his hand, waving and flaring it like a magician making something disappear. As the valet followed the movement with his eyes, Troy closed the final step between them and put a crushing right uppercut under his jaw. The valet's head crashed back and his legs went limp. Troy caught Charles beneath the armpits as he fell and dragged him back behind the podium.

Troy quickly stripped off his own tired rags and donned the valet's pressed white clothes. He was halfway there. Now he just needed a rental car to arrive before the bellboy returned.

Looking across the street from behind the valet stand, he caught Emmy's eye. As she gave him the thumbs up from the park bench, his plan hit another snag. Two cars arrived at the same time.

Both guests drove rental Toyota Camries, one white, the other gold. Thinking fast, Troy went first to one passenger door and then to the other. White was in front, and it contained another elderly couple, well dressed and fit. Gold contained a couple much closer in age to himself and Emmy but with waistlines two to three times their girth. Troy then went around to the driver's side of each car. He smiled and handed each man a ticket stub while repeating the same phrase: "Welcome to The Imperial, Grand Cayman's finest resort. Please proceed to reception. I'll see to your car and have your bags in your room before you've stopped soaking in the view."

To Troy's relief, neither sleepy-eyed gentleman gave him a second glance. They just pressed ten-dollar bills into his hands and grabbed their wives by the arms. Since the security camera looked in on cars exiting the circular drive, Troy hopped into the gold car and backed out.

"Well done," Emmy said seconds later as they pulled out onto the A1. "Now what?"

Troy accelerated, eager as always to put distance between them and their last stop. "You tell me. Find us a map."

She did. "The island is shaped kind of like an elf's shoe. We're on the long curlicue toe now, also known as Seven Mile Beach. West Bay is north at the tip of the toe and George Town is south at the base. Savannah is on the ball of the foot and Bodden Town and Breakers are both on the arch off to the east. Looks like West Bay is the biggest town after George Town. And it's not far. Let's turn around and head there, get off the road." She tilted the map in his direction and pointed.

"No good," he said with barely a glance. "The toe is a dead end. Besides, we'll be okay for at least another fifteen minutes. Let's use them to buy fifteen miles. We'll go there." He pointed to Bodden Town. "Major roads to the east and west, minor ones to the north, and a port to the south."

"Okay. I'm guessing it will take us about thirty minutes. Perhaps while we drive you can finally tell me why you think it's great news that there's a sniper after us?"

Troy looked over at Emmy and studied her face for a minute before answering. The sun was up now and it added a sparkle to her pale skin, giving him the impression that it really was made of alabaster. She met his gaze with her sprightly green eyes. "Two reasons," he said. "First of all, it means that we didn't kill the cop."

"How so?" she asked with dubious intonation.

"Because it confirms that a third party is involved—a third party with a gun."

Emmy pressed the tips of all ten fingers together and stared into space through the tent they formed. After a minute she said, "You're making a lot of assumptions."

"That's unavoidable. But I'm also applying Occam's Razor, going with the simplest, most obvious explanation."

"That's why you were so quiet these past few hours," Emmy said. "You were working all this out."

"I gave it my best shot."

"How about cutting to the chase."

"All right. I think someone tried to kill us because their attempt to have us locked up failed."

Emmy processed his assertion for a moment and then asked, "Why not just shoot us in the first place? Why lock us up instead?"

"There are lots of potential reasons," he said, bouncing his head slowly from shoulder to shoulder as he recycled various scenarios through his mind. Picking a favorite, he asked, "Did you ever read the Count of Monte Cristo?"

"Of course."

"Do you remember why Edmond Dantes was imprisoned in Chateau d'If?"

Emmy thought about that for a minute. "You think someone wanted us locked up on an island to keep a secret?"

"I don't know, but that makes more sense to me than anything else I can come up with. Anyhow, this brings me to the second reason I said it was great news."

"And what's that?" she asked.

"Neither you nor I have any idea how we ended up in that car, or on Grand Cayman, or even what we have been doing for the past six or seven years of our lives. But we do know one thing for certain."

"What's that?"

"The sniper has those answers."

Comprehension dawned on Emmy's face like a mountain sunrise. "So how do we find him and get him to tell us without dying in the process?"

Troy shook his head. "I have no idea."

Her countenance darkened a shade. "Wonderful."

"But I do know where we should start ..."

"Where's that?" Emmy asked.

Troy pulled off the motorway onto a scenic overlook and motioned backwards with his head. "In the trunk."

Chapter 14

Kanasis

OLIVER HORTON waited patiently for the willowy six-foot blonde to situate herself, his newfound appreciation for the simple-things-in-life attitude keeping his hand off the horn. First she stretched and leaned over her teal convertible this way and that, adjusting what must be Versace's entire fall collection until the shiny black bags lined up just so in the back seat. Then she moved on to set up her diamond-collared poodle with his treats and sippy cup in the passenger seat. Ridiculous displays like Miss Trust Fund's used to drive Oliver nuts, but now that he was faced with two-to-twenty behind bars, he lapped them up.

Oliver pulled his rented Mercedes into the parking spot as BRIANA3 pulled out, and then looked up at his destination's unlikely façade. Wendell had warned him that Kanasis was different. Different in style. Different in technique. Different in results. But aside from implying that Kanasis would charge him a seven-figure fee, Wendell had been uncharacteristically nebulous when pressed for details about the lawyer's work. It was as though his old Harvard roommate was at once proud and frightened, like a kid who found a loaded gun.

Dewey, Cheetam & Howe was not plastered high in bold letters as Oliver had imagined while boarding the plane in Vegas. Nor was Kanasis grandiosely displayed like the trademark of a French designer who had found a way to sell thread for more than its weight in gold. This Rodeo Drive address simply had KANASIS chiseled vertically into the black granite pillars that framed the armored glass door. Tasteful. Permanent. Proud.

Unlike the windows of its neighboring boutiques, which leading designers had painstakingly arranged to draw gazes and pull people in, Kanasis had fronted his office with mirrored glass. Passersby could still see in if the lights were on and they focused their gaze, but most of those who strutted past in their thousand-dollar shoes were no doubt pleased to see only their reflections. Oliver cupped his hands around his eyes and peered in.

Plants and sculpture occupied the foreground, bestowing a sense of virginal serenity. Not a bad tactic, he mused, given what Kanasis was selling. Beyond the Garden of Eden, Oliver saw legs. Two. Long. The perfectly sculpted flesh drew his eyes like a candle in the dark. His throat went dry as he followed them all the way up into the skirt of a twenty-something angel. She was sitting before a computer monitor typing away, oblivious to his stare. Two more points for Kanasis, Oliver thought. Having seen the reception, he was most eager to step inside.

He pried his eyes from the glass and took a firm grip on the thick brass cylinder that served as a door handle. His pull yielded no reaction at first, but after a momentary delay the heavy glass plate swung outward as though it weighed but a pound, and he stepped into an entry hall walled in mirrored glass. As a building contractor, Oliver recognized the system as one jewelers often used to inspect and approve their clients. The short, mirrored hallway ended in a second door, identical to the first except that it was hinged on the left. Again, he grabbed the brass cylinder and again the door released after a momentary delay. Another electromagnetic lock.

As the second door swung shut behind him, Oliver turned toward the heavenly receptionist. She smiled pleasantly back at him. "Good afternoon, Mr. Horton. I'm Kimber. Are you here to see Mr. Kanasis?"

Oliver stood there like a deer caught in halogen headlights, partly because Kimber was probably the single most beautiful woman he had ever met in the flesh, but mainly because the goddess knew his name. Apparently, Wendell had warned Kanasis that he might be coming. Kanasis had then passed that information along to Kimber, who had gone online to pull his picture off the Internet so that she would be ready when and if he walked through the door. Now that was the kind of service you expected for seven figures, not to mention a mark of great efficiency. Oliver was already thrice impressed and he had barely stepped past the threshold. This was a promising start. "Ah, yes. Mr. Kanasis. Is he available?"

"Just a moment and I'll check. Feel free to have a seat or enjoy the art." She made a sweeping motion with her long thin arm, forcing Oliver to rip his gaze from the natural beauty to the manmade variety.

As he was trying to form an opinion as to whether the watercolor in the opposite alcove was an original Renoir or a print, he overheard Kimber say, "I have an Oliver Horton here to see you."

He turned back around to find that she was again smiling at him. "May I ask who sent you?"

"Well, nobody, really. I—"

Kimber began shaking her head before he could finish. "I'm sorry. What I meant to ask was who referred you?"

"Oh, ah, Wendell Branson. But Mr. Kanasis obviously knows that."

Kimber's lips curled up as though reacting to an inside joke, but she just said, "Wendell Branson" into her headset. Then she nodded in agreement, giving Oliver the feeling of exclusive acceptance. "You're in luck," she said, standing as she addressed him. "Please follow me."

Oliver followed, working hard to keep his tongue off the Persian carpets that covered the hardwood floor. Watching Kimber, he was finally beginning to understand why a lawyer would spring for a Rodeo

Drive address. Aware that he risked meeting Kanasis in a state of full salute, Oliver gave himself a mental cold shower by diverting his attention to the decor. They passed several more alcoves, each adorned with an Impressionist watercolor, and several stately office doors, each flanked by pedestals supporting arrangements of fresh flowers. At the end of the hall, Kimber stopped before an elevator. She pressed a big brass button and stepped aside as the door opened.

Oliver thanked Kimber—most sincerely—before stepping inside and pressing the button labeled "K." The only button. Nothing happened after the door closed, at least as far as Oliver could tell. Either it was one of those incredibly smooth elevators, or it was just sitting there. He looked down at his watch. Fifteen seconds, thirty, a minute. He pressed the button again. Nothing. Two minutes. Three. Paranoia began to take hold. He sniffed the air for gas or smoke but detected nothing. He wanted to pound on the door and shout for help but did not want to appear cowardly to Kimber, so he focused on his breathing. In ... out ... in ... out ... After four minutes he backed into a corner and grabbed the handrails lest the floor should drop out to reveal a shark tank below.

After four and a half minutes, the doors slid silently open to reveal a palatial office. Feeling somewhat foolish but decidedly relieved, he stepped immediately inside.

Kanasis's workspace covered the same footprint as the entire first floor. A big hyacinth macaw greeted him with, "Welcome" from a perch directly across the room beside a granite bar. A floor-to-ceiling slate waterfall gurgled along the wall to his left between two exotic palms. To his right was a fireplace flanked with a suite of black calfskin chairs. Beyond them, beside a window that looked out over some of the world's most expensive real estate, stood Mr. Kanasis's enormous oak desk. It was unoccupied. The only person in the room with Oliver and the bird was another impeccably dressed assistant who was busy working the espresso machine behind the bar. This assistant was a good decade older than Kimber, and, alas, torn from the pages of Gentlemen's Quarterly rather than Harper's Bazaar.

"Espresso, Mr. Horton?"

Oliver looked at his watch. Ten fifteen. Normally he refused caffeine after breakfast, but he had been feeling pretty self-indulgent since learning that he was headed for the slammer. "Please."

The assistant nodded appreciatively and began brewing. Oliver noted that he moved with the grace of Baryshnikov and considered the possibility that he had studied to become a dancer. You couldn't walk your poodle from the spa to the psychiatrist in Beverly Hills without tripping over a beautiful Hollywood wannabe and spilling your chai infusion all over your Manolos. Perhaps that was why everyone drove. This guy had a face too—California surfer meets Wall Street broker, with carefully disheveled sun-bleached hair, a permanent tan, hazel eyes, and a square jaw, all topping a lean athletic build that was tastefully wrapped in a tailored suit. Dark chocolate with a caramel shirt. No tie.

After grinding the beans, the assistant asked, "What brings you to Kanasis?"

Oliver would not normally deign to discuss such personal business with an underling, but there was an intensity in the assistant's stare and a confidence in his voice that Oliver found at once compelling and disarming. "Two counts of manslaughter."

The man nodded as though he heard this every day. "What are you looking at?"

"My attorney back in Las Vegas, Tiberius Fitch of Fitch & Mathers, tells me that the best deal he can negotiate is four years."

"Minimum sentences for involuntary manslaughter, consecutively served. That's a very good deal, Mr. Horton. But not good enough, I take it?"

Oliver felt his hopes begin to fade as he nodded. "Concurrent cuts it down to two. I could live with two. I was expressing that sentiment to an old friend the other night over a bottle at the Sportsman's Lounge. He grilled me on the details for twenty minutes and then suggested that I pay you a visit.

"I'm glad he did," the assistant said, handing Oliver his espresso with a twist.

Oliver accepted the cup and saucer with polite thanks. It was delicious and the head rush immediate. "Wendell told me that Mr. Kanasis is something of a miracle worker."

The GQ model nodded graciously. "I appreciate the endorsement. In fact, I only work with referrals. Makes things so much more efficient, more … civilized." He took a slow, deliberate sip of espresso. "As a matter of fact, if I agree to consult on a case, I guarantee my client's satisfaction with the outcome. Why don't you have a seat and we'll see if we have a good fit." He motioned toward the calfskin suite.

The speaker's use of the first person hit Oliver like a slap in the face. This was Mr. Kanasis? Was it possible that the young Adonis who just fixed his drink had once been voted the California Bar Association's Man of the Year? Oliver looked down at the espresso in his hand as he reddened. He wondered what the beverage was worth at Kanasis's hourly rate.

Kanasis stood quietly through Oliver's moment of revelation. Clearly this was not the first time someone had mistaken his identity. Once Oliver had regained his composure, Kanasis held out his hand and said, "Call me Luther."

Chapter 15

Luv

TROY DROVE the coastal highway between George Town and Savannah while Emmy rummaged through the burgundy suitcases in the back seat. "I should have taken the other car," he said. "The couple was old, but at least their clothes would be wearable."

"No, you got it right," Emmy said. "Fat people can diet, but old people can't get younger."

"What are you talking about?"

She turned to meet his eye. "I'm talking about IDs."

"Did you get a look at the couple driving this car? They were enormous. We can't use their identification."

"Sure we can, if they were foolish enough to leave any in their bags. People rarely study ID pictures as long as the skin color is right and there's no glaring discrepancy. Who wants the bother? Not me. Next please. Trust me; I know a thing or two about using fake IDs."

An approaching truck kept Troy's eyes on the road, and it was probably just as well. He did not have the energy to keep up a convincing poker face while pondering Emmy's latest revelation. Struggling to keep his tone neutral, he asked, "How is it you know these things?"

"I'm a grifter," she said, with the casual, almost breezy air of a waitress mentioning the soup of the day.

Troy could hardly believe his ears. This bright, beautiful, courageous woman was a self-proclaimed grifter. Perhaps he had his definitions confused. "Like someone who cheats at cards?" he asked.

"Like an entrepreneurial actress."

"An actress," Troy repeated. That was rich. "And what do entrepreneurial actresses know about fake IDs?"

"We tend to run in the same circles as entrepreneurial artists."

"Oh, I see," he said, not seeing at all. He reminded himself once again that she was the one who awoke holding the murder weapon. He also recalled that the sniper had aimed for her head, not his. Maybe he had been wrong about her. His mental acuity was hardly at its best.

His tone must have betrayed his feelings, because Emmy snapped, "Don't judge me. I've been on my own since I was fourteen, doing what I had to do to survive. Just like you did today." She sat back, folding her arms across her chest.

Troy hated it when people said things like: I did what I had to do. There were always options; choices to be made. She may have lost her home at fourteen, but she still enjoyed fourteen more years than he had … Troy stopped himself. Got down off his horse. He reminded himself that he had been headed for jail rather than college until one kind soul intervened. Sure, he could swap stories with Oliver Twist, and he had worked incredibly hard after getting his one break, but it was that one lucky break that made all the difference. He needed to give Emmy one now.

Troy's thoughts were interrupted by the sound of Emmy rummaging around in the suitcases again. As he dared a look in the rearview mirror, a navy Nike baseball hat flew from the back and landed on the gear shift. A pair of sunglasses followed, then dark socks and black tassel loafers. "Size ten," Emmy said. "I saw that you're ten and a half but those should fit in a pinch."

"Are we in a pinch?" Troy asked, trying to lighten the mood.

"I think this counts."

Emmy continued to pull useful objects from the suitcases like a magician producing fluffy creatures from a hat. She got a white sun visor and Nike tennis shoes and a wraparound bathing suit cover-up that could replace her distinguishing pink shorts.

She made the change behind him and then climbed back into the passenger seat holding a fanny pack. She unzipped it and cooed. "Traveler's checks. Looks like about five-thousand dollars worth."

"Do you know a thing or two about those as well?"

"I do."

Troy was glad it was traveler's checks and not cash. He was feeling bad enough about stealing the suitcases as it was.

"Well, look at this," Emmy said, her excitement in crescendo. "Passports." She opened one and then the other. "You're Jeffrey Gordon. I'm Elizabeth. We're British, luv." She held Mr. Gordon's passport open so he could see the picture. As he looked over to examine it he saw Emmy go pale. She whispered, "Oh my god."

"What is it?"

"The issue date on these passports is July 19, 2005."

There it was, Troy thought. Confirmation. "What's the date on the Cayman Islands stamp?"

Emmy leafed through the pages until she found the right one. "4 September 2008," she said softly. "The day after Evan's petrol purchase."

Troy remained silent while Emmy digested the news. He had more or less accepted the fact that he could not account for the last seven years, that those memories were at least temporarily inaccessible. He had seen and felt his healed abdominal scar. But Emmy had apparently still been harboring hopes of a conspiracy theory.

"There's no way these were forged to fool us," Emmy said. "I really am thirty-two."

Troy reached over instinctively and rested his hand on her firm thigh in an offer of support. "Beats thirty-eight," he said. "And with the three-year gap since the Gordons' pictures were taken, your weight loss story becomes plausible. We can claim that we came to the islands to celebrate losing a hundred pounds."

He felt something wet on his hand and realized that Emmy was crying. He gave her thigh a little squeeze and she placed her hand over his. They entered Bodden Town in silence.

Troy kept his eyes peeled for the right kind of hotel, but did not have any luck. Before he knew it, they were seeing signs for Breakers. He pulled the Camry into a Marriott and started snaking through the parking lot.

"We should pick a smaller hotel," Emmy said. "The management is more likely to be flexible, and there will be fewer people to see us."

"I agree. But I wanted to stop here first." He parked next to another gold Camry. After ensuring that nobody was looking or headed in their direction, he got out and tried his key on the other car's door. It did not work.

"Did you really think it would open?" Emmy asked.

"You would be surprised at how few variants there are within a brand —at least there used to be when I was a kid, and more entrepreneurial. Regardless, the main reason I stopped was to switch license plates. Once the cops find a gold Camry with the license plate they're looking for, they'll call off the search. We'll be safe driving until they figure out they've been hoodwinked."

"So, you weren't always a high and mighty physician?"

"No. My life was once headed down a very different path." As he spoke, Troy used the tip of the ignition key to unscrew the clean Camry's plate and replace it with their tainted one. The procedure was so quick that he decided to take an extra minute to swap plates again with a neighboring Jeep's, adding another layer of confusion. "We'll be off the island by the time they untangle this triple play."

"You seem very sure of yourself."

"You should talk, Miss On your knees!" Troy said, sliding back behind the driver's seat.

As he was pulling out of the Marriott, Troy stopped suddenly and put the car in park. "Hold on a minute," he told Emmy. He got out wearing Jeffrey Gordon's sunglasses and ball cap and approached the driver of a waiting cab. He handed him the two tens he'd earned as a valet and said, "Pop the trunk."

The driver did as asked and Troy transferred the Gordons' suitcases to the taxi. Before closing the trunk he went back to the driver. "You got a pen and paper?"

"Yeah, mon," the driver said, handing him a clear Bic and a Post-it from a local real estate company. Troy went back to the bags and scribbled a note, slipping it inside the carry-on before wiping it and all the bags off with a rag from the trunk. "Please deliver those three bags to The Imperial. Mr. Jeffrey Gordon is expecting them. He's a big tipper."

"Jeffrey Gordon, The Imperial. Okay, mon."

Troy patted the roof of the cab and the driver pulled away.

"That was risky," Emmy said as he slid back into the Camry. "But very nice. What was on the note?"

"I told them that we'd mail their passports back to the hotel before they had to leave. You did say that their return tickets are for the twenty-second, right?"

"Yeah, mon," Emmy said with an appraising look in her eye.

They stopped just outside Bodden Town at a beachfront hotel called the Pirate's Cove. Troy pulled in when he saw the sign advertising private bungalows. "What do you think, Mrs. Gordon?" he asked, affecting a perfect British accent.

"Looks good to me, luv," Emmy replied in kind.

Troy nodded his head toward the CayMart convenience store on the other side of the street. Its windows were flush with bright, hand-painted signs boasting American Cigarettes, Cold Beer, Calling Cards, and Checks Cashed. "What about signing the traveler's checks? Are entrepreneurial actresses good forgers as well?"

Emmy donned Elizabeth Gordon's sunglasses, then pulled a pen from the glove box. "Give me two minutes to practice, luv, and Elizabeth herself wouldn't notice the difference."

Chapter 16

Tricks

AS HE ACCEPTED Luther Kanasis's firm hand, Oliver was struck by the thought that the attorney had encouraged his misperception. Luther had played to Oliver's preconceptions in order to slip behind his defenses and have an unguarded look around. No doubt this tactic served Luther well as an attorney, but Oliver suspected that Luther did it more for the sport.

"Tell me about your case," Luther said, motioning to the suite of chairs.

"What did Wendell tell you?"

Luther cocked his head. "Wendell? Nothing. A few days ago he phoned to say that I might be getting a client from Vegas, but he didn't even mention your name much less the details of your case. In fact, I had to call him while you were in the elevator to ensure that it was you he was vouching for."

Oliver noted that Luther used the word vouch like a Sicilian. He found himself fearing that this suave man might have a very rough side. He would follow up with Wendell on that point. For the time being, however, he was captivated by Luther's promise of guaranteed satisfaction—not to mention intrigued by Kimber's clairvoyance. "But your receptionist, she knew my name?"

"Parlor tricks, Oliver. Simple parlor tricks. Please. Time is money and the clock is now running."

Oliver laid out the details of his case over the next forty-five minutes with little interruption, selling it as best he could. Luther listened intently, using hand gestures rather than speaking if Oliver rambled or wandered to points deemed irrelevant. It was as though the lawyer found the sound of his own voice disruptive. Once Oliver had aired his whole sad story, however, Luther stepped in to summarize. "Given the facts as you present them, the prosecution's case hinges on the testimony of the site foreman, Matthew Lopez?"

"That was Fitch's conclusion as well," Oliver concurred.

"There's no physical evidence? No security video? No tape recording?"

"None." Oliver shook his head vehemently.

"So at worst they've got you for criminal negligence—until Mr. Lopez ups it to manslaughter by testifying that you specifically ordered the use of struts known to be faulty in order to complete the job on time."

"Right."

"In order to earn your bonus."

Oliver felt himself reddening despite the fact that he was talking to a lawyer. "Right. Look, Lopez is just a glorified construction worker. I, on the other hand, was a major contributor to the governor's campaign, and am a friend of the mayor."

Luther let that appeal sail past without a glance. "And this happened in Clark County, Nevada?"

"Yes."

"And the judge assigned to the case is Owen Rodgers?"

"Yes."

"And the prosecutor is George Hue?"

"Yes."

"And assuming that you don't take a plea bargain, your trial is set to start three weeks from tomorrow?"

"Yes."

Luther paused to think, staring into his espresso cup. After a long moment of silence, Oliver could no longer hold back. "Can you do it, Luther? Can you help Fitch get me two years?"

Luther looked up, his hazel eyes afire. "No."

The finality of Luther's verdict hit Oliver like a slap in the face. He suddenly felt dizzy. He had let his hopes rise. Two years was manageable. He had come to accept that. But four years, more than a thousand days: that crossed a line. He would be a different man when he emerged. If he emerged. He would not fare well in prison as a rich white man whose greed for a bigger bonus killed two poor Hispanic kids.

"No," Luther continued, "two years would be virtually impossible to plea-bargain in this political environment. Fitch was right about that. In fact, the four he already negotiated is a hell of a deal—no doubt due largely to your contacts. But if you place your faith in me, if you turn down the prosecutor's offer and go to trial, I can get you off."

Chapter 17

Scars

THE CAYMART CLERK was a skinny white male with a greasy ponytail and teeth that would have embarrassed an old mule. Troy watched him ogle Emmy unabashedly as she approached the counter.

"Good morning," she said, seemingly unfazed by the stare. "I'd like to cash some traveler's checks, Earl."

Earl said, "We charge three percent," and kept right on staring.

Emmy produced a plastic envelope from Mrs. Gordon's fanny pack, counted out four hundred-dollar checks, and then added a fifth as if by afterthought. "Do you have a pen I could use?"

Earl grabbed one from the side of the register and asked, "Do you have ID?"

"Sure," Emmy said, accepting the pen before withdrawing Mrs. Gordon's passport from the fanny pack. She laid it off to the side of the counter and began signing checks. When she finished, she stacked them neatly and handed the pile to Earl with a smile.

Earl accepted the checks with his left hand and scooped up the passport with his right. He opened the passport to the picture page and ripped his eyes from Emmy long enough to study the photo.

Emmy said, "Gotta love that Atkins."

Earl did not comment. He just shifted his attention to the traveler's checks and sorted through to the fifth one Emmy had signed. After another tense moment he said, "To my eye, the signature looks perfect. To my nose ... not so much. And then there's the picture ..."

Emmy reached over the counter and took the passport and checks from Earl's hand. He did not resist. He just gave her a surprisingly penetrating stare and said, "I could ignore my nose and cash all the checks you want, but there would be an additional fee involved."

Emmy stared back at him, her expression noncommittal.

Earl answered without further provocation. "Fifty percent."

Five minutes later, Troy and Emmy left CayMart with six Snickers bars, twenty-five-hundred dollars in cash, and the agreement that Earl would not process the checks until his shift ended at three that afternoon.

"You should check in alone," Emmy said. "They'll be looking for couples, and single women raise more questions than single men."

Troy did, and shortly thereafter he was admiring their bungalow's king-size bed. "You want the left side or the right?" he asked, testing the springs.

"What are you doing?" Emmy asked. "We don't have time to sleep."

"I'm not going to be much good without it," he replied, aware of the reversal in their positions but too tired to care. "Just a thirty-minute catnap to recharge the processor."

Emmy did not yield, and before he knew it Troy was behind a table in a semicircular beachfront cafe called The Grotto. He was looking out at sugary sand and crystalline water while a waitress informed him that, "Stingrays be swimmin' there at the edge of the shelf where the water changes from turquoise to indigo. Morays and octopi too. What will you be having? I recommend the lobster omelet with brie and papaya salsa."

Troy looked over at Emmy who nodded. "We'll take two, along with the bakery basket, orange juice and coffee."

She poured the coffee into waiting white mugs and disappeared. As Troy stirred in cream, he tried to find the best kickoff question for their let's-get-acquainted conversation. He knew a lot about Emmy's character, but little about her biography. Her choice of profession left him halfway between concerned and enthralled, and he could not help wondering if her work had somehow caused their predicament. It was on that sensitive topic that he wanted to start, but Emmy beat him to the punch. "I lied to you earlier—in the garage."

Troy managed to swallow his sip of coffee without choking, but only just. "How so?"

"I ... I ... I really couldn't have changed the tire in five minutes. I've never changed a tire in my life."

Troy exhaled.

Emmy smiled. "Just wanted to jump-start your processor."

"You did that."

"Good. Tell me, what's the last thing you remember?"

Troy added another creamer to his coffee and took another sip. "Afghanistan. I'm—I was—a military surgeon who was stupid enough to volunteer for the Special Forces after my first tour with a forward surgical team. I was tired of seeing corpses that had bled to death on the battlefield. Figured I could save a lot more lives if I was at the scene."

"That sounds almost suicidal," Emmy said, her face a mixture of admiration and concern.

"I convinced myself that it wouldn't be that much more dangerous because the Green Berets are so highly trained. But as time went by and death and injury thinned the ranks, replacements came from deeper and deeper down the barrel. Many weren't what we call tab qualified. Weekend warriors who had been given the beret without all the training. One such reservist, an accountant from Paducah called to active duty, made an amateur mistake and triggered a booby trap. He literally and figuratively kicked a bucket—one that the Taliban had packed with silverware and explosives.

"The accountant and two other soldiers were instantly shredded. I got a fork in my belly, and four others were similarly lucky. The last scene I remember is looking down at the inch of protruding aluminum handle as it siphoned off my venous blood like a spigot." Troy held up his fork with a piece of lobster omelet speared on the end. "I'll never forget the joy of pulling that baby out and stuffing gauze in its place to staunch the bleeding. I remember giving myself a morphine shot and running to help Captain Chapman, but nothing more.

"I must have passed out.

"When I awoke locked in Evan's trunk, my assumption was that I had been captured by the Taliban. But when I found the healed scar after seeing the dates on Evan's documents and evidence that I was on Grand Cayman, I put the pieces together."

"Incredible. Did you get the scars on your forehead then too?"

"I don't know when I got those, but they're fresher than this." For some mysterious reason, he felt uneasy talking or even thinking about his forehead scars. He wanted to change the subject. "Tell me, what did you think had happened when you first woke up?"

"I thought I had been kidnapped by some South L.A. gang. Waking up in a strange dark car spattered in blood, with a gun in my lap and a jackhammer in my head, it was ... horrible. Let's talk about something else. Do they teach you about memory loss in medical school?"

Troy nodded appreciatively as he worked to swallow the remainder of his croissant. "We studied the brain and the functions assigned to each of its various lobes. After combat I'm also very familiar with the psychological manifestations of cranial trauma. What we have is called episodic amnesia. We don't remember certain experiences—in our cases those from the past six or seven years—but we do remember biographical data and skills, so our semantic and explicit memories are intact."

"Is there a cure?" she asked.

"I don't know for sure. Memory involves billions of neurons and trillions of neural connections. Much of their function remains a mystery—or at least it was seven years ago. Anyhow, if the neurons themselves are damaged, the memories are likely gone forever. If it's a matter of bad connections, like what Alzheimer's patients suffer, we can get those memories back if we heal those connections or establish new ones."

"Is there a pill for that?"

Troy shook his head. "Unfortunately, it's not that kind of headache."

"I take it we can assume that we don't have Alzheimer's, or some other naturally occurring condition?"

"No, we can't assume that. For all we know, we could both be patients of the same clinic. If I got Alzheimer's or some other similar disease at this age, I would seek out the best clinic on Earth. Perhaps we both did and that's how we came to be together on Grand Cayman—you from L.A., me from Afghanistan or wherever the army had me."

"Do you believe that?" Emmy asked.

"No. Clinics don't dump you in a car with a dead cop ... unless perhaps they've injured you in some failed secret experiment and want to cover it up."

"I could never have afforded a fancy island clinic," Emmy interrupted.

"Drug companies often pay for your treatment during clinical trials, but I agree that scenario is a long shot. Still, it can't hurt to check the phone book for clinics when we get back to our room."

Emmy shrugged. "So you favor the alternative—that someone intentionally did this to us?"

"I think that's the most logical conclusion given the violence that has followed us. But to anticipate your next question, No, I don't know how they did it."

Troy finished off his omelet while Emmy digested his words.

Emmy finally set down her own fork and said, "In the movies it's always either a whack on the head or brain surgery."

"Every whack on the head is different. That could account for one of us, but not both."

"Well, then it's obvious what we need to do next."

"What's that?" Troy asked.

Emmy tilted her head to the side and flashed him a breathtaking smile. "Check each other for scars."

Chapter 18

Cop Killers

HONEY DISMISSED the last of the eleven couples his colleagues had scooped off the streets with a shallow word of thanks for their cooperation. Eight hours into the chase and he had nothing. The murderers had vanished.

"You get the security photos yet?" he asked, coming up behind the staff secretary.

"Shouldn't you be sleepin', Captain?" Susanna replied, swiveling around in her chair and looking at him over the top of her glasses.

"I'll sleep when they're behind bars. Meanwhile, I'll thank you to answer my questions without editorial."

Susanna's cheery features dimmed. Honey knew he was being a grouch, but didn't care. He would apologize when the job was done. "Oscar just sent them," she said, pulling a grouping of four photos up on her computer screen and proceeding as though he could not see them for himself. "We got three-quarter and profile shots of both the man and woman as they pulled out of the garage, but the resolution is poor. The low lighting and rain-streaked car windows didn't help either."

"I know what the lighting was like. I was there."

"Yes, captain."

"Take this down," he said, stepping around to the front of her desk. "He's mid-thirties, height about a meter eighty-five, weight about eighty kilos. Blue eyes, dark hair cut like a politician's. He's got two v-shaped scars descending just below the hairline above his right eye, and a big old dimple on the middle of his chin like Kirk Douglas. Last seen wearing running shoes, khaki shorts and an olive shirt. All bloody. Got it?"

"Got it," she said, her French-manicured fingers still tapping keys.

"Good. Now the woman. She's about thirty. Tiny, say a meter and a half high, forty-five kilos. Got bright green eyes and thick dark shoulder-length hair. Last seen wearing tennis shoes, pink shorts, and a white button-down top—also blood-spattered. Both are to be considered armed and dangerous, even though I did recover the guns."

"Got it. What you want me to do with the descriptions?" Susanna asked.

"Paste them beneath the photos and make me wanted posters. I want every law enforcement and customs officer on the island to have a copy within the hour. Put COP KILLERS on the top in big bold letters."

"What about taxis? I can drop off stacks at the cab companies, and they can pass them out to the drivers when they come in."

Honey was impressed. He took his fidgety fingers from his Adam's apple and said, "Good idea. But add a bold note that no civilian should try to apprehend them. They should just call 911 as soon as possible. Do the same for the marinas. And don't forget the charter flights to the Sisters," he added, referring to Little Cayman and Cayman Brac. "For once it will work to our advantage to be an island. If we get a lock on transportation, it's just a matter of time till they're rotting away in my jail."

Chapter 19

SBT

"WHAT'S YOUR FIRST NAME?"

Troy opened his eyes and looked down at the lady shaking his leg. She had roused him from a deep dreamful state, and he found himself struggling to resurface. As she came into focus, he had the strongest feeling that she was the wrong woman. She should be taller and blonde, and her eyes turquoise blue instead of emerald green.

Then, quick as a blink, the disorientation evaporated. Everything came back to him—the trunk, the sniper, the loss of seven years—and Emmy. "We didn't find matching scars, did we?" he asked, referring to their inspection of each other's scalps. He reached up reflexively and ran his fingertips across his forehead. "We've still got no clue as to the cause of our collective amnesia."

"I did find another angry scar on your scalp," Emmy said. "But unlike the forehead scars, you knew where it came from. You told me it was from a bicycle chain, the remnant of one of your weekly rows with Tommy McGuffin. As for me, I don't have any scalp scars at all."

Troy nodded, remembering.

"Then I crashed," Emmy added, "while you, apparently, went shopping." She stood up, held out her arms and twirled, exhibiting the jade Pirate's Cove polo shirt and khaki shorts that he had purchased in the gift shop. "You did a good job guessing my sizes."

"I had a pretty good look at your body."

The expression on her face told him that a change of topic would be a good strategic move, so he rolled up into a sitting position and said, "What was it you asked me?"

"Your first name. I had assumed Troy was your first name, but I see now that it's your last."

Troy wondered how she could possibly see that. When he hesitated, she mistook the reason and added, "You know my sizes; surely I can know your name."

"Sebastian. My first name is Sebastian."

Emmy nodded. "Not the best name for a skinny kid with mismatched eyes growing up in an orphanage."

"How'd you know I was skinny?"

"Lucky guess," Emmy said with a wink.

"I forgot," Troy said. "That's what you do. But seriously, how did you know Troy was my last name?"

"Your tattoo."

"I don't have a—" Troy stopped himself. He pulled up the sleeves of his Pirate's Cove polo to check his shoulders. Nothing. He checked his calves and ankles. Again nada. Where else could it be? Had she checked his butt while he was sleeping?

Emmy headed off that embarrassing train of thought by saying, "It's on the bottom of your left foot. Pretty strange place for a monogram if you ask me."

He crossed his left leg over his right knee and took a look. There it was, plain as day. Two palm branches arced around the initials SBT. The tattoo was in an unusual place, Emmy had been right about that, but the location was not the strangest part.

"Do you remember getting it?" Emmy asked.

"This is odd."

"That's what I said. Plus you don't strike me as the tattoo type. An officer and a gentleman and all that. Tattoos speak volumes, so I pay a lot of attention to them. It's not just what a person chooses, but where he or she puts it, the color, size, quantity. They're—"

"No," Troy interrupted. "I mean—I don't have a middle name."

Emmy put her hands on her hips. "Come on, it's Bartholomew, isn't it? Sebastian Bartholomew Troy. You can tell me."

"Seriously. No middle name."

"Huh. So you don't remember getting it?" Emmy repeated.

Troy looked back down at his foot. "There's no way that I could. This is a henna tattoo. They don't last more than a month."

"You're up on your body art," Emmy said, more to herself than to him. "That's surprising." She snapped her fingers after a moment of thought. "Henna is all over the place in Asia and the Middle East, including, I presume, Afghanistan. Am I right, doctor?"

"You are."

They both stared at the tattoo in silence for a minute. Then Emmy said, "Perhaps the initials are your wife's?"

"I'm not—" Again Troy cut himself off. Seven lost years … Was there a Sara Beth Troy out there somewhere, worried sick?

Emmy reached out and took his left hand. She held it up. He was wearing a gold band. How had he failed to notice it earlier? "Oh my …"

"I know," Emmy said, holding up her own left hand. She was not wearing a ring, but looking closely Troy could see the pale indentation where one had recently resided.

They both sat in silence on the edge of the bed as the implications ran the first lap of what promised to be a long course. Had they been having an affair? Was the dead cop moonlighting as a detective sent by one of their spouses to get incriminating photographs? Were they married? Was it possible that he did not remember his own wife? What if he had kids? The questions were maddening. A man could go crazy just thinking about the possibilities.

He ran his fingers over the tattoo in an effort to refocus his thoughts and another possibility entered his mind. "Is Emerald Green your real name? Or is it a professional name?"

"A professional name?" Emmy asked, her tone bordering on belligerent.

"Yeah," he added quickly. "Like Norma Baker's Marilyn Monroe."

"Emerald Green is my legal name."

"Oh."

"But it wasn't always," she added with a grin that betrayed her false indignation. "For the first fourteen years of my life I was Carly Jo Andrews."

Troy had wanted to hear her say Samantha Brie Andrews or Sandy Brooke Andrews more than he was comfortable admitting even to himself. To cover his embarrassment he turned his attention back to the tattoo. "Forgetting the discrepancy with the initials for a minute, why in the world would I ..." His speech trailed off as he spoke, leaving his last words barely audible.

"What is it?"

After a moment of silence, Troy looked up at her, excited. "If you knew that someone was going to erase your memory, what would you do?"

"Run. Fight. Hide. Depends on the situation."

Troy shook his head and then reached out to take her hands in his. "I would try to send myself a message. Wouldn't you?"

Emmy's eyes grew wider. "Of course. Like in that Schwarzenegger movie Total Recall."

"Or Christopher Nolan's Memento. That's actually the last movie I remember seeing."

They both turned their gaze to Emmy's left foot. She kicked off her new sandal and crossed her leg. Another henna tattoo stared back at them from her sole, this one a series of twelve digits: 004995625425.

Chapter 20

Impressions

LUTHER LOOKED OVER at his new client, thrilled, but hiding it. Contrary to all appearances, he needed Oliver's money. Desperately. And the greedy contractor's case fit Luther's rules to a T. "Did Wendell mention my fee?"

Oliver still had the glow of a man delivered from the gallows, and he answered accordingly. "Yeah. He led me to expect to pay seven figures. You got it."

"Good. You do understand that the million is just my consultation fee? Fitch will still be your lead council. You will still pay for his services as before. Just tell him that Mr. Lopez's testimony will no longer be a problem—without reference to me."

"I understand."

"Did Wendell mention anything about how you were to pay me?"

"How? No. But cash is no problem."

Luther held up a hand. "The million is payable immediately to an offshore account, and is fully refundable if you do not hear the words, not guilty."

"Fair enough."

"In exchange, I expect, I demand absolute discretion. Is that understood? You are never to mention this payment nor our agreement to anyone. Not Wendell. Not Mr. Fitch. Not your wife. Not your accountant. Not your priest. No one. Ever. Is that clear?"

Oliver nodded.

"Say it, Oliver."

"It's clear. No one is to know of our arrangement. Ever. But how are you going to—"

"Don't ask."

"It's my money, I have the right—"

"And I have the right to refuse your case. You are only here as a favor to Wendell. It's not as if there's a shortage of wealthy individuals needing legal miracles." Just those whose case hinges on witness testimony, and who have no other legal issues or addictions, and who are appearing before a prosecutor and judge I haven't already cheated.

Oliver responded by sitting silently with his head bowed and his fingers tented.

Luther saw the move for the hollow threat it was. Oliver might be one of Las Vegas's top building contractors, but Luther could make him jump on one leg and cluck like a chicken if he chose to do so. He was the only man on the planet selling get-out-of-jail-free cards.

"Are you in, Oliver, or out?"

"I'm in. I'm in. Just tell me this much: it's the judge, isn't it? You've got a relationship with Rodgers; an understanding, don't you?"

"I've never met the man," Luther said with a shake of his head. "Never even heard of him."

"Come on ... then why did you ask?"

Luther decided to throw his new client a bone. "I asked because, like any good magician, I never perform my trick twice before the same audience. It is precisely because I don't know Rodgers that I accepted your case."

"So it's some kind of trick?"

"Ask again and you'll never see it."

"Okay, Luther, okay. I just want to be sure it's reliable. A million dollars isn't what it used to be, but it's still a lot of money."

"It's not money, Oliver ... It's four years."

The words had their intended effect, and Oliver sagged back into his chair, slack-faced and nodding.

Luther let the sentiment sink in for a moment and then stood to end their meeting. "When you have everything set up on your end, give me a call and I'll give you an account number with strict instructions. Be sure you follow them to the letter, and then forget them—forever."

"Agreed," Oliver said, holding out his hand.

As Luther took it, the macaw said, "It's a deal. It's a deal."

"What's with the bird?" Oliver asked.

"Jury's my secret weapon."

"Jerry?"

"Jury. If he likes my speech, I know the jury will. I practiced all my arguments before him back in the day." Luther pressed the elevator button.

"I just need to know one thing before I go," Oliver said. "How did Kimber know my name?"

Luther bit back his reflexive reproach, deciding that a show of ingenuity would serve him well at this point. "Now that we're in business together, I'll share that little secret with you, Oliver ... if you'll promise to take it to your grave."

Oliver nodded his solemn acceptance of the terms.

Luther held up his hand, fingers spread. "Fingerprints."

"Fingerprints? How did you ... oh, the door! It was the door handle, that brass cylinder, wasn't it?"

"Very good, Oliver. The electromagnetic lock won't release until the cylinder has captured your prints."

Oliver began nodding his appreciation but stopped suddenly. "Bullshit. That's not how you do it. I've never been printed for comparison. Ever. In fact, I've gone to great lengths to avoid it."

Luther shook his head as if to say "Tisk tisk." "Then you've wasted your time, my friend. Believe it or not, the government doesn't tell us everything. With the Patriot Act, they don't have to."

"You talking about some big secret program?"

Luther smiled.

The elevator door opened.

Oliver stepped inside but did not press the button. "How's it work?"

"Quite simply, actually. Ever buy anything with plastic?"

"Who hasn't?"

"Ever use one of those electronic signature pads, the kind with a thick tethered stylus?"

"Sure."

"Did you know that most of them are manufactured by a major defense corporation?"

Oliver raised a skeptical brow. "I don't generally pay attention to things like that."

"Of course you don't. Nobody does," Luther said. "But think about it. The stylus on those signature pads is wired to a computer that has just verified your identity by both your credit card swipe and your signature. It covertly uploads your prints direct from your hot little fingers into a database. Over time, Homeland Security builds a complete set from those partial reads."

"And you have access to it?"

"Everything is for sale, my friend."

"That why those government laptops occasionally disappear?"

Luther smiled. "You just need to know whom to ask. Speaking of which, you owe Wendell a show of thanks. I'd suggest a case of Chateau Margaux '96; clarets are his favorite. Then you can get back to planning the next four years of your life—after you've transferred my money."

Chapter 21

Interpretations

THEY BOTH STARED at Emmy's foot for a moment as though hoping it would speak. Finally, Emmy said, "Looks like an international phone number."

"Yes and no," Troy replied. "Yes, zero-zero is international from Europe and, I assume, from the Caymans. Also, forty-nine is Germany, a big country, and twelve digits makes sense too. But there are no parentheses or dashes. Why leave it ambiguous?"

Emmy shrugged.

Troy continued to think out loud. "I don't know either. Maybe it's nothing. But it seems to me that in a situation like ours, where people are after you and you fear that your memory is about to be erased, that you would tend to be as clear and succinct as possible. You would leave yourself whatever link you needed to reconnect with your life, to pick up wherever you were before your memory got erased. A phone number to a confidant would be perfect for that." Troy felt his excitement mounting. "The owner of that number probably knows what happened to you."

"To us," Emmy said. "I'm guessing that SBT is the owner. And he or she is just as likely to be your friend as mine. Do you think it's safe for us to use the hotel phone?"

It was Troy's turn to shrug. A pay phone or the lobby phone would probably be safer, but the only credit card he had was Detective Sergeant Johnson's and he was not about to touch that. He should have ditched it long ago, but was keeping it for an emergency. "Let's find out."

His hand shook as he reached for the receiver, scaring him more than the sniper shot. Surgeons needed steady hands. He handed the phone to Emmy rather than attempting to dial, and hoped that his infirmity had gone unnoticed.

Emmy dialed 9 for an outside line and then 004995625425. When it started to ring she pressed the speakerphone button. The line picked up and a message came on, first in German, which neither of them understood but both could gist, and then in English: "The number you have dialed is not in service. Please recheck the number and try again." She dialed again as Troy read the numbers off her foot. The same recording repeated.

Troy stood and began to pace the room, his right elbow resting in his left palm, his chin between his forefinger and thumb. Emmy remained on the edge of the bed. "There are two logical possibilities," he said, as much to himself as to her. "One, the number was disconnected after the tattoo, presumably by the same people who wiped our memories. Two, the tattoo is not a phone number."

"What else would it be?"

"I don't know. We've been assuming that the number leads us to SBT. But if you think about it, it's equally logical that SBT leads us to the number."

"Or perhaps SBT is some kind of decryption code for the number?" Emmy ventured.

"Perhaps. But that seems awfully complicated. Why would we do that to ourselves?"

"So nobody else could read it."

Troy shook his head. "We have to assume that anyone clever enough to induce amnesia is also capable of deciphering any code that we can crack. Unless of course you're some kind of mathematical whiz. You never did specify what kind of grifting you do. I gather from your previous reaction that it's not card counting?"

"I'm pretty good with numbers, but not that good. I make my living as a counselor."

"Counselor as in psychic?" Troy asked.

"I'm good at reading people," Emmy said, prevaricating.

"I see. Does that really pay the rent?"

"I get by. Most people will gladly pay to have someone tell them what they want to hear—so long as the source is credible. In your world, credibility comes with shoulder patches, medals and letters after a name. In mine, it comes with getting it right. I'm careful to word things ambiguously enough that I can always claim to be right."

"How do you do that?" Troy was asking partly out of genuine curiosity, and partly to give his subconscious a chance to work the tattoo problem.

Emmy looked up at him, indecision in her eyes.

Troy did not press. He just watched her make up her mind.

She made it up quickly. "I just provide the words. I let the client provide most of the meaning and all of the significance."

"Like a fortune cookie?"

Emmy nodded. "Or a horoscope."

"And there are enough fools with money for you to make a decent living doing that?"

"I don't consult fools, Troy. In fact, counterintuitive though it may seem to skeptics like you, the more logical a person is, the better."

"Come on ..."

"It's true. Logical thinkers are by definition those best at connecting dots. I throw out an array of suggestions, and my clients aptly connect them in the way most meaningful to them—ignoring the incongruities as we all do when hope is involved, I might add."

"But the smarter a person is, the harder he is to fool."

Emmy shook her head. "A person's desire to find meaning in his life is independent of his intelligence."

"I don't buy it."

Emmy grew a crafty smile and crossed her legs before her on the bed. "Come on then, sit. Take my hands." She offered her hands palms up. "Put your money where your mouth is."

Chapter 22

Ava

TROY WAS NOT INCLINED to take time out of the investigation to play psychic games, but on second thought he decided that perhaps a little meditation was just what the doctor ordered. Besides, this kind of trickery had always fascinated him.

"Don't you need tarot cards or tea leaves or a crystal ball?"

Emmy crinkled her nose. "Most people do feel more comfortable if there's some kind of mystical medium involved, enough so that I keep the full spectrum in my office."

"The full spectrum?"

"Everything you mentioned plus runes, incense, the Ouija board and many more in my parlor. I charge differently for each, but the content of the reading is the same as when I go it alone."

"Which is the most expensive?" Troy asked, his curiosity peaked.

"Whichever the client wants most, of course. Come on," she patted the bed. "Have a seat."

He climbed onto the bed and mimicked Emmy's meditation stance. She took his hands and stared into his eyes, her face expressionless, her gaze disarming. Troy focused on the rich green color of her irises. They looked like Monet lily pads sprinkled with little flecks of gold. After a moment she closed her eyelids and began to move her head in circles, whispering "relax" with each revolution. Troy found the atmosphere incongruously soothing and stimulating at the same time.

After a minute, once his shoulders had turned to putty, she stopped and opened her eyes. Staring through him she began to speak, her voice melodic and uplifting. "Some of your aspirations tend to be pretty unrealistic, Troy. It is good for you to have dreams, but you need to be realistic, too." She paused, and took her head through another revolution. "I can see that at times you are extroverted, affable, and sociable, while at other times you are introverted, wary and reserved. You have found it unwise to be too frank when revealing yourself to others, yet sometimes you battle with the temptation to do so."

Another silence found Troy feeling mesmerized as Emmy rubbed her thumbs around the palms of his hands. She continued. "You pride yourself on being an independent thinker and do not accept others' opinions without satisfactory proof. You prefer a certain amount of change and variety, and become dissatisfied when hemmed in by restrictions and limitations. At times you have serious doubts as to whether you have made the right decision or done the right thing, although it usually turns out that you have. While disciplined and controlled on the outside, you tend to be worrisome and insecure on the inside. You must overcome those feelings if you are to grow to your full potential, a potential that I sense is great indeed."

Emmy closed her eyes and withdrew her hands, breaking the spell. Then she rolled her head through two more revolutions and asked, "Well?"

"Well what?" Troy replied, his voice uncharacteristically weak. "We may not have known each other very long, but we have been through a lot together. Of course you know things about me. I know things about you too."

"But was I accurate?"

"I suppose. But not helpful."

"I was just getting started."

"So finish."

"Would you like to hear more?"

"Sure."

"Well, there you have it then: Another fool and his money parted."

"But only because you know me." And because it's so pleasant to hold your warm hands, look into your brilliant eyes and listen to your sweet voice. "I trust you don't run naked through the jungle with all your clients?"

Emmy raised her eyebrows. "No. But I do use those very same words to open with all of them."

Troy could not hide his surprise. "What! Every client?"

"Yep. From doctors to dishwashers. Actually, I would normally modify it a bit, throw in a dozen more stock phrases based upon the client's age, gender, appearance and anything else I happened to know about him or her. But I didn't want to do that with you. I wanted to give you a reading I could have given if you'd walked mute into my parlor while I was blindfolded—although even under those circumstances I still would have modified my reading based upon your footfalls, smell, the way you sat, the feel of your hands, and your physical reactions—twitches and breathing—during the reading."

"So what do you know about me that's not canned?"

"Would you like to know?"

The way she said it, with an intriguing, almost sinister lilt, turned his mouth dry with apprehensive anticipation. "Yes."

"That's how I make my living. I keep them coming back every week."

Troy held his arms wide and bowed his head. "I'm impressed."

"Thanks."

"So, are you going to tell me what you genuinely know about me?"

Emmy surprised him with a sober stare. "Why don't you let me ask you a question instead?"

"Okay," Troy said, feeling inexplicably nervous.

"Tell me about the man who helped you make it from an orphanage to med school."

"How … how did you—"

"Come now, Troy. Don't make me repeat myself. This is what I do."

"There's more to it than that," Troy insisted.

To his surprise, Emmy said, "You're right. There is. The only reason I'm in good physical and mental health is because I wandered under the wing of a wonderful woman. Most runaways aren't so lucky. Ava Zamora was the queen of the con in L.A. back in the nineties. She's the proverbial person who taught me everything I know."

Troy took a moment to absorb this and then said, "Judge Others. That's his name, really. The third time I passed through his juvenile court, Others saw past my record and rough edges to what lay underneath—an ability you obviously share. He studied my file, gave me the brainteaser questionnaire that I later learned Mensa uses for admission, and then decided I had potential if given a good environment. He put me to work in the courthouse instead of sending me off to juvie."

Emmy nodded. "Was medical school your choice, or his?"

"His. I wanted to be a lawyer like him—as you've obviously already guessed. He knew me better than I knew myself, however, and steered me toward a military medical scholarship. Thank goodness he did. Tell me more about Ava."

"You always change the topic if I scratch beneath the surface," Emmy noted. "But that's okay. As for Ava, telling you about her would take hours."

"Hours we don't have," Troy concurred, feeling strangely disappointed to be getting back to business.

"So what do we do next?" she asked.

And just like that Troy had it. The meditation had worked. Excited, he asked Emmy, "What's odd about the tattoos?"

"What isn't odd. The location for starters."

"No, that's explainable. We just didn't want anyone to spot them— lest they try to remove them with a cheese grater or blowtorch. The answer to the question is: palm fronds."

"Palm fronds."

"Why would I have asked the artist to draw them? If I had wanted to make SBT look like a monogram I would have written the initials in the shape of a diamond, or put the T in the middle and drawn it bigger."

"I give. Why?"

"Because SBT is not someone's initials."

"It isn't?"

"No, SBT is a logo."

"Of course!"

"And where do you find logos?"

Emmy looked over at the nightstand. "In the phone book."

Chapter 23

Guests

AFTER LOCKING the elevator to prevent any chance of interruption, Luther removed his suit coat and rolled back the double-buttoned cuff of his right shirtsleeve. He plunged his hand into the cascading waterfall and said, "open sesame." An excited Jury flew from his perch to a rocky outcrop atop the falls, alighting just as Luther's fingers found their mark. The water stopped and the slab of slate backing the waterfall slid aside, revealing the door to Luther's massive safe.

Jury made a wolf whistle.

The safe like the electromagnetic door locks had come with the office, which prior to housing Kanasis had been a jewelry store. The jeweler had the cast-iron monstrosity built into the concrete wall at the time of the building's construction. Since replacing it with a more modern equivalent would have been a major ordeal and drawn unwanted attention, Luther had opted for rock-solid high-tech camouflage instead.

His designer suggested the floor-to-ceiling waterfall, and it was perfect. Luther had soon grown accustomed to the soothing sound (and gotten over the incessant urge to pee) and he now had a duplicate in his study at home, sans safe.

He took satisfaction from dialing in the five-digit combination. Spinning the cold steel between his fingertips felt like foreplay, foreplay that climaxed with the release of the mammoth door.

Today, Luther scored the first time around. He plucked his reward from a velvet-lined shelf. His fingers felt electrified as he flipped through the thick linen pages of the titanium binder to the next available space. This ritual never lost its luster. Entry forty-seven was going to feel every bit as good as the first.

He took a vintage silver Montblanc from its rack on the shelf and filled in the anxious line: Oliver Horton/Matthew Lopez, $1,000,000, September 4, 2008. Luther recapped the pen and twiddled it between his fingers. "Someday, Jury, this journal is going to be in a museum. In the meantime, we're going to have an obscene amount of fun."

"Girls and cigars," Jury replied. "Girls and cigars."

Luther put the binder back on its shelf. He pulled his key ring from his pocket and used a cylindrical vending machine key to unlock the refrigerated safe within a safe. The stainless steel box he withdrew had originally held one hundred and forty-four vials, each cocooned within its own small foam and fiberboard container. Ninety-six remained. Ninety-six. He had shown exceptional self-control in the use of his magic potion. Until now.

Aside from the single backup dose Farkas always kept on hand, Luther had never supplied Formula 456 to his operative without designating the recipient. This first deviation did not constitute the breaking of one of his rules per se, but Luther knew he was crossing a line. Furthermore, as an attorney he knew all too well that crossing lines was what got people caught, or worse. He promised himself that this deviation would also be the last.

He withdrew three vials and applied a label to each, designating them as a popular brand of rapid-acting synthetic human insulin. The ruby-red color might once have raised uncomfortable questions, but marketing knew no bounds these days. He placed the three vials in a padded manila mailer along with a corresponding package insert. He would go home early today in order to hit FedEx by three. Farkas would have his ammunition in the morning.

Luther returned to his desk and tried to work on one of the legitimate cases that provided his cover, but between the new case and Farkas's predicament, he could not concentrate. As a result, the front gate to Luther's Bel Air estate yielded to his Porsche just sixty minutes after he closed his safe. He pulled his convertible onto the circular drive and parked before the main entrance. Looking to his left he saw his gardener's perfect ass peeking out from beneath her kelly-green shorts. It swayed alluringly back and forth as she scrubbed the bottom of his Spanish fountain. Coming home early definitely had its advantages, he thought.

"Good afternoon, Giselle," he said from his car.

Giselle kept scrubbing, her tight ass wriggling away as if guided by a conductor's baton. After another silent moment he noticed the white iPod clipped to the waistband of her shorts. She had not heard his approach. Given the good mood Oliver had put him in, Luther was tempted to take her where she knelt. She had been with him for three weeks now. His anticipation was nearing its peak …

He got out of the Porsche and slammed the door, ending all chance of surprise and forcing his return to discipline. He had waited this long, he could last until the weekend when he would have the time to seduce her properly. Giselle jumped up at the bang and whipped her head around, a startled look on her glistening face. Luther reached out and hit the pause button on her iPod. "Good afternoon."

"Luther. You're home early." They kissed cheeks. Her blouse was unbuttoned halfway to her navel, exposing some world-class cleavage. She seemed to understand the unwritten rules, and appeared most willing to play the game—this far, anyway.

"Yes, I had a good day. Don't let me interrupt you," he said, turning toward the house. "Just wanted to say Hi."

The cook had the afternoon off, so the kitchen was quiet. Luther grabbed a Corona from the special fridge that kept his booze just shy of frozen and headed up the winding staircase to his study. He had a stack of mail to manage, and he wanted to see how the market was doing.

He found the arched double doors to his study closed, making the doorway look like the entrance to a castle keep. That was most unusual and a little disturbing. He wondered if Brandy was snooping around. That was one drawback to his revolving-door system of domestic help; no matter how well the agency tried to screen, you were bound to get people unworthy of trust. He would talk to her and then check the security tapes later to see if they corroborated her story—more out of curiosity than anything else. Brandy's transgressions or lack thereof would make little difference at this point. He was tiring of her. She had been with him for nearly four months, and three was usually his limit.

He flung both doors open wide, eager to catch her in flagrante delicto, but the sight that met his eyes sent his Corona to the sandstone tiles instead.

Jimmy Scapone—"Orca" as he was called by all unfortunate enough to know him—was seated ten feet in front of him. Another man roughly the size and weight of a Frigidaire stood silent guard off to Orca's right by the waterfall. And then there was Brandy. Poor Brandy. Orca had repositioned Luther's favorite leather armchair directly beneath the large domed skylight, center stage so to speak. He was leaning back in it with his hands behind his head, and his legs splayed out in front. Brandy was between them, her head in his lap. She jumped and spun at the sound of the shattering bottle. Luther saw that her left eye was swollen and turning black. She had obviously been crying.

While Luther's mind was still processing the incredible scene, Orca reached out and swatted the back of Brandy's head, displeased by her cessation. As Brandy turned to resume her forced servitude, Luther caught a glimpse of her project and saw that the rumors were true; the nickname was more than the figment of a wishful imagination. Orca really was a whale, a killer whale.

Orca gave him a smug smile. "Luther. Good afternoon. I wasn't sure when you would be getting home. Do lawyers play golf on Thursdays, or is that just doctors?"

Luther could not conjure up a response fitting to the situation, so he just stood there staring at the vile scene and praying that the WWF poster boy to his left was only there to watch.

"Aw, doesn't matter," Orca continued, speaking as though they were long-lost friends chatting on a chance elevator ride. "Fortunately, Brandy was here to keep me entertained." He patted her on the head. "What does matter is that you're here now. We have to talk."

Chapter 24

Support

WHEN THEY FOUND the Cayman Islands yellow pages to be four hundred pages thick, Troy purloined an extra copy from an adjacent bungalow so they could go at it from both ends. They ordered a whole pot of room-service coffee, but Emmy struck gold before Troy drained his first cup. "Solomon Bank & Trust," she said. "I found it."

Troy left his phone book on the desk and walked over to the bed where Emmy lay prone, reading with her ankles crossed in the air behind her. Sure enough, there it was, SBT surrounded by palm fronds. "A bank," he said. "Of course. Did you ever read The Bourne Identity? The classic Ludlum thriller."

"Afraid I missed that one."

"It's one of my favorites. The hero wakes up having lost all his memory. He doesn't know his name or profession or anything. His only link to his past life is a piece of microfilm implanted under his skin with the name of a Swiss bank and a numbered account. Arriving at the bank, he finds that all he has to do to access his account is write out the number longhand for handwriting analysis. It was perfect, because like us he had no identification. This gains him access to a safety deposit box where he finds passports, disguises, millions in cash, and a gun."

"Do you really think that we're going to be so lucky?"

"Somehow I doubt it. But the point is, I would have recalled that story when trying to figure out how to communicate with myself in the future. I can't believe that I didn't think of it immediately—probably because I know my identity. Anyhow, I'm sure that's it. There's a safety deposit box waiting for us at Solomon Bank & Trust."

Emmy was nodding along as he spoke, but Troy could tell that she did not seem to share his level of enthusiasm. "What is it?" he asked.

"How did it go for Bourne at the bank?"

Troy reached up to loosen a collar that wasn't buttoned. "Actually, by accessing the account he alerted the people who were after him that he was still alive. They tried to kill him on the spot."

"And let me guess, there was a woman with him who all the while was telling him to run away."

"Marie. Yes. Sort of."

"So maybe that was the message, Troy. Maybe this was your way of telling yourself to run."

Troy shook his head. "Why not just tattoo RUN then?"

"On the bottom of your foot? Lots of ways to interpret that, don't you think? I had a client with ARMY tattooed on his shoulder. Every time I saw it I wanted to look for LEGY on his thigh."

"I've got to go with my instincts on this one, Emmy. And they're telling me that the answers to our questions are at SBT."

Emmy stood and squared off her slender five-foot-two frame against his solid six. "But it's not just your instincts that matter. We put the other half of the puzzle on my foot, so obviously I'm supposed to have equal input."

"Okay, you tell me then. What do we do if not the bank? Mug a Chinese couple, steal their passports and spend the rest of our lives hiding in a rice paddy?"

"At least that way we'll get the rest of our lives! We've lost enough already. I can't stand the thought of us losing anymore."

Emmy's use of us stilled Troy's tongue. Her Freudian slip had spotlighted the elephant in the corner.

Judging by the mollification of her expression, she realized it too.

After a moment of strained silence he reached out and clasped both her hands. "As tempted as I am to run off with you, I can't do it until I know that I wouldn't be leaving someone else behind. I'm sure you can't either."

Emmy met his stare for a minute, her eyes misting over. Although no words passed between them, he knew that they were thinking as one. The foundations had been ripped from their lives, replaced by corpses, snipers, and guns. The only support each now had was the other. What would they do if the secrets within Solomon Bank & Trust somehow stole that too?

But in their hearts they both knew that there was no escaping the bank.

Chapter 25

Leasing

MESMERIZED THOUGH HE WAS by the surreal scene transpiring in his study, Luther still found himself feeling for Brandy. This emotional flare-up surprised him—given his own situation and the fact that he planned to fire her soon anyway. It also bothered him. He had to walk a fine line when talking with the Mafia boss. He had to act tough and superior yet subservient. Compassion had no place on that overcrowded landscape. Looking Orca in the eye, he said, "Our business is man's business. Let's not mix it with pleasure."

Orca gave an appreciative shrug and said, "Brandy, darling, we're going to have to finish this later."

Brandy backed her head away, hesitant, fearing another swat. When none came she stood silently and bolted for the door.

Orca made no attempt to cover himself after she left. Zipping up would be dangerous if not impossible given his engorged condition. He just left his flag waving in the primitive display of manly superiority that Luther suspected was the true objective of Orca's assault.

As Brandy fled, Orca said, "I was just getting ready to explain your domestic situation to Zero, seeing as how we was getting to know Brandy and all. I was telling him that I thought you had discovered a trend for the twenty-first century. Much better that you're here to explain it to him yourself though, don't you think?"

Luther looked over at Orca's steroid-stuffed companion. "Zero?"

"It's from sub-zero," Orca said. "You know, the big freezers?"

"I get it," Luther said, guessing from the dull look on the bodyguard's face that the nickname was a double-entendre.

"So tell him," Orca pushed.

Luther was perversely proud of his unique domestic arrangement, but he did not like to discuss it. He did not like to discuss anything revealing with anyone. Unfortunately, a bottle of Courvoisier had loosened his tongue while he was trying to secure his loan from Orca, and the braggart in him had escaped. Since then he only drank alone. "Let's not go there today."

"He uses domestic help as rent-a-wives," Orca said, ignoring the plea. "He has this employment agency that works with a lot of Hollywood wannabes who can't pay their rent. The agency sends him hotties like Brandy on a regular basis. They clean the house during the day and polish his knob at night. Ain't that right, Luther?"

Luther just nodded and tried to look bored.

"Come on Luther, show some pride. It's a brilliant system. Tell Zero how you came up with it."

Luther turned to Zero, accepting that the fastest way to end the game was to play along. "I got the idea while leasing a car. I only lease cars—never buy—so I can trade them in for a new model as soon as I get bored with my ride. The salesman got a long call from Vin Diesel while I was in his office, so I picked up an exotic car catalog. Looking at the different models astride each vehicle, I found myself wishing that I could get the same deal on the girls that I could on the cars they were advertising. Before the salesman hung up, I decided that there was no reason I couldn't.

"I drove my new Ferrari straight to Fernando's, a talent agency representing wannabe models and actresses and made a deal with the man himself. It's actually a very symbiotic arrangement. The women on my domestic staff get to live in a mansion and make good money doing easy work. I get to cut it off quick and clean whenever I want, with no backtalk, guilt, or alimony. And I don't waste time in pickup bars."

Zero opened his mouth for the first time. "Why not just call hookers?"

Luther gave the enforcer a double take. Despite being crude, it was a reasonably intelligent question. "Two reasons. First of all because hookers are dirty, bitchy crooks and I don't want them in my house. Secondly because there's no challenge in it. No conquest. I like the hunt. These girls don't show up at my door with their legs spread. They come to cook or clean or tend the grounds. I have to seduce them."

Zero nodded like a big dog appreciating a good bone. "So how long you keep 'em?"

"Depends. Usually about three months: One to seduce them, one to try everything out, one to tire of them. I keep three girls, so that makes for a new one every month which is just about right."

Orca slapped his knee and Luther looked back to see that he had managed to zip up. "He got the idea from leasing cars. Cars, can you believe it? Too bad you're not Italian, Luther. With a business mind like that you could be working for me. But then, you are working for me, aren't you?" Orca asked, his tone suddenly serious.

"You are working, right?" he repeated. "I'm asking because you are two weeks behind on this month's payment. Now, in principle, I'm not opposed to late payments 'cause the vig keeps right on giving. But I do need to make sure that there is no fundamental problem." He turned his head toward Zero. "One percent a week don't sound like much when yous borrow it, but when the principal is twenty-five million, that's a mil a month in vig alone." He let his gaze drift back to Luther. "We don't have a problem, do we, Luther?"

"No, we don't have a problem," Luther said, kissing Oliver Horton's fee goodbye. "You'll have your money within forty-eight hours."

Chapter 26

Invisible

THE NEXT MORNING Troy and Emmy watched a big brown UPS truck rattle to a halt in the alley behind Cayman Computing. The game was afoot. They had not broached the subject of their relationship since putting their plan together the previous afternoon. The elephant was back in its corner, but still very much in the room. If all went well these next few minutes, the safety deposit box would be in their grasp, and the elephant would be free to retake center stage. Until then, however, their focus was all business.

As Troy's eyes locked on the driver, he felt the same adrenaline surge that had preceded every combat mission. A familiar sense of calm wrapped him like a shroud. Time slowed.

The UPS driver left the radio blaring the melodic opines of an island talk show host as he disappeared into the back. He emerged from the side doorway a few seconds later with two small boxes and an electronic clipboard. As he disappeared through Cayman Computing's delivery entrance, Troy and Emmy tossed down the cigarettes they had been pretending to smoke, walked casually over to the truck, and hid inside.

No sooner had they taken up their positions in back than the driver reappeared. He started the truck and drove forward about forty feet, stopping again behind the Pet Palace. This time when he entered the rear compartment in search of the appropriate packages, he found himself looking down the barrel of a gun. "Hello Marvin," Emmy said, her tone calm and serious. "I need you to take off your clothes."

Marvin held up his hands, his look as much amused as concerned. Despite the gun, Tinkerbell did not appear overly threatening.

Troy stepped forward and pulled him into the back of the truck. "No worries, friend. We just need to borrow your truck and uniform for a few minutes."

"Tampering with the mail is a federal offense, you—"

"We're not going to touch a single package," Emmy interrupted. "As my colleague said, we just need to borrow your uniform and truck. You behave yourself and you'll be back on your route within the hour. We'll even give you five hundred dollars American for your trouble."

Marvin shifted his gaze from the gun to Troy. "No shit, mon?"

"No shit, mon," Troy replied as Emmy placed the gun in the pocket of her windbreaker. It was just a plastic toy, so she did not want Marvin getting a good look.

Troy was into Marvin's clothes and behind the wheel in no time. He drove the truck on a circuitous route from the Pet Palace to SBT so that Marvin could not track their movements in his head. Without the knowledge of their destination, the only evidence Marvin would have was the green kind, and Troy felt safe in assuming that he would not want to present it.

Troy double-parked the truck directly in front of the bank's door. He looked back at Emmy who nodded but said nothing. He said, "Just borrowing this," to Marvin as he hoisted a random package onto his shoulder to hide one side of his face from passersby. Already spending the evidence in his mind, Marvin said, "Good luck, mon."

The interior of Solomon Bank & Trust was solid but stylish, a gentleman's bank. Only big money need apply. The designer had selected white marble floors and cream-colored walls with a few oil paintings depicting classic island scenes. Troy headed for a central stone pedestal supporting an enormous bouquet of fresh tropical flowers. He recognized the birds of paradise and lilies but the rest were just yellows, oranges and pinks to him. He stopped as if to admire the arrangement while surveying his options. Beyond the lobby, four teller windows split the room off to his right. Centered across from them a clerk's desk stood guard before two glass-walled offices. The focus of the back wall was a very solid-looking door, presumably leading to the vault and the safety deposit boxes.

The clerk, Thomas Delacroix according to the nameplate on his desk, was an impeccably dressed man with a thick mop of blond hair slicked back atop his head. Although Troy suspected that he was only in his late twenties, Thomas already wore the permanent obsequious pucker of a seasoned executive banker. The office immediately behind Thomas's desk belonged to a haughty-looking woman named Agnes Andrews. Agnes wore her black hair up, her reading glasses on a gold chain, and apparently went to great lengths to avoid sun exposure. The corner office housed a thin fortyish gentleman named Gunter Gustafson. Gunter wore what Troy guessed was the only bow tie on the island.

Troy decided to start with Thomas.

As Troy approached his desk, Thomas stood and held out his hands to accept the package. "I'm actually here for personal business," Troy said. "I'm on my lunch break."

"I see. Well then, it would be my pleasure to help you," Thomas said, a little too halfheartedly by Troy's reckoning.

"I need to access my numbered account."

"Very well," Thomas said, a bit more interested. He pulled a white index card from a drawer and slid it across the table. The card was blank except for the SBT logo in the corner and twelve short lines printed across the center in the same golden-brown ink.

Troy's hand trembled as he reached for the pen. That was twice now. The infirmity was beginning to give him serious concerns. He would have to give up surgery if the shaking became chronic. His immediate concern, however, was passing the handwriting test. Praying that it was nerves and not nerve damage, he dropped his arm below the table and shook it out before penning a longhand number in each of the twelve blanks.

Thomas accepted the card with a polite nod, fanned it twice as if to dry the ink, and slid it into a machine reminiscent of a bill changer. "This will only take a minute," he said, but began frowning at his computer screen a few seconds later.

Seeing Thomas's face contort, Troy knew that the smart move would be to run, but he held his ground, met Thomas's eye, and asked, "Problem?"

"Yes, ah no, ah sort of," Thomas replied. "This is a valid account number, but not for a numbered account. It's a traditional bank account."

"A traditional account?" Troy repeated. "Not a safety deposit box?"

"No," Thomas said, his voice growing thin. Dealing with deliverymen who could not keep track of their pennies was obviously beneath him —the mighty clerk of Solomon Bank & Trust. "It's just a checking account," he continued. "That does not mean that the contents are any less secure or your privacy any less sacrosanct, it just means that your name is associated with the account rather than your handwritten account number."

Troy was flabbergasted. Why would he choose to make his lifeline the number of a traditional checking account? He must have sat there with a dumbfounded look for a bit too long because Thomas finally asked, "Is there anything else I can do for you?"

Troy ignored him as the old saw about the best place to hide a grain of sand ran through his mind.

"Anything else?" Thomas repeated.

Finally Troy looked up. "I'm sorry. It's been a while since I accessed this account—obviously. There was a fire and I had to move and ..." He trailed off, shaking his head. "Would you kindly call up an account summary?"

Thomas made "But of course," sound amazingly like "Piss off," but his attitude changed visibly a second after hitting the enter key.

"I have your summary here, sir, and I would be most happy to print you out a copy for your perusal. Perhaps some espresso and scones? We do have private courtesy rooms that you would be more than welcome to use."

"Just the summary report would be fine," Troy said, biting back both his excitement and the urge to leap over the table to study Thomas's computer screen. "It's most kind of you to offer, but I'm on a schedule."

"Of course. Now, I'll just need to see your identification."

Chapter 27

Guess who's coming to dinner?

FARKAS FINISHED sanding his fingertips just as the UPS truck pulled away. He leaned back in the balcony chair, put his feet up on the rail, and began sharpening the edge of his right thumbnail, pleased to have an unobstructed view of the bank's entrance once again.

He checked his watch. Eleven o'clock. Twenty-five hours down, five to go. He did not actually expect Troy and Emmy to appear in his crosshairs. The odds against their clambering back on Luther's trail were a million to one, not to mention that only fools would stick around an island plastered with posters of their wanted faces. These two were not fools.

The tinkling of a bell drifted to his ears through the open doorway to his back. The sound put a deep double crease between his thick eyebrows. He did not have time for George and Ilene right now.

He checked the street as far as he could see in both directions, looking for anyone the height and color of Troy or Emmy. Seeing no contenders, he walked to the bathroom, pulled the wedge from beneath the door and flung it open. "I told you not to ring if it wasn't a dire emergency. You've got your tea, your biscuits, and your toilet. So what is it? Do I need to give you another shot of sedative? Or do you want me to tie you down to the posts of your bed?"

George stood shielding Ilene behind his stooped body. "Yes sir, sorry sir ..." His voice cracked and he had to pause. Ilene put her trembling veined hand on his bony shoulder.

Farkas felt like a heel for terrorizing them, but he had learned long ago that in this world, you had to do what you had to do to take care of yourself and your own. Damn the rest. Besides, any trauma the Wootens were experiencing would soon be forgotten. And, since he was such a nice guy, not much else. He had set his UV-C flasher to its lowest wavelength so the radiation would only effect memories formed within the last thirty days. Given the Wootens' lifestyles, they probably wouldn't even notice the loss. No harm, no foul. Right?

George got his voice back and said, "It's just that, well, my son is going to be coming for dinner at six. I thought I should warn you so there wouldn't be an overreaction."

Farkas narrowed his reptilian eyes. "Overreaction?"

"Yes, you see, Martin is the Deputy Chief of Police."

Chapter 28

Reversal

EMMY LOOKED OVER at Troy as they waited at a stop light. He continued staring straight ahead down Elisabeth Avenue, looking at nothing.

"Well?" she asked, eager to hear what he had learned in the bank.

"I'm completely confused," he blurted, turning to face her. "It's not a numbered account. It's a traditional checking account."

"What about the safety deposit box?"

"There isn't one."

"The light's green."

"What?" His mind was spinning in a rut. He couldn't get past the fact that there was no box.

"The traffic light is green. Drive."

"Oh." Troy pressed the accelerator and continued north along Seven Mile Beach toward West Bay. He did not know where to go next, but wanted to keep them on the move.

"How much is in the account?" Emmy asked.

"I don't know. You need identification to access a regular account. I don't even know what name is on the account. The only good news is that there's a lot of money in it. At least I assume there is. The snotty clerk perked up considerably when he saw the balance."

"You don't even know what name is on the account," Emmy repeated sotto voce. At the next stoplight she said, "Troy, remember when you caught our earlier mistake, when we had been assuming that the number would lead us to the initials, rather than the other way around?"

"I remember."

"Well, maybe we've got it backwards again. Maybe the important thing is not what's in the account, but who owns it."

Troy chewed on Emmy's idea for a moment, liked the taste, and started thinking out loud. "So why not just tattoo his name on your foot, or at least his initials? Why write his bank account number?"

"Isn't it obvious?" she asked, clearly enjoying her moment of power.

"Not to me."

"We didn't know his name, just his bank account number. We came to Grand Cayman to learn his name. That's when we popped up on his radar and he erased our minds."

We came to Grand Cayman, Troy repeated to himself. Obviously Emmy was continuing to assume that they had been together prior to the erasure. Deep inside he wanted to believe that she had placed the ring on his finger. His attraction to her—emotional, intellectual, and chemical—dwarfed any compulsion he could recall. His little voice, however, was expressing big doubts. Until he could figure out why, he knew the prudent move was to keep his feelings locked inside.

Troy forced his mind back to business. Emmy's analysis of the clues was nothing short of brilliant. "You're a genius," he said, and had the pleasure of watching her light up. "As long as you're on a roll," he added, "why don't you hypothesize on why we would have done that."

"Hypothesize, huh …"

As she teased him, Troy knew that he had walked right into her trap.

"My pleasure. It's the oldest trick in the detective's handbook. We were following the money."

"What money?" he asked.

"I don't know. Is there an amnesia business? In any case, I vote that we keep following it."

That had Troy's vote too, but he decided to push back for the sport. "I might buy your scenario, were it not for one thing."

"And what's that?"

"We're not detectives."

Emmy's eyes telegraphed checkmate. "Are you sure?"

Chapter 29

Vogue

TROY AND EMMY spent the rest of the morning formulating their plan of attack over a basket of conch fritters and a pot of strong coffee. Then they drove to the heart of George Town's shopping district where Emmy disappeared to do her thing while Troy hit an internet café for his. It took him about thirty minutes and ninety dollars in information brokerage fees to get what he needed.

After another errand, Troy returned to their designated meeting spot and sat on the edge of a fountain to wait for Emmy. He was restless by nature, but the setting invited him to a respite long overdue. He enjoyed deep leisurely breaths of the jasmine scented air and listened to the medley of bird calls and cascading water. As he watched a passing woman pry her stiletto heel from the cobbled walk, his mind returned to Emmy's *are you sure we're not detectives* comment. He noted how naturally they were working together to plot what amounted to a covert operation and felt a strong and sudden sense of déjà vu. He knew it was a nonsense feeling, the dividend of reading a thousand thrillers. He would never have given up his scalpel and stethoscope for a cloak and dagger—even for a woman as amazing as Emmy—unless …

Troy rose and began circling the surrounding plaza, massaging his right forearm and thinking the unthinkable. After an indeterminate number of laps he found himself standing before the window of an upscale children's clothing store. They had the cutest pink and white outfit in the window, with a pleated skirt and white ruffled blouse and tiny matching shoes all decorated with bows. For some inexplicable reason, the display buoyed him with enough warmth to lift him out of his funk.

No sooner had he sat back down on the fountain's edge than Emmy called his name. She gave a twirl as he looked up, shopping bags sailing out to her sides. Her stunning appearance all but sent him toppling backwards into the water. She wore a turquoise and teal suit the likes of which he had only seen on news coverage of fashion shows. The top exposed her entire beautiful back as it looped around her neck and down in what was little more than ribbons over bare breasts to cross again just above her belly button before fastening in back. The pants started well down her hips where they clung tightly all the way down to her knees before flaring out for the remainder of the journey to her ankles. Troy was vaguely aware that she was wearing matching strappy high heels, but his attention was riveted higher. She had obviously spent some time at the makeup counter and now appeared to have blossomed from the pages of Vogue. "Wow," was all he could manage to say.

"Did you get the video camera?" she asked, holding up a small matching handbag while ignoring his stupor. "I picked one that will make the hole difficult to detect. Built the whole outfit around it."

"Not that anyone will be looking," he said, adding "Wow," again for good measure.

"Thanks. I'm glad you like it, but please don't say that again. Tactics like this make me feel cheap. Since we don't have a lot of tools in our bag, I'm not going to be foolish enough to ignore those that will work based on principle, but I still don't enjoy it."

Troy felt the shame of a chided schoolboy sweep over him, but just for a second. "Sorry. And thank you. I do appreciate your ... flexibility."

"Let's go. The bank closes at four. You can tell me what you dug up on Gustafson while we drive."

Chapter 30

Visible

THEY PARKED on a side street two blocks from Solomon Bank & Trust. Emmy gave her platinum-blonde wig a final inspection in the mirror before getting out. Between the new hairdo and four-inch heels that propelled her up to average height, she would not be easy to recognize. She was hiding in plain sight.

She would have preferred Troy's approach, but that did not fit with her need to be distractingly sexy. He had purchased a sweat suit and padded it with towels and a pillow. Together with a baseball cap and sunglasses, that left his chin dimple as his only tell. She could have disguised that as well with stage makeup, but the bank's four o'clock closing precluded its procurement.

"Yas ready?" he asked, his intonation reminding her of a Bronx gangster.

Emmy crinkled her nose. "First Irish, then the Bronx. What's with the voices?"

"Been doin' 'em ever since I's a kid." He switched back to his normal voice. "I don't want Thomas to recognize my voice if he overhears me talking."

Emmy nodded her approval while digesting the voices news. "So you used humor to compensate for the Waardenburg syndrome?"

Troy stopped dead in his tracks. "How on earth—"

"I can see that you only wear one contact, and that it's tinted cobalt blue to make your right eye match your left. And when I examined your scalp I saw the roots of the shock of white hair starting to show beneath the dye job. The rest is simple deduction. Kids are cruel. You're obviously very bright and you found a way to compensate."

"No one outside of the medical profession had ever detected my condition before. I don't have the hearing loss that commonly accompanies Waardenburg. My ailments are purely cosmetic, and in this day and age, that means they're easy to assuage. At least for an adult. Everything is harder when you're a kid—and double that for orphans."

"I hope I didn't embarrass you," Emmy said. "It's just what I do. I'm always observing people, compiling and analyzing little bits of data and history like that for use in my work. I need to learn to keep my mouth shut."

"No worries. My skin is far from thin."

"Psychologists do the same thing, you know. I just look for ties to your social desires or career aspirations rather than your mother."

"That's good, because I like talking to you, but I don't have any ties to my mother." He gave her his high-voltage smile. She would have swooned were the effect not diminished by his silly outfit. "I'm going to run on ahead," he added when she did not topple. "Why don't you slow down so that we arrive a couple of minutes apart?"

"Probably safer that way," Emmy replied, pointing to her flamboyant heels.

As he took off, she corrected herself. She had it backwards. The safe move was probably running—in the opposite direction.

Chapter 31

A Bird in the Hand

FARKAS USED his rifle scope to confirm the sighting. His eyesight was tip-top, but he wanted to be absolutely sure before making the call. Satisfied, he used the speed dial without taking his eye off the mark.

"Talk to me," Luther said.

"I've just spotted Troy. He's added fifty pounds to his frame with pillows, is walking with an altered stride, and has his face and forehead hidden with sunglasses and a baseball cap, but it's him."

"You're sure?"

"I'm looking through a rifle scope at his Kirk-Douglas dimple right now. No way to mistake that chin. A feature like that would be tough to camouflage on short notice. Troy obviously decided to ignore it and hope for the best. I'm about to give him the worst—assuming that's still what you want?"

"Where are you?" Luther asked.

"On a private balcony across from Solomon's. He's entering the bank as we speak."

"I can't believe it! How did he do it? How did he find the bank again? Are you sure you wiped his memory?"

"I'm sure. I did them just like the others. After forty-six straight successes, I'm confident in both my skills and the technology."

"And you're sure they're working alone?"

"Well, they were working with Detective Johnson. But as you well know, I've already plugged that hole. I never observed them in extended conversation with anyone else, but even if there was someone, they can't possibly remember him now. They must have left themselves a trail of breadcrumbs—although I can't imagine how. I didn't leave them with so much as a scrap of paper." Farkas kept the Hensoldt scope sighted in on the bank entrance as he spoke.

"Bloody Hansel and Gretel," Luther said. "Wait a minute. You only mentioned Troy. What about Emmy? Is she there?"

"Shit," Farkas said, realizing the obvious. He couldn't risk taking out one without the other. "I'll have to follow him to her."

"Do that. Then do what you have to do to find out what trail they're following before you kill them. I don't want to give anyone else the chance of picking up where they left off."

Farkas was already disassembling his rifle as Luther spoke. When his boss finished, he said, "Agreed," followed a moment later by "Hold on."

"What now?" Luther asked, his irritation showing.

"I just spotted Emmy. She's approaching the bank from the opposite direction, and ... incredible."

"What?"

"I would have expected her to wear a dumpy disguise like Troy, maybe even try to sneak past me as a teenage boy. Instead she's dressed for a Milan runway, and let me tell you, the effect is enough to make the Pope himself go dry in the mouth."

Farkas began reversing the disassembly procedure.

"It's going to be a shame to spoil that with an ugly red spot. Do you want me to drop them as they exit, or do you still want to go for an interrogation?"

Luther remained silent for a moment of contemplation, then said, "Better a bird in the hand than two in the bush. Go ahead and take them out."

Chapter 32

Aura

GOOSE BUMPS TINGLED Emmy's arms as the air conditioning blasted her exposed flesh. It seemed that Solomon's management feared their money would melt if the mercury crested sixty degrees. Now, if she could just stop sweating on the inside.

She glanced off to her left where Troy was distracting Ms. Andrews with questions about mortgages. Then she shifted her focus to Gunter Gustafson's office. He was alone. Had he not been, Troy would have headed her off at the door and they would have tried again a few minutes later. She made a beeline for Gustafson's door but Thomas intercepted her halfway, standing behind his desk and offering assistance in a tone that sounded more imploring than obsequious.

"Thanks for the kind offer," she said, flashing her smile, "but I have an appointment with Gunter."

Thomas nodded and returned to his seat, but she could feel his eyes caressing her flesh all the way to Gustafson's door. She gave the glass a light knock and then walked in and closed it without waiting for an invitation. "Good afternoon, Mr. Gustafson. My name is Maya. Maya Lamb. I have some money to put away and was told that you are just the person to help me."

"Really, well ah, quite so, yes. Please, have a seat." His pupils were dilated, his face beginning to flush. Despite some superficial evidence to the contrary, Emmy knew then and there that Gunter was not gay. She could still have worked him if he was, but that would have required a bit more verve. She didn't mind expending verve, but preferred to save it for special occasions.

Emmy took the cushioned chair before Gunter's desk, crossed her legs with her purse in her lap, and gave him her warmest smile.

"Do you already have an account with us, Miss Lamb?"

"No, no. That's why I'm here. I need help in selecting the right kind of account."

"I can surely help you with that. Why don't you tell me exactly what you're looking for."

Emmy rambled on a bit about inheriting some money and wanting to see it put to good use while asking enough questions to ensure that Gunter did most of the talking. After four or five minutes of back and forth during which she frequently crossed and uncrossed her legs, Emmy leaned forward and put her purse on Gunter's desk. "Excuse me for saying so, Gunter, but I can't help but be distracted by the life force you're radiating right now."

"The life force?" he asked, glancing down to assure himself that his force had not sprung free of his pants.

"Yes. Yours is most powerful. It's as though you're a tiger trapped in a man's body." She glanced around the office. "But then I suppose you do spend most of your day in a glass cage."

Gunter had no idea how to react to this, of course, so he just stared at her. Emmy leaned still closer. "Would you mind if I read your aura?"

"Ah, well, I ..."

She pushed her purse further back on his desk, adjusting the angle as if to get it out of the way. Then she reached out and took his hands. "Oooh," she gasped, as though they conveyed an electric shock. "Very powerful indeed. Capricorn obviously. You are going to be easy to read."

Gunter just stared at her in lusty disbelief. Apparently this did not happen to him every day.

She looked into his eyes for a good sixty seconds before beginning, allowing her gaze to grow vacuous, possessed. "You are extroverted, affable, and sociable at times, I'm glad to see that. But on other occasions, far too often, you are introverted, wary, and reserved. You also have a great need for other people to like and admire you, but you keep it hidden away."

She massaged the palms of his hands with her thumbs as she spoke, without looking away from his eyes. "I sense a great deal of unused capacity, both personal and professional, which you have not yet turned to your advantage. Perhaps this is because of your tendency to be critical of yourself. Much too critical, Gunter. While you do have some weaknesses, as we all do, you are generally able to compensate for them if you try. But you don't try often enough because, although disciplined and self-controlled outside, you tend to be worrisome and insecure inside." She cocked her head to the side and narrowed her eyes a hair before continuing. "At times you have serious doubts as to whether you have made the right decision or done the right thing but you worry in vain. You need to trust your instincts more.

"It's clear to me that you would prefer more change and variety than you currently have in your life. Monotony is at the core of your dissatisfaction. Sometimes you feel hemmed in by restrictions and limitations. You pride yourself as an independent thinker, but don't get to exercise that talent nearly enough.

"I get a strong affinity for numbers from you. I've got that too. They rule my life. I'm seeing twos, threes and sevens."

She released his hands and shook her head, bringing her eyes back into focus. "I'm sorry if I bored you, but I thank you for the indulgence. When I see an aura like yours I just can't help myself."

"My pleasure. That was … remarkable. I, I don't know what to say. My sister didn't send you, did she?"

"Your sister? No. Nobody sent me. It's just a gift I've always had. A gift or a curse—depends on how you look at it."

"I see, well, ah, where were we?"

"Oh, I think your Priority A account sounds perfect."

"Excellent. It is our most popular account. I have one myself."

"Tell me something, Gunter. Would it be possible for me to pick my own account number?"

Emmy could sense a surge of reservation, so she added, "Please. It's important to me."

"Well, uh, I suppose it might be possible if it's the right format and the number is not already in use."

"What format do you need?"

"It will start with two zeros and a four. After that the next nine digits can vary."

"If I give them to you will you try to make it work."

"Okay."

Emmy brought her index and middle fingers up to her temples and closed her eyes. "Nine, another nine, five, six, two, five, three—no wait, four, two and five."

She opened her eyes and looked up expectantly as Gunter finished typing.

"I'm sorry," he said, studying the screen. "That number is not available."

"Are you sure? Can you read it back to me?"

Gunter recited the correct number.

"And there's no way to get me that number?"

"I'm afraid not."

"Is it new? Perhaps I could—"

"No, it's an old account. I'm sorry, really. We'll have to pick another."

Emmy stood and extended her hand across the table to shake his. He looked at her in disbelief as he stood to accept it. An encounter like this would be difficult for any normal person to comprehend and impossible to forget, much less a fastidious banker. "Is the exact number really that important?" he asked, no doubt reluctant to end what was likely the only enchanting customer experience of his career.

"It is," she said, giving his hand a final squeeze. She released his hand and picked up her purse, doing her best to give the camera a clear and close-up parting shot at Gunter's screen. "You take care of yourself, Gunter. And try letting that aura of yours get a bit more fresh air before you become dangerous."

Chapter 33

Mist

"THAT'S REALLY THE BEST we can offer," Agnes Andrews rebuffed. "Perhaps you should try the internet." She spoke the name as though it would poison her tongue.

Troy shrugged and nodded along. He had toyed with the haughty banker for fifteen minutes now—the amount of time Emmy predicted it would take her to manipulate Gustafson. Clearly, the moment to retreat had arrived. He stood, said, "T'anks for ya time," and left her fishbowl office without further comment.

Glancing over his shoulder, he thought Emmy appeared to be wrapping up. She had the camera-purse in perfect position and Gunter shaking his head at the computer screen. Troy whipped out his cell phone as he shuffled his padded sweat suit past Thomas. He continued to the far side of the exotic flower arrangement where he spun back toward Gunter's office, said "Yeah?" and pretended to listen.

Emmy was standing now. Gunter's prim face was contorted into an unnatural combination of distraught and perplexed. Troy was so entranced by watching Emmy's smooth moves that he failed to notice the man approaching from his left. "Hey buddy, you mind giving me a hand for a second. This frickin contraption takes two."

Troy turned to find himself confronted by that all-too-familiar uniform. The police officer was struggling to stuff a flyer into the thin crevice of an advertising display. "Bloody thing is too tight," the cop added.

Troy's eyes darted from the COP KILLERS headline to the grainy headshots beneath without revealing the emotions that erupted within. It was he and Emmy, right there in black and white. His split-second appraisal was that it would take a pro to identify them from just the shadowy security shots, but combined with description of his forehead scars and dimpled chin, it was a no brainer. The question was: had the cop bothered to read it?

Troy turned an appraising eye to his adversary. Officer Jacobs was a handsome man, a ladies' man, the kind of guy who spent a lot of time at the gym and never gave you a chance to forget it. Troy hoped he pressed iron to compensate for a lackluster mind rather than a puny penis—otherwise it all ended right here.

Maintaining the Bronx accent, he said "Hold on," into the phone, and then "Pardon" to Jacobs.

Jacobs pointed to the display. "Just hold this doohickey open so I can slide this wanted poster in on top. Capice?"

"Uh, yeah, sure officer," Troy replied, pushing past the surreal nature of the situation. "Anything I can do to help." He pressed the phone between his ear and shoulder, keeping his dimple covered and scars in the shadow of his baseball hat while he pried the display's plastic lips apart.

Jacobs slid the poster in and stepped back to admire his work. Troy caught him doing a double take just as Emmy came around the corner. Turning toward her, Jacobs' eyes bulged and then bulged again.

He drew his gun.

"You're the two in the poster," Jacobs said, backing toward the door and cutting off their only means of escape. "Get down on your knees. Holy shit! On your knees."

Troy knew that this was the time to do something miraculous like they always did in the movies, but he had seen too many real gunfights to be stupid enough to try. Instead he primed himself to pounce. Despite the fact that Jacobs was holding a gun and sported more muscle than most cows, he was now a bundle of rattled nerves and thus prone to mistakes. Captain Honey must have talked them up as super-villains in order to keep from looking like a putz. Or perhaps, Troy would later reflect, Jacobs somehow sensed what was coming—just not from where. As he shouted "Down!" for the fourth or fifth time his head vanished into a red mist, exploding off his shoulders like a watermelon at a target shoot.

Chapter 34

But for a Nail

FARKAS WATCHED the cop's head disintegrate through the magnified perspective of his sniper scope. He found it more odd than gory, a magician's now-you-see-it, now-you-don't—except for the telltale red mist. Farkas had been expecting the magic, so he had the rifle collapsed and back in its shoulder canister before Troy and Emmy had fully registered their gift from above.

Popping the cap on the end of the canister, Farkas felt his blood pumping with a hunter's fury. He could not kill them where they stood, but there was no way he was going to let his quarry escape again.

As he slung the case over his shoulder and leapt over the balcony rail toward the soft grass twelve-feet below, Farkas never once took his eye off the ball.

He was halfway to the ground when he realized his mistake. It felt like a hollow-point round tumbling through his gut. He had been so focused on dealing with the cop and his quarry, that he had forgotten to flash the Wootens.

It would have taken him less than ten seconds to reach the bathroom door, throw it open with a violent smack, and meet the wide-eyed stares with a programmed UV-C flash.

The crucial mistakes were always just a matter of seconds.

Even before his feet hit the ground he knew that there was no going back. He did not have a key to the Wootens' front door and Troy and Emmy would get away in the time it took him to pick his way in or climb back up. "Govno!"

"What?" Luther asked. "Did you miss? Kill the wrong guy?"

Farkas had also forgotten that his boss was on the phone. He pulled the black helmet over his head before answering into the wireless mike. "I don't miss. The cop's toast and they're going to get the blame. I just twisted my ankle jumping from the balcony," he lied.

He hopped on his scooter and brought it to life.

"Don't let them escape," Luther said, adding the obvious. The man was more nervous than he was.

"No worries. Between Troy's padded clothes and Emmy's high heels they're not setting any land speed records." Farkas watched them disappear around the corner before the first police car arrived.

"What's your plan?" Luther asked.

"I'll follow them to wherever they were hiding out, interrogate them, and then end this whole fiasco such that they get the blame for killing the cop."

"How you gonna do that?"

"Make sure their bodies are never found. I'm leaning toward concrete galoshes."

"I mean the cop part. Won't ballistics prove that it wasn't them?"

"What ballistics? I'm on a tropical island. They've got known cop killers and another dead cop. These bozos aren't going to look further than that."

"What about the bank's security video?"

"Icing on the cake. Solomon's has cameras over the front door and behind each teller, but nothing in the entryway. Troy and Emmy will be identified walking in and running out right after the shot."

"I hope you're right."

"Where did that come from?" Farkas said to himself.

"What are you talking about?"

"They're getting into a car. A gold Camry. I didn't know they had a car. I'm going to have to let you go—"

"No! Keep me on the line. Go ahead and focus on them, but keep me on the line. Update me when you can. I'll keep quiet."

Farkas did not reply.

Luther broke his promise almost immediately. "You still on that scooter?"

"Yeah ... Shit."

"What is it?"

"I think Emmy spotted me."

"You said scooters were invisible there. You said—"

"I know what I said, but they weren't looking for tails before, and even the best tailing tactic is going to be far from perfect when it's one on one. The pros use teams, but you won't let me use anyone else."

"Shit."

"Exactly." Farkas sped up as the Camry did the same. There was no sense trying to hide anymore. "I'm not going to get that chance to interrogate them. They won't stop moving until they've lost me. I've got to take them out on the road." He reached for the Glock 36 in his cargo pocket.

"No. That will draw attention, raise questions."

"Do you have a better idea?" Farkas asked, pleased by the opportunity to avoid Luther's Monday morning quarterbacking.

Luther's one word response came after a surprisingly short interval. "Yes."

"I'm all ears."

"Did they see you shoot the cop?"

"Of course not. Nobody did."

"So this is the first time they've spotted you?"

"Absolutely."

"Then don't shoot. Shout. Pretend to be their friend. They don't remember anyone they've met in the past six years. Troy doesn't even remember his wife and daughter. Pretend that you were helping them on the case. Get them someplace alone and give them a soft interrogation. Then make sure no one finds the bodies."

"Luther?"

"Yeah?"

"You're brilliant."

Chapter 35

Second Chance

HONEY AWOKE to the ringing of his mobile phone. "Yeah?"

"Captain, it's Molly. They did it again. The couple. They killed Jacobs. Shot him in broad daylight."

Honey bolted upright on the couch, knocking a bag of chips to the floor. They were still on the island! "When? Where?"

"Just a few minutes ago, at Solomon Bank & Trust on Elizabeth."

"Are they still at the bank?"

"No. They got away."

Honey felt his adrenaline stutter. "In Jacobs' cruiser?"

"No. It's still at the scene."

"Damn."

"As far as we know," Molly continued, "nobody saw where they went. Information is still coming in. I knew you'd want me to call you right away."

"You did good." Honey looked at his watch. Four-fifteen on a Friday afternoon. His mind was churning like an outboard prop. "Okay, here's what we're going to do," Honey said, pressing the phone to his ear with his shoulder as he buckled his utility belt. "Contact the police stations on all the surrounding islands. Let them know that the blue brotherhood needs their help catching a couple of cop killers. Ask them to volunteer their weekend to the cause. We'll fly in everyone who can come tonight on the Coast Guard plane and bunk them at the Ivory Inn—old Morris owes me a favor."

"Okay," Molly said, drawing the word out. "Then what?"

"At dawn we'll launch the biggest manhunt in island history."

Chapter 36

Momentum

"CAN'T YOU GO ANY FASTER?" Emmy shouted. "He's still behind us."

"Faster isn't going to help. On these roads he'll still be able to keep up and we'll just run the risk of attracting cops. We need to go smarter."

"Smarter? What does smarter mean?"

"Getting him caught at a light. Finding a narrow alley where I can jam the car into reverse and back over him. Luring him close and then braking hard so he crashes into us and goes flying. I'm not sure what opportunity will present itself, but I figure that it's kind of like obscenity; I'll know it when I see it. Speaking of which, I don't suppose you recognize him?"

"He's a hundred feet away and wearing a black helmet with a tinted face shield."

"Kind of distinctive, don't you think?"

"You know what I mean."

"I do. I just thought that with your talent for reading people, you might recognize him by some other means."

Emmy was struck by Troy's insight. She made a point of learning to recognize her regular clients by the sound of their footfalls and the smell of their toiletries. It was always impressive to greet a client by name when he approached from behind. But all she had to go on now was the visual input of a man dressed in black on a scooter. "I don't recognize him."

"That's all right. I just recognized smarter. Hold on."

Emmy turned back to face forward just as Troy jerked the wheel hard to the right. The Camry jumped the curb onto a wide staircase whose yard-long steps connected the sidewalk along an upper business road with the lower beachfront one. He punched the gas and the horn simultaneously, evoking stares and screams from all around. "What are you doing?"

"Being smarter. The scooter may be as quick as the Camry, but it has much smaller tires and only minimal ground clearance. He won't be able to climb the stairs."

"Will we?"

"God, I hope so."

Emmy planted her feet flat against the floorboard and clenched her seat in a death grip. It was a good thing she did. The impact of the first stair would have given her whiplash otherwise. A series of bone-jarring jolts followed as the car bucked from stair to stair like a playground pony. By the time they neared the top their momentum was spent. She thought the car was going to stall out and reverse directions—crushing their pursuer with any luck—but then the rear tires caught and they bounced over the top.

She immediately turned back to see how the scooter was fairing but their trunk blocked her field of vision.

Troy got the car back onto a proper road without killing anybody and before she knew it the staircase and the scooter were both far behind. The whole maneuver had taken less than ten seconds, but fear had made them feel like an hour.

"Well done," she said, her dry mouth capable of only a whisper. "What now?"

"Finally—an easy question," Troy said, sounding considerably more chipper than she felt. "Now we find someplace out of sight to park. We need to have a look at your videotape. We need to find out if that close call was worth it."

The quiet place they selected some thirty minutes and fifteen miles later was the parking lot of Reefer's Dive Shop. Reefer's boat was out for a sunset dive so the place was deserted. An easel on the counter predicted calm waters for the eight AM boat dive to Ten Sails—no reservation required. There was a kid running about, but he was too busy washing out gear and filling up tanks to pay them any heed.

Troy busied himself swapping license plates again while Emmy used the zoom feature on the video recorder's built in three-inch LCD display to transcribe the information on account 004995625425 onto the margin of their map. The angle was a bit too sharp to make reading Gunter's computer screen a piece of cake, but working letter by letter while using the appearance of known words like *account* for reference, she had it pieced together by the time Troy plopped back into the driver's seat, his mission accomplished.

"Are we happy?" he asked, handing her a vending machine Snickers bar.

"We got what we came for. How happy that makes us remains to be seen."

"Do tell."

"It appears to be a personal account, with one Kostas Kanasis as the sole owner. I'm not sure if that's a man or a woman."

"It's a man," Troy said. "A Greek man. I don't suppose you got a meaningful address? Just a PO box in Delaware or Mykonos, right?"

Emmy smiled and it felt good to use those muscles for a change. She pointed to the coastal region of West Bay. "Actually, Kostas lives right here on Grand Cayman."

Chapter 37

Anticipation

"I SHOULD HAVE SHOT THE DAMN TIRES," Farkas cursed to himself. "Instead of struggling to ride, push, carry and toss a two hundred and fifty pound scooter up a staircase, I should have just whipped out the Glock and shot the damn Camry's rear tires. Then I could have walked up, put a bullet in each of their brains, and ridden straight to the airport never to return. Witnesses be damned."

He looked down at the satellite phone in his left hand and then over at the bottle of Tortuga rum in his right. He weighed the two like competing melons at a farmer's market. Then he thought about his sisters and remembered why he was working for Luther in the first place. "Perhaps later, my friend," he told Tortuga, and then turned on the phone.

Farkas expected Luther to start out cursing him for ending their call in the middle of the action. Instead, he simply said, "Tell me."

"I lost them. I fucking lost them. That bastard drove his Camry up a staircase. Up a staircase. The scooter wouldn't follow. I blew it. We're screwed."

"Do you know if they got any information at the bank?" Luther asked, the calmness of his voice surprising Farkas.

"I don't know anything, but I bet they did."

"Why so certain? The Caymanians are like the Swiss, secretive as pedophiles."

"You should have seen Emmy. Dressed the way she was, given her charms and talents, she could have gotten Cheney to confess why he really invaded Iraq. Anyway, do you want me on the next plane to Vegas?"

"No. Obviously we still have business to deal with there."

"Look, I know that my judgment has fallen far short of flawless lately, but we can consider our business here done. Troy and Emmy are far from fools. They've seen the wanted posters and are feeling serious heat. With a second cop killing now attributed to them, they know they'll get burned if they stick around. Either they already got what they came for or they never will. In either case, they'll run now."

"Where do you think they will run?"

"I haven't a clue."

"Well, fortunately I do."

"I can—" Farkas interrupted himself as Luther's words sank in. "What did you say?"

"I said I know exactly where they'll be running to—and it's right there on the island. So do us both a favor: quit your whining and pick up a pen."

Chapter 38

Kostas

"WHAT DID YOU LEARN? What's he like?" Troy shot the questions at Emmy the moment she closed the Camry's door. She had used a large bouquet of flowers and a FedEx envelope full of real estate advertisements to con her way past The Tropical Towers' guards and up to the luxury penthouse condo of Kostas Kanasis himself. This was primarily a reconnaissance mission to prepare for their impending attack, but Troy was dying to know if the owner of bank account 004995625425, the man who had stolen their lives, was more like The Godfather or Doctor Frankenstein.

"Kostas is not the man behind our misfortune. He is a harmless old man living out his golden years alone."

"What! That can't be. If this is a dead end then everything we've done since waking up in the police garage has been in vain. He must have pulled the wool over your eyes." Troy knew that assertion was nonsense even as he spoke the words, but his frustration had a mind of its own.

If Emmy took offense, she did not show it. "I did not detect a hint of deception the whole time we spoke."

Her tone was far too chipper for the news she conveyed.

Troy blinked twice as if to clear his ears and said, "And you saw no flash of recognition when you said the flowers were from Emerald Green and Sebastian Troy?"

"No. I don't think he's ever heard of us. When I handed him the envelope and explained that Troy and Green were with a real estate developer he deflated before my eyes. In my professional opinion, Kostas Kanasis is just another bored and lonely senior citizen."

"So that's it then," Troy said, his voice trailing off.

"Not necessarily. Just because he doesn't know us, doesn't mean he doesn't know the people who did this to us. We should be able to learn everything we need to know by asking him the right questions the right way."

"What questions? What way?" Troy had asked, his hopes rising. Two hours later, he was about to find out.

Emmy had explained her plan while they shopped for clothes. Yet again. Troy noted that Emmy's plans always seemed to involve buying a new wardrobe, and that was fine with him. By his amateur reckoning, her scheme was as brilliant as her smile.

Looking at the door to the penthouse of Tower A, he asked, "Are you ready for this? You sure look it."

She had her hair pulled back and knotted, and wore sunglasses that robbed her emerald eyes of their fire. Her gray suit, like Troy's, was off-the-rack, and her black pumps had three-inch heels. Unless Kostas had Emmy's talent for reading people, he would not recognize her as the Flowerama delivery girl who had knocked two hours earlier. "Absolutely," she said. Then she reached up, pulled his head down to hers and gave him a breathtaking kiss.

She turned and knocked on the door before he knew what hit him.

Now there was a first kiss he would never forget, Troy thought, even as he struggled to purge it temporarily from his mind.

Emmy cleared her throat and pointed to her lips.

He hastened to wipe the lipstick transfer off in time.

Troy's first thought when he laid eyes on the man who haunted his dreams was that Emmy's "harmless" appraisal had been an understatement. For starters, given the veins and age spots on his hands and neck, Kostas appeared to be well into his seventies. His gray cardigan sweater and thick dark-framed glasses, showed little inclination toward either the evil mastermind or backstage powerbroker stereotypes. Troy detected no hint of malice in his watery grey eyes, nor deepening crease between his long curly brows. The man slated to change their lives looked about as alert and intimidating as an old squirrel.

"Mister Kanasis?" Emmy asked, holding up her false identification.

"Yes."

"I'm Julia Sanders with Interpol. This is my colleague, Agent Harold Singer. May we speak with you for a moment?"

"I suppose. What is this about?"

"Perhaps we could step inside. It's personal in nature."

Kostas took a step back, pulling open the door. "Of course."

"Did you receive an unexpected delivery this afternoon?" Troy asked, noting the flowers on the dining room table off to his left.

"Yes. I got the bouquet of flowers you see over here and an envelope full of advertising materials."

Troy and Emmy gave each other grave nods for Kostas's benefit before turning back to him. "We're going to need to see your driver's license, passport, and latest bank statement, Mr. Kanasis."

"What for? Am I in some kind of trouble?"

"No, sir. You've done nothing wrong. Our purpose here today is to keep you and others from becoming victims of a crime."

"A financial crime," Emmy added. "If you'll show my colleague the documents he requested, I'll be happy to explain everything to you while he makes note of your information."

Kostas looked unsure for a few seconds, but then laid his suspicions aside. Motioning toward a doorway he said, "Why don't you have a seat at the kitchen table. I'll be there in a moment with the documents."

Troy and Emmy nodded appreciatively and headed for the kitchen. The moment they entered Troy understood why Kostas favored this room. The kitchen offered a spectacular view of West Bay and the Caribbean Sea. Looking down he could see four distinct shades of blue in the water, as though the sea was painted by numbers. The hues ranged from the faintest turquoise near the beach to a midnight blue further out. All of it looked inviting, and though it was just there beyond the glass, it seemed a million miles away.

They were still standing at the window when Kostas came back in. "Here you go," he said, handing over his passport and driver's license.

Emmy accepted them with a nod and immediately passed them off to Troy. Then she got busy distracting Kostas so Troy could photograph the documents without his noticing. "As I indicated earlier, it appears that you've been targeted as part of a financial scandal. The group we're after provides legitimate real estate documents to which they have no actual connection, and then they try to get you to invest in them through their organization. It's kind of like selling you the London Bridge if you're familiar with that expression."

"Why the flowers?"

"That's just part of the confidence game. They invest a hundred dollars so that you'll have a warm and fuzzy feeling while you listen to them ask you for a hundred thousand."

"But they did not ask for any money. They just delivered the flowers and an envelope."

"Yes," Emmy said. "That's all part of it. The request to hear them out will come within the next twenty-four hours—unless of course they spotted us and got scared off."

"So what am I to do?"

"Well, that depends. You can either just refuse them outright, and that will be it …"

"Or?"

"Or, if you'd like to help us bring them to justice, you could agree to meet with them and we'll catch them in a sting. It's completely up to you, and I don't want to pressure you in any way."

"I'll need to think about it."

"Yes, of course. In the meantime, we still need to see your banking documents. We're trying to figure out why they targeted you, so we know who to warn in the future."

"I don't have any banking documents."

"You don't have an account at Solomon Bank & Trust?" Troy chimed in.

"No."

Troy felt a chill run up his spine. He wondered if they'd gotten the wrong Kostas Kanasis. Perhaps this was senior and they needed junior? "Well then, if you don't mind my asking, how do you pay your bills?"

Kostas blushed. "I don't pay them. I mean, I do pay them, but not personally. I have an attorney who handles all my banking."

"Your children don't handle that for you?" Emmy asked, her thoughts obviously following the same track as his.

"No. I don't have any children. No family at all, as a matter of fact."

No family at all, Troy repeated to himself.

"Could you get us your attorney's name and number?" Emmy asked.

"Yes, of course. I'm sure I have his card somewhere."

Troy turned toward Emmy and they exchanged perplexed looks as Kostas got up and went in search of the business card.

"How often do you see your attorney, Mr. Kanasis?" Troy asked loudly, so Kostas could hear him from the other room.

"Oh, I never see him."

"What I mean is, how often do you speak?"

"Not very often. In fact, I don't remember ever speaking to him."

"Ever," Emmy repeated. "How is that?"

Kostas walked back into the room with a rumpled old business card. "I don't remember a lot of things. I've developed a problem with my memory."

Chapter 39

Arlen

LUTHER LAID his satellite phone down on his oak desk and let out a long sigh. Between Orca's visit and the Farkas fiasco, these last few days had been unnerving. Life was supposed to be easy when you made the kind of money he did, wasn't it?

The problem, he knew, was that the money just passed through his hands, teasing him. He never got to hold it, fondle it, revel in it. The bulk of his earnings went to Orca. The rest went to pay his mortgages, his social fees and expenses, and his professional and domestic help. At the end of the day, even with annual earnings well into eight figures, he was still living off credit cards.

A light two-toned bell intruded on his thoughts and Kimber's face appeared on his videophone. He could tell by the look in her eyes that she had good news. "You've got a visitor, Luther," she said, holding an embossed business card up to the camera. "Arlen Blythe, CEO of Savas Pharmaceuticals is here to see you." By stating his name that way, Kimber was signaling that she had confirmed Blythe's identity with his fingerprints. "He said to tell you that Bogart sent him."

Bogart, that was good news, Luther thought. "Please make Mr. Blythe comfortable and then send him up in five minutes."

Bogart had been Luther's best paying client. Whereas Luther charged a million dollars to erase a single witness's memory, he doubled his fee for each additional erasure on the same case, keeping the cost in line with the incremental risk. If the prosecution's star witness suddenly could not swear to what he had seen anymore, that was tragic, but not necessarily unusual. It was a different kettle of fish altogether if the prosecution's two star witnesses both "developed amnesia." Then the judge might smell something rotten and decide to take a closer look. Closer looks were exactly what Luther most wanted to avoid.

Rather than refuse multiple erasures outright, however, he had put a risk-reward matrix in place. Bogart had paid Luther a three million dollar fee for a double erasure. Given that Arlen Blythe was the CEO of a pharmaceutical corporation, Luther could imagine myriad scenarios for which he might require a double. Perhaps a couple of clinical investigators had observed regrettable adverse effects, or his security division had identified a couple of whistleblowers about to toot. Hell, it could even be a triple, Luther mused. Three wipes were worth seven million dollars. Four was worth fifteen. Dare he even hope? Luther shook his head. No. He dared not. Although a big job would not break the letter of the inviolable rules he had established in the beginning to keep from getting caught, it would certainly crack their spirit.

Still, to get Orca off his back …

Luther Googled Savas Pharmaceuticals. Scanning the summary posted on an investment website, he saw that Savas was a one-drug firm —but what a drug it was. Vitorol, their oral insulin, was the world's number-one best selling pharmaceutical, bringing in a staggering twelve-billion dollars last year. Twelve Billion. All from pills that probably cost a penny apiece to manufacture. That was the kind of return he had hoped to be earning when he plunked half his tort earnings into Aridon Biotech six years ago. He had hoped to cash in on the Alzheimer's pie the way Savas was cashing in on the diabetic. He had rolled the dice and taken his chances, and lost. Big time. Never again.

The elevator doors chimed, and Arlen Blythe walked into his office. With his radiant aquiline features and thick crop of gray-tinged hair, the CEO looked like his title: the head hired gun for one of the world's most profitable firms. At forty-six, he was young enough to represent the next-generation image that Savas sought to portray, yet experienced enough to impress the industry analysts and roundtable hosts with his acumen and gravitas.

Luther knew instantly that it would be a mistake to try to pass himself off as the hired help to this guy. Arlen no doubt knew his Shakespeare. According to the rumors Luther now recalled, the founder of Savas had spent eighteen months working with all three of the world's top executive search firms to identify the perfect man to assume the reigns of his company. The man whose identification and recruitment had commanded millions in fees was standing before him now. And he needed Luther's help.

As Luther walked from behind his desk to greet his potential new client, he could not help fantasizing about the fee they might be agreeing to the next time they shook hands—if only Arlen had the right kind of case. "Good afternoon, I'm Luther Kanasis. Please, make yourself comfortable," he said, motioning toward his suite of black calfskin armchairs.

Arlen nodded and complied, but did not offer an opener. Not even his name. Apparently, he wanted Luther to make the first move. His clients tended to do that for some reason, as though they thought it a clever way to test his oratorical skills. Little did they know that despite the nature of his business, oratory had nothing to do with Luther's ongoing success. "It truly is a pleasure to have you here, Mr. Blythe. I've been an admirer of yours for years. Your work at Savas has been little short of miraculous. Twelve billion last year. Now that is impressive."

When Blythe failed to reply or even nod, Luther added, "So, we have a mutual friend in Bogart ..."

"Yes," Arlen said. "I was most impressed by the resolution of his case."

Luther nodded.

"We had a long talk about it over a couple of splendid Padron cigars. I don't usually smoke, but given Bogart's affinity I joined him and actually enjoyed it immensely. Even ordered myself a couple of boxes of the same limited edition just to have around when the occasion warrants." Arlen kept his gaze riveted on Luther the whole time he spoke, giving Luther the impression that the words were just filler, packing peanuts around some greater purpose.

"He doesn't have the faintest idea how you helped him," Arlen continued. "His assumption is that you simply used bribes."

Luther kept his best poker face securely pasted throughout this speculation. His clients always wanted to know how he did it, but of course he never told them. He never even hinted.

"That's one of many areas where Bogart and I differ," Arlen added.

Luther waited for more but nothing came. Finally he said, "I don't follow."

Arlen's lips smiled, but his eyes continued with their dissecting stare. "You see, Luther, I have deduced your secret. I know exactly how you've been winning. You've been erasing memories—chemically."

Chapter 40

Cutout

EMMY LOOKED OVER at Troy as they waited for the elevator, trying to gauge his state of mind. She was not pleased with the results of their meeting with Kostas Kanasis, but judging by Troy's expression, his jury was still out.

Not hers.

All that work, all that exposure, all that danger … Discovering and deciphering the tattoos, hijacking the UPS truck, scamming Gunter, watching a cop's head explode before their eyes, impersonating Interpol officers, for what? For the name of Kostas's accountant, an attorney in Miami. What good was that to them? "I can't believe that after all this, all we have is the name of a lousy attorney."

Troy held up his index finger without turning toward her, indicating that he was deep in thought. When the elevator arrived on eighteen, he took two steps forward to enter but did not turn around. He just stood there, staring intently toward the back wall.

Emmy was about to hit the lobby button, when she thought better of it. She pressed seventeen instead. They descended one floor, the doors opened and closed, and then she hit sixteen, all with Troy barely blinking. And so it went: fifteen, fourteen, thirteen, twelve. On eleven, Troy suddenly turned to her. "It's brilliant. Bloody brilliant." He wore a smile a mile wide.

"What is?"

"The system."

"What system? What are you talking about?" Emmy asked, frustrated and anxious.

"Kostas Kanasis."

"Kostas Kanasis is just a sweet old man, a victim whose memory has been wiped—just like us."

"No, he's not like us. You were on the right track earlier, but you need to take it one step further. He's a cutout."

"What on earth are you talking about?" she asked, pushing the button for ten.

"Think about it, Emmy. Think about the chain of clues."

"The chain of clues?"

"Yes. Go all the way back to the tattoos. Why did we choose to make that bank account the one thing we told our future amnesic selves about?"

"I don't know. All we've gotten from it, besides a few attempts on our lives, is the name Alexander Tate, Attorney at Law, Miami. That hardly blows my skirt up considering our predicament and what we went through to get it."

"I'll tell you why we chose it," Troy said. "We chose it because that was all we had. Before our memories were stolen from us, we were following a money trail. You had it right."

"It sounded good at the time, but not anymore. What makes you so cocksure?"

"Cocksure?"

Emmy blushed, remembering the kiss. "I'm sorry. I'm just frustrated."

"Don't be. Here's your answer. It's the only sensible explanation that covers everything. As soon as you assume the money trail scenario to be true, then everything else falls into place."

Emmy did not feel everything falling into place, but seeing the conviction in Troy's cobalt eyes, she sensed inspiration coming. She pushed the buttons for floors nine through one to buy some quiet elevator time and said, "Do tell."

Troy began to pace, speaking to himself as much as to her. "For some reason—and I don't know what that was yet—we were following a money trail."

"A trail that we now know leads to a sweet old man whose mind has also been wiped," Emmy interjected.

"That's where we're wrong," Troy said triumphantly.

"It doesn't lead to Kostas?" Emmy asked, incredulity muffling her voice.

Troy shook his head. "It leads through Kostas."

"Through Kostas," Emmy repeated, not understanding yet. "Go on."

"Okay. But let me back up. I'm going to postulate that back when we were following the money trail before our amnesia, our investigation kicked up enough dirt to alert those concerned and make them nervous. At some point—I'm guessing when we showed up here on Grand Cayman—we crossed a line and they decided to make their problem go away."

"By erasing our minds and having us incarcerated for murder," Emmy finished the thought.

"Exactly."

"And Kostas is a cutout on this trail?"

"Right again."

"I'm not sure I know what that means."

Troy nodded his understanding. "Kostas is blindly holding the real criminal's money, perhaps laundering it as well. The money trail looks like it leads to him. And as far as the banks and tax authorities are concerned, it does. But this evening we learned that it really passes through him—without his knowledge."

Despite Troy's explanation, Emmy was not there yet. "You're going to have to explain that."

"Of course. And again, I'm speculating with assumptions that make everything else fall into place. Here goes. Mister X, the guy or guys or organization we're really after, is doing something illegal that makes him a lot of money—money that he has to launder. I don't know what that business is, but I think your earlier assumption that it involves erasing memories is a good one."

Troy paused for Emmy to nod that she was following, and then continued. "Like any smart crook, he's obviously very cautious, perhaps even paranoid about being identified and caught. And of course he's also well aware of rule one in the detective handbook. He knows that anyone coming after him is going to try to follow the money trail. So what does he do?"

"He sets up a blind middleman, a cutout," Emmy answered, seeing the light. "How do you think it works?"

"I think Mister X found a sweet old man with no family living on an island and offered him a deal. I think he offered to set Kostas up in a luxury condo and pay all his bills, in exchange for running his money through the account Kostas has maintained for the last twenty years. He gets Kostas to assign him full power of attorney over the account to him. Then he wipes Kostas's mind so he has no recollection of the arrangement. That's why all Kostas knows now is what Mister X's attorney told him afterwards: that all his bills are taken care of and he doesn't have to worry about money. And that's all Kostas cares to know. Why question it? He lives a good life."

"And Mister X is safe," Emmy added.

"Right."

"Because Kostas is a cutout."

"Right again. Except that we now know about Counselor Alexander Tate in Miami."

"And Tate will know who Mister X is," Emmy said, finishing the chain. "He has to know to manage the arrangement."

Troy shook his head. "Not necessarily. All he needs to know to run normal operations is Kostas's financial information."

"If that's true, then we've got nothing. But you look like the cat who swallowed the canary."

"Things aren't always normal. There have to be contingencies ..."

The elevator opened onto the lobby before Emmy could get Troy to elaborate.

They walked quickly past the concierge's desk so that he would not get another look at their faces. Emmy suspected that it would not matter if he did. She doubted that they would ever return to the

Tropical Towers—or Grand Cayman for that matter. Time to head for Miami.

Assuming they could find a way off the island before they got caught.

Back out in the balmy Caribbean air, they were making a silent beeline for the Camry when a bearded man in a Kangol cap stepped out from behind a garden bush onto the sidewalk before them. Emmy felt a shudder of shock as he locked on her with his copper-colored eyes.

"Emmy! Troy! Thank goodness I found you. I've been so worried."

Chapter 41

Something Big

DESPITE ARLEN BLYTHE'S specific language, Luther reacted to the CEO's allegation as he always did when a client claimed to know his secret. He maintained his poker face, assumed that the allegation was just a fishing expedition, and ignored it. "How can I help you, Arlen?"

"We'll get to that," Arlen said with a slow, confident nod. "We're not there yet."

Luther sat quietly and waited. He knew every trick in the interview game and was not about to fall for something as amateur as filling the awkward silence. Sixty seconds later he was feeling pretty good about his ability to project a relaxed, confident air when Arlen opened his mouth and took Luther's breath away.

"Jeff Landis came to me first."

Luther did his best not to react to the mention of his deceased former colleague.

"Looking for money that is," Arlen continued. "I was tempted to have Savas take the same minority ownership position in Aridon Biotech that you eventually did. A cure for Alzheimer's would be a blockbuster of Vitorol's magnitude, so even with the odds of a thousand to one against their taking the compound all the way to market, the financials were right. But I turned it down because I was committed to the strategy of maintaining Savas's laser focus.

"You know, ours really is an incredibly powerful strategy, for one so simple. When you've only got one product, there's no ambiguity or confusion about where everyone in the entire organization is to pour their best efforts. The efficiencies gained by cutting out all the superfluous crap and distractions and honing in on doing one thing better than anyone else in the world are staggering. Still, there are those on my board who worry about the risk of having all our eggs in one basket. But I digress …

"I'll be honest with you, Luther. When Aridon's facility exploded, taking out Landis and his entire research and development team, my first thought was: Thank goodness I walked away. Of course, by then word had already leaked within the biotech community that his compound had fizzled, that it destroyed neurons along with the plaque.

"Tell me, how much did you have invested, Luther?"

"Why don't you tell me, Arlen."

Arlen nodded his approval of the challenge. "Twenty million dollars. That gave you what, twenty percent?"

"And a seat on the board."

"Yes, the only outside seat," Arlen said, casually crossing his legs.

He knew. Luther could feel it. Arlen actually knew. Everything... Impossible. "Are you going somewhere with this? I do pretty well with my law practice, but four years later I can still feel that bite, so I would appreciate it if we could stop picking at the scab."

"Your law practice ... yes. I see the office—" Arlen said, holding out his hands palms up and looking around. "And like most leading members of the California business community, I know the name. But my researchers haven't discovered any substantial legal activity coming out of your law practice since you lost that Optiplase tort at trial—also four years back. Talk about a bad year."

Luther wanted to throw this guy out, toss him out on his ear. But something had him hooked. He knew what it was and the knowing made it bitter. Greed.

"You know," Arlen continued, in his increasingly annoying lilt, "I spoke to a tort attorney friend of mine who told me that for national medical torts like that, the lead attorney can expect to shell out ten to twenty thousand dollars per plaintiff in recruiting costs—given all the advertising and testing required to sort the diamonds from the rough. Ten to twenty thousand per. And my researchers tell me that you had three thousand plaintiffs. That means the not-guilty verdict cost you in the neighborhood of forty-five million out of pocket—versus what, the seven hundred million you would have won with guilty? Now that must have hurt. And that was what, two months before the twenty million you had invested in Aridon went up with Landis's team and their facility in a big ball of fire? I pity your accountant that year. Sixty-five million in the red. Sixty-five."

Luther did not take the bait. He left the ugly numbers sitting on the table like candied Brussels sprouts.

Arlen pushed on without missing a beat. "According to the GQ article Luther Kanasis, the California Bar Association's flamboyant Man of the Year, you only cleared forty million on the Iprophine tort that made your name. By my calculations that left you with a twenty-five million dollar hole.

A hole like that can put a lot of pressure on a man. Could force him to take steps that he might never otherwise consider ... drastic steps."

Luther felt his stomach turn somersaults as Arlen dissected his past with the cold surgical precision of a veteran coroner. Arlen had pulled everything from the air. He had no proof, could not convict, but he was spot on. Luther did not like where this was going. That was exactly the point, of course. Arlen wanted him to feel helpless and afraid. Arlen wanted Luther to tip his hand. "Forgive me, Arlen. But if you have a point, I would prefer that you get to it."

"Or what? You'll brush me off to get back to your thriving law practice? To servicing your clients? According to my sources—and I have impeccable sources—the fresh UCLA grads you have slaving away downstairs do all the work, and then it's only enough to make Kanasis look legitimate to the IRS. You asked about my point. My point is this: I know that you make all your money using Aridon's technology to rescue people like Bogart from impending crises. I know that you took a goose egg, added a dash of desperation, and turned it golden. And you know what?"

Luther could not resist biting. "What?"

"I think that's brilliant. I think that makes you exactly the kind of guy I want to do business with."

Luther tried to keep his face impassive as a granite bust, but he could not help cracking. Ever since he blew up the Aridon complex with all staff inside to secure exclusive alternative use of the failed Alzheimer's compound, blackmail scenarios like the one Arlen was surely about to propose had been among his worst recurring nightmares. A second whale was about to hop on his already overburdened back, and there was nothing he could do about it. "If you're so sure of your preposterous claims, why the dog and pony show? Why all the speculation? Why not just come out and tell me what you want?" Luther strained to convey casual indifference in every word, if not each facial expression.

"It's called courtship, Luther. I thought it appropriate, perhaps even necessary. You see, I'm not here for blackmail. Nor am I here to propose a penny-ante job like the one you did for Bogart. I'm interested in something big."

Chapter 42

Fritz

TROY STEPPED REFLEXIVELY between Emmy and the stranger, shielding her, even as the thrill of hearing his name coursed through his body. The man who confronted them by name wore a dark brown Kangol cap that matched his stylishly scruffy beard. Both the cap and the beard looked out of place, given the warm weather, and the thought that they were probably worn to hide a balding head crossed his mind. Perhaps Emmy's talents were rubbing off on him.

Kangol was a couple of inches shorter than Troy at about five-ten, but much broader. He projected the solid meat-on-bones look of a rugby player. Kangol's most notable feature, however, was his reptilian irises. They were the strangest coppery color and shimmered with an almost metallic sheen. Troy empathized with the stranger's ocular plight, but did not drop his guard.

"Whoa," the stranger continued, holding up his hands in surrender and offering what seemed to be a genuine smile. "Didn't mean to startle you. But I did, didn't I?"

Troy did not answer.

"Look, you guys came to me, remember?"

"No," Emmy said. "We don't."

Kangol's face took on a concerned expression. "Oh my god, it really happened. Didn't it? You lost your memories, just as you feared?"

Emmy nodded while Troy just studied the man.

"Wow. That changes things. Where do I begin?"

The question was rhetorical, but Troy answered anyway. "How about giving us your name and telling us what you're doing here."

"Yeah, sure. My name is Fritz. Fritz Morgan. I'm a reporter with the Miami Herald. We ran into each other a few times while doing similar research. Familiarity led to chitchat and eventually we became friends. These last few weeks we've had a contest going over who could find the best rum drink. Each night we hit a different bar. Last time we met you asked me to come find you if you ever dropped off the grid."

Troy thought about that for a minute. "So you think we're fellow reporters?"

Fritz weighed his words. "More like private detectives."

"How did you know where to find us?" Emmy asked.

"That's a longer story. I'll be happy to give you all the details and answer your other questions, but not here. I think someone has been following me. Why don't we go down to the West Bay marina? I've got a small yacht docked there. We can take her out where no one can overhear us and talk till dawn. You guys must have loads of questions."

Troy looked at Emmy. He wanted her read of this guy. She beckoned off to the side with her head. "Give us a minute, Fritz," he said.

"Yeah, sure. Whatever. I'll be right over there," Fritz said, pointing to a bench at the center of a nearby garden alcove.

Troy put his arm around Emmy's shoulder and they turned to walk in the opposite direction.

"What do you think?" he asked, as soon as they were out of earshot.

"I don't know. He's nervous and is definitely holding something back. That may be explained away by the situation, but there's one other thing."

"What's that?"

"I don't like rum."

"I'm not a fan either, or at least I wasn't last time I remember. I guess it all boils down to one question: Can we trust him?"

"Do we have a choice? His story sounded plausible enough within the context of our situation. In any case, it's great to meet someone who knows our names and isn't shooting at us. I'm dying to hear what he has to say."

"Yeah, me too."

They rejoined Fritz and Troy said, "Sorry about that. We're a bit jumpy these days. We'd love to talk."

"And we appreciate your doing as we asked. Finding us, I mean," Emmy added.

"No problem. Do you have your own car, or do you want to ride with me?"

Troy was about to confirm that they had their own car when Emmy said, "We do have a car but we'll ride with you. I just need a minute to get a few things." She thrust her hand into Troy's pocket, withdrew the car keys, and was off.

Troy looked over at Fritz as they turned toward his car, searching for the hints of nervousness that Emmy had found so apparent. All he saw was a mask of concern.

"So what's the last thing you remember?" Fritz asked.

Troy saw no harm in answering truthfully. "Afghanistan. 2001."

Fritz sucked in breath. "Seven years. That must have been one rude awakening."

"You have no idea," Troy said, wondering if Fritz actually did. Troy did not elaborate. He did not want to relive the joys of waking up locked in a dark trunk with a corpse. Fritz seemed to understand this.

They completed the walk to his Citroen in silence. Emmy showed up a minute later carrying the two beach bags that held their clothes.

"So how did you find us?" Emmy asked, once they were headed for the marina.

Fritz did not answer for a good thirty seconds, so Emmy repeated the question.

"I think we're being followed," Fritz finally replied, his voice low, his eyes on the mirror.

"Is it a man on a black scooter?" Troy asked, turning with Emmy to look out the back window into the night. No sooner had Fritz said, "Yes," than a side window blew out, sending glass everywhere.

"Duck down!" Fritz yelled. "He's got a gun!"

Troy pushed Emmy into the foot-well and lay down over her as Fritz accelerated and began weaving in and out of traffic.

"Stay down. I think I can lose him."

They complied, winding up face to face on the floor as Fritz continued to bob and weave. Emmy had a splotch of blood on her cheek. When Troy wiped it away and found no scratch, he realized that his own face was dripping blood. Emmy put her lips to his ear. "I don't trust him. I'm not sure why; it's just instinct. But on the other hand a yacht is exactly what we need—especially if he's heading for Miami."

"I was thinking the same thing—about the yacht," Troy whispered back. "There's no way we can go through the airport with our faces on wanted posters."

"Do you think it's safe?" Emmy asked.

"Getting on a boat with Fritz? I think so. I was skeptical before someone shot at us, but that erased most of my doubts. Besides, he could have shot us the moment he had us in the car if he wanted to."

"I hope you're right, but I have the nagging feeling that you're wrong."

"Why did you want to leave our car?"

"I wanted the chance to study him further before we got on the boat. That's a point of no return, so to speak."

Fritz brought the Citroen to a screeching halt. "I've lost him for now," he said. "But it probably won't take him long to spot the car. Let's make sure we're on the Lady Jane before he does."

Troy gave Emmy an inquisitive look as he straightened up. She just shrugged an I-don't-know.

Chapter 43

USSC

"BEFORE WE GET TO THE SPECIFICS of my proposition," Arlen said, "let me give you some background."

"All right," Luther said, pleased to shift the topic from his own woes to someone else's.

"Vitorol, Savas's blockbuster oral insulin and only product, is set to go off patent in December 2012. Vitorol's original patent actually expires next year, but thanks to a Hatch-Waxman extension, we've got another three years."

"A Hatch-Waxman extension?"

"Yes. Back in 1984 Senators Orrin Hatch and Henry Waxman sponsored what has become the defining patent legislation for the pharmaceutical industry. It includes provisions for granting patent extensions to corporations who perform the costly clinical trials required to safely extend a compound's approved indications to classes that would not otherwise be served. In Vitorol's case, we got a three-year extension for obtaining both a pediatric indication, and for proving Vitorol's safety and efficacy in a form of diabetes prevalent only among Native Americans."

"So without Hatch-Waxman, Vitorol would go off patent next year?"

"Eleven months from now."

"And since you are telling me this, I presume that your extension has come under scrutiny?"

"That's correct. It has been challenged by Braxton, the generic manufacturer who holds the patent on the buffering agent we use to get the insulin past the stomach to where it can be absorbed in a pH neutral environment."

Luther was not interested in the chemistry. He needed to know who the key players were, and how much money was involved. "How big a deal is this?"

"Do you have any idea what happens to a drug when it goes off patent?"

"I assume the generics move in to steal market share."

"When it's a blockbuster like Vitorol, they swoop in like rabid vultures. We will lose between sixty and eighty percent of our sales in the first year off patent. By the end of the second year, Vitorol's sales will be less than ten percent of their patent-protected level."

"So basically, once you go off patent, it's all over? Savas is kaput?"

Arlen nodded. "There are a few games we can play to squeeze more out of the lemon, but you're essentially right. That's it."

Luther did the math in his head. It was not tough. At twelve billion a year, every additional month of patent protection was worth a billion bucks. Three commas. Nine zeros. The three years Hatch-Waxman got them were worth a staggering thirty-six billion in sales, virtually all of it pure profit, no doubt.

Luther would have liked nothing more than to take a thick slice of that pie. In fact, this was exactly the kind of opportunity he had been waiting for. But alas, he could not solve patent problems with 456. Laws did not have memories. "I'm not confirming any of your earlier rampant speculation by telling you that my specialty is criminal law, particularly those rare instances where witness testimony is the lynchpin of the prosecutorial case. Your case is about as far from my center of competence as they come. I'm sorry, Arlen, but I really can't help you."

Rather than rising, Arlen leaned further back into the couch and spread his arms out along the top as if he owned the place. "You know, I spent a lot of time thinking about what I would have done if I were you, if I had complete control of 456. I think I would have adopted a strategy very similar to yours. I would have made secrecy my absolute first and highest priority. After all, there may be a lot of wiggle room for the rich in this great country of ours, but overly greedy or careless millionaires can still wind up in jail.

"As far as I can tell, you have managed to conduct your nefarious business for over three years now without a whiff of scandal by operating like a micro-mafia. You work only with known entities, and only by strict bona-fide referral. Your clients are people of means who have no bigger legal challenges hanging over their heads. And you only work with people whom you're sure you can get off, so they won't later point the finger your way in exchange for a reduced sentence. Nonetheless, you keep your clients completely in the dark as to your methods. And it works.

"Bogart did not have a clue that you were using a drug. As with everyone, I suppose, the notion did not cross his mind because he assumed that if a memory-erasing drug had been invented, he would have heard of it. Rumor would have gotten out. Yet it has not. Not a peep."

"Again, I have to ask you if this is going somewhere," Luther said.

Arlen smiled. He appeared to appreciate directness. "My point is this. Your adoption of an ultra-conservative business model has caused you to overlook what we in the pharmaceutical industry would call a major line extension." Arlen crossed his legs, giving pause to emphasize what came next. "Shall I tell you what I have in mind?"

Luther found himself staring at a fork in the road. He could either walk away now and end their meeting with his façade intact, pretending that Arlen's conclusions were nothing but wild speculation. Or, he could tacitly acknowledge that the pharmaceutical executive was batting a thousand, and learn more. Arlen had obviously put a lot of thought into this, just as he had said. Furthermore, his insight was little short of miraculous—judging by the clients, attorneys and judges Luther had worked with who had not a clue. Among outsiders, only Sebastian Troy had suspected the truth, and Luther had neutralized him before he got within three thousand miles.

Arlen might only be here because he was familiar with Jeff Landis's research, but he was here, and that meant he had serious needs. One way or the other, Luther had to deal with him.

Luther also thought of Orca, and what a relief it would be to have the killer whale off his back at last. That image was the clincher. He nodded. "Tell me."

Arlen's eyes flashed with the satisfaction of a chess master whose opponent made a long anticipated move. He got straight to the point, to the line extension. "You have focused exclusively on the witness stand. I want you to turn your attention to the bench."

Luther's jaw dropped and he gave up all pretense of control. "You want what?"

Arlen remained silent, allowing him to process.

Luther thought out loud. "If the judge loses all memory of evidence and testimony presented, all you get is a mistrial."

"Keep going," Arlen urged.

"A mistrial buys you time, perhaps months … months at a billion per."

"You're getting there."

"The exact outcome seems unpredictable. Is there any precedent for this?" Luther asked, certain that Arlen had checked.

"There is some. Judges have died, had strokes, or otherwise become disabled in the middle of trials. In a few cases a replacement judge has simply stepped in. But in the vast majority, a mistrial had to be declared and the whole proceedings restarted."

"How much time are you expecting to buy?" Luther asked, trying to gauge his fee for this new line of work.

Arlen shook his head. "You need to back up, Luther. You still haven't asked the critical question."

"Critical question?"

"By switching from the witness stand to the bench, you're only halfway there. You need to make one more leap."

Luther squirmed uneasily in his chair. He did not like having his intellect put on the spot like this. After a minute of drawing blanks, he got up and stared into his waterfall, determined not to give in. Arlen sat quietly while Luther tried to let his mind run free before the cascading wall of water. It took two minutes, a full hundred and twenty seconds, but the right question came. He turned around slowly. "Is your case already on appeal?" he asked, not bothering to hide the trepidation in his voice.

"Bravo, Luther. Bravo. Savas versus Braxton is about to go before the United States Supreme Court."

Chapter 44

Why

PEERING OUT from adjacent portholes in search of signs of pursuit, Troy and Emmy watched the West Bay marina fade behind them. All appeared peaceful and quiet, as indeed it was supposed to be in paradise, but whoever had shot out the window of Fritz's car minutes before was still out there. Had they lost him? Or was he watching them right now through binoculars, making plans to capture them at sea?

"Care for a drink?" Fritz asked. "I've got the autopilot set to take us to Jamaica. It's a hundred and eighty miles. We won't be there until morning."

Troy had been so intent on the view that he had not heard Fritz descend from the bridge. Judging by her jolt, Emmy had not either. He turned to see Fritz holding up a chilled bottle of Pinot Grigio in one hand and an Appleton Dark Jamaican Rum in the other. Troy was not much of a drinker, but given the circumstances ... "A cool glass of wine sounds great."

"Make that two," Emmy said.

"You guys have more control than I do," Fritz replied with a shake of his head before turning back towards the kitchen.

The forty-foot Lady Jane had a simple floor plan. Up top there was just the bridge with some extra seating and a large sundeck. Below there were two bedroom suites separated by a central lounge area and a kitchenette. You did not get a lot of room for half-a-million bucks, but then Troy supposed that the guys who bought these floating motels were not counting their pennies. "How does a reporter afford a ride like this?" Troy asked.

"Believe me, he doesn't," Fritz called back from the sunken kitchenette. "It's the publisher's, but he doesn't pay for it either. He writes it off as a business expense. My trip is just part of the justification. I'm doing a feature series on financial crime in the Caribbean. Nice work if you can get it."

"Is that how we overlapped?" Emmy asked. "You said earlier that we had run into each other a few times while working on the same story."

"That's right," Fritz said, unloading two wine glasses, two bottles, and two tumblers full of ice from a platter. After filling Emmy's wine glass he turned to Troy and said, "You sure you want to go with the soft stuff?"

"I'm sure. Rum gives me a headache."

"Fair enough," Fritz said, and poured accordingly. "Cheers."

"Why are you taking us to Jamaica?" Emmy asked.

"Because your pictures are on wanted posters all over Grand Cayman. Because someone is shooting at you. Because according to the news you've killed two members of the Royal Cayman Islands Police in the last forty-eight hours. Because—"

"We didn't kill anyone," Troy interrupted.

"I know, I know. That's why I'm putting my own neck on the line to help you. That said, I do need to know what's going on. Why were you at the Tropical Towers?"

"Did we tell you what we were investigating?" Emmy asked, throwing the question back at him.

Fritz cocked his head to the side such that his coppery irises reflected the glow of a candle, and Troy realized that he was wearing contacts. That observation struck a cord—why would anyone wear lenses that made his eyes look so reptilian?—but it was forgotten with his new friend's next words. "Not specifically. You implied that you were here because of a private grievance."

Troy felt his throat go dry as his heart skipped a beat. He brought the glass to his lips and took a long sip of the crisp white wine. Fritz was about to read them the latest chapter of their lives, the chapter that would link their past, their present, and their missing seven years. They were about to learn why someone wanted them dead, and what it was they had lost.

"Are we married, Emmy and I?" Troy asked, surprising no one more than himself as the words leapt from his mouth unfiltered by his conscious mind.

Adding to Troy's surprise, Emmy reached over beneath the oval table and took supportive hold of his thigh while Fritz shifted his gaze back and forth between the two as though he were watching a tennis game. "Ah, no. No you're not."

The proclamation hit Troy like a bucket of frosty water. As the chill reverberated, he wanted to look over at Emmy, to see if her features registered a pain akin to his own, but fear stilled his head. He was not willing to risk another crushing emotional blow at that moment.

As her hand slid limply off his thigh, Fritz added, "But then, you are both single."

Troy and Emmy turned to look at each other, and he saw hope nudging the pain from her eyes. He turned back to Fritz and held up his left hand. "What about this?" he asked, pointing to his wedding ring.

Fritz grimaced. "That's why you're here."

Chapter 45

Nine

"THE SUPREME COURT!" Luther shouted as Arlen confirmed his suspicion. "Are you crazy? The justices are guarded like the president."

Arlen remained on the couch, silent and apparently content to let his host vent his frustration by shouting and pacing before the waterfall. Luther took advantage of the opportunity to pull his thoughts together. After a full minute of pacing brought his blood pressure under control, he realized that despite Arlen's supernatural insightfulness in other areas, the otherwise clairvoyant CEO assumed the use of a traditional delivery system. He did not understand that erasing minds was not as simple as slipping someone a pill. "My work ... it requires physical contact."

"I appreciate that," Arlen said, breaking his silence in a calm, even monotone. "But you're wrong."

Luther stopped pacing and stared at his prospective client. "With all due respect for your deductive powers, I think I know my methods better than you do."

"Calm down, Luther. Listen to your waterfall. I'm not referring to your methods. I'll take your word for those. I'm talking about the supreme court justices. They're not guarded like the president."

"They're not?"

"No. In fact, they're not guarded at all—although I too had assumed they were. It's a common misconception. The truth is, if they're not looking at abortion, the supreme court justices receive fewer threats than your average federal employee. Makes sense if you think about it. Only a complete idiot would provoke a judge."

That did make sense, Luther thought as he sat back down across from Arlen. Why was he so tense anyway? He knew the answer, of course. Orca had him all riled up. The bastard kept him under both tremendous financial pressure and the threat of physical danger. Arlen would potentially be offering him a means of getting out from under the whale—but the risk would no doubt be commensurate with the reward. Luther hated risk. He took a deep breath, and said, "Tell me more."

A thin smile cracked Arlen's face. "Despite the extraordinary power they wield, the lives of supreme court justices are not that different from yours or mine. Believe it or not, Justice Goldstein actually had her purse snatched while walking near the Kennedy Center. And Justice

Stoffer was mugged while jogging the city streets. Both perpetrators got away. Getting to the justices is not going to be that big a problem."

"Then why not just shoot them?"

Arlen shook his head. Perish the thought. "You'd have to hit all nine at once, and that would be virtually impossible to orchestrate since the only time they're together is at the court or an occasional state function, and they are well guarded at those. Plus bullets and bombs are unambiguous, whereas mass amnesia opens up all kinds of doors to speculation and debate. Was it something in the water? Speculation and debate buy me time—months, at a billion per."

Luther began to relax as various scenarios danced through his head. Given Arlen's wealth and the profile of the target, Luther could probably ask for five million dollars, maybe even ten. Hell, with billions at stake, why not ask for twenty-five. Twenty-five million and he would be free of Orca.

That was it, he decided, drawing a mental line in the sand. Twenty-five million was his price. But wait a minute, he thought, recrossing his legs. Arlen had used the plural. He had said getting to the justices. Did he need two neutralized to sway the opinion his way? Three? No way. No way was Luther going to risk attracting that kind of heat. If more than one justice drew a blank, the cause was going to get some serious scrutiny. Just one on the other hand, and the court would probably try to cover it up. Hell, the justice might not even confess to having lost his or her memory—so long as it wasn't the chief. "Which justice do you have in mind?"

"Have you got any Scotch?" Arlen asked.

It was the chief, Luther thought. Otherwise Arlen would have come right out with it. That would make it easier to request twenty-five million with a straight face, but still ... "I've got a twenty-year-old Macallan. How will you take it?"

"Straight up."

Luther forswore drinking during business after his slip-up with Orca, although at the moment he was mildly tempted. If ever a situation needed a bit of lubrication, this was it. But he would not yield. Not until he was out of the woods.

He poured two fingers of Macallan into a Baccarat crystal tumbler for Mr. Arlen Blythe, and then gave himself an equal serving of similarly colored apple juice, adding a couple of rocks. He often did this with drinking clients. He would confess if the topic came up, but found that this minor deception made his guests more comfortable.

After handing Arlen his Scotch, Luther resumed his seat and sat in silence thinking, Please, not the chief.

"So, where were we?" Arlen teased, holding his tumbler appreciatively to the light after enjoying the first sip.

"You were going to tell me which justice, which member of the United States Supreme Court, you need neutralized."

"Oh yes, right. Actually, Luther, I need you to erase the memories of all nine."

Despite all his training, despite Julliard, despite gliding gracefully through countless courtroom surprises, Luther choked. He literally choked on his drink and began to cough uncontrollably. "All nine!" he screamed through a juicy mist. "You are crazy, Arlen. I'd like to help you, but really, there's no way." He stood and walked back to the bar for a towel.

"Of course there's a way, Luther. All we need is a will."

Luther stopped in his tracks. He knew code when he heard it. "It would take one hell of a will."

"I'm well aware of that."

I bet you are, Luther thought. But if you were fully aware, you wouldn't be here. Luther had calculated his fees for three, four and even five wipes during one particularly boring afternoon in court. By doubling his fee for each additional wipe, three wipes got him seven million. Four wipes netted fifteen. And five wipes earned him a cool thirty-one million dollars. For nine ... it would take him a while to do numbers like that in his head. And it was pure fantasy, so why bother. He set his tumbler down on the coffee table, knocking the daydream from his mind. It was time to stop flirting with disaster, time to be done with Arlen Blythe. He would find another way to rid himself of the killer whale. "Did Bogart explain my fees?"

That chess-master gleam flashed across Arlen's eyes again. "Indeed he did. He explained that your fee doubles with each additional case. I believe he paid you three million for his double."

"That's right. It's to keep the reward commensurate with the risk. I'm sure you understand."

"Indeed I do. In fact, I did the math."

"You did?" Luther asked, certain that Arlen had gotten the equation wrong.

"For nine erasures, you get five hundred and eleven million dollars. I've brought you a check."

Chapter 46

Balinorm

TROY DID A DOUBLE TAKE, trying to fully comprehend Fritz's last words. "What do you mean, the ring is why I'm here?"

Fritz did not answer immediately, taking an eternity to refill their glasses first. Finally he said, "As I understand it from bits of your conversation, you both woke up on the island with no idea where you were or what you were doing here?"

"That's right," Troy said. "I was in the trunk of a car with one of the dead cops you heard about. Emmy was in the front."

"And how did you get from the trunk of a cop car to the Tropical Towers?"

"It's a long story."

Fritz motioned toward the kitchenette with his head. "There's a couple of more bottles in the fridge, and we've got all night ..."

"We were—" Troy felt Emmy kick him below the table. "—tracking down the man whose business card was in my shoe."

"Why would you do that?" Fritz asked, his tone skeptical. "The card could have belonged to the man who attacked you. You could have been walking into the lion's den."

"Where else were we to turn?" Troy retorted. "We had no idea what was going on, why the cop was dead, or why we were on Grand Cayman. We didn't even know what year it was."

"Tropical Towers is a residential complex," Fritz said. "Did this man have his home address on his business card?"

"No," Emmy said. "But he gave it to us after we called his cell phone."

"The kind of discussion we required was hardly suited for the telephone," Troy added.

Fritz shook his head and pushed away his rum. "Look, I'm a reporter. I interview people for a living. I can tell when people are lying."

"I'm not lying," Emmy said.

"So why did you go to Solomon Bank & Trust?"

"How did you know we went there?" she asked.

"That's where they say you killed the second cop."

"That was the other card in my shoe," Troy offered.

"Show them to me," Fritz said, his skepticism on his sleeve. "Show me the cards."

"We don't have to show you anything." Troy said, wondering why Emmy had chosen to deceive their only friend, but willing to follow her instincts.

"And I don't have to take you to Jamaica. I can drop you right back on Grand Cayman. Look, I don't mean to be pushy, but I'm taking a big risk by helping you guys. I'm becoming an accomplice. In return, I think it's only fair to ask for all the details. Furthermore, I have to think about the story that's going to justify this to my boss." He motioned around the yacht. "Now be honest with me, or get off my boat."

Troy looked over at Emmy. She shrugged and said, "I'm sorry. I guess everything we've been through has us wound a bit too tight. Go ahead, Troy, tell him everything. I'm going to the bathroom—feeling a bit queasy." She stood and disappeared into the aft cabin.

Troy turned back to Fritz. "This is where it all started," he said, taking off his left shoe and sock.

By the time Emmy returned, Troy had laid it all out: the sniper at the Seagull's Nest, the discovery of the tattoo, Emmy's trick at Solomon Bank & Trust, the man on the motor scooter, and the meeting with Kostas. The only thing he left out was mention of Kostas's attorney, Alexander Tate.

Emmy returned as he was finishing up. Troy noted that the sparkle was back in her eyes.

"So what's your plan now?" Fritz asked.

"I don't know. I guess that depends on what you tell us."

"I'll be happy to tell you everything I know. Ironically, all that amounts to is what you told me before your amnesia. I've no new information for you, so I'm not sure how much it's going to help." Fritz took a long pull on his drink. "To be honest, I think it's going to hurt. If I were you, I think I'd rather live in ignorance."

Fritz set his tumbler down and it immediately slid across the table as the Lady Jane rolled over a large wave. He stood. "Tell you what. You think about my advice for a minute. I'm going to take my motion sickness medication. When I get back, tell me what you've decided." Fritz began walking to the aft cabin, but stopped after two steps. "Say, I've got extra medication, if either of you would like a shot. Could make the difference between twelve hours in the bathroom and a good night's sleep."

"Sounds good to me," Emmy said, placing a hand on her stomach.

"A shot?" Troy asked. "Not a pill or a patch? What is it?"

"The trade name is Balinorm. It's only been out for a year or so, but it works like a charm. Keizer is making a killing. I couldn't sail without it."

Fritz disappeared into the aft stateroom and came out a minute later with a black syringe pen resembling what diabetics use to inject their insulin. He pulled up his shirt, plunged the whisker-thin needle into his abdomen, and hit the button. Troy heard a click.

Fritz swapped needles and ruby-red cartridges, recocked the pen injector, and passed it to Troy. "Any fatty tissue is fine," Fritz instructed.

Accepting the injector, Troy felt a twinge of doubt even though he had just seen Fritz inject himself. A second later, however, that twinge was supplanted by a wave of nausea, and he pressed the button.

Emmy followed suit.

Fritz said, "I'm feeling better already."

Chapter 47

Bo

FARKAS COULD NOT HELP basking in the glow of his own cleverness as Emmy cleared the dishes from the table. Not only had he tricked his guests into injecting themselves with 456, but he had even managed to cover his tracks by lacing their dessert pudding with crushed Dramamine.

On the downside, he had used up his stash of 456 and was once again left with only a single dose in reserve. And he too now had the miracle drug shellacking his dendrites. But without the subsequent UV-C exposure, his system would flush it within forty-eight hours. No harm, no foul.

Now he just had to pump enough booze into them to dull their edge.

Fortunately, he had just the ticket.

Once Emmy retook her seat, Farkas asked, "Did you make up your mind? Do you want me to tell you what I know about your tragic backgrounds, or would you rather let sleeping dogs lie?"

"Tell us," Emmy said. "The good, the bad, and the ugly."

"As you wish. But first I'm going to freshen up our drinks. Trust me, you're going to need them."

After pouring healthy measures of rum and wine, Farkas said, "Ladies first," and began the unlikely task of telling Emmy her own story. There was no percentage in lying to her, no need to spice things up. He just told it like it was. "Back in 2005, having worked for years as an upscale psychic in L.A., you moved into the Beverly Hills estate of one of your former customers, a man named Bo Beaulieu, with whom you were in love.

"Bo was much older than you, and very wealthy. Needless to say, his relatives were displeased to see anyone without her own money coming between them and their inheritance. To make a long story short—your words, not mine—they pressured him not to marry you and he never did. That did not bother you because you were happy just to be with Bo, much happier than you had ever been before. You were a good 'wife.' That situation lasted for a year and a half, until Bo was killed while jogging in a hit and run.

"Adding insult to injury, Bo's family moved into his estate and kicked you out before the body was cold, claiming that you were just domestic help on par with the maid and gardener."

"Shall I continue?" Farkas asked, wanting to appear empathetic.

Emmy nodded as he knew she would.

"You did the only thing you could, not having any money of your own. You went back to working as a psychic. It was hard going. You had gotten used to living the good life and felt that your discontent affected the quality of your readings. Furthermore, all your old, hard won clientele had moved on during your eighteen-month hiatus, and so it was pretty rough going.

"You brought a civil suit against the man who was allegedly behind the wheel of the killer Porsche Cayenne, but you lost when the only witness to the crime developed amnesia and could not testify.

"After that you were back on the streets."

Farkas watched Troy reach over and pull Emmy toward him with both arms, using one to hold her tight, the other to stroke her hair. She looked limp as a rag doll, staring forward, her cheeks dry but expressionless.

One down, one to go.

Farkas turned toward Troy and said, "That's Emmy's story. Are you ready for yours?"

Chapter 48

Leapfrog

HONEY RETURNED to his office after four long hours at the bank. Getting nowhere was exhausting. He was hungry too.

"Any luck?" Molly asked.

"Luck? What's that?"

"Are they bank robbers? A new Bonnie and Clyde?"

"No," he said, wondering if she had peanut butter crackers in her big beige handbag today. "Their intentions remain a mystery. She spent fifteen minutes talking to one of the account managers, but then didn't open an account when the number she wanted wasn't available."

"That's weird."

"It gets weirder. She spent five of those minutes reading the account manager's aura. Did a hell of a job too, he said."

"What was her partner doing?"

"He was chatting up the other senior banker about mortgage rates. I'm guessing that they were waiting for Jacobs to arrive."

"You think maybe it was personal? Johnson and Jacobs both?"

"I don't know what else to think. Maybe they're just complete psychopaths. But then there's that anonymous tip ..." Honey shook his head. "How we doing with the blue brotherhood?" he asked, changing the subject.

"Got over fifty confirmations with more coming in all the time. Coast Guard will have them here around midnight."

"Great. I want them in place when the air and sea ports open. With the ports manned, our guys will be free to sweep the interior en masse."

"How can I help?"

"Oscar is getting us new mug shots off the bank's security cameras. They're much sharper than the old ones and in color. I'll need you to make up new wanted posters and several thousand flyers. Then I need you to get on the phone with channel 9 and the radio stations. I want them all broadcasting the description I gave you."

"Okay. I take it you're going to be leading the chase?"

"No."

"No?"

"No. I'm done chasing. This time ... I'm going to get out in front of them."

Chapter 49

Agent Simms

TROY STUDIED FRITZ for a long minute, trying to decide if he wanted this to be the man who narrated his life. Despite all appearances and what they had been through, he did not trust their reporter friend. In the end, however, he simply had to know.

"I'm ready. Give it to me straight."

Fritz nodded and took another sip of his drink. "I know quite a bit more about you than Ms. Green. I was planning to make you the subject of a separate human interest story."

"Just give me the highlights," Troy said, knowing that exposing his past would be like ripping a Band-aid off his heart—a very big and sticky Band-aid. Best to be quick.

"Very well. Three-and-a-half years ago you married an international correspondent for CNN. Her name was Sabrina Trevino. The two of you had met on several occasions in Afghanistan and then dated throughout two years of coincidental service in Iraq. When she got a job with CNN's Washington bureau, you resigned your commission, married her, and went to work at Bethesda Medical Center as a civilian.

"You sure you want to hear this?" Fritz asked.

"I am," Troy replied.

"As you wish.

"Sabrina got pregnant on your Hawaiian honeymoon. She gave birth to Alisandra nine months later. That was about two-and-a-half years ago." Fritz paused to let Troy digest this while he drained his tumbler of rum.

"Nine months ago," Fritz continued, "you were driving home from dinner when you were clipped by a drunk going sixty in a Hummer. The road was icy and your 3-series BMW spun out of control. It flipped over a railing and fell down into a ravine where it landed upside down on some boulders. The roof of the car caved in, killing your wife and daughter. The steering column shielded you from the brunt of the impact, and you walked away with a couple of gashes on your forehead and a smashed up arm.

"The drunk, Russell Rankin, never even slowed down."

Troy felt the room begin to spin. This could not be happening. He looked over at Emmy and saw tears rolling down her cheeks. She reached over and put her hand atop his.

Mercifully, Fritz kept talking, not allowing Troy to dwell. "You were pulled out of the car by an FBI Agent on his way home from work. Agent Simms witnessed the accident and saw the driver clearly, but did not get the license number. He lost his memory the day before the trial and could not testify, forcing the prosecution to drop the case."

"They dropped the case?" Emmy said. "What about the physical evidence, the drunk's Hummer?"

"It turns out that Rankin's wife had a matching black Hummer. When the police showed up the next morning and asked to see his vehicle, Rankin produced his wife's. Before the police figured out that they had been duped, Rankin reported his own stolen. He also had a group of friends willing to provide him with an alibi."

"And the man who killed my boyfriend?" Emmy asked. "What happened to him?"

"Similar story, I gathered. You didn't give me the details."

"Yet no one connected the dots?" Emmy pressed.

"Drunk drivers kill over ten thousand people a year in the US. You would have to be looking pretty hard to distinguish those two dots."

Troy slumped forward with his elbows on his knees and his palms on the back of his head. If more were coming, he did not want to see it telegraphed by slanted eye or crinkled brow. He wanted a blindfold for the execution.

Apparently Fritz was out of ammunition, because Emmy asked, "How did Troy and I meet?"

There was a long pause, during which Troy guessed that Fritz and Emmy were passing silent signals. Then Fritz cleared his throat, reloading so to speak, and took the next shot. "Troy lost more than his family in the accident. The nerve damage to his right arm cost him his ability to operate. With no job to pour himself into as he worked through the stages of grief, he devoted himself to obtaining justice. His first stop was Agent Simms, whom he assumed Rankin had bribed. But after a thorough interrogation and a month of follow-up detective work, Troy became convinced that Simms' amnesia was real.

"His next move was to look for similar instances."

"He connected the dots," Emmy interjected.

Troy looked up to see Fritz nodding. "He dug up an article on your case that made the society pages. He flew out to L.A. and the two of you clicked. While your situation was not as dire as Troy's, you were also very motivated to get to the bottom of what happened and eager for a break from L.A. So you joined forces.

"I don't know the specifics of how you ended up on Grand Cayman, other than that you were following the trail of payments made by the unconvicted murderers. I got the impression that you were using illegal means—stealing financial records, hacking into banking networks, things like that—because you avoided revealing your methods. That's about all I know."

"I see," Troy heard Emmy say. "Well, I think that's enough for one sitting. I'm going to put our friend here to bed."

Chapter 50

Recipe

LUTHER STARED at Arlen with his mouth agape as the number replayed in his mind. Five-hundred-and-eleven million dollars. Half-a-billion. Talk about life changing on a dime. After repeating the musical number five or six times to himself, however, the lawyer in him regained control and he settled back into the plush armchair. "What's the catch?"

Arlen spread his hands, palms up. "There's no catch, Luther. Just a few conditions."

"I see ... Do tell; I'm all ears."

"Is that an espresso machine I see over there?" Arlen asked.

Luther stood, more pleased to have an excuse to walk off some tension than irritated by the delay. "Single or a double?"

"I'd love a double," Arlen said, standing as well.

They walked over to the granite bar where Arlen leaned with one elbow on the countertop. After Luther ground the beans, Arlen began. "There's one thing we need to agree on up front. It will help everything else fall into place."

"Go ahead."

"Given the amount of attention that your history-making performance will garner, and the corresponding size of your payout, I trust you can see that it would be in everyone's best interests for this to be your swan song. After successfully wiping the entire United States Supreme Court, you, the compound and your five hundred and eleven million dollars are to retire permanently. Hell, let's make it an even five fifty, agreed?"

Luther's knee-jerk reaction was *no way*. He was not going to let a client dictate his life. But after a moment's thought, he realized that retirement was the only sensible move. After this job, the FBI would forever be on the lookout for new occurrences of wiped minds. Meanwhile, with *Who shot JFK?* getting old, conspiracy buffs would look at the amnesic Supreme Court as tigers do red meat. Thousands of closet nerds would begin digging through past cases, sifting the minutia for clues. Yes, Luther thought, he would be well advised to be living on a distant island when that happened—his own private island.

And it wasn't as though he enjoyed his work.

Feeling a profound if unexpected sense of relief, he said, "Agreed."

"Excellent, my friend. I'm glad we're of like mind. Now, let's discuss tactics."

"I work alone. Always have, always will," Luther replied. He was a proud man, the California Bar Association's Man of the Year for chrissake. He had to show some spine. He drew a line, and vowed not to let Arlen cross it.

To Luther's chagrin, Arlen's expression remained as cordial as could be. "Have you ever wiped anyone as high profile as a US Supreme Court justice?"

"My client list is confidential."

Arlen took a sip of his espresso and then set the cup back down on the saucer. "I'll take that as a no. Tell me this then; have you ever done more than two wipes for a single case?"

"No. Multiple wipes are just too dangerous. Despite the higher pay, I prefer sticking to singles."

"I see. So now that we've determined that the size and scope of your experience are both but a fraction of the task at hand, do you still find it reasonable to ask me to part with half-a-billion dollars without some kind of oversight?"

Luther recognized Arlen's tactic as one of his own courtroom favorites: framing. Luther had reduced the world of possibilities to a yes or no based upon an overly simple set of parameters. Luther also realized that Arlen had just run him through a subroutine. Luther had routinely prepared dozens of similar argumentative loops before his courtroom appearances. If the prosecutor says A, get the jury back on track with subroutine X, if he says B, use Y. Luther hated being on the receiving end of such tactics. Their use implied that Arlen was currently holding him in intellectual contempt. He resolved not to end up there again, and tossed out a framing question of his own. "Do you really want to involve yourself so deeply in something so risky?"

Arlen smiled as if to say touché, then changed his tack. "When I was negotiating with Landis, Aridon was on their 243rd compound. How much further did he get?"

Luther decided to play along. "All the way to 456."

Arlen raised his brows at the implied progress. "I trust that the compound still requires UV-C activation after implantation?"

"That's right."

"Is the amount of memory erasure constant?"

Luther could think of no reason to hold back that detail. "No. We can vary it from a minimum of around four weeks up to about the last twenty percent of a person's total episodic memory."

Arlen looked off into space for a minute, then nodded and asked, "Do you know why twenty percent is the limit?"

The pharmacology of 456 was a testy topic for Luther. He was embarrassed not to understand it. Landis had been Luther's only source for such information, but he flaunted his PhDs in Biochemistry and Molecular Biology every time he opened his mouth. No doubt that was part of the reason he had trouble getting financing. Initially, Luther had not given a crap about the science—he was in it for the money—so he had let Landis's explanations fly over his head with little more than a contemplative nod. Now that Compound 456 was the sun in his universe, however, Luther was very curious indeed. He sensed an opportunity, swallowed his pride, and said, "No."

Arlen gave an understanding nod and said, "Landis wanted to cure Alzheimer's. While the biochemistry of the disease remains largely mysterious, we know that the formation of plaque clusters in the neuron forest is key. The plaque clusters strangle nerve cells—like weeds in a garden. Landis's strategy was to devise a compound that destroyed the plaque.

"He had a patent on an enzyme that fluoresced with heat when exposed to ultraviolet-C radiation. So his tactic was to develop a carrier for that enzyme that would bind uniquely to plaque—a guided missile to deliver his heat bomb, so to speak. Once in place, he planned to expose the enzyme to UV-C via the optic nerve, and destroy the plaque. With the plaque gone, the progression of Alzheimer's should be halted if not reversed.

"Incidentally, this is exactly the kind of treatment the pharmaceutical industry loves, because you have to keep coming back at regular intervals to have the weeds pulled.

"Landis's problem was finding a carrier that would bind only to plaque—a very smart missile. Unfortunately, the plaque in question, beta amyloid, is a peptide comprised of the same amino acids that are the building blocks of the nerve cells storing memories. Thus after 456 attempts, he still had nothing that attached to plaque and only plaque."

Luther knew that last point all too well. An announcement to that effect had marked the second worst day of his life. He said, "Landis thought he had it with 456. It worked in monkeys—but not in humans. When 456 destroyed the memory of the first volunteer, he threw in the towel."

"Hard to get more volunteers after that," Arlen agreed. "Now, you said that you can wipe memories from a minimum of about four weeks up to around the last twenty-percent of a person's life, right?"

"Right."

"Do you regulate that interval based on the quantity of 456 injected, or the exposure to UV-C?"

"The exposure to UV-C."

Arlen nodded as though this was the answer he expected. "And the higher the frequency, the longer the erasure, right?"

"Right. So how does it erase memory?" Luther asked.

"Memory is another gray area—pardon the pun. We still know surprisingly little about how memories are created and stored. The building blocks of memory are neurons, and you have billions of them. Each neuron has myriad branches, called dendrites, which conduct the flow of information. Over time, the dendrites become more stable, like the branches on a tree growing thicker. You follow?"

"Sure."

"Good. Now, there are also different types of dendrites, and again they are not fully understood. But nonetheless, given your explanation, it's obvious to me that in addition to attaching to beta-amyloid plaque, 456 attaches to dendrites associated with episodic memory. When activated with UV-C, it heats up. The heat fries the more fragile dendrites, the thinner branches so to speak."

"And at the most powerful setting, the heat is high enough to fry the most fragile twenty percent of branches," Luther said. "Got it."

"Good."

"I'm surprised that the heating doesn't damage the rest of the brain."

Arlen nodded. "That's one of those things you never know until you try. Since no one has caught on to you, apparently not. But I do have to believe that it causes one hell of a headache."

"So I've heard," Luther said. "Thanks."

Arlen drained his cup. "Now, with that arsenal in mind, let's get back to the battle plan."

Chapter 51

Alisandra

EMMY SHUT the stateroom door behind them and turned the lock as Troy flopped onto one of the twin beds. She should have felt numb from Fritz's revelations about her own past, but pity for Troy consumed her instead. She had lost the man that she loved. That was tragic … and probably true. But at the end of the day he was just her boyfriend, not even her fiancé. Troy had lost his wife, his daughter, and his career.

Although Troy had neither expressed nor voiced his feelings, she knew that he was attracted to her—spiritually and romantically. She also knew that those emotions were now fueling fires of guilt. She should probably be feeling guilty too, but she was not. Bo Beaulieu was gone forever. Troy was there with her. He was the only man she knew. And she loved him.

She wanted to lie down next to Troy, to put her arms around him and hold him until he cried himself to sleep. No, she corrected herself, that wasn't exactly true. In fact, she wanted to rip off their clothes and make love to him all night.

Neither was in the cards.

They had work to do.

Which meant she had to bring her partner around. "I'm so sorry, Troy. I can't even imagine what you're feeling."

He looked up at her with tears in his eyes. "Alisandra. My daughter's name … was Alisandra. It's a beautiful name. I'd always wondered if I'd have boys or girls and what I would name them. Now I know."

Emmy did not want to risk the potential fallout from a supportive squeeze, so she offered a reassuring nod.

"Now that name is all I have," Troy continued. "I have no idea what she looked like, so I can't even mourn a picture. Was she a pony-tailed brunette or a pig-tailed blonde? Big blue eyes? Hazel? Brown? Did she inherit my condition? Was she an angel or a mischief-maker? Did her voice sound like little bells? Did she call me Papa, or Daddy, or some variant that was easier for her to pronounce? Will I ever know? She's not just gone from this Earth, you see, she's also wiped from my mind. So is her mother. So is … my wife."

Troy made eye contact once again, his eyes suffused with pain.

"May I make a suggestion?" Emmy asked.

Troy nodded.

She took his hands and pulled him up into a sitting position. Without releasing them, she said, "If I were Sabrina, if I had died in the terrible accident that somehow spared your life, I would want you looking forward, not back. I would tell you it's a blessing that you don't remember and I would urge you to treat it as such."

Troy blinked a few times but did not speak.

Staring into his eyes, trying to lend him strength, Emmy swore she could actually see Troy pulling his act together. She could almost hear the drill sergeant screaming Pull yourself together, soldier! in his mind.

And then the pain passed like a summer storm and the old Troy began to shine. "You're right, of course. And I'm being selfish. You lost someone too."

"That's not the same and we both know it."

Troy kept going as though she had not spoken. "I need to start thinking big picture. Someone out there can wipe peoples' minds at will. The sanctity of memory is at stake—and no one is truly safe. Right now he seems to be using his diabolic power to win court cases, but what if he decides to branch out? What if he begins selling his potion or whatever it is to terrorists? What if the presidential aide carrying the nuclear football suddenly forgets his job and thinks it's just another briefcase? What if he slips the Kool-Aid to the crew of a nuclear sub? The damage this guy could do is limitless. God, I've been so self-centered."

"No," Emmy said. "You've made tremendous sacrifices in an attempt to bring this guy to justice. The fact that you've been doing it for personal reasons is irrelevant. If you boil it down, everything everyone does is for personal reasons."

Troy did not look convinced. "We've got to get to Miami immediately. We need to track this guy down right away. Who knows what violations he has planned for tomorrow, and the day after. There's no time to waste."

"Well, I've got good news in that regard," Emmy said, amazed by the speed of Troy's recovery, but knowing that this was just a break in his psychological storm. "You're not going to have to wait until tomorrow to start tracking this guy down."

"How so?"

"It's time I let you in on a little discovery of my own...."

Chapter 52

Sharks

FARKAS WATCHED the second hand on his stateroom clock make the sweep that would turn two fifty-nine to three AM. He had tried to sleep for a couple of hours after sending Troy and Emmy to bed, but it was a lost cause. The knowledge that he would be feeding his guests to the sharks come sunrise, kept the sandman from calling.

He was glad that he had gone the extra mile to learn how Troy and Emmy had gotten back on Luther's trail. Tattoos. A couple of lousy henna tattoos. It was a clever and insightful insurance policy—but one that would disappear when their feet did.

As an added bonus, Farkas now knew Luther's bank account number. He had memorized it when Emmy showed him the bottom of her foot. One step closer …

As the second-hand hit twelve, Farkas rose from his queen-size bed, his eyes fully adjusted to the dim recessed light that bathed the entire yacht. He grabbed his special camera and crept toward Troy and Emmy's sleeping quarters. Given the gusting wind, sloshing waves, and ever-present hum of the dual Mercury inboard motors, Farkas found it easier to creep unnoticed about a moving yacht than any home. He would keep that in mind when planning future wipes.

Farkas paused outside the forward stateroom for a moment to listen. He pictured the stateroom's triangular layout in his mind. It consisted of little more than two twin beds and some storage, all arranged in a V-shape along the curvature of the ship's prow.

He heard no sound.

Farkas donned his custom sunglasses, gripped the doorknob, and began to turn. Troy and Emmy's heads would both be about seven feet in front of him when he entered. He would step in and shut the door loudly behind him in order to wake them with the noise and get them looking in his direction. Then he would hit them with the UV-C flash.

This time, they would awake on a reef infested with sharks.

This time, there would be no miracle escape.

The knob stopped turning. He took a deep breath, and threw open the door. He stepped in and slammed the door behind him. The blankets neither moved nor rustled. For a second he worried that his plan to inebriate them had backfired. Then he felt the cord bite into his neck.

Attempting to whirl about, Farkas felt the noose constrict. He dropped the camera and brought both hands to his neck, only to feel something hard crash into the back of his head.

~ ~ ~

When Farkas awoke, his head was pounding and his neck was on fire. He was seated in an aluminum chair, his forearms bound to the armrests with duct tape. The noose Troy had snared him with still encircled his neck. As he tested his bonds, the cord began to tighten.

"Stop moving your legs. You're only choking yourself," he heard Troy say.

Understanding at once that they had tied the end of the noose to his ankles—a tactic he and his brothers had often used to interrogate Serbs —Farkas pushed his feet back under the chair. The cord slackened, but his neck still burned. "What the hell are you doing to me?" he asked. "Is this how you treat all your rescuers?"

"You can cut the act, Rokus," Emmy said, stepping into view. "We found your passport. Rokus Farkas of the Republic of Croatia."

"And the sniper rifle," Troy added from behind Farkas's back. "And the flasher concealed in your camera."

Like any good field operative, Farkas had a cover story prepared. "Call me Farkas," he said. "Everyone does. I'm with Interpol. What gave me away?"

Emmy shifted her gaze away from him to look at Troy and said, "He's lying." Then, turning back to him she said, "We had our suspicions confirmed hours ago when I feigned motion sickness and searched your room. And just to be accurate, what gave you away was what I did not find, namely the tools of the journalist trade: a notebook, voice recorder, and laptop computer."

"Let me show you—"

"Save it," Emmy said, cutting him off. "I found this a few minutes ago." She held up her left hand as if giving him the finger. She was wearing her engagement ring. A three-carat brilliant cut set in platinum. Farkas figured he could sell it on eBay for at least thirty grand.

"You rigged the window in the car, didn't you?" Troy asked. "You blew it out yourself with a remote-detonated charge. It was a clever move. Made me a believer. Unfortunately for you, Emmy here wrote the book on cons. She saw right through it."

Farkas needed time to think of plausible explanations. Given their memory loss, there had to be a formula that would work, if only for a few seconds. That was all it would take to snap their necks. He churned the waters of his mind. Nothing surfaced. He could hardly pretend to be infiltrating them for Interpol after having told them their own sad stories. The ring was a real kicker. And to top it all off, Emmy appeared to be a human lie detector.

Realizing that he was out of time, he decided to stick near the truth, but minimize his own involvement. They weren't going to hurt him, after all. Were they? No. They weren't killers. And they couldn't take him to the police. All he had to do was cooperate until they made a mistake. They had a long way to go and it would only take one slip-up.

An idea bubbled up from his problem-solving center. A delightfully wonderfully simple plan. He knew how to escape.

"Yes, I rigged the car's window. What else do you want to know?"

Chapter 53

Revelations

TROY LOOKED UP from the greasy pair of pliers and ball-peen hammer he'd found in the yacht's toolbox. Farkas had given what sounded like an honest answer. As ironic as it sounded, Troy was not sure that an honest answer was what he wanted at that moment.

He had waited in the dark for five hours, steaming and scheming, waiting to see if Emmy's conclusion proved correct. When it had, when Farkas stormed into their room holding the camera that Troy now knew not to be a camera at all, Troy had boiled over. Now that Farkas was awake, the hickory shank of that hammer was itching his hand.

"What else do you want to know?" Farkas repeated.

Troy looked over at Emmy, hoping she would shake her head and tell him Farkas was trying to play them for fools.

She nodded instead. Farkas was not holding back.

Still thumping the hammer head against his open palm, Troy walked around to face his foe, then sat down to watch his secret weapon work.

"What were you planning to do with us?" she asked.

Farkas shrugged. "I was going to erase your memories again."

"With the Balinorm," Troy asked, stressing the phony name.

"You figured that out, huh?" Farkas said, sounding amused.

Looking into his captive's eyes, Troy realized that Farkas was the real deal. His bravado was not dependent upon superior firepower. Troy knew the type. They were rare. He'd probably be wearing a green beret or a SEAL's Trident if he'd been born beneath an American flag. As it was, the Croatian really was an army of one.

"And then what?" Emmy pressed.

"And then drop you off while you were still unconscious."

"Unconscious?"

"Yes, the erasure overloads the mind, knocking you out for about three hours. Gives you a hell of a headache, too. But I guess you already know that."

"Drop us off where?" Troy asked.

"Jamaica. As agreed."

"He's lying," Emmy said.

"On the island, or in the surf?" Troy asked.

Farkas grew a faint smile and looked Troy in the eye. "I know a reef —lots of sharks."

Emmy shook visibly as Troy felt a shiver run down his spine. He had not thought it was possible, but there actually was an experience worse than waking up in a trunk with a dead cop—and Farkas had planned to give it to them. The admission gave new meaning to the words brutally honest.

Troy changed the subject. "Who are you working with?"

Farkas's expression became uncomfortable for the first time. "I honestly don't know."

"Not good enough," Troy said, standing. "You've been doing this for years. Of course you know." He gave the hammer another thump. "The only question is how many toes we're going to pulp before you remember."

Farkas did not blanch as any normal person would. He seemed completely indifferent, and that sent a second chill up Troy's spine. What had this guy been through that the ball-peen prospect was not worth a rise?

"Think about it," Farkas said. "Everything you know. The big picture. This guy gets his hands on a drug that can erase memories. He's sitting on a vein of pure gold, and he decides that the best way to mine it is to use it to win court cases. What's his biggest challenge?"

"Sleeping at night?" Emmy suggested.

"Keeping things secret," Troy said.

"Bingo."

"So how did he find you?" Emmy asked.

"Another clever move. I lost my license to practice medicine while still in my residency. He called me the day after the notification was posted on an AMA database."

"He wanted a desperate doctor," Troy said, nodding.

"How'd you lose your license?" Emmy asked.

Troy could not care less about this scumbag's personal history, but he decided that letting Emmy probe for details might not be a bad idea. Perhaps she would trip him up.

"I went to medical school at SUNY-Brooklyn. It was a big deal for a Croatian. My family pooled all their money to send me, to get me out of the civil wars—where most of my family eventually died. They gave me everything they had, but it still barely covered tuition. Since foreign nationals are not eligible for student loans, I had to work nights. Full-time. Even then I couldn't afford so much as a dorm room. I rented an armchair to sleep on from a fellow Croat living in a one-room apartment in Queens. Long story short, I took a lot of speed to keep going. I had been up for thirty-two hours when I screwed up a diagnosis, mistaking congestive heart failure for an asthma attack. The kid died. A fellow intern—a man after my girlfriend—tipped the administration off to the fact that I was high at the time. They tested my blood, and I lost my license."

"You're lucky that's all that happened," Emmy said.

"The hospital wanted to keep things quiet."

"That kind of thing happens more often than you think," Troy added. "Just check the phone book for medical malpractice attorneys."

"I didn't know what to do," Farkas continued. "I went from hero to zero overnight. Nonetheless, my sisters were still counting on me for financial support. I was distraught and desperate. Then the phone rang. A man who called himself Luther offered ten thousand dollars cash for secretly administering a special treatment, just a simple two-step procedure. That was nearly four years ago, four years and forty-six procedures."

"Including ours?" Emmy asked.

"No. You weren't cases. You were cleanup. Forty-six witnesses. Although you, Ms. Green, were one of those too. You have the honor of being the only person ever flashed twice."

"Almost three times," Emmy added. "But we digress. Are you telling me that through forty-six jobs you never once met your employer?"

"Never. We just talk via satellite phone. I don't even know for sure what country he lives in, although I assume it's the US."

"What else do you assume?" Troy asked.

"I assume that he's an attorney, since he chose to use the drug toward legal ends, and people tend to stick with what they know."

"What's his last name?"

"I don't know. I'm not even sure if Luther is his real first name or not. I get the feeling that it is. It comes naturally to him."

"How old is Luther, judging by his voice," Emmy asked.

"Late thirties, early forties."

"Caucasian voice?"

"Yes."

"American accent?"

"Yes."

"What's the area code on his phone?" Troy asked.

"312. Chicago."

"You ever hear the El running in the background, or station announcements, like on The Fugitive?" Emmy asked.

"No. I don't think he lives there. He's too relaxed. Never mentions the cold either."

Emmy looked at Troy and nodded. She believed him.

"Tell me how the drug works," Troy said. "I want the details."

Farkas met Troy's eye, and nodded. Former doctor to former doctor. "It's a two-stage procedure. First the victim must be injected with a biopharmaceutical compound Luther calls 456. Within fifteen minutes of injection, 456 bonds to fresh dendrites. It—"

Troy held up his hand, cutting Farkas off and turning to Emmy. "Memories are stored in neurons. You have billions of neurons which interact through trillions of connections. Those connections have physical, electrical, and chemical components. Dendrites are the physical portion, the wiring so to speak. They're like the roots to the neuron plant."

Emmy said, "Thanks," and Farkas continued. "Once bonded to your fresh dendrites, a process requiring just fifteen minutes from injection, 456 is activated by Ultraviolet-C radiation. Depending on the wavelength used, I can erase anything from around four weeks' worth of memories to about the last twenty percent of a person's life."

"Is that range related to dendrite maturation?" Troy asked.

"Right. Dendrites, like roots, grow thicker with age and thus less vulnerable. Perhaps that's why Alzheimer's patients tend to lose their earliest memories last."

With a sinking feeling in his gut, Troy asked, "What, exactly, happens when 456 is activated?"

"The UV-C fluoresces the 456, causing it to emit heat that cooks the dendrites. The higher the wavelength, the greater the heat, the thicker the dendrites it destroys."

Hearing those words, Troy collapsed backwards onto the couch.

Emmy looked over at him, panic in her eyes. "What is it?"

Troy shook his head. "If what he says is true—and I have no doubt that it is, from a medical perspective it makes too much sense—then there is almost no chance of ever getting our memories back. All links to them have been physically destroyed.

"My family is gone forever."

Chapter 54

Half

"BACK TO THE BATTLE PLAN," Arlen said, apparently having explored the biochemistry of 456 to his satisfaction. "Tell me more about the mechanics of memory wiping."

"It's a two-phase process," Luther replied, holding up one hand and then the other. "First, we inject the 456. Then we flash the target with UV-C."

"Tell me about the injection," Arlen said. "How much is needed?"

"Like cyanide, a little goes a long way. One milliliter is enough."

Arlen arched his aristocratic brows. "Great. So darts work, and you can use the old Cold War devices like injector rings and umbrella tips?"

"We've used all of the above."

"Any special conditions? Does 456 have to be refrigerated?"

"For storage, but not for use. It's like insulin in that regard."

"Got it. How about timing? Any limits there?"

"On both ends. It takes fifteen minutes to activate—to bind to the beta-amyloid-like peptide as I now understand. You have forty-eight hours from injection to expose the 456 to UV-C. After forty-eight hours, its bioavailability drops rapidly, depending on a person's metabolism."

"Got it. Tell me, since the UV-C travels directly to the brain through the optic nerve, am I right in assuming that they have to be looking at the flasher when it happens?"

"You are."

"How do you manage that?"

"Simple. We usually imbed it in a camera flash. People tend to look at a camera when it's pointed in their direction—it's a subconscious reflex, if not a conscious one. And a camera provides perfect camouflage. The whole process looks as natural as can be—until the victim drops unconscious."

Arlen smiled. "Excellent. So once you've got the subject injected, it's all downhill from there."

"You got it."

"And for how long does the procedure render the victim unconscious?"

"Again it varies with metabolism. About three hours."

"Is there any way to tell if a person has been primed with 456?"

"There is. If you look at him through lenses that filter out all light above and below the 300 nanometer range, his eyes will appear to glow with a violet tinge."

"Excellent," Arlen said, sliding forward in his chair. "Okay, here's my proposal, the good stuff, the moment you have been waiting for ... I will pay you half your fee once you present me with an acceptable plan to flash all nine Supreme Court Justices. Then I will—"

"Hold on!" Luther interrupted. "You said earlier that you brought me a check."

"A figure of speech," Arlen said, splaying his hands. "As I was saying, I will pay you two hundred and fifty million dollars upon approving your detailed plan, and then the balance—we'll make that an even three hundred million after I verify that you have injected all nine justices with 456. That way you can be ready to disappear the moment you flash them."

Luther considered the proposal. He could try to insist on immediate payment of the first half, but what would be the point? It shouldn't take him more than a week or two to come up with an acceptable plan— assuming the task was possible. The only reason for insisting upon payment now would be to run off with the down payment if it wasn't possible, and Arlen had no doubt thought of that.

What if it wasn't possible? Luther wondered, beginning to worry. Now that he had half-a-billion dollars dangling before him, the thought of losing them was unbearable. He could not let that happen. He would find a way. "Your terms are acceptable," he said, holding out his hand.

"I'm glad to hear it," Arlen said. "But I'm not finished yet."

Luther felt his face going red and used his extended hand to reach for his espresso. "What else?"

"Just one more thing, and I'm afraid that it is a deal breaker. Non-negotiable."

Luther nodded as his throat went dry, then took a sip of his drink.

"Given the size and intensity of the investigation that we both expect, I am going to have to insist that you flash everyone involved in this and all your previous operations. The day after the justices go amnesic, you and I are to be the only two people on the planet who have a clue as to how it was done."

Finished and obviously pleased with himself, Arlen held out his hand to seal the deal.

Luther tried to look taken aback, as though the thought of betraying his colleagues offended him. In truth, Farkas was the only person Luther had ever worked with, and it had always been Luther's plan to flash him when all was done.

With visions of private beaches and Playboy Bunnies and Jury screeching "It's a deal" in the background, Luther took Arlen's hand.

Chapter 55

Unhealthy Returns

"SO WHO'S YOUR NEXT VICTIM?" Troy asked, resuming the interrogation without the benefit of having a human lie detector by his side.

"I don't know," Farkas said.

"Do I need the hammer?"

Farkas's expression remained calm, almost detached. "I'm supposed to fly to Boston when I'm done with you. Check into the Hyatt Regency and wait for an envelope. That's how it always works. Usually a different city. Always a different hotel. Never any details in advance."

Troy was not happy with that response, but it sounded reasonable given what he knew of Luther's operating style. He decided to stir the waters a bit to keep Farkas talking in the hope that something would slip out. "Don't you ever stop to consider the big picture?"

Farkas raised his bushy brows. "Big picture?"

"You're creating a world where one man can rob another of his mind."

Farkas shook his head and chuffed. "Samuel Colt created that world long ago."

"No. A bullet to the brain only keep's a man from moving forward. 456 reaches back in time to steal his past. You're opening up a whole new dimension of destruction."

Emmy shouted down from the bridge before Farkas could retort. "Farkas lied. We aren't en route to Jamaica. We're headed back to Grand Cayman. He took us in a big circle."

Troy shouted, "I'll be there in a minute" without taking his eyes off Farkas.

"I already admitted that my real destination was a reef," Farkas said. "You'll forgive me if I didn't point it out as we passed. I didn't think that would be to my advantage."

It was Troy's turn to chuff. He might well have been tempted to toss Farkas overboard if he'd seen a school of dorsal fins off the prow.

Troy decided he had all the information he was likely to get, and in retrospect there was no sense discussing ethics with a man who had no soul.

He reached forward to recheck Farkas's bonds. The duct tape had bunched up a bit around the ends overnight, but it had yielded little to the Croatian's best efforts at escape. Farkas may as well be in chains. "We're going to leave you now."

"Just like that?"

"Not quite." Troy reached into a drawer and withdrew Farkas's modified camera and special UV-C filtering sunglasses. "I figured out how your neuron-frying system works. Now you're going to learn how it feels. Got anything you want to get off your chest? Any message you'd like to leave for yourself?"

Farkas eyed the camera for a long moment, and then looked up at Troy. "I had expected the sharks," he said, his voice cool as glacial ice.

Troy donned the sunglasses. "You deserve the sharks. As does your employer, and for that matter all the lawyers who pull tricks to set guilty clients free. But I'm not starting down that slippery slope. I'm not going to become like you." He brought the camera to his eye and added, "That said, I will feed you to the sharks if you blink."

Farkas nodded his understanding, his approval.

Troy paused with his finger on the button, and then lowered the camera. He confirmed for the third time that he had set the wavelength to erase four years according to the chart taped inside the back cover. "When you awake, you will have no recollection of compound 456, or Luther, or the lives you have ruined."

Farkas nodded stoically. "I suppose you think I should thank you."

Troy pressed the button.

Farkas's head jolted back as though shocked when the UV-C bathed his face. Then his eyes rolled back and closed and his body went limp as a wet noodle.

"You're damn right you should. Four destructive years. Dozens of damaged lives. And instead of paying for your crimes, you're getting a clean conscience and a second chance. Make the most of it, you bastard."

Troy ran up the stairs without looking back.

As soon as Emmy saw him she pointed to the navigational display. Troy saw the elf's shoe silhouette of Grand Cayman dead ahead. They were actually coming at it from the northwest, whereas Jamaica was on the other side of the island, one hundred and eighty miles to the southeast.

"So we lose half a day," he said. "It could be worse."

"It is worse. We're low on gas. We have no choice but to stop at Grand Cayman."

"You worried about the wanted posters?"

"It's more than that," Emmy said. "I listened to the radio while you were below dealing with our friend. The whole island is looking for the Cop-Killing Couple. That's what they're calling us. No doubt they have our pictures—fresh color ones from the bank's security cameras—decorating every gas pump on the island."

"Maybe we could siphon off another yacht's gas."

"No good. They're intercepting and searching all outgoing vessels. Once we enter port, that's it."

"Can't we make Little Cayman or Cayman Brac?"

"They're both ninety miles away. Out of range."

"So you're suggesting that we dock and abandon the yacht?"

"I don't think we have a viable alternative."

"So be it."

"But what then?" Emmy asked. "How do we get to Miami with the whole island looking for us? I might be able to slip through the gauntlet disguised as a teenage boy, but not you. Those scars of yours are like bullseyes on your head—and I absolutely refuse to lose you."

Troy wrapped his arms around her. "So what's new? Personally, I'm glad to be back in the game—so long as I've got you by my side. Besides, I'm sure you'll think of something."

Chapter 56

Drama

"DUDE, YOU'RE BURNING."

"It's an experiment," Troy replied without looking up. "Coppertone pays me to do this. You should talk to them. Easy money."

"No thanks, man. But you have yourself a ball."

With the whole island looking for his famous dimple and scars, Troy was hiding in plain site like an ostrich with his head in the sand. Emmy had left him on Seven-Mile and told him to burn.

As the teenagers walked off down the beach, laughing among themselves, the sea breeze brought a familiar scent to his nose. A second later he heard, "This is going to hurt." Then he felt an icy blade slip between his shoulder blades.

Troy whipped his head around to see Emmy standing over him holding an inverted bottle of aloe vera. "I wasn't finished," she said. He saw her face crinkle and knew that she had winked behind her imitation Cartier sunglasses. He flipped back over and checked Ironman while she rubbed the freezing lotion into his scorched skin. She had been gone for over three hours.

"How did it go at Tropical Towers? Did you get the car?"

"I did," Emmy said, finishing with his back. "I also picked up some children's sunscreen for your face. It's thick and white and will camouflage your scars." She popped the top off a small tube and began dabbing lotion on his forehead as though she were finger painting. Satisfied, she moved on to his nose and ears. "It might look like a disguise if I only do your forehead. This way, you look more like a careless tourist." She finished and said, "Those ripe shoulders of yours complete the picture nicely, so long as you have your shirt off."

"Aren't you going to put any on my chin?"

"Too conspicuous. But I picked you up this lovely cognac cigar." She pulled a glass tube from her beach bag. The cigar inside was long and fat, and looked like it would burn for hours. Liberating the cigar, she popped it in his mouth and then stepped back to admire her creation. "Way too goofy to fit the cop-killer mold."

"Thanks. But this isn't going to get me past the kind of serious check they're bound to have at the airport."

"Sea port," she corrected. "I picked us up a couple of cruise ship IDs. And probably not. My sunglasses won't cut it either. That's why our next stop is the Cayman Drama Society."

"Cruise ship IDs?"

"They're like electronic hotel keys, except that they have your name and cabin number printed on them. You use them for identification when embarking and disembarking."

"And you just picked them up?"

"From a beach bag emblazoned with the Neptune cruise line logo. Now, get in the car."

Troy made the connection between the Cayman Drama Society and disguises as he hunkered down in the back seat. He closed his eyes as they drove, focusing on the hum of the Camry's tires and shifting as necessary to keep his back out of the sun.

Emmy turned on the radio and station surfed until she found news. The announcer was midway through a story about the impact of increased cruise ship traffic. Apparently, the island's 9,200-person cap on cruise passengers was routinely exceeded, sometimes by as much as two hundred and fifty percent. The bumper crops of tourists were a boon to George Town's working residents and business owners, but a bane to everyone else.

"Back to the day's top story. Sixty-two law enforcement officers from neighboring islands arrived on Grand Cayman this morning, volunteering their weekends to join in the hunt for the couple that brutally murdered two of their own. We advise all our listeners to be on the lookout for the unidentified pair, but not to approach them under any circumstances as they are considered extremely dangerous. He is Caucasian, approximately one hundred and eighty-five centimeters and ninety kilos, with dark hair, blue eyes, two v-shaped scars above his right eye, and a Kirk-Douglas dimple on his chin. She is around one hundred and sixty centimeters, forty-five kilos, with dark hair, fair skin and bright green eyes. Anyone—"

Emmy turned off the radio. "We're here. Just in time from the sound of things."

"Is it safe for me and my distinctively dimpled chin to emerge?" Troy asked, pulling Farkas's Kangol cap low on his forehead.

"Looks that way; I only see one other car, an old green pickup. The theater is sandwiched between a forest and a school, and it's Saturday afternoon."

He got out and asked, "What exactly are you hoping to purloin?"

"Heavy makeup, facial hair, tinted contact lenses. I figure that this is the best place on the island to get everything we need with minimal exposure."

"What technique do you have in mind?"

"You'll see." She knocked on the right half of the double door. No answer. As she began a second round the left door swung out and a tall black man of some sixty years asked, "May I hep ya?" He had a mouth bursting with white teeth, friendly eyes, and wore navy coveralls that had seen no fewer than a thousand washings.

"Hi. I'm Josephine Jamison. I'm a makeup artist at Universal Studios, Hollywood. I'm on vacation—here on a cruise—and I was hoping to talk some kind soul into showing me around your fine theater, particularly backstage." She flashed a heart-stopping smile.

"Well, I dunno how our li'l the-ater compares to what you got in Hollywood, but we's mighty proud of it. Come on in, Miss Jamison." He looked up at Troy. "Mista Jamison. Welcome. I'm William."

They stepped inside and the janitor secured the door. The theater was dark but for the light emanating from someplace backstage. The air smelled of freshly cut wood.

"I's been here since we opened back in eighty-seven. Know every inch of her, so I don't really need the lights 'cept where I's workin'. I can turn them on for you though if you'd like?"

"It's really the backstage we're interested in," Emmy said. "Particularly your costume and wardrobe facilities. That's my specialty."

"Right this way, ma'am. Right this way."

Troy had an uneasy feeling as he followed William back toward the source of the light. Emmy was good, but this struck him as too easy. Then again, he had not gone through life with a centerfold figure and a smile that opened doors.

William led them down a passage to the right of the stage which turned into a wide hallway that ran behind it. The hallway was as tall as the stage itself, and full of tethered ropes and electrical switches and miscellaneous props. Several doors lined the wall off to the right. "This is the room you're looking fa'," William said, opening a door marked Makeup. Troy held back as William ushered Emmy through.

Troy heard Emmy gasp as she entered and knew what she had seen even before he peeked around the doorframe. Officer Honey stood there with satisfaction beaming from his eyes. This time he was the one holding the Colt.

Chapter 57

Sketch

FARKAS WATCHED THE CLOCK, waiting for ten long minutes after hearing Troy and Emmy leave the yacht before moving. His plan had worked perfectly, but the jig would be up if Troy returned for something forgotten and found him awake.

Then the ball-peen hammer would come back out and stay out until Farkas revealed his secret.

Then Troy really would flash his memory away.

The upside of the whole bungled episode was that his custom contact lenses had been battle-tested. Now he could go forward without the nagging fear that some UV-C might still slip through. When Luther decided to terminate and erase their relationship—an end Farkas saw as inevitable—he would find the tables turned.

The downside of Troy and Emmy's escape was that it made him look like an idiot. Luther might now decide to end their relationship with a bullet rather than a flash, especially when Troy and Emmy showed up at his door. That too was inevitable—unless Farkas killed them first. To do that, he had to escape.

Troy had used duct tape to bind the entire length of Farkas's forearms to an aluminum deck chair. Farkas was going crazy trying to sever the thick gray coils. They were tough as steel gauntlets and Troy had removed every blade from the kitchen. Farkas tried everything from snagging the tape on shelf corners to puncturing it with drawer handles. Meanwhile, his quarry was slipping further and further away. Nothing worked. The legendary tape was just too resilient.

Since his only means of movement was hopping on two bound legs, and he could only do that while bent at an L-shaped angle, he was inadvertently giving himself a real beating. At a quarter past noon, Farkas finally conceded the inevitable. He would break his neck before breaking free.

He needed help.

He decided to scream.

Aware that he was more likely to break his neck than make it to the top of the stairs and through the door, Farkas positioned himself at the base of the stairs. Keeping his eyes on the wall clock, he began screaming "Help!" once every sixty seconds. After an hour, with his throat dry and sore, he switched to every two minutes. Then to every three. Four hours after his first scream, nearly six hours after Troy and

Emmy had fled, he finally felt movement on the boat. "I'm down here! Please, help!"

Farkas heard cautious footsteps, and then a black face poked around the doorway at the top of the stairs, followed immediately by a gun. "Thank goodness you heard me," Farkas said. "I've been robbed."

"Are you alone?" the officer asked.

"Yes. The couple who did this to me left hours ago."

The officer did not holster his weapon as he and his partner came down. After a brief visual inspection of his bonds, they searched the two staterooms in a manner much more professional than Farkas would have expected from paradise cops. Satisfied with their search, they began conversing in a language Farkas could not understand.

Farkas read their name tags. The senior officer was a sergeant named Brandell. Junior's name was Mertins. They seemed to be studying him while they spoke, and were paying particular attention to his eyes. Farkas frequently received double-take glances since the reflective nature of the custom lenses gave his eyes an unusual metallic sheen. They were kinda cool, he had always thought. They meshed nicely with his scruffy beard and Kangol cap to complete a tough-guy image. He half expected to start a Hollywood trend. But admiration was not written on the officers' faces, and an uneasy feeling overtook him. "Would you guys mind cutting me free?" he asked. "I'm getting pretty tired of this chair."

Brandell nodded to Mertins, who went to the kitchen in search of a knife Farkas knew he would not find. He brought back a pizza cutter instead. Eventually, Mertins cut through the tape on the inside of Farkas's right arm. The instant the final strand gave, Farkas ripped his arm free with a motion that would have made a veteran bikini waxer faint.

Farkas said, "Thanks," and had begun to rub his bloody forearm against his shorts when Brandell stepped forward and slapped a handcuff around his wrist. Then the sergeant linked it to his left wrist before slicing through one side of the tape and signaling for Farkas to repeat the depilatory procedure. Farkas looked Brandell in the eye, gauged his intentions to be serious, and complied without breaking eye contact.

"What's the problem?" Farkas asked. "Why the cuffs?"

Neither officer replied. They just pulled him to his feet and escorted him back to their squad car.

Perhaps Troy and Emmy had been captured and broken. He could think of no other explanation for this cruel twist of fate.

As they pulled away from the West Bay marina, he pressed his luck. "I deserve to know what this is all about."

Neither officer spoke, but Sergeant Brandell held his clipboard up to the Plexiglas partition without looking back. It displayed a police artist's sketch—of his face.

Chapter 58

Tango

STARING DOWN the barrel of Officer Honey's Colt, Emmy felt like her air supply had been cut off.

Then the lights went out.

In the blink of an eye the theater became dark as a cave. Before she could react, someone grabbed her arm and yanked her violently backwards. She careened into someone else and they both tumbled to the wooden floor. The makeup room door slammed as she fell, blowing wind across her face.

Lying there in the dark, Emmy pictured the circuit box they had passed in the hall. Troy must have flipped the big gray switch. His reflexes were amazing.

She waited through a moment of stunned silence for Troy to place a hand on her shoulder or whisper in her ear. Neither came. Had the slamming door drowned out a gunshot? Was Troy wounded? She reached out tentatively toward the figure beside her. She felt the soft fabric of old coveralls. William.

He groaned in response to her touch, his tone more winded than wounded. He was not shot, just stunned.

If William was with her, then Troy must be on the other side of the door. He had used the momentum of swinging her out to sling himself in. He had gone after Honey.

She braced for the gunshot that would change her life while picturing the two combatants blindly circling one another on the other side of the door. William stirred, breaking her trance with, "Oh Lordy." As he began rising to his feet, she knew instinctively that he was going for the circuit box. She had to stop him before he found the lever.

At five foot two and a hundred pounds, Emmy was not born into the warrior class. But she had come of age on predatory streets. She sprang up, wedging herself between William and the wall. Her left shoulder knocked his probing arm aside as she rose while her hands grappled for his neck. As William staggered backwards to slip her grip, she moved with him, getting her legs into position. When he brought his hands up to claw at hers, she brought her right knee up with full force. It found the soft target.

William let out an agonized, "Ooph," and doubled over, whacking his forehead against the top of hers. The wallop dazed Emmy, but she remained standing. William crumpled to the floor, where he began to rock and moan.

A gunshot boomed through the dark like a cannon as scuffling sounds erupted from the makeup room. Emmy froze and strained her ears. The noise peaked with a loud smack followed by a crash.

Silence ensued.

She got a splinter groping for the circuit box, but found it and pulled the central lever.

William lay off to her left, still rolling around much as she had envisioned. If only he had waited a few seconds ... As she reached for the knob of the dressing room door, it opened. Troy stood there, his face a mask of concern.

"Are you okay?" he asked.

"I'm fine." She poked her head into the room to see Officer Honey on the floor.

"He'll be okay," Troy said. "I just knocked him out."

"With your bare hands?"

"It's not that hard, medically speaking, if you know what to do. The tough part was doing it in the dark. I had to direct my blow by touch which meant grabbing before I struck. That was when he got the shot off. But enough history, let's get the hell out of here."

"Not yet," Emmy said. "We still need disguises. Pull William in here while I search for what we need. Then change into Honey's uniform. When you're done with that, tie them up together, back to back."

"You want me to impersonate a police officer?"

"It's the only way, Troy. You heard the broadcast. I'll explain as we get dressed."

Chapter 59

End of the Line

FARKAS UNDERSTOOD what had happened the moment he saw his composite picture. The old couple from Elisabeth Avenue had given his description to the police. He felt like kicking himself. If only he had remembered them a few hours earlier...

Lifting his gaze from his handcuffs to the patrol car window, he spotted the pier where Troy had dumped the detective's body. He only had a few minutes to escape. The first order of business at the police station—after calling the Wootens in for a lineup—would be to print him. Once they found his fingerprints sanded, they would know they had their man.

He had to attack while they still harbored doubt.

Using the sharp nail of his right thumbnail, he began slicing the skin of his left wrist just above the calloused lump. He had imagined this moment a thousand times since placing the implant, but found it much more difficult in real life. His skin did not yield so easily, and warm blood turned his fingers so slick that they could not wrench the key free. He clawed on in desperation, ignoring the pain as he dug into the scarred tissue. He had only seconds, only one chance, and it was slipping from his grasp.

He looked back up as they hit the curb to the garage where it all began. His eyes scanned the garage for other occupants while his fingers continued working.

"Let's see if we can't get this straightened out," Mertins said, getting out and opening the rear door.

Farkas stayed put.

"Come on, buddy," Mertins pushed. "It's time for the moment of truth."

"Where are we?" Farkas asked. "How do I know you're really cops?" It was weak, but the only disarming stall tactic that sprang to mind.

The question was surprising enough to buy Farkas another second of delay. That second proved enough to wrest the key from its encapsulation.

"We're at police headquarters," Mertins said. "Look at the other cars in the garage."

Farkas made a show of looking around from the back seat while mating key with lock out of sight. He continued to study one car in particular as he emerged. His puzzled stare prompted Mertins to follow his gaze.

That was all it took.

Farkas whipped the empty cuffs around like a flail, catching Mertins square in the temple. As Mertins fell, Farkas bounded off the doorsill, banked off the open door and lunged over the roof at the shocked sergeant. Brandell made the mistake of going for his gun rather than getting out of the way. Farkas slammed into him before he could raise his weapon. As the sergeant tottered, Farkas whipped around, windmilling the handcuffs into the back of Brandell's head. As Brandell slumped, Farkas saw that he had not been as lucky as his junior partner. The handcuff spur had impaled his neck around the second cervical disk. He would likely be paralyzed if he lived.

Farkas picked Brandell's hat up off the bloody concrete and placed it on his own head. Then, for the second time that week, he heaved two bodies into a patrol car trunk. Again, he had to arrange the unconscious forms like spoons in a drawer so they would fit. He slammed the trunk, got into the driver's seat, and uncuffed his right wrist. Time to fly.

Emerging from the dim and dreary garage into the freedom of the bright Cayman sunlight, Farkas felt like he was being born again. He drove straight for Owen Roberts International Airport with dark lights and a silent siren. It was only a few miles. He found a place in the corner of the lot where a good thirty meters separated him from the nearest other car. He needed the buffer. Mertins would soon awake and start making noise.

He stuffed the composite drawing of his face into his pocket for later study and got out. His first impulse was to lock the keys in the car to add further delay to the chase. Realizing, however, that this would limit his escape options if the shit hit the fan, he stuffed them into the exhaust pipe instead.

He walked to the terminal and scanned the departure board for the first flight out. He found one headed for Orlando leaving in just thirty minutes. With luck, he would be aboard. If not, the next departure was not for an hour and ten minutes, and it was headed for Mexico City.

Farkas made it to the gate with enough time to grab a cup of Blue Mountain Jamaican coffee. Boarding was just starting as the barista passed him his steaming beverage, so he decided to get the call over with.

Picking up a payphone receiver, he half expected to see Emmy and Troy walk past disguised as a nun and priest. He knew the odds of that were infinitely small given the manhunt, but kept his eyes peeled nonetheless. What was that quote about luck being at the intersection of preparation and opportunity?

"Hello Luther? It's me."

"You're not calling from your satellite phone," Luther said. It was a statement, not a question.

Farkas did not want to explain that the phone was now on a yacht, and that it would likely end up in police custody. So he just said, "That's right. The battery died."

"So let's have it."

"You want the good news, or the bad?"

"Start with the good."

"I figured out how they got back on your trail. Emmy tattooed your bank account number on the sole of her foot."

"Wiley sons-of-bitches. Well, at least once the foot is gone, the clue will be too. I suppose that's your bad news—that the foot has escaped with Emmy still attached?"

Farkas could hardly believe his ears. Luther's tone was calm and cordial. What had gotten into him? He was usually a prick even without cause. Now that Farkas had genuine bad news, he seemed unfazed. Perhaps he had finally gotten laid. Perhaps he was in love. "Yeah, I'm afraid so."

"And I suppose you have no idea where they are, or where they're headed?"

"Nope."

There was a long, painful silence ending with, "Get your ass on a plane to Las Vegas. You've got a job to do, and just forty-eight hours to do it. Instructions will be waiting for you tomorrow morning at the Bellagio."

"Okay. You got it. What's the rush?"

"I've got another project for you after Vegas, a big one."

"Sounds good. Where?"

"I'll tell you that when we meet," Luther said.

"Meet?"

"Yeah. Meet. In LA. Forty-eight hours from now. Call me when you know your flight details. I'll send a car for you."

Luther hung up the phone before Farkas could respond. It was just as well. Farkas was in shock. They were finally going to meet. That could only mean one thing: His gravy train was approaching the end of the tracks.

Chapter 60

Officer Jones

TROY—or Officer Jones as he would call himself for the next hour—dropped Emmy off a block from the cruise terminal and then backtracked in order to leave the patrol car halfway to the airport. It was worth a mile's walk to keep the clues ambiguous.

He moved like a man on a mission—which he was—having reverted to his military bearing the moment the cap hit his head. He spotted Emmy where she said she'd be, doing some convincing window-shopping, and made a swift approach. She was wearing brown contact lenses, stage glasses with silver frames, and a curly blonde wig that ended at her shoulders.

"Don't you look dapper," she said as he walked up beside her. "I've always been drawn to men in uniform. Not so sure about the mustache and goatee, though. Makes you look a bit too Pancho Villa for my tastes.

He touched the shiny black bill of his hat and then grabbed her beneath the elbow like a formal escort.

Turning toward the terminal he said, "Three ships, that's a blessing."

"I was hoping for more," Emmy said. "And where are all the people? Judging by what we heard on the radio, I had expected this place to be a virtual anthill."

"Don't worry about it. Everyone will assume that you can't be a fugitive if you're already with the police. Trust me, I've worn a uniform enough to know how people react to one."

Just then a pink and yellow courtesy trolley pulled into the terminal cul-de-sac. Before it had finished disgorging its jolly crowd, a second trolley pulled in.

"Ask and ye shall receive," Troy said.

"I wish."

They blended into the herd of beach bag-toting cruisers. Emmy flashed her stolen cruise ship ID at the terminal checkpoint, but the guard paid more attention to Troy. It was as if he expected Troy to point at her and mouth "prostitute" with a wink. Troy maintained his no nonsense expression.

As they approached the Neptune III, a pair of uniformed officers with binoculars rose from a table and began walking their way. Troy asked Emmy a question, using conversation to augment their camouflage. "So how do you think Honey found us?"

Emmy's cool and reasoned reply reflected her battle-ready state of mind. "He just put himself in our shoes and set an intercept course. I'm sure he orchestrated the media blitz just to make sure we were thinking about disguise."

"My thoughts exactly. I'm just embarrassed that I didn't play a better game of chess."

"You did okay," Emmy said. "Why do you think he came alone?"

"That's an easy one. Pride."

The officers were almost upon them now, and they looked serious. Troy could not see their eyes for their mirrored shades, but he felt their gaze boring into him. So close …

And then they walked past. He heard, "Would you two please come with us?"

"What's this about, officer?" a male voice behind them responded.

"Step this way, please. This will only take a minute."

Troy listened without looking back as the couple was toted off through the murmuring crowd. Fifteen steps later he and Emmy reached the Neptune's gangplank. A sailor seated behind a podium eyed Troy and then said, "May I see your Neptune ID, ma'am."

Emmy handed him her stolen credential and the sailor ran it through a reader. He smiled when he got the green light and handed it back.

Emmy turned to Troy. "Thank you so much for seeing me safely back. It means a lot."

"My pleasure," Troy said.

"You always hear about how scary such situations are, but you never really understand until it happens to you."

"Mrs. Beaumont was mugged," Troy said, addressing the sailor.

The sailor's eyebrows shot up. "So sorry to hear that, ma'am. Are you okay? Is there anything I can do for you?"

"No, thank you. Officer Jones has been most kind. Made me feel safe again."

"Can I buy you a drink," She said, turning back to Troy. "There's a beautiful lounge up on the, the …"

"Promenade deck," the sailor supplied. "You're thinking of the Atlantis Lounge on the promenade deck."

"When do you weigh anchor?" Troy asked the sailor.

"You've got ninety minutes till the whistle," the sailor said. "Plenty of time for a drink."

Chapter 61

Mix-up

HONEY OPENED his eyes to see big white teeth attached to an old black face. William, the theater janitor.

He sat up to rub the back of his head only to note that they had stolen his clothes. Rage and shame battled within him for emotional dominance—but pride was the real culprit. He had blown his perfect plan by attempting to bring them in alone.

"What time is it?" he asked, grasping at straws. "How long ago did they leave?"

"'Bout fifteen, maybe twenty minutes ago. They done tied us up back ta back, an' it took me a while to wrangle free."

Twenty minutes was too big a gap for Honey to overtake them, but he might still catch them if he could guess where they were going. He had no doubt that the theater was their last stop before leaving the island because that's what he would do. The only question in his mind was: By air or by sea?

"Have you got another set of coveralls?" he asked William.

"No, sir. These here is all I got."

Honey thought of making the old man give him his clothes, but he wanted to take him along. Another set of eyes was another set of eyes. After weighing the alternatives for a brief moment, the obvious struck him. "Where do you keep the costumes?"

Five minutes later Honey was racing William's old Chevy pickup toward Owen Roberts International Airport with the janitor by his side. He was dressed in the blue chalk-stripe suit coat and pants worn by the actor playing Willy Loman in Death of a Salesman. It was six inches too short and sixty pounds too fat for his frame. He felt ridiculous.

As he pulled into the airport's long drop-off drive, he saw a police car parked off to his left in the far corner of the parking lot. He made a snap decision and cranked the wheel left, taking the old pickup over the curb and grass toward the parking lot.

"What you doin', Captain?" William asked.

"Getting reinforcements," he said. If he was going to walk through the terminal in that ridiculous suit, he was going to do it with a shotgun over his shoulder like Elliot Ness.

He expected to find a couple of his men napping in their car. That seemed the only explanation for their remote choice of parking spots. To his chagrin, however, the patrol car was both empty and locked. As he whirled about cursing the precious seconds he had lost, he heard "Help!" coming from the trunk.

Honey felt his hopes surge.

He had guessed correctly.

They had come to the airport.

"Hold on!" Honey yelled back. "You got a tire iron?" he asked William.

"I got my tool chest. There's a hamma'"

William handed him the tool without delay. Honey took it and proceeded to wedge the claw beneath the trunk lock.

"Wai' Captain," William said, reaching for the instrument. "Betta' ta just break the window an' pop the boot."

Christ, Honey thought, even the janitor was outsmarting him today. He gave William back the hammer so he could do the honors. William did, and Honey popped the trunk.

Mertins scrambled out as soon as the latch released. Honey saw that his right side was covered in blood and asked, "Are you shot?"

"Not my blood. It's Brandell's."

Honey moved around to where he could see into the trunk. The man he had known for close to a decade, ever since he joined the force from the Royal Navy, was dead. "That makes three," he said. "First Johnson, then Jacobs, now Brandell. Unlock the shotgun and let's go get the bastards."

"Bastards?" Mertins repeated. "Captain, it was just one guy."

"Christ, Mertins. Haven't you been paying attention? He's got an accomplice. Pretty little she-devil. She must have been waiting out of sight."

"Captain, no Captain. This wasn't the couple that killed Johnson and Jacobs. This was the man who kidnapped the Wootens."

"The Wootens?"

"Yes, sir, Deputy Chief Wootens' parents. He held them hostage in their condo for two days—over on Elisabeth Avenue."

Honey felt his hopes dash. Not only did this make it less likely that he'd catch the pair who had twice humiliated him, but now he had another killer on his hands. The island was going to pot. "Shit."

"We'll get him though, Captain. Don't you worry. His prints are bound to be all over the car."

Chapter 62

Alexander Tate

TWO DAYS AFTER entering Miami as Jeffrey and Elizabeth Gordon, Emmy wheeled Troy toward the law office of Alexander Tate. The con was on.

"Twelve o'clock sharp," she said, looking at her watch. "Here we go."

"How can you be so sure he's going to walk through that door?" Troy asked. "We only have one data point."

"He's punctilious. You'll see."

"Punctilious?"

"You doctors have your vocabulary, we psychics have ours. Are you excited?"

"I feel like I'm going into combat."

"We are," Emmy said. "Really makes you feel alive, doesn't it?"

Troy looked back over his shoulder at his partner. "You know, you're right. I never would have guessed it, but I think I'm getting hooked."

On more than just the job I hope, Emmy thought, looking up at the building before them. Tate's office was not the penthouse floor of a majestic downtown high-rise as they had hypothesized while stowaways aboard the Neptune. Rather it occupied a few modest rooms on the third floor of a suburban office park, wedged between a podiatrist and medical billing firm.

The sliding glass door opened to their approach just as Tate stepped off the elevator.

Troy mumbled "Punctilious" just loud enough for Emmy to hear but did not look back to see her smile.

Tate was a handsome man for a back-office attorney, with a full head of chocolate hair and one of those semi-firm physiques that screamed club membership. She dropped her purse as their eyes met, sending pills across the pavement around Tate's feet. "I'm so sorry," she said, bumping into him once and then again as they both bent over to retrieve the spilled medication. "So clumsy of me."

"No problem," Tate said, giving her an appreciative once-over. "It happens to the best of us."

They worked together to reassemble Emmy's purse while Troy looked on from the wheelchair. Then she said, "Thank you so much," stood, and pushed Troy into the lobby. Tate said "My pleasure," and made for his car.

"How'd you do?" Troy asked, once the elevator door closed behind them. Emmy turned to him and produced Tate's cell phone in her hand as if by magic. Then she turned it off.

"Very impressive," Troy said.

"That was the easy part. Now, get into character. Remember, you're old-money rich and accustomed to getting your way. Your body may no longer be what it used to, but your mind is still sharp as a whip."

"Just who do you think you're talking to, young lady? I've been dealing with situations like these since before you were born."

"Perfect," Emmy said as the elevator doors opened. She assumed the fawning air of a pretty young nurse caring for a rich old man and began pushing him toward suite 3B.

During their two partial days of surveillance, Troy and Emmy had determined that The Law Offices of Alexander Tate and Associates employed just three people, including Tate himself and two women. Judging by their cars and carriage, Emmy speculated that the younger woman was a fellow attorney working for Tate, while the older one was a secretary—or legal assistant in the vernacular. Alice, the secretary, seemed mildly surprised to find that they had unscheduled visitors. "May I help you?" she asked.

"I certainly hope so," Troy said, in his best septuagenarian voice. "We're here to see Alex."

"I'm afraid Mr. Tate is not in right now. He has a working lunch."

"Not anymore he doesn't," Troy said, raising his voice. "Get him on the phone. Tell him Kostas Kanasis is here, and I don't have time to wait."

"Yes, sir. I'll see what I can do."

"Please do," Troy said, looking back over his shoulder at Emmy and shaking his head at Tate's audacity.

"I'm afraid his phone is going straight to voice mail. He must have it off. Would you like me to leave a message?"

Troy shook his head and raised his voice. "I need a person, not a message, and I need him now."

"Is everything okay out here," a woman asked, appearing from the back much to Alice's relief.

"Mr. Kanasis here has urgent business with Mr. Tate," Alice said.

"He should be back any minute," the woman said. "I can recommend a good restaurant nearby if you would like to get some lunch."

Emmy did not like the words back any minute—it would be a disaster if Tate returned before they left—but she sensed that Tate's coworker was just being diplomatic.

Troy said, "Look, Miss …"

"Sylvia," she said. "Sylvia Dashell."

"Well, Sylvia, any minute is not good enough. Can you guarantee me that it will be one of the next ten minutes?"

"No sir, I'm afraid I can't."

"Because that's all the time I have, I—" He held up a hand, cutting himself off and deflating a bit of pressure from the room.

"The problem, Sylvia, is that I have to be back on my plane very shortly. I'm hosting an important dinner this evening on Grand Cayman. The banking commissioner and three ambassadors will be there. Besides, I'm not really here for Alex's legal advice. I just need to review my records. Perhaps you could help me?"

"Mr. Tate doesn't like—"

"Mr. Tate doesn't like losing his best customers," Troy interjected decisively. "I'm sure we can agree on that."

Sylvia looked over at Alice who shrugged. Emmy sensed that they were about to hit a wall and chimed in. "We just need to make a copy of Mr. Kanasis's bank records. We don't need to make any transactions," she said, proffering a Cayman Islands driver's license with a picture of Troy made up to look like Kostas Kanasis. "It should just take you a minute. I'm sure Mr. Tate has the file in order."

After a tense moment, Sylvia reached out and accepted the license. She gave it a quick, cursory glance, and then said, "Please hold on a minute."

Emmy used the occasion to slip Tate's cell phone onto the corner of Alice's desk.

Sylvia returned three minutes later, wearing a smile. "Why don't you come back to my office."

Once they were resituated, Sylvia asked, "Which records, exactly, do you need copied?"

Deviating from the script they had rehearsed, Troy beckoned her over toward him so that he could whisper in her ear. Whatever he said, his improvisation worked. Sylvia backed away when he was done and said, "That should be simple enough. Just give me a minute."

Troy avoided Emmy's eye while they waited, trying to stay in character no doubt.

It did not take Sylvia long. When she returned she slid an envelope into Troy's hand.

Troy said, "Thank you" in his most sincere voice and then he added the phrase that Emmy had him memorize. "I'm a pretty good judge of character, Sylvia, and I get the feeling I can confide in you. Can I confide in you, Sylvia?"

"Why yes, yes of course."

"I have the strong suspicion that something funny is going on. No hard facts, mind you, it's more of a feeling. Given your tender young age, I don't suppose you know what I mean ...?"

"I think I understand, Mr. Kanasis."

"Please, call me Kostas."

"What can I do for you, Kostas?" Sylvia asked.

"I'd like you to keep an eye on my account for the next few weeks."

"Keep an eye on it?"

"Yes, I'd like you to be my eyes. I'd like you to monitor my account and call me at this number," he held out a thick, embossed card, "and only this number any time funds come in, or go out. Just till the end of the month. Could you do that for me, Sylvia? I'd be most grateful."

"Well, sure, I'd be happy to. But perhaps Mr. Tate—"

Troy held up his hand. "Checks and balances, Sylvia. Checks and balances. Let's just keep this between us."

Chapter 63

Redirect

"THE BALLISTICS REPORT IS BACK, CAPTAIN."

Honey could tell by the tone of Susanna's voice that he was not going to like what she had to say. The cop killers had somehow slipped through his massive dragnet and their trail was now seventy-two hours cold. More bad news would be a perfect cap to the worst five days of his professional life. "Give it to me."

Susanna held out the piece of paper, obviously not wanting to be the bearer.

"Why don't you just tell me what it says."

Susanna looked down at the floor for a moment, then looked back up and said, "It says that the couple in question could not have killed Jacobs. He was killed by a high velocity rifle round. The shooter had to be on the other side of the avenue at the very least."

What the hell was going on, Honey wondered. "Is that it?"

"The rest is technical." She proffered the printout again. "Perhaps you better read it."

Honey took the paper and gave it a quick glance. Ballistics wasn't his bailiwick and he was not in the mood to pretend. As he handed the report back to Susanna to file, his eyes landed on the address in the header. Solomon Bank & Trust was located at number nine Elisabeth Avenue.

He felt a warm glow fill his chest as clarity dawned.

He knew where he had seen that address before.

Chapter 64

Contingency Planning

AS SHE PUSHED Troy's wheelchair from Tate's office back to their
rental car, Emmy could sense his excitement. The mysterious document
he had procured with a secretive whisper was obviously both a major
clue and the confirmation of some theory. She had no idea what either
was. Despite her burning desire to know, however, she vowed not to
ask. She wanted to figure it out on her own.

"You did great," Emmy said, sliding into the driver's seat. "I think
you're a natural."

Troy said, "Thanks," in his normal voice after removing his wig and
nose prosthesis. Then he flipped down the sun visor to expose the
mirror, and began attacking his makeup with handy wipes. "I'm glad I
don't have to do this every evening. What a pain."

She put the car into drive and started fishing, "To the airport?"

Troy looked over at her with a mischievous smile. "Yep."

"Where are we flying?"

"I'm not sure yet. Kind of exciting, isn't it?"

"Because you haven't opened the envelope."

"That's right."

Now that Troy knew she was playing the game, Emmy was doubly
determined not to ask. She considered what she knew. Kostas Kanasis
was a cutout. He was laundering Luther's money without knowing it
and shielding him from his crimes. An attorney in Miami was their
middle man, but he was half blind. Tate only knew Kostas's identity. He
couldn't know Luther's identity because then there would be a chain
instead of a cutout. So what document could Tate have that would help
them? Emmy was stumped.

She tried another tack. Troy had figured it out. He had figured it out
right after making the cryptic observation that Luther had to have
contingencies. Contingencies for what? Tate did not know his name and
Kostas was a feeble old man. What was an old man going to do …?

And then she had it. Just as simple as that. She knew what was in the
envelope.

She looked over at Troy. All remnants of his Kostas disguise were
now gone, but the mischievous grin was still there. "Why don't you go
ahead and read Kostas's will. I'd like to know where we're going."

Troy's eyes bulged. "Don't tell me you can read through envelopes.
Wait a minute, did you read my lips?"

"I can read lips, but no, I didn't read yours. Like you, I realized that Luther needs a contingency in case Kostas dies. He can't have his life savings going to Kostas's cousin."

"More like the state," Troy said, unfolding the last will and testament. "I'm sure Luther picked someone without any relatives."

Emmy took the turnoff to Miami International Airport as Troy began to read. "This thing would easily fit on one page were it not for all the legalese. It's just what I expected, a single beneficiary for all assets of the estate. And there's a nice little twist," he said.

"What?" Emmy asked.

"Luther and Kostas do have one thing in common. I was wondering how he picked his mark."

"What's that?"

"A last name. Kostas's sole beneficiary is Luther Kanasis."

Emmy let out a long breath. "You think they're related?"

"If so, I'm sure it's distant. Makes sense though. Pick the same last name, especially an unusual one like Kanasis, and the inheritance seems natural enough to any casual observer or bureaucrat. But at the same time, you would never locate Kostas by studying Luther's family tree."

"Does it list Luther's address?"

"Oh yes, it certainly does."

"Well …?"

"You're going home, my dear. Luther Kanasis lives in Bel Air."

Chapter 65

New Light

LUTHER POUNDED the leather-wrapped wheel of his black Porsche 911 Carrera. "Damn! Damn! Damn!" he shouted into the breeze. "It just can't be done." He pounded the wheel again. He wanted the private island and lifetime supply of Playboy Bunnies.

From the minute Arlen left his office a week earlier, Luther had been scouring the internet and racking his brains, searching for inspiration. He was desperate to find a creative way of wiping the entire Supreme Court of the United States. If there were such a way, it eluded him. So he was going to pound out his frustrations on the heavy bag in his home gym.

As he drove down Wilshire, the feeling that he was overlooking something simple began nagging at him. After turning onto Beverly Glen, he lowered the Porsche's steering wheel so that he could grip it between his knees and began rubbing both his temples, trying to slip his mind through the loophole in his thinking.

Flashing was not the problem. He had found the perfect opportunity for Farkas to do that. The opening ceremony for the court's new term was just three weeks away.

The rub was the injections.

Farkas would need to inject all nine justices within the preceding forty-eight hours. It was a weekend devoid of any functions that might bring the whole bench together. That meant Farkas would need to inject each individually, and forty-eight hours simply wasn't enough time. With luck and meticulous planning he figured Farkas could do two in one day, maybe even five in one weekend. But not nine. Not undetected.

What was he missing?

A second operative? No. There was also no way Luther was going to bring someone new into his operation. Not at this stage. Not when the stakes were this high. Likewise, there was no way he was going to get dirty himself. Half a billion dollars was an awfully sweet prize, but no amount of money in the world was worth spending the next ten years of his life in prison. He would not survive one year of owing Orca twenty-five double-large.

He shook his head and repeated himself as he turned into his estate's circular drive, "It just can't be done."

As he pulled the 911 to a skidding halt on the drive's crushed stones, Luther resolved to call Arlen and tell him as much. Best to get it over with. Best to get temptation out of the way.

Giselle waved to him from across the yard and began walking his way. He had been too distracted by Arlen's offer to seduce her over the weekend as planned. And despite the enticing bounce beneath her tight white shirt, he did not see his ardor returning anytime soon.

The agency had not sent an automatic replacement for Brandy yet, as was their norm. Either she had told them about the forced fellatio, and Fernando's had blacklisted him, or she had not told them anything at all, and they did not know that a replacement housekeeper was needed. He assumed the latter, since the agency got too much business from him to cut him off over a blowjob. He thought about giving Fernando a call, but decided to put it off in case he was wrong. One unpleasant call a day was enough.

"Good afternoon, Mr. Kanasis," Giselle said, approaching with enthusiasm. She stopped just two feet away holding a trowel in her gloved hands and flashed him a big smile. Luther felt a stir and reconsidered his previous conclusion. Perhaps Giselle was exactly what he needed. Arlen could wait.

"How many times do I have to tell you to call me Luther?"

"I know. It's just that, well, my brother's name is also Luther. And I just can't think of you as my brother."

Luther took that as a good sign. "Well then, why don't you just call me Mr. K? Or better yet, just K."

"K. Yeah, I like that."

This was the time, Luther thought. "Giselle, as you know, Brandy's not with us any more. Would you mind coming inside to give me a hand? The yard already looks perfect."

Giselle's smile faded. "Maybe later, after your guests leave."

"Guests?"

"Yeah. That's what I was coming to tell you. You've got a couple of visitors. Big guys. The ones who were here a week or so ago. They said you were old friends and they just barged right in."

Luther felt the passion drain from his body and ice water begin to flow in its place. Two visits from Orca in as many weeks—that could not be good.

He turned toward the house without another word to Giselle.

"There you are, Luther. Zero and I were beginning to worry about you."

"I'm touched," Luther said, resolving to end this meeting as soon as possible and go beat the stuffing out of his heavy bag. "To what do I owe the pleasure?"

"An opportunity has arisen …"

"Opportunity?" Luther did not like the sound of that.

"Yeah. Opportunity. You ever hear of Jimmy Choke?"

Luther blinked. Every cop and criminal attorney in L.A. knew about Jimmy. He was Orca's primary rival, and the only person Luther knew who made Orca the Killer Whale look like a catfish by comparison. Jimmy Cortese got his nickname by slicing off men's penises and stuffing them into their mouths where, unwilling to chew, they usually tried to swallow it whole and choked. "I've heard of him," Luther replied, his voice wavering.

"That's too bad. Zero here was looking forward to telling you about him. Anyhow, Jimmy has gone and pissed off a mutual friend of ours back in Chicago. That transgression has given me the opportunity to take over Jimmy's territory, consolidate our operations so to speak."

"Congratulations. You need me to draw up a contract? Some new articles of incorporation?"

Orca turned to Zero. "You hear that, Z? Articles of incorporation. Now that's a lawyer for you." Turning back to Luther he said, "No. We don't operate that way. All I need to do is pay Chicago for Jimmy's franchise and it's mine. Well, almost all," he added, winking at Zero who nodded back. "So, as much as it pains me to say, I'm going to need to call in the principal on your loan. I'm going to need the full twenty-five mil. Plus the outstanding vig, of course."

Luther stared at the Mafia boss, unwilling to believe his ears.

Orca stared back.

The sound of grinding walnuts filled the silent void.

Finally Luther said, "That's impossible. I don't have—"

Orca held up his hand, cutting Luther off. "Believe me, I'm enjoying my fifty-two percent interest. If there was any other way, I wouldn't be asking. But don't worry, I don't need the money now."

"Well, that's good because I haven't—"

"I can give you a week."

As Luther stood there dumbfounded with thoughts of life in Mexico pecking around the edges of his mind, Zero held up the fist containing the walnuts and squeezed. The nuts cracked loudly in his paw. Zero worked his fingers until he had pulped them and then opened his fist to let the dust slip through his fingers and onto the tiled floor.

Luther felt his testicles give an involuntary tug. "Is there anything else?" he asked.

"Yeah, as a matter of fact there is. Do me a favor and go fetch me that pretty little gardener of yours."

Chapter 66

Timeless and Reliable

"I'VE GOT A FEELING this could be our break," Emmy said, looking over at Troy after the beautiful young gardener crashed through Luther Kanasis's front door and made a beeline for her scooter with tear-filled eyes. "Let's follow her."

Troy pulled the Honda Odyssey they had been using as their observation base out into traffic a hundred yards behind the girl's red Vespa. "What are you thinking?" he asked.

"I'm thinking she looks like someone who needs a friend."

"Don't you think she has a few of those already?"

"You'd be surprised, Troy. So many pretty young girls like her come out here to take their shot at a Hollywood dream only to meet with an endless stream of rejection. They end up living reclusive lives among people they don't like because that's the only place they can afford to be. Television becomes their only friend. I used to do readings for a lot of them when I was getting started."

"That sounds morally precarious. What did you tell them?"

"Morally precarious, eh? Are you a doctor or a priest?"

Troy shrugged, and she saw pain in his eyes.

"I'm sorry. It's a sensitive topic for me. To answer your question, I tried to help them. I would encourage them without making promises, trying to keep their spirits up, knowing that a good attitude could give them that vital edge. Most didn't make it, but a couple of them did— not to the A list, but far enough to be happy."

As they turned right off West Sunset onto San Vicente Boulevard, Emmy said, "She's headed for the beach." A few blocks later the gardener parked her Vespa before a liquor store. Troy stopped the car before the air hose of a neighboring gas station and stepped out for reconnaissance. He returned a few seconds later and said, "A bottle of Merlot and a single plastic cup."

"What brand?"

"Kendall-Jackson."

Emmy said, "I've got a good feeling about this."

The Vespa continued down San Vicente to Pacific Coast Highway where it turned left toward Venice Beach. A few blocks later it pulled into a beachfront parking lot and took the last spot in the motorcycle section. "There's nowhere for me to park," Troy said, frustration evident in his voice.

"There's no need," Emmy said, opening the passenger door. "Just go back to Luther's before she gets a good look at the car. I'll meet you there later."

As Troy pulled away, Emmy watched the gardener head across the sand with her purchase.

Confident that she would be easy to find, Emmy walked over to the Vespa and crouched down to adjust her sandal. After making sure that no eyes were upon her, she drained the air from the Vespa's front tire.

Next on her mental to-do list was obtaining the supplies needed for what psychics called mirroring. In order to help establish immediate rapport, she would replicate the gardener's actions and appearance. Fortunately, she already had the dress right: shorts, sandals, and a polo shirt. Mirroring body position, gestures, and even breathing patterns was second nature for Emmy. All she needed was the Kendall-Jackson.

Emmy found The Wine Cask just half-a-block away after asking a meter maid for directions. When she headed out across the warm sand, Emmy was just ten minutes behind her quarry.

She spotted the gardener near the base of the pier, sitting cross-legged in the sand just inches from the surf. She was staring out toward the setting sun with a cup of wine in her hand and a blank look on her face.

Emmy angled her approach to hit the surf line beyond the gardener's peripheral vision. She took off her sandals at the water's edge and walked through the swishing surf in the gardener's direction, her eyes staring out into space, the uncorked Merlot bottle hanging dejectedly from her left hand.

She trudged slowly past the girl, just inches in front of her, but stopped a few feet after passing as though struck by a random thought. Certain that the gardener's eyes were on her, Emmy backed up and turned to make eye contact.

They looked at each other in silence for a moment, and then Emmy let her eyes drift to the gardener's own Merlot bottle. "You having that kind of day too?" she asked, plopping down into the sand beside her new friend. "I just lost my job. It wasn't a great job or anything, but it was the only job I had."

Emmy filled her plastic cup with Merlot and then poured half the contents down her throat. Turning toward her new friend with her cup raised, she said, "I used to do this all the time, back when I was dating Kevin. We'd get into the worst fights." She shook her head slowly and smiled. "But when we weren't fighting … it was the best."

She set her cup down in the sand and waited for the girl to comment. She didn't.

After a long minute of silence, Emmy said, "I haven't been back here much since he moved on. Ironically, I kind of miss it. The sea, the setting sun, and a good bottle of wine. All timeless. All reliable."

Emmy picked her cup back up and took another sip. The gardener had yet to utter a single word. After more awkward silence passed and a group of teenagers walked by, she asked, "How about you: guy problems, or work problems?"

The gardener turned to look at her and said, "Guy at work problems."

Emmy knew she had her.

Chapter 67

Tails

IT WAS ONE-O-FIVE AM when Troy hit the button that automatically opened the Odyssey's left sliding door. Even before Emmy flopped into the seat beside him, Troy knew that she was drunk. She was moving with far less poise than usual and he could smell the wine on her breath. She did look happy though. "I got it all," Emmy said, her speech slightly slurred.

Troy poured her a cup of coffee from his thermos. Handing it to her he said, "Do tell."

"According to Giselle—that's her name—Luther Kanasis is using an employment agency to find himself a wife."

"What?"

"Yeah. He has a revolving door of cooks, maids, and gardeners cycling through. How's that for a novel approach. Apparently the potential-wife part is a badly kept secret. The agency just hints that that's his intention, indicating that he wants a genuine, all-American wife rather than one of the princesses that run in his social circles."

"A Mary Ann rather than a Ginger," Troy said.

"Huh?" Emmy asked.

"From Gilligan's Island. Before our time, I know, but it's still a classic comparison."

Emmy rolled her glazed eyes.

"So what happened?" Troy asked. "Did Giselle find out that she's not the one?"

"She sure did, but not directly. She was forced to pleasure Luther's guest, that mafia-looking toad of a man we saw entering with a bodyguard."

"Did she comply?"

"She did what she had to do until she got the chance to escape."

"So I take it she's not going back, even though it wasn't Luther who attacked her?"

"No, but she hates to walk away. She loved the job. Light work doing what she loves and she pockets triple what she'd get elsewhere. Can you believe Luther pays his domestic help ten grand a month? Plus she lives there, rent free, in a room over the garage."

"It doesn't sound rent free to me," Troy said.

"I agree. But I'm still going to give it a try."

"You're what?"

"Luther's maid quit a week or two ago for the same reason. The agency hasn't replaced her yet."

"So you're just going to show up, say the agency sent you, and begin dusting?"

"Why not?"

"Lots of reasons, the first being that he'll recognize you."

"I'm not so sure about that. Given what Farkas told us about Luther's operation, I figure there's a fifty-percent chance that the only thing he knows about me is my name. Remember, Farkas has never met the guy, and he's been working for him for almost four years. In any case, there's only one way to find out."

"What if your 50:50 bet comes up tails?"

Emmy's eyes suddenly sobered. "Then you'll have to rescue me."

Chapter 68

Brute Force

NUBILE NUDE BEAUTIES gyrated above Luther within gilded, glass-floored cages while a large-breasted caramel-eyed Asian frolicked before him on the stage. As he made his way across the floor toward the back, Luther felt a newfound appreciation for his creditor. While Orca's place of business could not be more different from Luther's own, they did share a commonality: both were best in class.

Although Luther knew for a fact that Orca kept no less than half-a-dozen knuckle-breakers on hand during busy hours, besides the paying customers there was not a pair of testicles around. Even the entryway cash register was manned by one of the gorgeous off-shift strippers. No doubt the muscle was all packed into a Vegas-style security room. Luther could picture them there, dressed head to toe in black and ready to react with decisive discretion as required. He was about to find out just how accurate that image was.

Approaching the camouflaged door to the left of the stage, Luther asked himself if he really wanted to go through with this. He could still back out. He could drive to LAX and fly off to a new life. Once he knocked on that door, however, once he let the Killer Whale into his world, there would be no turning back. Like a shark smelling blood, Orca's primitive instincts would take over the instant he sensed a possible kill.

Before Luther's knuckles even tapped the door, a steroid-stuffed security guard opened it and said, "This area is private." The black-clad teenager appeared to be nearly as wide as he was tall. Looking over fireplug's shoulder, Luther caught sight of Zero and looked into his lifeless eyes.

"It's okay," Zero said to Fireplug. "Mr. Kanasis here is a friend of the boss." Then, addressing Luther he said, "You're in luck; the boss is in."

Luther would not necessarily have called that luck, but it was efficient. "Lead the way."

"I'm going to have to search you first," Zero said.

Luther held out his arms once the door closed behind him. Sixty seconds later, he entered Orca's office. He had been there before, but the stark contrast to the rest of Lisa's Place still caught his eye. Rather than being dim and plush, Orca's environment was bright and harsh—kind of like a shark tank, Luther mused. Halogen lights beamed down onto glass shelves, while a black granite desk with matching coffee table and bar stood like oases on the thick, sand-colored carpet. Orca looked up, surprise registering on his face. "Luther, I half expected you to be in Rio by now. Glad to see that you're not so stupid. Did you bring my money?"

Luther ignored the question. He wanted to take control of the conversation, and going on the defensive right off the bat was not going to help him accomplish that. "Lisa's Place. You never did tell me where you got the name."

"The clientele we target don't want Pussy Palace appearing on their AmEx bills."

"Good point, but who is Lisa?"

Orca smiled. "There is no Lisa. The original owner was from Moscow. Before he died, he told me that Lisa means fox in Russian. He thought it was a nice pun. I don't care about puns, but I saw no reason to mess with a good thing."

Orca looked down at his watch. "You still got seventy-two hours to come up with my money, so that can't be why you're here. What is it, now that the maid and gardener are gone, you looking to get laid? I thought you still had the cook. What's her name, by the way? Great legs."

"I came here because I want to pay you what I owe you."

"I'm glad to hear that. Just don't be asking me for an extension. My offer from Chicago is going to expire, and I'd rather put my balls in a blender than miss that deadline." Orca paused to scratch his sack. "Well, maybe not my balls, but certainly your balls."

"You won't have to bother with anyone's balls."

"Good."

"All you have to do is provide me with a little bit of help."

Orca shook his head. "All I have to do is point Zero in your direction."

"I may be a lawyer, but I don't bleed money."

"That remains to be seen. In any case, I bet he can extract the deeds to your house and yacht in less time than it takes to say twenty-six million."

"I'm sure he could. But they won't help you with Chicago. They're mortgaged for all that they're worth. Don't you think I'd have sold them already if that was an option, rather than paying you fifty-two percent?"

"I thought maybe you was emotionally attached. People get that way. So tell me, counselor, what was this little bit of help you had in mind?"

"I need you to connect me—or rather a colleague of mine—with nine soldiers on the East Coast. I need top guys, ex-CIA or Special Forces, James Bond types. Guys who can do a sophisticated job with absolute discretion."

Orca nodded appreciatively. "And this is going to get me my money?"

"As long as they're the right kind of guys."

"What's the job?"

Luther shook his head. "All you need to know is that with their help, you get your money. You get Jimmy Choke's franchise. Without them, you don't."

"How long you need them for?"

"About two weeks."

"Starting when?"

"In forty-eight hours."

"What you going to pay them?"

"Enough."

"I need to be able to tell them what to expect."

"Tell them that they'll be well paid."

Orca cracked his neck, first on the right, then on the left. "And when do I get my money?"

"You get me the names today, I get you your money as requested."

Orca moved on to his knuckles. "Anything else?" he asked.

"Yes, one thing. No one besides you and I are to know of my involvement. No one besides you and I are to know that nine people are involved. Each man is to think that he's working alone." Luther handed Orca nine slips of paper. "Those are the times and places for nine meetings on Sunday. Have one man show up at each. That's all they need to know. Each man will get ten grand just for showing up—and taking a vow of silence."

"Very interesting, counselor."

"Do we have an agreement, then?"

"Yes," Orca said, his eyes alight with the glow of greed, "we do."

Chapter 69

The Extra Mile

EMMY LOOKED OVER her shoulder at Troy as she approached Luther's gate. "Wish me luck."

"You sure you want to do this?"

"With all we've been through, do you really need to ask?"

"Well, I—"

"You just keep your ears open and your eyes on the screen so you can come to my rescue if anything happens."

"Of course, but—"

"Don't worry; I'm going to run like hell the moment I sense that he's suspicious."

"With all due respect to your senses, we know they failed us at least once before."

Emmy crossed her arms across her chest. "Do we now?"

"Farkas caught us."

"Huh. Well, I guess that just makes your role all the more important."

"I guess it does," Troy said, climbing over the Odyssey's third row bench seat. Once settled in on the carpeted floor, he popped an earbud in his right ear and checked the screen on his Blackberry as Emmy whispered, "Testing. Testing."

"Loud and clear."

"How's the picture?" Emmy asked, placing a large sun hat on her head.

"With the phone clipped to your belt, all I see is the underside of the steering wheel, but the image is clear." They had rigged a cell phone to send streaming video clandestinely so Troy could see and hear everything Emmy did.

Emmy pulled the Honda into Luther's driveway and pressed the intercom button. Luther's voice came on a couple of minutes later. "Yes."

"Mr. Kanasis?"

"Yes."

"This is Vicky Dixon. The employment agency sent me over to fill the maid position." She looked ahead rather than into the camera. It was important that she be able to look into Luther's eyes the instant he got his first good look at her face.

"It's about time," Luther said, buzzing her in.

Emmy pulled in as the gate swung open and parked so that the minivan was facing the gate, just in case she needed to make a quick exit. To that end, she had decided to leave the keys with Troy as well.

"Good luck," Troy whispered as she tossed the keys over the back seat.

Stepping out, she removed her sun hat and placed it behind the driver's seat. It had done its job. She hoped the rest of her outfit would perform as well. Emmy had chosen to wear white shorts and a green shirt that offered a peek at cleavage and added flare to her eyes.

Luther answered the door just seconds after her knock. "Hello Vicky, I'm Luther Kanasis. It's a pleasure to meet you."

Emmy studied Luther's face for the slightest flash of recognition—flaring irises, contracting lids, increased blood flow to the cheeks. Nothing pinged her radar. The only suppressed emotion she detected was a hint of lust. "Likewise."

"Please, come in," he said, stepping back and pulling the arched door open wide.

"Your home is beautiful," she said, thinking, "so are you." Luther had a charismatic presence that gripped you right away—a powerful aura, people in her business would say. If she did not hate the man with every fiber in her being, she might well have been attracted to him. As it was, she found it hard not to spit.

"Thank you. Let me show you around. What did Fernando tell you about the position?"

"He said you needed live-in housekeeping for an unspecified duration."

"That's right. Anything else?"

"He said it was the best deal in town, and I was lucky to have qualified. Judging by the numbers he quoted, I'm inclined to agree."

Leading her up the sweeping semicircular staircase, Luther asked, "And did he tell you what those qualifications were?"

Giselle had primed Emmy to expect this question. "Of course there was the standard reference to diligence and hard work, but the real emphasis was on discretion. He told me that you demanded absolute discretion and rewarded blind loyalty."

"That's right. Does it bother you?"

"That depends on why it's an issue. Are you involved in anything illegal?"

Luther forced a chuckle that sent a chill up Emmy's spine. "Well, I suppose that depends on your definition of involved."

Emmy stopped walking and turned to face Luther. "How so?"

"I'm a criminal defense attorney. On rare occasion, the people I represent are convicted of illegal acts."

"I'm okay with that. But why the great need for secrecy?"

"Lives depend upon my discretion, and I must pass that requirement on to all around me. You are never to mention a word about your work here to anyone, nothing you see, nothing you hear. Is that understood?"

"Yes."

"No griping to friends, not even an I-love-my-job. Are we clear?"

"Yes, sir."

Luther's serious visage vanished in a millisecond and he was all charm again. "No need for sir. Please, call me Luther. Any questions?"

"Just one."

Luther nodded.

"What happened to the last girl? I mean, if I may be blunt, I can't imagine anyone giving up a job like this."

Luther shrugged. "I had to let her go. She was good at the day-to-day routine, but in a crunch, she wasn't willing to go the extra mile. Her devotion was not absolute, not congruent with the paycheck. You would be wise to keep that in mind, Vicky. We've only just met, but I already have high expectations for you …"

Chapter 70

Accounting Adjustments

"YOU FIGURED IT OUT," Arlen said, stepping off the elevator into Luther's office. "I knew you would."

"Good morning to you too," Luther said, just finishing up behind the espresso machine. He motioned his guest toward the suite of chairs before picking up the two piping-hot beverages. "You bring your checkbook?"

Arlen nodded in appreciation of Luther's directness. "As promised. Let's hope I'm impressed enough to open it."

As the two titans took their seats, Arlen looked around the room as if searching for something. Luther understood immediately, but chose to enjoy his first sip of espresso before commenting. When Arlen returned his gaze to his host, Luther said, "Expecting PowerPoint or flip charts?"

Arlen nodded. "Corporate habit."

"In my businesses—both my legal practice and my ancillary services —I'm well advised to commit as little as possible to paper. I have also found that juries are more likely to believe an attorney who speaks extemporaneously than one who constantly refers to notes." This was a ploy, of course, and a fairly clever one Luther thought. He had concocted it to help ensure that the bluff he was about to attempt would fly. Studying the skeptical reaction on Arlen's face, he felt a rumble of doubt.

"In my business, I'm well advised to always get promises on paper." Arlen paused, inviting Luther's comment.

Luther made none.

Finally Arlen said, "But I see your point." He settled back into the leather and added, "Do be advised that my checkbook and I will walk out of here at the first sign of smoke and mirrors."

"Fair enough," Luther said, resisting the urge to stand as he began his performance. Placing far more certainty in his voice than he currently felt, he said, "The wiping will occur Monday morning, September twenty-ninth, at the press conference preceding the annual opening conference. I trust you agree that the timing is ideally suited to create maximum chaos?"

"It's perfect," Arlen said, sliding forward in his chair. "And less than three weeks away." He was trying to play the role of the cool senior executive but he couldn't hide his excitement. Luther's news was worth tens of billions of dollars. "It will take months for congress even to figure out where to start when the entire court is found to be mentally unstable. By the time the president nominates replacements and congress approves them, they'll almost certainly lose the entire court year. Once sound minds are eventually in place on the bench, they'll have an additional year's backlog to deal with. My experts concur that our case will slip at least one additional year back in the queue if it isn't removed all together." Arlen rubbed his hands together subconsciously. "How, exactly, are you going to do it?"

"The activation itself is the easy part. That's how I can be so confident about the date. I'll get a man into the press conference with the necessary equipment. It's the implantation that will take real guile. To accomplish that, I've assigned a top man to each of the nine justices. They have spent the last few days studying their assigned target's routines, and have mapped out an implantation strategy accordingly."

"It only took a few days?" Arlen asked.

Luther nodded confidently as he spoke. "My men are pros at infiltration. It wasn't hard for them to get their hands on the justices calendars. All of them are men of habit, creatures of routine. The older ones are all pretty domestic, but each has regular outings. The younger guys, the ones in their fifties, both jog on a regular basis. They will be particularly easy pickings.

"Let me tell you what I've learned about the routines of each justice," Luther continued, preparing to let loose a long list of memorized bullshit. "We've got primary and backup plans for each, taking all foreseeable contingencies into account."

"Please," Arlen prompted.

And so Luther rattled off detailed plans of attack that resembled what he expected Farkas and Orca's men to compile in the coming days. He did it all without notes, drawing on skills developed during his courtroom days. Studying Arlen's features, he could tell by the time he got to the second name that the CEO was sold. Nonetheless, Luther continued with the same confident enthusiasm and attention to detail through all nine.

Arlen remained silent once Luther had finished, giving the appearance of one who was deliberating on the words he had just heard. Luther remained calm, trusting in his instincts and minding the old maxim to shut up once a person was sold.

Finally, without a word, Arlen reached into his pocket, withdrew his cell phone, and speed-dialed a number. "Make the transfer."

Luther waited in silence, very aware of the beat of his own heart.

Arlen smiled, closed his phone, and said, "It's done. Two hundred and fifty million dollars has been transferred to your account."

Luther found himself unable to speak. A quarter of a billion dollars. He held out his hand.

Arlen grabbed it and pulled Luther close. He whispered in Luther's ear, his voice cold as death. "I've got ten times this amount in my war chest, Luther. If you run, I will track you down."

Luther backed away as Arlen released his grip, acutely aware that he was exchanging one mafia boss for another. Orca was old school, Arlen new, but they were equally deadly. After a long silence, Luther found his voice. "I'm doing this exactly because I want to live the rest of my life in peace, rather than looking over my shoulder. You have nothing to worry about, Arlen. Our interests are aligned."

Arlen nodded, his cordial mask back in place. "I trust you haven't forgotten our agreement that all your colleagues are to share the justices' fate?"

"I'm a details man, Arlen. I haven't forgotten a thing." Actually, it was not the thought of additional wipings that was grating across Luther's mind. It was the impending murder.

With just one more deposit on the horizon, it would soon be time to close Kostas Kanasis's account.

Chapter 71

Oops

USING A MIRROR to keep an eye on the estate's front gate, Troy tried to get inside his enemy's head. Now that he had seen Luther's face, house, car, clothes, office and servants, he had a good framework from which to extrapolate.

While this exercise might pay dividends later on, he was really just killing time. Crouched behind the third row of seats in the Honda Odyssey Emmy had parked in Luther's drive, his options were limited. Meanwhile his need for distraction was severe. Emmy's video cell phone had run out of juice four hours earlier, leaving him in the dark. She had a regular cell phone as backup in her purse, but had yet to call.

As he checked his Nokia's battery level and signal strength for the tenth time, it finally began to vibrate. "Are you okay?" he asked.

"I'm fine," Emmy said, her voice free of duress. "Sorry to be incommunicado for so long. It's the cook, Desiree. She's been finding excuses to follow me wherever I go."

"Is it possible that she suspects something?" Troy asked. "Maybe you used to know her but don't remember."

"That's not my read. I think she's bought into the bullshit about Luther looking for a wife and is trying to find a way to eliminate me as competition."

"So where are you now?"

"In the basement. Kind of hard for a cook to justify popping down here. Wasn't easy for me either. I had to dust the rest of the house first so as not to look suspicious."

Troy could tell by Emmy's tone that she was excited about something. "You uncover anything interesting?"

"A lot of high quality reproductions—both artwork and furniture. If I weren't trained to spot a fake I never would have known that they weren't genuine."

"That skill come from another of your entrepreneurial acquaintances?"

"That one came from Ava herself. One of her favorite confidence games involved a switcheroo."

"Any conclusions?"

"Luther is not as wealthy as he wants to appear."

"Who is? Did you inspect the guest house?"

"No. I'll do that tomorrow."

"How about safes or hidden rooms?"

"I haven't found either yet. I used the laser tape measure just like you showed me. Got every room. We can study the results later, but I'm pretty sure that all space is accounted for."

"Anything interesting in Luther's study?"

"I spent a lot of time there, dusting every crevice. It's obviously the center of his universe. In addition to the normal desk and bookcases covered with pristine legal tomes, he's got a huge waterfall along one wall, an enormous fireplace on the other, a big domed skylight over the center, and sandstone tiled floors—all four elements converging."

"All four what?" Troy asked.

"The original elements. Water, fire, air, and earth."

"That tell you anything?"

"His subconscious is screaming for stability and balance."

"We'll have it screaming for something else soon enough. Did you search his desk?"

"I did. Picked my way in. Nothing unusual."

"How about the basement? Anything there?"

"I hope so. I've been working the lock to a closet for these last few minutes."

There was the source of her excitement, Troy thought. "How big a closet?"

"I'm guessing it's about five foot by eight."

"What makes you think there's anything more special than old knickknacks inside?"

"First of all, those are in the attic. Secondly, Luther installed a seven-tumbler lock on the door. That's exceptional. The vast majority of locks have only five. He's definitely hiding something here. Oh, hold on ..."

Troy waited through a long silence before Emmy said, "Got it, I'm in."

He refrained from asking the obvious questions. She would tell him what she saw.

"It's a computer room. The air is a lot warmer than in the rest of the house and it has that computer smell."

"Ozone," Troy said.

"Right. There's a narrow table running the length of the eight-foot side, and a single-wheeled armchair, a Herman Miller."

"So Luther spends a lot of time there."

"Or at least he did at one time. The room's fairly dusty, although that could just be because the maid doesn't come here."

"Except you."

"Except me."

"What do you see?"

"There are computer monitors all along the wall above the table, two rows of them, eight long. They're numbered one through sixteen. So are sixteen black boxes stacked at the far end."

"What kind of boxes?"

"They look like small DVD recorders. There's also a big computer with its own monitor and keyboard. All the DVD recorders are connected to it."

"Is there anything on the monitors?"

"No. Wait, one of them is coming to life. Number fourteen. It's a beautiful woman in an ornate elevator."

"Is DVD player fourteen doing anything?" Troy asked.

"All the DVD players have a green diode lit up, but fourteen has a red one too. Okay, the elevator door just opened. The woman is exiting. Now I see her on monitor fifteen. She's in a room with a waterfall like the one in Luther's study. There's also a granite bar in the background. She's walking toward the camera. Now she's on sixteen. So is Luther. He's seated behind a big oak desk. That must be his Rodeo Drive office."

"So the security system is motion activated," Troy said. "And everything that moves is recorded."

"Oh my god," Emmy said. "Monitor seven just came to life. It's Desiree. She just entered the kitchen from the pantry."

Troy understood the problem immediately. It was a monster. Everything Emmy had done that day, from searching Luther's desk to picking her way into his security room, everything had been recorded.

Chapter 72

Promotion

FARKAS REMOVED the safety cap from his injector ring and inspected the weapon. Three tiny needles glistened in the elevator light. The ring was ready; was he? He had no choice.

The doors parted to reveal an enormous office, complete with a granite bar, slate waterfall and one Luther Kanasis. Luther's appearance surprised Farkas—much more Hugh Jackman than Gene Hackman.

Crossing toward Luther's desk, Farkas tried to exude an image that would fit an iron grip. He knew that was not a stretch. He was much more Van Damme than DeVito.

"We meet at last," Luther said, coming around his desk and extending his hand.

Farkas did not reply at once. He looked Luther in the eye while catching his hand such that Luther's knuckles aligned. Then he smiled and squeezed like a vice, knowing the pain he inflicted would drown out any pin prick. "The pleasure is all mine."

Farkas saw a shadow flicker across Luther's eyes, but as predicted, he continued to smile. Men hated to appear weak.

The injection ring did its work in less than a second, so Farkas only pumped twice before releasing. He broke eye contact for a second to diffuse the tension and used his left hand for a diversionary pat on Luther's right shoulder. "Nice place you have here. Hardly the discreet hideaway I had envisioned."

"Sometimes the best place to hide is in plain sight. Please, have a seat. Tell me how it went in Vegas."

"After you," Farkas said, not wanting to give his boss the opportunity to inspect his injured hand.

Farkas had expected Luther to start out exactly thus, with a cordial question about Vegas. Best to be sure his affairs were in order before terminating Farkas's services with a bullet or a flash. For his part, Farkas was more than happy to play along. He needed to buy fifteen minutes— time for the 456 to activate. Then at the first sign of trouble, he would squeeze the remote concealed in his left hand and the UV-C strobe hidden in his Kangol cap would flash.

"Is that an espresso machine I see up there?" Farkas asked, glancing toward the bar.

"Yes. But it's nearly five o'clock. Perhaps you'd prefer a Scotch?"

"Naw, you know how Vegas is. This is breakfast time."

Luther nodded and made the drink, gobbling up enough time that Farkas figured he was safe. "So how is Mr. Rodriguez?"

"I'm pleased to report that he has no memory of the last twelve months of his life."

"Excellent. Does that mean you got your groove back?"

Farkas met his boss's eye. "After Grand Cayman, you mean?"

"Yes."

"I did."

"Good. You never did tell me exactly what happened there."

There it was, Farkas thought, the lead-up to the end. He had decided days ago to play it straight, no excuses, but with a bit of panache. "I was bested by a clever surgeon and an evil pixie."

"Evil pixie?" Luther asked, his tone more curious than condemning.

"It's from a Croatian fairytale. Emmy looks like a pixie, all petite and fiery with bright emerald eyes that can see into a man's soul."

Luther nodded appreciatively. "Yes, combined with a clever surgeon they do make a formidable team. I should have taken the time to learn more about them. They were, after all, the first and only people to ever suspect my existence. Some day you'll have to fill me in on the details. At the moment, however, we have more pressing matters."

Farkas raised his brows in genuine query. This was not at all what he had expected. He reminded himself that Luther's stock-in-trade was that you never saw him coming. He would remain wary despite his boss's cordial demeanor and collegial attitude. "So what's next?"

"What's next, my friend, is your bonanza."

"My bonanza?" Farkas repeated, finding the remote with his thumb. "What does that mean?"

"It means that you're about to become rich. Fifteen days from now I'm going to pay you ten million dollars. Eight figures. Tax free."

Farkas knew that was four hundred wiping's worth, having done the calculation many a time in his head. Keeping his tone neutral and his thumb poised, he asked, "And just what do I have to do to earn this bonanza?"

"Actually, you've already done most of it," Luther said. "By working dependably for me these past few years. I'm moving you into management."

"Management? Management of what?"

"A big job. A huge job. A job that will make history."

Luther's excitement appeared genuine. Farkas was actually starting to believe. "You have my undivided attention. Who is it, the president? One of the major party nominees?"

When Luther did not contradict him right away, Farkas knew that was it. A suicide mission. That made perfect sense.

"No," Luther eventually said. "Just the nine justices of the United States Supreme Court."

Same difference. "I see. Is that all? Just nine of the most closely guarded men on the planet?"

"Actually, they're not guarded at all. At least not when they're outside the courthouse."

"So you think that I can just walk up to them like anyone else?" Farkas said, not bothering to disguise his incredulity.

"You're not listening, Farkas. I told you, you're in management now. You're going to have help. Nine men as a matter of fact."

Nine men, Farkas thought. One apiece. That sounded good. Too good. "So what is it you aren't telling me?"

Chapter 73

Cleanup

THE PHONE SLIPPED from Emmy's grasp and clattered across the tabletop. As her nervous fingers fumbled to bring it back to her ear, she heard Troy asking, "Are you okay? Emmy, are you okay?"

"No, I'm not okay. I'm totally screwed. As soon as Luther checks the tapes, he's going to see that I spent the day snooping around. I'll have to quit. Run. And I still haven't found anything. All this has been a waste."

"Calm down," Troy said. "We'll think of something."

Troy's words did not reach her, but something in his tone did. If he was confident, she could be confident too. "Do you think there's some way to edit the tape? Take out the suspicious parts?"

Troy took his time answering her. She pictured him lying on the floor of their rented minivan, looking toward the ceiling with that contemplative thousand-yard stare she had grown to love. "I don't think you're going to have time to review and edit sixteen tapes before Luther returns. Even if you could, we probably wouldn't fool him. Security systems have a built-in time stamp."

Emmy glanced at an active screen. Desiree was rubbing spices into the skin of a duck. "You're right, the time and date are in the corner of every active monitor. Maybe we should cut our losses. I'll keep searching the house until Luther returns. Then I'll run. Maybe we'll get lucky."

"Hold on," Troy said. "I've got another call." He clicked off before she could ask who it was. She could not think of anyone who might be calling him. Probably a wrong number.

Turning her attention back to pressing matters, Emmy looked around for other discs. She found a box of fresh DVD-9s on the floor beneath the table, but none that were used. Either Luther stored the recorded disks in another location, or the system was set up to reuse the same disks. Perhaps she could just copy yesterday's video and paste it on top of today? Who really paid attention to a date stamp anyway? She discarded that idea immediately. She was not in yesterday's tapes, and Luther would specifically be looking for her.

"I'm back," Troy said. "You're not going to believe—"

"Oh my god!" Emmy said, cutting him off.

"What?"

"It's Farkas. Farkas just walked into Luther's office."

"How on earth?"

"I don't know. But that does it. Now I have no choice but to run. Can you imagine if I hadn't gotten into this room? If Luther had brought Farkas home while I was here? Should I bring all the DVD's with me?"

"No! You can't leave." Troy said, his voice emphatic. "That phone call. I've just learned something big. I don't want to go into the details over the phone, but now it's more important than ever that we stop Luther."

"But Farkas can identify me."

"Not necessarily. We don't know that he didn't lose his memory. All we know is that he found his way to Luther's. Remember our own experience."

"He told us he'd never been to Luther's. Never met the man. Obviously his whole spiel was a lie. I don't know how he fooled me so completely, but he did."

"Maybe, maybe not. Maybe he had the equivalent of a tattoo on his foot." Troy trailed off. His silence seemed to last forever.

Emmy knew he was thinking, but eventually could not take it anymore. "Troy?"

"I got it!" Troy said. "I know what we can do. I can fix this thing, but you're going to have to hang in there. I need an hour. Does it look like Luther and Farkas are going to be there for a while? Are they getting comfortable?"

Emmy could not imagine what solution Troy had found, but experience had given her faith in his genius and she found herself willing to make that blind leap. "It's hard to tell. They are sitting down, but they're talking with a lot of passion so it might be over quick. I don't have sound."

"Can you read their lips?" Troy asked.

"Not under these conditions."

"Did Luther give you any idea when he planned to be home?"

"No. Who called? What's your plan? Don't leave me hanging, Troy."

"I'll tell you everything when I get there. We don't have time to waste now. Just trust me. Forget about the cameras and get busy cleaning. You've got a whole day's legitimate work to do."

Chapter 74

Anticipation

LUTHER CLOSED the titanium notebook with a great sense of satisfaction. Two hundred and fifty million dollars. A quarter billion. He was tempted to take the money and run. True, Arlen would send an army after him—but would he send more men than the FBI and Secret Service combined? Actually, Luther decided, he might. And, unlike them, Arlen's mercenaries would know who they were looking for.

Then there was Arlen's point about the ambiguity of mass amnesia.

Deciding once and for all to move ahead, Luther began placing 456 ampoules into mailing boxes. He packed eighteen in total: nine for the Supreme Court Justices, nine for Orca's thugs.

Returning to his desk, he picked up his scrambled phone. Anyone tapping Orca's line would hear gobbledygook and think Luther's call originated in Iceland.

"Talk to me," the killer whale said.

"Did you arrange those meetings for me?" Luther asked.

"I did. All nine."

"You do know these guys personally, right? You can guarantee me that they're James Bonds, not Jack the Rippers?"

"They're on the East Coast, so I can't say that I know them all personally. But I'm told that they're primo. What else can I say? I did what you asked. Now get me my money." Orca ended the call before Luther could comment.

Luther sat there in silence, his stomach shriveling further with each breath. There was a reason he had never attempted to expand his operation before, and this was it. With the involvement of each additional person, the variables multiplied exponentially. His two-man operation had just expanded to twelve. Thank goodness this was the last hurrah, otherwise he'd be in prison within a year. And in any case, it was Farkas's problem now. The risk, hereafter, was all his.

Weaving his Porsche impatiently through Saturday evening traffic, Luther sought another train of thought and remembered that he had a new girl. She was a hottie. Fernando had come through once again, and just in time. With Brandy and Giselle both gone and Desiree too eager to please, he desperately needed a new source of release.

With his departure imminent, his normal rules no longer applied. He could begin to seduce her immediately. Hell, if she had snooped around as much as most first-day girls do, he could go straight to blackmail—

tonight. Wouldn't that be grand. He just needed a little something for which she would want to make atonement.

Naughty fantasies began running through his head as he gave his Carrera the gas. He pictured her pouty lips, her fiery eyes, and that hot little body of hers. She could not weigh more than a hundred pounds. He could bounce her around like a gymnast on a beam. She was almost … pixie-like …

Chapter 75

Rocky

FIFTY-THREE MINUTES after coming up with his plan, Troy crept into Luther's security room. After returning from his errand, Emmy had guided him past the watchful cook and down the basement stairs. Then she had pounced and begun squeezing the stuffing out of him.

It felt wonderful.

So did seeing the monitor showing Luther behind his office desk. And alone. "Did Farkas leave?"

"About forty-five minutes ago."

"So if he was headed this way, he would already have shown up?"

"Probably ..." Emmy's voice trailed off and she took a sudden step back. "What's in the box? I thought I heard something move."

"That, my dear, was the sound of salvation."

"It sounded more like a rat."

Troy patted the box, eliciting more scratching. "Salvation can take many forms. Rocky here is going to explain to Luther why his computer shut down in the middle of the night."

Emmy took another step back. "It really is a rat?"

Troy nodded and waited for her to get it. Emmy did not take long, and once she did, she switched gears almost immediately. "So who called you?"

"Sylvia Dashell."

"The attorney from Alexander Tate's office? The woman you bribed to keep you secretly appraised of activity in your account?"

"Kostas received a deposit today. Two hundred and fifty million dollars."

Emmy's eyes bulged like a mating frog's. "You sure you heard that right?"

"I'm sure. I had her repeat it. Twenty-five with a seven zero tail."

"The records we saw indicated that he only got one million for a job. Do you think he's going to flash two hundred and fifty people all at once?"

"I was thinking more along the lines of one very important person."

Emmy gasped. "Like the president?"

"Either him or one of the major-party nominees. Now you see why we can't run?"

"Of course."

"Good. Now, you get back to your cleaning. I'm going to erase all the DVDs back to the time when our nocturnal friend here supposedly stepped on Ctrl-Alt-Delete. I'll call you when I'm done so that you can distract Desiree long enough for me to get back to the Honda. Then you find an excuse to run an errand."

"I can't believe that we might be working to save the president," Emmy said. "My whole life I've been operating in a moral gray zone, just trying to get by. Now for the first time I'm working in the white, and it's for the president. It feels different. It feels good."

"Let's hope it's the start of a new trend," Troy said, giving her hand a squeeze. "Now get to it. We're probably short on time."

Troy had just finished erasing the twelfth DVD back to 2:43 AM when Luther rose from behind his desk and crossed the room to stand before his slate waterfall. A big blue Macaw watched him attentively from its perch off to the right. Why were rich people always so flamboyantly eccentric?

As Troy watched, Luther removed his jacket and scrunched up his right shirtsleeve, sending the Macaw to a new perch atop the waterfall. Then Luther plunged his hand into the water.

The flow stopped almost immediately and the slate backing slid aside. Troy found himself looking at the black iron door of a mammoth safe. No wonder Emmy had found nothing upstairs. Luther's office safe was large enough to hold Hoover's secret files.

He watched Luther work the combination with practiced ease. Troy could see the dial, but the camera was too far from the door for him to read the numbers. He found himself expecting to see bars of gold stacked inside, but when Luther hauled the heavy door open Troy saw only empty shelves.

Luther pulled out a metallic binder that his body had hidden from view. He opened it and made a careful entry using a thick silver pen. When he finished writing, he stared at the page as though it were the picture of a long-lost lover or firstborn child. When he finally closed the notebook, he laid it back down lovingly. Next, Luther pulled a key ring from his pocket and crouched down to reveal what appeared to be a mini refrigerator. This he unlocked with a short, round key like the ones typically used on vending machines and bicycle locks. As he swung the insulated door open, a light went on inside, confirming Troy's initial hypothesis as to its nature.

Luther used both hands to extract a box made of the same metal as the binder. He laid it gingerly atop the refrigerator, opened the lid, and began removing small ruby-red ampoules. "There it is," Troy said. "That's what we've been looking for.

"Now all we have to do is get it."

Luther proceeded to place the extracted ampoules into a book-sized cardboard box lined with thick foam padding. Troy counted nine ampoules total. Then Luther repeated the procedure with a second box. Once both boxes were full and sealed, he reversed the procedure to close the safe and restore the waterfall.

When Luther took the package back to his desk rather than the elevator, Troy seized the opportunity to rewind the tape with the hope of deciphering the combination using digital zoom. He paused with the cursor over the rewind button. Perhaps it would be better to just make a copy of Luther's entire visit to the safe and interpret it later.

Using the software's convenient drag-and-drop procedure, he burned the ten minutes from 17:42 through 17:51 off camera 15 onto a fresh DVD. Sliding that backup into his breast pocket, Troy felt a sense of accomplishment. Now even if the shit hit the fan he would not leave empty handed.

Checking the monitor, Troy saw that Luther was still at his desk. He decided to attempt to decipher the combination while all the equipment he needed was at hand.

Troy had the first four digits of the combination scrawled on a notepad when he looked up to see that screens 15 and 16 were both dark. Luther had left his office.

That was when he remembered that he still had four DVDs to erase.

Praying that the DVD in his pocket contained the same high-definition video as the original, Troy forgot about the tape he was watching and began furiously erasing the remaining hard drives back to 2:43 that morning. Questions cascaded through his mind as he worked, but his surgical fingers did not fumble. How long ago had Luther left? Was he coming straight home? Did he carry a gun? Troy knew he should call Emmy to warn her, but he could not risk the time. Besides, she was just cleaning. There was no harm in Luther catching her doing that. Troy was the one out on a limb.

It took him seven minutes to erase the remaining four DVDs back to 2:43 AM. Then he simply turned off the computer. The DVD recorders' green diodes extinguished along with the computer monitor. The wall monitors showing Emmy and Desiree remained lit. Apparently they were part of a separate system.

"Now for the finishing touch," he said, slipping a peanut butter cookie into Rocky's box. With the rat's mouth gainfully engaged, Troy pulled Rocky out and set him on the table. Then he inverted the box and shook it over the keyboard. Several rat pellets dropped out. Two landed on the desk and the third wedged between the F and R keys. This simple ruse probably wouldn't fool Sherlock Holmes, but Troy did not expect Luther to bring in a forensic consultant. As the lawyer himself would put it, this was enough for reasonable doubt.

Reassuring himself that the safe-cracking DVD was in his pocket, he stood just as monitor one lit up and Luther's black Porsche approached the gate. Talk about cutting it close. He tossed Rocky another cracker to keep him distracted, and slid out the door. He used Emmy's tension wrench to re-secure the bolt and then picked up his phone to give her a call. Now, all he had to do was make it out the back door and into the Honda unobserved.

Chapter 76

Tips

EMMY'S CELL PHONE finally began to vibrate. Troy had taken much longer than she'd expected. She moved out of Desiree's earshot and brought the phone to her ear.

"I'm ready," Troy said. "And I've got what we need." He sounded excited.

"You can't come up yet. Desiree is rearranging the pantry near the top of the stairs. It's almost as though she knows you're down there."

"Luther just pulled through the gate. Think of something." Troy hung up.

Emmy walked back toward the pantry, thinking fast. Inspiration tended to strike her on the fly, and her muse did not let her down today. "Have you got a minute, Desiree? I'd love to get your opinion on something."

Desiree looked silently down on her from a step stool. It was a gaze meant to intimidate.

Emmy was unaffected. She was used to talking up to people who tried to use their relative height to tactical advantage. And as a psychic she was accustomed to dealing with skeptics. The trick in both cases was to alter the antagonist's perspective. Right now Desiree saw her as competition for Luther's affection. "It will just take a minute. While dusting I noted that Mr. Kanasis has a nice collection of Swiss chronographs. One of them is the same model Breitling that I was planning to get my fiancé for his birthday. I'd love a second opinion."

The effect on Desiree was instantaneous. She brightened up and said, "Sure." But as her first foot hit the floor she paused and asked, "You're getting him a Breitling, and he hasn't gotten you a ring?"

"Oh, I got the ring. Two carats. But I'm not about to wear it here. I learned in my waitressing days that men treat you much better when they think you're available."

Desiree's smile returned and she finished her descent. "They still don't treat you all that well."

"You're right about that."

They had just reached the top of the sweeping semicircular staircase when the front door opened. Emmy felt as though an icy hand had gripped her heart. Had Troy made it out in time? "Maybe tomorrow," she whispered to Desiree as they both turned to greet their master.

"What are you two ladies up to?" Luther asked, depositing his keys in a vase on a knickknack shelf to the left of the door. Although his tone telegraphed lighthearted banter, Emmy detected suspicion in his eyes.

"Desiree has just been giving me some tips on your preferences," Emmy said. "She's been very helpful."

"Glad to hear it," Luther replied, a penetrating look in his eyes. "Why don't you join me for a drink, Vicky. You can tell me about your first day and I can give you all the tips you need."

Chapter 77

Accommodation

FARKAS PUSHED OPEN the stairwell door with a little too much vigor. It slammed into the cinderblock wall and ricocheted back at him, but he stepped through in time to avoid its ire. His first day in "management" was not going well. Time to bring Luther into the loop.

Luther answered on the second ring. "How's it going?"

"Neanderthals. Your business associate sent us Neanderthals."

"All of them?"

"I've seen eight so far. You wouldn't trust any of these guys with your dry cleaning, much less 456."

Luther paused as though winded, confirming Farkas's suspicion that this was bad news on several levels. "What did you tell them?"

"Not a word about the plan, that's for sure. As soon as it became clear that I'd eaten meals with more brainpower, I pretended to receive a call telling me that the job had been called off. I acted all pissed and gave each guy ten grand for his time and his tongue as agreed. But hey, for what it's worth, your plan of alternating the meetings between the sixth and seventh floors worked like a charm. No one suspected that this would have been more than a two-man op."

"Swell."

"I take it you went this route due to a lack of alternatives?" Farkas asked.

Luther prevaricated with a collegial, "How about you? Know any talent?"

"Farkas means wolf in Hungarian. Like my namesake, I work alone."

"Maybe number nine will work out. Maybe he'll have friends."

"Maybe monkeys will fly out of my ass and do the job for us, Luther, but I wouldn't count on it."

"You sure you went to med school?"

"You sure you're an officer of the court?"

After another long pause, Luther said, "Tell me something. How many people do you really need to do the job?"

"Nine people, one city, forty-eight hours … If I had four people, each could do one a day and I could pick up the ninth."

"What if it was just you and two others?"

"Three apiece … yeah, that should be possible with enough planning."

"Two weeks good enough?"

"If they're good people."

"You're being awfully accommodating."

"I want my ten million bucks."

"Glad to hear it. I want to give it to you. In the meantime, go ahead with your last meeting. Maybe we'll get lucky. In either case, I want you to come back to LA when you're done. We'll finish the recruiting here."

"You sound like you have someone in mind."

"As a matter of fact, I do."

Chapter 78

Craps

"SO THIS IS THE FAMOUS RODEO DRIVE," Troy said. "I'd expected Chanel No 5, but this smells more like Eau de Armpit."

"This isn't Rodeo Drive," Emmy said. "This is the alley behind Rodeo Drive. Now, do you want to let me know why you're interested in the fashion boutique three doors down from Kanasis rather than Kanasis itself?"

Troy turned from his appraisal of the back wall toward his co-conspirator. Boy did she look good in black. "According to the sticker in their front window, Balthazar uses the same security company as Kanasis. I figure it's perfect for a dry run."

"Uh-huh. And that mysterious black box I saw you slip into your backpack; you going to tell me what that's all about?"

"The Y400? According to Pedro-the-Procurer, it blocks the full commercial spectrum of cell phone transmissions within a two hundred foot radius."

"And you think that's going to keep the armed response away when we key into Kanasis?"

"Pedro wasn't sure if the full commercial spectrum included the frequencies used by security companies. That's why we're going to try it out here first, just to be sure."

"Well, be quick about it. Luther expects me to be on hand to greet his guests when they arrive at ten."

"Is that all he expects—the sight of your pretty face and a few welcoming words?" Troy had been so busy preparing for tonight that they had hardly spoken since the close call in Luther's security room.

"That's what he said. He is very image conscious, and a pretty maid answering his door exemplifies his preferred persona."

"Well, if the next few minutes go as planned, then the only people opening Luther's door from now on will be foul-breathed federal employees with sadistic streaks and penchants for sodomy." Of course, if the next few minutes went badly, Troy and Emmy would be the ones going to prison, but he left that caveat unsaid.

Highly motivated by both carrot and stick, he used a dumpster and then a drainpipe to climb quickly atop the two-story building. Troy wanted to put the Y400 beside the alarm's antenna to maximize its jamming effect, but he found only air-conditioning equipment. Aware that the clock was ticking, he planted the jammer atop the air handler's fuse box and climbed back down.

"My cell phone is drawing a blank," Emmy said. "That's a good sign."

Troy shook his head. "The only good sign is no sign of Atlas Security."

"How are you planning to test the alarm—put a brick through the window?"

"Something a bit more surgical. Come see for yourself."

All the businesses on North Rodeo Drive were closed at this hour, leaving the street relatively deserted. A group of young tourists meandered loudly about, drinks in hand, but at the moment they were clustered across the street, taking pictures before the entrance to Ralph Lauren.

"Keep a discreet eye on them," Troy said, checking to ensure that his cell phone was still searching as they approached Balthazar's front door. He pulled a long thin white clown's balloon from his pocket, secured the neck to a manual pump and gave it just enough wind to make it rigid. Then he pushed the balloon through the brass mail slot and finished the inflation. Fixing his eyes on the motion detector's green diode he released the neck of the balloon, sending it in a spiraling flight around the store until at last it came to rest on the shoulder of a black-clad mannequin.

The diode turned red.

Pleased with the result he said, "Whoever finds that in the morning is going to wonder what goes on after hours at Balthazar."

"Not here," Emmy replied. "This is Hollywood."

Troy linked his arm through hers. "Let's walk toward Santa Monica Boulevard to wait for the response that we hope won't come."

They did—and it did.

In just five minutes.

"That was quick," Emmy said.

"Yeah. So much for the Y400 and that thousand bucks. Pedro doesn't have a return policy." In Miami they had pocketed a pretty penny by pawning Emmy's engagement ring, but that money was running short. Troy still remembered the number from the AmEx card he had always used, but was keeping it as an emergency reserve. Credit cards put you on the grid.

He watched over Emmy's shoulder as a security car screeched to a halt before Balthazar and three armed men burst out. Two of the guards drew their guns and converged on Balthazar's entrance while the third sprinted for the smelly alley. "They're using the same tactics my Special Forces unit did when clearing buildings in Afghanistan. Must be ex-military."

"Judging by the way they move," Emmy said, "one has to wonder if they sit on the edge of their chairs all night, drinking Red Bull and waiting for the horn." Once they disappeared inside, she added, "What's plan B?"

"You'll see," Troy said, extracting a handkerchief and two small atomizers from his backpack. "Once they leave."

She gave his tools the once over and then said, "I can't wait more than fifteen minutes. If we haven't opened Luther's safe by then, I'm going to have to go back. If I'm not there when Luther's guests arrive, he might get suspicious, look around, and notice that his keys are missing."

"That reminds me," Troy said. "Did you manage to turn the contrast to black on Luther's security monitors?"

"Numbers fourteen through sixteen."

"Great. And don't worry. It shouldn't take them long to clear a small fashion boutique."

The three guards emerged a few seconds later, no doubt having already reported a false alarm. Troy and Emmy began walking toward Kanasis as soon as the Atlas Security Jeep pulled away.

Emmy unlocked the door with Luther's key and Troy pulled the handle. "It's still locked," he said, checking the crack between frame and door for bolts. "Are you sure you turned the key all the way."

As Emmy said, "I'm sure," the door yielded to Troy's tug. "There's some kind of an electromagnetic lock in place. I'm not sure what that means, but it can't be good."

The alarm keypad began to beep and glow yellow. Troy went to work with the handkerchief and spray bottles. "First we give it a cleaning with some good old Windex … then once it's clean and dry … we give it a thorough misting with bottle number two."

"What does bottle number two do?" Emmy asked.

"It's a micro-granulated tacky powder that fluoresces under black light."

"You don't say."

Mid-way through the misting the beeping turned frantic and then flatlined. The keypad began to flash red. "Sixty-seconds," Troy said. "Not bad. I was afraid we might only get thirty. Let's go."

Troy led her back across the street. They concealed themselves behind a potted azalea bush halfway down the block.

The Atlas men arrived in just three minutes this time, no doubt because they had already been on the road, but they spent much longer inside than they had at Balthazar.

"I can't wait any longer," Emmy said. "I have to get back to Luther's."

Troy looked at his watch: Quarter to ten. "I'll call you as soon as I've got it and you can run." He bent his head to kiss her. "Good luck."

"You too."

The Atlas men left shortly after Emmy. Now that the time pressure was off, he waited fifteen minutes to be sure they were back at base with their boots off before going back in.

He spent the time mentally rehearsing his next steps in order to maximize their speed. The first key the guard had pressed would show a clean fingerprint under his black light, because it was touched by a clean finger. The second key pressed would display the outline of the first number on it, because the numbers themselves were recessed within the buttons and thus would not transfer powder. The third number in the code would have the second number outlined strongly over a weaker first, and so on.

Troy had practiced the deciphering exercise a hundred times back in his hotel room on a similar keypad. He knew he was safe as long as the code was just four digits in length. Five was still possible, but six was the next likely length after four and that was too much. If it was six or more, or if the guard had used multiple fingers, he was SOL.

Sometimes you just had to roll the dice.

Checking to ensure that he was not being watched, Troy crossed the street and keyed back into Kanasis. Again, the alarm console began its sixty-second countdown. He turned on the black light and bathed the keypad. Given all his practice, he could tell immediately that the guard had pressed the three, four, five and seven once apiece. That would have been fine, except the guard had also pressed the eight, twice.

Sometimes you crapped out.

Chapter 79

Green Light

LUTHER'S GUESTS WERE LATE, but not late enough. They arrived before Troy called. Emmy could not skip out.

Luther had not told Emmy who was coming for cocktails, but when the two monsters emerged from the black Mercedes S600 she recognized them from Giselle's descriptions. Orca and Zero—the killer whale and his refrigerator-sized bodyguard.

At Troy's suggestion, Emmy had unlocked windows at various strategic locations throughout the house in case she ever needed to bolt. As she walked toward the front entrance, she went over the escape routes in her head like a paranoid preparing for a hotel fire. When she reached the door she paused to take a deep breath. Things could be worse; it could be Farkas. Where was that weasel?

She slipped into character and opened the door before the bell's echo had died. "Good evening, gentlemen. Mr. Kanasis is waiting for you in his study, if you'll please follow me."

"So you're Luther's new girl," Orca said, giving her a slow inspection from head to toe. "I'd be happy to follow you, dear. What's your name?"

"Vicky," she said, turning toward the stairs.

"Vicky as in Victoria, or just Vicky?"

"As in Victoria," she said, without pausing or looking back.

"I'm glad to hear that. These days, parents have a tendency to be cute —at their kid's expense. I figure you gotta give a person a choice, you know. After all, what if ya'd wanted to be a lawyer, or run for president."

Emmy knew she should remain silent, but could not resist the tempting barb. "I'm so glad you approve, Orca."

"Cute and feisty too. I bet Luther keeps you around for more than the normal couple of months. Still, when he does let you go, stop by Lisa's Place if you want to make some real money. Ask for James, that's my Christian name."

Emmy did not so much as turn to acknowledge the offer. She just knocked on the arched double doors to Luther's office and announced, "Your guests have arrived."

Orca pushed past her without waiting for a response. As he walked in with Zero following the requisite four paces behind, Luther rose from his armchair and said, "So glad you were able to come, my friend. Please, have a seat. We have a lot to talk about. A lot to talk about."

Emmy heard two hundred and fifty million dollars' worth of excitement in Luther's voice, so she made the split-second decision to advance rather than retreat. Walking to the corner bar she asked, "May I pour you gentlemen a drink?"

"Don't worry about it, Vicky. I'll pour the Scotch," Luther said. "You just make sure the door is closed. We don't want to be disturbed. Feel free to go out or to bed if you wish. We won't be needing you anymore this evening."

Emmy nodded and left without comment. This was it. Her chance to foil an evil act worth a quarter-billion dollars. She stepped to the side of the study doors and perked her ears. She could hear muffled voices, but the thick oak garbled individual words. Thinking fast, she ran down the hall to snatch a glass from the bathroom. While pulling it from the gilded holder, however, an even better idea popped into her head.

The ceiling of the closet off Luther's study had a trapdoor accessing an unfinished portion of the attic. She had peeked up there her first day on the job while searching for a safe. What's more, the closet door was louvered. She would be able to see and hear everything Luther and Orca said—if she could get inside.

She had to hurry.

Emmy raced down the hall and up the attic stairs. She yanked the chain that switched on the bare bulb and wove her way through the piles of dusty boxes. The finished part of the attic ended where the angle of the roof brought it close to the floor. She ducked under the low beams and found herself disoriented in a dark jungle of wooden rafters and blown fiberglass insulation.

Maybe she should have stuck with the glass.

Emmy worked her way in what she thought was the direction of the study, stepping rafter-to-rafter, ducking beams and avoiding nails. She had hoped that boisterous voices would guide her, but heard only the wind whistling through the tiles above. While glancing back toward the light of the finished section, trying to orient herself and judge distance, a familiar rat scurried over her foot. Emmy reared back in shock and punctured her scalp on the tip of an exposed roofing nail. She let out an involuntary scream before slapping her own hand over her mouth. Now she had to add a tetanus shot to her to-do list. With her luck she would survive all the trauma of the Kanasis investigation only to succumb to lockjaw. Then she wouldn't be able to kiss the very man she was fighting for.

Emmy continued her quest for what seemed like hours even though she knew it was barely minutes. It was maddening, knowing that she might miss the big payoff by seconds. Her skin began to itch from some kind of allergic reaction. She finally found the trapdoor on the far side of a ventilation duct. She brushed the insulation back from the edges so no telltale crumbs would drop inside and hauled it open.

The voices drifting up from below were muffled. Distinct, but indecipherable. "In for a penny, in for a pound," she whispered, and lowered herself through the hole. She dropped to the ground knowing that the shelving would serve as an escape ladder.

Once inside the closet, she pressed her ear to the door and tried to peer through the slats.

"... kill the president?" Emmy recognized Orca's voice.

"Fifty million dollars. Not a penny less," Luther replied.

"That's a bit steep, don't you think? I mean, I got friends who would give it a try for ten and would throw in the Pope for free."

"Enough of this," Luther said. "I see that our guest has finally joined us."

Emmy strained to see who else had joined the meeting, but the slats in the door were too narrowly spaced. She was attempting to widen the angle with her pinkie when the door flew open beneath her fingers. Two gorilla paws reached in, grabbed her beneath the armpits, and hoisted her off the ground as though she were weightless.

Zero carried her over to the suite of chairs where Luther and Orca were sitting and held her out like a cat. Unwilling to look Luther in the eye, she looked down and saw that her toes were a good two feet off the ground.

"Miss Green," Luther said. "My little pixie. So glad you could join us."

They knew her real name, Emmy thought, still trying to comprehend the sudden twist of fate.

Orca stood and did a full circle around her and Zero.

She felt like a slave being appraised at auction.

"I'm a bit concerned," he said to Luther. "She's so tiny. I don't think it's going to fit."

Emmy tried to wriggle free as Orca unzipped his pants, but she was wrestling with iron. For the moment at least, it was up to Troy to save her. She thought of the horror story Giselle had relayed, and prayed that he would hurry.

Chapter 80

Fade to Black

THE TEMPO of Troy's heart increased with the alarm's warning beep as the implications of a six-digit security code sank in. He could attempt to read the keys and hope to get lucky, but he had another avenue to try first. He had used a mnemonic device to make a few likely codes available for quick mental access. Converted to numbers, LAWYER had two 9s, MEMORY two 7s, and another likely candidate the two 8s the Atlas guard had pressed. Troy keyed in L-U-T-H-E-R, 5-8-8-4-3-7, and the beeping stopped.

Troy heard the waterfall before the elevator doors opened and he smiled. He knew why Luther chose to keep it working even at night. Regardless of the reason, the cascade was beautiful. It shimmered like a silver veil in the dim light filtering through the far window. Troy was not there for the aesthetics, however; he had come for the ledger and ampoules on the other side.

He removed his backpack and withdrew a camping lantern that he had cloaked on one side. He angled it so that no light would shine toward the window and turned it on. The moment he did, the macaw began to rustle in its sheet-covered cage. Troy felt similarly excited. It was time for the moment of truth.

Standing where Luther had stood, Troy pulled up his right sleeve and plunged his hand into the waterfall just as Luther had done. As spray misted his face, he explored the slate backing beneath with his hand. No matter where he pressed, nothing happened.

Feeling around more carefully, Troy thought he detected the outline of what could be a button, but it would not depress. He began to worry that the waterfall was on some kind of a timer, that it could not be opened when the office was closed. What a shame it would be to have come this far yet be able to go no further. "Not a chance," he mumbled. One way or the other, he was moving that mountain.

Returning to his backpack, Troy pulled out a portable DVD player and booted up the video of Luther opening the safe. During the second playing, he realized that he had fallen for a classic magician's trick. He had focused on the hand that appeared to be working all the magic, the hand reaching through the waterfall. He had failed to pay any attention to Luther's left hand, which rested on the structure's rocky left edge.

Troy set the player down and then mimicked Luther's moves with both hands. He felt the rock hinge in a quarter inch beneath his left hand, but still got nowhere with the button beneath his right.

Again he watched the video.

This time he figured it out on the first pass. The bird. A three-point trigger. Very clever indeed.

Troy removed the sheet from the macaw's cage and opened the door. The bird climbed down to the doorway, but went no further.

Troy walked over to the waterfall and reached for the buttons. The bird did not move. "Fly, bird, fly." He pointed to the perch atop the falls.

The bird just scratched his beak and began to preen.

Again Troy watched the tape. Luther made no special movements that Troy could detect. He must have said something, but the recording had no sound and his back was to the camera. Troy had never owned a bird. What was the avian equivalent of fetch? How did you get a bird to help you open a safe? How did you bring Mohammad to the mountain?

And then he had it.

Reassuming his stance, Troy said, "Open Sesame."

The bird flew.

The water stopped.

The slate backing slid aside.

Troy wiped his right hand off on his jeans and then rubbed both hands together vigorously before attempting to work the combination. Fourteen, ninety-two, seventeen, seventy-six, sixty-four. He got it open on the first try. Studying a digital magnification of the video, Troy had not been entirely certain of the numbers he thought he saw Luther dialing until he recognized the pattern. 1492, 1776, (19)64: three great dates in American history, the last being the year of Luther's birth.

The massive black door surely weighed more than he did, but the hinges were balanced so perfectly that it moved with little effort. The view that the swinging door revealed was identical to the one on the tape. They were in time.

Troy pulled the titanium binder off the black velvet shelf and flipped it open. Jeffrey Randal/Lionel Esposito, $1,000,000, June 16, 2005. Wendell Branson/Gregory Harris & Paul Culleton, $3,000,000, July 2, 2005. Archibald Martin/Wendy Caffrey, $1,000,000, July 26, 2005. He ran his finger down the list until he came to Isaac Goldfarb/Emerald Green, $1,000,000, November 27, 2007. That confirmed it. A warm pulsing glow suffused his body from head to toe. This was the end of the journey, the payoff for all the risk, the damning evidence for which he had traded the memories of his wife and daughter.

Flipping the page with sweaty hands, he found another familiar name three entries down. Russell Rankin/Charles Simms, $1,000,000, February 15, 2008. Charles Simms was the FBI Agent who had witnessed Russell Rankin claiming the lives of his wife and daughter and robbing him of his ability to operate. Charles was the fourth victim of that wealthy drunk. Troy and Emmy had decided that they would take whatever evidence they found to Agent Simms, retired or not. "We've done it, Emmy," he said.

With a heart that was at once victorious and sad, Troy tucked the ledger into his backpack. Turning back to the safe, he crouched and used the circular key on Luther's ring to unlock the refrigerator. Opening it, he found just one item: the metal box he knew to house ruby-red vials. Peering inside, Troy found the box divided into a twelve-by-twelve grid, one hundred and forty-four chambers. About half of them were empty. So many stolen memories. Troy pulled one of the remaining vials out and held it to the light. "Liquid amnesia."

Troy considered the option of smashing the whole lot then and there on the rocks of the waterfall, but realized that this would be destroying evidence, evidence that he would need. Besides, for all he knew, Luther had gallons of the potion stored away in some underground bunker. Deciding that the sensible move was to take them all, he pocketed the ampoule in his hand and slipped the box into his backpack.

As he secured the box, another thought struck him and Troy pulled the binder back out. Flipping it open to the last page with entries, he found a surprise. Instead of seeing the name of the president or one of the major party nominees, he found a list of nine names he did not recognize following the contractor's. Arranged in alphabetical order, he read, "Alverado, Brewer, Goldstein, Lincoln, Reynolds, Secada, Stoffer, Stevenson, and Thompson."

The dollar amount also knocked him for a loop. Instead of the two hundred and fifty he had expected, the ledger listed five hundred and fifty million.

He was still staring at the enormous number when another thought hit him and he reread the names. A few struck bells this time through and he found himself supplying their first names as well. "Anthony Secada, Daniel Stoffer, Charles Thompson." Some of them were completely unfamiliar, but then he would not recognize any name from the last seven years. He counted them again to be sure. Nine. "The Supreme Court Justices," he said aloud.

"That's right," a familiar voice boomed behind him.

Troy whirled about to find Farkas glaring at him over a shifty smile. First Troy focused on the beaming, metallic eyes, and then his eyes drifted down to the instrument in his nemesis's hand. Before he could react further, a crackling sound broke the silence and a burst of blinding pain invaded his chest, turning his world white before it faded to black.

Chapter 81

Choke

"PUT THAT AWAY, you're scaring the girl," Luther said.

"But I like it when they're all aquiver," Orca replied, rubbing his rising manhood between his fingers.

"I need her."

Orca rolled his eyes. "Wait your turn. There will probably be something left."

"For the job. I need her for the job."

Orca rolled his eyes, stopped rubbing, and asked, "How so?"

"It's a surprise."

"She looks surprised enough already. But hey, now that you mention it, I've got a surprise for you, too. You owe me nine hundred grand on top of the twenty-six mil."

Luther had seen this coming, but he wanted to make Orca work for it. "How do you figure?"

"I got you nine guys. The fact that you chose not to use them is not my problem."

"Your men were unacceptable. I asked for James Bonds, you sent me buffoons."

"Make it an even million, or I just might let them know you said so." Orca walked over and stood toe-to-toe with Luther.

He was good at playing tough with Zero around, Luther thought. But then, who wouldn't be. For the last couple of minutes the giant had been holding Emmy up with such relaxed ease that you would think her weight was on par with a glass of beer. Take Zero out of the equation, however, and Luther could wipe the floor with the fat, balding thug. "Even if they were acceptable, a hundred grand is a bit steep for a referral fee, don't you think."

"I'm not renting apartments. I'm a banker. We work on percentages. If you paid me twenty-six double large without breaking a sweat, I figure the operation's got to be worth at least three or four times that, say an even hundred mil. At one percent, I'm letting you off easy."

Luther nodded as if in defeat and walked over to his desk. "Tell you what, James, let's make it an even two."

"Now you're talking. I knew you could be reasonab—"

Luther whipped a Beretta from his desk and put a round in each of Zero's eyes.

The giant collapsed without a sound—or so Luther guessed. It was hard to tell over Emmy's screams. He had the gun leveled at Orca's chest before the mafia boss fully comprehended the amazing turn of events.

Keeping his eyes on Orca, Luther said, "Shut up, Emerald!"

She did.

Beckoning toward the heavy wooden armchair he had brought to his office in anticipation, he told Orca, "Sit down."

"So you do have a pair," Orca said. "I'm glad to see it. I was beginning to get worried. You know, now that my territory is expanding, I'm going to need a legal advisor with balls, a true consigliere."

"Sit down and shut up."

"You ever read the Godfather?" Orca asked, ignoring the command to shut up as he took the seat.

Luther brushed off the question and addressed Emmy instead. "You'll find some thick black zip ties over there on the bookcase. I want you to use them to bind my guest's wrists and ankles to the chair."

Luther had expected Orca to make a bolt for the door at this point, but he remained seated. Now he realized that Orca probably interpreted the bindings as a sign that he was not going to be killed. It was a reasonable hypothesis, but it was wrong.

When Emmy had all four zip ties in place, Luther put the Beretta in his pocket and gave each of the bindings an extra tug to be sure they were tight. Not one had an extra ratchet left. Emmy had done a good job. "Sit down and cross your ankles," he told her, motioning to the floor.

Emmy complied.

Luther bent down and bound her ankles together with another zip tie. "Can't have you running off on me while I'm busy."

"Busy with what?" Orca asked. "Don't you go doing anything stupid, anything you're going to regret. Zero, we can forget about. Water under the bridge. I was planning to get rid of him soon anyway. He knew too much. Besides, as I said, I can use you by my side."

Satisfied that Emmy would not be able to slip free and relatively certain that she was too traumatized to try, Luther turned his full attention back to Orca. He found the look of panic seated there to be immensely satisfying. After three-and-a-half years of sweating his monthly vig payment, he had a lot of hard feelings built up inside. The Killer Whale's latest extortion attempt had put him over the edge.

"You shouldn't have gotten greedy, Orca. You should have left well enough alone. I was just about to give you twenty-six million dollars. Twenty-six million on top of the forty-two I've dished out these last three-and-a-half years."

"Hey, Luther, it's my nature. You ever hear that anecdote about the scorpion and the frog?"

Luther ignored the pitiful attempt to lighten the atmosphere. "I've got good news for you, James, and I've got bad. The good news is: I'm not going to shoot you."

Orca let out a big sigh and Luther actually saw a tear trickle down his cheek. "You're making the right choice, Luther. If for no other reason than that you wouldn't last a day if you did."

"My thinking exactly," Luther said. Then he stopped talking and waited for Orca to ask.

The grandfather clock along the west wall ticked off a good thirty seconds before Orca could not take the waiting any longer. "So what's the bad news?"

Luther walked over to Zero's corpse and pulled the racquetball from his pocket. He knew that Zero always kept one there for practicing his favorite walnut-crushing trick. Standing, he put the ball in Orca's lap so it would be handy for shoving into the pig's mouth the minute he began to scream. Then he reached into his pocket and pulled out a switchblade. He flipped it open and tested the edge with his thumb. It sliced off the outer layer of dermis without drawing blood. You couldn't get a blade any sharper than that. Looking up from the mirrored finish to Orca's eyes, he said, "The bad news is that Jimmy Choke is going to get the rap for your murder."

Chapter 82

New Shoes

TROY DRIFTED BACK toward consciousness feeling woozy. His first jolting thought was that Farkas had erased his memory again, but he dismissed it with a quick sigh of short-lived relief. If his memory had been erased, he would recall neither Farkas nor the erasing procedure. Then his chest protested to the accompanying deep breath and he remembered the Taser.

When the floor did not stop moving as his grip on consciousness improved, Troy realized that his wooziness was seasickness. He was on a boat.

Opening his eyes, he found himself seated in the dark cabin of what he guessed was a thirty-foot boat. Farkas had bound his hands securely behind his back and his feet … What had happened to his feet? They were cold and he couldn't move them at all. He was weighing the medical likelihood of a Taser blast to the chest doing nerve damage to the feet when the hum of the engine changed. A moment later a door opened behind him and moonlight streamed in, casting his shadow over a grungy wooden floor. The door closed as quickly as it had opened and a florescent bulb flickered to life overhead.

Troy blinked twice, looked down at his feet, and felt his heart drop through the floor. Unfortunately, the cold numb sensation was not the result of nerve damage.

As reality sank in, Troy actually pined for the time he had woken up back on Grand Cayman, locked in a dark trunk with a cop's bloody corpse. A quote from Dean Acheson leapt forth from the abysses of his mind: "The manner in which one endures what must be endured is more important than the thing that must be endured." He suspected that the former Secretary of State would recant his famous bromide if he found himself in Troy's shoes, but nonetheless Troy vowed not to give Farkas the satisfaction of sensing the fear that gripped his heart. "Concrete galoshes. That's hardly original."

The coppery-eyed perpetrator of all Troy's woes walked around him in silence until they were face to face. "True, but then I'm an old fashioned kind of guy. And there's nothing more reliable. I decided that reliable was high on my list of priorities this time around. I'm sure you understand."

Troy did understand. And Farkas was right. He was helpless as a newborn kitten. In a strange kind of way, he found that thought comforting. It took the tension out of the situation to know that there was absolutely nothing he could do to change things—short of getting Farkas to change his mind... There. He had gone and done it. The tension was back. And for what? The slimmest thread of hope? Better to go out calm than flailing. At least he would look like a man. Drowning wasn't supposed to be such a bad death, was it? After all, you did spend your first nine months floating in a bag of water. And your body was ninety percent water. So how bad could it be?

"It's your contact lenses, isn't it?" Troy asked. "That's how you retained your memory."

Farkas raised his wiry brows. "Very good. I'm impressed. Even Luther hasn't figured that one out."

"You sure about that? I mean, if he did figure it out, would he tell you?"

"Why wouldn't he?" Farkas asked.

"Oh, I don't know. Maybe because you're wearing them for him. I mean, I was thinking, why would you be wearing protective lenses? Yours is the only game in town. But then it occurred to me. You figure that once Luther has his mattress stuffed to capacity, he's going to erase your memory and walk off into the sunset, knowing that all evidence linking him to his crimes has been destroyed."

"As I said, you're very good."

Farkas walked back behind Troy, grabbed the top of his chair and tilted it back on two legs. This put the full weight of the concrete bucket on the back of Troy's calves at the point where they hit the steel crossbar. Nerves Troy did not know he had screamed in agonized protest, but pride kept him from crying out. Once Farkas had dragged him clear of the cabin door and out onto the deck, however, he forgot about the pain. This was it. The last stop. The end of the line. Go forth and feel no more.

Troy looked up at the heavens. Out on the water far from the lights of L.A., the night sky reminded him of Afghanistan. In the category of last-thing-you'll-ever-see, the pearls-on-black-satin shroud of the Milky Way would be near the top of his wish list. Emmy, he realized, was number one. At least she wasn't there with him. He prayed that she had gotten out. Praying was all he could do. He was powerless to help her now.

The deck of the old wooden craft stunk with the odor of rotting fish. Just as they had flailed about here, drowning by the thousands, so he too was about to perish in the depths below. That was what Farkas had reduced him to, a fish.

He scanned the peeling decking as a desperate thought surfaced, searching for a stray scaling knife or pair of wire-cutting pliers. His eyes found nothing but a scrap of old netting—and a sledgehammer. The gleaming twelve-pounder stood propped against the cabin wall, near the doorway Farkas had just dragged him through. The price tag was still attached.

"That's in case you decide to get too lippy," Farkas said, following his gaze. "Works much better than stuffing a sock in your mouth."

"Charming place you've got here. Is this the boat from the original Jaws?"

"No, I think the shark ate that one."

Farkas had stopped the boat near a buoy that was taller than the boat itself. Troy pictured himself clinging to it for dear life and wondered if there was a radio beacon aboard that he could rewire to send out an SOS. "You stop here to ask directions?" he asked, motioning toward the buoy with his head.

"I just wanted to make sure that when you go down, you stay down."

"Huh?"

"Trawling is not permitted within a hundred yards of a buoy," Farkas said, sliding open the prow gate to reveal the black water below.

Troy realized that he only had seconds left. If he was going to act, this was his last chance. "After you zapped me with that little toy of yours, did you take a look at your boss's accounting ledger? Did you see how much he's making? I mean, Wow!"

"It's a good business."

"Yeah, but that's not my point."

"What is your point?"

"My point is this: You think you're his partner, but partners make fifty-fifty." He shrugged. "Maybe sixty-forty or even seventy-thirty. But I'll bet you're not even making ten percent. You're just a tool. But then you already knew that, as your special lenses suggest."

"I am well paid," Farkas said. "Sometimes I even enjoy my work. I'm not falling into the American trap of comparing what I earn to others. I make enough."

"Nice speech. Who you trying to convince?"

"Did I mention the sledgehammer?" Farkas asked, moving toward the gruesome tool.

"You can't get a refund if it's been used."

As Farkas drew in a breath to retort, his satellite phone rang. He pulled it from the pocket of his dark slacks and brought it to his right ear, covering the left against the wind. "Yes … Are you sure?" He hung up without saying anything else.

"God calling?" Troy asked.

"Change of plans," Farkas said, putting the phone back in his pocket. He picked up the sledgehammer before Troy's preoccupied mind could churn out another wise crack.

Hoisting the sledgehammer over his shoulder with both hands, Farkas said, "This is going to hurt."

Chapter 83

In the Bag

EMMY SAT in the corner of Luther's study, ankles bound together with a zip tie that felt like it was made of steel, trying to make sense of her world. The giant who had effortlessly held her aloft for what seemed like ages was now lying dead a few feet away in a pool of blood.

Luther and Orca were arguing loudly just a few feet away, but their words reached her ears like a television coming from another room. She was in shock. The bullets that entered Zero's skull through his eyes had flown just inches above her head. And Luther had fired twice. Had he intended one of those bullets for her, and just not gotten around to fixing his mistake? No, she decided, if that were the case he would not have bound her ankles. Still, why did he fire twice? It wasn't as though anyone could survive one bullet through the eye.

Orca's voice crescendoed, drawing her out of her dazed stupor. She looked up to see Luther shove a racquetball into the mafia boss's mouth. While that struck her as a dangerous thing to do, Luther's next move left her flabbergasted. She stared in morbid fascination as Luther unzipped Orca's fly, reached inside, and pulled out an organ the size of a tennis ball can. Then he picked an open switchblade off the floor and proceeded to … She couldn't watch. Clenching her eyes as tight as they would go, she put an index finger in each ear.

When she opened her eyes again, Orca was thrashing about in the chair like a man who … well … exactly. After a minute his movements got sluggish, and then he passed out. That was when Emmy noticed the waterfall of blood cascading off the edge of his chair onto the tiled floor. The crazy thought actually shot through her mind that as Luther's maid, it was her job to clean up the spreading mess. When she pulled her eyes off the morbid pool, she saw that Orca's face was a deathly pale. She also saw the bloody stump sticking out of his mouth. That was when she passed out.

When Emmy drifted back into consciousness, Luther was not in the room. The clock on the wall registered two AM; she had been out for a full five hours. Either her body had finally yielded to the accumulated stress, or Luther had injected her with a tranquilizing agent. Somewhere deep inside Emmy knew that this was her chance to escape, but she still felt spent. The ordeal on Grand Cayman had been the worst she had ever heard of, much less experienced, but even that was tame compared to tonight's experience. Her senses were fried. Her adrenal glands wrung out like the season's last lemons. But then she thought of Troy, and that gave her strength.

The image of Luther's switchblade danced through her mind. If he had left it behind she could free her legs. Then escape would be easy. Emmy worked herself onto her knees and then her feet using the back of Orca's chair. Because of the way Luther had bound her feet, with her ankles crossed, it would be difficult if not impossible for her to hop around. She did not even think that she could stand for more than a few seconds unsupported. But she did have a better view. The switchblade, however, was nowhere to be seen. Luther must have taken it with him.

Inspiration struck when her eyes fell on Luther's desk. Desks had scissors. She even knew where Luther kept them. She tried hopping toward the desk, but the zip ties bit painfully into her ankles and cost Emmy her balance. She caught herself on the edge of the desk as she fell. She pulled herself up onto the desk so that her ankles dangled freely over the side, and opened the center drawer. The scissors had been removed. Of course they had, she told herself. Luther had taken them when he left her alone in the room. The man was a lot of things, but carefree and foolish were not two of them.

Sitting there like a shipwreck survivor on a deserted island, looking across a scene of carnage that belonged only in a gangster movie, Emmy enjoyed another flash of inspiration. Maybe it didn't matter that she couldn't escape. If Troy now had Luther's journal and supply of ampoules, he would bargain them for her release. Luther would do anything to get them back, she was sure of that. But was it worth the price? Was her freedom, her life, worth the price of letting Luther continue with his business? Could she allow him to continue with a quarter-billion dollars' worth of destruction?

She did not have the time to process that question before Luther burst back into the room with a bag full of paper towel rolls, a package of heavy-duty trash bags, and a pair of handcuffs. Seeing the latter, Emmy wondered momentarily if Luther was working with a crooked cop, but then she realized that the cuffs were probably from his box of sex toys.

After setting down his load, Luther picked her up off the desk and carried her over toward the closet Zero had snatched her from. Emmy assumed that he was going to lock her in the dark, but he set her down outside the door and cuffed her right wrist to the doorknob instead. "I take it you're not going to make me shove that racquetball in your mouth," he said. It was not a question, but she shook her head anyway.

Emmy clenched her eyes as Luther went to work with the bags and tape. She forced her mind to go elsewhere, and focused on the memory of breakfast in The Grotto with Troy. She tried to taste the conch and brie omelet and hear the swishing surf. She succeeded in blocking out the grotesque noises coming from a few feet away until a new sound registered from below. Someone was coming up the stairs, and judging by the thumping sound, he was dragging something heavy.

She opened her eyes to see that Luther now had both bodies in thick black trash bags. He had placed one bag over the top of each corpse and another over the bottom, joining them in the middle with duct tape. A fifth bag, this one full of blood-sopped paper towels, stood off to Emmy's side.

Luther had obviously heard the noise too, but he did not seem concerned. The thumping moved closer until the door to the study flew open—and Farkas walked in. He was pulling a rope as though dragging a sleigh, although this rope connected two ankles. Emmy felt all hope drain from her body when the shoes came into focus and she knew that those ankles belonged to Troy.

Chapter 84

Live Another Day

TROY'S HEAD was pounding like a small nuclear war after Farkas dragged him feet first up Luther's marble staircase, but that was nothing compared to the pain that erupted in his heart when he saw Emmy handcuffed to the closet door.

Luther said "Welcome" as Farkas let go of the rope. Troy's feet dropped to smack against the parquet floor, prompting a reflexive "Aargh" instead of his customary "Hi." While having one's feet sledgehammered out of a bucket of hardened concrete beats the hell out of the alternative, it was not how Troy would recommend spending one's Sunday night.

To Troy's surprise, Luther looked over at Farkas and said, "I told you not to hurt him."

"Nothing is broken. He's only bruised."

That was true, Troy thought. Farkas had been somewhat less than reckless when wielding the twelve-pound mallet of steel. Still, that trip up the stairs had felt like a bout with Muhammad Ali. Didn't they have the fireman's carry in Croatia or wherever the hell that bastard was from?

Troy made eye contact with Emmy and mouthed the words, "Are you okay?"

She nodded and mouthed back, "And you?"

Troy said, "Never better," and then turned to his host.

Luther said to Farkas, "Help yourself to a drink. I need to have a word with our guests." Turning back to Troy and Emmy he said, "Do you two have any idea how lucky you are?"

Troy was not sure if it was the post-traumatic stress talking or if he was just too slaphappy to give a damn, but his mouth just sprung open and words started tumbling out. "You know, that's just what I was thinking. A quiet Sunday evening, four old friends, and your beautiful home. But if I could make a tiny suggestion: have the trash carted off before inviting company in."

Luther did not bother attempting to camouflage his amused expression, and Troy took minor comfort in having caught him by surprise. It did not last.

"You make my point for me," Luther said.

"Why are we lucky?" Emmy asked.

"Were I any other person, or were this any other moment in history, there would be four sets of trash bags on my floor now, instead of just two."

"Because you can erase our memories," Emmy said. "With chemicals instead of bullets."

Luther spread his hands in a magnanimous gesture. "Not to mention the fact that the memories you'll be losing can hardly be your best. Of course, if you prove to be more trouble than you're worth your luck will change." Luther pulled a Beretta from his pocket. Then, turning back to Troy he said, "She's a lot quicker than you are. I see why you chose to make her your partner."

Troy was thinking that actually the memories of his time with Emmy were the most precious in his head. But he did not want to give Luther a glimpse through that window into his soul, especially given the scenario that he expected was about to unfold. "I get the feeling that there's more to it than that. Perhaps you need our help with something first?"

Luther smiled and Troy knew that he was right. "Well, this is a quid-pro-quo world we live in. Tell me, now that you've been to my office, do you have any idea what that help might entail?"

Troy looked at Emmy. "He's planning to erase the memories of all nine justices of the United States Supreme Court. No doubt that's a bit too tall an order for our friend Farkas here. So he figured, why not involve the clever pair who already know what he's up to. Nothing to lose ..." Troy shifted his gaze back toward Luther. "Half-a-billion dollars to gain. That sound about right, old friend?"

"I'm glad to see that we're on the same page," Luther said.

"I'm not going to help you make anybody an amnesiac," Emmy said.

"Don't be silly," Luther said, his voice honey but his eyes ice. "Of course you are—although perhaps not in the way you think. And besides, it's no big deal. Even Shakespeare wanted to kill all the lawyers."

Troy said, "First of all, Shakespeare was defending lawyers by suggesting that killing them was the first step toward tyranny. Although to be honest with you, Luther, I can think of one lawyer worth killing. Secondly, the United States Supreme Court is a cornerstone of the greatest democracy the world has ever known. Weakening that foundation could have disastrous consequences, consequences that will be far reaching and impossible to predict. I'm with Emmy. Go fuck yourself."

Ignoring the last of Troy's remarks, Luther said, "Well then, I guess I'll just have to leave the country when we're done." He walked over and held the Beretta to Emmy's right temple. "But that's then. Let's talk about now. Now you and Farkas are going to go to Washington to begin stalking your prey. Meanwhile, Emmy and I are going to take a little vacation, a retreat so to speak. During which it's not myself I'll be fucking."

Troy resisted the bait and remained silent.

"Once you wipe all nine justices," Luther continued, "I'll set her free —less any recollection of these past few weeks, of course. If you're really nice, I'll even set her free in the same place we flash you. It will be just like old times all over again—except there won't be any tattoo on your foot, and by then it wouldn't even matter if there were."

Emmy said, "Don't do it, Troy."

Luther pulled back the slide on the Beretta and said, "Your choice. I can always get someone else. You've seen the ledger, you can do the math. This is going to happen."

Now that he thought of the possibility of having all memory of her erased, Troy could not bear the thought of losing her.

He decided to seek comfort and guidance from those who had endured even worse. Those who had persevered through the Holocaust, those who had lived to tell their heart-wrenching tales, had done so by holding on to life through any means available. They had done whatever it took to live another day. Only by clinging to life with an iron fist, no matter how shameful, no matter how selfish, had they made it to Nuremberg. To justice. If he took the high road now, they would both be dead but nothing else would change. If he complied, they still had a chance.

He looked over at Emmy who was shaking her head. As tears ran down her cheeks, he said, "I'll do it. I'll help you flash the justices."

The contemptuous look that crossed Emmy's face scorched his heart. Then Farkas grabbed the rope between his feet and began dragging him out of the room. He prayed that would not be the last he saw of his beloved's face. Luther had obviously seen Emmy's venomous glance, because he said, "You should be kinder to your colleague, Emmy. After all, your life is now in his hands."

Chapter 85

House Call

"THE REPUBLIC ENDURES, and this is the symbol of its faith. Those words were spoken by Chief Justice Charles Evans Hughes on October 13, 1932, during the laying of the cornerstone you see before you." The elegantly dressed African-American tour guide spoke with more reverence than Troy would have thought possible, considering that she repeated her spiel twenty times a day. Troy continued past the group following the red umbrella. He already knew too much about the "symbol of faith" he was about to destroy.

He caught sight of Farkas, who was still talking on the phone with Luther. Farkas had to check in every eight hours with updates, and Troy made sure he never forgot. Luther had warned him that if Farkas missed a call, Emmy got a bullet.

The first words Troy made out as he approached were, "... forged credentials worked out fine. They didn't give us a second glance." Farkas paused while Luther spoke. Then he replied, "Only Stevenson's is left. The man's eighty-eight, so his social life is minimal. We're probably going to have to inject him in his house. We're still finalizing the details of that plan." Again Farkas listened. "Okay, I'll tell him."

Farkas ended the call, opened a text message and then the attached photo. "Here's today's eye candy," he said, holding out his BlackBerry. The screen showed Emmy sitting cross-legged before a white wall. She held a printout of the current USA Today out before her as though reading a proclamation. She looked tan and radiant and wore her breathtaking smile. Troy knew that her smile was almost certainly forced and intended to cheer him up—but it worked anyway. "Thanks. What did Luther say?"

"He said that you weren't going to be getting any more pictures until we figure out how to implant Stevenson."

Troy shook his head. He had racked his brains for a way to get to the eldest justice, and he had come up blank. The other eight justices all had habits that took them outdoors where Farkas could either get close enough to hit them with a dart while they were moving, or bump them with a needle that he swore most people would never feel if they were moving. "Even if they do notice it, they'll assume that it's just a bug bite if you don't act suspicious," Farkas asserted.

Unfortunately, Stevenson spent virtually all of his time at home. "The trouble isn't so much getting to him, as making the injection indoors without his noticing," Troy replied.

Farkas shook his head. "That's not entirely correct. It's all right if he is aware of the injection, so long as he doesn't report it."

Troy understood the power of Farkas's insight the moment he heard it. Although it pained him to admit it, Farkas had impressed him over the course of these past nine days. Of the eight plans they had finalized thus far, Farkas had developed seven. He brought the trademark deductive reasoning of a doctor to his new profession. He approached his operations with the same callous precision as a brain surgeon, focusing entirely on the mechanics of the physical task he was performing without allowing himself to be distracted by emotional factors.

Troy, meanwhile, had spent the bulk of his waking hours trying to devise a way out of this mess. So far, he had nothing concrete, and time was running short.

Switching his processor to the task at hand, Troy deduced that Farkas's latest so-long-as-he-doesn't-report-it insight opened up two new potential avenues of attack. They could look for a way to prevent Stevenson from reporting the injection, or they could look for a way to make him not think to report it. To accomplish the former, some sort of coercion would be the most likely tack. Troy guessed that the Secret Service, even though they did not protect the justices on a day-to-day basis, would have devised the means to immunize them, and thus the Republic, from such threats. So he focused on the second angle: figuring out how to make Stevenson not want to report the injection. "Are you thinking of trying to swap out one of his regular injections for 456?"

"No. That leaves too much to chance. I'm thinking that one of us physicians needs to play doctor."

"To do that we would have to get around Stevenson's regular nurse, McGrady. And if we tried to substitute her, they'd put him through every modern diagnostic available the moment the skullduggery was discovered."

Farkas got the sly look in his eyes that Troy had seen a few times before. "True, but suppose McGrady were to invite one of us for consultation."

Troy had studied Justice Stevenson's personal life backwards and forwards, but did not see where this was headed, unless ... "Did you happen to go to medical school with Mary McGrady?"

"No. Nothing like that. Tell me, how old is Nurse Mary?"

"Thirty-two."

"And she's a looker, right? Safe to assume that Stevenson finds it pleasant to have her around."

"Sure, I guess."

"And how long has this pretty young nurse been working for Stevenson?"

"Eight months."

"Pretty good gig, don't you think? Days off, good pay, prestige ..."

"Sure."

"So suppose Nurse Mary were to wake up with no memory of the events of the last month. Do you think she would report it right away? Or do you think she would try to cover it up, you know, hope it was just a temporary glitch that went away?"

Troy did not like where this was going. On the other hand, he did not have a better suggestion. "I suppose most people would do whatever they thought was necessary to protect their job, if they saw no harm in it. But how would that help us?"

"Suppose you showed up at Stevenson's the first day of Mary's memory loss, pretending to have an appointment—an appointment Mary won't want to admit she has forgotten?"

Even though he already knew the answer, Troy asked, "What kind of appointment?"

Farkas held out his hand, mimicking a shake. "Hello Mary, I'm Dr. Davis from Georgetown University Hospital, here for that consultation you requested ..."

Chapter 86

An Old Friend

"THAT'S IT THEN," Troy said, looking up from a desk blanketed in hotel stationery and Post-it notes. "We've got all nine implants planned down to the last detail. We're done until Friday."

Farkas brought his hand up to stroke the beard he kept forgetting was no longer there. "You don't sound pleased. You should be. You're saving your girlfriend's life."

"She's not my girlfriend. She's my ..." Troy paused. What was his relationship with Emmy? Thanks to the mind wiping, she was his only friend. She was also his partner, his confidant, and, he suspected, the love of his new life. "I don't know what she is, but obviously she does mean a lot to me. I'm going to go crazy waiting around for two days with nothing to do but speculate on what Luther might be doing to her."

Despite the fact that Farkas had flashed away his memory of his wife and child, and that they were now working together only because Troy was under the cruel heel of coercion, a semblance of camaraderie had developed between them. They were both doctors, soldiers, men of the world, and participants in what would likely become the most famous caper since the Rosenberg kidnapping. As much as he hated to admit it, he could understand Farkas's arms-length point of view—even if he didn't respect it.

"Don't you remember anything from Afghanistan?" Farkas asked.

"What does any of this have to do with Afghanistan?"

Farkas leaned back in the hotel armchair and laced his fingers behind his head. "You've seen war, right? You've seen men rape breastfeeding mothers before shooting them through the heart? You've seen prepubescent boys hacked to death with machetes to keep them from growing into vengeful men? You've witnessed—"

"Okay, okay, I get the gruesome picture. Yes, I have seen war. What is your point?"

"My point is that whatever Luther may be doing to Emmy, it's insignificant. She's a grown woman. And besides, four days from now she won't remember a thing."

Troy bit back a sharp retort in favor of a more subtle thrust. "I was wondering how a man with the intelligence to get through medical school could do what you do—voluntarily. Now I understand. Civil war lobotomized you, robbed you of your ability to feel. You've become little more than a crocodile with a brain."

Troy thought that would either shut Farkas up or bring him to his feet. Truth be told, Troy welcomed a fistfight with the bastard, although it was anyone's call who would win.

Farkas surprised him again. "Like most creatures on this planet, humans included, I do what I have to do to survive. And like the best of those, I do it more for my family than for myself."

"You have a family?" Troy asked, incredulous.

"I have sisters. Their husbands are worthless, the leftovers of a generation that lost its best to war, so they count on me. With the money I make from this job, they will be free to pursue happiness, as you Americans like to say, and I will be able to start my own practice, settle down."

"How much are you getting for this job? What's the collapse of the US judicial system worth to you?"

"The US system did not bring me justice. It robbed me of my career. So as far as I'm concerned, it's not worth a penny. Luther, however, is paying me ten million."

"Of the half-billion he's pocketing?" Troy chided. "That's what, two percent? Not even a bad tip. And you're doing all the work."

"It's as Karl Marx warned a century ago: The man who owns the means of production reaps the lion's share of the rewards." Farkas shrugged. "But when the production is as big as this one, the crumbs are big enough. I'm happy with my ten million."

Troy was still digesting that when Farkas began to squirm in his seat. "Speak of the devil and he appears," Farkas said, pulling the vibrating BlackBerry from his pocket. "Yeah."

As Farkas listened, Troy studied his face for any indication of the news. But as always, the hired gun was a blank slate. Farkas said, "We're confident that we've got all nine nailed. We've even developed backup plans for most." After another pause, Farkas said, "No, he's cooperating. In fact, he's anxious to get this over with. I'm not sure what I'm going to do with him for the next two days. Run up the pay-per-view bill I guess." Troy thought he saw a look of mild surprise flash across Farkas's face after Luther's next question, but it could have been gas. The Croatian doused everything in Tabasco sauce. After a minute, Farkas simply said, "Okay," and then he held out the phone. "He wants to talk to you."

Troy snatched the phone and said, "Let me talk to Emmy."

"Soon," Luther replied, not missing a beat. "In the meantime, I understand that you're bored, that you've got two days to kill?"

Rather than take the bait, Troy waited for Luther to get to the point.

Luther did. "I've got an assignment for you to complete before this weekend's finale. I'd like to say that it will keep you out of trouble, but that's not entirely accurate."

"We've already got our deal. I'm not doing another thing for you, unless you have something else to offer."

"You'll do whatever I tell you to do, or—"

"Or what? You're not going to do anything, so don't make idle threats. You need me to complete this mission. In fact, it's safe to say that at this point in the operation, or more precisely at this date on the calendar, you need me more than I need you." The words just flew from Troy's mouth without forethought. He knew that it was foolish to challenge a top courtroom attorney to a verbal joust, but the frustration pent up inside him demanded release.

"I'm only getting money out of this, Troy. You are getting two lives; your own, and Miss Green's here. Shall I let her know how little you think she's worth?"

"Why don't you just get to the point, and tell me what you want?" Troy said, trying to sound aggressive as he retreated.

"That's more like it. I want you to take a trip—back to Grand Cayman. Have you been missing it?"

"That depends, are you going to send Emmy to join me? It just wouldn't be the same without her."

"I'm afraid not. I need Emmy here, with me. But you are going to get to see an old friend."

"And who would that be?" Troy asked, now genuinely curious.

"Kostas Kanasis. If he doesn't die of natural causes within forty-eight hours, Emmy will."

Chapter 87

Dinner Arrangements

"PHONE FOR YOU, HONEY," Susanna yelled across the bullpen.

Honey looked up from the report he was perusing with Mertins. "Who is it?"

"I don't know, but he's obviously Irish."

Honey felt his heart skip a beat. Could it be? The manhunt had dropped to passive status ten days ago, and he had all but given up hope of redemption.

"You okay, Honey?" Susanna asked, reading his face.

"Fine. Just give me the phone," Honey said, crossing the room. He snatched the receiver, took a deep breath and said, "Captain Honey."

"Have ye put it together yet, Captain?" asked the voice he would never forget.

"I still have a few questions. Why don't we meet for lunch to discuss them?"

"Actually, I did breakfast on yeer fine island. But I'll be lunching here on mine. I will, however, be arranging for you to dine with another person of interest."

Honey's throat went dry. He took a sip from Susanna's cold coffee cup before replying. "The shooter?"

"Precisely, the man who assassinated Jacobs. May the saints bless that quick mind of yours. Of course, after ye anticipated our escape strategy, I expected no less. Tell me now, have ye tied him to the Johnson murder as well? I suspect that took more than simple ballistics. He sands his fingertips, you know."

Honey had surmised as much after finding Brandell's car clean despite Mertins' insistence that the perp was not wearing gloves. "He wore a helmet throughout that operation, but I managed all the same—used a computer to uniquely identify his skeletal measurements. We've got him for the whole trifecta, Johnson, Jacobs, and Brandell."

Irish paused, leading Honey to infer that he did not know about Brandell, then said, "Good. So, if I get him to you, will that get my friend and me off the hook?"

Honey's impulse was to lie, but intuition told him to play it straight. "I've still got about twenty charges with your names set squarely beside them. Everything from assault with a deadly weapon to desecrating a corpse."

"I regret that those actions were necessary. The shooter put my friend and me into a bind we couldn't escape without violence. So I guess this is where quid pro quo comes into play?"

Honey thought about the proposition. He could legally promise anything and renege. No doubt Irish was aware of that. Irish wanted a gentleman's agreement, implying that he was gambling on Honey's need to restore his dignity. A fair wager. Again, Honey asked himself the question he had been mulling over these past two weeks: Would he have done what they had done, if he were in their shoes? The answer had not changed since the last time he asked: Of course. "When can I expect this dinner?"

"Monday. Perhaps you'd like to meet him at the airport? He'll be arriving on a private flight."

Chapter 88

Call Forwarding

FOR HIS RETURN from Grand Cayman, Troy booked the flight that maximized his layover in Miami. Four hours on the ground—less the ten minutes he used to call Honey and the ninety it had taken him to procure a Miami cell phone—left him about half an hour to conduct his business with Tate.

"You mind waiting?" he asked the taxi driver as they pulled to the curb. "There's an extra hundred in it for you. My flight is at two."

The Russian driver just nodded and cranked the volume on his ABBA CD.

Troy recognized Alice from his first visit, but since he had been a wheelchair-bound seventy-year-old then, she did not recognize him. "I'm Arthur Adams," he said, holding out his hand. "I've got a twelve o'clock appointment with Mr. Tate."

"Yes, I know he's expecting you. I'll just let him know that you're here."

"Thanks. Tell me, Alice, is Sylvia here?"

"Sylvia, no, she's out to lunch. Is that a problem?"

"No, no, nothing like that," Troy said, closing the subject.

Just then a man entered whom Troy had last seen picking up pills off the downstairs floor. He said, "I thought I heard someone arrive. He held out his hand, "I'm Alexander Tate. You must be Arthur Adams."

"A pleasure to meet you, Mr. Tate. I've heard good things."

"Please, come on back to my office," Tate said, gesturing.

"Sure, but first, I was hoping that I might be able to impose on your charming assistant to pick me up a sandwich? Say corned beef on rye, or even better a Reuben? I've got a lot to go over with you, and a crazy schedule the rest of the afternoon."

Troy was no Emmy, but he knew voices, and he definitely detected a strain of embarrassment in Tate's when he asked Alice, "Would you mind running down to Lenny's for a couple of Reubens?"

To her credit, Alice said, "Not at all." She opened the filing drawer on her desk, pulled out her Sak purse, and walked out quickly enough that Troy suspected she was hiding either a scowl or tears.

Turning back to Tate, Troy said, "Lead the way."

When Tate opened his door, Troy was delighted to see a long couch residing beneath an oil painting of what he recognized as Miami's South Beach. "Lovely painting."

Tate looked over at him and said, "Yes, when I told my realtor what my budget was and expressed my desire for a view of the beach, this was what she suggested." He winked and then settled down into his high-backed burgundy chair as they both chuckled perfunctorily. Sitting across the cherry desk in a similar chair with a lower back, Troy scooted forward so that the lip of the desk hid his lap from view. That would make things easier.

"Now, Arthur, what is it I can do for you? On the phone you mentioned the need to establish a number of offshore accounts?"

Listening with practiced ears, Troy began to dissect the lawyer's syntax, tone and cadence. Tate was obviously of British origin, and had made no attempt to lose his accent. No doubt that was at least in part due to the fact that Americans were subconsciously more trusting of a British voice. This was good news for Troy, since they also tended to identify a voice by that foreign accent without much regard for its subtler features. "Yes, I've just come into a substantial inheritance," Troy said, using words he wanted to hear repeated.

"An inheritance? So you made your money the really old fashioned way," Tate commented with a chuckle.

"Yes. My uncle's estate on Grand Cayman." He paused, ostensibly for a reaction, but really in order to focus on palming the syringe tucked beneath a rubber band up his sleeve.

"We do a lot of work on the Caymans. And for that matter, a lot of work with rich uncles." Another chuckle.

"That's wonderful. Say, Alex, would you mind showing me to the restroom before we get into the details?" Troy asked. "That will give you a couple of minutes to come up with some specific recommendations."

"Yes, of course," Tate said standing. "Can you give me an idea as to the size of the opening deposit?"

"I don't know for sure yet, since some of the assets have yet to be liquidated, but it will be well into seven figures, perhaps eight."

"I see. I happen to have several outstanding opportunities in that range. But I'm getting ahead of myself. Please, follow me."

Troy slipped the syringe into Tate's left buttock as the lawyer held open his office door. The sedative worked instantly, and Troy had to whirl about to catch the lawyer before he crashed to the floor.

Holding Tate under his arms, Troy dragged him over to his couch and laid him out as though he were taking a nap. Hopefully, that was not an uncommon position for the lawyer. He toyed with the idea of taking off Tate's shoes for effect, but decided not to push it.

Pressed for time both because of the plane and because he did not know how long it would take Alice to return from Lenny's, Troy recited a few practice phrases to get Tate's voice right, and then picked up his phone. He dialed the number he had memorized weeks ago.

"Luther Kanasis." The lilt in Luther's voice betrayed his subscription to caller ID.

"Yes, Mr. Kanasis, this is Alexander Tate calling from Miami. I'm afraid to be the bearer of bad news. Your uncle Kostas Kanasis has passed away."

"Oh, no. So suddenly? Did he have an accident? He didn't fall off that beloved balcony of his I hope."

"No, nothing like that. It appears that your uncle died of natural causes. The coroner will know for certain early next week."

"I see."

"Yes, well, my sincerest condolences."

"Thank you."

"Now, as the executor of your uncle's will, I am pleased to inform you that he has named you as the sole beneficiary of his estate. In addition to his condominium on Grand Cayman, this includes an account at Solomon Bank & Trust worth approximately two hundred and forty-eight million dollars.

"I would be happy to help you—"

Luther cut him off with, "I thank you, but the only assistance I will be needing is for you to open a numbered account for me in Switzerland. I would like the entire balance transferred by close of business today. Less your fee, of course."

"I see, well, the Swiss account will be no problem, but I'm afraid you will have to wait a few days for the transfer. Your uncle's assets are frozen as per legal requirements until the coroner gives the all-clear. I should be able to have your money in Switzerland by close of business Tuesday."

"Are you certain?"

"Well, no. We can't be one-hundred percent sure until the fat lady sings, but you can be certain that I will be on top of it. I'm planning on going to Grand Cayman personally to ensure that this and a few other affairs are handled properly. I'll call you if it looks like there's going to be any delay. Meanwhile, since I won't be reachable here at the office, let me leave you the number of my mobile phone."

Chapter 89

Dog Day

TROY DIALED a number from memory and then cradled the payphone receiver between shoulder and chin while Farkas watched from ten yards to his left. Pretending to make a call at this time on this phone was part of the plan he and Farkas had concocted for injecting Justice Brewer. Still, Farkas was eyeing him suspiciously. Was it the nature of the Croatian beast? Or was Troy's deception easy to spot?

He pushed his fears aside and continued to follow the script, unscrewing the cap from his mineral water and emptying it over an indentation in the sidewalk to create a puddle.

"Seaborn's. Sean Seaborn speaking."

"It's Sebastian Troy calling, Sean. Is my order ready to go?"

Troy kept Farkas in his peripheral vision as he spoke. The Croatian sat on a park bench with three French Bulldogs tethered at his feet, watching him over the top of his newspaper. He had been dissecting Troy with his eyes nonstop since Troy's return from Grand Cayman an hour ago. The logical conclusion was that Farkas thought he was now looking at a bona fide assassin, but Troy's little voice was screaming that Farkas somehow knew his secrets.

"It's four-thirty on Friday, right?" Sean Seaborn said, his squeaky voice conjuring up the image of a thin man in protective goggles and a white lab coat. "I promised you it would be ready by Friday afternoon and it is Friday afternoon, so yes, it's ready."

"And the FedEx—"

"The FedEx guy is due here in a few minutes—also as promised. I do still need the shipping address however, and of course your credit card number for the balance of the payment.

Troy dictated the AmEx number he had memorized years ago and the address of the Italian restaurant next to their hotel. He and Farkas had eaten late dinners at Benvenutos half-a-dozen nights during the past couple of weeks, not because it was particularly good, but rather because it was convenient. Their marathon of surveillance had them up early and out late, so they were always tired when the job was done. As a result, Troy knew their usual waiter well enough to make an arrangement. "Make sure you specify Saturday morning delivery, care of Benny Azara. If you just do regular priority overnight, I won't get it until Monday, and they're useless to me then."

"I am filling out the form as we speak," Sean squeaked, "and will place it in the courier's hands personally. Thank you for your business."

Troy severed the connection while continuing his pretense of talking on the phone. Amazing the service you could get by offering a ten-fold price premium, he thought. Still he was cutting it close.

Glancing casually back to his left, Troy saw Farkas pull his sunglasses down from atop his head to cover his eyes. That was the sign that a two-year-old mittelschnauzer named Dory had entered the far side of the park—with Justice Stanley Brewer in tow. They knew from prior stakeouts that it would only take Dory sixty to ninety seconds to drag her master to this end. Troy felt the familiar adrenaline rush. It was showtime. Kickoff. The start of a nine-game season.

He moved his paper grocery bag a pace to the left so the corner rested in the puddle his mineral water had created. As the water wicked up the side, his mind drifted to the gamble they were taking with the science.

According to the bioavailability calculations of scientists murdered four years ago, Friday afternoon was too early to implant a dose that would not be activated until Monday morning. The drug's doomed inventors had estimated forty-eight hours to be the outer limit of its bioavailability. MDs Troy and Farkas had revisited that conclusion after determining that they could not fit nine risky implants into just two days. Knowing that medical treatment in general and drug profiles in particular were required to be conservative, and given the slowed metabolism of a man in his seventieth year, they agreed to risk an eighteen-hour extension. Brewer might not lose as many years' memory as the other eight, but even one year would be more than enough.

Troy cradled the payphone receiver as Dory and her owner strolled into sight from behind a bushy mound. He stooped to gently lift the brown bag by its handles and set off on an intercept course.

The small city park was fairly crowded, this being a sunny fall afternoon and D.C. being a walking town. To Troy's chagrin, Dory was proving to be one popular bitch. Every dog has her day. As she stopped to exchange sniffs with one purebred after another, Justice Brewer exchanged reserved pleasantries with their owners. Meanwhile, Troy was literally left standing there holding the bag.

He glanced around casually, careful not to shake the bag while acting like a vacationer soaking up the view. Soon Dory resumed her quest for fresh scents and pulled Justice Brewer toward ground zero. As Dory passed Farkas, the Croatian kept his French bulldogs heeled by stepping on their leashes. Once they were midway to Troy, however, he stood and followed. The three slobbering hounds strained at their leashes, eager to get a snout full of Dory's scent. Farkas was still about fifteen feet behind Brewer when Troy, closing on them from the opposite direction, tugged sharply at the handles of his brown bag.

The two-pound package of ground beef broke through the paper and split open on the ground, just as it had during his practice sessions in the hotel. This time, however, it was only inches from a schnauzer's nose. Dory's tail began whirling like a propeller and she dove at the feast from heaven before Brewer could rein her in. As Troy bent to reassemble his other rolling groceries, Farkas's three French Bulldogs leapt into the mix.

The startled justice bent over the writhing mound in a frantic attempt to extract his feasting pooch from the sixteen-legged tangle. He failed to notice the mosquito-like prick on his rump amidst the torrent of flying spittle, flapping leashes, and disappearing meat.

Chapter 90

Brinksmanship

LUTHER HAD SLIPPED a needle into Emmy's shoulder as she watched Farkas drag Troy from the room. With her heart breaking, she had not felt the prick.

When Emmy awoke, she was already imprisoned.

Twelve days later, nothing had changed.

The *Brinkman* was sixty-eight feet of floating luxury, a gleaming pearl gliding gracefully through an azure ocean. Emmy felt like a princess locked in a tower while black and white knights battled for her in a land far far away.

She hated it.

She wanted to pick up a sword and fight her own battles.

Brinkman's opulent atmosphere felt hauntingly familiar. She had no memory of ever setting foot on a yacht, or showering in a head, or having a private chef to cook whatever she wanted for breakfast, lunch, and dinner. Yet she had slipped into the lifestyle like a well-worn slipper. This was her first sighting of the ghost of Bo Beaulieu. Oddly enough, it did not spook her. She didn't feel a sense of loss or longing or remorse. The only emotion she had experienced aplenty these past twelve days was guilt.

Seated before her lacquered burl-wood vanity in burgundy shorts and a sleeveless honey-colored top, preparing her makeup for today's photograph, Emmy would rather have been in San Quentin. She tried to imagine what Troy was doing at that very moment. Was he lying in wait with a dart gun beneath a cold wet bush? Passing himself off as a DC cop? Rappelling off a roof? Whatever it was, she knew Troy was doing it for her. He was performing acts he would rather die than commit, all in the hope of saving her life. And there was painfully little she could do about it.

Emmy was attempting to assist Troy through her daily proof-of-life photos, but feared this was like passing him a garden hose and expecting him to squelch a volcano. Still, she felt better for the trying. For starters, she did everything she could to appear optimistic and happy in the photos, hoping to bolster Troy's mood. Luther, of course, encouraged this, as it played into his hand. But she was also telegraphing clues to her whereabouts. Every day she sunbathed on the *Brinkman's* long bow, so that Troy would come to realize that she was being held in a tropical climate, with access to the outdoors. Luther may have figured this out, but he didn't seem to care. Either he figured that "sunny climate" wasn't much of a clue, or he decided that it was worth the risk to watch her lie about in a bikini.

Luther had been surprisingly gentlemanly with her. Despite Giselle's mention that Luther liked the hunt more than the conquest, Emmy had fully expected him to come to her cabin the first night and take her anyway he liked. On the ocean there was no one to hear her scream. She had lain awake until dawn, a steak knife poised to thrust, but Luther had kept to himself.

The one clue to Troy that Luther would surely have stopped had he noticed, was her use of sign language. Unfortunately, the odds of Troy figuring it out were not good either. On her first day aboard the yacht, Luther had photographed her holding a computer printout of the LA Times article on Mafia Boss James "Orca" Scapone's brutal death. The author led with the suspicion that rival boss Jimmy "Choke" Cortese was behind the execution, given the signature method of asphyxiation. That night she had come up with a plan. The following day and every day thereafter, Emmy held the daily newspaper headline with her left hand positioned so that her fingers spelled out one letter of SS-BRINKMAN in sign language. There was no detectable pattern in any one picture, but she figured that Troy might study them en masse— hopefully every night before bed.

Today she would dangle the printout from her fist with her thumb clenched between her ring and middle fingers, signaling N, the final entry in her code. Her hope was that Troy had devised the means to escape Farkas and would do so the moment he knew where to find her. Luther had implemented the system of thrice-daily checkups as a countermeasure, but Troy had the voice talent to get around that.

Setting down her tube of lip gloss, Emmy rose from her vanity and walked upstairs to the main deck. Luther sat lounging on a semicircular couch, reading the latest issue of Caribbean Lifestyles. He set the magazine down as she approached, and said, "My, you do look lovely."

"It's for Troy," she said, immediately regretting her words. Distasteful as it was, she wanted to keep on Luther's good side. There was no telling when the opportunity to escape might arise, and she wanted the split-second advantage that a cordial relationship would give. Changing her tone to one more friendly, she said, "I've been meaning to ask you a question."

"Yes."

"Why did you choose to use 456 the way you have? Why erase the memories of witnesses. I'd think you could market such a drug legitimately to trauma victims, women who have been raped and soldiers returning from battle. Then none of this would have been necessary."

Luther gave her a look that she interpreted as half suspicion, half admiration. "I owed twenty-five million dollars to the mob. The interest, the vigorish as Orca called it, was a million a month. Given all the delays that a controversial new product like that could expect from wedge-issue politicians, evangelical Christians, and Scientologists, just to name a few, I'd have been worm food before I saw a dime."

Emmy nodded, trying to show understanding, sympathy.

"And then there's the fact that I had to kill everyone at the company who invented it," Luther added. "That inclined me toward avoiding the public eye. Shall we take that picture now?"

Emmy tried to keep her face impassive as she said, "Yes."

She took her seat on the other end of the semicircle, and raised the fresh printout as prescribed. Luther raised his digital camera and was just about to snap the photo when a call came in on his satellite phone. Emmy checked her own watch and saw that it was four hours too early to be Farkas. When Luther answered, however, she heard the Croatian's distinctive voice ringing from the phone. She strained to hear his side of the conversation.

"We've done it!" Farkas said. "We've implanted all nine."

Luther's face burst wide open as a childish smile welled up from within. "That's fantastic. Did all the implants go as planned?"

"More or less. We had to use our backup plan on Goldstein since she came down with a cold. We caught her at her hairdresser rather than synagogue."

"With priorities like that, she doesn't deserve the bench."

"Speaking of deserve ..." Farkas prompted.

"Don't worry, my friend. Your seven zeros are but a flash away."

Clapping his phone shut, Luther thrust his right fist up into the air and shook it three times in victory.

"You're that happy about disabling the country's judicial branch?" she asked.

Luther shook his head. "I couldn't care less about those nine old farts. Did you know that former Chief Justice Rehnquist spent a decade on the bench as a drug addict? Millions of Americans were incarcerated for using drugs while the chief justice was popping fifteen hundred milligrams of Placidyl a day." He waved a hand dismissively. "What I do care about is this." He flipped his phone back open, pressed seven on his speed dial and then engaged the speaker for her benefit.

"I just got the word," said a voice Emmy did not recognize. "My man has seen the whites of their eyes. Is everything else set for tomorrow morning?"

"Absolutely everything."

"Excellent. Well then, congratulations are in order. As agreed, I'll order the transfer as soon as we're off the phone. You'll have the remainder of your fee within an hour of banks opening in Europe."

"Three hundred million," Luther prompted.

"Three hundred million. Don't forget to tidy up."

"I won't."

"Good. And Luther ..."

"Yes?"

"Have a nice life."

Luther sprang from the couch as he closed the phone and sashayed over to the galley. He opened the cabinet on the far end and pulled an emerald-cut burgundy box off the top shelf. Tucking it lovingly under his arm, he grabbed two tumblers from the bar and brought his loot over to the table before her. He sat down with his hips abutting hers and laid the treasure down before them. Scrawled atop it in gold lettering were the words: LOUIS XIII by Remy Martin. After giving her a moment to digest the words, he drew back the lid with both hands, exposing the famous Baccarat crystal decanter that housed the world's finest cognac. "It's time to celebrate."

Looking over at the lust radiating from her keeper's eyes, Emmy felt a paralyzing chill creep up her spine. Her free pass had finally expired.

Chapter 91

Fireball

"I HOPE your plan for getting us out of here will work as smoothly as your ploy for getting us in," Troy whispered, fishing for information once they were far enough down the Supreme Court's Grand Hall to be out of the guards' earshot.

Farkas ignored him. The payout of a lifetime was just a few steps away, and he was not going to say or do anything that might jeopardize his fortune.

They walked in silence behind the small crowd of reporters to the West Conference Room. Once they had reached their destination, however, Troy leaned toward him and whispered, "Don't you think it's time to brief me on the details of our escape plan? I mean, within seconds of the justices all fainting, security is going to come down like an iron curtain. I don't want to be locked inside while they investigate."

Farkas had kept out of jail by keeping his mouth shut. If somebody did not need to know something, he did not tell them. Period. Troy did not need to know that Farkas had simple smoke bombs hidden in the cuffs of his trousers. When the smoke erupted, he would still run for the doors like everyone else. Likewise, Troy did not need to know about the dozen tiny blasting caps secreted outside, the "gunshots" that would send the evacuating crowd running in all directions. At the same time, however, Farkas did not want to alienate his co-conspirator. They had nine sets of pupils to focus their flashes on. His chances of success improved markedly if he could go at them from two angles. He needed Troy's unflinching participation.

"Did I ever tell you how I got us press credentials?" Farkas asked.

"No. You ignored my questions on that as well," Troy replied, still avoiding his eye. Farkas had found him uncharacteristically diffident all morning. Even after taking out Kostas, Troy still lived in a world of ideals—a world where survival-of-the-fittest was not the presiding rule. His amnesia was going to be a blessing. It would allow him to look in the mirror after this morning without flinching. It would let him forget what he had done.

Farkas needed no such balm.

"It couldn't have been easier," Farkas whispered. "Wearing a black suit and earpiece, I approached a group of reporters waiting to gain access to the Capital and flashed forged Homeland Security credentials. I asked to see all of their credentials, and one-by-one ran each through a portable scanner which I described as "the latest advance in counter-terrorism technology." Then I pressed a button that made the scanner beep and pronounced each to be legitimate. I gave the scanned files along with our pictures to the same lady who made my Homeland Security creds, and voila, we were golden."

Troy shook his head. "That's the problem with conditioning people to follow procedures, to bowing to authority; you train them not to think."

"And you reduce everyone's operating performance to that of the weakest link," Farkas added, "making loopholes easier for us to exploit. Speaking of which, you go set up toward the right edge of the press area. I'll stay here on the left. Between our two angles, we should catch the gazes of all nine justices simultaneously."

"How about you take the right, and I stay here on the left," Troy countered. "Closer to the exit."

Farkas smiled. He didn't do that very often, but knowing that an overflowing bank account was just minutes away, he was feeling giddy around the edges. "All right. But no comebacks if you get trampled in the rush to leave."

Farkas had trouble keeping his smile down as he set up his camera and pretended to calibrate it for the distance and lighting. This was the most-serious, highest-risk assignment he had ever undertaken, but all he could think about was his triumphant return to Croatia, flush with ten million bucks. He would set up each of his sisters with enough cash for them to leave their deadbeat husbands. Then he would buy the country estate he had always dreamed of, and set up his own medical practice. It would be as though he never lost his license, better even, for he was years ahead of his original schedule. "Whoever said there were no second chances?" he mumbled.

The press conference prior to the Supreme Court's opening conference was far less organized than Farkas had envisioned. People were just milling about the hallowed room waiting for the justices to appear. It was almost like a cocktail party, but for the casual dress and absence of booze. There were also fewer photographers than Farkas had expected, only about twenty in all, including C-SPAN's videographer. In retrospect, he figured that was more than enough. Elderly people wearing baggy black robes were hardly a feast for the eyes—unless they were the victims of a tragic attack.

A camera flash to his left alerted Farkas to the arrival of the first Justice. It was Jack Reynolds, the Chief. Troy had implanted him during his habitual Sunday morning jog around the ellipse. The others followed behind in procession.

Farkas used a camera fitted with a special viewfinder to check their eyes. All nine pairs glowed with a violet tinge.

Farkas switched to the UV-C flashing camera and waited with a hungry finger poised patiently on the button. Eight figures were just a flash away. He and Troy had agreed to wait until all nine justices had taken their seats behind the long mahogany table. They couldn't have anyone fainting too early and triggering an evacuation procedure. He dared a glance to his left to ensure that Troy was in position, and then it was time.

He pulled the string that ran up his pant leg and looped around his belt, releasing the smoke bombs and activating their sixty-second timer. As they rolled in different directions across the floor, he aimed his camera at Justice Reynolds. A tremendous spike of adrenaline hit his bloodstream as he pressed the button that sent three pulses of UV-C per second flashing toward attentive pupils. He swept first to Reynolds' left and then back across the table to the far end, nailing each justice one by one.

None of the Justices reacted.

They just sat there, smiling for the cameras like seasoned politicians. Ideas began to flood his mind about what had gone wrong. Had Troy somehow replaced the 456 with a harmless fluorescing chemical? What about his UV-C flasher? Perhaps the security scanner had somehow disabled it? If so, then Troy's had to be malfunctioning too.

Turning toward his coconspirator, Farkas saw Troy staring back at him. Pointing his camera back at him. Then Farkas felt a fireball consuming his brain, and everything went black.

Chapter 92

Visual Aid

"HE'S DIABETIC," Troy said to the neighboring reporters as he gave Farkas a shot of epinephrine disguised as insulin. "Don't worry, he'll be fine."

Troy had tried to reach Farkas before he collapsed to the floor, but too many tripods had blocked his path. Fortunately, he had the stimulant ready as backup. Now he had to get Farkas out of there before someone called an ambulance.

Farkas's eyes fluttered and then opened without focus.

Troy slipped an arm under his shoulders and pulled him into a sitting position. "Come on, buddy, let's walk it off." He exerted more upward pressure and Farkas rose to his feet.

"What happened?" Farkas asked, his voice weak and uncertain.

"You forgot to take your insulin, again. Come on, let's get you home." Troy needed to get Farkas out of there before someone overheard Farkas ask the inevitable question: "Who are you?" And it was inevitable. There was no doubt in Troy's mind that this time Farkas was not faking it. 456 had literally fried Farkas's mind. His memories of Troy and Emmy and Luther and even his eight-figure payday were all up in cranial smoke.

What wasn't smoking was Farkas's bombs. Troy had disabled them in the middle of the night, along with Farkas's flasher.

Farkas moved as though he was sleepwalking, his legs supporting his weight but his mind relying on Troy for all guidance. Troy piloted him out the visitor's entrance into the back seat of a limo waiting on Maryland Avenue. "Hyde Field," he told the driver, referring to Washington's executive airport.

"That will only take us about thirty minutes. You got me for the whole morning."

"The airport is just the first stop. My friend has a plane to catch."

"Is he all right?" the driver asked, pulling out.

Farkas had slipped back into unconsciousness the moment the weight came off his legs.

"He's a diabetic. Gets this way when his insulin level is off." Troy would have to give him another epinephrine shot when they got to the airport. Officials tended not to scrutinize those who flew private very closely, but there were limits.

The limo driver shrugged and pulled out into traffic.

He had done it! He had taken Farkas out of the picture and saved the United States Supreme Court. Sitting there on the cool black Naugahyde with Farkas slumped against his left shoulder, Troy felt mildly relieved but was not all a tingle with the thrill of victory. He was still a long way from converting his epic tragedy into a romance.

One hour later, after watching Farkas fly off on a charter jet to Grand Cayman and faxing the flight details to Captain Honey, Troy took the first step toward achieving his primary goals. Using Farkas's satellite phone and mimicking Farkas's voice, he made a call.

"Give me the good news," Luther said right off the bat.

"It's done."

"Fantastic. Congratulations. It hasn't hit the news yet."

"And it won't. Not for forty-eight hours. They swore everyone to silence for national security reasons."

"And nobody is going to risk angering the entire Supreme Court," Luther added, half to himself.

"I want my ten million wired immediately."

"Not until it hits the news. I need proof," Luther insisted.

"I've got proof. A video."

"They didn't confiscate it?"

"They kept my camera. Even made me show them my pictures so they could see that I hadn't swapped out memory disks. But they didn't know that it has a video feature that writes to a separate memory disk. I got that disk out."

"That will do. When will you be here?"

"Are you at home?"

"We just arrived."

"We?"

"Emmy's with me, remember?"

"Right. Well, I've decided that it's in my best interests for us to never meet again. So I'm just sending Troy with the video. You watch it and transfer my money this afternoon, understood?"

"Are you sure you—"

"I'm sure. You just transfer my money. Ten million. Today."

After a long pause, Luther said, "Okay."

"And Luther?"

"Yes?"

"If we do have to see each other again, it's not going to go well for you."

Chapter 93

Dirty

BENEATH PORTENTOUS CLOUDS and a blustery wind, Troy pulled his rented Chevy into a BP station a half-mile from Luther's estate. He did not need gas, but he wanted to hide Farkas's effects where Luther would not discover them if the next hour did not go entirely as planned.

Glancing down at the wallet, satellite phone, and remaining 456 vials as he slipped them beneath the spare tire, Troy realized that Farkas would be in custody now—his situation virtually identical to the one he had arranged for Troy four weeks earlier. Whatever followed next, Troy could at least feel good about that.

Settling back into the car, he rechecked the seals on the double-bagged portable DVD player occupying the passenger seat. He found that particular detail squared away, but knew there were countless others that might not be. Emmy would be lost to him forever if he failed to deal with a single one.

He could still call the police, he realized, and report a hostage situation. But the odds were that Luther had Emmy primed and ready to flash at the first sign of trouble. Dialing 911 would likely lobotomize her and land Troy in the cage next to Farkas.

He spit a surge of bile out through the window, and punched the gas.

Arriving at Luther's gate, Troy slipped one of Farkas's covert injector rings onto his right middle finger. This was it. An hour from now the world was going to seem like a very different place—either for Luther, or for Emmy and him. He crossed the fingers of his unloaded hand and punched the intercom buzzer.

The gate opened without a word from within, and Troy pulled the Chevy onto the crushed stone drive. He parked directly between the front entrance and the Spanish fountain and threw open the car door like a man meaning business. While turning toward the door, he reached over his head and slipped the DVD player atop the fountain's third tier where it could not be seen by anyone shorter than a Laker.

He marched up to the massive front door, and rather than using the bell or oversized brass knocker, pounded on the oak with the heel of his left fist. This was where it got tricky, he knew. He fully expected Luther to answer with a gun in his hand, but was committed to pushing ahead regardless.

"Troy, long time no see. Please, come—"

Troy pushed open the door before Luther could finish. Squaring off with the man toe-to-toe he pushed Luther back with a challenging open-palmed double-blow to the chest. Luther was a hard body, his chest all muscle, but the force of Troy's shove still landed him on his butt. "Where is she?" Troy asked, glowering down.

Luther locked Troy's eyes as he rose slowly to his feet. "She's the same place you are: at my mercy." Luther rubbed his left pectoral muscle subconsciously. "You would be wise not to forget it."

"Answer my question," Troy persisted without blinking. "Where is she?"

"I'll take you to her."

"Good."

"Once you show me the proof Farkas promised."

"You see the proof once I see the girl."

Luther shook his head. "Remember the details of our agreement. You don't just get to walk away."

"I'm not asking to leave. I'm asking to see her."

"Very well," Luther said. "Wait here. I'll be right back."

The instant Luther disappeared down the hallway at the top of the semicircular stairs, Troy pulled the injector ring off his finger to confirm that it had delivered its contents. Empty. Smiling to himself, he plunged the ring into the potted palm to the left of the doorway. The soil was still moist from a recent watering, so it left dirt on his fingers. With no other option at his immediate disposal, Troy licked off the evidence.

Luther reappeared almost instantly, dangling a pair of handcuffs from his right index finger. "Turn around and put your wrists together," he commanded. "Then I'll take you to her."

Troy complied, reckoning that the score was now tied at one apiece. Still anybody's match.

Luther walked around to face Troy once his hands were cuffed. "That's better," he said. Then he punched Troy fast and hard in the solar plexus.

Troy doubled over in agony, his lungs craving air.

"Well, come on then," Luther said, heading for the door to the backyard. "Time's a wasting."

After forcing himself into a pose that was more exclamation point than question mark, Troy followed along a cobblestone path through a manicured garden to a guesthouse that was nicer than anything he had ever lived in. Like the Spanish-style master estate, the guesthouse boasted numerous white stucco arches and black-railed balconies and a red-tiled roof. Troy gauged it to be about eighteen hundred square feet, spread over two floors.

Luther pushed open the front door like a cowboy entering a bar and then bounded up the tile stairs two at a time. Troy wanted to keep on

Luther's heels, but he needed to run out the clock. 456 required fifteen minutes of activation time. So he took the stairs deliberately, one by one, his hands still cuffed behind.

Luther had the door to a secondary bedroom unlocked and held open by the time Troy reached the top stair. Troy looked in and felt his heart melt. Emmy was spread eagle on a twin bed with a gag in her mouth. She was clothed only in lacy red underwear. Luther had secured her wrists and ankles to the bedposts with padlocked chains.

"I thought you'd like her this way," Luther said with a crocodile smile.

Locking eyes with Emmy and seeing the glow of recognition, Troy felt a warm surge of relief. "Take the gag out of her mouth." he said, struggling to keep his tone civil.

"As you wish."

As Luther pulled the gag from her mouth, Troy saw that it was a pair of pantyhose, secured in her mouth by tying the legs. The moment Luther backed away, Troy bent over and kissed her hard, full on the mouth. He didn't stop until Luther pulled him backwards by his handcuffs.

"You taste like dirt," Emmy said, an inquisitive glimmer in her eye.

"You taste great."

"You've seen her," Luther said. "Obviously, she's fine. Now, back to business."

"It's in your fountain," Troy said, maintaining eye contact with Emmy. "The DVD player Farkas instructed me to give you is in your fountain."

Troy heard the door shut behind him and a key turning in the lock. "Don't get too comfortable," Luther shouted. "I'll be right back."

"Farkas told me to remind you to transfer his ten million immediately," Troy shouted back. "He told me to warn you that Rambo has nothing on him. Having watched him in action these last few weeks, I would have to agree. You don't want him coming for you."

Chapter 94

Backfire

"YOU HAVE TO GET OUT OF HERE, NOW," Emmy said, as soon as Luther was gone. "For both our sakes."

"Luther knows I'm not going to leave without you," Troy replied. "That's the only reason he left us here alone. Besides, the door is bolted, the window is barred, and my hands are cuffed behind my back."

"Kick the door down and run," Emmy pleaded, tears streaming unbidden down her cheeks. "Find me later. Remind me that I love you. If I know that you'll do that, then I can take it. Go now. You've only got seconds before he comes back from the fountain."

Rather than doing as she asked, Troy just stood there staring back at her through misty eyes. She wanted to yell at him again to go, but his face beamed with such a loving glow that she could not do it. Finally, he said, "I think he's going to be gone a lot longer than that."

"Don't be a fool, he's—" She cut herself off. "What do you know that I don't?"

"There is no video of the wiping of the Supreme Court Justices. We didn't do it. Well, we did, but I sabotaged Farkas's camera. I also rigged the DVD player to flash Luther with UV-C. As we speak, he's losing his mind."

Emmy could not believe what she was hearing, and for a moment she thought this was another of her dreams. But Troy was there, using his foot to open the door to the closet. "And Kostas? Luther told me what he had ordered you to do ..."

"Kostas is fine. We had a long talk and then he went to Greece for a month."

Emmy felt a huge weight lift from her heart. She still had lots of questions, but Troy had allayed her chief concerns. "How did you manage to inject Luther? When?"

"I picked a fight minutes ago when I first arrived and injected him then. Farkas had custom built a lot of clever mechanisms for delivering 456. I inherited them. Can you pick handcuffs with a wire? There's a coat hanger here from a dry cleaner."

"I can pick them with the right wire, but that's too thick. Did you know that all handcuff keys are the same?"

"No. Really?"

"Pretty much. How about a bobby pin? I don't suppose you have one of those?" Emmy asked, trying to ease her own tension. Despite what

Troy had told her, she expected to hear Luther's footfalls any second. After spending two weeks with the man, she knew not to underestimate him. Luther was the sharpest tool in the shed.

"I'm fresh out. But this obviously used to be a woman's room. Maybe we'll get lucky. I hear Luther's maid leaves something to be desired."

As Troy scrounged, the implications of his earlier statement finally registered. Emmy asked, "What did you mean about inheriting Farkas's tools? Is he dead?"

"No, he's alive."

"You're confusing me, and I'm mixed up enough already. Where is he? Do you know? Luther was furious that he wasn't coming back with you. He tried to hide his anger from me, but I could tell."

"I zapped him too and sent him back to Honey. I'm sure they're having a lovely chat as we speak."

Emmy could hardly believe her ears. How had Troy managed to do all that? "You're a wonder."

"Will this do?" Troy mumbled, picking up a miniature gold paperclip with his lips.

"That's probably too weak to work as a pick, but it just might do as a shim if the cuffs are a knockoff brand. I'll give it a try."

Troy dropped the paperclip into her hand.

"How on earth did you manage to flash Farkas?" she asked, while working the paperclip into a straight wire. "Before Farkas flashed you."

"I found a specialty optical shop on the internet while supposedly researching the justices. I e-mailed them a rush order for two sets of custom contact lenses."

"Two sets?"

"A blue UV-C filtering pair for myself, and a metallic-brown non-filtering pair for Farkas. Saturday night while Farkas was sleeping contently with the knowledge that five of the nine justices were already in the bag, I swapped his lenses."

"I hope they were in a case at the time, rather than his eyes."

"Of course."

"But how did you inject him? I mean, he must have been wary about that."

"I let him inject himself. I mixed 456 in with his anti-insulin last Thursday. He's been giving himself tainted injections ever since."

"Didn't he notice?" Emmy asked, satisfied at last that the paperclip was sufficiently straight. "I'd think he'd feel different without his medication?"

"Oh, he was still getting two-thirds of his usual dose. And blood sugar levels are always in flux anyway. I'm sure he wrote any unusual feeling off to stress."

Emmy maneuvered the handcuffs around Troy's wrists so that she could access the tiny gap between the teeth and the housing. "Hold very still now," she said. Then she began pushing the wire into the gap. The wire was just thin enough to fit. She worked slowly, careful to keep it straight and parallel to the swinging arm. She hit resistance when it was about a quarter of an inch in. "Perfect."

"What's that?"

"Don't move. I'm at the junction between the teeth and the ratchet. Now, if I can find the seam ... and the wire's stiff enough ..." She felt the ratchet give, and it was all over. The handcuffs swung open.

"That was amazing. You are amazing," Troy said, turning around and giving her another big kiss. She kissed back, hungrily.

Luther had not returned.

"It's your turn," Emmy said, when they came up for air. "You think you can break this bed apart?" Catching the look on his face she added, "Not that way."

The bed was an antique, made of sturdy oak, but it was no match for Troy's pent up frustrations. Within five minutes, he had both her hands freed. They were still in chains, but no longer attached to the bed. When he moved toward the foot of the bed to start working to free her feet, Emmy said, "Go to work on the door. Now that my hands are free I can use the paperclip to work the padlocks."

"Okay," Troy said, picking up a bedpost and testing it on the air like a bat.

"What's our next move?" she asked. "Assuming you can get the better of that door."

"Oh, I'll get the better of the door. And then you're going to be the busy one."

"How so?"

"You've got some important calls to make," he said, his eyes all a twinkle. "As Luther Kanasis's personal assistant."

Chapter 95

Rewriting History

LUTHER FOUGHT his return to consciousness. In stark contrast to the monster headache throbbing between his temples, the soft mattress and warm sheets seemed to be sucking him in for a warm embrace.

"Good morning, sir," came a soft sweet voice just inches from his face. The tone was so soothing that it took Luther a moment to realize that he had no idea to whom it belonged. He flashed back to college, where he had often awoken with girls of whom he had no recollection. Usually after a night of partying. Usually with a hangover. He had virtually stopped drinking when he started practicing law, but nonetheless his headache was of that unforgettable variety. Last night's Fourth of July party had obviously gotten out of hand. He hoped she was worth it. Grudgingly he opened his eyes.

Standing beside his bed—dressed, dammit—in a peacock Chanel suit was a gorgeous sprightly nymph of a woman. Her body screamed sex, his kind of sex, but her beautiful face was all business. Her enchanting emerald eyes seemed to study his—a bit too intently for the hour, he thought—as she shot him a smile. "I'm sorry to wake you," she said. "But we've got another big day ahead of us. The media will be here in an hour for the press conference."

"And I wanted to go over the latest poll numbers with you first," came another unfamiliar voice from the other side of his bed. An unfamiliar male voice. Startled, Luther whipped his head around only to be rewarded with a volcanic throb. He clenched his eyes for a second, and then opened them to see a thirty-something man in a conservative suit. He had penetrating cobalt eyes and a pronounced dimple on his chin. Luther had never seen him before either. Yet here he was, in his— Luther interrupted his own thought to scan his bedroom. It too was unfamiliar, although opulently furnished to his taste. "Are you okay, sir?" the man asked before Luther could process the situation.

"I've got one whale of a headache."

"Another one?" the woman stated. "You really should start taking something for the stress, as Dr. Martin has repeatedly suggested. Is this one worse than yesterday's?"

Luther had no idea, but it must be. He'd take just about anything to get rid of this headache, and apparently he had resisted medication thus far. At least it wasn't from booze … or a tumor. But stress? What stress? The man had said something about poll numbers. Perhaps they would shed light on the source of his stress. Ignoring the woman's question he said, "Give me the numbers."

The man cleared his throat. "Our latest poll pegs your name recognition within two points of the Lieutenant Governor's, thanks no doubt to coverage of the Rigby case. You are also neck-and-neck with Kramer on favorables." The man handed him a printout with several numbers circled in red pen, and +10 to 20 written beside them in the right margin.

Luther still had no clear idea what was going on. The whole situation resembled a dream. But given that he was a bullshit artist by nature, he decided to play along until something clicked. Pointing to the handwritten numbers, he asked, "Where do we get the bumps?"

The man and woman exchanged pleased glances, and then she said, "The press conference, of course. Speaking of which, you really have to get ready. I've selected a suit and tie that will play particularly well on camera. I've laid them out in your dressing room. You choose the shirt, so long as it's white. I'll see that your breakfast is waiting by the time you're out of the shower."

"And here's the final copy of your speech," the man said, handing him another several sheets of paper. "Along with your answers to the most likely questions. Memorize everything over breakfast. We need to make sure this comes off as sincere rather than conniving, so you won't want to carry notes."

"Fortunately, your record over these past couple of years should make that a relatively easy sell," the woman added.

"And regardless, this will generate a ton of publicity. I have every confidence, sir, that just forty days from now, you'll be waking up as California's Governor Elect."

"No doubt, sir," the woman Luther now presumed to be his personal assistant reverberated. "This will end the debate once and for all. Luther Kanasis wants to be governor so he can help improve people's lives. It's not about the power, prestige, or money. You've already got enough of those to burn."

Luther looked down at the paper, his aching brain grasping the fringes of a remarkable situation—or rather, nested situations. He was days away from achieving his life's dream, from becoming Governor of California, but the stress had finally overwhelmed him. He had once successfully sued UCLA for exposing a Mathematics PhD student to so much stress over his thesis defense that he suffered a staggering loss of memory. The poor guy basically forgot that he was a doctoral student and everything associated therewith, including where he lived and who his friends were. Luther's expert witness had called this episodic amnesia a natural defensive mechanism, and compared it to a house blowing a fuse. As he told the jury, the UCLA mathematics department had obviously tried to run an unhealthy amount of current through his client, and his body had responded accordingly.

Studying the two faces hovering over his bed, Luther had to wonder if he had been subjected to enough psychological current during his gubernatorial bid that he had blown a fuse. Was there any other explanation for the fact that he did not recognize his staff, his house, his— "Where's the paper?" he asked.

The woman whose name Luther craved to remember exchanged another brief look with his aide before turning to retrieve the Los Angeles Times from the writing desk behind her.

Luther accepted the paper with a nervous hand, his eye darting immediately to the date: Tuesday, September 30. His mind had blanked out three whole months. It was hard to process. He recalled that in addition to PhD students, combat soldiers were the most common victims of stress amnesia. Perhaps it happened to campaigning politicians as well, but they just covered it up. As he had to do.

Three months seemed at once to be too long a period of time to black out, and too short a period for so much to have changed. Impossibly short. He let his eyes drift back to the date, this time focusing on the year. The last digit was not the 3 he had expected, but an 8. He had blacked out five whole years.

"Are you all right, Luther?" the woman asked. "You're looking a little pale."

Analyzing dates for the first time, he realized that he must have had five amazingly successful years if he was already at the doorstep of the governor's mansion. He had been doing well as an attorney, but not that well. Perhaps he had caught the next O. J. Simpson case. No wonder he had blown a fuse. Regardless, he was not about to throw his life's dream away now. He would play along—bullshit, deduce, and investigate— until he connected enough dots to function appropriately, or his memory returned.

Calling on the nimble ability to compartmentalize his thoughts that served him so well in the courtroom, Luther donned a smile, looked up at his secretary, and said, "I'm just hungry."

Chapter 96

Philanthropy

"YOU REALLY PEGGED HIM," Emmy said, studying Troy with admiration. "I'm supposed to be the people person."

"It wasn't much of a stretch," Troy replied. "What successful, charismatic, ambitious attorney doesn't dream of using Capitol Hill or the governor's mansion as a stepping-stone to the White House—especially here in Hollywood? Let's just hope that the rest of the morning proves to be as predictable." Troy trailed off his speech and then snapped his fingers. "Oh shit. What if he turns on the TV? I say we get back in there and manage the situation."

Emmy's instincts told her that Luther would find it suspicious if they appeared too clingy, and it was key that they keep him in a trusting mood. But to Troy's point, if she were Luther, she'd reach for the remote the first chance she got. "Why don't you go downstairs and wait for the press, help them get set up. I'll manage Luther."

Emmy was a bit nervous that Troy might lash out at her suggestion. Neither of them had slept much during the past forty-eight hours, and the weight on their shoulders was gargantuan. But Troy just leaned forward and gave her a warm soft kiss. Then, without a word, he turned and headed downstairs.

She was going to marry him, someday.

Emmy knocked on the door to the master bedroom suite, said "Luther," and then entered without waiting for a reply. Since Luther did not know what their relationship was, she might as well let him assume that they were intimate. That would deepen his level of trust. She found Luther dressed in the blue suit and red tie she had laid out. He was seated at the secretary, studying his prepared remarks.

When he looked up, she said, "You look perfect. Very gubernatorial."

He nodded and returned his focus to the remarks Troy had given him. Something about the intensity of his gaze piqued Emmy's fears. She wondered if they had gone too far. They had discussed the option of handing him the speech at the last minute, but ruled that out as appearing unprofessional. Well, she decided, it was too late to take it back now. All she could do was press ahead as planned.

The plan was for her to plant a couple of key thoughts in Luther's mind before the press arrived. She cleared her throat and said, "We've got fifteen minutes before we need to go downstairs. I thought you might want to use them to practice for the Q&A?"

"Does this look right to you?" Luther asked, ignoring her question. He held out his copy of the remarks without pointing to any sentence in particular.

Emmy instantly recognized Luther's query as general and open-ended. She used such questions all the time when she needed to obtain guidance from her client without losing her authoritative air. She pretended to study the sheet for a minute, and then said, "It looks perfect." she added. "This is it, Luther. This press conference is what pundits will call the tipping-point moment. And you're going to do great."

"You're sure about the figures?" he asked.

Emmy glanced down for a split second. "The five hundred million? Yes, we've run the tests. The additional press and wow factor you would get by taking it up to a full billion are marginal. As long as the word billion is in there, be it one or a half, most people's reaction is virtually identical. And at ten percent of your personal net worth, a half-billion will play well with churchgoers. They'll see that as your proper tithe. We have definitely got the right number."

She smiled and handed the paper back to him with a reassuring nod. Luther did not meet her eye. His mind was obviously riveted on the glorious revelation that he was worth five billion dollars. By her calculation, he would stop questioning things at that point. If the dream was that good, you did not want to wake up.

And she still had the icing to layer on ...

"Remind me why we chose UNICEF?" he asked.

"That question is addressed on the second page, in the Q&A prep."

"Yeah, I saw that bit about the shrinking world and the neediest among us. But what's the real reason?"

Emmy shrugged. "Well, for starters, you tug at absolutely everyone's heart strings by reaching out to children. It's the only universal demographic. Had you donated it to a children's group here in California—as the old saw: All politics is local might dictate—you would raise questions and perhaps even animus because of who you did not choose. Other politicians have fallen victim to that trap. By donating to the United Nations Children's Fund, however, you avoid all that while showing yourself to be appropriately worldly." Studying Luther's eyes, Emmy saw that he endorsed her calculations. She decided to move in for the kill with the two words that would make him a puppet. "That worldliness image will be invaluable four years from now, when we're looking on upgrading the governor's mansion to the White House."

Chapter 97

Headline News

ALONE AND BEFUDDLED, Luther wandered about his enormous estate, exploring rooms, looking for familiar objects. With each step, the events of the morning replayed uncomfortably in his mind. The press conference had lacked the pizzazz he would have expected, given the dollar amount and political stakes. When he mentioned to his executive assistant—he really had to learn her name post haste—she had assured him that this was normal for anything short of a presidential campaign, and that in this electronic age, a little went a long way. "Newspapers habitually pick the majority of their stories off the wire," she added. "And television networks routinely show pool video clips."

Not wanting to parade the very ignorance he was struggling so desperately to hide, he had let the subject drop. Then she and his aide had excused themselves to "go ensure maximal coverage" while suggesting that he "rest up."

Resting up was, of course, exactly what he needed given his mental condition. Obviously they had sensed as much but had the tact not to mention it. He would not be able to rest, however, until he got a grip on his situation. His search of the house had yielded enough familiar objects to convince him that he wasn't completely bonkers. Space aliens had not beamed his soul into someone else's body. But most of his surroundings still looked unfamiliar, even if they didn't feel foreign. And on the bright side, it would not take long to get used to calling such luxurious surrounds home. Of course, he might be moving to the governor's mansion before he got the chance.

Completing his tour of the main house, he returned to his study, the room with the most familiar objects, and turned on the television. Perhaps, he thought, current events would jog something loose. One of the local network affiliates showed his picture and made mention of a prominent L.A. lawyer's half-billion dollar gift to UNICEF. There was no mention of his campaign to succeed Schwarzenegger. He supposed that this might be intentional. His team had hoped to keep the politics out of the news coverage so that it would play like a pure act, and to that end there was no mention of the gubernatorial race in his speech. Perhaps that linkage would come with the evening news, once the political editors and pundits had time to digest his momentous philanthropic act. Still, he thought they should at least have mentioned his candidacy.

Luther's concern grew when he got all the way through a cycle of CNN's Headline News without hearing mention of his phenomenally generous gift. Was the population at large really more interested in some B-list celebrity's racial slurs, or just CNN's news director? "Hello, people. It's half-a-billion dollars. Wake up."

A crashing sound downstairs brought Luther out of his doldrums. Leaping out of his armchair he ran out onto the hallway and looked over the rail. Two police officers the size of linebackers were running up the stairs at him, weapons drawn. Luther froze, rooted to the spot by confusion and fear. The policeman on the right, the first to the top of the stairs, pointed his weapon at Luther's chest and fired without word or hesitation.

Luther felt his chest erupt in flames as white heat blinded his eyes. As his whole body began to spasm, the understanding that he was being Tasered jolted through his besieged mind. Then everything went black.

Chapter 98

Bad Robot

LUTHER AWOKE to find himself strapped naked to a bed beneath a blinding spotlight that was focused on his bare belly. No, not a bed, he realized, a table, an operating table. The skin on his stomach felt as parched as a rotisserie chicken's, while his hands and feet were frozen. He began to shiver, although whether from cold or nerves he was not sure. Had he gone into cardiac arrest when the trigger-happy cop zapped him? He looked around the room but saw only darkness in every direction. No walls. No people.

Two jointed stainless steel constructions rose around him like robotic arms. The right arm terminated in a menacing set of pincers. The left arm supported a video screen, which although less sinister than the neighboring pincers was no less disturbing. Dark and lifeless, it mocked him. A link to the outside world was just inches away, but given the grip of his restraints, it may as well have been miles.

Shaking like a rehabilitating addict and feeling desperately alone, he strained against his wrist and ankle shackles with all the strength he could muster. Drawing blood or even breaking bones were of little concern to Luther. The physical pain this caused was negligible compared to the torment in his head.

He needed to be free.

But the broad straps of thick leather running tautly across his chest and hips robbed him of all leverage. He called out like a madman howling at the moon and received a hollow echo in return. An echo. The sound sobered him. Wherever he was, it was much more expansive than your typical operating theater.

Luther cried out for what seemed like days. Perhaps it was just hours, but it was definitely longer than minutes, for his voice faded to a gravelly whisper and he began to suffer from thirst. Lying there, immobile, with nothing but the spotlight for company, he began to wonder if the Taser had killed him. This place certainly felt like purgatory. If not for the overwhelming sense that he was waiting for something, it would qualify as Hell.

Somewhere in the swirling haze of passing hours, he figured out what had happened. Someone had seen the news story on his charitable contribution and figured that he was literally worth a king's ransom. He was being held until the ransom was negotiated and paid, kept under maximal stress so that he would readily agree to any demand when the screen finally came to life.

Yes, that was it. He would be asked to authorize a transfer via videophone, and then the robotic arm would release his bonds. With no human contact, the crime was virtually perfect.

As if in answer to his speculation, a dark voice echoed forth from the void, "Hello Luther."

Luther craned his neck and tried again to pierce the blackness, but it was useless. The spotlight spoiled his vision. He strained his ears, searching for a footfall, the rustle of clothes, breathing. They found only silence.

"Who's there!" he shouted, his mind too garbled to manage anything but the cliché.

After the echo of his own cry faded without hint of another noise, Luther began to fear that he was hallucinating. He was so lonely. Food, water, yes he wanted those, needed those, but there in the sterile blackness of that vast space, companionship was what he most craved. He did not want to die alone, a naked chicken roasting on a cold iron spit.

Mocking laughter erupted from silence as the video screen before him sprang to life. When his eyes came into focus, he found himself face to face with a mid-forties male. "Remember me?" the talking head asked.

Luther strained his brain for any trace of recollection, any hint of a memory of the handsome aquiline features that were contorted into a vengeful mask. Never before had Luther wanted anything so much, needed anything so desperately. He felt as though his very sanity depended on his ability to make that single connection, but he was betrayed by his own mind. It offered nothing, a complete blank.

Almost as bad as the cognitive failure was the realization that he would never be able to explain his condition to his captor, at least not convincingly. Stress-induced episodic amnesia. Yeah, right. He hardly believed it himself. Staring into the eyes he now feared would be the last he'd ever see, Luther found a glimmer of hope and latched onto it: The eyes were intelligent, the face dignified, and the skin white.

"You don't remember me, do you?" The intelligent eyes narrowed.

"No." Luther said, his voice hoarse and shallow. "I don't remember a lot of things."

The head nodded slowly as the lips thinned. "My name is Arlen Blythe. I'm the Chairman of Savas Pharmaceuticals."

"Pleased to meet you."

Arlen inclined his head perfunctorily, acknowledging the sentiment. "You do remember giving five hundred million dollars to charity though, right?"

Luther simply said, "Yes." He wanted to say more, but did not know where to start.

Arlen's face hardened as though instantly turned to granite. "It was mine."

Despite Arlen's sinister expression, Luther felt a surge of hope. If this was only about money, he could deal with it painlessly enough. He was a wealthy man. A billionaire. With power. "I'm sorry. There was an accident. I, I just don't remember. I will pay you back though, of course. With whatever interest is appropriate."

"I really wish you did remember, Luther. That would make this so much more satisfying. But alas ..." he shrugged.

"What? Make what more satisfying?"

"The news."

"What news?"

"You're broke, Luther. Wiped out. You owe far more than you own."

"No, no. That's not true. I have five billion. Well, four billion five hundred. And I am about to become the Governor of California. I'm sure we can work this out."

Arlen sprouted an amused look and nodded three times. Seeing this, Luther let out a sigh of relief. Everything was going to be okay.

"So that's how they did it," Arlen said. "I was wondering."

"How who did what?" Luther asked, the knots recapturing his stomach.

"Got you to give my money away, irrevocably."

"It was a scam?" Luther asked, even as the implications sank in. "I really am broke?"

Arlen nodded. "And you know what that means?"

Luther slowly shook his head, dreadfully confused and utterly terrified.

The robotic pincers above Luther whirred to life. They disappeared beneath the table only to reappear a second later clenching a scalpel.

"It means I'm going to have to extract half-a-billion dollars from your flesh."

Chapter 99

Teamwork

TROY LOOKED OVER the sweating silver bucket toward the strawberry sky, and smiled. Aruba's famous green flash had been beautiful, but it had nothing on Emmy's eyes. Had he ever been so happy? He'd never know. And he was okay with that.

As the couples without beachfront bungalows turned to walk back to their rooms, Troy picked the cordless phone off the rattan table and looked over at his breathtaking companion. "You sure this is the way to go?"

Emmy set down her champagne flute and accepted the receiver. "Absolutely. Especially now that Luther's dead." She grimaced while speaking the last word, and Troy knew she was picturing the grotesque scene that had made tabloid covers all over the world. The world's first robotic homicide.

"I mean the part about keeping it anonymous," Troy clarified. "Perhaps it would be better if they knew where the money came from? Perhaps knowing about Luther and his fate would give them closure?"

Emmy shook her head. "It will only raise painful questions, reopen wounds, and make the gift feel like blood money. Best to just let a little good fortune rain on those who have endured so much bad."

Troy raised his flute in a toast to her wisdom as Emmy dialed the first number.

"Hello."

"Good morning. Mrs. Jane Michaels, please," Emmy said, affecting a British accent.

"Speaking."

"Born January ninth, nineteen sixty-six?"

Hesitation. "Yes, who's asking please?"

"Mrs. Michaels, I'm calling from the All Saints Bank in Geneva, Switzerland to inform you that an anonymous benefactor has opened an account in your interest."

"Come again? Geneva? Anonymous benefactor? I'm afraid I don't follow."

"Yes, I understand your confusion," Emmy continued. "It's to be expected. Do you have a pen and paper handy?"

"Is this some kind of trick?"

"No, ma'am. I'm not going to ask you for a thing. I'm just giving. Do you have that pen?"

"All right," Jane Michaels said after a pause, her voice markedly suspicious.

Emmy read off a twelve-digit number, and then added, "The password is WALTER64. With that information you can access your account in person or over the phone, so don't share it with anyone you do not trust completely. In fact, I would strongly suggest that you keep everything I've told you strictly to yourself. There are a lot of vultures out there, with beaks tuned to sniff out money. Best to be discreet."

"What account is this again?"

"Your new account. The gift of an anonymous benefactor. The balance is one million dollars, American."

Emmy's revelation was greeted at first with silence, and then, "Come again?"

"That's right, a one followed by six zeroes. A gift, all yours, tax free, to do with as you wish. Enjoy yourself, Jane. You won't be hearing from me or anyone else about the money ever again."

"Thank you, I think …"

"You are very welcome. Please, enjoy yourself. You deserve it," Emmy said, and severed the connection.

"That seemed to go well," Troy said. "And only forty-four to go—plus Kostas Kanasis."

"You going to call him tomorrow?"

"He's scheduled to arrive home from Greece at noon. I'll call him shortly thereafter." Troy took another swallow, happy to have lived up to the promise he'd made the old man. Then he looked back at Emmy to find that her face was rife with a different kind of emotion. She looked nervous.

"Is something wrong?"

Emmy stood and ran her polished toes through the sand. "When are we going to sit down and figure out what we'll do with our share?"

Troy was about to say "No time like the present" and suggest ordering another bottle of Taittinger when his instincts kicked in. He wasn't as quick as Emmy yet, but he was learning. "Tell me what you're thinking."

"Combined, we've got two million dollars. That gives us a lot of options."

Emmy's use of "combined" and "we" was worth far more to Troy than the money. For the past four weeks, while they used Luther's titanium ledger to backtrack to all his victims, they had managed to avoid any talk of the future. He had hoped all along that they would want to remain together after their last duty was done, but all the same he had worried that the bonds forged under fire would slacken once the heat was off. Hearing her confirm his unstated desire, he couldn't believe that he had ever harbored doubt.

"I've already got it all figured out," he said, standing and taking her chin in his hand.

"Oh you do, do you?"

Troy nodded sheepishly.

"Out with it," she said, poking at his belly with both index fingers.

He stepped back and shook his head.

She held up a fist and looked at him sideways. "How about a hint?"

He dropped to one knee. "We are a pretty good team, you and I ..."

AUTHOR'S NOTE

Dear Reader,

Although the characters in FLASH do not yet appear in any of my other novels, I do have thoughts regarding their futures. If you email me at Flash@timtigner.com, I will be happy to forward you my unpublished thoughts on what happens to them next, and keep you informed on my new releases.

If you enjoyed FLASH, I think you'll find the characters and plots in my other novels to be similarly engaging. I hope you'll give them a try.

Thanks for your kind reviews and attention,

ALSO BY TIM TIGNER

Kyle Achilles Series
PUSHING BRILLIANCE, THE LIES OF SPIES,
FALLING STARS, TWIST AND TURN

Be among the first to learn of new releases by signing up for Tim's *New Releases Newsletter* at timtigner.com

~ ~ ~

Turn the page for a preview of PUSHING BRILLIANCE, book #1 in the Kyle Achilles series.

Kyle Achilles Series, Book 1
PUSHING BRILLIANCE

Chapter 1

The Kremlin

HOW DO YOU PITCH an audacious plan to the most powerful man in the world? Grigori Barsukov was about to find out.

Technically, the President of Russia was an old friend—although the last time they'd met, his old friend had punched him in the face. That was thirty years ago, but the memory remained fresh, and Grigori's nose still skewed to the right.

Back then, he and President Vladimir Korovin wore KGB lieutenant stars. Now both were clothed in the finest Italian suits. But his former roommate also sported the confidence of one who wielded unrivaled power, and the temper of a man ruthless enough to obtain it.

The world had spun on a different axis when they'd worked together, an east-west axis, running from Moscow to Washington. Now everything revolved around the West. America was the sole superpower.

Grigori could change that.

He could lever Russia back into a pole position.

But only if his old rival would risk joining him—way out on a limb.

As Grigori's footfalls fell into cadence with the boots of his escorts, he coughed twice, attempting to relax the lump in his throat. It didn't work. When the hardwood turned to red carpet, he willed his palms to stop sweating. They didn't listen. Then the big double doors rose before him and it was too late to do anything but take a deep breath, and hope for the best.

The presidential guards each took a single step to the side, then opened their doors with crisp efficiency and a click of their heels. Across the office, a gilded double-headed eagle peered down from atop the dark wood paneling, but the lone living occupant of the Kremlin's inner sanctum did not look up.

President Vladimir Korovin was studying photographs.

Grigori stopped three steps in as the doors were closed behind him, unsure of the proper next move. He wondered if everyone felt this way the first time. Should he stand at attention until acknowledged? Take a seat by the wall?

He strolled to the nearest window, leaned his left shoulder up against the frame, and looked out at the Moscow River. Thirty seconds ticked by with nothing but the sound of shifting photos behind him. *Was it possible that Korovin still held a grudge?*

Desperate to break the ice without looking like a complete fool, he said, "This is much nicer than the view from our academy dorm room."

Korovin said nothing.

Grigori felt his forehead tickle. Drops of sweat were forming, getting ready to roll. As the first broke free, he heard the stack of photos being squared, and then at long last, the familiar voice. It posed a very unfamiliar question: "Ever see a crocodile catch a rabbit?"

Grigori whirled about to meet the Russian President's gaze. "What?"

Korovin waved the stack of photos. His eyes were the same cornflower blue Grigori remembered, but their youthful verve had yielded to something darker. "I recently returned from Venezuela. Nicolas took me crocodile hunting. Of course, we didn't have all day to spend on sport, so our guides cheated. They put rabbits on the riverbank, on the wide strip of dried mud between the water and the tall grass. Kind of like teeing up golf balls. Spaced them out so the critters couldn't see each other and gave each its own pile of alfalfa while we watched in silence from an electric boat." Korovin was clearly enjoying the telling of his intriguing tale. He gestured with broad sweeps as he spoke, but kept his eyes locked on Grigori.

"Nicolas told me these rabbits were brought in special from the hill country, where they'd survived a thousand generations amidst foxes and coyotes. When you put them on the riverbank, however, they're completely clueless. It's not their turf, so they stay where they're dropped, noses quivering, ears scanning, eating alfalfa and watching the wall of vegetation in front of them while crocodiles swim up silently from behind.

"The crocodiles were being fooled like the rabbits, of course. Eyes front, focused on food. Oblivious." Korovin shook his head as though bewildered. "Evolution somehow turned a cold-blooded reptile into a warm white furball, but kept both of the creature's brains the same. Hard to fathom. Anyway, the capture was quite a sight.

"Thing about a crocodile is, it's a log one moment and a set of snapping jaws the next, with nothing but a furious blur in between. One second the rabbit is chewing alfalfa, the next second the rabbit *is* alfalfa. Not because it's too slow or too stupid ... but because it's out of its element."

Grigori resisted the urge to swallow.

"When it comes to eating," Korovin continued, "crocs are like storybook monsters. They swallow their food whole. Unlike their legless cousins, however, they want it dead first. So once they've trapped dinner in their maw, they drag it underwater to drown it. This means the rabbit is usually alive and uninjured in the croc's mouth for a while—unsure what the hell just happened, but pretty damn certain it's not good."

The president leaned back in his chair, placing his feet on the desk and his hands behind his head. He was having fun.

Grigori felt like the rabbit.

"That's when Nicolas had us shoot the crocs. After they clamped down around the rabbits, but before they dragged 'em under. That became the goal, to get the rabbit back alive."

Grigori nodded appreciatively. "Gives a new meaning to the phrase, *catch and release*."

Korovin continued as if Grigori hadn't spoken. "The trick was putting a bullet directly into the croc's tiny brain, preferably the medulla oblongata, right there where the spine meets the skull. Otherwise the croc would thrash around or go under before you could get off the kill shot, and the rabbit was toast.

"It was good sport, and an experience worth replicating. But we don't have crocodiles anywhere near Moscow, so I've been trying to come up with an equally engaging distraction for my honored guests. Any ideas?"

Grigori felt like he'd been brought in from the hills. The story hadn't helped the lump in his throat either. He managed to say, "Let me give it some thought."

Korovin just looked at him expectantly.

Comprehension struck after an uncomfortable silence. "What happened to the rabbits?"

Korovin returned his feet to the floor, and leaned forward in his chair. "Good question. I was curious to see that myself. I put my first survivor back on the riverbank beside a fresh pile of alfalfa. It ran for the tall grass as if I'd lit its tail on fire. That rabbit had learned life's most important lesson."

Grigori bit. "What's that?"

"Doesn't matter where you are. Doesn't matter if you're a crocodile or a rabbit. You best look around, because you're never safe.

"Now, what have you brought me, Grigori?"

Grigori breathed deeply, forcing the reptiles from his mind. He pictured his future atop a corporate tower, an oligarch on a golden throne. Then he spoke with all the gravitas of a wedding vow. "I brought you a plan, Mister President."

Chapter 2

Brillyanc

PRESIDENT KOROVIN REPEATED Grigori's assertion aloud. "You brought me a plan." He paused for a long second, as though tasting the words.

Grigori felt like he was looking up from the Colosseum floor after a gladiator fight. Would the emperor's thumb point up, or down?

Korovin was savoring the power. Finally, the president gestured toward the chess table abutting his desk, and Grigori's heart resumed beating.

The magnificent antique before which Grigori took a seat was handcrafted of the same highly polished hardwood as Korovin's desk, probably by a French craftsman now centuries dead. Korovin took the opposing chair and pulled a chess clock from his drawer. Setting it on the table, he pressed the button that activated Grigori's timer. "Give me the three-minute version."

Grigori wasn't a competitive chess player, but like any Russian who had risen through government ranks, he was familiar with the sport.

Chess clocks have two timers controlled by seesawing buttons. When one's up, the other's down, and vice versa. After each move, a player slaps his button, stopping his timer and setting his opponent's in motion. If a timer runs out, a little red plastic flag drops, and that player loses. Game over. There's the door. Thank you for playing.

Grigori planted his elbows on the table, leaned forward, and made his opening move. "While my business is oil and gas, my hobby is investing in startups. The heads of Russia's major research centers all know I'm a so-called *angel investor*, so they send me their best early-stage projects. I get everything from social media software, to solar power projects, to electric cars.

"A few years ago, I met a couple of brilliant biomedical researchers out of Kazan State Medical University. They had applied modern analytical tools to the data collected during tens of thousands of medical experiments performed on political prisoners during Stalin's reign. They were looking for factors that accelerated the human metabolism—and they found them. Long story short, a hundred million rubles later I've got a drug compound whose strategic potential I think you'll appreciate."

Grigori slapped his button, pausing his timer and setting the president's clock in motion. It was a risky move. If Korovin wasn't intrigued, Grigori wouldn't get to finish his pitch. But Grigori was confident that his old roommate was hooked. Now he would have to admit as much if he wanted to hear the rest.

The right side of the president's mouth contracted back a couple millimeters. A crocodile smile. He slapped the clock. "Go on."

"The human metabolism converts food and drink into the fuel and building blocks our bodies require. It's an exceptionally complex process that varies greatly from individual to individual, and within individuals over time. Metabolic differences mean some people naturally burn more fat, build more muscle, enjoy more energy, and think more clearly than others. This is obvious from the locker room to the boardroom to the battlefield. The doctors in Kazan focused on the mental aspects of metabolism, on factors that improved clarity of thought–"

Korovin interrupted, "Are you implying that my metabolism impacts my IQ?"

"Sounds a little funny at first, I know, but think about your own experience. Don't you think better after coffee than after vodka? After salad than fries? After a jog and a hot shower than an afternoon at a desk? All those actions impact the mental horsepower you enjoy at any given moment. What my doctors did was figure out what the body needs to optimize cognitive function."

"Something other than healthy food and sufficient rest?"

Perceptive question, Grigori thought. "Picture your metabolism like a funnel, with raw materials such as food and rest going in the top, cognitive power coming out the bottom, and dozens of complex metabolic processes in between."

"Okay," Korovin said, eager to engage in a battle of wits.

"Rather than following in the footsteps of others by attempting to modify one of the many metabolic processes, the doctors in Kazan took an entirely different approach, a brilliant approach. They figured out how to widen the narrow end of the funnel."

"So, bottom line, the brain gets more fuel?"

"Generally speaking, yes."

"With what result? Will every day be like my best day?"

"No," Grigori said, relishing the moment. "Every day will be better than your best day."

Korovin cocked his head. "How much better?"

Who's the rabbit now? "Twenty IQ points."

"Twenty points?"

"Tests show that's the average gain, and that it applies across the scale, regardless of base IQ. But it's most interesting at the high end."

Another few millimeters of smile. "Why is the high end the most interesting?"

"Take a person with an IQ of 140. Give him Brillyanc—that's the drug's name—and he'll score 160. May not sound like a big deal, but roughly speaking, those 20 points take his IQ from 1 in 200, to 1 in 20,000. Suddenly, instead of being the smartest guy in the room, he's the smartest guy in his discipline."

Korovin leaned forward and locked on Grigori's eyes. "Every ambitious scientist, executive, lawyer ... and politician would give his left nut for that competitive advantage. Hell, his left and right."

Grigori nodded.

"And it really works?"

"It really works."

Korovin reached out and leveled the buttons, stopping both timers and pausing to think, his left hand still resting on the clock. "So your plan is to give Russians an intelligence edge over foreign competition? Kind of analogous to what you and I used to do, all those years ago."

Grigori shook his head. "No, that's not my plan."

The edges of the cornflower eyes contracted ever so slightly. "Why not?"

"Let's just say, widening the funnel does more than raise IQ."

Korovin frowned and leaned back, taking a moment to digest this twist. "Why have you brought this to me, Grigori?"

"As I said, Mister President, I have a plan I think you're going to like."

ABOUT THE AUTHOR

Tim began his career in Soviet Counterintelligence with the US Army Special Forces, the Green Berets. With the fall of the Berlin Wall, Tim switched from espionage to arbitrage and moved to Moscow in the midst of Perestroika. In Russia, he led prominent multinational medical companies, worked with cosmonauts on the MIR Space Station (from Earth, alas) and chaired the international industry association.

Moving to Brussels during the formation of the EU, Tim ran Europe, Middle East, and Africa for a Johnson & Johnson company and traveled like a character in a Robert Ludlum novel. He eventually landed in Silicon Valley, where he launched new medical technologies as a startup CEO.

Tim began writing thrillers in 1996 from an apartment overlooking Moscow's Gorky Park. Twenty years later, he's still writing. His home office now overlooks a vineyard in Northern California, where he lives with his wife Elena and their two daughters.

Tim grew up in the Midwest. He earned a BA in Philosophy and Mathematics from Hanover College, and then an MBA in Finance and a MA in International Studies from the University of Pennsylvania's Wharton School and Lauder Institute.